PRAISE FOR
THE SPELLKEY TRILOGY

"The author, who began the book when she was thirteen, has an unusual style, a fiendish command of plot, intriguing characters, and a fine fresh imagination."

—*The Horn Book*

"Downer's skill works its magic here as readily as before. Even her minor characters are wonderfully alive. The temptation is to pause and become lost in wonder at minute details. The sensuous richness of Downer's writing extends even to the very scents. The story reads like a fairy tale with its light and dark sides, delicate descriptions, and down-to-earth humor."

—*School Library Journal*

"The numerous characters, including Caitlin and The Badger, a traveling troupe of acrobats, and Ylfcwen, the elf queen, are solidly and appealingly presented. . . . The freshness of invention and the beautiful, poetic style make the book a rewarding venture for fantasy lovers."

—*The Horn Book*

"Circus and Fairie are elements in an exciting tale of reclaiming a changeling and defeating an evil wizard. This sequel to *The Spellkey* stands on its own as a brilliant fantasy that will please devotees of McKillip and McKinley."

—*ABA Pick of the Lists*

Ann Downer
The Spellkey Trilogy

THE SPELLKEY TRILOGY

Copyright © 1994 by Ann Downer

Previously published in different form as *The Spellkey*, © 1987 by Ann Downer, *The Glass Salamander*, © 1989 by Ann Downer and *The Books of the Keepers*, © 1993 by Ann Downer. This edition is reprinted by arrangement with Atheneum Publishers Inc., an imprint of Macmillan Publishing Company, a division of Macmillan, Inc.

A Baen Books Original

Baen Publishing Enterprises
P.O. Box 1403
Riverdale, N.Y. 10471

ISBN: 0-671-87644-9

Cover art by Darrell Sweet

First printing, February 1995

Distributed by
SIMON & SCHUSTER
1230 Avenue of the Americas
New York, N.Y. 10020

Printed in the United States of America

Author's Note

The author wishes the reader to know that the novel
that follows is in fact three novels, conceived sepa-
rately and written over a span of eighteen years.
They appeared in print between 1987 and 1992 as a
series of three related novels. For this new omnibus
edition, much of the first part, "The Spellkey," has
been rewritten, and two chapters are entirely new.

The Spellkey

*To my mother
and to the memory
of my father.*

Contents

Contents

1

THE CAT IS BELLED

That morning the old witch Abagtha had set out to gather mushrooms, the silvery, fragile kind that spring up in the night and are gone by the time the sun is very high. She went out, her meager shawls clutched about her against the damp, to gather what she needed before they could vanish. Her quick, curranty eyes soon spied a white shape among the dried leaves and pine needles, and with a grunt she stooped to pick it. But something about it made Abagtha snatch back her fingers and suck in her breath and peer more closely. It was not a mushroom but a toe. At that moment the toe wiggled, and Abagtha swept away the leaves and twigs to uncover a sleeping baby. The child opened its eyes and smiled at the old woman bending over it. Abagtha saw the child had one blue eye and one green, as true black cats do. Considering this no trifling omen, the sibyl placed the baby in the bundle on her back, with the mushrooms and herbs, and brought it away to her home in an oak, with a red door, in the heart of the forest. The tree was an ancient as she was herself, and among its roots she nursed the child on wild honey and goat's milk.

As long as her memory served her, Abagtha had lived in the Weirdwood. She knew a little of the grey arts, if not the black ones, and could make up a spell or two if the sack of copper was heavy enough, but she didn't have a license to practice the weightier magics, for the Necromancer alone held the franchise for magic in that kingdom.

So, with the foundling on her knee, the old woman sold paltry spells to those brave enough to venture into the wood, taking cockles and eels in return for spells to raise the wind, and barley and oats in return for spells to bring rain.

The child grew at a wicked rate. When she had cut her teeth, Abagtha taught her bird lore: how to tell their eggs and calls apart, and then all their names, the man-given ones such as nightjar and nuthatch, and then the names in the language of the birds. Abagtha taught her how unlucky it was to kill a wren, how owls' eyes could be eaten to cure night blindness. And when the child was late in learning to speak, the old woman made her eat the tongues of birds.

The girl cried, swallowed, pushed the plate away, and spoke.

"No."

This gave Abagtha satisfaction, and she ate the rest of the tongues herself.

When the child had been with her seven years, Abagtha summoned her and told her to make cakes of millet and honey: "Make them round, mind." Then, putting on her many shawls, she instructed the girl to put the cakes in a napkin and bring them along.

They went out. The child trotted obediently at the old woman's heels. It was growing cold—the bears had already taken to their dens—and she was barefoot. But never having had shoes, or a name, she did not miss them. They walked a long time, long enough for the light in the wood to change, the birds to stop singing and the crickets to take it up again. The trees came farther and farther apart until, just as the sun was beginning to disappear, they came to the edge of the wood.

The girl had never seen the sun set; indeed, she had never seen the sun except as long streaks of light that fell from the treetops and dappled the forest floor. She stood and squinted at the fiery egg in its nest of purple clouds and said not a word.

Abagtha inspected the cakes, found them to her liking, and pinched the child for being inattentive.

"Roll one down the hill."

"But aren't they for our supper?"

She got another pinch. Abagtha took one of the cakes and set it bouncing down the hill. "There! Roll it, so."

The child's cake rolled down the slope, flew over a pebbled ford in the stream, and disappeared. Abagtha chewed her fingers thoughtfully.

"Yes, yes, yes," she muttered. "As I thought. Come," she said to the girl, settling her old body under a tree and spreading the cakes out in her apron. "We'll eat the rest."

"Why did we roll the cakes, 'Batha?" the child asked, her mouth full of sweet millet cake.

"You can tell a fortune by the way the cake rolls."

"And what was my fortune?"

But Abagtha ate another cake, and would not say.

After the day they rolled the cakes down the hill, Abagtha began to change. She had taught the girl all she dared, lacking a license to do more, and her pupil's aptness in the ways of magic began to sit ill with her. Abagtha became quarrelsome, forgetful. Without warning she would speak to the girl in foreign tongues, scold her without cause, howl at her in tempests of hilarity and tears. She stopped working her spells: the farmers came less and less often, so that there was less and less to eat. The old cat, Mambo, became melancholy.

Still, the child soon forgot these episodes, until the unlucky day the old woman discovered her scrawling runes of great power on the scullery wall.

"Have you been looking at my book of incantations, you meddlesome little toad?" Abagtha hissed. "Didn't I forbid you ever to put your dirty paws on it?"

The book of incantations never left its wooden stand by the hearth. Three ribbons marked its pages—one silver, one blue, and one green—and its pigskin binding was stamped with the shapes of herbs and animals: mandrake and hyssop, crocodiles and hedgehogs. Wary of its iron clasps, the child had never looked inside, except to catch a glimpse while Abagtha was reading from it. All she had seen was a dog curled up asleep in a capital *P*, monkeys swinging in the margins, and thick, scowling letters that meant nothing to her.

The girl shrank into the corner. "I didn't touch it! I couldn't! It's locked . . . you wear the key."

"How else could you learn to make runes like that, you nasty little liar?"

"I dreamed them, 'Batha, truly!"

And the child did dream things. She would dream of a farmer with a toothache, riding a spotted horse, and the next day such a farmer would arrive at the oak with the red door. Other nights the girl dreamed things less simple: men in black on horseback, battling; fire in the air; a garden under glass, full of birds; two people kissing by a hedge. One of Abagtha's other books had pictures of knights, and people kissing, but the girl liked the one with colored pictures of beetles better.

Abagtha was in no mood to hear about dreams. "Lies!" she spat. "Even *I* don't know the workings of those runes, and you scrawl them with no more care than if they were a game of crosses and oughts! Now, get a pail and rag and scrub this wall, and the floor, too, while you're about it! Mark this wall again, and you'll rue it."

When the old woman had gone the child cried silently for a bit, out of fright and relief. After a while she fetched a pail and wrung out a cloth. Kneeling before the wall, she paused with the rag in her hand, knitting her brow at the runes. Abagtha had never taught the girl her letters, so that the runes meant less than nothing to her. But some urge moved her tongue for her, made her hand trace the elbows and tails of the letters as she said softly:

"Spellkey . . ."

After the incident with the runes the girl kept her dreams to herself, playing quietly with the dried lizards she took from Abagtha's jars.

* * *

Years passed, and the girl grew tall and slight, a seedling seeking light among the upper branches. Her skin was smooth and white as almond meat, for it never saw the sun, and her dark hair fell past her waist, heavy as wet silk and tangled with burrs and cobwebs. In winter she wove it about her into a cloak to ward off the cold. Abagtha, now fearful of her charge's powers, kept her in the thinnest muslin well into the winter, and fed her on a nasty porridge of ground acorns, to keep her submissive. But the girl sought out berries and roots to sustain her, and suffered not too much from Abagtha's abuse. This is what Abagtha had dreaded most dearly of all.

Abagtha knew the girl's eyes to be those of a seer, the eyes of an otherworld daughter. For this reason she hesitated at outright cuffs, resorting instead to sly pinches. The girl met this malice with wit and quickness, doing the endless chores set for her without complaint. Where kindness is not known it is not missed. This even temper maddened Abagtha beyond endurance, and she withheld even the acorn porridge, even a blanket.

It was because she had no bed that the girl found the catstone. The bottommost room under the oak tree was a nut-cellar among the roots. From her youngest days the girl hid there, for though it was dark the cellar was warm, and Abagtha had forgotten its existence, so that the girl crawled there to escape both the cold and Abagtha's rages. This time, as she bit into a nut, the girl chipped a tooth. She lit the lamp, a dish of fat with a bit of rag for a wick, and held the nut to the glimmer curiously.

It wasn't a nut, but a pebble, shaped oddly like a cat, carved by some hand to enhance the chance resemblance. The girl made a cord out of strands of her hair, and put the catstone around her neck, hiding it well under her rags.

After she found the catstone, the girl began to dream in daytime. She would see faces in the basin as she did the dishes. The songs of the birds were as clear to her as human speech. And the ancient cat, who had always resented the girl, suddenly took to her with a fierce affection, rubbing against her legs and making a curious, croaking purring.

As the cat had a history of scratching and spitting, the girl continued for a time to kick it away. But the cat's affection began to wear away her resistance, and one day at last she picked up the cat and stroked it clumsily.

"There, old Mambo," she said to it softly.

The cat burrowed its head under the girl's chin, purring. Then an extraordinary thing happened: the cat, tapping the catstone with a paw, suddenly let out a great yammering that brought Abagtha at a trot. Her gaze soon fixed on the catstone, and she stood before the girl, eyes bright with greed, trembling with a more obscure emotion. The girl waited for a slap, but it did not come. Instead Abagtha warily stretched out a finger to touch the stone.

She was rewarded with a shock for her pains, blue sparks edging her arm with pale light. Abagtha gave a short shriek and stuck her fingers in her gums, noisily sucking the burn.

Then her countenance changed, and she smiled a toothless smile.

"Give it me!" she crooned. "Sweet childling, give it to your 'Batha, your old gran, who has cared for you this many a long year. Can you grudge her it? It is a cheap bauble, a nothing. Give it me!"

This speech, so against Abagtha's nature, terrified the girl more than would have an unreasoning rage. She fled.

She crept back that evening, driven home by cold and hunger. Her keeper extended a civil greeting, and set before her hot mutton broth and barleycakes—unimagined delicacies. The girl ate, too starved to be wary, the firelight picking out the stone where it lay nestled in the hollow of her neck. A white cinder appeared in each of Abagtha's eyes as she cracked her toes with quiet glee.

The girl's spoon clattered to the floor, and the room rippled and swam. Flushed and numb, she slid senseless to the floor.

"The pepper! The pepper!" chortled Abagtha. "A subtler herb, that." The old woman knelt by the girl and unknotted the cord of hair, depositing the charm tenderly in a box of carved horn. She then wrapped the box in a bit of rag and hid it in her bosom.

The girl came to a great while later, the arm twisted under her all pins and needles. Her hand went to her throat and found it bare, and she sat up with a cry. She went to Abagtha's chamber and found the old woman in her bed, the blankets clutched under her chin. Her eyes were staring, their malice replaced by bright fear. The box of horn lay open on the covers, and she held the catstone in her hand, worrying it ceaselessly with her thumb. She did not resist when the girl pried it gently from her grasp.

After she had replaced the catstone around her neck, the girl steeped herbs for poultices and nursed the tiny form in the bed. But Abagtha no longer had the will to live: she seemed intent on some distant vision, and the girl could not interest her in food, not even in cakes of millet and honey, perfectly round.

Inside a week the sibyl was dead. The girl without a name tucked the covers well around the body, and left a candle burning nearby. Then she put on a clean blouse and smock belonging to Abagtha and went away from the oak tree with a red door, locking up carefully and hiding the key under a stone.

∽∾

The Blue Toad in Moorsedge was crowded. The stranger stood on the threshold of the tavern looking for a seat. At last he spied an empty stool in the corner and struck out through the noisy throng toward it. He was weary, and wanted to sit awhile and nurse a cup of mulled ale. He managed to flag down one of the alewife's daughters and request his refreshment. The serving girl looked at him askance, informing him that he could have beer or ale, neither mulled. Supper was eight coppers: rabbit stew or hen pie. The stranger ordered his meal and gave instructions for a room to be made up for him at the adjoining inn.

The stew, when it came, tasted more like squirrel than rabbit. He chased it well with ale to keep it down, then pushed the empty pannikin aside and drew his seat into the shadows.

At the next table a cluster of men conversed in low tones. Seven strained to catch the eighth's whispered words.

". . . a light in the wood and went and found the old witch locked in her lodgings, deader than a doorknocker."

"It's not a sound mind that shuns its own kind to live alone in the Weirdwood."

"They say madmen lurk there, and deserters."

"And Direwolves."

There was a universal shudder, then a lull for drinking. One of their number wiped his mouth and spoke.

"You'll think me drunk or mad, but hear me out. Between the taxman and the toothpuller, I've been feeling the pinch, so I'd hired myself out to the charcoal burners to pad my wage. I was working on the edge of the Weirdwood one day, away from the others, when all of the sudden I get gooseflesh all down the back of my neck. I turned around in time to see a girl run off through the trees. And she were no village miss. No, she were as wild and dark a creature as I ever seen. Mark me: She had seer's eyes.

"Well, she threw me such a look it made my heart go cold, and the next day I went out to my stock and found my best milk cow writhing with colic. There now, what do you make of that?"

Now it did not matter that they had, to a man, at one time or another treated themselves or their milk cows or their children with Abagtha's tonics.

"I say the old witch has only shed her skin."

"What does she live on in winter, d'you think?"

"Whatever's unlucky enough to cross her path."

"I lost a ewe last week. . . ."

"The miller over Stillwine way told me his last lot of grain was full of rats, and he had to burn it."

In his sooty corner, the stranger lit a pipe. The smoke curled toward the timbers in pale ribbons, obscuring his face with a silver cloud. His hair glinted copper bright in the firelight, and his grey eyes never turned from their thoughtful contemplation of the speakers. He spoke, and suddenly the whole room was still.

"She sounds a regular menace."

Every head in the tavern turned and took in his profile, carved by the shadows to an eerie gauntness. The traveler gazed back unblinking.

"It's not safe to go abroad anymore, if you ask me." He said this very softly, but so piercing was his tone that even the cellarer among the vats woke and was afraid.

"He's right," said the charcoal burner with the colicky milk cow. "We'll lose our livestock at first, but when she's done with that, what's to stop her plying her spells on our wives and children?"

There arose an ugly muttering.

"It's an unpleasant task, but it must be done. I'll fetch torches. Who'll bring stout rope?"

They spilled out into the street. As the tavern emptied, the stranger signaled to the serving girl, and called for another ale.

The girl without a name was raiding squirrels' caches for her supper, her keen eyes spotting the signs of hiding places, her roughened hands digging through the snow and earth to find a nut or two the squirrels had forgotten, worms missed. Her hand kept returning to the catstone, no larger than any of the nuts piled in her lap, that hung around her neck. Suddenly she leapt up and around, the nuts scattering on the snow.

Behind her two dozen men brandishing spades and torches advanced through the trees, shouting and calling to their dogs. The girl swore under her breath and began to run through the snow. She splashed through an icy stream and, clambering up the bank, remembered the foul-smelling musk she carried to keep the Direwolves at bay. She took the vial from her pocket and uncorked it, but before she had a chance to smear herself with the oil she tripped on a tree root and sprawled headlong in the snow.

The dogs were on her in a minute. The men sheared her tresses from her and pared her fingernails to char and make into an antidote for her magic. Then they bound her hand and foot and slung her from a pole like a carcass of venison. The blood rushed to her head, and before they were out of the wood the girl had fainted.

Someone prodded the girl with a broom handle until she woke. At the sight of her eyes, one blue, one green, a single gasp escaped the onlookers gathered in the village square.

"A potent witch, no doubt about it." He was the wealthiest shopkeeper in the town and was expected to know such things. "We're lucky she hasn't done greater wickedness."

"Yes, but what do we do with her now?" They had never caught a witch before in Moorsedge, and were wondering how to proceed.

"We can't drown her. It would taint the wells."

"Burn her then," someone said uncertainly.

"What, are you mad? And have unholy ashes over every farm in the county?"

"We could . . . hang her."

"No, we can't kill her at all. Any fool knows that a witch's blood revenges itself."

"Just what are we to do, then, answer me that!"

The man with the red hair and grey eyes unfolded his arms and lit his pipe. "Are you men not even mice enough to bell your own cat? You needn't kill her, only render her harmless."

"And how are we to do that?"

"Weren't you listening? I just told you."

2

THE TANNER'S
DAUGHTER'S SON

After prayers the Badger fled to his loft quarters over the stable to savor an hour free of horses, prayers, and the growlings of a demanding stomach.

It was a season of religious feasts, and there had been a steady stream of pilgrims to the Abbey of Thirdmoon See, so the Badger had spent the morning mucking out stables, hauling water for the stable troughs, and putting the horses to graze in the pasture above the belltower. It was tiring work, and he had been tempted afterward to raid the abbot's spice orchard, not just for the sport of it, but because the abbot's oranges were an important supplement to a diet of suet pudding and black bread. The abbey had lost its last stableboy to scurvy.

But yesterday he had caught a bat in the forge chimney, and he hurried back to feed it, his pocket full of the crickets that had caused the abbot much puzzlement during prayers.

The Badger took out a pencil and notebook from under the mattress of his cot and began to draw the face of the bat as it hung upside down from the top of its cage. The boy whistled as he worked, a lively ballad, secular bordering on bawdy. Certainly if the abbot had heard the tune and divined its questionable origins, it would have meant trouble indeed—almost as much trouble as the purloined pencil and paper, pinched from the desk of the abbot's secretary.

He had finished the bat's head and was starting on the wings when a monk appeared in the entrance to the loft, the veil of a beekeeper's hat turned back to reveal a florid face made more so by regular doses of medicinal brandy.

"Now, where did you learn a song like that?" said Asaph, hoisting his considerable self up into the room.

"From the knifegrinder," said the Badger, covering the bat's cage with a cloth. "How do you know what kind of song it is, anyway? I was whistling."

"I can certainly tell a bawdy-house ballad from a hymn! Just be careful you're not overheard by someone with less than my abundant charity."

"You didn't come to tell me that."

"No. The abbot wants to see you."

The Badger made a face. "So, he's still trying to get me into a cowl and tunic, is he?"

"Yes, and he'll need nine strong men and a shoehorn to do it! Come, come. You'd best resign yourself to it, my lad. The abbot is as stubborn as you are. He's ninety-seven, but he isn't about to die until he's seen you shave your head and take the oath of the Pentacle."

In the margin of his drawing the Badger rapidly drew an unflattering, and cannily true, portrait of the abbot. Then he slapped the notebook shut. "Then he'll live to be one hundred and ninety-seven! Why does he want me, anyway? Why not the butcher boy or a beggar off the street?"

Asaph's glance slid discreetly over the other's wild hair, stable-mucked boots, and sorry clothes. "Perhaps he can't resist a challenge."

"I see." The boy's laugh was easy, but his eyes had clouded. "If he can save the tanner's daughter's bastard, he can make the very devil tell his beads like a regular pilgrim."

"Don't take that tone with me. You know very well what I meant."

The Badger reddened. "Sorry."

"You'd better go. And be careful how you choose your words. His Grace is in a holy temper."

The abbot was giving dictation to his secretary, a rabbity monk with a harelip that exposed prominent front teeth. The abbot himself was knife thin, with brilliant eyes sunk in a wizened parchment face. His gaze fell on the Badger, who was standing just inside the doorway, twisting his cap in his hands.

"Ah, young Martin."

"It's Matthew, your Grace."

"Yes, yes." The abbot waved him to a seat, arranging his own slight form in the chair opposite.

"I will be blunt. Your presence at the abbey has become a trial to me, and I am at an age when I must economize my trials. When I contracted with your grandfather to undertake your bringing-up, I assumed, when you came of age, that you would take the vows and vestments of our order. It is now painfully clear to me that you will not willingly do so."

Here the abbot paused as if anticipating a reply, but the Badger only stared at his feet.

"Furthermore," said the abbot, "it has been brought to my attention that you have taught yourself to read. In doing so, you not only reached above your station in pursuit of a gentle education, but doubled your offense by reading poetry and other forbidden writings. You knew such behavior went against all the tenets of the Pentacle, and yet you persisted. Was this how we were to be repaid for taking you in and offering you our protection?"

The Badger remained fascinated with his bootlace. When the abbot saw no answer was forthcoming, he sighed.

"I am therefore persuaded to let you go. I have secured a place for you with the apothecary in Moorsedge. You will go tomorrow."

The Badger leapt to his feet. "The apothecary? Really?"

The abbot made the merest of gestures, and his secretary scurried to the desk, took a fresh sheet of paper, and covered it swiftly with writing. Then Brother Hare (for so he was known while out of earshot) blotted the page, folded it, and held it while the abbot pressed his signet into the blot of wax on the seam.

"Your letter of introduction." The abbot pressed a small felt purse into the Badger's hand. "For expenses, mind you. And you may take a horse."

"Well, your pack will certainly be light," said Asaph.

The Badger surveyed the few things ranged on the foot of his cot: apart from a change of clothes there were only a few tools, the notebook, and a box of well-worn dominoes Asaph had made for him years ago.

"I'll be lodging with the apothecary. I won't need much, starting out."

Asaph was looking at him with great seriousness, picking his words as if he were paying for them by the letter.

"Badger, be careful what friends you make. You have been very sheltered here. I took the vows late in life, but before I did I saw much of the world. Things are different, outside these walls."

The Badger laughed. "Do you think me such a simpleton as that!"

"Yes," said Asaph. "Simple, good, and much as you hate it, still very young. Live you well, Badger. Love you well. We may not meet again. So will you promise your old friend that you will be a miser with your trust, and take care?"

Badger unhooked the cage and carried it to the window, giving the bat its freedom. He turned and looked thoughtfully at Asaph.

"I promise," he said, but already his thoughts had turned to his new freedom, his new life, suddenly so near at hand.

∽⌒∾

The next morning the Badger saddled his favorite horse, a piebald he had named Motley, and rode out the gate before the dew had burned off the grass. The abbot's letter was pinned inside his shirt, the purse of coins struck his hip in time to the horse's gait. As soon as he was out of sight of the gatehouse, the Badger nudged the horse's ribs with his heels and sped down the road with a quickening heart.

He made Moorsedge by early afternoon and turned the horse's head toward the marketplace. The shops lining the square were crowded, the people close and agitated as bees in a hive, with the same murmur and hum among the stalls of plucked chickens and new shoes. Motley picked his way neatly between merchants, servants buying their masters' dinners, and dirty urchins begging. The Badger spied a woman setting out a carpet and some tiles, which she was marking with colored chalk. She had seer's eyes, but the green one was glass. She looked up and gave horse and rider an appraising blue stare.

"Do you tell fortunes?" the Badger called down.

Fear flickered briefly across her features, and she glanced quickly around.

"Not so loud. And rein him in, will you?"

Motley had begun to mouth the fringe of the carpet. The Badger swung down from the saddle and felt for coins in his pockets. "How much?"

"Twelvecent." Her good eye roamed him up and down.

He extended his hand. The fortune-teller removed, polished, and replaced her glass eye before taking his hand in her own, which was surprisingly smooth and cool. She peered intently at the lines in his palm.

"You will make a perilous journey, lose something you prize above all else, and come into a great inheritance."

"What, a fortune with no talk of love?"

But she abruptly dropped his hand, hastily covering the tiles with a ragged cloth and pocketing her glass eye. The Badger looked up and saw a figure in distinctive dark purple robes, with a pentacle of dull iron. An Adept Noble, whose job was to make sure the laws of the Pentacle were kept in letter and in spirit. He was turning over merchandise in a stall, but his eyes were on the fortune-teller.

"And fivecent change, sir," she said, pressing some coins

into his hand, and handing him a length of cheap printed muslin.

As he led Motley away, he wondered what the penalty for fortune-telling was. Still, she was shrewd, he thought. She told someone dressed for hard riding that he would make a difficult journey. Nothing much in that. And every man loses something he values, if he loves his life.

A knot of young men had gathered to throw a game of bones. The Badger knew one of them: Cullen, the smithy's son, who came with his father when there was more shoeing than the abbey could handle alone. Once he had tried to hold the Badger's head under the water from the forge sluice, and another time, out of sight of his father, he had held the Badger's hand on a hot iron. When they were younger, he hadn't needed a reason. Recently his father had scolded him for shoddy work, and held the Badger up as an example of what he should be. It didn't help, either, that Cullen had caught his sweetheart flirting with him outside the abbey gates.

Catching sight of the Badger, Cullen elbowed his neighbor, who had been about to toss the bones. Silently the group watched him pass. And then he began to hear the low chant: *bastard, bastard.*

It was a stale enough taunt, but this time for some reason it stung, and the sting stirred an old memory. This same market, when he was only six, before his mother died and he was sent to live with the monks. Grandfather had entrusted him with some small errand and that word, *bastard,* had dogged him as he made his way from stall to stall.

But he had been too little, too innocent, to hear it for the taunt it was meant to be. When at last one pitying merchant, pushing coins at him across a countertop, had smiled and asked him his name, he had said, without hesitation, "Badger."

The Badger exhaled and shook his head and found that Motley had stopped to drink from the trough beside the public well. He slid down from the saddle to drink from the common gourd. Then he knotted the horse's bridle around a post and went to find a bite to tide him over until his new master might choose to feed him dinner. It occurred to him that the apothecary might be a little vague about meals. At the abbey, the suet pudding and black bread had at least appeared at clockwork intervals.

He let his nose lead him to a stall that sold penny loaves and stood in line flirting with the girls kneading bread at one end of the shop, up to their elbows in dough and gossip. When his turn came, the Badger bought ten penny loaves and ate three on the spot while the baker, her face pink from the oven's heat, wrapped the rest in greasepaper. Suddenly the laughter wilted in the throats of the girls, and the Badger saw the ruddiness drain from the baker's face. Everyone waiting in line fell silent, and in the eerie quiet the Badger heard a shop bell peal. Remembering that the stall had no door and no bell, he turned, curious.

The crowd had parted, and in the rift stood a woman, tall and dark and dressed in what once had been a garment, but was now a collection of rags pieced together with what looked like animal skins. Her extraordinary blue-black hair tumbled past her waist and all but hid her face, but the Badger could see that her eyes were a strange, pale blue. Just then she put up a hand to push back her hair, and the Badger saw the hidden eye was green. He was less astonished by this than by the collar—also hidden and now exposed—that was fastened about her neck.

It was made of leather and iron and was hung with sleigh bells. Her hands, too, were manacled and belled, so that her every move caused the bells to sound. The Badger had heard of bellings. They were a form of punishment reserved for severe crimes—blasphemy and witchcraft.

The creature stepped up to the counter, drew something from a pocket, and threw it into the balance. It tipped the scales noisily. The object was crusted with mud but here and there the Badger thought he saw the gleam of a gem. The baker filled a napkin with loaves, trembling in her haste, and handed the bundle back across the counter. Without a word, the belled woman took up her bread and left.

Once she had gone, the power of speech returned to the onlookers.

"Wanton!"

"Devil's woman!"

"Call a priest!"

"Are you mad?"

"I'd as soon use an asp to cure an adder's bite!"

"Hold on, I've a little holy water." The vial was passed like a jug among thieves. Everyone was anointed, and there was a smell like celery. Soon the girls were back to kneading bread and the baker was scowling at the Badger.

"And what else?"

"That's all."

"Then on with you. You're holding up the line."

On his way out the Badger paused by the girls wrestling with the bread dough. Their mother's reproach of him had put a luster on the Badger, and they answered his questions eagerly.

"Oh, yes," said the shorter and plumper of the two, "she comes in regular. Always pays with bits and pieces of swords and things, all stuck with rubies the size of chestnuts."

"One of the pearls was the size of a goose egg," said her sister.

"Oh, Hannah! Tell me another tale," said the first. They fell to bickering, and the Badger took up his bundle and left.

He dragged Motley from the shade so he could get a foot in the stirrup. He was headed for the district where the apothecary had his shop when he saw the belled woman surrounded by Cullen and two of his loutish friends. The woman was trying to ignore them, but they had circled around her and were slowly advancing.

"Here, kitty—"

"Ho, darling, isn't our cream good enough for you?"

"She's been to see the queen—the faerie queen—and won't talk to the likes of you and me."

"Did you sit under the queen's chair at court, kitty?"

Cullen seized her around the waist, wrapping her hair around his hand and pulling her head back. Her teeth were bared, but she didn't struggle or cry out. The Badger had seen animals like that, tensed for the dog's spring.

"If she doesn't like cream, maybe she'll like fishes' heads. What do you say, pet? Would you like that?" Out of the corner of his eye, the smithy's son suddenly caught sight of the horse and rider. He grinned.

"Look who's joined us. Good afternoon, bastard."

"Let her go."

"Ask me nicely, bastard, and maybe I will."

"It wasn't a request."

Cullen let her go and ambled slowly over to the Badger, taking hold of Motley's bridle. In his eyes the Badger could see him making the calculation: three on foot against one on horseback. Or three against two? It occurred to the Badger that the smithy's son might be afraid to turn his back on the witch.

"Let's continue this conversation some other time, bastard," he said, squinting up at the Badger. "I'm fascinated."

At a gesture the other two followed him out of the square.

"Are you hurt?"

The woman didn't reply, bending silently to retrieve the bread, which had been trampled in the dirt. She dusted off the loaves and wrapped them up again. As the Badger approached, she straightened and hugged the bread to her tightly.

"Stay away."

"Here, why don't you let me see that collar," he said gently, putting out a hand.

She bit it. There was a quick exchange of blows as the belled woman swore: "Dog! Dead dog! Worm in a dead dog!"

"Worse and worse!" the Badger said, parrying her attempts to land a blow. He managed to grab both her wrists and was getting a good look at the collar when she gave a howl of fury and brought her knee up sharply. He yelped in pain and dropped to the ground, cursing.

She was suddenly perfectly still, though her eyes were bright. She hiccoughed softly.

"Get up," she said.

"No—stay away from me." The Badger rocked on the ground, hooing softly.

"Here, get up," she said, and hauled him to his feet with more strength than he had credited her with.

He shook her off. "You're a madwoman," he informed her. "What were you trying to do, geld me?"

"You'll mend." She began to walk away, loosing dust and a faint music of bells as she made her way across the square.

"Stark staring," muttered the Badger.

❧

The abbot's directions led the Badger to a disreputable district of the town. He stopped a man carrying a wicker cage of cats and a large sack.

"Can you tell me the way to the apothecary? I'm a stranger here."

"Well, you needn't bother to advertise it," replied the man. The cats paced in the cage with a swift restlessness, crying loudly. "And if you're wise," he added, "you'll carry your money under your tongue instead of in your pocket."

"But the apothecary?"

"My, aren't we in a hurry? Straight on, past the bawdy house and the baths. Can't miss it."

"I'm grateful, I'm sure. Your cats are certainly full of quick."

"They smell the rats," replied the rat-catcher, hefting his sack.

Suspended above the door of the apothecary's shop was a stuffed crocodile, patched here and there with green oilcloth. It revolved slowly on its cord, grinning none too endearingly. There was no answer when the Badger knocked, so he gave the bell a good pull. The second-story shutters banged open, and a head, bald and snaggle-toothed, popped out like a cork.

"What do you want?" screamed the head.

"I was sent by the abbot of Thirdmoon See to take a place with the apothecary."

"Take a place? Take a place? At table, do you mean? In a witness box, in the jailor's house, on the gallows?"

The Badger wondered whether every single inhabitant of Moorsedge was insane. "No, man, an apprenticeship," he said, seized for the first time by misgivings.

"The apothecary is in prison, I tell you. Jail. Ha! ha! They'll hang 'im. A fine holiday, a hanging. They close the banks, and there's free rum punch."

"Hang him? What has he done?"

"He's a debtor, a loathsome debtor, a poisonous, villainous debtor. Oh, sir, a scurrilous sinner, wallowing in debt. Debtor's prison. Ha!"

"Now what do I do?" the Badger asked, of no one in particular.

"Do? Do? Stay out of debt! Ha! ha! Stay out of debt!" The shutters slammed shut, but the Badger could hear whooping from somewhere within.

"Well," he said to Motley, "I don't know what I expected, but it wasn't this." His thoughts turned to the lodgings he had outfitted in his mind, the suppers with new-made friends, the amusements in town.

What to do? Back to the abbey, he supposed. The thought of it made debtor's prison seem a holiday.

If anyone had happened to be in the apothecary's shop just then, they would have witnessed an extraordinary transformation. Into the fire fell some bits of black wax, and lo! the snaggleteeth were gone. The wax was followed by some putty, and the warts and ragged ear disappeared as well. Some serious scrubbing with a strong soap restored the unshaven face to a flawless pink. The red-haired man with grey eyes stirred the fire to make sure all of the disguise was consumed, then went out the back door just as the apothecary was coming in the front.

Old Caraway returned in a temper. A note had called him to the potter who sold him his jars; the potter knew nothing of the note. Furthermore, there was no sign of the boy he had been told to expect. At least he would be able to work in peace.

The apothecary, thought the stranger as he donned an unremarkable costume in the alley, would have been very surprised to learn that he was in prison for debt.

The penny loaves were long gone and the horse's pace had slowed when the Badger stopped that evening at an inn halfway to Thirdmoon. He was no sooner down from the saddle when the tavern doors flew open and a number of drunks stumbled into the street and into the Badger.

"Can I believe my eyes?"

"He's following us. Go home, bastard."

"What's that smell, the horse or the rider?"

"Do you *sleep* with your horse, or just bathe with it?"

The Badger had escaped a brawl twice already that day and knew it was useless to hope for such good fortune a third time, especially when a match would have set the breath of any one of them alight. Besides, now it was six to one, odds not even Cullen could pass up.

Many of the blows were poorly aimed, but he was well thrashed all the same. As he lay sprawled in the gutter, revelers spilled from the inn to see what the din was about. They complimented the Badger on his cowardice, and with great mirth emptied their tankards over his head. Drenched and stinging, the Badger sat on the paving stones and thought that by now he couldn't argue with the insult about the smell. Then someone brought a bottle down on the back of his head and he saw a burst of brilliance, and then nothing.

3

THE BARROW DOWNS

The Badger came to his senses in total darkness and had to blink several times to know whether his eyes were open or shut. The close air of the place filled his nostrils with an awful stench, and his veins with a cringing fear. He did not know this place, so why was it so familiar?

He groped around him for something that would tell him where he was. He felt earthen walls, then something else. He snatched back his hand, the hair rising on the back of his neck. His hand had closed on a bone.

He was in a grave. They had buried him alive.

Alive—the Badger felt cold air move against his cheek, and his pounding heart slowed. There was air, at least. Perhaps they had only bundled him into a cellar after all. His eyes had begun to sort out faint shapes from the blackness, and he saw the bone was a mutton leg. Now he could make out niches in the earthen walls. He scrambled up to examine them; by peering hard he could just make sense of the labels on the porcelain jars: *Confect of Canthar, Oil of Mastic, Solutive Honey of Roses, Pillular Extract of Cassia*. Nets hung from the ceiling—full of onions, by the smell of them; the Badger shuddered as he brushed against a ham suspended like a hanged man. This was no grave, but

no ordinary cellar, either, for all the hams and onions it
might contain. His head ached, and he still heard bells.

As he struggled to remember why bells were important,
he saw an approaching light cast a glow on the earthen
walls.

Someone rounded the corner carrying a lit dish of tallow. Before the light showed her face, the Badger remembered what it was about the bells.

The village witch silently placed a bundle on the ground
beside the Badger and lit a lamp from the dish in her
hand, not spilling any of the tallow despite the manacles
on her hands. The Badger found he had been lying on a
bed of dried heather and that his head had been skillfully
bound. He touched the bandage gingerly and winced,
remembering the bottle splintering in his ears.

"Where am I?"

"In my barrow."

That made him sit up. "You mean . . ."

"On the moor, yes." She untied the bundle, which contained the heel of a loaf of bread and two eggs.

She handed the latter to him. "They're boiled. Would
you rather they were raw?"

"No! Thanks," he said quickly. "They're fine this way."
His hunger won out over his curiosity, and he barely
looked at her as he peeled and ate the eggs. She watched
him eat without comment, handing him the loaf when the
eggs were gone. The Badger paused, chewing, and looked
up, wiping the crumbs from his mouth with the back of
his hand.

"Why did you help me?" he asked, and swallowed.

"You didn't seem to be very good at defending yourself.
And as long as I was taking your horse—"

"Motley? What did they—"

She firmly pushed him back down on the mat and began
to undo the dressing on his head.

"He's fine. He seemed distressed at the thought of leaving you, but he's eaten a dinner of moor heather and finds
it quite to his liking. The village idiots didn't touch him,
but if they had thought of it they might have made him
into a mock-venison dinner, for spite." She held a rag to

the mouth of a jug and tipped it twice. A smell of vinegar assailed the Badger's nose.

"What of the Direwolves? They might have made a meal of him."

"Yes, but they don't much like the smell of iron. They mostly leave alone any creature that's been shod with it. Or belled with it, for that matter. This is going to sting, but if I don't clean it, it will fester." She looked at him closely. "How did you manage to get into the good graces of that lot, anyway?"

"Oh, we're old childhood mates. I'm a bastard, you see. No better reason for a drubbing. Not that they need one."

"My eyes are the wrong color for their liking—though the rest of me seems to suit them. There, I'm done with you. Your shirt is in the other room, drying by the fire."

The other room of the barrow was dominated by the bronze bier of some warrior long since dust. The stone likeness had been detached and now stood in a corner; in its place was a nest of blankets and cushions. One corner of the room was taken up by war chests overflowing with armor, much of it broken up by grave robbers themselves long dust. A pail of water was steaming in front of the stove.

"I would have given you a bed in here, only you smelled so much, of beer and, well, piss."

"So that's the stench," he said ruefully.

"Yes. I thought I'd leave the bath to you. Your shirt is on the chair by the fire. Mind the bees."

His pants were as beer-and-piss soaked as the rest of him, and in order to bathe he would have to take them off. After a minute he gave up waiting for her to go into the other room and stripped, not knowing what else to do. While he bathed she sat on the bier, tying herbs into bundles with the appearance at least of complete unconcern. Near the hearth an old suit of armor was serving as a beehive. One of the bees exited through the visor and flew by the Badger's ear. He gingerly removed his shirt from the chair and put it on. As he did up the buttons, he thought of her, with her manacled hands, putting him across Motley's back, lowering him into the barrow, dressing him—undressing him, for that matter. He turned to face her.

"You're no witch, whatever they say. What are you, exactly?"

She turned on him a cool, blue-green gaze. "But I am a witch. Make no mistake about that. I am full of all sorts of volatile magics. I might slit your throat from behind while your back is turned, and have you for supper." She laughed, yawned, and stretched. "I know a little of magic; call me what you like. I was never named. At least, I was never given a name I cared to keep."

"Your parents never named you?"

"I never knew my parents. The woman who raised me called me lots of things—Lizardling, Underfoot—none of them names, really." She seemed to have a thought. "Call me Catling."

But was having trouble with her accent, with its undertones of crone and birdsong. "Caitlin?" he said uncertainly.

She laughed. "Yes. Call me that. Caitlin." Her hand went to the small stone that hung around her neck. She gave him a sidelong look. "It was quite a blow. Does your head hurt? I can give you something for the pain."

She seemed harmless, but he didn't like the idea of drinking a witch's potion. "I really just want to see my horse," he said.

"The trapdoor's here."

He hoisted himself out onto the moor. Motley neighed a greeting and the Badger passed his hands over the horse's legs with no little relief.

"Hey, you ugly old thing," he murmured under his breath. "Don't get any ideas about this being a holiday, just because you get to dine with a view." He beat the dust and sweat from the horse's coat as best he could, and saw that the tether ropes were secure. Then he stepped down onto the rafter and swung onto the floor of the barrow, cheerfully rubbing his head, which had begun to ache right on schedule.

"I believe the moor agrees with him."

"It will have to. You'll both have to stay until morning. The moor isn't safe at night."

"Then why do you stay?"

"The smith's son and his lot, they think the moor is haunted; it keeps them away. It's the grave robbers and wolves that keep me in."

"How did you come to be belled?"

She paused so long he thought she would not answer. "There was a sickness among the children," she said at last, "and some cows went dry. Nothing very remarkable in that, except it happened all at once. I grew up in the Weirdwood, alone with my guardian. That would have been enough, even if she hadn't dabbled in spells. So they blamed her, and when she died her blame was my inheritance. They were too great cowards to kill me, so they belled me instead, to know when I was coming."

"Why didn't you go seek refuge in the temple?"

She looked at him strangely. "There is no refuge in the Pentacle for the likes of me," she said at last. He thought, not for the first time, of Asaph's words: *Things are different, outside these walls.*

"How did you carry me, anyway?"

"With these." She shook the manacles so the bells rang, smiling bitterly. "I have learned to live with these, even to use them."

"I could take them off."

"Why should you?"

"Well, why should you have helped me?"

"Because I hate the ones who beat you—not because I bear you any love."

"And I bear no love for those who belled you."

Several emotions fought to fix themselves on her features.

"You're not doing this out of kindness?" she said at last.

"No."

At this reassurance, the fierce mask the fire had made of her features fell away. For the first time he realized she was not much older than he was.

"Can you really get them off?"

"I can try. To spite them."

"Yes, to spite them." But when the tools were fetched from the saddlebag, and the manacles and collar fell to the barrow floor, Caitlin rubbed her wrists, tears starting up in her eyes.

"It's so quiet," she said, her voice full of surprise. "I never could muffle them completely."

He watched her make a salve for her neck and wrists. Then Caitlin settled herself among the cushions on the bier.

"Tell me a story. Tell me where you come from, Badger, and then tell me a story with dragons in it. Then we will sleep, and in the morning I will show you off the moor."

∽⌒∾

The rat-catcher was in his rooms, placating his cats with scraps of mackerel after a day spent deratting a brewery and a judge's chambers. The cats swarmed over his legs, joggling for the fish. The rat-catcher chortled and helped himself to a few mackerel, teasing the cats on his lap by dangling the fish near his lips.

"Oh, yes, delicious, my pretties, yes! There, go on; have it. I bought liver sausage for my dinner." He stood, scattering the cats, which yowled and fled to the corners of the room with greasy bits of mackerel.

"Do I have mustard?" mused the rat-catcher aloud, going to the cupboard with a heavy tread. One foot was shorter than the other where a rat bite had festered; he had had to have his heel off. The cupboard held nothing but broken traps and some old cheese suitable for rat bait but not human consumption. His search was interrupted by a knock, and he limped to the door. Through the shutter he could see a clean-shaven cheek and a grey eye.

"What do you want?"

"I want some rats caught."

"Come back tomorrow." The rat-catcher started to close the shutter, but before he could his visitor slid a coin into the gap. It was gold, newly minted, and the rat-catcher felt his palms itch and his mouth water.

"There are more like it," said the stranger, "if I could remember where I put them."

The rat-catcher opened the door, motioning the man in.

The cats came clambering, and the man with grey eyes picked up a particularly noisy one, languidly stroking its fur.

"How ratty are you?" asked the rat-catcher as he put the liver sausage in a pan and looked for a knife with which to pare some potatoes.

"Not very. There are only two, but they are very *large.*"

The rat-catcher looked up sharply and spat with disdain. "I don't do that kind of rat-catching. I have no ambition to put my neck in a noose, thank you very much. If you want your wife and her fancy man sent to hell by the short road, you needn't've come to me. There are cutthroats aplenty in the street, and you wouldn't have interrupted my dinner."

"You mistake me. I don't want them killed. I merely want them displaced. You aren't going to eat that sausage without mustard, are you?"

"Haven't got any," said the rat-catcher ruefully.

A small felt sack appeared on the table, its contents settling pleasantly, coin against coin.

"That will buy a considerable amount of mustard. Watch for me in an hour by the tavern and I will direct you. Enjoy your supper."

∽◦∾

Above on the moor Motley whinnied nervously. A man, his hair glinting like tarnished copper in the moonlight, stepped up to the horse and stretched out a palm full of lump sugar. Faced with such a treat, Motley's wariness deserted him and he nosed eagerly at the sugar offered in the outstretched hand in its black glove. The man stroked the nap of the horse's broad nose, speaking in a lulling tone.

"Nothing to be anxious about; my fine fellow. We're going to be famous friends, very famous friends indeed."

Below in the barrow Caitlin woke and lay crouched on the bier, listening intently with her ears, her bones, her very skin. She heard nothing but the light snore of the Badger asleep in front of the fire. Some coals settled into ash, and overhead on the peat the horse shifted his weight.

Slowly Caitlin relaxed, her cheek reluctantly coming to rest against the cold ancient metal. At length, she closed her eyes, and at greater length she slept.

She did so fitfully, and dreamed. They were uneasy dreams, dreams of being punished by Abagtha, being locked in the smokehouse where Abagtha dried her herbs, being locked in a cellar full of rats.

Caitlin stirred, then woke with a shudder and start. The barrow was full of hundreds of rats, panicked by the thick tar smoke that choked the rooms. Gagging on the foul, stinging air, Caitlin felt along the wall, breaking the backs of rats all the way, and found the Badger. He hadn't woken, though the rats had crawled onto him where he slept, and begun to chew his boots. The smoke, thought Caitlin, and she hauled him to his feet.

The trapdoor was shut and the tunnel was full of smoldering rags soaked in tar. Everywhere the rats scurried in panic, making an awful noise. Caitlin's clothes began to smoke, and there was barely room in the tunnel to put them out. At last, their eyes streaming and throats raw, the two stumbled out into the black, cool, blessed night.

When the fits of coughing had subsided, they saw Motley standing a little apart, a large red handkerchief tied over his eyes.

"Our friends," said the Badger.

"No—they would have stolen the horse, or killed him."

The Badger knelt to pick something from the moor at the horse's feet, turning it in his hands, puzzled.

"What did you find?"

"Some footprints. And—it's odd—a sugar lump."

Caitlin's hands went to the amulet around her neck.

"Badger. You must leave at once."

He heartily agreed. "But you're coming with me."

She didn't argue.

❧

The abbot of Thirdmoon See rose at his usual hour, said his morning prayers, and awaited the arrival of his secretary.

Brother Hare arrived bearing a tray with a razor and a bowl of lather, and the abbot settled into the chair for his morning shave. The monk lathered the abbot's sunken cheeks and began to sharpen the razor. That instrument raised, the monk cleared his throat.

"Your Grace."

"Yes?" said the abbot, careful of the lather.

"The tanner's daughter's son is returned from Moorsedge."

"What happened?"

"We have not yet put any questions to him, your Grace. We thought it best to leave any interview to you. But as far as we can ascertain from his remarks to the hosteler who met him at the gate, the apothecary was unavailable." The monk began to scrape the abbot's beard. When he had reached the abbot's chin he spoke again.

"Your Grace."

"Hmmm?"

"He has brought a young woman with him."

"Dear me. What sort of young woman?"

"A witch."

The abbot was forced to spit lather in a most unseemly manner. "A *what*?"

"A young woman who works magic, scorning the creed of the Pentacle. As I said, your Grace: a witch." The monk rinsed the razor and wiped the traces of lather from around the abbot's ears and throat.

"Send them to me," said the abbot with unaccustomed energy. "Send them to me—but first make sure the woman is free of vermin."

The woman from the dairy and her niece were recruited to wash Caitlin. They came with brushes in many sizes, meant for cattle and carpets, and with strong lye soap and specially blessed pentacles to ward off evil eyes and other spell-spinning. Caitlin was led away, and from the dyehouse where they had readied her bath there could be heard at first shouts and short screams and splashing. Later, voices singing in rounds issued out over the courtyard, followed by laughter and then again screams.

While Caitlin was being readied for her audience with the abbot, the Badger went in search of Asaph. Knocking on the door to the monk's cell, he got no answer; when he knocked harder, the door swung open under his hand. The room had been stripped: the beekeeper's hat was not on its peg. A young monk not much older than the Badger was sitting on a bare cot by the window, reading a missal.

"Sorry . . . I . . . I must have taken a wrong turn. I was looking for Asaph."

The young monk looked at him strangely. "This was his cell. Did you know him?"

"Why, where is he?"

"They took him to the asylum yesterday."

The Badger left the block of monks' cells and wandered to the spice orchard, but he had no heart for stealing oranges. At last he went to his old room above the stables. At first he thought they had given over his room, too, but then the figure sitting on his cot turned, and he saw it was Caitlin. She was very pink, and someone had braided her long hair and dressed her in a robe of bluegreen stuff that couldn't decide whether it wanted to be the color of her right eye or her left. She was holding his recorder in her hands.

"Do you make music on this?"

"Sometimes—to amuse myself."

Her eyes widened a little, then narrowed. Caitlin had never heard of music for amusement, only for charming things. She saw the Badger was troubled.

"What's the matter?"

"Nothing for you to worry about." He had rescued some of Asaph's things from the forge coalbox: a small gilded missal, a manual on beekeeping, the barnyard animals carved from honeycomb Asaph made for village children. The Badger ranged them now on the foot of the cot.

Caitlin picked up a hen and a rooster; she thought of Abagtha, and an old spell to make hens lay. If you said the spell backward as you roasted a brown egg in the fire, the same spell would make hens stop laying. Most spells were like that, Caitlin mused. They could be turned inside-out as easily as a stocking.

"You're worried about someone," she said. "It's all right; it doesn't take a seer to see it in your face."

"I'll tell you about it later. Right now we have to go to the abbot and convince him you're not the devil incarnate."

"Ah." She made a face. "Perhaps I should have picked the robe of virginal white, after all."

The abbot let his gaze take in the curiosity before him. He noted the unsettling eyes, the blistered skin on the neck and wrists, the unholy amulet. After rolling his words around on his tongue like a mouthful of wine he might spit out, the abbot spoke.

"Are you a believer, my daughter?"

"I don't believe you are my father."

"Don't be impudent. You have had no religious instruction, then?"

"On the contrary. I am very well acquainted with your Pentacle. When the Necromancer succeeds in turning lead into gold, all faithful souls will be made pure and incorruptible. Yes—I know your Pentacle, very well." Caitlin had kept her voice low, but the Badger thought that if her hair had not been bound it would have thrown off sparks.

"Hush," said the abbot, stretching out a hand to touch the cat amulet. "You flirt with blasphemy, and I am too old for such nonsense. This is an amulet of the black arts. Are you a witch?"

"I am an herbwoman, and an interpreter of birds. I have been known to converse with cats. I am an otherworld daughter. Would you have me dye one eye to match the other, and take in laundry?"

The abbot pulled at his ear. Then his consternation seemed to lift.

"There are two courses of action open to me. You see, I have the duty of saving your soul from damnation while setting the populace at ease. The simplest way in which I might accomplish this is to have you burned at the stake." The abbot coughed; Caitlin didn't flinch. "But I am willing instead to offer you this option: confinement for the rest of your natural life in either a convent or an asylum. I leave the choice to you. Come to me before lauds tonight and I will hear your answer.

"Now, Matthew. Kneel, and explain yourself."

The Badger knelt. Caitlin arched an eyebrow.

"What is this about you trying to apprentice yourself to a witch?"

"The apothecary was in debtor's prison, your Grace."

"Does that excuse your subsequent behavior? You disappoint me. You will remain here until I decide what to do with you. I shall make inquiries of the muleskinner and the renderer." The abbot extended his hand, and the Badger touched his lips to the large ring of holy office, rose, and jammed his cap over his red ears.

"You may go."

In the courtyard, it seemed to him Caitlin looked at him with mocking eyes. "Are you a badger, Badger, or a mouse?" she murmured.

He turned on her like a dog that has had its tail pulled one too many times. "Mouse!" he shouted, and the word rang in the courtyard. Monks poked their heads out of casements to look quizzically at them as they passed.

"I've worn a collar, too, invisible, perhaps, but no less hard than yours! Only there is no getting mine off. Muleskinner! Boiler of lard! Heaven help me!" He strode off toward the garden without waiting for her.

When she caught up with him he was sitting on the fence at one side of the pumpkin patch, seemingly intent on a busy anthill. Caitlin sat on the fence beside him.

"Then why kiss his ring, if you feel that way about it?" She reached into his shirt and took hold of the pentacle that hung around his neck on a lace. "Or do you really believe third-rate alchemy is going to save your soul?"

"How can I not believe it? I've had it drummed into me day and night since I was six years old."

She let the pendant fall back upon his chest. "You didn't tell me you were a monk," she reproached him. "I thought you were going to be an apothecary."

"It seems I'm to be neither." He lifted his eyes to Caitlin's. "I haven't believed for a long time, if I ever really did. But if the truth is not in this, where is it? I really thought it lay outside these walls. I was a fool."

"Yes, you were, but no more a fool than anyone else."

They went to the kitchen gate, where the Badger spoke to the knifegrinder.

"Yes, I saw them take him away, in the back of a cart. He was raving so, it took three men to hold him down."

"You're sure it was Asaph?"

"Yes—the fat one, the drunkard who kept bees."

The Badger walked away without answering, though he wanted very much to sharpen his knuckles on the knifegrinder's back teeth. Caitlin followed, but not before she had cast a small spell dulling the knifegrinder's whetstone.

4

The Journey Begins

The Badger took Caitlin back to the stables to outfit her
for the journey. In her haste she had taken nothing from
the barrow, if there had been anything fit to snatch from
the smoke and rats. While the Badger searched for a pair
of boots to fit her, Caitlin picked up Asaph's missal.

"This book. It was your friend's?"

"Yes. Why?"

"Well, it's pigskin."

He looked up; half the time she seemed to read his
thoughts, the other half she acted like a simpleton. "That
it is."

"But it has gilt edges. You gild vellum, not pigskin. It's
as though someone made a jeweled waistcoat for a pig."

He took the missal from her hands. "He must have
added the gilt himself for some reason."

"I don't think so."

"Why not?"

"The gilt is poisoned."

The Badger dropped the prayerbook. "What!"

"Some belladonna or foxglove, maybe a little mistletoe."

"How can you tell?"

Caitlin pointed to a corner of the book where the

pigskin bore the marks of tiny teeth, then to a dead mouse on the floor by the foot of the cot.

The Badger shook his head. "But poison! He's supposed to be mad, not dead."

"It probably wasn't meant to kill him. Most likely he kept it in his pocket, and ran his hand along the spine when he was thinking. Just a little of the poison through the skin and his brain would begin to get foggy. After a while he would be the picture of a madman."

"But he was fine the last time I saw him."

"Perhaps someone decided not to wait for the poison to do its work."

The Badger stared at the prayerbook. What was he to believe, that there had been a plot to drive Asaph mad? It crossed his mind that she might be playing a game with him, for reasons of her own.

"Enough of this. The abbot's waiting."

The abbot was ready for his midday nap. He was wearing a nightcap, and Brother Hare stood ready, holding a small glass of herb cordial. The abbot looked balefully at Caitlin.

"Well, which shall it be? Convent or asylum?"

"Convent."

"Very well. You shall start today for the convent at Ninthstile." The abbot reached for the glass and took a sip of cordial. "It is a great distance, some months' journey, and I would not have you travel it alone. Matthew here will go with you."

The Badger was dumbstruck. "But the muleskinner . . ."

"This suits my purposes. Do you question my judgment?"

"Of course not, your Grace."

"You ought to have a chaperone, but I can spare no one to go with you."

"Not a eunuch to spare?" Caitlin said under her breath.

"Confound you, go as you please, so long as you go," said the abbot, whose hearing was acute despite his advanced years. "But mark me: I will not tolerate witches. I shall send word to the sisters at Ninthstile to look for you in the new year. If you have not arrived by then, I shall have the sergeant set a price on both your heads. If either of you fails to arrive in Ninthstile by the appointed day, the other shall die. You will be sent to the muleskinner, and not to be apprenticed. Now go."

While Caitlin chose a horse from the stable, the Badger had only to add a few things to his bundle: his recorder, which he had forgotten, and some marbles that had been the only thing in his pockets the day he first came to the abbey. Hesitating, he added Asaph's missal to his bundle. The monk's pentacle he hung from the rafter over the cot, then took the star from around his neck and hung it from the same nail.

Caitlin returned leading the grey mare, Maud. They saddled the horses and the Badger left the Abbey of Thirdmoon See for the second and, as it turned out, the last time.

∽∾

The messenger squinted through the eyepiece of his spyglass, trained on the dimple in the wood where Caitlin and the Badger had stopped for the night.

"Elric," he said, without turning to the red-haired man behind him, "are you sure she is the one?"

"I should hope to heaven she is, or I'll have seriously misspent the better part of twenty years. But look at those eyes, man. Look at those cockatrice, those seer's, those otherworld eyes!"

The messenger shut the spyglass and joined Elric by the fire. "She is striking," he said thoughtfully. "But I wouldn't exactly call her beautiful."

"No, but something about her would make a man forswear beauty."

"Just don't fall under her spell, or I'll have to report you to the High Council."

"Under her spell? My dear fellow." Elric knocked the ashes from his pipe into the fire. "I haven't forgotten what I was sent to do."

"Are you sure you can take care of them?"

"If you mean, can I carry out my orders, yes. But I'm

not sure I like this line of questioning. Stop it, will you, and hand over that tobacco."

The messenger tossed him a pouch. Elric caught it neatly and refilled his pipe. It was a blend of his own invention, smelling when lit of wet earth and dead leaves, so he could indulge his habit without giving himself away. His pipe lit, he walked to the rim of the hollow and gazed down on the pair below.

◦◦◦

As soon as they crossed into the woods the Badger had been seized with powerful misgivings. A few days ago he had been eating stolen oranges and arguing with Asaph. Suddenly all that, the whole tired and tiresome but familiar world of Thirdmoon had vanished, and there stretched in front of him only this dark wood. What in the name of sweet heaven was he doing, anyway, with this half-witch on the way to Ninthstile? Ninthstile, a convent so remote that it would take them half the winter to reach it. It was madness. If they lost time, if they were delayed in reaching the straits at Little Rim, they would be forced to wait until spring to cross, and by then every bounty hunter in thirteen kingdoms would be looking for them. And Asaph, poisoned and vanished? It was too much.

And then there was Caitlin. The first night in the wood the Badger had bolted upright to a bloodcurdling scream and found himself across the fire at her side, shaking her awake.

"You were having a nightmare." He spoke calmly, but the hairs on the back of his neck were standing up straight.

Her face was white as death, the hair against her brow damp with sweat. She turned away and drew the blanket to her chin. "Go back to sleep."

He hesitated. "What did you dream?"

She was already asleep or feigning it. Either way, she didn't answer.

This was not the Weirdwood, so there was no need to fear the Direwolves, but there might very well be deserters or robbers, so they rode as swiftly as they could without leaving the path. The Badger looked over his shoulder.

He could have sworn he saw something move behind them, off to the right. They came to a stream and paused to fill the waterskins.

"I don't mean to alarm you," he said, "but we're being followed."

"I know. He's been back there since early yesterday." Squatting in the middle of the stream Caitlin was washing with neat, catlike movements.

"I don't suppose you thought to tell me!"

Her eyes widened. "Why, what could you have done?"

"You should have told me, that's all," he said lamely.

They rode on in silence.

In the shadows, Elric was having a rest, leaning on the hunter's bow that came up to his shoulder. He was wishing for ointment; his last stint, masquerading as a jester at court, had made him soft. It was going to be hell keeping the two of them in sight. He was on foot now.

Elric was annoyed, and a little worried. He was sure of the girl, but he had his doubts about the boy. It was a nuisance and no little danger, but when the time came he would have to act. If someone got hurt who wasn't meant to, well, there was no helping it.

It happened the woods in question belonged to Milo, known to his subjects as the Boy King, though he was a strapping man of thirty-three. Milo was riding through his woods with a small hunting party of two hundred, consisting of his old nurse, his consulting astronomer, fifty courtiers, several dozen servants assigned to lunch detail, some sixty hunters and bodyguards, and a yammering pack of dogs that led the way through the dense thickets.

They were going to kill the first creature they saw, whether furred or feathered, great or small. It didn't matter what kind of animal, Milo insisted.

"You see, it says: 'Kill ye the first beast ye shall find, and cook it with the heart of a fox, and ye shall understand the voices of the birds and beasts.' "

"Nonsense," said Nurse, who was riding alongside.

"Oh, no," said the astronomer, "this has very recently been proven to be so."

Milo was reading aloud in the saddle from a small, illuminated book of wonders, so that two grooms had to ride at either side of their king, poised to seize the reins if his majesty's horse should suddenly try to unseat his rider and bolt through the trees.

"It's nonsense, nevertheless," Nurse proclaimed in her rich baritone. The astronomer was about to protest that he himself had witnessed such a case, but Nurse cut him off with a belch.

They had the fox already. All the roads in Milo's realm were in disrepair, the money for mending them having been spent on expeditions to capture ever more exotic creatures for his menagerie, the largest in thirteen kingdoms. Milo yawned. He hoped they would find something soon. Once he had gained the speech of animals he wanted to test it on the tame carp in the palace fountain.

The king's First Huntsman swore as he rode ahead with the hounds. He could hear old King Max turning in his grave. It was a good thing the old monarch had died when he had. And they had all thought the prince would outgrow this monstrous foolishness! They would have to turn back in an hour or two, and they hadn't seen a thing.

Apart from the king's party, and from the pair traveling to Ninthstile, the woods held a small party of the king's guards, looking for poachers. These were bad times in Milo's kingdom, and no game was safe. It happened that there was only one poacher in the woods just then, an old rascal by the name of Purley, and he had concealed himself for the afternoon inside a hollow tree. The woods were crawling today; he hadn't seen it this bad since Prince Milo, aged six, had gotten lost hunting dragon's nests. The only thing for it was to stay put and have a nap. When all these busybodies had gone home he would come out and tend to his lines.

The patrol consisted of five guards, each of whom had been hoping to be assigned to hunt duty. That was easy work and a good day's outing, with better meat and drink than they got at home on feast days. As it was, they had only been given brown bread, red and white cheese, and beer—"not even a little hot wine!" they grumbled—and they were all in a nasty temper. Heaven help any poacher they caught.

❧

Old King Max had loved to hunt. These woods had once been his deer park, before his son's indifference had condemned them to rack and ruin. They were thick with deer, but the king and his party were making such a racket that every living thing for miles gave them a wide berth.

Caitlin and the Badger were making far less noise, and now and then as they rode they would spy a hind drinking.

"We're coming to the edge of the forest," Caitlin said. They had not stopped to rest all that day, for they were still being followed.

The Badger reined in Motley beside her. "If we do a little hard riding, we might reach a town before dark."

Just then a huge stag crashed through the thicket, hurtling across the path. In midair it shuddered and gave a groan awful to hear, and fell thundering to the ground, making the horses rear in terror.

Swearing, the Badger tried to calm his horse. Motley was skipping and snorting at the smell of fresh blood. The shaft of an arrow emerged from the stag's side.

Elric stepped from the underbrush, fitting another arrow to his bow. He had tied a kerchief about his face, but he thought he saw Caitlin put a hand to her amulet.

"Oblige me, madam, and climb that tree. Yes, that one. Come, come, you can do better than that."

"What in the name of—" said the Badger.

But the hunter stepped up, putting a finger to his lips. "Hush!" he said, pressing the bow into the Badger's hands. "You oughtn't to be hunting here, my friend. These are the king's woods." With that, he flung the quiver at the Badger's feet and vanished.

As if on cue, the patrol galloped through the gap in the trees. The point of a sword pressed lightly into the base of the Badger's throat.

"You're under arrest in the name of the king."

In the tree Caitlin crouched very still, watching the Badger being trussed like a piece of game. She was helpless.

If she revealed herself, they would both be lost. Caitlin saw the Badger's face strained with the effort of not looking in her direction. She was afraid the pounding of her heart would give her away.

"Two horses," said one of the guards. He gave the Badger a kick. "Where's your friend, eh?"

Getting no reply, he aimed the next kick at the Badger's head. Then they led him away, with the horses in tow.

"Come on," said their leader as they rode off, "I think he went this way."

Elric escaped. One minute the guards had him in sight, the next he was gone. He was still smiling over his marksmanship when he neared the edge of the forest and saw the town road stretching out before him. Carelessly, he took a step forward. A poacher's snare closed tight around his foot, the sprung trap hauling him up by one leg to dangle in the treetops.

The dogs had found Caitlin. They sat beneath the tree, panting and howling by turns. Coming up to them the First Huntsman gazed up into the branches and began to laugh.

"Well, sweetheart," he called up to her, "I hope you fancy fox for dinner!"

Caitlin was too weary to answer. Let them climb up and get me, she thought.

The rest of the hunting party rode up and reined in their mounts. Necks were craned, eyes shaded as everyone looked up into the treetops.

"A princess!" crowed Milo in delight.

And a princess Caitlin became, despite the best arguments put forth by Nurse, the astronomer, and the First Huntsman. Milo ordered Caitlin retrieved from her perch and placed before him on his horse. "Or is it behind?" he fretted aloud. One of his books had a picture of such a scene, if only he could remember it. "She is a mute princess," he explained to Nurse. "All her brothers have been changed to ravens by a wicked stepqueen, and to free them she must keep a vow of silence for seven years. Let me see: we will have to devise a system of hand signals." Milo loved this sort of puzzle.

"She needs a bath," said Nurse.

Caitlin held her tongue. The First Huntsman helped her into the saddle, muttering under his breath, "Ah, you can talk as well as I can!"

And so the three of them arrived in Milo's kingdom in three very different styles. The Badger entered slung across the back of a horse and was promptly thrown into Milo's dungeon. Caitlin entered like royalty and was immediately submerged in a hot bath, on strict orders from Nurse. And Elric was cut down past midnight by Purley the poacher, who revived him with rum and helped him into town on foot.

5

THE MAGPIE KING

The richest men in Milo's kingdom were the money-lender, the hangman, and the rat-catcher. The capital was sooty, full of dark, sour smells, and the streets rang with an unceasing din. It was hard to tell the houses from the taverns; they alike stank of beer, with arguments spilling out into the streets. In Milo's kingdom, the man next to you would as soon slit your throat for a piece of bread as a piece of gold. On every street corner there were fist-fights, and people took their children to see the public hangings, since there were no puppet shows.

Caitlin saw none of this. Certain peasants were paid an allowance to keep up a rustic touch along the king's road: Children hurried home from their shifts at the glue works; their mothers smeared their faces with rouge to give them a healthy pink. Then the whole family would drag father out of bed so that he could be leading the cow on a rope and smoking a pipe when the king rode by. It was this picture Caitlin saw.

Now she lay floating in the second proper bath of her life. The water had issued from an unseen source, steaming and perfumed. Caitlin lay back in the water and thought.

45

She wondered where they had taken the Badger, and whether they hanged poachers in this kingdom.

She wondered, too, about the man who had shot the deer. She had an uneasy feeling that she had seen him before. In the Weirdwood? Moorsedge? She stared through the vapor at the bathwater, willing the scene to take shape in the colored swirls of oil.

Nurse entered, hefting a huge pile of towels. A string of handmaidens followed, bearing an assortment of gowns and shoes, and caskets of jewels.

"Wash your neck, and then out of the water with you! So you can't speak, is that your story? We'll see about that. You, dry her off, and you, put that gown on her. We'll see how she looks in blue."

After she was dressed, Caitlin was led to a banqueting hall. It was an indoor garden, with a hundred evergreens lit with uncountable tapers. Cages of songbirds were suspended from the ceiling, which was painted with clouds; on fair evenings the dome opened an oval eye on the stars. Tame deer wandered among the diners, begging for tobacco, and a bear in a lace ruff capered clumsily to a piper's tune.

If the courtiers were disconcerted by Caitlin's eyes, they hid it well. Everyone was intent on Milo, who had cocked an ear to a nightingale in a cage. On the king's plate was what Caitlin supposed was the unfortunate fox's heart, and a poached egg; the first animal they had seen had been a hen, but the owner had refused to part with it, finally taking a sovereign for one of the bird's eggs.

Milo shook his head. "Nothing—nothing—it's really very disappointing. Perhaps it has to settle in the stomach. I will try again in the morning."

If there had been no need to keep mute, Caitlin could have told the king what the bird was singing. It was one of the first songs Abagtha had taught her: *My love has flown to the moon, the moon, and there is no consoling me.*

Milo spied Caitlin and stood, beaming.

"Princess!" A place had been set for her beside the king, and as she slipped into it Caitlin wondered what was expected of mute princesses whose brothers had been turned into ravens.

Kissing his hand seemed a good beginning, and she surprised herself by summoning up a few tears. The whole court was touched, no one more than the young king himself. He could hardly eat his soup. Between the courses they played Twenty Questions until he had pieced together the whole of her tragic story.

Her name, Caitlin pantomimed, was Emeralda (here she pointed to Milo's ring). For his benefit she relived her arduous journey over the terrain of her plate, through forests of asparagus, treacherous custard seas, baked plains of beef. Pity welled up in Milo's heart.

The astronomer and Nurse traded dire looks. There was no mistaking it: The king was smitten.

∽∽

The Badger breathed in the smell of filthy straw and tasted the foul mattress beneath him. He closed his mouth and tried to swallow, but his throat was too dry. Every bone in his body ached, and his eyes burned. This was not his room in the abbey, or the barrow on the moor. It stank, it was small, and he was not alone in it.

The Badger sat up, clutching his pounding head. He blinked, trying to train his eyes on the three uncertain figures across the tiny room.

The first face he sorted from the gloom was pale, topped with a shock of grey hair, although the face was not particularly old. The eyes were pale, too, made even less substantial by the thick lenses secured with wire and string. The second face he could make out was young, its handsome features fixed in a scowl. It was unpleasant to hold the dark gaze beneath their thunderclap brows. The Badger released it and turned to the third face. This one was very old, a mass of wrinkles that all but hid the eyes. It was hairless and toothless; a set of false teeth hung around the old man's neck on a cord. The Badger looked from one to the other to the third again. His head was killing him.

"Hello," said the first.

The second nodded grudgingly.

The third put in his teeth, as if that would help him see better.

"I'm Fowk," said the first, handing the Badger a pitcher of water. It was warm and unpleasantly fusty, but it was water. The Badger drank, washed his face, and thanked him.

"You can call me Badger."

"This is Ulick—don't kick me! Why shouldn't I tell him your name?—and this here is Old Dice. How did you manage to get thrown into our good company?"

The Badger felt the back of his head, wincing. "Poaching." To his surprise he saw Ulick's face light up into a pleasant smile.

"Good for you! We'll get on, you and I."

"Ulick here helped himself to one of the king's peacocks and was fool enough to put the feathers in his cap," said Fowk. He himself, he explained, was a lockpick. "I'd have us out in the blink of an eye, too, if it wasn't for those bolts." The iron bars in the door and window were thick as a man's arm.

Old Dice took out his teeth again. "Pleased to meet you. Pleased indeed. I myself am a purveyor of antiquities. Relics. A victim of circumstances, I assure you—I lacked a license—most unfortunate oversight. I expect to be released shortly."

But when the Badger asked how long he had been there, Old Dice fell silent. Fowk took the Badger aside.

"Best not to take that tack with him. He's been here fourteen years."

⌯⌯

It was a fine morning and Milo took Emeralda on a tour of his menagerie, the best in thirteen kingdoms. There were creatures Caitlin had only seen in Abagtha's books: lizards the size of a large dog, goats with great twisted horns, horses banded black and white, a creature part duck, part mole. There was a golden bear that could fit inside a teacup, and a white bear that was twice as tall at the tallest man. There was a bull with heavy armor and a horn on the end of its nose. They passed a pool of great tusked sea-boars and came to a golden pavilion. Milo took a key from his ring.

"These are the rarest animals of all," he said. "Wise men thought they were creatures of fancy. But I have a mermaid," he whispered, "and a unicorn."

And, after a fashion, he did. Caitlin had to admit they were marvelous fakes. The unicorn was some sort of exotic deer. You could see where the other antler had been sawn off, and the fur bleached and horn gilded. Now the dark roots had begun to grow in, and the gilt was chipping off. But to Milo it was a creature of legend.

The mermaid, too, was no mermaid, nor was it any creature Caitlin had ever seen. It was whiskered like a pig with the fins of a turtle and the tail of a fish. It had no golden scales, no gossamer hair to comb, and it seemed doubtful that its song, if it had one, could have lured sailors onto the rocks. It seemed sickly, pining for its own kind. Caitlin was glad when the pavilion was locked again behind them.

"My menagerie is famed throughout Pentacledom," Milo said proudly, linking his arm in Caitlin's. "I send expeditions to the ends of the earth, even in the waste of winter, to find every shape of beast, and dig them out of their dens when they are at their meekest. I spare no expense. And charlatans try to sell me fakes. Why, only last week a man came to court with what he claimed was a gryphon. He said it had died on the long journey from its eyrie, but you could plainly see it was half a housecat, sewn to a crow."

They came to an unused summerhouse, with spacious porches and a grove of fruit trees that in the spring scented the air. Milo led Caitlin through the suite of rooms.

The king showed her how to fill a silver cup with water by turning a handle in the wall. He sat on the wide bed to show her how soft it was, and opened the cupboards to display the rich clothes that hung there. He seized a little bell from a table and rang it. Three handmaidens appeared silently in the doorway. He waved them away again.

"Just ring that, and they will bring you anything you want. I know you must be eager to begin your task, and free your brothers all the sooner." A boy appeared with a large basket of flowers, which he emptied on the floor. A second boy appeared and did the same. Milo handed Caitlin a little box.

"I thought twelve reels of silk thread to start. If you need more, you must tell me. And there are steel needles, as well as silver. I didn't know which you would need."

Caitlin looked at all the flowers, overwhelmed.

Milo had taken off his crown and was turning it in his hands. "Well! I'll leave you now. I know you have a lot to do."

Caitlin sat still for a long moment after he left her. Then she threaded a needle and began to string blossoms into a chain. She was reaching for the sixth flower when she fell back onto the bed laughing. This would have surprised Milo enormously, for everyone knows that to free a prince from enchantment, a princess may not speak or laugh for seven years, all the while sewing a shirt of aster flowers. But then, Abagtha had never kept books of fairy tales around, so Caitlin could not really be faulted.

❦

"Every penny in this blasted kingdom goes to buy freaks and monsters for the king's amusement. Children starve, women go in rags, men die of nosebleed for want of a surgeon! I say, to save the body, we must remove the festering limb."

As he watched Ulick pause and tear a great mouthful of bread from the common loaf, the Badger thought that a king was usually the head of the body, and decapitation probably wouldn't bode well for the health of the kingdom. Ulick washed the bread down with water. It was that day's ration, and as a result was a little cooler, less musty than the day before. The Badger watched Ulick drink; when it came his turn he hoped there would be some left.

Fowk was digging a tunnel. The outer wall of the cell tapered; higher up, at the small grated window, it was a foot thick; at the bottom, near the floor, it was three times that. All Fowk had for a shovel was a bent spoon, which he was using to scrape the unyielding earth away little by little from underneath the wall. The dirt then had to be hidden: pushed out the grate, stuffed in the mattresses, or, if the guard was coming, swallowed. Fowk had been in Milo's prison for nine months. It had taken him six months to make the tiny coach and horses, sized for fleas, from the hairs of his own head; these had been traded to the urchins through the grate for a spoon. He had been hard at work for the last three months, and now the tunnel was nearly finished. This put Fowk in high spirits, and he whistled softly as he worked. This habit had contributed to his arrest in the first place.

Old Dice was arranging the relics in their tray; each time the guards confiscated the petrified tears in an ivory vial and all Dice's other curiosities, the urchins outside the prison grate would retrieve them from the gutter and pass them through the bars. It was a good collection, and there had been a time, not so very long ago, when the Badger would have exhibited keen interest in it. But he was uneasy. He had been wondering, ever since his head had cleared, what had happened to Caitlin. Those eyes were going to get her in trouble wherever she went.

"This," said Old Dice, "is the head of a talking turtle that once belonged to the oracles of Chameol."

"Shut up, old man," said Ulick. "Chameol doesn't even exist!"

Dice bristled. "The king sends an expedition there annually, sir. Six ships every year."

"And none of them has ever come back. There isn't a soul in the whole kingdom who hasn't lost a father or a brother or been taxed to starvation to outfit those ships. It's criminal."

"You two," said Fowk, "stop it, or you'll bring the guard, and we'll never get out."

"This," Dice went on, "is a beetle in amber that used to belong to a sorceress in the spice mountains."

Ulick started to say something, but caught Fowk's eye, and thought better of it. He moved to the grate and stared out, muttering.

"And this—this is the most precious of all," the old man

said. "A lock of hair from the last woman of full elvish blood. I think you'll agree it's in a state of remarkable preservation."

The Badger handed it back, trying to mask his disgust. If it was elvish hair, then elves smelled very much like goats.

"It's very remarkable, but I haven't any money on me at the moment."

This pacified the relic-seller, and the Badger was at last able to drink from the jug, passing it to Fowk.

The lockpick paused only long enough to take a swallow. "Can't stop now," he muttered. The earth was as hard as stone and yielded slowly, slowly to the scrape of the spoon.

"Why don't you get Nix to bring you a pick?" the Badger asked. Nix was a tiny boy, one of the countless urchins who swarmed the streets of the city. He made daily visits to the grate, which opened on a dingy alley.

Fowk shook his head. "Then we'd have to make our way through the rest of the dungeons. Besides, I'm none too sure Nix would understand. He's a little touched."

The Badger had to agree. Nix was exceedingly small, a wisp of a thing, paler in every respect even than Fowk, with hair light as milkweed down and the barest flush to his skin to show he was alive. He came to the cell every day, pressing his face to the grate, chanting singsong nonsense, and passing little gifts though the cracks, treasures culled from tavern sweepings: snuff, apple peelings, corks that still tasted of wine.

Ulick launched into another speech on the rule of King Max's only son. The Badger took out his missal and opened it.

He had taken to wearing it in his shirt, out of some sentiment for Asaph, he supposed. He was surprised the guards hadn't taken it, but perhaps it had gone unnoticed. Asaph's missal fit easily into the palm of the hand. They probably had taken his money and been satisfied with that. The Badger, in his boredom, had read the prayerbook through twice, a feat he had never accomplished in all his years at the Abbey of Thirdmoon See. He opened the missal again, quailing at the prospect of a third reading, and only riffled the pages idly. And that careless action revealed something a thousand more careful readings would never have uncovered. On the fore-edge of the pages, where the gilt was, there was something written, something only revealed when the pages were spread slightly beneath the thumb. The Badger carefully held the missal up to the light at the grate, fanning the gilt edges out carefully. The ghostly writing reappeared.

> *It unlocks no doors,*
> *Empties all prisons,*
> *Unbolts no shutters,*
> *Yet clears all visions,*
> *It turns no lock,*
> *But topples all towers,*
> *The SPELLKEY unlocks the lock of Hours.*

∽

"I'll give you my necklace, if you'll trade with me."

"I wouldn't trade with you for a mountain of rubies and the best-looking husband in the world."

"Today she broke everything in her room and wouldn't eat until we brought her raw meat. If you had seen her! She cracked the bones and sucked out the marrow. I'm afraid to go into the room—"

By now Caitlin was wide awake, but the handmaidens had moved out of earshot. Apparently she was not the only enchanted princess quartered in Milo's summerhouse.

The next morning Caitlin saw the meat-eater. Breakfast had brought poached eggs, Milo, and Nurse.

"Nurse has come to help you with your sewing," Milo announced cheerfully. Since the failure of the fox heart the king was distrustful of eggs and called for popovers.

One of the handmaidens hurried up and whispered anxiously in Nurse's ear. Nurse frowned, folded her napkin, and heaved her great bulk out of her chair. She padded away after the servant, and Milo and Caitlin shortly heard a crash, followed by a shriek. Nurse reappeared, looking grim. All she said was "Milo." Before he could get up, a creature dashed out onto the porch.

It was a young girl of uncertain age—she could not have been more than twelve—with matted hair and a brown complexion much marred by scratches and bruises. She moved about very quickly on all fours like a dog, which she in all respects resembled. Her teeth were bared and she snarled and whimpered, resisting all attempts by the gathered household to subdue her. Caitlin suddenly reached down and placed her breakfast on the flagstones. The creature snuffled the air, spied the dish, and thrust her face into it, devouring the eggs with a snap or two of her jaws. After that the gardeners managed to chase her back into her quarters with rakes and hoes.

The handmaidens vanished. Nurse sat and drained a cup of hot wine. Milo pushed his plate away and began to play with the salt cellar.

In the commotion Caitlin had nearly forgotten her oath of silence. Now she tugged on Milo's sleeve imploringly, making a question of her eyebrows and hands. He sighed and spoke.

"You see under what a bitter enchantment she suffers. We found her as we found you, during a hunt. Some sorcerer had worked a spell on her, so that she believed herself to be a wild creature. The dogs traced a wolf to its den, and when the hunters went in after it, they found this child living among the brood as one of them."

Caitlin was weeping, her tears falling unchecked to the tablecloth. She made no attempt to wipe her eyes. She was thinking of Abagtha. However terribly the old woman had treated her toward the end, it was thanks to her that Caitlin had not met a similar fate. Her tears were not wept out of sentiment. Rather, they were wept out of fear of what might have been.

Milo saw them solely as the mark of a sweet and gentle soul. He took her hands in his. Nurse watched him lose his heart and called for another cup of wine.

❧

Even Ulick was asleep. He had been quiet all evening, since Nix had brought him a message scrawled on a wrapper. Fowk and Dice had seized happily on the slivers of fresh pear the boy handed through the grate. Now they, too, were asleep.

But the Badger couldn't close his eyes. He was thinking about the mysterious message concealed in Asaph's missal. Whatever the secret to the riddle was, it must be something valuable. For it, a man had been driven mad or, as he feared more and more, murdered.

He kept thinking about the sugar they had found outside the barrow on the night of the fire. The horse had not so much as whinnied the whole time the culprit had been setting the trap: lighting the rags, sealing the trapdoor. Through it all Motley, the horse he would trust with his life above any man, had not made a sound. It made the Badger wonder if, given a chance, he might have found some sugar in the stables, where the missal had been left in the woodbox. Or if the hunter-bandit's pockets held any sugar lumps. Had the same person poisoned Asaph, set fire to the barrow, and set him up as a poacher? The Badger feared that prison was making him a little mad. He also feared his crazy imaginings might be true. But it seemed the answer lay in the riddle in the missal.

He got up and went over to the pallet where Fowk lay sleeping.

"Fowk." He shook him gently. "Fowk. What's a Spellkey?"

Fowk opened his eyes and yawned, not seeming to find this middle-of-the-night conversation at all unusual.

"Not sure. I've heard of them, but I don't know anyone who's ever seen one. Legend has it they were forged long ago in a lake of fire in one of the lost kingdoms before Chameol, even—"

Ulick grunted in his sleep and rolled over.

"—and that anyone who possesses one can open any lock, any chest, any prison. You see how it is."

"Yes." The Badger sat back on his heels and thought about that. Then he seemed to come to himself again, and blinked. "Good-night!" he whispered, and went back to his own pallet.

Dice was awake. His eyes glittered in the dark. It could

have been glee, or it might have been greed. There was no telling. His hands toyed with his teeth on their cord for a long time before he slept.

◇◆◇

Nix ran through the palace grounds. In his hand he clutched two marbles, one green and one blue.

They were his prize possessions. He had owned them for ten minutes now. The man had given them to him through the grate. "Find her," he had said.

The little boy halted, clutching the edge of a stone wall. The flagstones were nice and cool beneath his feet. He would find her and give the marbles to her. Then maybe she would give him a nice drink with ice in it. At the tavern, he had seen rich people put ice in good things to drink. Or she would give him cake, and a kiss.

But he would find her.

The astronomer, who was the king's old tutor, was in his laboratory mixing up a love-powder.

"Though I can't fathom why," said Nurse. "I should think that was the last thing we needed. He means to marry her! Then where will we be?"

The astronomer slowly ground earthworms in a mortar. "But what can we do, my pet? He may be simple, but once he is set on something he cannot be swayed. He resembles his father in that."

"You can explain it, then, when the Adept Royal comes, and wants to know why Milo is still on the throne, and a prince in swaddling clothes, waiting to succeed him!"

At the mention of the Adept Royal, the astronomer went a little pale.

Nurse had gone to the window, where she could see to the summerhouse where Emeralda was quartered. The wolf-girl was on the lawn, testing her chain and eyeing one of the palace swans. Nurse mused on swaddling clothes, and all the accidents infants could fall prey to. But it seemed to her there was a simpler way out of their difficulty. With the right injuries, the death of one enchanted princess could be blamed on the other.

* * *

The mermaid had died, and Milo was sunk in despair. He hung around the summerhouse, refusing to attend to court functions, sitting instead at the foot of a tree, clutching a locket that held one of the mermaid's whiskers.

Caitlin had finished one of the shirts. One sleeve was longer than the other, and surely no head would fit through the opening she had left at the neck, but it was done. Caitlin took it to where Milo sat brooding under a pear tree. He looked at it, smiled wanly, and drew her down on the lawn beside him.

"Oh, Emeralda! All I wanted was to learn the speech of the animals, to learn a little of the ways of magic. My father had no use for it. To him, what was invisible was of no use here on earth, unless it was the breath in your lungs."

Caitlin stroked the flowers in the little shirt. They were faded with longing for the branch, but still gave off a heady scent.

"I dined on the heart of the fox," Milo said, "but the barking of the dog mocks me still. They say it is a marvelous thing, the speech of animals. They say it can be passed on by a kiss."

And, against her better judgment and instinct and all her long history with the ways of men, Caitlin kissed the king. It seemed to improve his mood substantially.

When Nix found Caitlin later that day, the handmaidens were measuring her for a dress, and Caitlin was growing suspicious.

"He told me to give these to you," whispered the boy.

Caitlin took the marbles in surprise. Then she let him take her hand and lead her away.

"Badger!"

Her voice brought him to the grate.

"Where in the name of sweet heaven have you been?"

"At the king's palace. I can't stay. Are you all right? What are they going to do with you?"

"Let me rot, I suppose. Look, can't you charm the lock, or something?"

"Not unless you have the legbone of a roan mare on

you. But I can manage it eventually, if you'll keep. And there's something else. I think the king means to marry me."

"Well, let him. The abbot can't confine you in a convent if you're married to one of the High Thirteen, can he?"

"Then who will get you out, goose?"

"Do that first. Oh Cait—what's a Spellkey?" He told her about the missal.

She shook her head. "I don't know. But the king has a library. I'll see what I can find."

"Hurry. I've been thinking about things, and the more I think the less I like all this. Get me out soon?"

"As soon as I can."

Nix lived in a barrel outside a tavern in the heart of the town. He was napping when he overheard the men. They had set down their tankards on the barrel-head, and Nix could hear them clearly.

"During the harvest festival, we'll do it."

"How?"

"The wicker king. We'll fill it with our men, and when the king steps out to put a torch to it, we'll have our chance."

The men went away. Nix knew them. The first had given him a note for Ulick. Nix was climbing out of the barrel when a man came up to him. He was tall and thin and had red hair. He put his hand on the boy's shoulder.

"I'm looking for a girl. One blue eye, one green. Dark hair to here. And a youth, not tall but not short. Fair. Do you know where they are?"

Nix nodded.

"Take me to them."

But Nix ran away.

Caitlin was asleep in the garden. She was having a dream, and as she dreamed her fingers ripped out the stitches in the shirt of flowers in her lap.

She dreamed of a magpie that had a tree all to itself. It gathered in its nest brilliant objects, silver combs plucked from behind the ears of grand ladies, coins snatched from fountains, snuffboxes stolen from window-sills. But it gathered no food, and grew weak. Soon it was too weak to fly, and the other magpies drove it from the tree, and tore it apart.

Caitlin sat up, a cry in her throat. Nix was sitting beside her in the grass. In his hands he held a little man woven out of willow branches.

"Hello," she said softly. "What have you got there?"

"A wicker man."

Caitlin went to the palace and found what had been the old king's library. Among a great many books on the hunt, and the building of waterways, she found a book on magic.

She ran her finger down the columns. *Sneezing . . . soot-fall . . . soul cake . . . speedwell . . .* "Ah, here it is."

But the facing page, with the rest of the entry, had been torn out, and the next page, and the next.

6

A WICKER MAN

It was damp and dark in the bottom of the barrel where Nix crouched, nibbling the crusts, cast on the floor by a wealthy woman breaking her journey at the tavern.

It was harvest time in the countryside, but in the town it was merely an excuse to drink to excess. There was little enough of a harvest to celebrate. The best of the crops went to the king's table, and the rest was sold to merchants who would find eager buyers across the sea.

So it was that most of the wheat in Milo's kingdom was milled not into bread but cakes, cakes that would never fill the stomachs of urchins like Nix. But he ate his second-hand crusts and was glad to have them. Tomorrow he could warm himself at the bonfire. And the giants would be there.

They were built of wickerwork, taller than the belltower of the temple, moving through the streets as if they had will and life of their own. Nix knew there were men inside them, working the ropes that made the giants move. But knowing the secret of the giants didn't stop Nix from shrieking at them as loud as the next boy. They were a sight to see, moving down the streets, through the wild holiday crowd to the bonfire that flared in the distance.

Thinking about it made Nix shiver again. That, and the two men talking: "During the harvest festival, we'll do it."

The crusts were gone. Nix felt for the little willow man, clutching it while he waited for it to grow as dark outside as it was in the barrel, for the workmen to leave the giants and go home to bed. Then Nix knew what he would do.

∽∾

Whether it was because of the cat amulet, or because of her eyes, or because her heart was full of confusion, it seemed that magic plied the needle, and not Caitlin's clumsy fingers. The seven shirts of aster flowers were almost finished. Only the right sleeve on the last remained undone. The task had taken eleven days.

The handmaidens had almost completed the gown. All it lacked was its buttonholes, and the left sleeve. There were seven veils, fashioned of sheerest net, light as cobweb. Everything was nearly ready. Still, Milo put off asking her.

He had tried many times. Breathlessly, he watched her walk through the grove near the summerhouse or bend her head over a book in the library. And each time he opened his mouth it was as if he were mute instead of she.

Caitlin wondered if you could refuse a king's offer of marriage. How easy it would be to stay, she thought, a little surprised. It was not that she fancied the rich life at court. It was just that Milo's fashionable and devoted cortiers viewed nothing about Caitlin as extraordinary. Not once had anyone stared or made the sign of the Pentacle out of fear, or remarked on her seer's eyes. They were too used to Milo's collection of grotesques and curiosities to look twice at a mere witch. So she saw visions, did she? Well, who didn't, these days? Everywhere you went there were people setting out carpets and offering to tell your fortune for some outlandish price.

It would be easy to stay, except for the other enchanted princess, and the dead mermaid. It made Caitlin very melancholy to think of the mermaid, and whether it might have lived if she could have somehow gotten it to the sea. But it was the memory of the wolf-girl, nose to the ground like a dog, that drove all sleep from Caitlin's weary limbs, all dreams from her brain. In the morning, she would go once more to her silent task, swiftly threading the fading flowers onto the silken thread. She could look out the window of her room and see where the dark hills met the sky. There was something in her that needed to walk and meet those hills. Then, too, there was Ninthstile, and the Badger. I must get away today, she thought, and go to the prison.

∽◦∾

Why hadn't she come?

The Badger lay on his pallet while Ulick paced the cell. Fowk was digging the tunnel, as usual, and for once Dice seemed to be asleep, relics momentarily forgotten.

What if she married the king? There would still be a price on his head even if he did get out of this hell-hole. After that it seemed he could choose between muleskinning and the gallows.

"Stop pacing," he said to Ulick.

Ulick ignored him. He was thinking of his sweetheart. Two summers ago Milo had spotted her in the marketplace and had brought her back to his palace to spin straw into gold. Ulick saw her now and then, from a distance, amid the king's party leaving the theater, or on a country outing to sample the new wine. She wore an elaborate wig now, and rouge, and applied a false mole to her cheek. When they met she looked right through him.

After tonight, she would have to come back to him.

Dice seemed to have lost all interest in his relics. They lay in a forlorn jumble in the tray. He slept and snored a little, but whether sleeping or waking, he seemed intent on something wonderful, smiling faintly to himself. If Fowk had not been digging, or the Badger brooding, or Ulick pacing, they might have heard him mutter to himself between snores, something about a key.

∽◦∾

The royal goldsmith had finished the ring. It was an opal, set in a wreath of laurel leaves wrought in gold. Milo's instructions had been very specific. An opal wrapped in laurel leaves was supposed to confer invisibility on the wearer. It was a very large ring, for it was an exceptional stone. On Caitlin's hand (which though finely made was not small), the ring reached the first joint of her finger.

The astronomer had seen the ring, and he and Nurse arranged to meet in the old king's study.

"It is worse," said Nurse, "than the time he kept that white mule in the court, convinced it was a princess under a cruel enchantment."

"Worse even," said the astronomer, "than the time he went hunting for emeralds in gryphons' nests."

"I have finished the love powder. I will arrange it so that he becomes enamored of you."

"But what about you, my pet?"

"I shall remain one of the king's closest advisers."

Nurse laughed, a rumble deep in her chest, and pulled the astronomer into her lap. If the love powder didn't work she had another plan. She had found a gardener's tool that left quite credible claw marks.

～～～

Caitlin stared at the ring on her finger. She opened her mouth, but remembered in time to close it. Wildly she pantomimed to Milo, who beamed up at her from where he knelt. She shook her head firmly, removing the ring and pressing it into his hands. This only made him smile at her more tenderly still.

"I know your every objection, my love! Do you think I haven't thought them all to myself a thousand times? Do you think that before I first saw you I ever thought to marry a princess under a vow of silence? A wife who, night and day, must work at her task of selfless love? Do you think I have not said to myself, 'Fool, how can she think of a husband's caress as long as her dear brothers labor under such a cruel sentence?' "

If I remain with him another second, Caitlin thought desperately, I will be lost. This simpleton will convince me.

"Tomorrow night is the harvest bonfire. I have had a gown made for you, that I may show you off properly to my subjects." He took her hand and replaced the ring on her finger. Quite overcome, he kissed her, and through the kiss Caitlin thought, At the bonfire I can steal away and free the Badger.

That afternoon while the handmaidens were drowsing she crept away from the summerhouse and retraced her steps to the prison.

The Badger was uncheerful.

Caitlin saw him look at the ring. "I'm sorry I didn't come sooner," she said. "I couldn't get away."

"Neither could I."

Caitlin was annoyed, even a little astounded to feel herself blush. She told him about the pages torn from the book of magic.

"I don't like it." He was irritable and exhausted, less able to quell the creeping terror he felt. "Why haven't you gotten me out?"

"I'm sorry—it's just that he's such a child, and I have to pantomime everything. Every time I try to make him understand, he thinks it's another tale about ravens and enchantresses. Besides," she added, "have you ever thought that you might be safer where you are?"

The Badger had not forgotten about the redheaded stranger.

Through the grate Caitlin closed her fingers around the Badger's. "Take heart. At least I haven't dreamed about you yet."

∽∾∾

Milo was very fond of oyster soup, and his favorite way of eating it was to have it served in a golden soup-plate shaped like an oyster shell, garnished with real pearls he would dissolve in his wine and drink for good luck. He seemed to recall he had read about it in a book of the ancients, but Nurse maintained it was an old test devised by the only King Max to make sure the court jeweler was honest: real pearls dissolve in wine.

On the night that the king was accustomed to having his favorite soup, the astronomer made up some of his love powder into a pearl and placed it on the king's soup-plate. Nurse hummed, applying her womanly secrets, chewing on a clove and tying up her second chin in a piece of pretty silk.

But it was all for nothing. Milo didn't even drink the pearls, but pocketed them to have made up into a necklace for Emeralda. Nurse's fine lace sleeves trailed in her soup, which she ate without savoring. Nothing the astronomer could say afterward was any comfort.

That night the stars were thick in the sky, and no one could sleep. Ulick's sweetheart lay awake, thinking of her family left behind. The wolf-girl shuffled swiftly around her room on hands and knees, whimpering and growling by turns. And in her own room in the summerhouse Caitlin twisted the heavy ring on her finger.

The king, too, was awake. Milo went to the window and looked out to where the summerhouse gleamed in the night. He had not undressed yet; he had stayed up later than usual to read his fairy tales. They did not entertain him as they once had. The king sighed and rattled the pearls in his pocket. Perhaps they would help him sleep. He poured himself a cup of wine. How pretty the pearls were in the dark, slipping into the wine as if into the sea. After all, he could always get more pearls to make Emeralda a necklace, and nicer ones, at that. Yes. It would help him get to sleep. He drank the wine and looked out the window again. The wolf-girl had escaped. There: she scampered across the lawn, and there! she reappeared by the arbor-seat. How happy she seemed out of doors. Milo was wide awake now. The love-potion had begun to work through his blood like a bee-sting. He would build her a run, so she would get plenty of wholesome air and gain the strength she needed to fight her enchantment. Perhaps they might even teach her to eat with a spoon. He would ask Nurse in the morning. Milo went to bed, and the wolf-girl loped through his dreams.

∽◦∾

From the moment the sun rose the next morning, Ulick willed it to set.

"Set! Set on the day, and on the king's life!" he muttered.

Dice had put his teeth in. He was suddenly very interested in Fowk's tunnel and offered a great deal of advice on how it might be finished more quickly. Fowk kept digging steadily and silently while the relic-seller fidgeted at his elbow.

It was dusk when Fowk broke through to the other side. Then they had to wait while the guard brought their evening meal. As the guard's footsteps receded along the passage they threw aside their bread and began to enlarge the opening.

"Where's Nix?" Fowk wondered, mopping his brow.

The Badger rocked a large stone back and forth to loosen it. "He hasn't been around for a day or two."

Ulick pushed him aside. "Better leave the hard work to the men, boy."

The Badger opened his mouth, but caught Fowk's eye. Without a word he began to hide the rubble in his mattress.

"It's an improvement, at that," he said under his breath. He wondered what sort of bed they gave Caitlin to sleep in. Goosedown, probably, and wide as a barn door.

The relic-seller sidled up to him. "I have a business proposition for you."

The Badger kept putting the smaller stones into his mattress. "What's that?"

"Your friend, the one who comes to the window. She wears a charm. I would like to purchase it."

The Badger laughed. "What, the ring? I don't think she'll part with it."

"No, not the ring. The charm around her neck—a little cat—I would be willing to make an exchange. Any one of my relics for the charm she wears."

"I'm afraid it's not mine to sell."

"But you will ask her?"

"All right, I'll ask her." Foolish old man, he thought. We'll never see each other again.

The Badger was wrong on both accounts. Dice was no fool, and they were to meet again.

❧

When the handmaidens went to dress Caitlin they could not find her. She was with the wolf-girl. A bit of bread soaked in the juice from a bloody piece of beef had brought the wolf-girl in from the grounds, where she had been terrorizing the gardeners. Now she lay with her head in Caitlin's lap, licking the last traces of the treat from Caitlin's fingers. Caitlin saw that the girl was covered with hundreds of small scars and scratches, and her hands and knees were heavily callused from traveling on all fours.

"Was that good?" she asked softly, stroking the wolf-girl's coarse, matted hair. The wild creature bared her teeth a little, yawned, and was asleep.

And do you dream, I wonder? Caitlin asked herself. Watching her sleep one could never imagine this was anything but a slightly dirty child.

The handmaidens knocked and entered, bearing the dress and its veils wrapped in silk tissue.

"If you please, we have been sent to dress you."

Is it time already? Caitlin thought. But she nodded her consent, and gave herself over to be dressed.

Night transformed the town into a weird and fantastic place. The air was intoxicating, yet laced with fear and danger, part carnival revelry and part nightmare. As the flames of the bonfire rose higher, they cast huge, grotesque shadows along the sides and roofs of the ramshackle buildings. The flaring fire cast the alleys into the deepest of blacks, picked out the glittering, dripping dampness on the gutters and rainspouts, and turned the familiar into objects from a world that ran on rogue magic, a world in which the laws of kings and nature were set aside until the fire went out and the sun rose again on the dour and the real.

The giants circled the town seven times before the approaching the wickerwork altar where Milo sat with Caitlin. The light from the bonfire caught the thousands of pearls on her dress, and drenched her in sparks that cascaded down the length of her hair. It made Milo's cheeks rosy as a little boy's, and shone on the gold circlet of his crown. From afar they could see the giants' heads above the rooftops as the wicker king and his court approached through the din in the streets.

Milo pressed Caitlin's hand. It was the hand with the ring, and the heavy stone pressed into Caitlin's flesh painfully.

∽⌒∾

When they crept out of the prison it was dark. Ulick was the first to go his own way. Then Fowk said his good-byes and went in the other direction. Dice hung back with the Badger, who was in a spot.

He had arrived at the prison slung unconscious across the back of a horse, and now had no idea where he was, or how to find Caitlin. The old relic-seller made him uneasy, but he would need his help to find Caitlin and Nix was nowhere to be found.

"Will you take me to the palace?" the Badger asked. He wondered where Nix was. He couldn't help but feel that Nix would have made a better guide.

"Perhaps, yes, I might, for a trinket—"

It was getting cold, and the Badger was running out of patience. "Yes, yes, you'll get your trinket. Come on."

Dice led him off down the alley.

Ulick made his way to the middle of the throng, to the giants at its heart. It seemed the very fire was in his veins, he felt himself burning, burning, towering above the crowd like a wicker man.

"A new world for wicker men!" he hissed. "And death to kings!" He spoke quietly, but his words pierced the wicker armor, and the ears of the shivering Nix. Why had he hidden himself here? He was only a boy. If they found him they were sure to thrash him, or worse. He must hide a little longer, until the giants had come up to where the king was waiting.

But he must not wait too long. After his audience with the wicker men, Milo would set a torch to them and usher in the harvest.

The once merry crowed had turned ugly. Some knew of the plot, and even if they didn't agree with the method, none had any great quarrel with the outcome. With the king dead, the army would be thrown into confusion.

Many would desert, or loot themselves. It would be a thieves' holiday, and there was nothing wrong with that.

Caitlin felt the hairs on the back of her neck stand on end. She knew a mob when she saw one. She felt a sudden sharp longing for her barrow.

Milo beamed, and put his arm around her waist to pull her close. "Look, my dove. Look what a stir you have made among them. They can see what a queen I have chosen." In the firelight Emeralda seemed to him as lovely, as enchanted as ever. Why, then, did his thoughts keep returning to the poor wolf princess?

His strength was no comfort to Caitlin. I have only traded an iron ring for one of gold, she thought. Why is this one so hard to cast off? Why was the crowd making her so nervous? It was more than the edge of violence, sharp and dangerous, beyond the shadows and the firelight. The women who had dressed Caitlin had tried to take the catstone from her, but she had hidden it, reknotting it around her neck once they were gone. Now she fingered it lightly, and it seemed to the king that her green eye gleamed greener, and her blue eye bluer. But surely that was firelight, nothing more.

Elric slunk through the crowd, swearing as he picked his way through knots of revelers. The stableboy had seen him. His foot was still killing him, and the last thing he needed was a chase through streets full of drunks with daggers and short tempers. He ducked into the shadows to catch his breath. It was all because of that damned snare in the woods. It was more than just twenty years' hard work, he reminded himself. There was much more at stake.

The Badger got a stitch in his side and had to stop. He hung on to the side of a tavern, heaving with exertion, until the pain subsided. The redheaded man was gone. Worse, so was Dice. He could tell he was near the palace. The streets were full of people carrying torches and shouting. The Badger was swept up and carried along with them for a distance before he saw the giants.

He used to wonder, as he daydreamed in the abbey

orchard, what marvels and wonders were to be seen out in the wide world. Never had he imagined anything like this. The giants with their torchlight eyes were the dark figures of his oldest nightmares. For a moment, he was again a boy of six, screaming in his sleep, with Asaph shaking him awake, lulling him to sleep again with a story about a poor man's youngest son.

He had lost the stranger with the red hair, but this occurred to the Badger only feebly. His thoughts were all for the giants. This was fear, fear as strong as that he had felt waking in the barrow, but a fear edged with something else. Danger, and excitement. The giants were were very close.

Ulick was wishing that he were inside the wicker man, so his could be the hand that thrust the knife home. But he would have his consolation. With his queen he would take the crown, the throne, the kingdom.

Caitlin's hand was on the catstone, which was sending tremor after tremor of fear through her fingers. She could not move, she was held firm by the dreadful gaze of the advancing giants. I must do something, she thought. I must act. But it was as if they were thoughts she had had very long ago when she was a young girl. Her hands and feet would not obey.

Just then, inside the wicker king, the assassin working the giant's head with a pulley drew an evil-looking knife from his sleeve.

Nix uncurled and launched himself from his perch, landing on the man's shoulders.

The knife flashed through the wicker armor. The crowd gave a single shout and the simmering riot came to a rolling boil.

The Badger caught sight of Caitlin but was quickly buried in the crush of the crowd.

Milo, who had been about to pluck a bunch of flowers from the wicker shield of the giant, felt Emeralda shove him roughly to the ground. To his astonishment and dismay he heard her cry, "Milo!"

* * *

So the plot came to nothing, and the expectations of Nurse and the astronomer were dashed. Undone also was all the good of the aster flowers. Caitlin gave Milo back the ring. He took it without seeming to grasp what the gesture meant. When he was presented to the king, the Badger was more than a little puzzled to hear himself addressed as one of the princess's brothers.

"You managed to save one of the shirts, at any rate," said Milo. "Although it was the one that lacked a sleeve."

The Badger's arm, cut with a broken bottle during the mayhem, was tied in a sling of black muslin, looking very much like a raven's wing.

They left the king and walked in the garden, and Caitlin told him how Nix had taken the knife meant for the king.

"The soldiers came out of the confusion with the assassin and this tiny creature, like a little white dog run over by a cart in the road."

"Will he live?"

"If he does, it will be no thanks to the astronomer. He's put leeches to him."

"Save your worry for the leeches," said the Badger.

But Milo's diviners and toothpullers put their wits together and between them managed to stop the bleeding. A clean bed and plenty to eat worked wonders, and Nix grew stronger.

Milo put aside all his books of fantasies, boarded up the palace, and went to live in the summerhouse with Nix and the wolf-girl. The three of them made a cunning picture in the evening, walking along the brow of the hill at dusk, the tiny boy, the broad tall man, and a creature like a dog scampering at their heels. Only if you were to look more closely, you would see the boy was the wolf-girl, walking uncertainly upright, with Nix playing mascot behind her.

With Milo away from court, Nurse once again had hopes of ruling. But the courtiers had all fled to find other livings, and one morning she found even the astronomer had gone, taking his telescope with him, in search of another situation.

The moneylender, the hangman, and the rat-catcher,

being the wealthiest men in the town, formed their own council, but to their chagrin the old king's huntsman and the lockpick Fowk soon joined them, along with the poorest men in town, the toymaker, the bookbinder, and the soapmaker. Among them, they managed not to rule badly, if they didn't exactly rule well. The town still stank, but everyone ate a little better, and the pickpockets only came out after dark.

Months after Caitlin and the Badger had left the kingdom, a fisherman's youngest daughter pulled a mermaid from the sea. Her father was in bed with influenza, and her brothers were all at market-day in the next town, so it fell to her to tend the nets.

It would be hard to say which was more surprised, the mermaid or the girl. They stared at each other for a long moment, each thinking the other a marvel of ugliness, and then the girl unfastened the net, and the creature slipped into the cold sea and was gone.

7

ORIEL'S FOLLY

Their horses were nowhere to be found, and the Badger was inconsolable. They continued their journey to Ninthstile on foot.

As they reached the edge of Milo's kingdom, they met the old relic-seller, carrying his tray of scarabs and charms. His teeth on their dirty cord swung to and fro like the bell on a goat's neck.

Dice fell in beside them. At first, he didn't remember the Badger, but once reminded was glad enough to see him. He put in his teeth to favor Caitlin with an ill-fitting smile, remarking at once on her amulet.

"A pretty trinket." His eyes glittered beneath their cataracts like filmy gems. "An heirloom, is it?"

Caitlin put her hand to the catstone. "No, just a luck-piece."

That made the relic-seller wheeze with laughter. "Where are you journeying?" he asked when he had recovered a little.

"To the coast," said the Badger.

"And after that?"

"To Ninthstile."

Behind their cataracts the old eyes smoldered. "Ah. The

good sisters! You must give them my regards." And for the next mile he told them a yarn about a wonderful relic, the teeth of a nun that, when shaken and spilled from a cup, spelled out the answers to weighty questions.

At last Caitlin broke in gently. "You know so much of relics. Have you ever heard of a Spellkey?"

Dice removed his teeth and ran his tongue over his tender gums. "Well, well. Where did you learn about such a thing as a Spellkey?"

"Every child is lulled to sleep with tales of magic rings and keys of power."

"I have heard of them, true. Keys that will open any door, unlock the truth from a man's lips. I have never seen one, but then, there are so few genuine relics since the Necromancer outlawed the guildhalls and placed a tax on relics."

Magic occupied a curious place in the kingdoms where the Pentacle and its tenets were kept. Reasonable people saw nothing wrong with having their fortunes told at the fair, or buying a trifling spell to make it rain on the turnip crop, but they harbored a deep-seated fear of spellsmiths, seers, and other unsavory types deemed dangerous to the public health. Magic was a fine thing, as long as it was licensed and practiced by people who had undergone a proper apprenticeship under a necromancer or apothecary. If you started letting changelings and simpletons and unmarried women meddle with spells, where would it end? So there were laws banning the study of the old rune tongues. You couldn't copy a map without a permit from a sub-necromancer. The sale of certain substances and objects was carefully controlled: spinning wheels, mirrors, tinderboxes, cauldrons—all could too easily slip over the threshold from household commonplace to object of magic. And cash bounties were paid on all cats with suspicious markings, goats with two heads, and dogs with forked tongues.

Bribery ran rampant, as might be expected, and spells were to be had on any and every street corner, if you knew whom to ask. All the same, if your fine new baby just happened to have a beautiful white star in the middle of its forehead, you didn't shout it in the streets at noon, and you might pay the midwife a small sum each month not to say anything about it.

Caitlin was very quiet as Dice finished a tale about the oracular tortoise's head. She shot a sidelong glance at the Badger. Intent on the old man's tale, it was plain that he liked nothing better than a tale, no matter how unlikely, no matter how disreputable the teller. Did he just like a good story, or did he believe some of his Thirdmoon lessons still?

They had crossed into Fifthmoon, and there was no town in sight. It was agreed that they should make camp by the roadside, each taking a turn at watch, in case of highwaymen. None of them had eaten, but it was an unspoken agreement that none should mention the fact.

The Badger took the first watch. It was quite cold, and he pulled his blanket closer, stirring the coals to life with the toe of his boot. He was worried about the crossing. Storms sometimes came early to the straits, making crossing impossible until spring. Then what would he do, with a witch-girl on his hands (for so he thought of Caitlin, when he was tired and underfed), and a bounty on his head? Old Dice snored a little, but Caitlin tossed, clenching and unclenching her hand around the amulet as she slept. *So dark*, he thought, *What is that old saying about eyes like hers? Otherworld daughters, that's it.* To his surprise the Badger saw how high the moon had risen. In a little while it would be time to wake Dice.

The next thing he knew it was morning, and Caitlin was roughly shaking him awake.

"He's gone, and my amulet, too."

They breakfasted on regret and silence, and went on down the road.

A short distance away, hidden by the swell of a hill, Elric watched them go. When they had gone far enough down the road, he began to follow, riding Motley, Maud in tow.

❧

Old Dice ran through a field of ripe corn. His teeth on their cord had fallen from his mouth; now the string snapped, and the teeth were lost between the rows of stalks. The relic-seller panted in his terror, whimpering and casting wild glances backward as he ran, but never letting go of the amulet. He clutched the catstone so hard it made a welt in his palm.

"They shall never have it!" he muttered. "It is mine, it belongs to Dice the Wise, the Keeper of Relics." Here the old man got a stitch in his side and paused for breath beside a scarecrow, leaning on the bundle of rags and straw. But the arm beneath his hand was real, and before Dice realized the scarecrow hid a man, the knife had done its work. Dice crumpled under the thrust like a withered stalk under a sickle. The stone flew from his hand and vanished.

Elric turned the old man over to make sure he was dead. After closing the relic-seller's eyes, he pried open the hands. The amulet was gone.

"Damn!"

To his credit, he thought of doing something with the body. But there was no time to even glance around for the amulet, much less dig a grave in a cornfield. Someone was coming toward him through the corn, and he was forced to leave Dice to the crows and run for it.

◦◦◦

At first Caitlin attributed the dreams to thirst, hunger, and exhaustion—surely, they would otherwise have ceased with the disappearance of the amulet? But soon she was forced to allow that the dreams were coming as strong and as clear as ever, catstone or no catstone.

She imagined that the hedgerows on either side of the road were growing taller, and at the same time pressing in, so that the road was narrower. The more she resolved not to look at them, the more she could see them out of the corner of her eye. When she did look, the hedge looked as a hedge should look. But as soon as she glanced away it would begin to creep toward her, a thing of menace, full of thorns, spiders, gleaming eyes. Once she even imagined that a claw had reached out from the hedge to snatch at her, and she leapt aside with a muffled shout.

"Let's stop," said the Badger at last, trying to keep the worry out of his voice.

But that would not do, no, not at all. She pictured the evil so clearly when she was awake that she could only imagine how it would terrorize her when she slept.

"There's no shade," she said.

"We'll find some."

But now that Dice was gone he was not sure that they were still on the right road. They had little money, even if they did find a farmhouse whose occupants might sell them milk and bread. Caitlin must rest, that was plain enough. It made him uneasy to watch her. She was beginning to look like the hunted, haunted thing he had met in the square at Moorsedge.

There was a break in the hedgerow, and he helped her through it. She flinched and gasped as though she was being led through a wall of fire, and then they were through, standing in a field of wildflowers, only a meadow away from a low stand of trees.

"There's water there," he said. "Come on. We'll rest a bit."

When they reached the small brook, Caitlin sank to her knees on the mossy bank and bathed her face in the cool water, then sat up to dry her face with her shirt. She looked up at him, and it was as though she had been roused from a nightmare, crouching there blank-eyed in the dappled light and shadow under the trees. It made her look quite unearthly.

"Go on, lie down. I'll keep an eye out."

Reluctantly, she stretched out with a bedroll under her head. She watched the brooklet rolling past, letting the sound and sparkle of it wash the memory of the hedgerow from her mind. She let her gaze wander from the water to a dragonfly's darting path, to a basking frog, to the waving reeds. But what was making them wave? She sat up.

"Badger," she whispered.

A young girl was sitting on the bank opposite, almost

hidden in the weeds, crowned with a circlet of flowering rushes, staring at them with frank interest.

"Hello," said Caitlin.

"You're trespassing," said the girl, matter-of-factly. "This is the king's private land."

"Well, then, you're trespassing, too," said the Badger.

"I am not," she said. "It's my land, too. I'm the king's daughter."

"Are you, now?"

"She *is* wearing a crown," Caitlin said.

The girl untangled herself from her hiding place and waded across the stream. They saw her hair was not pale gold but silver, though she was no more than nine or ten. She was wearing a nightdress and over that toy armor, gilt on leather, and she carried a wooden lance. Her mouth, hands, and hem were stained pink with plum juice.

"I'm Oriel," she said, with incongruous hauteur. "Daughter of Linus, King of Fifthmoon, House of the Green Lion. Who are you?"

"I'm Matthew Tannerson," the Badger said quickly, "and this is my sister, Kate. We were set upon by highwaymen. They took our horses and all our money."

"Well, then you must stay the night in my tower."

She led them across the fields, which changed to lawns and then gardens. The Badger was expecting her to show them to some crook in a tree, but at the edge of the king's wood, in a small circle of birches, there stood a small stone tower. It appeared to have been abandoned, but while the weeds on one side had been allowed to grow waist high, on the other what looked to be a wild tangle proved to be a cleverly disguised garden.

Oriel opened the small door, and led them into the single round chamber decorated with bright hangings in a crude, lively style. The room was crammed with furniture: a low cot covered with furs; a table piled with books, and another chest of books on the floor; a sewing frame; an inlaid dressing table: the castoffs of a royal chamber. Visiting dignitaries may once have been quartered here, but for years it had served as nothing more than a storehouse.

A fire was laid in the grate, and Oriel bent to light it. Then she took a snuffbox down from the mantelpiece, helped herself to a pinch of clove, placed it on the back of her hand, and inhaled it expertly. She held out the box to the Badger.

"No thank you," the Badger said, inwardly marveling.

Caitlin was studying the tapestries. "These are from the further-lands, aren't they?"

Oriel nodded. "My mother was from Thirteenmoon. To keep her from being homesick, my father built her this house, so she could pretend she was back in her father's palace."

Of the five kingdoms that lay across the straits, Thirteenmoon was the most distant, a land of ice palaces and perpetual snows so remote and forbidding it seemed a land of fables. Some of the hangings showed scenes from daily life: wolves pulling a sledge through the snow, a race between sleek ice-boats with brightly patterned sails. Others seemed to be scenes from legends told to pass the unending winter night: the Fool letting the narwhal bore a hole in the hull of his boat, the Fool marrying the sea-maiden.

Caitlin came to the last tapestry and found, recessed in the wall, a small shelf flanked with sconces, which were empty.

"My mother would light candles for her ancestors," Oriel explained, "and burn ambergris and musk on their anniversaries. Our Lord Chamberlain said she was worshipping false gods."

The Badger glanced through the books on the table. Their pages held not cautionary tales or hymns or religious strictures, but adventures. The child obviously had a keen imagination, and no doubt such tales kept it sharp. All that about Thirteenmoon, and a bride house. The tower was probably an old countinghouse. Still, it was a bit of luck, he thought. Tonight they would sleep in comfort, out of the wind and rain.

"Listen," he said to Caitlin. "You stay here. I'll go out and see if I can find us anything for supper."

"But you can come back with me," Oriel said, "We're having partridges, I think."

"I don't really want to raid the king's larder, thank you very much."

Oriel made a face at him, and turned to Caitlin. "I don't think he believes I *am* a princess."

"You musn't mind him," she said. "He doesn't believe most things."

Oriel turned and stared at the Badger with an expression of such perfectly mingled fascination and horror that he laughed out loud.

"All right!" he said. "I accept your invitation—so long as I may bring some supper back for Kate."

"Of *course*," Oriel said, as though he must be thick in the head.

Then she made him go change his shirt and wash his hands and clean his nails and when he returned from this toilet he discovered she had changed her muddied night-dress for clothes more befitting a princess: a richly embroidered smock over hose, and gold kid slippers. Her mouth and fingers still bore faint pink stains, but she had combed most of the rushes from her hair.

"Father won't let me wear armor to dinner," she explained.

The Badger traded a glance with Caitlin.

"Maybe you should come," he said.

"I couldn't. I can't," she said. And it was more than the journey, or the hedges, or even the loss of her amulet that morning. Something about the tower, about the small bare shelf flanked by the empty sconces, in the way she had felt when Oriel said the words "Our Lord Chamberlain"— something told Caitlin she and her otherworld eyes would not be welcome at the king's table.

❧

King Linus of Fifthmoon was seated on the terrace overlooking his gardens, a vantage point from which he could watch the progress of the gardeners as they trimmed the topiary menagerie wrought in privet and quickthorn. He was dressed all in shades of ivy, and his reddish beard grew close to his face, rusty lichen on a stone. On a table in front of him was set a living miniature of the topiary menagerie. As the gardeners moved from one green animal to the next, the king observed them through a pair of opera glasses and made corresponding changes to his miniature with a pair of manicure scissors. Behind him stood a row of courtiers and attendants, likewise dressed in green, observing the action and murmuring among themselves.

"My dear," said Linus, without looking up. "Did you do all your lessons?"

"Only the natural history. May I have real armor?"

"I suppose you may, if my Lord Chamberlain thinks it wise."

Oriel made a face. "Papa," she said, "this afternoon I found this young man wandering around. He had been set upon by bandits. They took all his money and made him change his clothes for theirs. May he dine with us?"

"By all means," said Linus, tearing his gaze from the gardeners to look at the Badger. He frowned slightly. "But he must be changed!" At the wave of his hand a footman stepped forward.

"See he is changed," said the king.

The footman took him to a barber, who barbered him, and a valet, who clucked over the Badger's fingernails, and his clean shirt. The Badger had to admit that his nails were cleaner when the valet was done with them. He was dressed in black trousers, and a white shirt faced with green silk at the neck, and fastened with green stones at the cuffs, and a vest of a dark leaf green with carved emerald buttons. He was annointed with something sharp and green-smelling, and then the valet nodded to the footman, and he was led to the great hall.

Up and down the length of the long room were spaced small orange trees in pots, and the walls were festooned with garlands of greenery. Greyhounds wandered among the company, jeweled collars around their necks, their toenails clipped and capped with gold. From its perch high in a chandelier ablaze with candles, a falcon watched the proceedings, as if it might suddenly swoop down to snatch the rabbit from the serving dish.

A place had been laid for him beside Oriel, and the Badger slipped into it. No one seemed to take any notice of him, except Oriel, who poured his wine for him and showed him what to do when the pageboy came by with a silver bowl of napkins that had been wrung out in hot water.

The king sat alone at the head of the long table. The Badger saw with relief that the table was laid with a white cloth, and that the wine that was being poured was red. Perhaps the partridges would not be green after all. The king's color was still much in evidence, however. All up and down the table the lords and ladies of the court were dressed in shades of ivy, moss, and emerald. The lords wore beards, trimmed into points and forks, and all the ladies dressed their hair in a towering style of curls and intricate plaits, with flowers tucked into them. The Badger wondered that Oriel was not made to wear green, then he realized that the princess was the flower in this strange garden, the fairest bloom in it. But where was the queen?

One other person at the table was not wearing green. The king's Lord Chamberlain sat at the king's elbow, dressed in grey, a handsome man with dark hair and beard lightly streaked with silver, and lively dark eyes. Lines at his eyes and mouth suggested he was a man who smiled easily and laughed often. Then the Badger noticed the ornament that hung around the man's neck on a heavy silver chain.

It was a silver pentacle, and at its center gleamed a single dark stone, black as onyx, but with a scarlet glimmer at its heart that showed it to be a bloodstone. The king's lord chamberlain was an Adept Royal, a high alchemist who represented the Pentacle to kings. The mottled red stone was a sign that he had been inducted into the Necromancer's inner circle, and answered to him alone.

The Adept Royal was seated at the king's elbow, and he had the king's ear. At this moment he was filling it with plans for a new abbey to be built adjoining the palace grounds. The king nodded, but all the while his hands played with the pair of manicure scissors that hung from his neck on a ribbon, as though he knew, elsewhere, that his miniature garden was growing unkempt.

"Plans for the abbey have been drawn up," said the chamberlain. "I could show them to your majesty after prayers."

"An abbey," the king said mildly. "Is that monks or nuns? I think I should prefer nuns, you know, in my wife's memory."

So her mother is dead, thought the Badger, glancing at Oriel, then around at the company. No one was dressed in mourning, so her death could not have been recent.

The king did not appear at all devout, but this did not seem to worry his Lord Chamberlain. He waved away the servant who appeared with the wine, but made sure the king's cup was kept filled.

"An abbey may have monks or nuns. If monks it is a monastery, if nuns, a nunnery. The necromancer had thought to place a monastery here, but I shall put your proposal to him. It would be most ideal, as I think of it. Your daughter might pursue her studies with the good sisters."

"It will take some time to build an abbey. In a few years she will be fourteen, and of an age to be married."

"True, very true," said the chamberlain. He smiled at Oriel, who looked down at her plate. She does not like him, the Badger thought. He had noticed that the greyhounds grew quiet near the chamberlain, and drew their tails between their legs. If a scrap of meat fell from the chamberlain's knife onto the floor, they let it alone.

But the man is likeable, the Badger thought. Though a religious man he seemed quite worldly. When he was not pressing the king for a commitment to the building project, he was leaning over to speak in the ear of the lady on his other side. All the time the pentacle around his neck turned this way and that, catching the light, making the dark red stone wink.

❧

In the tower Caitlin stood and gazed out the narrow leaded window at the king's gardens. Dusk was gathering rapidly, sinking the topiary animals into gloom. The sight made Caitlin uneasy, and reminded her somehow of the sinister hedgerows, and she turned away.

The furs on the cot were tempting, yet weary as she was she could not sleep. Her gaze kept straying to a tapestry on the wall opposite. It depicted a woman standing in a garden. She was dressed in royal robes that glinted with golden threads: the queen, no doubt. Oriel's mother? She was flanked by a gryphon and a unicorn, worked in greenery but strangely animated.

At last she got up and went to the table to see if any of the books were in a rune tongue she knew. She pulled out a simply bound book in which were written tales of the Fool. The copyist—a royal scribe? no monk would have wasted ink on such silly, profane tales—had decorated the margins with pictures of the Fool. There were others, portraits of monks that were not very flattering. The writing seemed to be a northern rune tongue. Perhaps this was a favorite book of tales the queen had brought with her. Caitlin found the runes difficult, but with the pictures she managed to piece together a tale.

In this adventure the Fool was sent into the cave of a giant to steal the riches he hoarded there. The giant was blind, but used a magic eye of glass to see. The Fool won the magic eye in a game of dice, and used it to see where all the gold and gems of the world were hidden in the seams of rock. The Fool became the richest man in the world, and used his wealth to build a magic ship, and in it the Fool sailed off the edge of the world, where he was rescued by creatures of the air. They returned him to his pigsty, all his wealth gone, but with the giant's glass eye in his pocket.

There was another tale, but the effort of reading such unfamiliar runes had given Caitlin a headache. She put down the book and went to the makeshift washstand Oriel had fashioned of a tarnished silver bowl and an ornate but cracked pitcher. As she bent to splash her face, she stepped back with a start. Reflected in the surface of the water she saw not her own features but the mournful face of the woman in the tapestry.

8

A Dram of Wormwood

By the end of the feast, the chamberlain had secured the king's promise that he would look at the plans for the abbey after chapel. The table had been cleared and the sweet course brought out, a towering edifice of preserved fruit mortared together with nougat and sweet almond paste, and decorated with nutmeats and leaves of real gilt. The diners' cups were refilled with spiced wine. The Badger found the smell familiar; the abbot had been fond of a glass, and the brothers of Thirdmoon See had made a nice income from selling it. He remembered watching the cook add spices to the kettle simmering over the abbey hearth: angelica and nutmeg, juniper and lemon, violets picked from the shade of the garden wall. And something else, something he couldn't remember.

At last the king folded his napkin and rose from the table, the signal that the meal had come to an end. Behind the king, the courtiers filed from the hall two by two. To the Badger's great surprise Oriel whistled loudly, sending the falcon plummeting from its perch to land on the back of her chair.

"Do you like him? His name is Gyrfal. He was a birthday

present. I am teaching him to retrieve my shuttlecocks. Would you like to see my other presents?"

It struck him how lonely she must be, with her mother dead and a father who would have had more interest in her if she had been fashioned of boxwood. Little wonder she ran off to slay dragons. "I've stayed too long as it is," he said. "Cait will have been expecting me these last two hours."

"You must meet me tomorrow, then, by the stream." He promised and, when he had filled a napkin with the food he had saved for Caitlin, she led him down one corridor and then another.

"If we meet my father's chamberlain he'll make me to go to chapel, and you, too."

"Is it chapel you dislike, or the chamberlain?"

"He says my mother did not believe in the Pentacle, and so she cannot be in heaven."

"When did she die?"

"When I was five."

"Was she ill a long time?"

"Oh, she was not ill at all! They tried to tell me she was, but I don't believe them."

The Badger saw he was treading on dangerous ground, and stepped cautiously. "Is that when your hair went white, when your mother died?"

"Yes," she said. "Here's the way out. It used be to the head draughtsman's quarters, when father kept draughtsmen, before he went mad for gardens. I come here when it's too cold to go to the stream."

The Badger could see why. The room was used to store scale models of various building projects: guildhalls, almshouses. To judge from the dust on everything, they had been abandoned before they could be completed or perhaps even begun. The room overlooked the stables.

He swung a leg over the windowsill and looked down at the courtyard below. He wondered how far down it was. The last thing he needed was a sprained ankle.

"You will come tomorrow?" Oriel said.

"Yes," he said, and jumped.

The moon had risen, and as the princess leaned from

the window, she was caught for a moment in a shower of silver light. The moonlight revealed something that had so far escaped the Badger's attention. Oriel was blind in her right eye.

∽∾

Caitlin had just decided to leave the tower to look for the Badger when he came in the door, wearing borrowed finery and carrying a napkin tied into a bundle and a bottle under his arm. He shot her a guilty glance as he went to the table and began clearing aside the books.

"I had almost given you up," she said.

"I'm sorry. I didn't mean to stay so long. You must be starved." He moved the candle to the table and dragged over a chair. She went and sat down, amused at his solicitude. The reflection in the basin had so unsettled her she was just grateful to hear another voice filling up the silence. And she *was* starving, now she thought of it.

"Oh, and here," he said, drawing the cork and setting the bottle at her elbow. "Close your eyes."

She did, and he popped a strange small fruit into her mouth, oily and salty and slightly bitter. As she bit down on it Caitlin felt a flush come to her cheeks. His voice echoed in her mind, *Close your eyes*, and she imagined a kiss so vivid it made her stomach flutter. She began to cough.

"Don't choke," he said.

"What is it?"

"An olive. They grow in warm places. At least that's what Oriel told me."

"Oh."

"I didn't like it, much, either," he confessed.

While she ate, he described the king and his court, the royal dress code, the king's chamberlain and his plans for the abbey.

"Very strange," said Caitlin. "I should like to see this chamberlain."

"Well, that's not the strangest thing by half. Had you noticed that Oriel is blind in one eye?"

Caitlin dropped her knife. At his words she had a sudden glimpse of Oriel as she had been when her mother was yet living, a dark-haired girl with one blue eye and one green. And then again, the mournful face, the grieving mother. But now the face was blurred, as though she were seeing two faces, the image of one laid upon the other.

The Badger's hand was on her shoulder, shaking her gently.

"Drink that wine," he said. "You look like you need it."

"I'm all right. You must find out, tomorrow, what happened to her."

"Well, ask her yourself. She'll be at the stream again."

There was only the single cot, so they pulled the bedding onto the floor for Caitlin, and the Badger stretched out on the frame. She was instantly asleep, only the top of her head visible among the furs. The Badger stretched out on the bare canvas with a sigh, laying an arm over his eyes, too tired to sit up to blow out the candle. At least he was not sleeping on the wet ground. His mind began to turn from the events of the day to random imaginings of what he would do, once he had delivered Caitlin to her convent. He would have a living to make, and a plan had been taking shape in his mind, on those long stretches of road when they both fell silent. He had many dreams— joining the crew of a ship or a caravan headed north—but only one plan. He would find a smithy somewhere who needed someone handy with horses. The sooner he was apprenticed, the sooner he would be able to buy a forge of his own. Independence, that was the main thing. No more having to answer to someone else. No more obligation.

As he drifted off, he remembered what else went into the abbot's cordial: a dram of wormwood.

◆◇◆

Caitlin was already deep in dreams. She was sitting on the floor in the dark—where, she could not tell. Someone was there with her. Not Abagtha; not the Badger. Whoever it was rattled something in a box, and passed her an object, cold to the touch: a small metal box on a chain. She fumbled with the catch in the dark and when she lifted the lid the room was suddenly flooded with light from the giant's glass eye, nestled in velvet in the small silver snuff-box. The light showed the place to be the bride house, and the person who had passed her the box was the woman from the tapestry. Her face was no longer sorrow-ful, but full of anguished love and dreadful resolve.

Then Caitlin was walking through the knot garden as dusk was beginning to fall. In the failing light the great topiary animals rose around her on all sides. As she walked she noticed rings on her hands, fabulous gems in heavy settings. The woman in the tapestry had worn such rings. Looking down she saw that she wore skirts fashioned of a rich brocade shot with gold thread. She began to run, gripped by the same terror she had felt among the menac-ing hedges. But she was not merely fleeing danger. She was searching for something, and must find it before some dreadful thing happened.

Turning a corner she came upon a small tiled courtyard. In its center, beneath a sundial, lay a sleeping child: Oriel, yet dark-haired, and no older than four.

She caught her up and ran with her out of the garden, the garden she had lovingly planned as a green and fra-grant retreat, a haven for birds and small creatures. It had been planted with love, but the garden was hers no longer. Evil dwelled there, luring her small daughter toward one deadly trap after another. Already she had climbed one of the topiary animals and only just escaped breaking her neck. She had eaten a handful of tempting berries and nearly been poisoned. No matter how they scolded and punished her, Oriel was always drawn back to the sundial at the heart of the maze.

There the dream abruptly ended. Caitlin woke up and lit the candle, then rose and went to splash her face with water. But the surface of the basin was adance with rip-ples. Caitlin knew she had not jarred the table, and cross-ing the room her footsteps had been light. She stood, barefoot, mesmerized by the pattern of ripples. At last she reached out a finger to touch them.

At once the surface of the water was smooth as glass. The queen stared back at her, no longer mournful, but as though she wished to speak and was mute.

"Yes," Caitlin whispered. "I promise. I will."

She went back to bed but it was an hour before she slept.

❧

The next day they returned to the stream to wait for Oriel. Sitting against the tree, and without looking at him, Caitlin haltingly told the Badger of her dream. He hardly seemed to be paying attention, gazing sleepily into the reeds, but when she had finished her story he spoke.

"So you think this ghost, this face in the basin, is the queen?"

"Sometimes. The rest of the time it seems to be someone else."

"And you think she did something to Oriel that made her go blind in one eye?"

Caitlin did not answer for a moment. "I think she was trying to change the color of her green eye to blue, using some half-remembered remedy, to hide the fact that she had seer's eyes. I think Oriel only lost the sight in that eye slowly."

There was movement in the reeds and Oriel appeared, armorless, but carrying a newly captured cricket in a tinderbox cage.

"I can't stay," she said. "Father says I must have lessons, and not be so wild." She drew a gold-slippered foot through the weeds. "It is all the doing of his Lord Chamberlain, because I would not go to chapel! But I brought you this, so you can come to the garden." She handed Caitlin a rumpled green bundle. Unrolled, it proved to be a gown of watered silk, bottle green. "I will try to get out later to see you. If they catch me, I shall say I am hunting crickets."

Caitlin smoothed out the folds of the dress thoughtfully. "Where is your father's chamberlain?"

"He rode out this morning with father to look over the site for the abbey."

"I should like to see the chamberlain's room. Can you take us there?"

Oriel's eyes flashed. "Oh, yes!"

Caitlin disappeared with Oriel into the weeds and, after

some rustling, emerged wearing the silk gown, her hair put up in the fashion of the court, though if you looked closely you could see that short lengths of reed had been pressed into service as hairpins.

The three began to make their way across the meadows to the palace. From the top of the tree against which Caitlin had been sitting, Elric watched them. He was still wearing a gardener's smock; his hands were callused from the garden shears and there was a wasp sting on tho back of his neck. He waited until they had gone a safe distance, then swung down from the lowest branch and went after them.

❦

The king's chamberlain had his own apartments not far from those of the king. They were decorated in a style that seemed monkish at first glance. On closer inspection, however, it proved anything but plain. A modest coverlet of rough blue cloth, when turned back, revealed a fur lining and fine damask sheets. The chest beside the bed held a small book—a cycle of Pentaclist morality plays—and an unadorned cup.

The Badger held the cup to his nose, then handed it to Caitlin. There was still discernable a faded, flowery perfume.

"The chamberlain likes his brandy," said the Badger. "Plum, I'd wager."

Caitlin frowned. She could almost make out a faint note of something else, beneath the distilled scent of overripe fruit ready to drop from the branch. Sweet and lulling. She set down the cup.

Oriel had found a book at the back of the wardrobe. It was a simple ledger, and it was locked.

"I can undo that," said the Badger, reaching for it.

"No, don't," said Caitlin. "If the lock is charmed, he might be able to divine who broke it. Let me think." She nibbled her thumbnail a moment, then turned to Oriel. "Set the book down on that table by the window. And let me have your cricket."

Oriel surrendered the tinderbox. Caitlin said a charm on it and set it, opened, on the table beside the ledger.

With a chirp the cricket hopped from the tinderbox onto the table, and then onto the ledger. The lock sprang open.

"Now he will only summon up a cricket. No, don't touch it! Let the wind turn the pages."

The covers were warped, and the breeze from the window had soon opened the ledger. The pages were covered with writing in a careful hand, double columns of dates and place names, a record of births, all of them extraordinary: *Boy with caul. Girl, blind. Girl, widow's peak. Boy, extra toe. Twin girls, sharing a caul. Girl, crossed eyes. Girl, seer's eyes.* And on and on, page after page. Each time the birth of a child with seer's eyes had been recorded, there was a small mark in the margin—not an X, but a twisted rune.

Caitlin had gone deathly pale. The Badger took one look at her and grabbed the ledger, quickly thrusting it back into its hiding place.

"Oriel, let's get out of here."

"My cricket!"

"I'll catch you a dozen. Come on!"

Caitlin protested she was all right, but at last admitted some fresh air would do her no harm. Oriel led them to the terrace, and stayed until a little color had returned to Caitlin's cheeks.

"I must go back," she said reluctantly. "My handmaidens will get in trouble if I'm missing too long. But I'll meet you at the sundial, an hour before sunset."

They started into the garden, arm in arm to blend in with the other pairs of courtiers out for a stroll among the topiary. They passed some ladies all in green, seated in a circle around a gentleman playing the lute.

"You're awfully quiet," said the Badger.

"I'm worried about Oriel."

"There's nothing for her here, that's certain."

"No, more than that. I fear for her if she remains." She caught his glance and withdrew her arm from his, quickening her step. "I know you think I'm mad! It's not that the chamberlain will harm her. It's something else. I can't explain."

"But what can we do? We can't take her to Ninthstile with us."

"No."

"Then what?"

"I don't know. I thought—" She shook her head. "I thought my dreams might tell me."

"If I hadn't fallen asleep and lost your amulet, you mean."

But she left the bait untouched, slowing her step to slip her arm back in his. "Let's not quarrel," she said. "We have too far yet to travel together."

They came to a stone seat and sat down. The Badger broke off some twigs of boxwood and began fashioning a horse from them, as Asaph had taught him to do with straw. He glanced up and saw her watching his fingers as they wove the green twigs into a horse's head. One of the reed hairpins had come loose, and some strands of her hair had fallen around her face.

"The thing is," he said quickly, "we're only here because you had to rest. So, as long as you're rested, we can go on our way. Can you travel?"

She nodded.

"Then let's get out of this place. I'll see if I can get a pair of horses."

"I don't like to think of Oriel here, once that abbey is built."

"If they—it, whatever it is—were going to harm her, wouldn't it have done it by now?"

"Yes. Yes! It sounds reasonable, the way you put it. But I just know she is in danger. And I think somehow I am meant to help her."

"Well, you and your dreams work on that. I'll see to getting us some horses."

The Badger already had a plan. He had noticed some of the courtiers playing a game with small carved pieces on a board marked out in colored squares. It didn't look very different from monks and nuns, a down-and-dirty form of checkers he had learned from one of the abbey turnspits. The Badger had been very good at monks and nuns.

Caitlin wanted to go back to the tower for another look at the book of tales. They agreed to meet back at the entrance to the garden, and walk to the sundial together to meet Oriel. Then they walked on, leaving the twig horse behind on the stone seat.

It was easy enough for the Badger to sidle up to one of the tables where they were playing monks and nuns. He grew so absorbed, watching the progress of the game, that he was startled to find he had drained a cup of spiced wine without realizing he even held it. He let someone refill his cup. He was sure he could play, and win, but what could he stake? He was officially a gentleman, but a gentleman who had lost everything to highwaymen.

The game ended, and the loser stood up, shaking his head, leaving the contents of his purse and a note promising the balance.

"Who will play?" fluted a silver voice. The winner, one of the mor⸢ striking ladies of the court, cast her bright sparrow's eyes around the company, but no one would rise to the challenge. At last her eyes fell on the Badger, widened, then narrowed. She smiled.

"You, then. Will *you* partner me in a game?"

"Alas, my lady, I have already been taken for everything."

The onlookers laughed, but the lady held her seraphic smile. Between the towering arrangement of her hair, stuck with feathers and jewels, and the layers of her rouge, it was impossible to guess her years. She might have been his age, or twice that.

"Surely not *everything*," she said, ranging the ivy-green pieces on her side of the board, and inclining her head slightly at the seat opposite.

The Badger found himself sitting down and ranging the white pieces—nuns, as he thought of them, but roses, as they called them in this game—on their squares.

"Everything worth having, madam. I have lost my gold,

my jewels, anything I had of any value. Even these clothes are borowed."

"Then let these be the stakes," she said. "For each piece of yours I take, you shall forfeit an hour's leisure, to be spent in my company as I shall dictate."

The laughter rose all around them, but as though at a signal, the crowd had begun to disperse. Soon the Badger and his opponent found themselves alone, except for the wine steward, the fly-swatter, and the fool. It occurred to the Badger, as he contemplated his first move, that he had not noticed the fool at the banquet the night before.

And he reminded himself, not a little sternly, to win.

∽∾

Caitlin set aside the book of tales with a sigh. She was not sure what she had hoped to find, only that it had eluded her. And she felt sure that she had precious little time to think of some way to save Oriel from the evil she felt in the maze and, strongly, in the chamberlain's room.

Maybe, she thought, it has nothing to do with the tales after all. Maybe I have been looking in the wrong place. If Oriel's mother were alive, what would she do to protect her?

Caitlin looked around the room, and noticed for the first time one of the bright hangings. It seemed to depict a scene from a tale not included in the collection she had been struggling through. The Fool, dressed for hunting and with a hawk on his wrist, stood beneath a fir tree. What was remarkable was that the branches of the evergreen were bare, the needles falling in a shower to dapple the snow.

She hunted through the chests until she found some tapers and small, fragrant lumps of some resin she guessed could be burned for incense. The tapers fit perfectly in the sconces on the wall, and when she lit the lump of resin it gave off a spicy, animal perfume, all musk and smoke.

The incantation came to her as suddenly as the inspiration to light the candles. It was a spell Abagtha used to use when she wanted to get even with farmers who shortchanged her for services rendered, or paid in shoddy goods. It was a flexible spell, equally good at making trees drop their fruit prematurely or melons rot on the vine. Caitlin repeated the incantation as long as she dared. She did not want to draw the Adept Royal's attention to the bride house. For all she knew, that pentacle with its blood-stone center could find the source of spells.

Then she went to the door of the tower and called out a long summons in the language of the birds. She was not at all sure it would have the desired result. She knew a little hawk, but gyrfalcon was another dialect entirely.

Out of nowhere, the tame falcon flew down to perch on Caitlin's bare wrist, making her gasp as his talons drew blood.

Many pardons, said the bird, choosing a better perch on the back of a chair.

Your mistress is in grave danger. You must be her eyes and ears, and warn her. I will tell her to heed you, and never to part with you.

It shall be done as you say, said Gyrfal.

There was a little rabbit left over from her dinner the night before, and Caitlin gave it to Gyrfal as a seal of the promise. Then the bird flew off and disappeared among the trees.

The Badger came up, leading by the bridle two sad-dled horses.

"Well done," she said, noticing as he drew near a scent, too faint for a nose less keen than hers, of wine, mingled with a woman's perfume. An emerald stone was missing from his cuff. "What did you have to give for them?"

"I won them, at checkers," he said, a little crossly. "But Cait, it's the oddest thing. The garden—"

The strange frost lay thickly over Linus's garden, blan-keting the green menagerie, covering the stone seats, obscuring the hours on the sundial at the center. Already most of the topiary animals were skeletons of twisted branches and wire, their leaves littering the paths and benches, marking out the maze in evergreen.

The king stood on the terrace, looking out at the strange scene, as though he was newly wakened from a dream. He looked down at the miniature garden, and at the scissors in his hand, as though he had never seen them. At last he turned to the courtiers, and lifted his voice in a roar.

"Don't stand there gawking like a bunch of ninnies! Go and get changed, all of you! And I forbid anyone to come into my presence wearing green!"

Oriel was at her window, elbows on the sill, chin in her hands, watching the courtiers scatter. Gyrfal, perched on top of the wardrobe, kept a keen eye on his young mistress.

Though, it occurred to Caitlin as they rode away, she will not need him so much now.

9

FOUR LETTERS AND A MAP

It took three days for the Badger to sicken. On the third night, as they sat around the fire, Caitlin saw him wince.

"All you ill?"

He shook his head. "It's nothing. My gut's all in knots, that's all. Must be this rich food doesn't agree with me after prison rations." He made light of it, but when he raised the cup to his mouth his hand trembled.

The next morning when she walked across the cold fire to wake him he would not stir. Panic gripped her as she felt for his pulse and laid an ear to his chest.

"Dead to the world, but still in it," she muttered. She dragged him behind a thicket of brambles out of sight of the road and made him a sickbed out of their bedrolls.

She was too busy at first to fear the worst. There were herbs to gather, good, clean clay to dig from the bank for a poultice, and green twigs to peel and burn for their healing vapor. But still she did not guess, and for all her efforts he worsened. When she had done all she knew to do she had at last a spare moment to sit and eat a heel of bread by the fire. It was then that fear seized her and she began to shudder with a noiseless crying.

"If you die," she said to the Badger's still form, dashing the tears from her eyes, "the ground's too hard to bury you, so think of that! Wolves will scatter your bones over thirteen kingdoms. . . ."

At last she thought of the brandy in the chamberlain's room, and the bitter note beneath the perfume of the plums. Wormwood. The signs had been there, even if she had been blind to them: the racing pulse, the stomach pains.

Now it was a simple thing to gather the right herbs, to roast a knobby root over the coals and grind it into a bitter powder. By the morning of the third day the Badger woke bathed in sweat and complaining of a headache. Caitlin sat by the fire, her face streaked with soot, and smiled a weary smile. There could have been no better news than if he had awakened bathed in nectar, with a celestial melody and not an anvil-headache teasing his brain.

The Badger sat up, with no idea that he had lain near death for two days and nights. "It must be almost noon," he said resentfully. "You might have awakened me."

"I've been doing my best to wake you for two days," she said, and told him as much as she thought he ought to know, but not enough for him to guess how close to the grave he had come.

But he did guess. As they were saddling the horses he saw her lean on the broad neck of her horse, burying her face in its mane, and while her expression was hidden from him, the way her shoulders relaxed in relief and exhaustion made everything clear.

"Here, put these on," he said, handing her a pair of gloves he had brought from Thirdmoon. "It's too cold to ride all day without them."

It had grown much colder, and they were two days closer to the first storm of the winter.

∽∾∽

They kept to the main roads after that, and when they had to take a side track it was with many a backward glance. As they rode they passed carts bringing the last of the harvest in from the fields, and the Badger seized his chance to lighten the wagonloads a little. They supped in the saddle, on apples, yams, and turnips, and stopped to sleep in snatches, for it was cold at night, and it was easier to stay warm riding quickly beneath the harvest moon along the empty highway to the sea.

Or nearly empty. Elric was still behind them, although he was being careful not to let Motley get too close to his master. At night as they slept, Elric stole up to their horses, distracting the animals with lumps of sugar while he pressed their hooves into a box of powder ground from blind cave salamanders. As the horses went down the road they would leave phosphorescent footprints Elric could follow easily hours later in the dark. He would wake late and wait until nightfall before taking up the chase. He had much to occupy him, notably the writing of a letter.

Cousin,

I'm afraid I will need my allowance early. My expenses have been much higher than anticipated. There have been the horses to keep (you know what they eat), a friend's gambling debts to pay, salve for a wasp bite, and after being bent double for days pruning hedges I am afraid I bought myself a massage and a manicure. And will you look in on our brother and his daughter in Fifthmoon? All was well when I left them, but until their houseguest departs I will not rest entirely easy.

Everything else is as well as can be. Give my love to my sister.

Your loving cousin, E.

~∞~

Elric was not the only one writing a letter. That same morning the abbess of Ninthstile looked out the window at the nuns in their brown smocks digging potatoes in the convent fields.

"Has the messenger arrived?" she asked one of the sisters.

"He has not."

"Bring me my writing things," she said without turning around.

The sister fetched a small lapdesk containing paper and a steel pen. The abbess began to compose her letter.

> Convent of the Sacred Pentacle
> Ninthstile, Ninthmoon
>
> Abbey of Thirdmoon See
> Thirdmoon
>
> My dear brother in faith,
> As I have not had a message from you in some weeks, I am in the dark about whether to expect the young woman whom you have sentenced to our order. Having conceded to your greater wisdom in this matter, I am anxious to have her among us, for an extra pair of hands would be of use to us now in getting the crops in before the first freeze. As it is, I have had to turn away a robust and pious young woman from the town who wished to make her living with us, as I am holding our only spare cell for your postulant. May I have a word from you?
> Yours in the Pentacle,
> Clovis

When he received this message, the abbot of Thirdmoon See was in bed with an earache. The abbess's letter did nothing to succor him. He read the few lines grimly and called for his secretary.

"Take a letter," he snapped at the harelipped monk.

> Abbey of Thirdmoon See
> Thirdmoon
>
> Convent of the Sacred Pentacle
> Ninthsile, Ninthmoon
>
> My dear sister in faith,
> You shall receive by messenger from our brothers in Eighthmoon an allowance sufficient to hold a place for my charge until such time as she arrives. You may feel free to use it, if you feel so compelled, to hire a robust maiden from the village, to pull up onions in the

meantime. I impress upon you the extreme displeasure that will be brought upon you by the Necromancer should you fail him in this office, a displeasure from which I should be quite unable to shield you.

"Yours in the Pentacle, and so on," said the abbot, applying a compress to his ear.

Upon receiving this reply the abbess went out into the garden and pulled up onions, twisting each out of the ground viciously, as if it were the abbot's head.

There was another letter, one the Badger had never unsealed. It was the letter of introduction to the apothecary. Upon his brief rise in the world at the court of Fifthmoon, the letter had arrived at the royal laundry still pinned inside the Badger's shirt. A shortage of bluing had caused a pileup at the laundry, and the shirt was not laundered until long after the Badger had left Fifthmoon. It was then that the abbot's note was discovered by an illiterate presser. Dutifully, he pressed it, admiring the handwriting.

THE SANCTITY OF THE PENTACLE DEPENDS ON THE DEATH OF THE BEARER AT ALL COSTS.

❧

They were nearing the coast. In the morning the Badger woke to the taste of salt on the air. When they left the abbey the leaves had just been starting to turn after the long summer. It was now seven weeks since he had ridden out the gate of the abbey so cocksure and joyful, to become apprenticed to an apothecary. It seemed seven years. Still, it was good news: it was still a week or two before a storm could be expected to close the straits, and even that would be freakishly early. They had made good time, and if they made a good passage and had no more adventures, they could expect to reach Ninthstile by the first snow.

Having made these calculations, the Badger saw no need to rise early. He rolled over, hugged the bedroll to him, and drifted back off to sleep.

Caitlin's eyes were wide open. It was not a dream that had disturbed her sleep, but an uneasy feeling that they were being watched. She rose quietly so as not to wake the Badger. As she pulled on her boots she looked at the shock of tow hair that was all of him that showed; it made him look like a little boy. Caitlin felt a wave of helplessness. In many ways he was an innocent. If things went on as they had, that innocence could well end up costing him his life.

She walked to a clearing, her heart beating faster, the blood loud in her ears. There was someone watching her and listening. It was so still, no bird called, not a cricket offered a chirp to the morning air. Listening with all her might, all Caitlin could hear was a distant crop of the grass as the horses grazed.

Caitlin didn't know that she had spoken until the words were already hanging in the frosty air.

"Why are you doing this? What do you want from me?" Her words, and the thought that someone might really be listening, made her turn and run.

She shook the Badger awake roughly. One look at her face compelled him to hold his tongue and saddle the horses.

"Dream?" was all he said, when they had gone some distance down the road.

"Yes, but I was awake."

In the clearing Elric had had a nasty shock. *Her sneaking up on me like that,* he thought. His hands shook as he lit his pipe, and he wondered whether he was feeling his age. In his occupation, it wasn't uncommon for men to retire early. Like the Badger, he had thought to sleep in, but now sleep eluded him.

Still, he knew something the Badger didn't, something that would throw all the Badger's calculations to the four winds: sailors who took passengers across the straits were a highly superstitious lot, and the sum that could persuade them to give passage to a young woman with raven hair and seer's eyes had not been minted.

They reached the port of Little Rim that afternoon. The horses, used only for an occasional hawking outing, took the scent of the sea immediately to heart and trotted toward it with heads lifted to the salt air, ears up like signals of good weather.

Caitlin and the Badger stopped at the first good-sized inn. Because they were being followed, they had not for some days dared to light a fire, and it had been longer than they cared to remember since they had eaten a hot meal. They ordered the fish muddle, and while they were waiting for it the Badger inquired about a ship for the crossing.

"*The Golden Mole* sets sail tomorrow," the tavern keeper told him, "and *The Wavetrimmer* two days after that. The next ship won't weigh anchor until late next week."

"And after that?"

"After that you'd best settle in until spring. Most of the berths have been spoken for months since. You'll be lucky to bunk with rats in the hold."

The Badger returned to the table to find Caitlin making great inroads into a platter of fish and potatoes. He took the knife, scraped a third of what remained onto her plate, and began to devour his own meal from the serving platter.

"We shouldn't have any trouble crossing to Ninthmoon."

Caitlin didn't answer, and the Badger set down his knife.

"Look, Cait. You had better speak now. If you don't want to go I won't take you. I'll say you cast a spell over me and left me wandering around the docks with the net menders. And you can go where you will."

"And the bounty hunters?"

"By the turn of the year, I can be back in Thirdmoon See to explain myself."

"I have come to believe with all my heart that if you return to Thirdmoon See with me undelivered, the abbot will not go easy on you."

"But better muleskinning for me than Ninthstile for you." As he said it, the Badger bent over his plate so his face was hidden from her.

"No," said Caitlin, "you must deliver me, and on time. I begin to see a pattern in it."

"Pattern?"

"Only that there is more at work in this than one stable-boy and a village witch can account for."

He raised his head and met her gaze with growing suspicion. "You know a great deal more about all this than you're letting on. Have you dreamed the end, is that it? It is, isn't it? You know what's up, and you're not telling! Sweet heaven, but you'll drive me mad before this is over!"

"That is one thing of which you can be sure," Caitlin said. "But you'll find, I think, a serenity in lunacy. At least, I have always found it so."

They settled their bill and went in search of *The Golden Mole*. As they went, a man approached the tavern keeper.

"Were they asking after passage to Big Rim?"

"What if they were?"

Something gleamed in the man's hand. It was too dark to tell if it were silver or the blade of a dagger. In either case the tavern keeper thought it in his own best interest to answer.

"Yes. He asked about ships making the crossing this week."

"Did he say where he was bound?"

"No." To his relief, the tavern keeper saw a silver coin appear on the barrel-head beside him.

"Obliged," said his questioner.

"Don't mention it."

"You had better not, if you know what's good for you, and if you don't, by the Pentacle. I'll teach you!" And with that he made his exit. The tavern keeper suddenly wanted nothing to do with the coin, and dropped it into the apron pocket of a passing serving girl.

Reaching the street the man saw Caitlin and the Badger headed to the dock where *The Golden Mole* was moored. Satisfied, he stopped a passing vendor and bought a bag of steamed mussels. Before long Elric came into view.

The two men greeted each other silently, with a sign each understood. The other handed Elric the bag.

"The Golden Mole."

Caitlin and the Badger had already been turned away. The ship's first mate took one look at Caitlin and refused to let them on board.

"And if you come around here again you can make the crossing tied to the keel!" He spat to stave off the evil eye. "Sainted Pentacle, I've never seen a petrel black as that."

The Badger was shaken, Caitlin only sullen. When he started to ask directions to *The Wavetrimmer*, she protested.

"What's the use? You'll never find a ship willing to take me on, not unless you find a way to dye my blue eye green."

As it turned out, there was no need for that: *The Wavetrimmer* had sustained considerable damage from rats and in ridding them from the hold it had been discovered that many of the ship's timbers were rotten. *The Wavetrimmer*, a sailor told them, was in dry dock, and would trim no waves until spring.

It began to rain. They pulled their cloaks around them and bent their heads to the wind, walking back to the tavern. Suddenly Caitlin stopped stock-still and stared. Almost hidden by a pile of nets was an old woman selling eels. She could have been Abagtha, risen from the dead.

Caitlin's lips went blue, and she was so much more than usually pale that the Badger put out a hand to steady her. She shook off his arm and went up to the old woman.

"What a ghost you are!" she murmured. "As if you had come to take me back, or warn me."

The old woman merely narrowed her black eyes and held out a basket, lifting the lid to show a squirming mass of eels. Caitlin drew back with a shudder. Was it all a trick of the light? Now the old woman's eyes didn't seem so dark, and her face seemed younger, with something eerie about it.

"Eels, missie? They are very fresh," said the old woman, shaking the basket so the eels slithered to the other end of it. "Or is it something else that you are looking for, daughter? A ship, perhaps?"

The Badger stepped forward. "Cait, I don't like this."

Caitlin didn't hear him. "And do you know of a ship?"

"Something better! A way to walk on water, for a price."

"Name it."

The Badger began to pull on her arm. "Come on, Cait. Can't you see she's mad?"

She shook him off so fiercely he let go.

"Your price, old woman."

"Your hair, my dear. Nothing less."

That gave her pause, but only for a moment. "Show me, first."

The Badger made a noise of disgust and walked a short distance away, standing with his hands thrust as far into his pockets as they would go.

The old woman brought out an eel, freshly killed, and slitting it with a knife she drew out a map. This she unfolded and presented silently for Caitlin's inspection.

It was beautifully made, the product of ancient skill, drawn on the finest vellum in colors that seemed to swim beneath the eye. She could clearly see the woods and streams of the countryside through which they had just passed. But all the markings were in runes Caitlin had never seen, and half the map was missing—the half with Ninthstile. Before she handed the map back to the eel-seller Caitlin noticed a gruesome sea-monster on the part representing the straits. Just a flourish of a bored mapmaker's pen?

"Where is the rest?"

The old woman laughed, a sound as dry as driftwood. "You are thinking that it is little enough for the rich price! Your glory, your crown, for half a map in a rune tongue no one has spoken for seven times seventy years!"

Caitlin kept her gaze level, but in the winter light off the water her eyes blazed, the blue one making the green greener, the green one making the blue one seem the thing they named the color for. She was not vain about her hair, but she well remembered a time it had been cut against her will.

The eel-seller relented. "There is a harpmaker who has the other half, and they say he knows runes from before the Pentacle."

"And the Spellkey?"

The black eyes glittered, and the old woman reached up with a withered hand to touch the blue-black silk that tumbled to Caitlin's waist. "Perhaps. Your hair, first. Then I will tell you the way."

The Badger bit his lip as Caitlin bent her head and let the old woman saw off the thick rope of her hair with a rusty fish knife. The length that remained began to curl in the salt air, and the sight of her pale face with its dark halo made the Badger's throat go dry.

Caitlin seized the map and tucked it inside her belt. The hair glittered in the old woman's fist like strands of jet. "Where will I find the harpmaker?"

The old woman pointed up the sheer face of the cliffs.

They left the old woman to her eels and baskets. Caitlin moved as if in a dream, deep in thought, not so much about the map and the promised Spellkey, as for Abagtha and the early days when the old witch's indifference had most resembled kindness. And she was hoping fervently that she had not surrendered her hair for nothing. She had let the eel-seller shear her in the hope that the map would prove all she guessed, but also that the loss of that seal of womanliness might drive from the Badger's eyes a certain look she had seen in them lately.

The Badger walked behind her, his eyes fastened on the bare nape of her neck. He was greatly afraid she was going mad, and he wanted both to run away from her as far and fast as he could, and to seize her and shake her to reason. For he had not even recognized his own symptoms, and he sickened ever more as the hours wore on.

∽

The eel-seller sank back among the nets and closed her eyes for a long moment. When she opened them again they were grey. Elric's calling was giving the beholder what the beholder wished to see, but this latest deception had called for a sorcery outside the boundary of his license and power. The mercurial potion he had drunk made him queasy, and he turned his head to retch. When he raised his aching head Elric saw atop one of the baskets the lively heap of Caitlin's hair. He let his fingers run through its silky mass and shuddered.

"Ah," he breathed, "that I could buy your eyes as well!"

10

A LIAR'S TALE

As they climbed the steep path up the cliff, they spied the wreck of a ship on the rocks, ghostly beneath the water, its timbers bleached like ribs, the broken hull a shattered breastbone.

"They must have tried to make the crossing after the first storm," the Badger said.

"Walking on water."

"What?"

"It's what the old woman said, about the map. I can't think what she meant."

"She might not have *meant* anything. What I don't understand is what she wanted with your hair."

"She may think she can get some sort of power from it."

"Well? Can she?"

"Don't be superstitious."

When they reached the top they were suddenly afraid they had climbed the wrong path, for there was no dwelling in sight. Then Caitlin pointed, laughing. Up through the sod of the clifftop rose a chimney, and from the chimney a wraith of smoke. "Though it seems a much more mannered barrow than mine."

There was a trapdoor in the ground, and after looking

for a bell (for some reason he thought there would be a bell), the Badger stamped on it with his boot.

The door immediately swung open, as if the harpmaker had been waiting for him (which he had). He beckoned them in.

"Call me Leier," he said, "as in one who tells untruths, or as in a kind of harp."

Leier looked glued together out of driftwood and catgut, all sinew and weathered grey. He wore what must once have been a bard's tunic of bright green; now it was a harlequin pattern of varnish, wine, and gravy stains. The room was crammed with harps, the smallest no longer than your thumb, the tallest seemed to hold up the roof. The single table was crammed with curling foolscap sheets of music, newly glued harp frames drying, and skeins of unstrung harp strings.

Leier gave them cups of hot bogberry wine, laced with gin, to warm them from the inside out.

"You have come looking for a map, and hoping to find the Spellkey, but you haven't been told what it is. So you are frantic to know, and you have sold your hair to find out. Did it mean much to you, your hair?"

"No more than it weighed."

"Ah, but you would be surprised. Hair can weigh a great deal. A young woman not far from here drowned, washing her hair in the river. Sank like a stone. Perhaps that is what you meant after all, that your hair meant a great deal to you?"

"It was no sacrifice. You seem to know a great deal about our quest."

"It is my calling to know such things. I am no seer, mind. My eyes are of a color. But I am a storyteller, and a storyteller must have an eye for detail. All morning and afternoon I have seen signs of visitors: Part of the cliff fell into the sea, and I saw a little cloud the shape of a cat chasing its tail. Which is an odd thing, for it's dogs that chase their tails. But it was a sign nevertheless, for here you are. But wait." Leier disappeared among the harps, reappearing with a scroll tied with string.

"The other half of the map?" said the Badger.

"He's quicker than he looks, isn't he? Well, we'll put the halves together and see." Leier spread out the map on the table. Once the corners had been weighed down with gluepots, it was clear the halves matched exactly. Caitlin's eyes immediately fastened on something penned faintly in one corner, in runes she knew.

"Chameol!"

"Then it's real, after all," said the Badger.

"Who ever said it wasn't? Don't tell me you're a Pentaclist!" Leier peered at the Badger suspiciously.

"But it's just a map, after all—we can't sail across the straits on it."

"Just a map? Who said it was anything *but* a map? But it is a very good map, perhaps the best in thirteen kingdoms. Believe me, it is worth the best you have to give." Leier's eyes went to Caitlin's shorn head. "And you have already given your best, or very near to it."

"Well, that settles it. Let's go, Cait. Heaven knows we haven't got anything to give him for it." In truth the Badger had a little money, but he didn't mean to spend the last of it on a crazy hermit whose brain was half pickled with gin.

"Oh, but you mustn't judge it by what you can see in it. It's what you *can't* see in it. But here—you have nothing to lose! You say you have nothing to give me for it. We will work it this way. I will tell you every tale I know; if you fall asleep before I am done, I keep the map. If I run out of tales before dawn, the map is yours."

Caitlin considered. "Will you read the runes to us, if we win?"

"Ah, milady, you drive a bargain hard. The runes, too, and more, but only if I'm tongue-tied before day is broke."

"Cait," said the Badger, "we've got to get back to the horses."

"Then go to them!"

"And leave you here, to kill yourself on the rocks in the dark?" The truth was that the Badger did not relish making his way back to the inn alone.

"I had managed to keep myself alive without your help

before you came, and I shall manage without it when you are gone," she said tartly.

"Brute luck, that's all." Then he and Caitlin drew their chairs away from the fire, so they would be a little chill, and emptied their cups into the jug, so the gin would not make them nod. Then Leier reached for one of the harps hanging overhead and let his fingers skim its strings.

"Long ago, before the Pentacle, for there are some things so old, before things became as they are now and there was still magic abroad in the land, an old woman had a field of enchanted potatoes. As there was no Pentacle, and no Pentaclists to tax her for growing enchanted potatoes, the old woman grew as many as she wanted, without having to give half to the temple.

"Now it happened one fine autumn that the crop was larger than she could ever remember, and the old woman had a very good memory indeed. She grew calluses on her hands the size of soup-plates from digging up the crop, her cellar was overflowing with potatoes, and the barn, and the corncrib, and the house, until the potatoes threatened to fill the chimney. At last the old woman threw up her hands in despair. Much as she hated to do it, she loaded the cart with potatoes and drove it to the rubbish pile on the edge of town. Then she went home and had her supper of ordinary potatoes, for enchanted potatoes are unpredictable things, and the old woman wanted a good night's sleep, and no surprises.

"But enchanted potatoes are full of all sorts of arbitrary magics, and even in the dump pile they waited in their jackets of silvery brown, and before long there came wandering a soldier home from the wars, lame and ready to drop from hunger. He had been turned away from every inn in the town, and all he wanted was to curl up on the rubbish heap among the broken crocks and parings and catch a few hours' sleep. If he found a morsel fit to eat, or half fit to eat, the poor soldier was starving enough to eat it.

"Now right after the old woman had dumped her load of enchanted potatoes, a sweep had come up with a cartload of live coals and ashes, so that when the soldier curled up on the heap he was surprised to find a warm spot at his feet. What should he discover but a potato, roasted in its jacket and piping hot! He devoured not one but seven—for he hadn't eaten in as many days.

"At first the enchanted potatoes had no effect except to plunge the soldier into a deep slumber, and he seemed bound for that in any case. But he had no sooner shut his eyes than he began to have the most extraordinary dreams—"

Caitlin was jolted awake by the Badger's elbow in her ribs. "You'll have to do better than that," he hissed. He himself was an old hand at staying awake, having been awakened every four hours throughout his boyhood for prayers.

Leier told them the rest of that tale, and then another, and then he stopped. "Are you hungry? Can I offer you a bite? Perhaps a potato? Well, if you're sure—"

He told them the story of a blacksmith's youngest son's great kindness to a cricket king, and the inheritance it won him; the curious history of a girl who climbed down a staircase under a hearthstone, and the strange things she found there; of a fisherman who pulled a locked box from the sea, and many more. . . .

"There was a simpleton who built a castle of butter in an icy waste, and there he ruled in summer, crossing to the desert in the winter, where he built a castle of biscuit. And he made himself a wife all of butter, and a wife of biscuit, because he found the one of butter cold. . . .

". . . there was a beauty whose father promised her to a beast. And living with him, she grew to love him, and changed into a beast herself. . . .

"Once upon a time there was a dairyman, and he and his wife were childless. The wife was so jealous of their poor tabby that she drowned the cat's litter. Not long after that the wife conceived and bore a small son with a cat's face, and they called him Catswhiskers. . . ."

Leier paused. It was the middle of the night. He

reached for another harp and began his seventy-second tale, when Caitlin stopped him.

"We've heard that one already."

"Are you sure?" Leier frowned.

"Yes." Caitlin yawned. "He kisses the princess, and when she wakes he finds she is his stillborn twin."

"Mmm." Leier put the harp in the pile of finished tales. The next harp gave out a weird chord that made the Badger shudder.

"A prince loved to ride in the fields outside his father's palace. He would leave his mare under the trees and go walking into the broad golden meadows, discarding his fine embroidered coat and glossy boots to walk unfastened through the bowing, fragrant hay. One day he met there a lovely girl, all mute, naked but for her red and golden hair and a skirt of straw and flowers. She beckoned him to the bank of the stream, and he followed her and lay with her there all day in delight until dusk, when she left him. He met her there for many days, neither of them speaking a word, she mute, he mute with desire for her."

Caitlin's eyes were narrowed as if in sleep. The Badger seemed hardly to breathe as the harpmaker's voice washed over him.

"She always was the first to leave, and the one demand she made, imploring him with her eyes and a shake of her head, was that he never follow her to watch where she went. For weeks he was only too willing to comply, to admire her neck and rosy flank from behind as she left him.

"But as time went by the prince began to convince himself that she went from him to another lover. He hid his mounting rage from her, determined to follow her and catch her unawares.

"At their next meeting she seemed full of tenderness and sorrow, and kissed him upon parting as though sending him to his death. As soon as she was out of sight he struggled into his clothes and stole after her. The setting sun seemed willfully to blind him, the grass to reach up to trip him. She was in his sight one moment, gone the next. He fell, rose, stumbled after her. She had gone back to the grove of trees where he left his horse. He thought he saw her stepping from some ermine mantle, her body gleaming in the last rays of the setting sun. Then the sun left his eyes and he saw she was stepping into a horse's hide, her human foot already knitting with the hoof and shank and fetlock. Turning and seeing him, she rent the air with an inhuman cry of grief and vanished through the trees, leaving the prince to mourn forever the loss of his beloved roan mare."

Caitlin nudged the Badger, who seemed in a trance, and he drew away at her touch as if from something hot. He went to the pail of icy water by the door and splashed his face until some color returned to it. Out the single window carved into the cliff-face it was still dark: It might be one hour until dawn, or six.

Leier strummed a gentler chord, staring at the ceiling. "There was a young queen, newly wed, who rose every dawn while her husband was still sleeping and let a ball of wax fall from her taper into the basin. One day the wax formed the sign she was waiting for, and the queen knew she was with child. Now, it did not sit well with the king's advisers that he had married a woman from a land so far across the sea. What was known about her? And did not women from strange lands work magic and devour their own children? The young queen had not been married a week when she overheard the king's wise men plotting to steal her firstborn and stain the queen's robe with blood, so that the king would have her put to death.

"Now the young queen did indeed work magic of a benevolent variety, and she used all her ingenuity and quickness of wit to devise a means for outwitting the royal advisers. So when the wax curdled tellingly in her basin, she lost no time going to the palace apiary, where she made a secret cradle of beeswax and said a spell over it. She visited the apiary regularly, and in the spring she surprised her husband with a daughter. . . ."

When Leier finished this tale he could tell by the sound of the sea on the cliff where the tide was, and what hour it was. The pile of harps that had already given up their stories filled the room. Leier picked up a harp that had some strings missing, but he was unable to remember the ending, and Caitlin refused to allow it as a tale.

"There's one left in that corner," said the Badger.

"No, not really." Leier shifted in his seat.

"What do you mean? It looks like a harp to me. Either tell us that tale, or hand over our half of the map."

Leier looked at them a little wildly, his eyes glazed from a night's tale-telling, the cords in his neck standing out in concentration. He crossed the room and picked up the last harp. It was made from a different pattern than the others; when Leier picked it up the candle on the table guttered, and the pile of finished harps settled with a musical sighing.

"Once—" Leier cleared his throat, licked his lips, and started over. "Once there was a tanner's daughter's son—"

He got no further. The Badger had him by the collar, pinned to the floor, growling, "How could you know that, if you are any good thing?"

Caitlin dragged him off. "Stop—look, it's light—we've won."

But the Badger had paused, mind racing, hand on the purse of money in his pocket. To hear the rest of that tale—to know how this journey should end. But Leier had seized his chance. Snatching up a knife, he cut through the strings, and for good measure cast the now mute frame on the fire.

Then he held the map over a candle.

"Careful," Caitlin said, her hand going to her bare nape, "that cost us much."

As Leier held the map over the flame, writing that had been invisible to them darkened by degrees until at last it could be made out: the figure of a key in the seas between the Eight Moons and the Far Five.

"The Spellkey?"

"No—but you are not far from the truth. It is the key to Chameol."

"That's uncharted water," the Badger said uneasily.

"Only if you have a Pentaclist map. A few nights of the year it is shallow enough at ebb tide for you to wade across. Tonight is one of those nights. It will take you three hours, and once you've begun there is no turning back, or you'll be caught in the incoming tide."

"Say no more." Caitlin reached for the map and took it over by the fire to study it. Leier seized the Badger's arm.

"Watch over her. She is the stronger of you, and because of that, she is in the greater danger."

The Badger nodded, then shook his head. "How can I protect her, when I don't even know what the danger is?"

"Only know it is in your power to save her, as she has saved you."

Caitlin came back with the map. "You promised to translate the runes."

Leier had barely taken the map from her hand when a knock sounded on the trapdoor. "Quickly," cried the harpmaker. "This way!"

Under the rug there was a crawlspace as dank and unwholesome as could be imagined. "It leads to the beach at the base of the cliff, here," he said, showing the place on the map. "Go, I tell you. I know that knock, and they mean you no good."

When Leier opened the door to admit the bounty hunters, there was no one else to be seen. There was only one cup of hot gin on the table, and the two spare stools were being used to hold a harp frame while the glue dried.

"Two strangers traveling together? No, no, I can't say I have. But there were two bodies washed up on the beach just last week, though it would be stretching the truth to say they traveled together."

11

THE DEVIL'S SIEVE

Elric had lost them. They had gone up the cliff, he had watched them, but neither he nor anyone else had seen them come down. To go and visit the harpmaker would be too great a risk, exposing them both. It was when he stopped for a hot toddy that he overheard the bounty hunters.

"Washed up drowned, the two of them, just like Flotsam and Jetsam in one of them romancers."

"But will they pay? That's the thing."

"They're in sacks out front. After my dinner I'm going to find the notary and get 'em notarized. Then it'll be back into the sea with them, with some lead weights this time, and a prayer, if I can remember one."

Elric set down his tankard and went outside to where the sacks with their unlovely burdens leaned wetly against the tavern stoop.

He felt curiously light, looking down at them, thinking, Will I end that way, when it is my turn? And he could not really believe she was dead, that it was over, his job was done.

This was not how any of them had imagined it would happen.

～∽～

Caitlin and the Badger had descended into the Devil's Sieve, a network of caverns that honeycombed the cliff. From the moment the trapdoor slammed shut above their heads they were assailed by an eerie moaning, deafening at times, but most frightening when it was barely audible. Now it was low and mournful, now a raging wail that threatened to deafen them, shrieking and howling around their heads like a loathsome spirit denied rest.

The howling made the Badger increasingly confused and dispirited. Caitlin, who was a harp upon which all manner of otherworldly notes could sound themselves, was driven half mad by it. The Badger had never seen her so frantic, or looking less human. She was like a cat trapped in a burning building, so paralyzed with fright that she shrank against the walls of the cavern, incapable of moving forward or backward. At last the Badger blindfolded her with his handkerchief and led her along.

If you can call it leading, he thought to himself, *for a leader knows where he is going.* The darkness and the echoing, eerie cry of the sea drove his sense of direction from him. He felt, as he led Caitlin inch by inch through the chill, pitch-black caverns, as if he were an unwilling player in a giant game of Blind Man's Bluff. All the time Caitlin clutched his arm silently, shuddering. The Badger had never seen her so devoid of spirit, and it frightened him.

After wandering for what seemed hours they came upon a landmark—a curious projection from the ceiling of the cave oddly like a human hand. The Badger realized with a sinking heart that they had been this way before. His panic passed through his hand into Caitlin's like a spark, and she thrashed out, striking at him blindly, and making a terrible, catlike moaning. The Badger tried to calm her but ended merely parrying her blows. They kept up a frantic wrestling for a moment in the dark before the Badger slipped and fell. They hit the cavern floor together. Caitlin, suddenly calm, took the blindfold from her eyes.

"We're lost."

He knew she meant it in both senses of the word.

Unspoken between them hung the knowledge that the tide had long since turned. They could not make the crossing now.

Caitlin laughed, and the sound was so unexpected it sent a shudder up the Badger's spine.

"I must be going mad," she said. "I feel as though the caverns have eyes."

The Badger suddenly jumped to his feet with a cry. They had been surrounded by a dozen brown and wizened faces, all studying them with intense curiosity.

They were children, but so strange in their speech and attire they might have been members of some distant tribe. They were dressed in rags fashioned from the clothing meant for grown men, held on with crudely fashioned belts or suspenders. These strange outfits had been further adorned with shells and feathers, giving their wearers a wild aspect.

None seemed much older than eight, except for a boy who was taller than the rest. He alone of them seemed to be able to speak, and he told them they were the Cavekin, children cast off when their sailor fathers returned to the sea and their abandoned mothers returned to the farm. Put to sea in casks, they had been spat back on the rocks by the waves. Rejected by both land and sea, they took to the caves, which were part land and part sea but really neither.

Their guide led them to a chamber deep in the heart of the Sieve, and spread before them a feast of crabs and mussels roasted in the shell, and all sorts of dainties rescued from a chest tossed up by a storm. There were potted meats, preserved figs, cake in tin boxes, cheese, and a lone bottle of wine the rocks had spared. One of the jars bore a wax seal with the crest of Milo's kingdom.

Caitlin and the Badger ate at first merely to show their hosts respect, unsure still whether they were hosts or captors: while the children were small, most carried sharp daggers.

But these they used to cut fish, which they preferred raw, and washed down with great quantities of a salty beer made from dune grass. They also ate with great relish skewers of meat that the Badger refused with a shudder, fearing it was roasted bat.

After this strange feast, the Cavekin fell asleep in a pile, "like so many puppies," the Badger said.

There was comfort now, in the warm, sooty chamber, in lingering by the fire and feeling the tension of the previous hours drain from them.

The Badger relit one of the torches and, stepping over the sleeping children, held the light to the chamber walls at the edge of the fire's circle.

The walls were covered with runes and fantastic pictures of strange creatures: winged elk, and lions with human bodies. The Badger traced maps of cities lost in the clouds, or hidden beneath the waves, where women leaned from watery balconies, singing back to the whales their own songs.

Caitlin found, scattered among the broken sea chests and fish bones that covered the chamber floor, objects of wonderful workmanship, such as she had not seen, even in Abagtha's books, nor among King Linus's treasures. There was a clock in a bronze case that told not just the hours but the phases of the moons and the procession of the stars across the heavens. There were maps showing great mountain ranges on the bottom of the sea, and fine instruments whose use they could not guess, wrought in such steel as the Badger had never seen.

"These are never from any shipwreck," said the Badger. He waved a hand. "Glass, pottery—none of it would have made it over the rocks in less than a hundred pieces."

"Yes."

"Well, then where did it come from? Those children never stole all this. If they somehow had, they would have sold it for food."

"It must have been here all along, then, from before these catacombs were formed, or when they served a different purpose." She pushed away the tattered flag of a ship long since splintered into driftwood, and exposed a niche in the wall.

"This was a fitting for a torch. Besides, you don't think

the children carved those runes, do you? They probably can't write in any living tongues, let alone a dead one."

The Badger was studying intently the runes on the far wall. "Let me see the map," he said suddenly.

Caitlin took the halves from their waterproof packet inside her shirt.

"Yes," he said. "See, they match the ones on the map, here, and here. They're the same as the *L* in Chameol."

"And there are three letters before, and three after— as in Spellkey." Caitlin's eyes were shot with gold from the torchlight.

The boy who had served as their interpreter woke, and dashed the sleepy-sticks from his eyes. The runes and "pretties," as he called the treasures, had been here as long as he could remember. He led them to a spot where part of the cave had collapsed. Through an opening they could see an ancient chamber, lined with what Caitlin guessed were stone biers, and here and there the glint of further treasures.

The Badger remembered their engagement with the tide, and the boy led them swiftly through the tunnels. As they went, their guide would stop and snatch a blind white salamander from its hiding place, kill the creature with a quick bite to its skull, and sling it from his belt. By the time they reached the cave entrance, a tassel of salamanders hung from the urchin's waist, and the Badger was feeling queasy.

It was a steep drop of forty feet to the narrow strip of rocky beach that had been left along the base of the cliff by the incoming tide. The boy lowered them to it by means of a rope, hauled it back up, and disappeared.

They found themselves alone on the beach.

"It won't be out again for hours," said the Badger. He squinted at the sea; the moon had risen, and there was a light wind. Caitlin settled herself on the sand.

"We ought to sleep," she said.

But although he was so weary and cold he was ready to drop, the Badger found he couldn't sleep. Instead he sat and watched Caitlin sleep, dreamlessly, it seemed, for she tossed and muttered not at all. She lay curled as flexible as a cat, the sea breeze stirring the roughly cut hair at the nape of her neck. The Badger closed his eyes, and when he opened them he was a little surprised to see her there still, sleeping so soundly.

This was no beauty he had ever been taught to admire. Beauties had winning smiles, shy glances, breasts as ready to roost in the hand as a dove. Caitlin was as tall as he, or taller, probably stronger, yielding in nothing, contrary in everything, beetle-browed and stormy.

But for all that he was conscious of nothing so much as the desire to kiss her, and not very gently.

"God help you," he said to himself, "if you fall in love with that!"

She was awake now, rubbing the sleep from her eyes, pulling her clothing closer around her against the cold.

"How long have I been asleep?"

"I don't know. A few hours. The tide is almost out. We should wait a few minutes more."

She nodded dumbly, and he watched her stand and walk toward the surf.

"Where are you going?"

"I'm thirsty." She knelt, scooped up some water, and quickly spat it out, completely dumbfounded.

"It's salt!"

He laughed. "And what else should it be?"

It was a defeat for Caitlin, if a small one. She hated these confrontations with facts alien to her, common knowledge to everyone else. Most people do not live in oak trees with red doors; most children do not dream the future; the sea is salty. The worst thing was always thinking each humiliation would be the last.

"Here," he said. "I saved the wine. The children seemed to prefer that beer."

She accepted the bottle from his hand, and as her fingers closed on the neck they brushed his own.

She handed back the wine and he drank, too.

"I've never seen the sea either," he confessed, "and if Asaph hadn't told me, I wouldn't have known it was salty. He was a sailor once, and he used to tell me—"

"Badger. I think I should go alone."

His heart froze. "What?"

"I want you to leave me here."

"And what will you do?" He spoke calmly, but his heart was hammering.

"Swim across on my own."

"Don't speak nonsense. And don't tell me half-truths, either! You've had one of your dreams, haven't you? You had a dream just now."

Caitlin was silent so long he thought she might not answer. Then she said. "Yes."

"Cait—"

In the moonlight the tears ran down her face unchecked. "Don't you see? I don't want you killed over nothing."

"Don't talk nonsense."

"I don't want you killed over me."

"Well, I don't plan on paying you any such compliments, don't worry. I think we had better start out." He began to take off his boots, then his jacket. "You'd better do the same. When these get wet they'll be like lead weights."

They waded into the shallows with their teeth chattering. Hands shaking with cold, they held the halves of the map together.

"Yes," said Caitlin, "this is the place."

"All right." The Badger watched her go out into the waves, and then, with a heavy heart, he followed.

⤜⤛

Leier stood on the cliff gazing out to sea. The moon was bright, and a stiff breeze made sails of his cloak and shirt. He paced to the edge and back, muttering under his breath.

"Not good! Not good, I fear, not good at all!"

A storm was coming in, and the Badger had miscalculated the tide.

⤜⤛

The map was folded and pinned in Caitlin's shirt, and as the water came higher and higher she took out the packet and clenched it in her teeth. They were not halfway across when suddenly Caitlin could no longer feel the bottom.

The Badger saw Caitlin founder as a wave hit her. *Sweet heaven, she can't swim.*

So this is how I die, she thought. It was not at all as she had dreamed it; she was so numb with cold she hardly felt it anymore. The salt was bitter, but now the water seemed to her as warm as tears.

The Badger fought through the waves toward her. There was no way he could swim to either shore and hold her head above water. He might gain the shore alone, but he did not think of it. He reached her and pulled her head out of the water, but a large swell drove them apart.

When he broke the surface again she was nowhere in sight.

"Cait! Cait!" His calls were useless, lost in the vastness of sea and sky more quickly than a tern's cry. Then the water was over him, and he remembered nothing.

❧

The first bounty hunter paid the fisherman. As he got out his wallet he made rather a show of a dagger he carried. "And a little extra, eh? for the wife and babby, and because you're a man what knows how to hold his tongue."

He and the second bounty hunter pushed the fishing boat into the waves.

"There's a storm coming," said the other. "I don't like it."

"Well, neither do I, but it's a damn good thing I thought to check her eyes, isn't it?"

❧

Gently, gently, the dolphins nudged the still forms. Working in pairs they kept their burdens steered toward the island that lay before them, shrouded in mist and ringed with rocks. They chattered between themselves of the coming storm, still a distance off, and to the north. On the shore someone was waiting with a lantern, for the storm had made it dark again. There would be mackerel for them, and their warm, watery pen. Closer and closer they nudged the two forms.

Although the coming foul weather had made it dim,

there was enough light to show the gold collars the animals wore, and the strange runes upon them.

On shore the two bodies, apparently lifeless, were put on litters and carried off to the building, white as coral, that rose above the others on the island. As the procession of lanterns and hooded figures wound toward the fortress, the storm closed in.

Caitlin woke to find herself alone in a wide bed in a shuttered room. *Am I in the convent, then? No, I must be dead. This is heaven, or hell, or some such place.*

A woman entered the room bearing a tray. Caitlin could not tell, looking at her, whether she was angel or fiend.

"Where am I?"

The woman did not reply, but placed the tray on the table beside the bed. She held a cup to Caitlin's lips, and gratefully Caitlin emptied it of a liquor, clear as water but thicker, sweet with honey and fragrant with honeysuckle and an herb she could not name. No sooner had she finished it, than Caitlin felt strength coursing through her limbs and at the same time a profound weariness. Her eyelids closed of their own accord.

When they opened once more there were two women in the room, the one who had ministered to her and another—taller, her hair hidden by a headdress.

"Is this the convent?"

The women looked at each other and laughed, but did not answer her. They helped her out of bed and dressed her in clothing that was light and soft yet marvelously warm.

Caitlin was led down an open corridor with arches facing the sea. To her right she could see a low orchard and fields falling away to a bay. Then they turned a corner and the women let her into a room.

Lost in the bed at the other end of it lay the Badger, his head bound, his cheek cut.

Heart beating swiftly, Caitlin thought, *He isn't dead, or they would have put coins on his eyes.* There: the sheet had moved. He had breathed.

"Leave us."

When they had gone she went and undid the dressing with trembling hands. Satisfied that they had treated the injury competently, Caitlin turned back the covers. She meant only to feel for broken bones, or at least that was what she told herself as she ran her hands lightly over the Badger's limbs.

He seemed cold to her touch, so there seemed nothing wrong with slipping in beside him, to warm him.

She realized he was awake.

For a long moment, she lay tensed beside him, pretending to be asleep. But his arms tightened around her, and he shook her gently.

"Cait—"

When he recalled it later, it seemed to him he had moved from deepest sleep into the throes of an agile, feverish passion quite unlike waking. He had imagined what loving her would be like more often than he liked to confess, but never the way it happened: halting questions, to learn whether she was in the bed by design or accident; the first kiss, careful of the bandage, then a needy one, in which all the breath was drawn from his body through the top of his head like a fire, leaving him light as ash. The first shock, and then abandoning themselves to it, like falling and burning and drowning all at once. Who would have guessed that a tongue so acid could taste so sweet, that one so rough could be so tender? Bewildered but not inclined to question this turn of fortune, he kissed the nape of her neck and drifted off into a healing sleep.

Caitlin lay beside him, silently reciting her surprise: the sea is salty, and this is sweet. Sure now this was neither convent nor hell, and that they were safe for the immediate future, Caitlin let herself be lulled off by his heartbeat.

12

THE ISLAND

In the morning they woke to find breakfast had been set out at the foot of the bed: fresh fruit in winter, melon and strawberries that seemed hot from the sun, steaming cups of wine, bread and butter. Two sets of clothes had been laid out as well, identical except for size. Caitlin had the longer legs, and got the longer trousers. Someone had left a basin and razor, and the Badger let himself be barbered. She didn't cut him at all, and when she had finished, bent her head and quickly kissed him under the chin. She got lather on her nose doing this, and while they were laughing, the door opened to admit a woman.

She was taller than Caitlin, and unlike the women they had seen the day before she wore no headdress. Her hair spilled in a bronze riot over her shoulders and down her back. Her clothes, too, lacked the restraint of the sick-nurses' uniforms: over black trousers and boots she wore a flaring coat of black velvet and turquoise silk that came to her knees.

She went to the window and threw back the shutters.

"Good morning! I trust you spent the night well." Mischief leapt in her eyes.

"We did, thank you," said Caitlin coolly.

"Good, good. I am your guide and interpreter, Iiliana. Now, tell me your names and how you came to be in such a cold sea during such a nasty storm."

"We couldn't afford passage to Big Rim, so we thought we would swim across at low tide," Caitlin said.

"And what awaited you in Big Rim?"

"Our parents wouldn't agree to our getting married," said the Badger.

"Why didn't you stow away?" asked Iiliana, opening her eyes very wide. Caitlin shifted uneasily; the eyes were very blue, and very knowing.

"If we'd been caught, they would have put us ashore again in Little Rim, and then our parents would have kept us apart forever."

Iiliana burst into laughter. When the hilarity had subsided she put on a pair of spectacles and read from some papers she drew from her pocket.

"Matthew Tannerson, born to Margaret, the unwed daughter of a widower and tanner by the name of Thomas in the town of Moorsedge, Thirdmoon See. Remanded by maternal grandfather to the guardianship of the abbot of Thirdmoon See to be apprenticed as a monk or else taught a trade. Apprenticed briefly to an apothecary in Moorsedge but returned in semi-disgrace."

She looked at the next page. "No given name, familiarly known as Caitlin; abandoned as a child in the forest known as the Weirdwood, raised by a recluse and spell-seller named Abagtha. Little known of early years until the death of the old woman. At about the age of sixteen the girl left the wood and went to live in a burial chamber on the moor. During this period she may have suffered abuse at the hands of local men, although this is undocumented. Allegations of witchcraft, and so on."

Iiliana looked at them over the rims of her glasses. "Shall I continue? There is more."

Caitlin could only shake her head.

"What do you mean to do with us?" the Badger asked, his arm stealing around Caitlin's waist.

"Only what it is my duty to do," Iiliana said, pocketing her glasses. "Show you our beautiful island."

                    *   *   *

"No one else has spoken to us," said the Badger as they followed Iiliana through the gardens to the street. "Is there some vow of silence?"

"Not exactly. The women attending you have been with us a short time, one less than a month, the other not yet a year. They cannot speak to outreefers until they have been on the island a year. It is one of the things we are most severe about." Iiliana burst into laughter. It was hard to imagine her severe in anything, or to feel they were in any danger on this island.

It was very beautiful. On the low hills in the distance they could see flocks of goats and scattered cottages of thatch, and behind that a mill set against the gnarled trees of an orchard and the dark green of a vineyard.

Iiliana took them away from that peaceful beauty to the sea's edge, where hundreds of crested lizards sat basking on the rocks, diving into the rough surf to fish, looking for all the world like old men taking a cure at the mineral wells. Iiliana seized one and scratched it under the chin, so that it fell into a stupor.

In the distance on the far end of the beach, they could see figures in grey smocks moving around the sand with wooden hoes.

"What are they doing?" Caitlin asked.

"Sweeping the sand back into the sea," said Iiliana. "Actually, they are combing the seaweed to dry, but that doesn't have the same appeal."

"Is the seaweed used as fuel?"

"No, there's peat for that. We call this sea-flax, and we weave a fine linen from it."

"I can't imagine it," said Caitlin.

"You're both wearing it."

There were surprises for them all morning. Cellars stretched for what seemed like acres beneath the town, the sea kept out by a system of pumps and locks. Then there were the guildhalls where the sea-flax was woven into everyday fabric and intricate tapestries on enormous looms.

"Wouldn't it be simpler," the Badger said above the racket of the looms, "to import things? Surely Fourthmoon wool would be cheaper than weaving your own linen this way."

"It might be, if we had a port."

"Do you mean to say," said Caitlin, "that you make everything you require on this island?"

"Yes."

"If you have no port," said the Badger, "how did you bring us ashore?"

Iiliana turned from the bank of looms to the doorway. "Come. I'll show you."

She led them to an inlet that widened into a lake, its surface paved with water lillies. On its shore Iiliana stood and lifted a whistle to her lips. The Badger heard nothing; Caitlin held her hands to her ears as if against a painful sound, and six beautiful creatures broke through the carpet of water lilies with ease and grace, leaping in arcs and falling back into the water.

A woman appeared, hauling a pail.

"G'morrow, Iiliana."

"G'morrow, Haana. Is that their breakfast? Allow me. It will be like old times, when I went around smelling like a bait box." She turned to Caitlin. "When I first came here, it was my job to feed them, or rather, to feed their mother and their aunts. Here, do you want to feed them?"

The creatures, gentle and curious, pressed up to the bank, making a strange and happy music, turning somersaults for the fish.

"Are they fish?" asked the Badger.

"No, they breathe as you do. See that one over there? She's nursing her calf."

But among the wonders they were shown, they were told nothing of the island's history, and saw nothing of the workings of its government. Besides the low white building where they had spent the night, there was no central structure that seemed to serve as a palace, and they saw no one in a uniform who could be a soldier.

"No soldiers—no men, for that matter," said Caitlin. But when she questioned Iiliana about it, their guide pulled out a pocket watch.

"It is that late? I will miss all my morning appointments." She walked on ahead and the Badger slowed his steps, so that he could speak to Caitlin without being overheard.

"What do you think she means to do with us?" said the Badger.

"I'm not sure. Nothing bad, I think. We've been treated well enough."

"But to what end?"

Caitlin only shrugged. Iiliana had stopped a little distance ahead.

"Come along, you two gossips! Yes, gossips! My ears are buzzing with all you're saying about me. And none of it true, none!" She broke out in another peal of that extraordinary laughter.

Their survey of the island had used up the morning. They were given a simple meal of soup and bread, and afterward Iiliana summoned a young girl and told her to take the Badger to see the island's horses. He was reluctant to leave Caitlin, and Iiliana smiled at the struggle written so plainly on his features. In the end he didn't say anything, but turned and went with the guide.

"Now," said Iiliana, casting down her napkin and pushing back her chair. "I have more yet to show *you.*"

Whatever Caitlin expected to find on the other side of the door Iiliana opened, it was not the sight that confronted her: a dozen girls, standing at easels arranged in a ring, taking a lesson from a woman in a blue smock. It seemed to be a natural history lesson, for the models they were painting ranged from fronds of seaweed to a troublemaking crab that would not sit still for its portrait.

When the door opened they all looked up, but returned to their painting. Their tutor looked questioningly in their direction, but at a sign from Iiliana resumed her circuit of the room, commenting on her pupils' technique.

"All of their lessons are held in the round this way," said Iiliana. "That way no one is ahead of or behind anyone else. And they only take lessons in the afternoon. Mornings are spent at their tasks in the fields or dairy."

But Caitlin had noticed something about the pupils intent on their painting lesson. Every girl around the room had piebald eyes. Not seer's eyes: not one girl had one blue eye and one green. But each had eyes of different colors or hues: two shades of brown, brown and blue, grey and green.

The effect this had on Caitlin was not lost on Iiliana. She led her from the schoolroom and along the corridor to a suite of rooms. From the way she casually kicked off her shoes and collapsed onto a sofa, these were obviously Iiliana's private apartments. They were as curious as their owner, a combination of the moor barrow, Abagtha's pantry, and Milo's conservatory all at once.

Everywhere there were wonderfully made books, all illegal under Pentaclist law. Wall space not devoted to books was covered with tapestries, paintings, and maps. The floor was covered in a mosaic of women swimming in a circle with dolphins. The sea mirrored the stars painted on the ceiling. There were cases of stuffed birds, most unfamiliar to Caitlin for all her bird lore; slabs of rock thick with silvery shells; coins with their portraits worn away by time; a curious sphere painted with maps, and a long tube on three legs, which was pointed out the window. Caitlin saw all these wonders, but could barely wonder at them.

"Those girls," Caitlin said at last. "Their eyes. How did they all come here?"

"One or two accidentally, as you did. The rest were brought, to save them from almost certain death, either at the hands of the Pentaclist soldiers or of their own superstitious parents."

"Are any of them like me?"

"You mean, are they seers? No. They are taught something of the otherworldly arts: herb lore, some of the lesser rune tongues, the meaning of dreams. But their dreams are not like yours." Iiliana leaned her chin on her hand, studying Caitlin. "Are your dreams troubling you?"

Caitlin turned away. "You seem to know everything about me. Then tell me, when have they not?" It was not anger that made her voice tremble, but fear.

Iiliana still lay upon the couch, in an attitude of unconcern, but her eyes were shrewd and bright.

"You are worried about him. In fact, you are making yourself sick with worry for him."

"I wish to heaven I had never met him!" Caitlin pressed the bone above her breast, as if to quiet her heart.

"That won't help," said Iiliana quietly.

"Then tell me a remedy for it."

Her pose was so languid, Iiliana might have been asleep, except for her eyes, which caught and threw back the light from beneath their copper lashes.

"Time, and distance. So you must either have patience, or a cunning, swift boat. Would you maroon him here with me, if I'd let you?" She laughed gently. "I think not. You were so busy cringing from the sting of the fang, you never felt yourself treading further and further into the web."

"Yes! It is a web, leading inward, with no way out but—"

"Are you already caught?"

"You yourself said it."

"Do you wish yourself free of him?"

Quite unwillingly Caitlin remembered striking out at him that day in the market square, hauling him from the tavern gutter, nursing him through his fever, clinging to him in the catacombs, so that remembering their nakedness in the dark, it seemed the least of their intimacies. "I can see no good coming of it," she said at last.

"Can see or have seen?" Iiliana's eyes were barely open.

Caitlin's heart was still beating rapidly, and her breath came as gasps.

"Yes," said Iiliana, "I think you have already had a bad dream, a nightmare, and it has frightened you badly. Are you so exalted an oracle, that your dreams must always come true?"

"They tend to," Caitlin said unsteadily.

"I don't doubt it. But remind yourself from time to time

that we sometimes make our dreams come true, whether we mean to or not."

Tears worked their way gently between Caitlin's eyelids, and she moved her mouth silently, in pain.

From the couch Iiliana offered her arms.

"Come! Come here, and tell me all. I know everything about you, everything. But I would hear it again."

∽◦∾

The Badger followed his guide through field and marsh until at last the girl put up a hand and signaled for him to stop.

"There! Do you see them?"

Across the misty clearing a herd of mares, all white and grey, moved almost noiselessly through the shallow water.

"They're wild!" the Badger exclaimed.

"Of course. If they were tame, I daresay we would have put the stables closer in."

"None have been broken to saddle?"

"In breaking them to saddle, we would also be breaking their spirit. Distances here are short. They are more useful to us here than behind the plow."

He nodded. He knew that kind of usefulness. There was a tangle of wildflowers that covered the garden wall by the abbot's orchard, that one of the old monks left wild, when it might have been planted in climbing beans.

The horses had stopped to strip the younger myrtle trees of their leaves, some stretching their necks down to nuzzle colts.

"How did they come here?"

"We don't know. They have been here as long as anyone can remember. They may be descended from the survivors of a shipwreck, horses meant for the Far Moons, as breeding stock."

In the failing light of the winter day the horses seemed to him ghosts of his own life, or the part of it irretrievably gone. As the herd turned and moved off through the mist the Badger felt he was watching something of himself move away from him forever.

He felt the guide shaking his arm, and realized he had been standing there a long time, and had grown quite cold.

"Come on," said the guide. "It will be dark before we get back, and they will be waiting for us."

In the herd a stallion, the only piebald, turned his head and whinnied in distress, but the the eldest mare gave him a nudge, and he followed.

～～

Dusk had gathered in the room, but Iiliana did not get up to light the lamps.

"Do you remember anything more?"

Caitlin nodded.

"Tell me."

"I can't."

"Yes, you can. You must."

"It hurts—"

"You have hurt before and will hurt worse than this, I promise you. Life is a hurting business. But it will pain you less if you tell me."

Caitlin turned her head as if to avert her eyes from the vision in her mind.

Iiliana took hold of her hand. *"Tell me what you see."*

The words came at last, in a whisper. "My own death."

～～

He turned on Iiliana. "What have you done with her?"

"Put her to bed. No harm has come to her, but she is exhausted. See for yourself."

They left him with her. She was cool to his touch, sleeping a bottomless sleep. He felt for her heartbeat at her temple, then kissed her carefully.

Oh, Cait, he thought. He had made a count of the days in his head. There were not many left.

When Caitlin woke she felt as if all her blood had been replaced with nectar and quicksilver. She sat up in bed with a laugh in her throat. The Badger, asleep in a chair by the bed, woke startled and stiff-necked.

"Are you all right?"

"Mmm. Wonderful. Shouldn't I be?"

"When I came back, Iiliana had put you to bed, and wouldn't tell me what had happened."

Caitlin frowned. "I hardly remember myself. We talked."

The Badger felt a small hiccup of jealousy leap in his throat. "Oh? About what?"

"You, among other things."

"And you had only good things to say, I hope?" he said a little coldly.

She grabbed him by the collar and pulled him onto the bed beside her.

"Look in my eyes, you idiot, and tell me what you think!"

He was not to be put off so easily, and pulled away. "Where you're concerned, I sometimes think I don't know anything."

"But I'm simple enough to read. Here," she said gently. "I'll show you."

Late in the morning they were summoned by Iiliana, led this time to a long hall with an empty throne on a dais at one end. Iiliana sat waiting for them, in a chair below the throne and to the left of it, befitting an ambassador.

"You wanted to know about our history and government. I had hoped to introduce you to our head of council, but she has been unexpectedly called away. She did leave word that I was to extend to you her most heartfelt greetings, and her sincere regret that she could not see you off at your departure. For depart is what you must do."

At the mist-shrouded bay they were put blindfolded into a boat without a rudder.

"She means to kill us on the rocks after all," said the Badger in a low voice.

"Nonsense," said Iiliana, standing on the shore. "There is a charm sewn into the sail, and besides, the boat knows its way to the far shore. When you have been put off at Big Rim, it will find its way home again."

"Home to Chameol," Caitlin said. "The fabled island. Aren't you supposed to give us a draught of forgetfulness?"

"Dolphins' tears and lotus nectar? That's just an old

sailors' yarn. But you gratify me. I thought you would
never guess."

"I am sure I haven't guessed all."

"No, but I think you have guessed enough. The dolphins
will stay with you, to nip at the heels of the sea-monsters."

As the waves got a grip on the boat's keel and steered
it into the current, they heard the golden laughter of Iiliana, queen of Chameol, pealing in the salt air like a toll
of fair weather.

13

ELRIC'S CALLING

Elric might never have caught his mistake if it hadn't been for a rat-catcher's terrier. The dog was worrying two sacks on the tavern stoop, where the bounty hunters had left them in their haste. In kicking the animal away, Elric saw the sack had come untied. Feeling his gorge rise, he knelt to refasten it.

But the bodies had dried a little in their patient wait on the stoop, and the corpse in the open sack had the wrong color hair. With trembling fingers Elric undid the other sack and began to laugh.

"By all that's holy!" he said, "I hope I am not too late."

By dusk he was safely stowed away aboard *The Golden Mole*, bound for Big Rim.

On his arrival he went to the tavern, looking for a man with a thin wallet and no weapon but a small dagger. There were a handful that fit the description, but in each Elric saw some trait that made him turn away: The man was drinking on credit, or gambling, or talking too loudly. At last Elric spied his man in the corner, back to the chimney, smoking quietly, and avoiding scrutiny of any kind. If he had turned his gaze away, Elric would have

139

been hard pressed to tell what the man was wearing, or the color of his hair. Which was as it should be.

"May I join you?"

"There are two stools, and I only have one ass."

When the innkeeper had brought him his ale, Elric drank deep and stared into the fire.

"What news?" he said, without looking up.

"Banter's dead."

Elric was silent for a moment. "How?"

"He was found at the base of the cliff, at the Devil's Sieve. Strangled, then thrown off."

"Had he shown at his last tavern?"

"Yes. He had found her amulet."

Elric's heart leapt. "Did he hand it in?"

"No. It must have been on him when he was killed. It wasn't on his body."

Elric made a small sign, and they fell silent for a while as the innkeeper passed nearby, gathering up empty tankards.

"Well," he said at last. "Here's to Banter." And they drank to the repose of his soul.

"What of you?" said the other, looking at Elric for the first time. "I heard you had found them both drowned, and had been recalled."

"Our pigeons have flown, and after that storm two days ago, heaven knows where they will come to roost."

"They haven't been seen here. They may not have made land."

"Or landed to the east," said Elric, "and made for the woods."

"The silk forest? If they've reached it, we'll never find them."

"If they've reached it, we'll have to."

Elric left the tavern and went to a certain house in the town. After a night in the hull of the ship with the rats, he needed a bath and a meal that hadn't been cooked in a tavern back room. Even more, he needed a pretty face and some conversation.

He got little enough of the latter. The woman who

opened the door seemed to know him, for she let him in without a word, and before very long Elric was bathed and seated by the fire eating a fine mutton chop.

"Ah, Emma. You can still cook."

"And why would I forget? I get enough practice."

He nodded toward a jar on the mantelpiece. "Can I fill my pipe?"

"You're broke, aren't you?"

"Well, yes."

Emma put her hands on her hips and shook her head.

"Don't worry," he said. "I have enough for the bath, and dinner."

"And the after-dinner?"

"I thought we could do without the after-dinner, if it's all right with you."

"Suit yourself."

She left him, and Elric placed his empty plate on the hearth. She had left a pouch of tobacco for his pipe, after all. But as he lit his pipe he caught sight of his reflection in the mirror over the fireplace, and it seemed to him his eyes had turned green and blue.

Hearing him curse, Emma came back into the room.

"I've broken my pipe," he said, showing her the pieces.

Emma gave him a long, hard look, took the fragments, and set them down. Then she turned and began to unfasten his vest.

"Look, sweet, I told you. I'm bust."

"Never mind about that," she said, kissing him. She had calculated that no one would know the ring in the tub was his, and the chop would not be missed.

In the morning she let him sleep late, and he cursed her for it, scrambling into his clothes and only pausing to give her a quick squeeze and a bite on the ear. He walked off down the street without a backward glance, as was his habit. Emma watched him go without a pang. Strange egg, she thought, though handsome enough, in a funny sort of way. She wondered who the girl was. She had slipped him a sleeping powder in his toddy (she kept such things on hand), but even in his deep sleep Elric had called out a name.

∽◦∾

In the streets of Big Rim, Elric suddenly felt his pocket being picked. He whirled around and caught the offending hand in a beartrap grip; at the same instant he recognized the pickpocket. Elric let out his breath, pocketed his property, and walked on down the street without looking back. The pickpocket followed.

"What's up?" Elric said, stopping to turn over apples in a stall.

"You've been recalled."

He fought the urge to turn around. "Recalled?"

"Not so loud. You're to report to the Council tonight, an hour after dark, back room of the Mole and Toad."

"Twenty years, they count for nothing?"

"It's happened to the best of us."

Elric had no answer to that.

At the appointed hour, he made his way to the tavern and was shown to the back room. He knew every man around the table, although some of them he had not seen since he was a boy of twelve.

"Sit," said one of them, curtly.

Elric folded his arms. "I'll stand, I think."

"As you wish. We have it on reliable advice that you are too close to your quarry, and your judgment is affected."

"In ten words or less."

"Iiliana herself has ordered it." He pushed a letter across the table at him.

Slowly, Elric lowered himself into a chair. After a long moment, he picked the letter up. At first the words in the familiar hand swam. Then a single phrase rose up from the rest, like treasure worked free of a shipwreck, rising up through the waves.

> In short, my dear Elric, you can no longer keep the vows you made to me, and I must call you home again.

*   *   *

He looked around the circle of faces in confusion, thought, *Banter isn't here*, then, *Banter's dead*.

"I'm sorry," said the man who had handed him the letter. "There's nothing we can do. And there's more. The abbot of Thirdmoon See has met a rather spectacular end, and we can only take it as a warning: We have been found out. We simply cannot trust this case to someone whose allegiance has been compromised."

Elric opened his mouth, but either thought better of it, or couldn't summon the words. He turned without answering and left.

For some hours he walked the streets of the town. His calling had been taken from him, and suddenly he, a man of all trades, had no trade. He had no family, no country, no wife, nothing to claim him and nothing to claim. The one thing he longed to claim was the one thing forever denied him. As the night grew deeper and he wandered into the part of town where the lamplighters dared not go, he saw before him always those eyes, a sapphire and an emerald, specters in the dark. He stumbled and fell, cutting his kees on the broken paving stones and gasping a curse.

He sat a long time where he had fallen. When at last he picked himself up, Elric stood looking back on the lights of the port, where the ships rose and settled on the waves.

"All right, you've called Elric back, and Elric you shall have!"

The next day, Iiliana was interrupted in her letter writing by a knock on the door.

"What is it?"

"It may be of no importance, but it was so strange. A boy was foundering in the waves, and the dolphins went after him. But he fastened his box to the collar of one, and swam to shore."

After the messenger had gone, Iiliana sat looking at the oilcloth parcel for a long time. She started once or twice to open it, but both times her hands fell back into her lap. At last, with an impatient cluck of her tongue, she seized the box and tore off the cloth and twine.

Lifting the lid, Iiliana collapsed on the bed in helpless laugher, and a tear or two of relief.

Nestled on a wad of copper wool sold for scouring pots was a pair of grey marbles. There was a note.

> You have recalled me, and I have come. Did you think
> I would give up my quarry after twenty years? Then
> your brain has gone soft. I will come home when I
> have done what you sent me to do.
>
> Your servant,
> Elric

"All right!" she said, wiping her eyes and holding one of the marbles to the light. "All right."

～◈～

By the time they had worked loose the token bonds and lifted the blindfolds from their eyes, the island was already lost in mist. On either side of the boat they glimpsed from time to time the blue and silver of a dolphin's back. There seemed to be little enough wind, but whether it was the charm sewn in the sail or the guidance of Iiliana's dolphins, the boat without a rudder seemed to be steering a steady course.

"Yes," said the Badger, "but where?"

Upon waking that morning Caitlin had felt that the weight of a lifetime's nightmares had been lifted from her, and when she washed in the basin she was surprised to see that her eyes had not been changed in the night to a blessed, ordinary brown.

So it was with some startlement that she woke from a dream of the man with red hair and grey eyes. As visions went, it was not in the least foreboding. He was standing on the shore in full sunlight, smiling a little smile, looking into the distance after something. Caitlin opened her eyes and looked into the Badger's blue ones. She frowned.

"Bad dream?" he asked.

"No—just strange."

He was learning not to press her. "I think I can see the shore."

They reached the Far Moons to the east of Big Rim, on a steep and rocky beach that rose to meet a stand of trees stretching as far as the eye could see. No sooner had they waded to shore than the boat began to drift back out to sea, against all logic, and the tides. The last they saw of it was the sun flashing on its sail, and the bright back of a dolphin leaping in a sparkling arc.

Iiliana had returned to them their own clothes, piecing out their gear with warm vests, cloaks, and boots to guard against the winter. As they walked up into the dark wood, they were glad of them.

"Well, it seems you lost your hair for nothing. The map's gone."

"We reached the other side, and that's all we hoped the map would do," she pointed out.

He bowed deeply, and swept an arm grandly, indicating what path there was into the woods. "You first, since you're so full-up with confidence."

She disappeared before him into the trees. Before he followed her, the Badger paused, afraid he was turning as uncanny as she, for his heart was full of foreboding. What you should do before you take another step, he thought, is catch her up and run somewhere, far away, to safety.

But safety from what, and where? The red-haired man, and anywhere but Ninthstile.

The silk forest was nothing like the Weirdwood where she had grown up nor was it like the seedy deer park where Milo had chanced on her. As the snow swirled and fell around her, Caitlin remembered the wood where she had spent her first seventeen years: stands of ancient oaks, and beneath them, hemlocks, everything chewed by rodent teeth, nights thick with the flight of owls and the sentry calls of the Direwolves.

The trees here were smaller, spaced as though planted long ago by a single hand, their trunks silvery in the winter light that was like a perpetual dusking: birches arched in girlish yearning, black elders darker, bent in wisdom. And then the trees seemed to be calling back and forth to each other, and then to her. My daughter, said the elders, my daughter.

Caitlin resisted the calling of the trees. Madness, she thought. Don't give in to it. The Badger had fallen behind, and the speaking of the trees grew louder, so that she imagined she felt whispered breath on her ear. Stumbling in the snow, Caitlin clutched at one of the trees, and as her gloved fingers closed around the smooth bark she saw clearly as waking a young man in springtime, bending down the catwillows and smiling, lifting up a young woman and laying her upon the bed of branches, while her fingers undid the ribbons of her shirt. Caitlin knew the woman's face: she had seen a ghost of it reflected in the washbasin, twinned with the face of Oriel's dead mother.

The Badger's hand fell on her shoulder, and Caitlin started with a word on her lips. He looked at her curiously.

"What did you call me?"

Her eyes were full of wonder as she looked up at him. "I don't know."

"Yes, you called me something. Tyb-something."

"Tybio . . ."

The Badger shuddered uncontrollably. "Don't go so far ahead next time. I don't want to lose you."

She nodded, and they went on together, side by side when the narrow path allowed it.

Everything slept. Where the owls of the Weirdwood would have been watchful, and Milo's deer nervous, everything in the silk forest slept. In the roots of the trees the bright-eyed things with their coats of winter fur were curled in a deep December sleep. If you had taken a spade and turned over the frozen mud of the creek bed, you would have found in it a fantastic lode of living gems: frogs green as emeralds, salamanders milky as moonstones, turtles faceted like onyx. Most birds had fled to southern islands, and those that had wintered over tucked head under wing. Deep underground, among the slumbering worms and the drowsy mole, the cicadas were halfway through their seventeen-year sleep.

Everything slept, except for the cat and the badger, stealing forward through the snowy night on human feet. The snow fell steadily, thick as a curtain, lacy as a wedding veil, and upon its silvery screen they saw painted countless wintry visions, dreams upon the eyelids of the sleeping earth.

They felt they were the only living, waking things in the world, and then suddenly the snow stopped, the curtain was torn, and they saw before them a sight that brought them to their knees, and to their eyes the tears of speechlessness.

In the clearing was a hunting party, frozen in time, wrapped in silky gauze transparent as breath, so that at twenty paces they could see the light down on a young man's cheek, the stubble on the chin of the gamekeeper, the delicate ivory-work of the saddles. The riders were looking east, over their shoulders, with expressions of wonder, and everything about them, every look and gesture and inclination of the head had been captured by the light silky stuff in which they were enrobed. As they watched, Caitlin and the Badger saw that the silk was being mended and restored by a thousand tiny spiders, moving tenderly across eyelid, lip, and wrist. They remained for a long time kneeling in the snow, watching the wakeful spiders go about their ageless task.

"Are they living or dead?" the Badger said at last.

"Neither. Or both, I don't know," she said. "Look. Behind them."

There was a hunting lodge. They had to free gently the handle and hinges from the clinging silk and shoo the anxious spiders away as the door swung inwards.

The air inside was itself like silk, clinging, warm as if it had just left the spider. At first they couldn't see very far into the room, and made as if to brush the air from their hair and eyelashes. Then they saw, asleep at a spinning wheel, the spinner.

She was the one thing the spiders had not touched. Everything else in the lodge wore a net of silk, and the thousand spiders, like their sisters tending the hunting

party, crept slowly from eave to eave, mending the silk.
What they lived on Caitlin could not guess: not a midge
stirred.

While not old, the spinner seemed of another age. Her
hair was dressed in the ancient way, and her clothes were
not merely old-fashioned but archaic: wooden sandals
laced over painted leather leggings, a skirt and tunic of
silken wool trimmed with bells.

But the face itself was not ancient, not a quarter as old
as the clothes, no, not even as old as Abagtha. She was
only just past that age at which women are still counted
young, and time had just begun to carve its traces around
her eyes and sleep-softened mouth. The spinner was a
woman of wealth, her rank woven in the border of her
robe and stamped in the signet of her rings. But wealth
had not come easy; the hands themselves were callused
by the thread, red from work they were used to.

Caitlin moved through the gauze of silk toward the spinner, not knowing she did, heedless of the spiders that
scurried desperately from her tread.

Just as she was reaching out a hand to touch the sleep-
er's shoulder, the eyes opened.

"Ah, how I have been watching for your coming!"

14

THE RIDDLESPINNER

"No, ask no questions. I have little enough breath in me; let me save it for the telling. You are wondering what I am, and how I came to be here, and what befell those outside. They are living yet, do not fear. Hold a mirror to their lips, and it will mist even now."

The spinner seemed hardly to move her lips, yet her voice filled the room, low and clear. It was the sound of silence at dawn, when you are alone in the dark, waiting for it to be light. They sat spellbound, listening to that voice, and found they could not speak or move. And they did not wish to. They wanted nothing but to sit there in the lodge in the middle of the forest while around them the spiders spun, and the spinner's breast rose and fell with her breathing, and outside a fresh snow fell softly all around, fell silently and eternally on the hunting party and the wood.

Everything she said to them was like a memory restored, and as she spoke she began to spin, working the wheel so it sang and whispered beneath her words.

"Such a way you have come, farther than you even know. And you think you are lost, and fear you are past saving. Tell me, boy, what you know of the swallowwort."

The Badger was tongue-tied.

"You, tell him."

Caitlin had to wet her lips before she could answer. The wise eyes, now young, now ancient, seemed to look through her, and then into her soul of souls. "It is a plant. When you place it on the forehead of a sick man, he will laugh or cry. If he cries, you know he will live."

"Yes," said the spinner. "The saving tears. You must remember this, when you leave me. For you are not lost; I will tell you the way, in a little while. But first you shall hear a tale. It is not my own story, but it is the story of one like me, who is now dead."

And this is the tale she told.

"Long ago a brother and sister were born to poor parents. They called the boy Myrrhlock and the girl Myrrha. One day a strange woman appeared in the doorway of the cottage and announced that she had come to take the boy away, for he showed a talent for the shifty arts. But the father wanted the boy to help in the fields and said, 'Take my daughter, for we have no dowry money, and no man will ever marry her.'

"The old woman was ill-pleased, but she took the girl, who followed crying, for she was frightened and stricken with grief at leaving her home. 'Do not cry,' the woman said. 'They did not want you, so it must be that you are going to a better place.'

"Now, her mother had always told her that you went to a better place when you died, so the girl only cried harder. At that the old woman (who was a powerful spellcaster) picked her up, though the woman was frail and the child heavy, and carried her along as if she were a feather, telling her stories until she stopped crying and fell asleep.

"So the girl was brought away to a distant land and raised up in a fine house in the countryside, where she was set to the study of all the arts the old woman thought fit to teach her.

" 'It is well you did not bring the boy after all,' they told the old woman, 'for this child is so bright and quick and kind we can imagine no better.'

"But the old woman regretted leaving him behind.

Tilling and sowing, she feared, would not fire his mind, and when she thought of the flints there were for such tinder, she did not sleep well.

"She was borne out: Myrrhlock grew broad and strong from the hard work, but resentful of his father, for he well remembered the day they had taken his sister away. At first he missed her, but after a time he began to imagine the life she led away from them. As he planted potatoes in the hot fields he thought of her in a summerhouse, eating sherbet; while winter winds howled about the house, and he huddled in his cot beneath a rough blanket, he imagined her in a featherbed.

"And the boy's heart became poisoned with hate, and ripened with it until it was so full it overflowed into his eyes, which became the color of quicksilver and just as changeable.

"One day, ten years after she had taken the girl away, the old woman returned to the house where the poor farmer lived with his wife.

" 'I have come for the boy as well, if he will go with me,' she said.

" 'You're a day too late. Yesterday he made off with my only drafthorse. I hope he's thrown and breaks his neck!'

"The old woman journeyed homeward, thinking nothing good would come of it. Indeed, the boy had not been gone a day when he fell in with a Necromancer, a magic worker who had betrayed so many kings he was an exile, welcome nowhere, compelled to travel the highways in all weathers, never resting. He took the boy as his apprentice, teaching him no art but magic, for it was in his eyes the only art, and then only dark magic, for he thought it crowned the others. Since the boy's thirst was the thirst of hatred, he drank up these bitters greedily and never longed for the waters of true knowledge.

"Myrrha his sister had grown up bright of mind and countenance, graceful and excellent in all things, fluent in seventeen tongues and renowned for her spinning and weaving. Any fool can spin thread of wool, and even flax is no trick, but silk! There, she thought, is something to spin.

"It was said she could spin a thread before the silk had left the silkworm. Now, that is truth-pulling, but her tapestries were wonderful to look at: portraits of long dead kings and queens, none larger than your fingernail, but marvelously lifelike. When she wove a tapestry of a unicorn with its head in a maiden's lap, you could see the eyelashes on the unicorn, and the freckles on the maiden's nose. Word of her skill traveled through all the kingdoms, so that a cat that had slept on scraps of her cloth was rumored to be the best mouser in the kingdom, and its kittens fetched a pretty price in silver.

"At last word of the spinner reached Myrrhlock, and leaving the magician he went to the kingdom where his sister was living. There he inquired after her, pretending to be a lovesick admirer, and the townfolk smiled on him, and bade him welcome to the ranks of her army of suitors.

" 'Has she many lovers, then?' he asked.

" 'They are as stars in the sky, but the chief among them is Tybio.'

"Tybio!" Caitlin cried.

"Let me finish," said the riddlespinner. "Then many things will be clear to you."

Caitlin sat back, and the riddlespinner went on.

"Tybio was one of the workers who tended the mulberry trees and gathered the cocoons from the silk forest. It was there that the spinner had met him. It was the springtime, and they were not long falling in love, and often as she sat spinning Myrrha would smile, thinking of him, how he had bent down the branches of catwillow and made for her a bed, soft! Unimaginably soft.

"Myrrhlock vowed that his revenge should start with Tybio. One day as the young man came to the grove of mulberry trees the magician's apprentice fell upon him and killed him and hung his body from a tree, so his sister should see it as she came to meet her lover in the grove.

"For a time Myrrha would take neither food nor comfort, and it was feared she would starve her body or her reason, for she did not eat enough to keep the one or the other. But one day the old woman came to her in her chamber and found the spinner once more at work, her tresses cut and coiled on the bed.

" 'They were what he treasured most,' Myrrha said. 'Bury them with him.' And she kept up her spinning, her hand steady on the wheel, foot true to the treadle.

"Now her brother had taken up catoptromancy, which is magic with mirrors, and many of the other mancies, and such magics that were so dark that black was too light a color for them. And when he gazed into his mirrors and saw his sister at her work, Myrrhlock became so enraged that his teacher, the magician, left the house, taking nothing with him. For he feared his pupil, and justly."

Here the riddlespinner paused, sinking back to catch her breath. A minute golden spider, no bigger than a honey-drop and as transparent, hung suspended from her earlobe like an amber earring. Then the riddlespinner opened her eyes and continued her tale, setting the wheel spinning faster just as it was about to slow to a stop.

"So Myrrhlock set out for the place where his sister was living. As he set off he caught up a lump of myrrh from the table and mile after mile he worked the lump in his hands, working the poison of his hatred into it, saying over and over:

Sister, know a brother's love
Everlasting as myrrh and the grave,
Sweet as a tomb-posy,
This love portion shall you have.

"Now it happened that not all that had been Tybio went with him into the dark earth. Not long after he had been buried the spinner learned she was carrying his child, and before the first snow she bore an infant girl. And in the child was all the spinner's love of life born again. Her eyes were full of light and gladness, and her laughter rang once more in the marble hallways.

" 'Work your ruin!' she cried, as her daughter pulled the cloth from the table, scattering the silver dishes. 'Pull all the world down around its ears! You will make it again, you will, my little world-maker.'

"On the road, Myrrhlock saw the child in his mirror, and he saw the means of the mother's undoing."

At this Caitlin shuddered uncontrollably. The spinner beckoned her closer, and although there was no fire on the hearth, Caitlin felt heat warming her blood, heat that seemed to come from the spinning wheel, or the spinner herself.

"One day the court went hunting. It was harvest time and they were on the luck-chase, to catch an animal and let it go in barter for a good harvest, fidelity in love, and bounty in all good things.

"Now Myrrhlock disguised himself as a huntsman and worked the lump of myrrh into something like a baby, swaddling it and hiding it in his saddlebag.

"The custom was, when the quarry was caught, to exchange a kiss between neighbors instead of the first blood, and these kisses were bestowed regardless of sex or station. It happened that when the deer was caught and the garland placed around its neck, Myrrha turned and bestowed a kiss upon her brother, not recognizing him, but as their lips met she felt cold, and cried to the old woman, who rode near her, 'Where is my daughter?' The old woman reassured her, but as Myrrha watched them cut the luck-tuft from the deer's tail and present it to her, her heart was cold with foreboding.

"As they rode back to the palace, Myrrhlock cast a spell so that they should lose their way and ride deeper and deeper into the forest. Myrrha became separated from the rest of the party and called out for her daughter and for the old woman and lastly for the huntsman. Suddenly she saw him before her, holding out a bloody bunting. With a cry in her throat, the spinner reached for the bundle, and when she touched the myrrh-baby she was held fast, and fell down dead.

"But her brother's victory was not without its price. As his sister fell dead at his feet, Myrrhlock's lip where she had kissed him split, and his hair went white.

"Now the old woman came upon them with the baby in her arms, and when she saw Myrrha lying dead she cried out, 'I knew long ago no good would come of you. See what a thing you have done.' Myrrhlock spoke a terrible spell, but because his lip was cleft the old woman and the child were not killed, but the rest of the party was cast into an endless slumber, and the baby made deaf and dumb and blind. Having done his worst, Myrrhlock left the wood.

"The old woman took the child to a lodge, and with her skill gave the child new sight and speech, giving her the eyes of creatures of the night and the speech of the whippoorwill and the cars of the owl. And knowing that the time of her own death was near, the old woman cast a last spell, so that all the spiders in the wood came and cast a silky pall over all the company. The child grew up alone in the wood with only the spiders for company, so it was they who taught her to spin. She lived out her life under Myrrhlock's curse, spinning all winter, asleep all the summer, so as never to see the springtime, when love is abroad in the world.

"To this day they say that if the spinner in the wood is ever awakened, that murder of love and life shall be avenged, and the world set aright. The eyes of the world will be opened, and everyone will understand the speech of the birds, and the creatures of night and air, and the wisdom of the ages shall become the bride of the future.

"All this I say, but it is not my tale, but the tale of one like me, and she is dead these ninety-nine and nine hundred years. Child, are you yet cold?"

"No, warm."

"Then you shall spin for me, and I shall rest. Here, the distaff, and the spindle. Ah, the thread has cut you. Your hands are tender, though not unused. Is your heart so? You must put it in a box and have a key made for it." The spinner laughed softly. "Yes, you shall have a key made, or make one."

The thread Caitlin was spinning was a little rosy with her blood, and it seemed to the Badger that she had slipped into some kind of trance. He rose and started toward her, words caught in his throat. As his hand closed on her arm, he felt a shock and found he could not pull his hand free. The sensation was neither pleasant nor painful. One had only to give in to it. He surrendered to the whispering of the wheel and let himself be pulled in to its skein.

Scenes from his past and scenes beyond his imagination spun before his eyes. There was Asaph, hiding the missal beneath his cot and looking over his shoulder. There was his own mother, her face so lovely and full of the sorrow that half made it so, looking at him and weeping, and grandfather, angry. A young woman weeping as she hid a baby in a heap of moss in the wood, and an old woman finding it. A young girl being led along a hillside by an old woman, her small hands clutching something in a cloth. Then the child turned her face toward him, and he saw that it was Caitlin. He saw her putting coins on the old woman's eyes and fleeing through the snow, and then they were leading her out, tied to a pole like the spoils of a hunt. They cut her hair from her, and there, at the edge of the fire, was the man with the red hair. And there he was again, in the field of corn, turning over a body, and it had the face of the relic-seller.

But now it was Caitlin again, her clothes torn, her face bloodied, being held down by two of the toughs from Moorsedge, while Cullen stood over her, smiling. Then the scene changed again, and he saw himself lying as if near death, with Caitlin bending over him. And then, scenes of horror: Asaph's eyes, staring in death—the Cavekin lying heap on heap, horribly slain—the bay of Chameol red with the blood of Iiliana's dolphins. And finally, Caitlin herself, pale in death, decked with flowers as if for the grave, a man in a black mask bending over her with a slender knife.

With a cry he wrenched Caitlin from the wheel, and she collapsed in his arms in something between a faint and death. He raised his eyes to the spinner.

"Is that her future, then?"

"Some the past, some the future. Some is what might be, some, what will be. You have not seen all. Some happy things—"

"Is this a happy thing?" he asked over Caitlin's head, her senseless weight pressing on him. "You've nearly killed her."

"No, she only sleeps. The vision passed through her into you. She will recall nothing."

"What are we to do?"

"You journey to Ninthstile. I will tell you the way."

"No, not there. Tell me how to find the Spellkey."

"And what will you do with it if I do? Do you even know what it is?"

"Her life, and her death."

The spinner looked at him a long while. She seemed much older now, as if each word of her tale had aged her. At last she spoke.

"In the heart of this wood there is a cave, and in it a dragon. He is older even than I, and they ran out of numbers for my age long ago. Tell him his name, and he will have to answer you three questions. But be careful he does not trick you of an answer."

The Badger nodded. "What is his name?"

"Ormr."

He picked Caitlin up and carried her out into the snow. The cold woke her, and before long she was walking through the deep snow beside him, holding his hand tight in her own.

When they had passed out of sight of the lodge and the hunting party, an extraordinary thing occurred. The silk that covered everything began to take on a gloss and hardness, as if it were spun glass, and the whole grove began to ring like a tuning fork, a single exquisite note that shattered the silk coverings. Inside them there was nothing but some quicksilver motes and ash. Where one moment the hunting party had stood wrapped in their silky dream there was nothing but a dusting on the ground that was soon covered up by fresh snow.

In the lodge the spinner smiled and worked the wheel faster, so that it made the same pitch that could be heard in the clearing. Then she, too, was gone, leaving nothing but the wheel and the spiders. At first agitated, the spiders gathered in one corner, golden and quivering, and then they, too, began to die. At last there was only one. She crept to the highest rafter and began to spin. When she had done, she suspended herself beside the new egg case and went to sleep, waiting.

15

ORMR

When he was a boy, before his grandfather had sent him away to live with the monks, there had lived in the same town a woman whose husband had been killed by a dragon. At least, that was what they said. You used to see her at the well, being shunned by the other women drawing their water. It was bad enough, they said, that she was a dragon-widow, but she had stopped wearing mourning after only a month, going about with her head uncovered, and when the mayor's wife spoke to her about it she only laughed.

On the streetcorners, the Badger remembered, the spell-sellers sometimes hawked dragons' teeth, but you were never sure what you would get for your money, as this was also the name for a peppery, preserved-plum sweet given to children who were being weaned from the teat.

And then there was the time, not long after they had sent him to the abbey, when they pulled a man from the bog. He must have been there for a thousand years, but he was perfectly preserved, his skin as soft as a baby's. There was a noose around his neck, and he wore the death-sentence of a dragon shirt: a black tunic emblazoned with a red dragon. No one was sacrificed to dragons any-more; such barbarism had died out with the advent of the

Pentacle. Besides, dragons had all but vanished in the great drought, the population scattered to the distant mountains and caves to avoid the ravages of the settlements: chimney and plow, forge and mill.

The Badger didn't even believe in dragons, though, as they went farther into the forest, he began to. They walked through the snow, threading their path through the trees, from time to time watching the silent flight, quite close by, of an owl. Every once in a while the Badger would turn and look at Caitlin, as if he walked in fear of her suddenly vanishing in this strange forest that was so much more her province than his own.

Caitlin walked in a dream of dragons, the withered lizard soldiers that had been her usual playthings back in the oak with the red door, fighting battles for her, their queen, against Abagtha's rages, against the long darkness of the night in the Weirdwood.

She remembered the books Abagtha had of the natural history of dragons: what they ate (veal on the hoof, still nursing; young pigs and lambs; melons, when they could get them back to the cave without breaking them), where and of what they made their nests (suspended from the roofs of caves, made of their own scales, shed, and the softest bat-down), how they chose their mates and raised their young, and the songs they sang to one another in winter, when their thin blood was in danger of freezing, songs said to be more lovely than any birdsong, more stirring than any of the songs of men. When she had asked Abagtha why the trees lost their leaves in the winter, the old woman told her it was the dragons' breath on the wind that blew the leaves from the branch, blasted by the heat to all the colors in a flame.

Once, when Caitlin was very little, she was walking alone in the wood, gathering mushrooms for Abagtha, when she spied a man a little way off through the trees. This was before she had looked into the book with pictures of people kissing in it, and for some reason she did not connect this man with the farmers who visited the oak with the red door to barter with Abagtha for potions and

powders. This may have been because the man she saw
now was naked, or because he was clean-shaven, or
because he had red hair. Whatever the reason, Caitlin hid
behind a tree for a long time, watching him take a bath
with a cloth and a kettle next to a fire in the clearing. He
did not see her, so she had got a good look at him. He
resembled her lizards more than he did either Abagtha or
herself, so she decided he must be a dragon.

Even when this notion had been dispelled, she continued to regard men with some of the awe, fear, and revul-
sion she reserved for dragons. Little of her experience of
men since that long-ago day had changed her impression,
so that once in the Badger's arms she fought the urge to
free herself, imagining in his kiss a dragon's tongue, scales
on his back beneath her hand. From her earliest days, she
had been slaying dragons, and harbored some still, in the
furthest caves of her mind.

❧

Elric had followed them into the wood, tracking them
easily through the snow. Having them well in sight on the
second day, he paused for a brisk sponge-bath. Melting
some snow in a cup over the fire and using a nearby tree
as his valet, he washed and shaved, feeling sure enough
of himself to sing, which was nearly his ruin.

It was only luck that he heard the rustle of a fleeing
wood creature. He had the fire out in an inkling and hid
himself inside the tree. Too late he saw his razor in plain
sight on a stump, but the bounty hunters thundered past
without noticing it. Elric waited a long time before emerging to dress, cursing because his hiding place had undone
the good of his bath. He moved off quickly through the
trees, and there rose before his eyes upon the black and
white screen of the snowy forest a vision from the past:
Caitlin being chased through the snow, the dogs at her
heels. Elric's breath caught roughly in his throat; he stumbled and nearly fell.

"Let me have done the right thing! For her sake—"

The night didn't answer: the snow only fell, the owl
looked at him, then over him, searching the snow for signs
of life.

∽∾∽

At Ninthstile, the onions and potatoes had all been dug, and the fields lay under new snow. The abbess stood at her window and looked over the white fields to the fringe of trees to the south, her fingers playing on the silver pentacle she wore around her neck.

After a time a bit of darkness detached itself from the darkness of the trees. It was not the pair on horseback she was hoping for, but a cart with a single horse.

It was the last day of the old year, which held a special significance for the villagers of Ninthstile. It was Riddance Day, a day for housecleaning and cleansweeping, getting rid of unlucky encumbrances. It is unlucky enough to own a cat with one eye, more unlucky still to kill the cat—except on Riddance Day.

So it was on this particular cold morning that the carter was driving a load to the convent. The single passenger was a girl of five, named Winna. She was the one mouth too many to feed. Her parents scraped a living by gathering ends of tallow from inns and taverns and melting them down to make new candles. It was Winna's job to cut the wicks. But then her older brother had run away to war, and she had to hold the mold still while her mother poured the hot tallow.

It was only a matter of time before she was burned. The hand healed so she lost the use of it, and now her father had to hire a boy to pour the tallow, and her mother had to do the wicks and care for the new baby, so it was off to the nuns with Winna. Her parents wept at the gate and handed up a meal for her in a box, and as the cart drove away her father swore that they would get her back, just as soon as things were paid up. But secretly, and he was ashamed to tell his wife this, he felt a burden lift from his shoulders, the weight of loving this odd child with her one blue eye and one green eye. Perhaps, he thought guiltily as the cart turned the corner and was lost from sight, perhaps now their luck would turn.

The carter reached the gate and gave a shout. Two nuns hurried out through a little door in the high gate. Having ascertained the carter's business, they gave Winna a hand down from her perch and led her through the door into the convent. The carter turned his horse, one hand on the reins, the other exploring the box that held Winna's dinner. She had picked at it and fed the rest to the birds. The carter grumbled, then sighed.

"Ah, she's welcome to it. God knows when she'll eat as well again."

∽

The Badger had turned in the doorway in afterthought. "How shall I know the cave when I find it?"

The riddlespinner was already spinning. "Just go through the forest as if nothing interested you but getting to the other side. Then you are sure to fall into it, headfirst."

Which is what happened: One moment they were walking through the wood and the next the Badger had vanished from sight, and before Caitlin could cry out she had fallen after.

They fell along a passage not much bigger than a badger set, suddenly landing unhurt on the smooth floor of a large, long chamber. One of the tiles had come loose; Caitlin frowned, turning it in her hands. It shimmered, irregular and ever so slightly curved. She raised her eyes to the Badger's.

"Dragon scales?"

He shrugged, but in his mind he swiftly calculated the likely height and breadth of a beast with scales a foot square.

"What I want to know," he said, standing and brushing himself off, "is how it gets in and out. This place is smaller than your barrow."

"Perhaps this is the back door." She was thinking of a certain spider in the Weirdwood that built its trap like a silky dungeon, a tunnel that grew narrower and narrower, ending in a web. She shot a look at the Badger and sent up a silent prayer to that sweet heaven of his that they would not shortly be food for worms.

At the end of the passage there was a low archway, and beyond that only darkness. If there was another way out of the cave it lay on the other side. While both saw the arch at the other end of the passage, each perceived the tunnel leading to it differently.

The Badger saw it black and sooty, the shadows crawling with large grey beetles—tomb scavengers. The pieces of an unfortunate adventurer's backbone were scattered up and down the passage like the tokens of a grisly game. As he neared the end of the hallway the Badger kept looking over his shoulder, chill sweat pearling his lip.

That part of her life not lived in the Weirdwood Caitlin had spent in a soldier's grave: none of the Badger's imagined horrors would have made her shrink. She saw the passage clean and well lit, and through the archway a light. She herself was suddenly garbed in a white gown and crowned with snow poppies from a mountain meadow. The Badger no longer walked beside her. With each step she took Caitlin knew she could not go backward, and that through the archway lay her own death.

They knocked against each other and came to themselves once more. The Badger saw the tunnel free of terrors, and Caitlin found the white gown of sacrifice had vanished, and she was clad once more in riding clothes.

"Is this a dream?" the Badger asked, his hand tight on her arm. "Or is it real?"

"If it is magic," she said, "we are making it."

"Then we are mad—mad together, but mad."

"Hush."

They had come to the archway, which was so dark now they could not see through it. Then they realized it was not darkness before their eyes but a curtain of black velvet. Caitlin drew it aside, and they passed into the room beyond.

It was piled high with treasure, piles of gold coins and gemstones, uncut, heaped carelessly as coals, but with a hint of the precious luster—scarlet, azure, verdant—hidden inside. The treasure seemed alive, sliding over and under itself like a seething cauldron, pearls tumbling over rivers of coins and medallions. Then the whole pile gave a great shudder and from the center there rose the dragon, the head all fiery eyes and dreadful teeth ranged like an army of spears. Then there were the wings, such terrible wings, clawed, and large enough to blot out the sky. The wind that rose from him tore their clothes, pressed their lips tight against their teeth, seared the buttons painfully to their flesh, forcing them against the wall. Then the fire came, hot as a furnace, singeing the breath from their lungs. But through their terror, through the sensation, they realized there was no pain.

The illusion was gone as soon as they thought it. The dragon was gone, and the treasure with it. They found themselves in a room lined with prints of strange plants and animals. A low table was piled with books, and on the floor there was a basin of water and a bowl of wine. In the grate a log of cinders collapsed, sending up a shower of orange sparks.

Then they noticed a small horsehair couch with clawed feet, about the size of a dog's bed. On it there lay a creature no bigger than a spaniel, with black wings like a bat's. The trunk of the creature was a deep turquoise, and soft, without either scales or fur, and it rippled as though some mysterious engine were at work within. The head had a muzzle like a dog's and huge golden eyes. The brow began in iridescent scales of black and blue-green, ending in a few rich plumes on the back of the otherwise naked creature. Besides the wings against its sides, it had an assortment of other limbs; human hands, beetle-like pincers, broad paws, neat cloven hooves. The creature's tail was long, slightly flattened, and pebbled like a turtle's.

The creature regarded them with a calm expression, blinking its lovely eyes, two winking coins. It folded and unfolded its wings, and they made a funny sound, like someone working a bellows. The creature opened its maw in a gesture like a yawn and they saw that it was toothless. It coughed a little cloud of soot, crossed its hooves over its breast, and addressed them.

"Who are you?"

"Badger of Thirdmoon See, and Caitlin of—of—"

"—Barrowmoor," she finished for him. "We are bound for Ninthstile."

The creature beat its wings, coughing again; this time sparks flew out. It ran a pointed, lavender tongue over its chops. "You can't get there from here."

"We are looking for Ormr," said Caitlin. "We were told he could guide us."

"I am Ormr," said the creature.

"But we were told he was a dragon," she protested.

"So I am: Ormr the worm; also, wyrm, wirm, wirme, wyrme, virme, weorm, werm, wurm, wurem, wurrum, wourme, weirme, woorme, waurm, and vermis. As in serpent, snake, dragon; anything that crawls, insect or reptile. I am many things. I am one of the pains of hell, or so they tell me. I am the grief that gnaws; I am your conscience and your madness. I am your most perverse fancy and desire; I am indeed a very worm of your own brains."

"But we saw a dragon," the Badger pointed out.

"An illusion conjured by your own minds, by your own fears." The creature worked its bellows, then folded its wings neatly. "What you saw in the passage, the dragon, the treasure—it was all what you expected to see. I did not invent it." Ormr coughed, a shower of soot and sparks. "Your brains have been ripe for dragons since you were children. The idea crept in through your ears, too small to notice, and bored its way to your brain where it slept, causing no pain or discomfort, for many years. Then one day it hatched as a dragon, and there was ruin in the land. Your brains are full of dragons. Here comes another! Can't you hear the tap of the egg-tooth on the shell? But you can starve them out, as if they were a fever."

During this speech Ormr's voice had become softer and softer, so at the end of it they thought he had fallen asleep. Caitlin and the Badger looked at each other, as if to confirm what had happened in the tunnel. When they looked back at Ormr his golden eyes were open again, regarding them with what could only be called amusement, even though this was a dragon before them.

"She who told you my name," it said thoughtfully. "Did she also tell you that I must answer three questions of your choosing?"

The Badger nodded.

"Well, then," said Ormr.

The Badger remembered the riddlespinner's advice not to ask about the Spellkey first.

"What is the way to Ninthstile?"

"It depends on where you begin. If you are lucky, it will be a long journey, and if you are very fortunate indeed you will never reach it."

"That is no answer," said Caitlin.

"True. Ninthstile lies a day's journey from here, due north, on foot."

At this they traded a glance. The Badger's heart sank, but Caitlin's beat faster. So close to the end.

"Who are the men pursuing us?" Caitlin asked.

The dragon closed its eyes and snorted, giving off a lot of steam, like cold water poured on dying coals. "I can tell you the name of one, the red one, for his face is clearer than the rest. His name is Elric."

"Is that all you can tell us?" asked Caitlin, dismayed.

"If you would know more, you must ask a third question," said Ormr. The black slits in its golden eyes had narrowed.

"Tell us what the Spellkey is," said the Badger.

Ormr shifted his body on the couch, the beautiful turquoise body rippling. "The Spellkey, the key of hours. That which unlocks a spell."

"That much we know," said the Badger impatiently. "That doesn't explain how it can empty prisons. And what is the lock of hours?"

"That is a fourth question." And Ormr closed his eyes.

The Badger put out a hand to shake the dragon awake, but as soon as he touched the creature his hand was stuck fast. Caitlin took hold of his arm to pull him free and found herself held fast with him. Ormr opened his eyes.

"You will reach Ninthstile safely," he said, "but there all safety ends. You are in greater peril than you guess, and you must arm yourselves against it well." They found they were able to move.

"We carry no swords," said the Badger.

"Such arms are useless in a battle such as this. You must go armed in fear, in human fear."

"You tell us we are in mortal danger, and then speak to us in riddles!" the Badger cried. "Why won't you help us?"

"There is help and help. I could tell you all I know,

and your peril would not be reduced, and many things would be ruined."

"Many things will be ruined if you do not!" said the Badger. "Our lives, our happiness."

"He is rash," Ormr said, training his golden eyes on Caitlin.

"Yes."

"It may yet save you both. If it does not first kill you. Here, there is yet a little gold in the room, if you look, and gems. Take them, if you wish."

But they could be persuaded to take nothing with them.

"Then take this stone from my mouth. It is lodged in the back and hampers my eating. Can you see it?"

The Badger peered into the dragon's open mouth. At the back of its throat a heart-shaped stone gleamed dully.

"I think I can reach it."

Caitlin remembered something dimly from Abagtha's dragon book, but it was too late. He had already pulled out the stone, which glittered in his palm, ruby red.

"His heart—" Caitlin cried. Horrified at what he had done, the Badger dropped the stone and it clattered to the floor.

Ormr's breathing was labored, and he worked his wings stiffly. "Pick it up: think of the cost. My task is done. Now I sleep."

That was how Ormr the dragon died, head curled to his breast, his limbs drawn up and tail wrapped around them.

As they went out once more into the snow the Badger looked at the strange stone in his hand, bewildered, wrapping it carefully and putting it in his pocket.

After a short time they came to the forest's edge and looked down on the town of Ninthstile, and in the distance, the convent itself. He gave her a grave look.

"How is it with you, love?"

She shuddered, turning from the sight of the nunnery in its fields of snow.

"I'm just thinking of what Ormr said." If they were to go forth armed in fear, she was well armed.

16

NINTHSTILE

Winna had been roughly wakened at dawn, given a harsh bath with stinging soap and ice water, and dressed in a robe that was too big for her. A nun came to inspect her once she was dressed. She had a kind face and eyes blue as cornflowers. She placed a lead pentacle around Winna's neck, ". . . for you are lead, basest lead, but in a year's time, if you are obedient and work hard at the tasks given you, you will earn one of tin, then copper, then brass, and, if you persevere, one of silver. Think of that!"

Winna was then given her breakfast. She was not allowed to sit with the nuns because of the impure influence of her eyes, so she took her milk and bread in the pantry, with the cats. While they ate, one of the nuns read to them from *The Five Points of the Pentacle* and other holy works, exhorting them at intervals to "chew slowly, and contemplate your mortality."

After breakfast Winna was led to the windowless cellar of the convent and set to making sacks out of string.

"When they are finished, you can start filling them with potatoes from that heap," the nun told her. She was left with a lamp of mutton tallow that did little to dispell the gloom.

Winna took up the string and began to make a sack, but soon she had made a cat's cradle instead. Staring into the web stretched between her fingers, Winna was soon intent on a vision: two people kneeling in the snow. She tried to see what they were doing, but the vision was gone. Instead she was staring through the web of string and fingers at a chink in the wall. Pressed to the gap was an eye. Winna inhaled softly, out of surprise rather than fear, for the look of the eye told her there was no need to be afraid. Winna went up to the wall, and as she approached the eye disappeared and was replaced by two fingers of a hand. Winna took hold of the fingers, and immediately pictured the man on the other side of the wall, not the gaunt figure he was now, but as he once had been, standing laughing in a grove of fruit trees, wearing a funny hat. Through the stone she heard him weeping.

Winna took out the heel of bread from her breakfast and passed it through the crack. The man passed it back.

"No, it is your ear I am hungry for; press it to the crack, and listen."

❧

"What are you stopping for?"

Caitlin was standing stock-still, staring at the grouped buildings of the convent which lay directly below them along the snowy road. She turned suddenly and buried her face in the front of the Badger's coat. He put his arms around her.

"I'll take this as a sign that you've had a change of heart, and mean to run off with me like any sensible woman."

"Sensible? I'm all numb. But I mean to finish what I have begun. Only allow me a little reluctance."

"I only wish you had more of it, reluctance. Or less, where I'm concerned."

Caitlin broke away and stood looking at him with dismay. "Is that what it must always come down to, where you are concerned?"

"Isn't that only natural, considering what you are to me?" His voice left him unevenly.

"Yes, what am I to you? A wolf-girl you found living in a barrow, that you have taught to eat with a knife and fork and to imitate the speech of men. You have cut its collar off, and the law says you may keep it."

They stood and stared at each other, both appalled at what she was saying, but unable to prevent the words from being uttered or taken in. Caitlin watched him go a deathly white and thought, Sweet heaven, you're killing him. She went to put her hand on his arm, but her marrow was frozen in her bones, and her limbs would not obey her.

"Perhaps it is as you say," he said, "what if it is? I never meant you any harm, Cait. You know that."

"Do I?" The words were out of her mouth before she could bite them back, and the taste of them was bitter.

The Badger dropped the pack he had been carrying and sat in the middle of the road, folding his hands over his bowed head. At last he looked up, eyes brimming with undisguised pain and love, and the sight cut her to the quick.

"Why? Did you mean to end it this way, from the start? If this was the way you felt, why did you bother to save me? If it was for this, it was no kindness."

She could only shake her head.

"Look," he said at last, "you have to tell me what you're thinking. I'm not the mind reader."

She was beside him in a heartbeat, speechless, tearful, kissing his face and mouth, pulling off his glove to kiss his hand. For a long while they held one another, kneeling in the snowy road.

"The Weirdwood. They would never find you there."

"No."

"You could go alone." He did not look at her as he said this. "They would never track you by yourself."

"They would find me. Maybe in a year's time or in twenty, but they would find me."

"Chameol, then."

"No, I have to go. I must finish this."

"I don't understand—"

"But it's so simple!" She stood and pointed toward the gates of the convent below. "Once I am through those gates, I will never see you, or hear of you again, unless I dream of you, or say your name myself when I ought to be praying."

He turned her toward him, holding her fiercely, but there was no undoing the words, or the past, or, it seemed, the near future. They divided the burden between them and started down the steep road to Ninthstile.

❧

"Send him in."

The novice left the room to fetch the visitor. While she was gone, the abbess removed a mirror and comb from their hiding place and combed her eyebrows smooth, tweezed a hair from her upper lip, and rouged her cheeks with pinching. When the rabbity monk entered the room, the mirror and the comb were gone, and there was a slight scent of anise seed.

The abbess was annoyed. "I was told to expect the Necromancer."

The monk's harelip made his voice come out with a slight whistle. "I am his messenger."

The abbess found this difficult to believe, but, on the outside chance that it was true, she held her tongue. "What is your business with me?"

"You yourself. May I say that you are a most pleasant business to behold?"

"I am sure I do not know what you mean."

"Only that such outward beauty must evidence surpassing beauty of the spirit." The monk ran a finger through the fine film of talcum on the writing desk.

"I am as a crystal vessel only, and any pleasing aspect is that of the Pentacle, any beauty its own."

The monk licked his harelip surreptitiously. "Quite so."

The abbess looked at him expectantly. "Your business . . . ?"

"The Necromancer himself sent me ahead to settle matters with you about the foundling girl, the one from Moorsedge. Has she arrived?"

"She has not, though if being looked for counted for anything, she would have arrived before she departed."

"Your dedication does you credit, but it is not only to learn of her that I have been sent. I must tell you that the abbot of Thirdmoon See is dead."

The abbess didn't blink. "Tell me what I must do."

"The situation is now so grave that the Necromancer himself must put matters to rights. To this end he has sent me ahead as his emissary, for he trusts me as he trusts himself. I need hardly tell you it is a delicate business. A barleygrain in the balance and—disaster."

"I see your meaning."

"Then you will see your duty to honor what will seem an odd request."

"Assuredly."

"There are on the grounds, I believe, underground chambers, outfitted for certain ancient ceremonies."

∽◦◦∽

A shutter was slid to one side in the high gate, and an eye pressed to the opening. The eye had a tendency to drift, which distracted the Badger as he stated their business.

"Badger Tannerson and Caitlin Barrowmoor. We have come at the bidding of the abbot of Thirdmoon See."

The gate opened and the walleyed nun regarded them with interest. "You have been expected this past full moon."

"Yes, we were detained unavoidably." Caitlin turned to the Badger. "The shearing is next, I believe."

"Yes." He looked at her, wanting to take her arm but aware of the nun's eyes on them. The nun took hold of Caitlin's ears and turned her head this way and that, frowning.

"Hardly your crowning glory, is it, my girl? Well, there'll be that much less to cut. You, boy. Don't go. The abbess has a word or two for your ears."

Caitlin and the Badger exchanged a startled look.

"What can she have to say to me? I'd as soon start on my way again."

"I am hard of hearing," the nun said. "Did someone ask you your druthers?"

"What's up?" Caitlin whispered as they followed the nun into the compound.

The Badger didn't reply. His heart was brimming with a peculiar mixture of dread and joy. Joy, that he had not been immediately sent away from her; and dread that he soon would be. This was torture, then: never to know which look, which word between them was to be the last.

The abbess was alone. She rose and greeted them, if the cool civility with which she met them could be considered a welcome.

She went to Caitlin and examined her closely: first her eyes, as though they might be counterfeit. Then the abbess's gaze moved deliberately over the cropped hair, wind-roughened complexion, stableboy's clothing.

"You have traveled together as man and wife, or something not as good," the abbess said at last. "That is regrettable. I will leave you with a moment, so you may say your farewells. Tell him, for me, that if he tries to meet you, or climbs these walls it will go hard with you both, hardest on you." She turned to the Badger. "You are to return to Thirdmoon at once. The new abbot awaits your arrival."

"Why, is the old one dead?"

The abbess paused with her hand on the doorlatch and looked at the Badger strangely. "Yes. Quite dead. You have a minute."

"I have nothing to give you——" The Badger felt in his pockets for some token, but there was only a stone.

She took the abbess's scissors from a table and cut a lock of his hair, hiding it in her shirt, a piece of gold, and gave him his change, a kiss. "Listen to me. Do not go to Thirdmoon; go anywhere else. But you must not go back to the abbey."

"It's no good, Cait. You can't stay——"

"But I do, I do stay. This is what happens, there is no changing it."

"The spinner said——"

The abbess had come in, had heard the word spinner. They turned to meet her gaze, their hearts beating wildly. But her face held nothing to alarm or reassure them.

"Come along. Sister will show you out."

The walleyed nun reappeared and showed the Badger the way out. He did not glance back; there was no need.

Caitlin's face would not begin to fade from his memory for a long time to come.

When the door had closed on him, the abbess turned to Caitlin.

"It is usual with us here at Ninthstile to attend first to the cutting of the hair. As you have taken that into your own hands, let us walk in the garden."

∽∾

The walleyed nun led the Badger out a different way than they had come in. As she led him through the convent the Badger took in the drabness of the place, the timber buildings with walls of daub and straw. The only building of any beauty was the temple, whose bell tower rose pink and silver in the winter afternoon. To this the nun led him. As she opened the heavy door, the Badger protested.

"Look here, this is not the way out and I am in no mood for prayer."

The nun made the sign of the Pentacle and plucked the Badger's sleeve. Her breath was unpleasant, and that eye would drive him wild. He wanted to shake her loose, but something about her checked him.

"What do you want with me?"

"I have something to show you, concerning Brother Asaph."

She led him into the temple, through the great hall and up a winding staircase to the choir stalls. From the bottoms of the wooden seats carvings of grotesque figures leered at him, the same hideous faces that had haunted his childhood, taunting him, keeping him from sitting down during the night-long vigils of hymns and prayers. He would be returning to just such a place as this, to a life empty of anything he loved. It was that thought that made the Badger follow the nun up into the vaulted timbers of the temple. Surely, she could not really know anything about Asaph, though it was odd she should know of him. The Badger followed her merely to postpone the moment he would be on his way again toward Thirdmoon, and ever away from Caitlin. Who was he, now, to care where he went and what he did?

Ahead of him the nun walked with more speed than he had guessed she had in her, bent over, sniffing like a rat after cheese. She stopped now and turned from him, busily adjusting her habit. The Badger realized suddenly they were quite alone, out of earshot of the rest of the convent. It occurred to him that the nun could have no good reason to know about Asaph's disappearance, no holy reason for leading him here.

"Enough of this," he said uncomfortably. "What do you have to tell me?"

To his horror, the nun turned to him, seized her left ear, and seemed to tear off her face. Beneath the mask of putty and gum was the face of Elric.

For a long moment they stood and faced each other, rooted to the spot. Then Elric realized he had made a miscalculation. Suddenly, this was no stableboy or failed apprentice before him, but someone far more dangerous. What's more, the Badger had a knife.

"Easy," Elric said, backing up. "Give me a listen, first!"

"Easy! Easy!" The Badger punctuated the air with thrusts of the knife. "Who would know better than you about Asaph's death? You killed him! And if you didn't fasten the bells around Caitlin's neck, you watched whoever did, you filthy—"

"Hear me out!"

"Hear you out—! Hear you out, you—no I won't libel dogs for you, that's too good for you. You're worse than a bastard, and that's not a word I use lightly."

"I'm unarmed!"

"Then arm yourself, or watch me cut out your liver before I take your eyes!"

Elric caught up a candle-mount, its massive candle held in place by a sharp spike. But this proved heavy and unwieldy, and after a few parries and thrusts Elric was forced to abandon it, vaulting over a row of stalls and sprinting up the aisle. Elric had speed over the Badger, but was hampered by the habit. They reached the rail of the gallery together and Elric found himself using a prayerbook to fend off the Badger's jabs. Who would have guessed a stableboy to be good with arms? Again Elric had to retreat, this time over the railing, swinging down a few flights faster than the Badger could follow on the stairs. By that time Elric had shucked the robe and was lost to sight among a thousand glowing tapers at the altar. It was too dangerous to swing here, and miss, thought the Badger; he could set the whole place on fire. He stepped forward cautiously. Was that a footstep, or his own steps echoing? His breath, or Elric's? But no, there he was, a gallery above, ever up, to the bell tower.

By the time he reached the staircase to the bell tower Elric was nowhere in sight. The stair rose out of sight at a dizzying angle. There was nothing for it but to climb them, even though it meant leaving himself open to attack from above. If he jumps from that height, the Badger thought, he'll kill us both. The Badger moved up, climbing ever to the left in an unending spiral, prepared at every turn to duck a pikestaff, or a falling block. At last there were no more landings, only a trapdoor leading to the bells themselves, a skeleton of scaffolding and ropes.

It was all striped light and shadow. Nothing stirred except a barn swallow, which darted gracefully into the open air of the courtyard. The ropes rose up out of sight, and the Badger could see the dim gleam and swell of the bells above him. It's so peaceful, he thought. The knife slipped in his moist hand.

"Give it up," he said under his breath. "You won't get past me, not without wings."

All he got by way of answer was the padding of feet on wood high overhead, and the single sleepy toll of a bell. Something fell from above, and the Badger turned it over with his foot, keeping a wary eye on the bells as he bent to pick it up. It was a drawstring bag; inside it was a braided circlet of hair—Caitlin's hair. Suddenly the bells began to toll, and the Badger looked up.

Elric landed on the Badger's back, the force driving the Badger's chin into the landing with a terrible crack. The knife skated across the sawdust of the floor. The Badger reached it first, seizing Elric by the collar and pressing the point of the blade to his throat. Elric did not plead for his life; he gazed calmly at the Badger, a fox with human eyes. But from the stairs below someone pleaded for him.

"Stop!"

It was Asaph.

∽

There were white roses in the garden. The abbess paused at the entrance to the yew walk and cut one with the scissors suspended from her waist by a ribbon. With care she placed the rose behind Caitlin's ear. Caitlin trembled, for she remembered the dream of snow poppies and the vision in Ormr's chamber. The abbess had not trimmed the thorns from the rose, and they pierced Caitlin's temple.

It was not a yew walk only into which the abbess led her, but a maze. Caitlin started to protest but with each step she felt fainter. As the snowy rose behind her ear slowly grew rosier, Caitlin's skin became as white as wax.

They came to the heart of the maze, and the walls of thick yew fell away. In the clearing there was a design worked in black and white and red marble: thirteen moons circling a five-pointed star. The pentacle itself was painted on wood: a trapdoor. This the abbess lifted, and as Caitlin was now too weak to follow (the bloom behind her ear was bloodred), she took her by the hand and led her into the gloom beneath the yew maze.

At the bottom of the stairs the abbess let go of Caitlin's arm.

"The Necromancer himself has asked for you. Wait here until you are fetched. There is a gown over there: put it on." The abbess's foot was already on the first step when she turned back.

"It will go easier with you if you do not resist." Then the trapdoor opened and shut, and Caitlin heard the bolt being shot home.

Outside the abbess shuddered and made the sign of the Pentacle. She hurried along the path, concentrating on the turns of the maze. The old abbess had become lost in the maze and when they had finally found her she was quite mad. The present abbess did not mean to meet the same fate, so she put Caitlin and the Necromancer from her mind.

Caitlin was too weary to put on the gown. Her head was throbbing; she put a hand to her temple and it came away bloodied.

This is the way I die, she thought. After a short time she fell into a delirium, and in it she saw a figure coming toward her, the face obscured and uncertain.

"Badger?" she said, and then, "Abagtha? Oh, 'Batha, have you come for me after all?"

The Necromancer came up to her carrying a wand. Now he struck the ground with it, and it flared up blue and silver and showed his face.

He wore a mask of black obsidian that made his eyes and mouth into black holes. His hood slipped back and she saw he wore a skullcap of goblinstone, silver-shot blue.

"You do not fear me," he said.

"I have foreseen this."

He nodded and put out a hand in a black gauntlet to touch the milky pallor of her skin.

"It is past time," he said, and plucked the red rose from Caitlin's ear.

She fell at his feet as if dead.

17

THE HEART OF THE MAZE

Caitlin woke to see her old cat amulet swinging slowly in front of her eyes. I am in the nut cellar, she thought, but it was not so. Gradually the things that lay beyond the amulet's arc swam into focus: cages of animals and shelves of books such as she had seen in the dragon's chamber. But the clasps that bound the volumes had no keyholes, and the pages were sealed forever beneath a film of gilt. Then Caitlin saw the plants ranged beneath in bell jars: foxglove, hemlock, buttercup—all deadly. She realized she was not alone. Her eyes focused again on the amulet, then on the hand that held it. At the sight of the mask, glittering black, she gave a cry and wrenched her head to one side.

The Necromancer went to one of the cages and removed the animal inside. As he stroked the badger's fur, the Necromancer's mask was streaked with silver, spitting light from a flame that blazed up, consuming some gassy fuel.

"Consider the badger," he said. "The feet and eyes of the animal are supposed to confer invisibility, though it is not specified whether the parts are to be ingested or worn as an amulet." His voice was not muffled by the mask;

rather, it seemed louder and clear for passing through the absolute, fire-born blackness of the obsidian.

"They are also said to make a powerful charm for instilling fear in and persuading one's enemies. It may be true; I have never seen it. It is also said to be a love-charm, which may be hearsay, but I like to believe it. What is love, after all, but the persuasion of the enemy?"

The badger squirmed in the Necromancer's arms, but did not bite. It was as if it struggled against the jaws of a trap and knew the end of its struggle was near.

"Don't hurt him." Caitlin meant, and did not mean, the animal in the Necromancer's arms.

Set your fear aside. Go armed in fear, in human fear. The black mask glittered, seamless, flawless. It revealed two pale, ancient eyes, the white flare of a tooth, the purple ghost of a tongue when the Necromancer spoke.

He turned and replaced the badger in its cage, picking up a mortar and pestle, from which there carried such a reek that Caitlin turned her head into the table where she lay.

"Romantics say that if you cut open a lark you will find its tune scrolled there, like the works of a music box. It is not so, but lovers will cut the birds open, anyway, out of fancy. But if you open a swallow, you will find a stone, the swallowstone, also called chelidony. This must be pulverized with some few other things: tortoise bile, the white of an egg, a certain purple dyestuff. And what do you think it becomes when it is snatched from the fire?"

She could not answer. Like the badger, Caitlin knew death, or something as good as death, lay around the edges of the room and hour, expectant.

"It is not the answer you suppose." He set down the mortar. "It is only a paint, a compound for labeling glass vessels. Did you think it would be an elixir? A love potion? Or perhaps a poison, sold to star-crossed lovers in a play?" The Necromancer paused, gazing down at Caitlin. "They thought boiled honey and barleysugar were powerful medicines, once."

"Who are you?" she whispered.

"I am the Necromancer."

"If that were all I would not fear you as I do."

The eyes clouded behind the mask, moons suddenly obscured. "You may call me Greykys."

Though she could not see him smile Caitlin knew he had. She shook with the same cold terror she had felt falling in the snow, hearing the dogs behind her.

"You have been drugged, otherwise you might have injured yourself struggling. For my purpose you must be unmarked. A delicate procedure: a bruise would ruin it."

Caitlin struggled to remember what she knew of the old rune tongues. *Greykys. Grey kiss*— She raised a hand, as if she would have removed the mask, had she the strength. Her hand fell back. "Elric—"

"You are trying to puzzle me out, are you? Where is the harm—no one shall ever learn it. Here is half the riddle, then. When I was a boy, long ago, the old language was still spoken, and *grey* was the word for hare. Consider it your wedding gift."

So that was it. He meant to keep her here, alive, if it could be called a life.

He read her look. "The idea repulses you. That surprises me. You have lived in such a chamber before, indeed you chose it, and I flatter myself enough to say I would make a better bridegroom than a corpse in a barrow grave.

"But that is not the kind of marriage I have in mind for you."

It was only then that Caitlin saw the velvet cloth he had laid out, and upon it the slender silver knives.

⤜∽⤛

The abbess saw three figures running through the snow to the maze, one tall and thin, red head like a match; the second shorter and broader, hair light as dun; the third a shaggy madman.

"Good! To it, gentlemen! By spring we will send the little ones in after you, to gather up your bones."

She frowned. Deep in the flesh of her thumb was embedded the thorn of a rose.

⤜∽⤛

Heaving with effort, the Badger fell to his knees, clinging to a stone seat, afraid he would break his ribs with breathing.

"Hold on—we've lost Asaph."

They drew ragged breaths of frozen air.

"How will we ever find her?" said the Badger at last.

"Perhaps she broke off twigs as she went." But they both knew she had probably been drugged, could even now be dead.

"No." This was said by Winna as she was carried up in Asaph's arms. For Elric, it was as if he were once again a boy of twelve, beholding a child in the wood for the first time, seeing his hope, her seer's eyes, the saving of the age.

"Here," said the Badger, kissing the top of the child's head. "You know your right hand from your left, don't you? Tell me, as we go, where to turn."

Elric started to protest but the Badger silenced him. "No, it must be me—someone must stay with the child and Asaph is too weak. Yes," he said, more to himself this time, "it must be me."

"The drugs are wearing off. That is good; you must be sentient when the cut is made. 'In full knowledge,' the old text says. It will take some minutes yet. The abbess was overzealous with the dose. While we wait I shall tell you what I am.

"Have you guessed my little riddle yet? No? You surprise me. You have such a talent for surmising things. It has cost me much, more than you know.

"I stumbled out of the wilderness, looking like an old man, though I was young. Only lately the wilderness had been fertile land, and I wore upon my face the singular mark of my misfortune. Those who found me made of it the mark of a prophet. I was glad to oblige them. Taking up a stick I drew a pentacle in the sand. I needed a heaven myself and was glad enough to invent theirs for them.

"As the new faith attracted more followers I became a high priest and a rich man. I filled my apartments with the apparatus of alchemy, for I had found my homemade heaven hollow and was searching for another immortality.

"Others have documented the quest—I trust you are familiar with it? Then I need not repeat it. I brought metalworking in the kingdom (for it was a single kingdom then, the moon yet unshattered) to a high art.

"I had become a skeptic, disbelieving in everything, when I made a discovery. Through long work with poisons (quicksilver, mostly, and some arsenic) I had become impervious to them. I could boldly eat them as if they were sweetmeats, for I had unwittingly taken in so much of them through the years I suffered no effect.

"Have you guessed it yet, that riddle of mine? Well, I will go on. I took up my studies with new enthusiasm, for I had stumbled on a provisional immortality. While the temples spread across the kingdom, I spent the gold from the temple coffers to buy every manner of killing drug known to surgeon and cutthroat. After a while I began adding other ingredients to the mixture: the tears of the tortoise, yew ash, dust from tombs.

"My age became so great I declared myself Necromancer and in a year's time announced my own death, appointing myself my own successor. I kept up this fiction for lifetimes, so that now time shrinks before me. Your own journey, a winter's span, is for me no more than an eye's blink. . . ."

His voice was lulling Caitlin to sleep, but as her eyelids tugged shut, the silver knives would wink and she would jerk awake again. In its cage the badger paced. Caitlin fixed her gaze on it, and, unused as she was to praying, began repeating a little prayer: *Go armed in fear, in human fear.*

"I did not age; rather, as my age increased so did my knowledge and my strength. This drew many to me, both men and women. I had no need of them; my secrets were my own, what need had I for the companionship of inferiors? My only mistress was my work, and there was no earthly woman to usurp her. Until she came.

"Her name was Tybitha. I saw her first at the temple, stealing offerings from the altar. How to tell you how I felt, seeing her kneeling there, slipping the coins into the lining of her blouse? Her face was in shadow, and the only parts of her the candlelight showed were her bowed head, her bare arms.

"I took her by the shoulder, asking her why she stole from the coffers of the holy Pentacle. 'Hunger,' she said. 'Have you no husband to keep you?' I asked. 'No,' said she, 'I have no husband, for I can neither weave nor spin.' I searched her face and found in it no trace of fear or desire, loathing or longing. So, while the law entitled her hand to be placed on the block in payment for the silver she had stolen, I took that hand in troth instead and placed on it my own ring of gold.

"After the marriage, I showed my bride the bachelor's apartments that were to be her married home. All that was mine was hers, I told her, except the locked room under the eaves, to which I alone kept a key. She nodded and asked whether a carpenter might be hired to install an airing cupboard.

"My wife was true to her word, and neither wove nor spun, contenting herself with tending the herb garden and teaching herself to fashion the blown-glass vessels I used in my work. I waited for her to disobey me, as I thought she must, by taking the key and opening the locked room. This she did not do, rapt instead on the installation of her cupboard.

"This tore at me in a way you cannot imagine. Having so rashly married her, I was frantic to discover something undeserving in her. But a wife with a more even temper no man ever had. She seemed content to spend her days working glass in the fire, afterward giving me my bath before taking her own. She catered to my appetite in everything: I never went off to bed unsatisfied. Surely, no better wife!"

Caitlin shuddered. Through the drug her mind worked the name over and over, turning it inside out: *Tybitha.*

"One day I discovered my stock of poisons was depleted. Not by a large amount, but some hand other than my own had tampered with the drug jars. I challenged my wife; she admitted taking it and claimed it was to kill rats. I let the matter drop. What was she, after all, but a lovely thief? If she had guessed the secret of my longevity, she ate the poison herself only out of vanity, to stay time's march on her beauty.

"It was nothing so womanly as that. How slowly the realization dawned!

"She was my enemy, come out of the wilderness to finish what she had begun. She had taken a new guise, arming herself with youth and beauty, to steal from me my inheritance, a precious touchstone of past and future. She had come, so bold as to take the name *Tybitha*, taunting me with the simplicity of it. And I was too drunk with her to see the meaning of it, a wasp trapped in honey.

"How witless I was, not to see it sooner! I had set the locked room as a test for her, and while I waited for the trap to spring she had turned the airing closet into an alchemist's chamber fit to rival my own. While I slept, drugged with love and trust of her, she turned my house inside out, searching out my secrets, forcing herself to eat the poison as I ate it. In her airing cupboard she gazed into a crystal of her own making, for she had told me one untruth. Where her mother had spun silk, the daughter spun glass.

"At last one day I discovered her in my most secret hiding place, about to set her hand upon the stone. I could not kill her—not only had love made me incapable, the poison had brought her a little of my own immortality. So I took her name from her, her youth and beauty, and her reason, and sent her off into the wood."

"*Abagtha.*"

"Yes. The word for an old woman's winding sheet. Two things should have taught me she was of Myrrha's blood. She was named after Tybio, and she had those same eyes, owl's eyes, as her nine-time-great-grandmother. Did you never guess? Think: Kiss—lip. Grey—hare."

Harelip, thought Caitlin. "Myrrhlock."

The eyes behind the mask gleamed. "None other. Not long after Abagtha's banishment my touchstone told me an assassin had been dispatched to waylay me. This despite the precautions I had taken." Caitlin thought of the book in Milo's library, with the pages torn out.

"I awaited him with pleasure; here at last was a test of my immortality. When the assassin arrived, I was surprised to see a girl of no more than thirteen, unarmed, remarkable for the fact that she had one blue eye and one green. This was before the nature of the threat had made itself clear. She did not suffer too greatly. But each year thereafter came a child, until one day as I was at my books I read in an ancient text how a prophet should come out of the wilderness and be undone by a child with one green eye and one blue. The runes were remarkable: *forest* for green, *sky* for blue.

"I saw now what I was up against and acted quickly, but those who had already gathered against the Pentacle saw to it some of the children were spared. So I have waited, for a hundred years and again another hundred, knowing every year will bring its circle of seasons, and perhaps a child, one eye on the forest, the other on the sky. But my patience, my poison, is running out. I need more and more of it, so that there will never be enough. Without my killing food I will die. But you offer me another way." Myrrhlock picked up one of the silver knives.

"I had long ago read of a creature that has aspects both of the male and female and is capable of recreating itself endlessly. Here, I thought, was the way to escape the limits of my poisonous addiction.

"But this, too, presented a problem. In each new infancy, I would lose memory and leave myself vulnerable to my enemies. I needed to create a perfect vessel into which I could transfer my thought, my soul, my self." He reached a gauntleted hand to caress Caitlin's cheek. "And where was there ever made a more lovely urn?"

The drug had nearly worn off, but Caitlin could hardly tell, she was so paralyzed with fear. The Necromancer's voice washed over her like ether.

"But first, a few adjustments. Your heart, for instance, must be filled with a mixture of sweet resin and lead, and your blood must be replaced with quicksilver. Then I will go in your body to Chameol and destroy my enemies once and for all. They will crown me queen, and the very straits will run red with blood." The knife skimmed over Caitlin's trunk, making a light cut, and Caitlin's gasp was like the sound of the flesh parting, the blood beading in the gap.

"*No!*"

The Badger started for Caitlin, as if to stop the welling of all that blood. He was flung across the room by a powerful blow, although Myrrhlock had not touched him. Dazed, the Badger took in the retorts and crucibles, the animals pacing in their cages. Wiping a little blood from his mouth, he turned to the Necromancer.

"What unnatural thing—"

"Unnatural?" Myrrhlock laughed. "Shall I tell you what is unnatural? Shall I tell you of your own birth? It is well known to me. A curious economy of forefathers, in that your grandfather served as your father as well. The word, I think, is incest? Unfortunate that the girl should have hung herself, especially since she waited until the child had reached maturity to do it. You have proved a nuisance to me."

Caitlin was slipping under the edge of a darkening mist. "Don't listen to him. Badger, my eyes. Look at me."

The Badger stood in the middle of the room, mute. Then he lunged at the Necromancer, only to be flung the length of the room. There was a sickening crack of a bone, and the Badger cried out.

"Do not try to save her. Save yourself. Turn now and leave while it is still charity that I extend to you." The Badger clutched his arm and said nothing. Myrrhlock grew angry; the darkness upon the mask shifted like a thundercloud. The Necromancer set the silver knife beside the amulet on the table where Caitlin lay.

"Do you really believe the life you intend for her would be saving her? Yes, I can see it. You will make a wife of her, a brood animal for the getting of your mooncalves. For such they would surely be. You yourself have seen it, the blight passed on through the blood. They carry the brood to the river in the dark of night and drown them."

The Badger saw in Caitlin's eyes that human armor, fear of evil, which is also the love of life. He could not stand the sight and looked away. It's not true, he thought, but could not summon the voice to say it. And feared it was true. The pain in his arm was not to be borne; he clenched his teeth and closed his hand on the stone in his pocket, the stone he had taken from the dragon's throat.

As his fingers closed on it—so hard it cut his palm— the Badger felt strength beginning to return to him, the pain itself charging through him like the anticipation of disaster, or desire.

Caitlin's own hand closed around the catstone. No sooner had her fingers tightened around the amulet than she felt the Badger's strength flowing into her, her own will passing into him. For the dragon's heart and the catstone were pieces of a single stone. His thoughts rang clearly in her mind.

Damn it, you're the strong one!

Now it's your turn to be strong.

And if I fail? We're done for!

No. We have not come this far to fail.

Myrrhlock perceived nothing of this, intent as he was on the white-hot mixture in his crucible. "When I am done with her, I will tend to you. In the meantime, think well on this: If you do not cooperate, I will pluck from you all memory and thought except the vision and sensation of her eternal agony. If you are reasonable, and I hope you will be, a place will be made for you in the temple. Did you not once wish to be apprenticed to an apothecary?"

I can't get near him, the Badger thought frantically. Caitlin's own answer slid into his brain, pushing aside the pain.

The stone! Armed!

With a single movement of his arm the Badger hurled the stone into the center of the mask. Myrrhlock gave an inhuman shriek as the mask shattered into a thousand fragments. The Badger caught a glimpse of a face he knew—the abbot's harelipped secretary. The riddlespinner's voice came back to him: ". . . the magician's lips where his sister had kissed him split, and his hair went white." Then the Necromancer gave a terrible shudder, his figure distorted into something out of nightmare, an apparition of wings and sightless eyes and a maw of purple flame. The horrific thing wavered in the chamber, as if in a death spasm, and vanished.

&ce;

Neither of them could recall later how they left the collapsing chamber with their lives. They woke in the snow, to the ache of healing, to see little Winna bending over them, the saving tears standing in her seer's eyes.

18

THE SPELLKEY TURNS

So far had the thorn pierced there was no retrieving it.
The abbess sank into a fever and could not be roused.
The nuns circled around her bed in confusion.

A woman was riding boldly through the gates of the
convent upon a piebald horse. She was dressed like a soldier, and her copper hair shone in the winter sun like a
shield. The dogs and children of the village danced around
her as she came, and strange figures in rags, shoeless—
inmates from the asylum. They could even pick out the
figure of the old abbess. All wore garlands of flowers,
though where they had come from in the heart of winter
there was no telling.

The nuns watched her approach, not knowing what to
do. They had been warned against her coming: Beware of
witches, they were told, and with hair like that she must
certainly be a witch, as surely as if she had seer's eyes.
Every four hours through the night the sisters were accustomed to being wakened, assembling in the choir stalls to
pray for protection against the legion of unbelievers.

But the abbess lay in a fever, and they knew not what
to do. Witch or not, the woman on the horse had an air of

command. Though their hearts leaned over the windowsill toward the banner of copper hair, still they hesitated.

Then the youngest remembered the old rhyme her grandmother had used to say to her when she was a girl:

> *Dogs and madmen dance around*
> *Coppercrown is come to town.*
> *She'll ride a pie horse in the gates*
> *To carry away the child that waits*
> *Hie me up so I can see*
> *When Copper-Copper-Coppercrown*
> *Comes riding through the town.*

The bowl of compresses broke on the floor. With impatient hands the young nun wrested the wimple from her head and let it fall on the stairs. Out into the snow she ran, heedless. This was the thing that had been foretold. The young girl knelt at Iiliana's feet, raising a flushed and ardent face to her queen.

The eldest nun had followed. Iiliana helped her to loosen her wimple and cast it off, the hairpins sinking into the drift and vanishing, the grey hair tumbling around the old woman's head as insubstantial as smoke.

"I thought I would not live to see this day," said the old nun, weeping. "After so many years it seemed as if they must only be legends after all."

"Iiliana!"

Elric came up with Winna in his arms. He caught Iiliana in an embrace, Winna and all.

"Enough," Iiliana protested. "You'll crush the child."

He handed Winna over. "Can't I be glad to see my sister?"

"Is she all right?"

It was understood she meant Caitlin.

"You had better have a look at them both."

"I will examine her—as for him, I think you and Asaph had best tend to that."

❦

"Have a little pity!"

The Badger sat across from Asaph and Elric at a table

in the abbess's chambers. At the Badger's outburst the others traded a glance.

"Everyone has been treating me like a child who's too young to know what's going on. I'm not a fool; I know I'm not part of your plans for Caitlin. But I do think, before you turn me out with a fresh horse and new suit of clothes, that you could tell me what it was all *for*."

There was a silence before Asaph answered. "There is an ancient brotherhood, the knights of Chameol. I am one such knight, as is Elric. You have met others, though you did not know it: Fowk the lockpick, and Leier. We are knights without armor, no arms but our wits, and in swearing fealty to Chameol we forfeit our bloodline, our names, our right to marry, to own more than we can carry in our pockets. So you see it was not so much a lie, my playing a monk. The vows are the same.

"We are sworn to Iiliana, pledged to defeat Myrrhlock and destroy the Pentacle. The verse on the missal and the runes in the Devil's Sieve tell of a great seer, an other-world daughter, who will come with a knight-without-a-sword to destroy the Pentacle and restore the age of knowledge and light."

The Badger stared into this face he knew so well, and not at all. This was an Asaph he had never seen, sober in fact and humor. His wounds ached, and when the Badger spoke it was in pain.

"That all sounds noble, but it explains nothing. Why? Why the gilt on the missal? Why pretend to go mad, and let me believe you were dead? Why kill the deer in the forest and leave me to rot in prison?"

"We are sworn to serve the Spellkey. Often we must serve in ways that seem cruel. But we are sworn to—"

"—let suffer and die."

"No—"

"Yes!" The Badger rose from his seat, trembling. "I tell you, yes!" He pointed to Elric. "I saw him turn over the relic-seller's body. You are sworn to murder, and worse, all of you. And you, Asaph, you pretended to be like a father to me—" The Badger's voice broke off.

Elric had risen, too. "I'll go."

* * *

"Are you telling me what the riddlespinner showed me was a lie?" the Badger asked when the door closed behind Elric.

"No—when Elric found him Dice was already dead, by Myrrhlock's hand, or at his bidding."

"And the wormwood in the wine?"

"Myrrhlock. We had no hand in that."

"And if Caitlin had not found a remedy? I suppose my death would have been unfortunate but necessary."

"You don't understand. Some deception was necessary, but it was not all a lie. How can I say where my vows left off and love began? You could either be a son to me, Badger, or a prophecy fulfilled. Who was I to claim you? We are all of us clay, mold for the Spellkey."

"So this had all been for Caitlin's amulet?"

"No. It is a stone of power, but your sacrifices were not made for it. The Spellkey is the journey from Thirdmoon to Ninthstile. As the runes tell it, the road is the shaft of the key, and each stopping place along the way a ward for unfastening the lock. The Spellkey is the test for telling the true seer and her knight. You might have succumbed anywhere along the way, swayed by love or wealth or the call of the Pentacle itself.

"It was Elric who had to see you thwarted and tempted at every step. But he was also to watch over you: it was he who saved you from the apothecary. Had you become an apprentice there you would not have lived out the week. Elric's task was to tease out the weakness in you, to trip you up. If you were not the ones, we had to know before you reached Ninthstile. We could tell you nothing, nor reveal ourselves, because you had to act out of what was in you, and in you alone."

The knight rose. "Now it would be best if you slept. A room has been made ready for you."

The Badger paused at the door. "I was rash—I'm sorry."

"No, be glad we are both still here quarreling!" The face changed briefly into the one Asaph had worn in his cups, then it was again this new face, the one the Badger did not know.

But he would grow to know it.

In the hall outside his room Elric was waiting. The two
men stood and faced each other and not for the first time
Elric felt this was no longer a stableboy before him. There
was something in the way the Badger winced and arranged
his arm in its sling—the gesture of an old man. Looking
at him, Elric felt a curious twinge.

"You were at Caitlin's belling."

Elric was too startled to answer.

In the dim light the Badger's eyes gleamed. "Yes, the
riddlespinner showed me that, too."

"Does Caitlin know?"

"She may have guessed. I haven't told her."

Elric nodded. "Myrrhlock would have killed her if he
had found her; it was before he knew her value to him
living. So I had to protect her, hide her where they would
never think to look. And I had to keep the village of idiots
from drowning her in a ducking chair. So I hid her in
plain view. Myrrhlock would think she was a village witch
and madwoman, nothing more. And with the bells, the
villagers would feel safe and let her alone."

"Let her alone? Did you never think, never really think,
about what they did to her? Did you think it stopped with
the *bells*? No, don't answer. There was nothing you could
do to stop it, I know; it was perhaps even necessary and
besides, it is all in the past, all for the best—"

Elric's gaze was grey and level and betrayed nothing of
what was in his heart. "I might have done something about
it, if I had known. But I did not, and whatever happened
to her—yes, even that—was better than death at
Myrrhlock's hands. And if I need forgiveness, isn't it from
her I need it?"

They fell silent, each thinking of Caitlin, newly belled,
falling asleep in the barrow that first night, waking hour by
hour to the sound of her own bells. Elric broke the silence.

"We were raised on the hope, Iiliana and I, that in our
lifetime the two would come, the otherworld daughter and
her knight."

The Badger laughed. "A tanner's daughter's bastard."

"No, a knight. The rune can mean simply a servant or companion, so we never knew what we were looking for. Whenever there was word of a child born with seer's eyes, a knight would be dispatched. I was twelve when I was sent off to the Weirdwood."

"It's finished then. You've found her."

"You still don't see. Not her, the both of you. The otherworld daughter *and* her knight. You have found the Spellkey, and unlocked it."

Iiliana had put the catstone on a ribbon and tied it once more around Caitlin's neck. Caitlin put up a hand to touch it.

Her heart was full of contrary emotions, wine and oil that would not mix. She had not expected to leave Myrrhlock's chamber with her life and was marveling yet at her escape. In all her experience Caitlin had found that others usually rescued you with an end in mind. Abagtha had taken her in and raised her to be a nameless slave. Even the Badger had unfastened the bells only to place a collar of another kind around her neck.

It looked as if she had been saved again, and Caitlin looked up, wondering what would be asked of her now. Iiliana's face was frank and kind. Caitlin worried. She was wary of honesty and kindness. They were a rune tongue she had never mastered.

"This stone—how often I tried to part with it, so the dreams would stop! But it was as if it owned me, not the other way around. How could it kill Abagtha and not me?"

Iiliana touched the stone she wore around her own neck.

"The old stories say that when Myrrha fell dead, her spinning hand struck a stone. The old woman saw this and came looking for it, and with a simple spell gave it the power of a dreamstone. You know that some stones seek out water; this stone seeks out dreams. It cannot spin a dream, only magnify the dreams within the dreamer, making them clearer and stronger, and burning them into memory. After Tybitha became Abagtha she was full of hollowness, and when she put on the amulet the hollowness consumed her. When you put it on, you began to remember your dreams. Myrrhlock knew the dreams would lead you to him, but he also knew the stone could give you the power to destroy him. So long ago he sought out the stone and shattered it. This was his undoing: the pieces fell down wells, were ploughed into fields, carved into necklaces— even fed to dragons. Each piece has the power of the whole and, once scattered, Myrrhlock could never gather them together again."

"And is he destroyed?"

"For the present he has retreated. Our battles against him have only begun, I fear. But they need not be your battles."

"What do you mean?"

"You have a choice. You may come to Chameol and be honored as our seer. All our secret arts will be open to you, and the ancient runebooks. You will be prepared to take your place as a high oracle. Or, if it is what you want, your otherworld sight can be taken from you, and you may go back into the world as an ordinary woman. But if you choose Chameol, you must come alone."

Caitlin nodded. "Would I be blind, then, if I chose to remain in the world?"

"No, you would see and dream as other women do, but you would not be able to move between the dream world and the waking one as you do now." Iiliana paused. "You would lose all memory of what has happened, of me and of Chameol, and of the tanner's son. No doubt that seems unduly cruel, but if you were allowed to remember even a little it would jeopardize our fight against the Pentacle. The Badger is part of what you must forget if you do not choose to join us."

"Then it is no choice at all."

"Have you not often wished your dreams away?"

"Daily! What good have they been to me? They never spared me pain or warned me of danger. When they did show me the future it was contradictory. In one dream I would see myself laughing, happy—in the next I would see my own death."

"The dreams mirrored your confusion. On Chameol,

you can learn to master them, to make them come at your bidding, and to tell what will be from what might be."

"When must I decide?"

"I set sail for Chameol in a week's time. If you come at all, you must come then."

❧

Morning found the Badger seated at a table. He had not been to bed, although he might have put his head on his arms for an hour in the darkest part of the night.

He cut a very different figure than he had when he set out for Moorsedge on a late summer morning months before, his thoughts on the new life he would make as the rising young apothecary. It would be too easy to say he looked older, though he did. He was leaner, and his face bore the traces of travel through unfriendly climates: briar scratches, winter sunburn, and a glaze to his eyes as if he could no longer sleep through the night—a trait found in soldiers long after they have returned from battle.

This morning the Badger's jaw glittered with a gold stubble; there were lines around his eyes, and his hands lay a certain way on the tabletop. He had not merely become a man, he had become mortal.

In his hand he held two marbles, one blue and one green. His thoughts were on the fortune-teller in Moorsedge. What had she said? He would make a perilous journey and lose what he valued most.

Caitlin had come into the room, and stood looking at the marbles in the Badger's palm. Suddenly she stepped forward and scooped them up, as if to throw them into the fire. The Badger caught her hands and stopped her and they struggled silently for a moment. Each soon saw neither was about to gain the upper hand, and the fistfight generated into a kiss. The marbles fell from Caitlin's hand and rolled forgotten into a knothole in the tabletop, nesting together cockeyed.

The Badger broke away, and the look on his face so appalled Caitlin she turned away.

"Don't—don't look at me that way."

"Not you, me! How can you stand to touch me? When I think of what he said, it makes my flesh creep."

Caitlin remembered Myrrhlock's version of the Badger's birth.

"You don't believe him?"

"In my heart I think I have always known and never wanted to believe it. And I can never know it's not true. Everyone who ever knew the truth is dead."

"What does it matter to you and to me? It is a terrible thing, if it's true, but a thing of the past. Anything can be forgotten. Love, look at me." She gently turned his face to hers. "I of all people know that."

"Don't you see? A mooncalf, that's what I am. Now do you see? The blood is bad, bad blood will tell. Monsters breed only monsters."

Caitlin said nothing. She was thinking how that morning a drop of wax had curdled in the water of her basin, making the rune for *acorn*, and the one for *kindle*. How to tell him?

The Badger had set a wider space between them, looking at her soberly, as if to paint her every feature on his brain. "I had come to think that it was only a matter of winning you over, making you care. I never thought it would mean giving you up."

Her heart was beating fast. "And are you? Giving me up?"

"It won't come to that. You're going to Chameol."

"Yes." To Chameol, to the moon, from waking to dreams. It is a terrible thing, sometimes, to watch someone you love asleep, Caitlin thought. It was as if you were watching yourself, afraid your soul would not be able to rejoin your body. Terrible, to be ever after alone, separate even from yourself, your own thoughts a stranger's.

"What will you do?" was all she said.

"I don't know. I won't say it doesn't matter; it does. But I'm not sure I can care about it today."

Caitlin went to see the shutters and door were latched. When she turned, he saw her hands unlacing her shirt.

"Is that wise?"

"No, but I want to be foolish a last time."

She came over to him, her shirt slipping from her

shoulders where her heavy hair should have lain. He put a hand up to touch the warm skin at the back of her neck.

"I can't," he said, shaking his head.

But her kiss persuaded him, and desire burned off the last of his reluctance. He pulled her onto the narrow cot.

It was her turn to be reluctant. "Oh, no! Not a *nun's* bed . . ."

Laughing and swearing he dragged the blankets onto the floor. "Myself, I could lie down on coals."

It was sharp and sweet and not without grief. In the end, too, there was no past and no future in that room, only the two of them.

She realized she still had not told him.

Outside, Elric put his hand to the latch. He had a proposal to put to the Badger, and he had not seen Caitlin go in. Iiliana had; she appeared beside her brother and gave a little shake of her head.

"Here, I wanted you anyway." She snapped a pair of shears in her hand, sharp and handy jaws.

"Your hair wants cutting. No arguments!"

∽◦∾

In a few days they had reached Big Rim. A ship was found, one even the rats had abandoned. Iiliana was well pleased, and bought it for a niggling sum. In the morning the ship was nothing but an unseaworthy hulk; by late afternoon, whether by skill or charm, the ship shone, straining at its moorings as if eager for the journey. The sails billowed though there was no wind, and all along the waterfront people stopped to stare at the ship and her odd crew. Every hand was a woman, her hair shorn from convent or asylum.

On the dock, Caitlin stood in the cape Iiliana had given her, its blackness sweeping around her like the hair she had given up. Elric, outfitted for hard riding, stood before her and held out a box.

"A repayment," he said, with a smile.

In the box lay his copper hair, nested in the braided black coil of her own.

"When your hair is grown to the length it was, we'll

meet again." He wanted to tell her of the bells that often haunted his sleep, but Elric knew there was no saying it. Some vows he must keep.

Iiliana put her hand on Caitlin's shoulder. "Farewells all said? The tide's not at my bidding, and this one is on the way out."

The Badger stood holding the bridle of his horse. His eyes met Caitlin's.

"There have been enough farewells, I think."

"Yes," Caitlin agreed, thinking there was something in his eyes she had not seen before. It made him look like Elric.

She did not know that Elric had held back part of the measure of her hair. A braided circlet of it cinched the Badger's wrist, hard and black as ebony, hidden by his sleeve.

The Badger was impatient to make a start, but Elric watched until the ship was out of sight. He squinted a little, looking into the sun.

At last he swung into the saddle and they headed out of town. When they had reached the edge Elric reined in his horse, turning to the Badger.

"Still want to go on?"

The Badger nodded. It was little enough to give up. His name, Matthew Tannerson, was easy enough. It was not as if he ever used it. And never having had a house or money he would hardly miss them. The third requirement of the vows was the reason he had accepted Elric's offer in the first place.

"It's not monkhood, mind," Elric said. "It's just that you can never marry."

The Badger doubted he would want to, between dreams of mooncalf children and dreams of—

"I'm ready."

Looking, Elric thought for the first time that the odd name suited him. At last the Badger had the look of a badger: a quick animal way of glancing around him, poised, keen, hungry. Yes, Elric thought, you are ready. "Do you see those woods?"

"Yes."

"When we pass into their shadow, you will be a knight of Chameol."

The Badger nodded.

"There will be no turning back," Elric warned.

"When is there ever?"

So the stableboy of Thirdmoon See died that day, and a knight of Chameol was born. In the days that followed the Badger learned to ride so that his horse's hoofprints hid those of Elric's horse, and the path showed nothing of their passing. As Motley picked his way through the light snow, his rider hoped he would learn in time to make his heart like the path: unmarred, betraying nothing of trespassers there.

◆◆◆

The *Double Dolphin* made good time to Chameol. Iiliana and Caitlin stood together on the deck as the shroud of mist fell away to show the island before them. Winna came up, yawning, and Caitlin took the child in her arms, wrapping the cape around her. She was surprised when Iiliana spoke.

"You are trying not to think of him. That's not good. You must think of him often, even speak of him. Hearts are more fragile than glass, for glass resists acid."

"I wasn't thinking of him, to tell the truth." To tell the truth? The wax, then, a single drop, falling in the basin, spinning a thread. Caitlin hugged Winna closer.

The dolphins came up to the side of the ship to greet them, leaping from the waves in the mist, calling their greeting. The crew pressed to the rail.

"See, Winna?" said Iiliana. "Your new home."

Winna's lip trembled, and she raised a troubled face to Caitlin. "Will I see them again, my mother and father?"

Suddenly Caitlin had a clear vision of herself sitting in an arbor in autumn. There was a cradle at her feet, and Abagtha's old book of spells lay open in her lap. Before her the leaves of the arbor shook, giving up a figure dressed like a thief and wearing the face she loved best in all the world.

"Yes," she said to Winna. "You will see them again. I'm sure of it."

The Glass Salamander

For Judy

For there is no friend like a sister. . . .
To cheer one on the tedious way. . . .
Christina Rossetti, Goblin Market

Contents

Contents

THE CHOICE

A tall, dark figure in a cape stood at the rail of the *Double Dolphin,* gazing out at the sea in a pose of princely meditation. Then the figure turned, swaying to keep balance on the deck of the pitching ship, and one could see it was a young woman, her hair cropped at the nape and curling softly in the salt wind off the sea. But what was most startling was the sight of her eyes, one blue and one green, set like jewels in her pale face, focused now on some scene only they could see, out over the waves.

What those remarkable eyes saw was a rider on a piebald horse, a golden head flashing between the white snow and the black trunks of winter trees. Lines, traces of harsh weather and harsh travel, made his young face seem older than it was. If his eyes saw some vision before them other than the snowy path, the rider's face did not betray it.

The young woman hung her head over the rail, suddenly dizzy, not from seasickness but a stab of loneliness. Though her eyes were the eyes of a seer, and the *Double Dolphin* was bearing her to Chameol and to an education as an oracle, the young woman had no idea when she would ever see the rider again.

It was only a few days ago that she had stood before the queen of Chameol, had stood before a choice.

"You may come to Chameol and be honored as our seer. All our secret arts will be open to you, and the ancient runebooks. You will be prepared to take your place as a high oracle. Or, if it is what you really want, your otherworld sight can be taken from you, and you may go back into the world as an ordinary woman. But if you choose Chameol, you must come alone."

205

Caitlin nodded. "Would I be blind, then, if I chose to remain in the world?"

"No, you would see and dream as other women do, but you would not be able to move between the dreamworld and the waking one as you do now." The queen of Chameol paused. "You would also lose all memory of what has happened, of me and of Chameol, and of the tanner's son. That will seem unduly cruel to you, but if you were allowed to remember even a little it would jeopardize our fight against Myrrhlock. The Badger is part of what you must forget if you do not choose to join us."

In the end, it had been no choice at all.

Far off, the rider on his piebald mount shivered. He had only just taken the vows of a knight of Chameol, thus surrendering his real name, his money and home, and the right ever to marry.

"It's not monkhood, mind," Elric had said. "It's just that you can never take a wife."

The Badger had nodded. He had no home and nothing to his name except his name; it had not been much to give up. If he could have, he would have surrendered his memory with it.

1

THE HAUNTING, OR
WHAT AILED HIM

Sleep, when it came to the Badger at all, was at best a
catnap from which he woke stiff and cursing, at worst a
night's vigil spent wrestling with demons.

Every night it was the same. He had tried gin, a tea
brewed of poppies, even the weird, aromatic pipe of mandrake. He had cast himself like a man shipwrecked on the
shores of a countess's bed, followed innkeepers' daughters
up the ladder to the loft as if to oblivion. He haunted the
alleys where half-witches sold spells of forgetfulness; on
their counsel he had begged a cup of madmen's piss from
the keeper at the asylum gate, had drunk it down with
the ashes from a lock of hair. When he had retched the
foul toddy up again he swore off debauchery and took up
self-denial, going for days without water, food, or sleep,
shaving his head so that only a rough gilt glittered on his
scalp and chin.

But every night it was the same, and this night no different from the others. As soon as his eyes closed in sleep,
the ghost came to spoil his rest, so that he woke in a

sweat, damning the name and face of her who would give him no peace.

Elric watched this and said nothing. What good would it do to say forget her, when the wretch would sell his soul to do that very thing? So, for the time being, Elric suffered the Badger his exotics and purgatives. After all, hadn't there been a time when he had done the same himself? And, too, the elder man wondered how much the younger one really wanted to forget her, for around his wrist the Badger wore still a braided circlet of that matchless ebony-and-indigo hair.

It was odd to think that only a few months ago circumstances had found the companions in a convent far to the north, playing a dire game of cat-and-mouse through the stalls and lofts of the temple. He had found himself, Elric remembered, in a nun's habit, the Badger's knife poised at his throat. That misunderstanding had been cleared up, and they had now spent nine months in the saddle, the Badger playing pupil to Elric's tutor, learning the arts of disguise and artifice that were their trade and profession.

Some knights there were, the Badger knew, who studied archery, falconry, and fencing. "No such education for you," Elric had said, setting the Badger to work by the fire with pots of paint, black and white and red, to change himself from horse thief to innkeeper to prince and back again. He taught the Badger to mix the uncanny, unreliable potion that could change his blue eyes to black or merely make him sick as a dog. Other times Elric would lounge by the fire, a switch in one hand, while the Badger stood stork-fashion on a nearby anthill. At the slightest movement of the Badger's foot, Elric would tap the anthill with the wand to excite the red swarm within. A variation of this exercise involved painting the Badger's upper lip with honey and bidding him sit impassive while the wasps came to collect it.

"Torturer," the Badger muttered once, early on, through a badly swollen lip.

"Not at all," Elric said, lighting his pipe and offering the Badger a clove poultice in a red-checkered handkerchief. "You must learn these things, absorb them utterly, or the lack of them could kill you. A twitch of the lip, a sneeze, a careless footfall could be your undoing. We're the opposite of most knights, you and I. We can't wear our colors for all to see."

Now they were journeying through the fens and marshes of Oncemoon, where there had been reports of hauntings of another kind. Word had reached Chameol of a merchant, respected in the town for his sobriety, who had fastened a live piglet to his head and insisted it was a hat. In another incident, a judge had sealed the windows and door of her house with pastry while her family slept. More cause for amusement than alarm, except for the young girl, clad in nothing but swanthistle and rushflower, who had wandered off into the marsh and was presumed drowned. Indeed, most of the sufferers seemed to be children: Reports had reached Chameol of children worried and bitten by unseen demons. Iiliana, Queen of Chameol, had dispatched the two knights to see what could be made of it.

They were ready to set out when Elric found the Badger, his head wrapped in buttered cheesecloth, about to lay his head on the hot coals and "roast the ghost out," and realized things had gone far enough.

"Come on," he said, hauling the Badger to his feet and unwinding the turban, "you're no good to me if your brain's been roasted like a chestnut."

Elric knew a conjurer who lived in the marsh, and he brought the Badger to her, careful to let him think it was their mission for Chameol that called them there.

∽∾∽

Grisaudra watched Elric row the boat toward the small island where a hut accommodated herself, a cat, and some wild pigs trained to nose out edible roots from the marsh. The conjurer of Oncemoon Marsh was ugly, not in a manner to arouse disgust, but because she came so close to being not ugly at all. She was wraith-thin, an urchin's height, with hair grey before its time that stood up along her scalp as if singed. One eye, through birth or accident, was swollen shut, the other was peculiarly clear and bright, as if it held the vision of both. Grisaudra had taken the blade of a sword in the face as a girl and lived, and the scar cleft her mouth from ear to chin.

But the sorcerer's voice made up for all that, a sweet, sad music that had once brought tears to an executioner's eyes. It was a pity, Elric thought, that Grisaudra of Oncemoon Marsh did not say much. A blind man or two might have fallen in love with her.

Grisaudra nodded without really listening to the Badger's inquiries about the drowned girl. While the Badger was making fast the boat, Elric had slipped into the hut to whisper his real purpose in coming. Now Grisaudra studied her patient with interest, noting the haunted stare of the eyes without seeing their fetching blue. She read the Badger's eyes for a long moment, as if gathering from their depths the particulars she needed for this illusion. Then, turning to the fire, Grisaudra spoke.

"I didn't see the girl you describe. Wearing only swan-thistle, you say? Too prickly a petticoat, to my taste." With her back turned, Grisaudra quietly took up a wand of birchwood. She struck the side of the chimney with it, and a fluttering, batlike cloud of soot flew into the Badger's face. From her pocket, Grisaudra removed a droppered vial of mixed venom, blood, and tears. The Badger tried to twist away as she seized his head in a purposeful grip.

"What's that?"

"Salve for the sting. Look up."

Coughing and rubbing his eyes, the Badger allowed the conjurer to minister to him. Grisaudra put a hand to the side of the Badger's head, steadying it for the drops, her palm slyly reading the knobs of his skull, the ledger of his memory.

Elric drew into the corner. He had seen this once before, and the memory still made him shiver. The smoke clung only to the Badger's face, leaving Elric's eyes clear to take in the unfolding scene.

The Badger swore as the drops went in, trying to dash the stinging stuff away. Then, through the rosy film in his eyes, he got a look at Grisaudra and blinked in disbelief. He murmured a name and with it something between a curse and a prayer, putting out a hand and raking his fingers through the air by Grisaudra's shoulders, as though something lay there, heavy and indigo, besides her rough garment. Grisaudra let herself be pulled into his arms and struggled for only a moment before she let the Badger close the inch that separated his mouth from hers.

Before she came to the marsh Grisaudra had made her home among a troupe of vagabond actors and acrobats and, before that, dressed as a boy, among the hired swords of the border wars of Tenthmoon. It was as much her dramatics as the drops that enabled her to work her magic. Seeing her from behind, as the Badger spread his cloak on the rush floor of the hut, even Elric could believe she was Caitlin.

Elric went outside to have a pipe. It was more morning than night when Grisaudra finally joined him. He passed her the pipe, for which she was grateful.

"He'll sleep now, ten hours, I'd say, maybe more." She darted him a glance through a wreath of clove smoke. "It'll be extra this time, you know. Triple for anything past a kiss—and it went rather beyond that."

"Of course," Elric said.

Her eyes were off, through the bracken to the moon. "Well, you know how I dislike it. Besides, my shirt's rent." She squared her thin shoulders against some memory, or against the chill. It occurred to Elric that the welt on her face was the least of Grisaudra's scars.

❧

When the Badger awoke, he showed no surprise at finding himself in Grisaudra's hut, no memory of his delusion of the day before, and no trace of his past ailment. He gave Grisaudra a piece of silver in payment for bed and breakfast, which made her color with embarrassment. While those dosed with the drops were usually content merely to gaze upon their heart's desire, Grisaudra more than occasionally was called to lay down her body to effect a cure. It was all right in her mind, as long as the "sufferers," as she thought of them, did not pay her. When the Badger had gone outside to untie the boat, Grisaudra pressed the money into Elric's hand. He took it without saying a word, but later, when she had watched the boat disappear into the mists, Grisaudra found another coin in the corner, beneath her sleeping cat.

That night, as she slept alone, strange visions from her patient's memory played themselves out in her dreams. A young woman, hair cropped and dressed for hard riding, knelt in the surf at the base of a cliff. The same figure, but her hair past her waist this time, wearing a collar and manacles of bells. And again, sitting in a maze, wearing a green dress, blue rushes in her hair.

Grisaudra rose and lit a lamp of firefly weed. In the greenish light it gave she roused yesterday's fire and, when the kettle boiled, brewed some sage tea—good for disorders of the brain and trembling of the limbs. She went back to bed and indeed dreamed no more that night, lying awake instead, feeling all over again the desperate embrace, the rasp of his unshaven chin on her throat, and how hot she had felt, there on the cold rush floor.

Grisaudra rubbed her head; all entwined, they had rolled under the table, and she had cracked her noggin. Funny, she hadn't felt it at the time. Now she was going to have a nice, egg-sized lump there. Silly fellow! Whatever had there been for him to cry about, afterward, until he fell asleep in her arms?

⋙⋘

The two knights reined in their horses and asked directions of some children who were swarming over the roof of a house.

Elric hefted his purse. "There's something in here for the one who can tell me the way to the shoemaker."

A freckled girl with skinned knees shinnied down the waterspout, barely on the ground before her hand was out for payment.

"It's down the hill, by the granary what was all burned up." Seeing that the purse was not forthcoming, the girl hopped from foot to foot impatiently and added hopefully, "It's an old brick house, you'll see, with green shutters." This won her the purse and the half pound of lemon drops inside, gold enough to make her the richest child there—

and to make her lose interest instantly and completely in pastry, even if it did come from the roof of a house.

They found the shoemaker's by following the smell of wet ashes. Three doors down from the burned-out shell of the granary, they turned in at a house with green shutters and a shingle in the shape of a shoe.

By the fire an aproned woman sat bent over her work. The Badger called out, "Will you tell the cobbler we are here to see him?"

The woman turned, and they saw she wore an apron of leather, and that she held not her darning, but a last and awl.

"When I was made a widow, I was made a cobbler, too," she said, setting the half-finished shoe down on the bench and waving a hand to some chairs. "Forgive me: I have given up more wifely things; I think I can still boil water. Can I give you a cup of something hot?"

A teapot was hunted up that, when the dust was washed off, revealed itself to be blue. The cobbler considered the Badger's question, or she might have been reading the pattern of leaves swirling in the hot water. As if to put a lid on her thoughts, she quickly covered the teapot and poured out the tea, answering.

"It was the geese we noticed first. Or Tillie noticed them, running around the yard as if a fox, or a fox from hell, were after them. The next day the whole flock was dead.

"Then we all came down with the fever. And Tillie nursed us all. I helped with the sheets and the gruel, until I came down with it, too. When the fever finally broke, she was gone. Someone had seen her wandering in the marsh, it seems." The cobbler laughed, put up a hand to cover a crooked smile, her eyes bright with tears.

"My Tilda! You never saw a child more sober, as practical, less given to fancy. And beautiful—what puzzles me is, if she was wearing nothing but some thistledown when she walked into the marsh, why half the men in the county didn't walk in after her."

The cobbler suddenly gave a cry and dropped the piece

of leather she had been holding. She had not been working her shoemaker's awl into the leather, as she meant to, but into the flesh of her palm.

How will she manage now, Elric wondered as they left her, her hand bandaged, staring into the fire. The Badger cursed, spun on his heel, and went back into the house.

"Forgive me—I would not press you except that it may prove useful. How did your husband die?"

The woman looked up. "Fighting the fire in the granary, last harvest. And what have we had since then but rain?"

The Badger could bring himself to ask her no more questions, only drew the wine within her reach, as she asked, and left her.

After he had swung into the saddle, they rode awhile in silence.

"What an awful thing," the Badger said at last, "to lose first one to fire and another to water."

They doubled back to the judge's house, where the beleaguered husband had just chased the last of the children off the roof with a broom and a volley of coal. His wife, he told them, was greatly improved.

"She's finally gone off to sleep—three weeks without so much as a wink, and if she wasn't plastering the roof or painting the floors with almond water and egg white, singing hey-nonny-non, and then hey-nonny *back*ward ..." The judge's husband leaned on the broom handle. "We've only just got the youngest unsewn from the cradle. And the smell. We haven't been able to get it out of the house."

"A smell?" asked Elric.

"Well, I hate to say it. You see, normally my wife is the sweetest of women, and sweet smelling. But the whole time she was ailing she sweated like a blacksmith. It ran off her—we had to change her bedclothes every hour, and I had to boil them to get the smell out. Like dead mice, dead mice in a chamber pot."

"This lasted three weeks?"

"Yes. It began just after the harvest. The town council had just sent over her salary, a sack of grain for the next quarter. I remember, she complained it seemed like sweepings off the threshing floor. My wife is a very particular woman."

"What to make of it?"

The knights had made their way to the town's only tavern, the Bandit's Thumb. The mulled ale could not totally dispel the chill that gripped the Badger as he thought of the waters of the marsh closing over the girl's eyes, over her mouth.

Elric shook his head. "I can't say I see any diabolical agent at work. But I can't believe they all took leave of their senses out of coincidence."

"They all said the same thing: the sleeplessness, burning and freezing by turns, hallucinations. Some*one* or some*thing* is at work in it. I just don't understand how it could affect them all so differently and not touch the rest of the household."

"There's something we don't know yet, a missing piece. Here—there've been some reports in Twinmoon. Perhaps we'll learn what we need there."

The two knights rode out along the high road, the Badger on the piebald, Motley, Elric on a roan mare. One of the carts bound for market caught the Badger's eye; there was something about its cargo. Nothing amiss, really, just very odd. It was the way the sacks were piled strangely upright in almost human forms, and the strange way the driver sat, as if he were Death himself.

As their horses drew alongside the cart, the Badger had to laugh at himself. They weren't sacks of grain after all, or not all of them. They were beggars in sackcloth.

"Lepers," said Elric. He chirruped to his mount and urged her forward with his heels, and the Badger followed, as Elric had meant him to. It would do no good, the red-haired knight had thought, for the Badger to look too hard. Each of the lepers wore a bell fastened around the neck, and the last thing Elric wanted was for the Badger to relapse into his haunted state.

But Elric was wrong after all. They were not bells but small, hollow globes of blue glass. And whatever else the silent figures in sackcloth were, they were not lepers. The cart hit a rut in the road, and the jolt loosened the hood of one of the silent human cargo. The hood fell back to reveal a face unmarred by leprous lesions, a face so uncommonly beautiful that if its owner had walked into Oncemoon Marsh, a man would like as not walk in after her. Her hair was the color of clouded honey, and there were broken twigs of swanthistle caught in it.

The driver was gaunt and grim-faced, his countenance remarkable for the utter coldness of its eyes and the harelip that split the mouth. He turned in his seat, barely taking his eyes from the road, and raised the hood once more so that the face and its beauty were eclipsed by sackcloth. Then the cart and its strange freight continued on into Twinmoon.

2

THE SECRET, OR
WHAT CAITLIN KNEW

The Queen of Chameol sat on her balcony, her bronze hair falling out of the braided circlet that was her only crown. A small table on her left held sealing wax, a paper knife, an inkwell, and a mound of unanswered messages. A twin table on her right held her cold tea and some fruit, bitten once and forgotten. Iiliana gazed out over the orchards to the sea, absently stroking a bird in her lap, the pigeon that had brought her morning's mail.

In the distance, off the swells where the sea-flax grew, Iiliana could see bobbing a dozen or so sleek black floats of the kind the fishermen used to mark their nets. Iiliana sat up straighter, then rang a little bell on the left-hand table. A young girl appeared silently in the doorway.

"Fetch my spyglass," Iiliana ordered, "and here—take this." She pressed the pigeon into the girl's hands.

A few moments later Iiliana lowered the spyglass with a low *yes!* of triumph. The seals had returned from their winter pastures in other waters to birth their pups in the seas off Chameol. Iiliana threw off her shawl and drew on a heavy, waterproof cloak.

"Maarta, Iida, come quickly! And Iilsa, put on a kettle of soup. You had better make it fish," she shouted back over her shoulder, already running down to the beach.

As the queen and her handwomen goat-stepped down the slick stairs carved out of the cliff face, they could see that one of the seals had separated from the rest and was swimming toward the rocky surf. A cry reached them, half seal bark, half human laughter. The seal cleared the sharp rocks with inborn skill, then collapsed in the shallows, suddenly helpless and clumsy out of the water.

Iiliana reached the creature first. It seemed to have been deformed by some accident, its flippers and tail misshapen, torn in a net or in a sea dragon's jaws. The seal raised its head and gave Iiliana a knowing look. It had human eyes, one blue as the sky, one green as the sea. Iiliana knelt by it and with a knife began to cut through the gleaming black-and-silver pelt.

And it was not a seal, after all, but a young woman. Under the tar that coated her face she was naturally pale, made unnaturally so by her winter's sojourn in the cold sea with the seals. She had been sewn into a seal's pelt tighter than her own skin, a layer of mutton fat her only undergarment. The reek was fierce. They washed her there on the beach and threw her chattering into a heavy woolen robe before hauling her up in a pulley and basket to the top of the cliff, where a wagon was waiting.

They brought her back to the modest low white buildings that were the island's palace. There Caitlin was fed hot soup, which Iiliana had to send back for more crab claws and fish heads before it would suit Caitlin's seal tastes. It took a week before her seal voice began to fade and they could again fathom her speech, and even then, when extraordinarily excited or amused, she would now and again lapse into barking.

At the end of the week Iiliana appeared in Caitlin's room with a strange parcel: two large shells bound in sea-flax.

"This was left for you on the beach."

Caitlin turned the contents out into her lap: some iridescent fish scales; a piece of black coral polished by the sea into the shape of a seal; some coins crusted green, kings made into ogres by time and salt water. Curious, Iiliana reached over and turned over one last object. It alone was not of the sea, and it alone was unchanged by it: a long-dead glassworker's brag-piece, a glass salamander, all red-and-purple transparency, curled in on itself as if in sleep.

"This is from the Elder Age," Iiliana said.

Caitlin nodded, rubbing the glass so it winked. Her own treasure, a cat amulet, had been lost in the sea. "It's a seer's glass."

Caitlin had come to Chameol to become a seer. Raised by a witch in the heart of the Weirdwood, she had endured a cat's belling at the hands of villagers, spending the remainder of her girlhood on a barren moor, making her home in an ancient warrior's barrow.

Her promise had survived all that, had survived trials at the hands of the ancient and powerful necromancer, Myrrhlock, though for her first weeks at Chameol, Caitlin had left a light burning all night beside her bed.

When the night terrors had ceased, Iiliana had summoned Caitlin to begin her apprenticeship, the honing of her gift. In the beginning, Caitlin had had her doubts.

"You want me to make *cheese?*"

Iiliana's laughter had pealed in the underground chamber.

"Don't tell me you've never divined with cheeses? Oh, someone, hand her a dowsing fork, and we'll dig a well of buttermilk!" The queen sat on a barrel, chuckling.

Caitlin put her hands on her hips. "Well, what am I supposed to think?" Iiliana had wakened her at dawn, bade her put on a smock and tie her head in a white cloth, and handed her a small, curved knife, for all the world as if they were going to cut mistletoe.

"The cloth is to keep your hair out of the milk, and the knife's for tasting. Here, work at this a few weeks, and if you can in truth tell me you've learned nothing worthwhile, you can stop."

For a month, then, she had labored in the cheese caverns, learning to mix the milk and rennet, to salt and strain

the curd, to know by a rap of her knuckles on a red wheel
of cheese if it was ready to be rolled up out of the dark
to the table. One day Caitlin cast off the smock and kerchief and went knocking at Iiliana's door.

"I have had enough."

Iiliana was at her sewing; her shears made a light, dis-
approving click as she set them down. "Oh? What makes
you think so?"

"This morning I found myself talking to a cheese."

"And? Did it answer you?"

"It's funny—it did, in its way." Caitlin had long divined
with candle wax in a basin of water, but in her lonely
weeks alone underground she had started to see runes
everywhere, in the swirling milk as she stirred it, in the
curds that formed, in the red-and-black wax in which she
enrobed the great wheels. They had spelled out her secret,
declared the thing that she must, for now, tell no one.

"What am I to try next?" she asked Iiliana. "Wine
making?"

"Not quite." And Iiliana had held up to the light the
glossy sealskin.

From Caitlin's window there was no sign of the storms
that had worried the straits of Chameol all winter. From
the balcony of her bedchamber she could see the fleecy
waves skip to the base of the cliff and back again, like the
lambs in the meadows above. The trees of the orchards
were lively with birds, and there were new foals among
the herd of wild horses that came by moonlight to graze
on the salt grass. In the greying of the night Caitlin woke
to the whickering of mare to colt. Once she was roused,
the smell of the night-blooming vine outside her window
kept her awake until dawn.

For spring had not come to Caitlin's heart; it was heavy
and cold, cracked open with swelling ice. She could not
seem to get warm, even on these balmy nights, and when
she pressed a hand to her heart it felt sore. She did not
try any of the remedies, the herbs and charms, at her
disposal. She knew what ailed her, knew where the cure
lay, knew the cure was the one thing she could never seek

out. How could she forget the Badger, when every day her body was being remade with the memory of him?

Among the seals, she had felt some relief. Anchored fast in a bed of sea-flax among the sleeping clan, she had forgotten human speech, had dreamed seal dreams. One of the seals had become as infatuated with her as any human lover and was not content unless Caitlin took fish from his mouth and slept all night beneath the watery stars, clinging fast to his fur, her face pressed to his bristly cheek. Now when she walked along the beach, Caitlin could hear him crying, calling for her in the seal name she had taken. Sometimes, in her dreams, Caitlin was in the Badger's arms again, but he had a seal's face. Just as often she clung in her dreams to the seal, only to have him turn on her a blue-eyed, human gaze.

Caitlin turned from the window and peevishly took up her hairbrush, lashing at her hair as if she meant to teach it a lesson. With each stroke she muttered a charm, a spell for lengthening, but she forgot to say a charm against tangles. Her brush caught on a snarl and with an oath Caitlin hurled the brush at the door.

It missed Iiliana by a hair's breadth. With a cluck of her tongue the bronze-haired queen of Chameol shook the ivory brush at her apprentice.

"Now, now! You know the rules! No spell casting during your probation, not even to make your hair grow faster."

Caitlin turned away with a scowl and quickly drew on a robe to hide her softly swelling middle from Iiliana's sharp eyes. She had been lucky no one had noticed on the beach, when they had cut her out of the sealskin. But already she thought her tutor was suspicious of Caitlin's newfound passion for cake and sweets, her sudden loathing of being attended when she dressed and bathed.

Iiliana looked thoughtfully at her young oracle-in-the-making. "We'll skip your archery and geometry this morning. I think the best thing for you would be a nice, lazy breakfast in the garden."

Under the spreading branches of a tree in bloom, Iiliana pulled Caitlin's favorite chair into a sun-dappled spot and piled it high with cushions. Once Caitlin was settled, Iili-ana produced bowls of scalding tea, a platter of buttered toast, and a covered dish. Her stomach had been fickle lately, but suddenly Caitlin was starving.

"Ah—that smells wonderful. What is it?"

Iiliana whisked the cover away to reveal calves' brains and pigs' feet on a bed of tripe. Caitlin sprang up with a cry of disgust, but the wave of nausea beat her to the hedge. For several minutes she was violently sick. Iiliana silently chafed her wrists and, when Caitlin seemed some-what recovered, helped her back to her chair. Someone had removed the covered dish. Iiliana seized Caitlin's chin and turned her face gently, but firmly, to her own.

"How far gone?"

Caitlin twisted away. "I don't know what you mean."

"Oh, but I think you do, my girl. I wasn't sure until this morning, and even then I thought we'd better have a little test. Normally, you have a cool enough head and a strong enough stomach. But then, things aren't quite normal with you, are they?"

Caitlin sighed. "About four months, by my reckoning."

Iiliana nodded thoughtfully. "Will you tell him?"

Caitlin folded a napkin into smaller and smaller trian-gles. "How can I?"

"He could be found, if that was what you wanted. But that is not what I asked you."

There were no men on Chameol; the price of becoming a seer had been to leave her past, and the Badger, behind.

"And if it is a boy?" Caitlin said, lifting her head. "Will you put him off the island, to live with the seals?"

"You know the answer to that as well as I do." No boy was made to leave his mother until his voice had changed.

Caitlin fell silent. She did not tell Iiliana that, gazing into the salamander glass, she had seen a fine, black-haired baby boy, that she had next seen an empty cradle.

It was harvest time once more when she was delivered of her son. Iiliana placed him, black-headed as a seal, in Caitlin's arms. He howled. Iiliana beamed and covered her ears.

"Ah, what a wonderful racket."

Caitlin smiled. "He favors his father in that, at least."

The child had his mother's dark looks but not, to Caitlin's relief, her seer's eyes.

"They're almost always passed from mother to daughter," Iiliana said. She was braiding Caitlin's hair into a heavy rope, weaving in a silver ribbon as she went. The child slept in a basket at Caitlin's feet. He was three weeks old, and she had not been able to settle on a suitable name. It had become a great contest among everyone on the island. Caitlin was opening dozens of the paper twists that collected every day in a designated jar outside the buttery.

"Ugh," she said, tossing them into the fire as she went. With one foot she jiggled the basket lightly. "Listen to these! Derward, Galt, Adalard. Sweet heaven, what names!"

An old woman drew near. She was new to the island; her fisherman husband, sorely tried by her quarrelsomeness, had set her adrift. Her face was red without being rosy, her hands sharp without being nimble. She burned the bread and the shirts alike and was as useless at gardening as she was at weaving. At last, out of desperation more than pity, Caitlin had agreed to have her as a maid while the child was nursing. The old woman squeezed one of her pawlike hands into the jar and drew out a paper twist. It had a singed look, as if it had been snatched out of the ashes, where Caitlin had thrown it. Oh, why wound her feelings, Caitlin thought. It can't hurt to read it again. She opened the paper twist.

"Bram," she read.

"A little black bird," Iiliana said, taking the paper from Caitlin's hand. "That he is, certainly." The queen of Chameol wrinkled her brow. *Bram.* It meant a black bird, but whether a blackbird or a crow, Iiliana couldn't remember. It meant something, if she could only remember what. There was a book in the library somewhere, if she could put her hands on it. The makeshift nursemaid had put in a stint there, too, more's the pity, and Iiliana was not at all sure where the book of names was. But what did it matter? Looking at Caitlin's face, Iiliana could see the matter was settled, and she swallowed the mild caution that had been on her lips.

Caitlin jiggled the basket with her foot. "Well, what do you think, my fellow? Are you a Bram?" The baby opened his eyes and gazed solemnly at his mother. She lifted him out to kiss him. Bram, she thought. Bram. She laughed sheepishly.

"How silly—but he's quite simply a Bram."

The old woman laughed and showed her bad teeth. She picked some hot cinders out of the fire, even though they burned her fingers; she used them to singe the hairs on her chin. The old woman's name, which no one could seem to remember, was Ordella, an elf-sword, something otherworldly and sharp.

∽⋙

Caitlin woke the next morning with the feeling that something was wrong. She lay in bed, listening for a moment before she realized Bram had not cried to be fed. That old woman, Caitlin thought, has been giving him a sugar teat, and I've told her time and time again she's not to.

She got out of bed and got the baby from his cradle. "Look at you," she said, shaking her head. "That Ordella's got you swaddled so tight you look like a loaf of bread from the baker." She unwrapped his dark head and put him to her breast.

But it wasn't Bram. It was a goblin baby. Its ears were pointed, its complexion a little too ruddy, but most of all it had yellow cat's eyes and small, sharp teeth. It did not cry but regarded her with a goblin's dispassion through large eyes of molten gold.

The household was roused and the palace searched, but Ordella had vanished without a trace. It was remembered that when she had been discovered adrift in the fishing boat, Ordella had in her possession a wicker eel trap, just the size for concealing a goblin child. Iiliana received the news grimly, her eyes red-rimmed. A little sweet gum and thistle to pacify the baby, and no one would think to search an eel trap.

Caitlin herself was beyond tears. She stood looking at the changeling, where it lay in Bram's basket, and terror seized her heart. Will they keep him warm? How will they feed him? she wondered.

"How will we feed him?" she heard herself say aloud.

Iiliana looked at her strangely. "It will take milk, if it can get it. But it would be better to give it a little beef broth. It's not a human child, Caitlin. It's not of this world at all. You must be careful of it."

When some broth had been warmed and brought, Caitlin reached over and removed the thistle teat from the changeling's mouth. Somehow, she thought it would not bite.

3

CHANGELINGS

Every morning, when the first pale bars of light slanted through the shutters and fell on her pillow, Caitlin would rise sleepless from her bed. Silently and swiftly she dressed, slipped the glass salamander into the pocket of her cloak, and stepped over the mastiff asleep in her doorway.

Over the fields she went, through the high salt grass wet with mist, following the sighing of the waves down to the sea. There, for hours on end, she remained as motionless as the rock on which she sat, deaf to everything but the surf on the rocks, blind to everything but the seer's glass she held cupped in her hands.

For a long string of days the glass refused to speak. Caitlin began to think her seer's gift was gone, lost to her now as the seal's speech that mocked her. Perhaps it was not a real seer's glass after all, but a clever fraud; after all, the Elder Age had had its talented swindlers along with its skilled artisans. One morning Caitlin's patience came to an end, and she raised her hand, poised to return the seer's glass to the waves that had given it up.

"It seems you speak only to seals. Well, they can have you!"

The vision struck her with the force of an icy wave so that she nearly dropped the salamander. What the seer's glass chose to show her at long last was Bram, cradled in a pair of arms. But they were not the arms of the Necromancer, at least not Myrrhlock in any shape he liked to take. These arms seemed living marble, pale and cold as frost on glass, bones as light and small as a hummingbird's—and were those *wings* behind?

Caitlin leaped up from the rock, the wind tugging back the hood of her cloak, setting her hair leaping about her face like an unruly dog, dark and sleek. The wind tore her voice from her throat as she let loose a shout of twin relief and frustration. Myrrhlock didn't have Bram—but who did?

Iiliana listened carefully as Caitlin related the vision the glass salamander had shown her. When she had finished, the queen of Chameol sat a moment in silence, as if a stone weighed on her tongue and made it too heavy for speech. At last she sighed and spoke.

"Caitlin, how much sleep have you gotten since Bram was taken?"

"What has that got to do with it?" Caitlin's color was already high from the salt air, her hair wild around her face, and she pushed it back, suddenly aware that she must look and sound more than a little like a frantic mother gone mad. "So you think this is all a fantasy brought on by too much worry and too little sleep?"

Iiliana smiled and shook her head, putting up a hand to smooth the furrows from Caitlin's brow. "No one is denying your seer's gift. But you must question whether you are summoning what you want your eyes to show you. Myrrhlock was nearly destroyed by you. We know he is abroad again. We have reports of his doings. In his weakened state he dares not strike at you. But your child: That is another matter; that would be a sweet revenge indeed. Does it matter in the end whether the agent was Ordella or this creature with wings?" Iiliana's mouth trembled, and her eyes were bright as she gripped Caitlin's hand. "I am afraid, Caitlin, very much afraid that Bram is—gone."

∽⌇∾

By its very nature, Chameol was an island of misfits, a place where a woman the outside world had deemed mad might find herself not only believed but honored as a seer, where a lonely recluse could work the herb beds or tend the beehives in peace. Widows with no one left to them in all the world could find contentment tending the flocks of goats or transcribing the songs of birds.

The cases of the younger islanders were somewhat different. Often they had made a misstart in life, destined to scrape a living from the gutters and alleys of the towns, until at last they had the luck to run afoul of a knight of Chameol.

Thus Midge had come to Chameol. Her brothers had given her the name because "she buzzed in your ears and bit." At seven, she was already an experienced pickpocket. That particular morning she had been working the flop-houses, where beggars and drunks could buy a bed of clean straw for six coppers, day-old straw for three. Pickings were slim, unless you knew where to look. She spied a man whose clothes, beneath the dirt, were finely made and whose snoring showed the glint of a gold molar: a gambler who might still have some of his winnings on him. She slipped her hand into the pocket of his vest only to find her wrist seized in an iron grip.

Instead of turning her in, he had bought her a currant bun and a pint of milk and a ten-copper hot bath at an inn. A woman brought her clean clothes and a heavy cloak. By evening, she was asleep in a small fishing boat under the stars. And in the morning, she had awakened on Chameol.

On the island she was called by her real name, though they spelled it Chameol-fashion: Iimogen. In the beginning she missed the clamor of street life and old deaf Mistress Peekie, who ran the flophouse. And she missed her lame tabby cat, the one that used to hold a live cricket gently between its paws just to hear it sing. But the island grew on her: a field of white daisies basking in moonlight, baby goats romping on the hillside, the dolphins. Iimogen woke one morning with a strange feeling and spent the whole morning doing her chores, wondering whether she was geting the flu. Then she realized what it was: She was happy.

And so she had been for seven years, until she turned fourteen and came into the awkwardness. Suddenly she seemed to be all elbows and knees and couldn't move without knocking over something or hitting her funny bone.

It was her turn that year to enter the lottery for tasks on the island that required new hands. Iimogen seemed to have a talent for none of the arts prized on Chameol, and when she drew a high number in the lottery her name went to the bottom of the list of those waiting to become dolphin keepers. Iimogen sighed when she thought of her lottery number. Eighty-nine! She would be raking sea-flax until she herself was eighty-nine before she ever became a dolphin keeper.

Then Iiliana herself had summoned her, and Iimogen had been told she was to be sent away, if she liked, to be trained to be something quite different: a page of Chameol. The knight who had brought her to Chameol seven years before had remembered and recommended her. So Iimogen went away in a boat with nothing but the clothes on her back.

What a blow it had been, after all, to find that the camp was no different from Chameol and that she was just as hopeless at the new chores she was given to do. She had unlearned her pickpocket's skills too well and seemed unable to summon them back now that they were wanted again. Not even in this way could she be useful! Iimogen feared she would be sent back to Iiliana in disgrace.

One night Iimogen slipped from her bunk, took her bundle from its hiding place, freed a pigeon cage from its hook, and crept out into the cool darkness. Some of her lessons, at least, she had learned well; she woke no one. Outside, she crouched in the shadows and considered her next move; she could not go back to Chameol, so it would be back to the alley, and to Mistress Peekie. The pigeon would take word to Chameol, once she was safely away, to tell them not to worry.

The town road was empty in the slowly lightening darkness. The first wagon to pass was not headed to market; the sides were red and bore a picture of a fierce lion and the words ROLLO THE GREAT. The second wagon, also red, was painted with a picture of a man eating a fiery brand.

From this cart there issued sleepy banter and sweet pipe smoke that made Iimogen pause, weighing whether to try her luck with the troupe of players. Then she saw the third wagon, grey as the dawn, piled with sacks of grain. Without a noise, Iimogen pulled herself aboard.

It was not long before she realized her grave mistake. The sacks held not meal but still, silent figures that looked right through her with the eyes of ghosts. Iimogen did not cry out, and made no sound to give herself away, crouching among the sacks. The knights had taught her how to write a message in the dark, using a pin for her pen. Iimogen pricked her fingers as often as the paper in her dread and haste, but the message took shape, and it was only a matter of fastening the capsule to the bird's leg. Then, with a thudding heart she felt the cart stop, heard the driver's footsteps approach the back of the cart. From the shadowy depths of a hood, cold eyes picked her out from among the rest in their sackcloth and eerie glass bells.

"What have we here, a runaway? Or something more?" The eyes, pale but cold and lightless, turned their gaze to the small cage Iimogen clutched in her lap. "What do you have there?"

"A—a bird. Please—it's just my pet," she stammered.

"More than a pet, I think. A pigeon. The very sort Iiliana favors as her messenger." The icy gaze turned up again, to search Iimogen's face. "A girl, in truth. For a moment I thought you just a reckless boy. Iiliana is choosing her pages younger and younger these days."

His hand reached for the bird, but not before Iimogen had flung it away. As the knights had taught her, she had weakened the catch with careful twisting, and the cage broke open in the road. The bird was off like a stone from a slingshot.

The cold, bloodless hand closed on Iimogen's throat, and she was sure he meant to throttle her, but it was only to fasten on a collar with a glowing bell of blue glass.

⤜⤛⤜

The pigeon winged its way homeward to the dovecote on the Chameol palace roof. The old woman who kept

the pigeons tended to this latest arrival, giving the bird its
fill of seed and water before removing the leg capsule and
sending the message down to the queen's chambers with
the rest of the morning's mail.

Iiliana read the topmost message and pushed the rest
of the pile away. Caitlin glanced up from her book by
the window.

"Bad news?"

"Of a kind." Iiliana silently held out the message. Caitlin
took the slip and read: HELP TWINMOON RED WAGONS.

Caitlin furrowed her brow. "It's not signed. And written
with a pin it's hard to tell whether it's Elric's hand or
the Badger's."

"Neither, I think—the mark of a child is strong both in
the words chosen and the way the pin formed them."

Caitlin remembered the message recently received from
the school for would-be knights. "You think it is from
Iimogen?"

"I fear it is." Iiliana rose from her chair and began
to pace. "Red wagons! Red wagons! What on earth can
she mean?"

"Do you think she was watched as she wrote it?"

"Oh no. Myrrhlock would never have let her finish it,
much less let the bird get past the sill. No, Iimogen is a
very literal-minded child, when her head's not clouded
with fantasies of derring-do. If she said red wagons she
meant red wagons."

Caitlin pressed her hands to her temples, remembering
a marketplace and a smell of spent firecrackers and stale
toffee. Red wagons. "A traveling troupe?"

Iiliana looked up. "Yes—I think you're right. Twinmoon—that is where Elric was, last we had word from
him."

Caitlin left Iilliana to dispatch her message, returning
to her own chambers to sit and ponder. Everything had
the mark of Myrrhlock, the necromancer she had thought
destroyed. She wanted to believe with all her heart that
Iiliana was wrong, that Myrrhlock had been defeated. At
length Caitlin rose and went to the basin of water at her

washstand; looking into the surface, she sent out a silent summons with her mind for a vision of Iimogen's captor. Just as an image was forming on the water's surface, her concentration was broken by a silent, keening call, a mute, insistent crying.

Caitlin drew aside the curtain and looked into the cradle, where the goblin baby lay. Its great yellow eyes reproached her. It did not cry, but Caitlin's mind filled with its complaint as with the silent pitch of a pipe that makes a dog cuff its ears.

With a sigh, she lifted the child—if it was that—from the cradle and put it to her breast, not without guilt, for she remembered Iiliana's warning. It did not bite; she had known that it would not, even as she knew that neither milk nor beef broth would long sustain it. Abagtha's old book of incantations had proven maddeningly vague on the subject of goblins, and what there was of the short entry had been nearly obliterated by a stain. Caitlin looked down at the sucking child. It held her gaze unblinkingly, and with hands that were too large for a baby it kneaded her chest with a kittenish motion that pricked with the same sharpness.

Caitlin knew she should not name it, knew all that naming it would mean, both for it and for Bram. But quite unbidden its name rose in her mind, a cipher in wax, spinning in the water of her basin: *Grimald*. The huge yellow eyes seemed to will her to say it aloud.

"No," she said to the goblin firmly, and abruptly returned it to the cradle. It pursed its mouth in disapproval.

"And that's the closest you'll get to a howl, I suppose."

In answer, the golden eyes blinked deliberately, and the goblin curled its hands docilely over the counterpane.

❧

Elric and the Badger had ridden into Twinmoon, sleeping in ditches, to which practice Elric attributed the strange ailment that felled the Badger their third night out.

It started with wakefulness, an inability to shut his eyes, that lasted seven nights. All night, while Elric slept, the Badger filled page after page of a notebook with strange runes, to get them out of his head. On the third night of his ailment the Badger woke Elric with a scream of terror, claiming demons on the other side of the campfire were going to spit him and roast him alive. The next morning Elric missed him, only to find him inside a hollow tree, a crown of mushrooms around his head, counting backward. It was with a sinking heart that Elric recognized in the Badger the symptoms of the same malady that had claimed the townfolk of Oncemoon.

"Hell, I'm no nursemaid," he muttered, and dealt with the problem in the simplest way he knew. He bundled the Badger into a sack so that only his head protruded and trussed him up like a sausage. They went on down the road like that, the Badger singing silly nonsense. At last, fearing he was going more than a little crazy, too, Elric found himself joining in, adding the harmony.

That night, made sleepless by the Badger's feverish wakefulness, Elric feared he, too, had begun to halluci-nate. At the edge of the campfire he saw a shadow flit, a beggar child one moment, something fetched from a tomb the next. But as soon as he wheeled to face it, there was nothing but a ragged branch tossing in the wind to mock him.

The Badger was in a calm mood, and Elric had left his arms out of the sack, his wrists in a loose hobble so he could write in the earth with a sharp stick. Over and over he wrote the same verse, "Master Donkey-Ears and Mis-tress Catawauler/Caught more fish than they could swaller." This did not satisfy, and the Badger rubbed it out, then chewed on the end of his stick to sharpen it. This blackened his mouth and chin so he seemed a tooth-less beggar, tied in a sack by an innkeeper tired of keeping him in drunkenness.

Elric was afraid to let sleep overtake him. To keep awake, he set his brain at a tease, to put the Badger's lunatic lyric to a song, biting his knuckles to stay awake. Madness, he was sure, lay in repose. In the middle of the fifth refrain, "Donkey-Ears, Donkey-Ears, Dame Cata-wauler's got the shears," sleep overcame his best defense, and he sank into it as a stone.

And here was madness after all, waiting for him, come this time as a girl. Elric bolted up, biting the air for fright.

"Damn you, you little witch," he said, when he saw it was Grisaudra.

The stuff of her dress shimmered; that was what had caught his eye outside the fire's circle, all ghostly. She moved, and Elric saw she wore a soldier's coat of mail, belted with a rope of flowers, borage for courage, and motherwort to ward off mischief. Grisaudra held a stoppered flask out to him; he sniffed the steam suspiciously.

"One of your potions?"

"Mint tea. It's for him, but you look as though you could use some yourself."

He could have, but Elric wouldn't have admitted it for anything. It was bad enough she'd scared him out of a nightmare, as if he were no better than a boy too small to send for eggs.

She went and kneeled by the Badger, who was too intent on his scratchings to care that she pressed a thumb in his kidney and turned his eyelid inside out. Her hand crept around his neck and up the nape, feeling his skull, reading the blind man's letters for memory.

"What are you doing?" Elric asked uneasily.

"When you left me, not all of him went with you."

Elric let out his breath, relieved it was anything so earthly as that. "Is that all you want? Well, he can't marry, but there *is* a special fund. . . ."

"Not *that*, you idiot! His brain, that's what the poor devil's left behind, and I wish to hyssop I could get him out of mine."

Elric was standing beside her now, wrapped in his blanket, for the scare had chilled his blood. "I've yet to hear a word of sense come out of your mouth. How can he have left his brain behind?"

Grisaudra released her grip on the Badger's head, and he quickly began to trace letters on the ground. "When I read him to do the drops, I had to read his memory in order to get a picture of his ghost."

"Her name is Caitlin, and she's very much alive."

Grisaudra shrugged. "But a ghost, all the same. You

yourself called him a haunted man. Well, something's gone awry, and I haven't been able to get his memories out of my head. They're becoming a real nuisance, and I'm here to give them back."

A nuisance indeed; she woke that morning to find her neck and wrists sore and blistered, as if a rope or some other bonds had chafed them. The cat, formerly immured in indifference, now swarmed over her, purring, so that Grisaudra would have staked her life there were a dozen cats instead of one. And the dreams. Not unpleasant, no, to the contrary! Very pleasant, so that when she woke from them she could have wept from disappointment.

Well, it had to stop! The shirt of mail she wore held the cold and made Grisaudra toss in her sleep, to keep the dreams at bay. But it kept sleep from her just as efficiently, and in the morning the cat looked at her mistress curiously, as Grisaudra swore at the wet matches and kicked the kettle.

She had finally lit the fire and set the kettle over it when the ghost overcame her. She found herself kneeling by the Badger while he lay near death, only it was winter and she was not Grisaudra, but the ghostly beauty, Caitlin. Surely as she knew Caitlin had once saved the Badger's life, the spell-seller of the Oncemoon Marsh knew that selfsame life, or the best part of it, lay in the balance again. What's more, she knew with more certainty than she liked that the soundness of her own mind was now caught up with the Badger and his ghost.

"Damn those drops!" she'd said, setting out a bowl of water for the cat and piece of cheese to draw mice. "The old man warned me about them." Grisaudra had then set off for Twinmoon, where she had heard the madness had spread and where she knew she'd find Elric and the Badger.

"He's got the same sickness," Elric said.

"Or at least the same strain. Unless I've missed him in his swanthistle petticoat. Now, *that* must've been a sight!"

"I don't see anything to laugh about."

"Sometimes laughter's the only poultice that will draw out the poison."

"Well, mint tea certainly isn't going to purge him, I guarantee you. Look at him! I should never have taken him for that cure of yours. I'd rather he were merely mad with love than mad for madness' sake."

"Well, it's some mischief other than my drops. He was right enough in his reason, wasn't he, when you left me?"

Elric had to admit it was so.

"Then it isn't a ghost in his brain that's bothering him. It's the beast on his back."

As if on cue, the Badger suddenly began to howl in terror, beating desperately about him so that the sack toppled over, rolling perilously close to the fire in his panic. In order to protect him from his own frenzy, they had to bind the Badger in his sack once more.

A beast on his back: The thought made Elric shiver, for in his mind he could see something—shaggy, taloned, fierce—clinging to his own shoulders with a deadly grip. Whether the creature was madness in store for him or the offspring of his own fear, the red-haired knight was not willing to wager. For hadn't he slept where the Badger had and eaten of the same dishes? Elric was afraid with every passing moment that his own mind would begin to slip from reason's grasp.

In truth, however, the two had not eaten the same. At the judge's house, the husband had offered them a meal. Elric thought the bread moldy and had fed it to the dog, but the Badger had been hungry enough to dip his in the sauce and eat it anyway.

Not six hours after they had ridden off, the dog had begun to behave in the most peculiar fashion, barking and snapping at the air, chasing its tail as if demons were after it. In the morning the husband had come out to find it lying by the well house, quite dead.

By the end of the third day on the road, the old nurse, Ordella, and the baby had reached the Weirdwood. It would have taken a person with an inexhaustible number of fresh horses, riding night and day at a breakneck pace, at least a week and a half to go the same distance, yet Ordella never broke into a jog that would have awakened the baby. The elf-woman knew one of the old tricks from the Elder Age, before the Necromancer had banned the elvish tongues. Half of it was a simple charm, placing feathers inside the felt of her shoes. The other half, the elder charm, Ordella's mother had called "skeining": You looked at the end of the road unfolding in front of you and imagined it as a piece of yarn. In your mind, you wound it up as fast as you could, so that it made a ball in your hand, hard and smooth as a stone.

When she had reached the Weirdwood, Ordella stopped to rest and take the feathers out of her shoes. There was no need to hurry now; this leg of the journey was nearly over. Bram slept soundly, having been dosed with some of the stonecrop cordial Iiliana kept to treat her occasional insomnia, and Ordella had tied a cat's whisker about the child's left toe, an elvish remedy, just to be sure.

When she was rested, Ordella put her shoes back on and stood up. Standing in the middle of a small clearing in the thick growth of trees, she sniffed loudly, sounding for all the world like a pig rooting for acorns. Evidently she smelled what she was seeking, for she gave out a satisfied grunt and set the baby down at the roots of an ancient oak. Set in the trunk and grown over with moss was a red door. Below it, skillfully covered over so no human eyes could detect it, was a second, smaller door that came only to Ordella's knees. She knelt down and drew a silver key from one pocket, slipping it into the lock. Ordella did not know as she put her shoulder to the task that another old woman had once carried a baby to this very oak or that the other baby had grown into the mother of this one. Ordella knew not and cared not, just muttered a mild curse at the rusty hinges.

Inside the oak it was black as a chimney sweep's fingernails and smelled of a feather pillow that had been left out in the rain. Ordella did not light a lamp or kindle a fire but carried Bram straight down a winding stair, past a small nut-cellar, to a trapdoor deep among the roots of the old oak tree. The elf-woman drew a key from around her neck, and it turned in the lock smooth as butter. When she opened the trapdoor, the damp, earthen passage was flooded with a warm orange glow. At this, Bram awoke and began to whimper.

As well he might, or might any human child waking hungry, far from his mother, to find himself on the back stoop of the Otherworld.

4

How Many Ravens?

Tillie shivered where she slept, though it was warmer in the tent than it had been in the wagon. She was dreaming of the day she had walked out of the house to feed the geese only to find them all dead, the smallest gosling floating in the horses' watering trough.

She dreamed of her mother in the throes of the fever, screaming in terror that the walls of the bedchamber were wolves' jaws, snarling and snapping. Tillie could hardly believe the madwoman in the bed was her mother. Her mother, who used to sit by the fire, stitching a golden vine and leaves all around a pair of dancing slippers, while Tillie read aloud. Now she struck the spoon from Tillie's hand, seeing maggots in the bowl instead of gruel.

The dream—which was a memory also—always ended the same way. The fever seemed to break: Her mother sat up and asked for her needle and thread. Weeping with glad relief, Tillie brought them, and while her mother began to embroider the felt of the slipper, the dream-Tillie would lay her head on the blanket by her mother's knee and sleep for the first time in days.

In the dream, she woke to find her mother still stitching, the whole slipper by now completely encrusted with

239

thread, so thick with a pattern in gold and scarlet that none of the slipper underneath could be seen. And her mother had not stopped with the slipper. When that was done, she had continued the pattern onto the blanket, sewing her nightshirt fast to the bed sheet. All the same pattern, in red and gold, a pattern of wolves' gullets, opened wide.

Tillie woke with a muffled scream. By the fire the Necromancer looked up from the maze of glasswork, where he was distilling a purplish essence. At his feet, like a pet greyhound, slept Iimogen. At her neck a hollow glass bell gave a purple glint.

"You have had another nightmare," Myrrhlock said mildly. As he spoke, he drew off some of the purplish liquid into a glass pipe. Removing his thumb from the end of the tube, he let the liquid fall into a small silver-and-crystal cordial glass.

"Yes, a nightmare," Tillie answered. The firelight on the glasswork, the Necromancer's goblinstone skullcap, the way Iimogen lay in some enchantment—all this might be some strange dream, too.

For Tillie was remembering a music she had heard, music she had at first thought was the kettle singing or her mother's feverish humming, high and melodic, the way golden stitching would sound if it were given a voice in music, a bright and twining thread of sound.

Then Tillie remembered the strange figure with a flute, wearing a cloak lined with silk in a pattern of poppies, leading the children out of the town, a goose leading goslings, a fox leading geese.

"You—" Tillie started to raise herself from the pallet to pull the twigs of swanthistle from her hair.

But the Necromancer's hand was already on the back of her neck, the glass pressed against her teeth like a steel bit, and she must drink the stuff down. In a minute, she was curled at the Necromancer's feet with Iimogen, her eyes blinking as the drops fell through the glass apparatus, collecting in the wide-bellied flask like liquid amethyst.

Myrrhlock's eye was caught by something in the corner. It was a hollow glass ball.

Ah, he thought, *so that explains it.* Myrrhlock picked up the ball and refastened it around Tillie's neck.

࿇

Caitlin could not sleep. She had drunk a cup of wine, but it had left her even more wakeful, playing game after game of geese-and-foxes until Iiliana pushed the board away, protesting that she would drop from weariness. After Iiliana went off to bed, Caitlin played a few more games against herself. The clock showed its pinched, small-morning-hour face; the trees tossed and turned outside her window; somewhere, far off, the sea snored.

Caitlin picked up and handled the small vial of purple stuff by her bedside, the ergot Iiliana had dosed her with to ease the pain of her labor with Bram. "Heaven knows the wine's not working," she muttered to herself. Not bothering to hunt for a spoon, Caitlin filled the hollow stopper with a thimble's measure and tossed it down like brandy.

The glass salamander shone softly on the stand next to the vial. Caitlin had fallen into the habit of petting it, rubbing her thumb along the curve of its coiled head and tail. She picked it up now and immediately felt soothed. Though the seer's glass had shown her nothing since the day on the rocks, Caitlin could not help silently beseeching it to show her Bram. She squeezed the glass tightly.

With a cry, Caitlin flung the salamander to the floor. She could have sworn it had bitten her, if she hadn't known well the delirium brought on by sleeplessness. As she bent to pick it up, Caitlin again admired the skill of the ancient glassmaker; true to life, the salamander's belly was white and the legs better modeled than she remembered them. You would swear the thing was real.

The ergot was having no better success than the wine. Caitlin paused in her prowling to peek into Grimald's cradle. The changeling was sleepless, too, or else its keener hearing had perceived Caitlin's light tread on the carpet as she paced. It gave a silent whimper and cry, and she knew it was hungry. Caitlin lifted the changeling from the cradle and walked the floor with it.

"The kitchen's closed, my little goblin. Besides, you've had two bowls of beef broth for your dinner. At that rate, you'll be needing a rowboat for a cradle before long."

Grimald *was* growing. It was his mind, his silent, insistent voice that was getting stronger every day. *Feed me*, he demanded. *Name me. I am Grimald. I am yours, as you are mine.*

Well, it has teeth, she thought. Perhaps it will let me sleep if I give it some solid food. Iiliana had given her macaroons to coax her appetite. At the first crinkling of the paper, Grimald opened his eyes. As Grimald bit into the first one, he gave a grunt of pleasure, like a baby pig, and made Caitlin laugh. The golden eyes glowed, the small pointed tongue ran around the wide goblin mouth. The macaroon was gone, and the goblin fell asleep in her arms. Caitlin lay down on the bed. It was nearly dawn. With her eyes closed, but for the light pricking of the goblin nails, it was almost possible to believe it was Bram asleep at her breast.

"Go to sleep, Grimald," Caitlin murmured as she drifted off.

On the nightstand the glass salamander had uncurled. One by one it slowly worked free its legs, uncoiling from its long sleep. As Caitlin spoke the goblin's name aloud, the salamander opened its eyes.

～∽～

The passage down which Ordella carried her stolen baby was covered with carpets of otherworldly workmanship and walls hung with tapestries surpassing human skill. The orange glow was cast not by rough torches but by lamps fueled with underground ethers. From time to time the elf-woman would pass a spot along the passage that showed signs of recent repair, where human trespassers—miners, eloping lovers, prisoners escaping their cells—had dug through into the Otherworld. On the human side of the wall the searchers would not know what to make of the wadded remains of torn clothing and a few mementos, like the pellets an owl makes out of the mice on which it dines. The search party would return to the light and air to report that the search had come to an unhappy end.

The missing were not dead, but neither were they wholly living. On the otherworld side of the wall the fugitives were taken in as half-castes, able to dimly recall the human world but never to return to it. Oddly, it was these interlopers who made the most beautiful tapestries, more highly prized than anything of elvish hands.

Some humans, however, could freely pass from the one world to the other. These were seers, oracles born with one blue eye and one green, who could see into the future at will. Caitlin was one such otherworld daughter, and it was for this reason that Ordella had been dispatched to fetch away her firstborn son. Bram's name, "little raven," was itself a charm to guarantee the plot's success, for the raven was the messenger of the Otherworld. For how was a group of such birds known but as *an unkindness of ravens?* When a number were sighted roosting in a leafless tree, shrewd folk knew a door to the Otherworld, and its attendant dangers, could not be far away.

Ordella did not pause either to admire the tapestries or to examine the patched portions of the walls. Both were well known to her, and she hurried Bram past them without a thought either for the fate of the weavers or that of the trespassers. Ordella was in a hurry; babies were the most resilient, yet the most vulnerable, of the human interlopers in the Otherworld. Bram must be brought quickly to the court and given mole's milk boiled with elves' rosemary, which unlike its earthly cousin was the herb of forgetfulness, not remembrance. This brew was effective in making human children forget their mothers, and without it they quickly pined away. As soon as he woke from his drugged slumber, Bran would be dosed and the drops would be put in his eyes to accustom them to otherworld light. It had once been the fashion to dye the human changelings' eyes goblin yellow, but this only turned blue and green eyes a murky amber, and the practice had all but fallen out of favor.

The corridor spiraled downward. The farther Ordella went into the caverns the brighter the light became, until at last the long corridor emptied into a large chamber. Here all the tapestries were wrought in silver, the work of a young woman who had thought to elope with her beloved, only to wake and find herself in the Otherworld. The light came from hundreds of translucent crystal lamps, lit with a different gas that perfumed the chamber and burned with a cooler, more silvery light. One whole wall was covered in a white flowering vine, the underground cultivation of flowers being one of the foremost elven arts. Next to the flowers, on a silver chaise fashioned in the shape of a grasshopper, reclined the elf queen, arranging blossoms in a vessel of ether. Ylfcwen was molting, and her new set of wings lay wetly across her back. The process was not painful, but the tedium of immobility to prevent tearing her wings had left the elf queen lethargic and more than a little peeved.

Ordella surrendered Bram to the nurses, who quickly gathered round. As they were about to give the baby the tonic of forgetfulness, Ylfcwen raised her hand.

"No, don't. Oh, put the drops in his eyes, all right, but don't give him any milk."

"Madam, the day-child will pine away if we do not."

The elf queen shrugged, as much to dry her wings a little as to express her indifference. "Day-child, night-child, he could be a four-in-the-afternoon child and you'd still have to set aside the mole's milk. There has been a change in plans. Drusian would have the child."

Yet Ylfcwen pushed the flowers away and tipped her head to one side. "But do set him by me, just for a bit."

Iiliana's stonecrop cordial had worn off, and Bram looked around him, his gaze held by the colored paper orbs of fireflies that lent more decoration than light. But he quickly gave his attention to the pretty lavender blood to be seen flowing beneath Ylfcwen's transparent skin, her iridescent wings and opal eyes without a dark center. The baby remembered his mother and would have cried for Caitlin except for the cat's whisker around his left great toe.

"Poor thing!" Ylfcwen cried, and bent forward to kiss his brow. "You look like you're going to explode from not crying." The elf queen looked up in sudden alarm. "He can't really explode, can he?"

"No, madam, though madam might tickle him, so as to vent him a little." Ylfcwen picked Bram up, fascinated by his smell of mingled sugar and salt, talc and milk and wet diaper, with a hint of that woody-musky human smell so unlike the cooling-jasmine-tea smell of an elf baby or the hot-sealing-wax-and-burnt-paper smell of a goblin.

The cat's whisker had loosened and fallen off, and Bram began to whimper with hunger, then cry with it in earnest. Ylfcwen nearly dropped him. "What's that?"

"He's hungry, madam. Since he's not to have the mole's milk, perhaps madam would like to give him a little nectar."

Ylfcwen breathed in Bram's smell, narrowing her opal eyes. "Yes. Let's give the day-child some nectar."

❧

Caitlin woke from a deep sleep, not at all surprised to find the glass salamander on her pillow. She was surprised that it now seemed to be alive, but perhaps not so surprised as she should have been, and was only mildly astonished to find that it could speak.

"My name," the salamander explained, "is obscure and nearly unpronounceable by human tongues. So it will suffice if you call me Newt."

Caitlin raised herself up on one elbow. "But why should I need to call you anything? This is a dream, and you're nothing more than a pretty piece of glass that I happened to look at as I was falling off to sleep."

"Oh? You think I'm part of your dream, do you? Go to the window, then, and have a look."

Caitlin got up and went to the window. The brilliant sunshine blinded her at first, but as soon as her eyes adjusted she could see Iiliana walking around the garden, bouncing the goblin baby in her arms to amuse it. The fly that buzzed in her ear, the smell of the flowering vine, the heat of the sun all conspired to convince her.

So I am awake, Caitlin thought.

"Just so," said Newt.

"Don't be rude," she said, alarmed that a glass gewgaw could read her thoughts.

It's all right, said the salamander, *you can read mine, too.* "Let me up on your shoulder, though, and I'll speak in your ear."

Caitlin lifted him gently to her shoulder, and the salamander twined his feet in her hair to hold on.

"When I was little," Caitlin said, "I used to play with lizards, dried ones, from Abagtha's jars." Her old guardian had kept a strange pantry full of such things for brewing potions and other mischiefs.

"There was a book, too," said Newt.

"Yes . . . her book of incantations. It's here in the palace, in Iiliana's chambers. She had it fetched here from the Weirdwood with some other things after I came, while I was with the seals." Iiliana had brought the book to her room to restore, taking to it with soft brushes and a magnifying glass when her other duties vexed her.

Caitlin went to the sill and looked out. Iiliana was still in the garden, picking feathers out of the birdbath; she had left the goblin baby on the arbor seat, and a raven had flown down to perch by Grimald's feet.

"Let's go find it." For Caitlin suddenly felt an overwhelming urge to see Abagtha's book of incantations, and her training as a seer had taught her to respect her urges. She was not entirely sure whether she was in the middle of a vision or just a very odd dream, but the worst thing that could happen, she supposed, was that she would be caught sleepwalking. "I don't think Iiliana's taken it to the library yet. Let's have a look in her chamber."

As she walked along the gallery that opened on the seafront, no one seemed to notice Caitlin or the salamander perched on her shoulder. They slipped unseen into Iiliana's chamber. The book of incantations lay under a glass dome borrowed from the kitchen, meant to cover cheese. Caitlin removed the dome and set it on the floor beside Iiliana's worktable. It was a heavy tome on a carved wooden stand, three ribbons marking its places, one blue, one silver, one green. The runes were thick and tangled like the thorny hedge around an abandoned castle, the gilt of the miniature paintings dulled by dust and worn by the bookworm's tooth.

The queen of Chameol had been restoring the entry on dreams. The illustration in the margin showed a fair young man with golden hair asleep under a tree in which there roosted three ravens. The young man's horse could be seen in the distance, where it had wandered off to gorge on windfall apples.

"Oh!" Caitlin jumped, so that Newt had to tighten his grip on her shoulder. "Now there are four ravens."

"Five," said Newt.

Something very strange was happening to the book. Before Caitlin's eyes another raven joined the other five, and soon there were seven. Though the window to Iiliana's chamber was closed, the pages of the book began to turn over rapidly, as if blown by a strong wind. There were no runes anymore, only a swarming mass of brilliant color, color that overran the page, filled the room with vines and birds and apes riding donkeys, making such a racket Caitlin expected all the palace to break down the door any minute.

"Quickly," said Newt. "The door."

And there *was* a door, right in the spot where a moment ago had stood Iiliana's washstand. What's more, it was a red door, very like the one in the ancient oak where she had lived with Abagtha so long ago. Indeed, the walls of the room had grown rough and woody like bark, the wallpaper peeling off in green leaves.

Caitlin stepped forward and bent to open the small red door, and in a moment she had stepped through it into the Otherworld.

5

GHOSTS AGAIN

In the dream, Grisaudra was fifteen again. She let herself into her parents' cottage with the key that hung around her neck. The silence got up to greet her. The dogs did not run out barking "Grr-g'morrow!" Her sisters were not fighting over whose turn it was to feed the pigs. She listened, but there was no hushed murmur of rushes as her mother sat by the fire, making baskets.

She went into the yard. The sight made Grisaudra sadder than the fact that there had been no one home to greet her. The yard was full of mud and soot from the forge, blackened parings, broken dishes, and empty bottles. Her father's blacksmith's tools were gone. So were the horses.

"Father?"

A lone goose stuck its neck out from under the cow shed. Grisaudra recognized it as the goose that laid no golden eggs: it laid no eggs at all. The family had taken everything of use with them. Even the weather vane, the girl could imagine her mother saying, could be sold for shoes. It was perfectly good brass.

Then the girl noticed a marker not quite covered over with mud and soot, in one corner of the yard.

REMEMBER GRISAUDRA
LOST IN THE BATTLE FOR TENTHMOON
YEAR OF THE PENTACLE
NINE HUNDRED TWENTY-FIVE

Grisaudra woke choked with the terror and furious despair she had felt those fifteen years ago, returning from the wars to find her family had moved on, giving her up for dead. Still wearing her vest of chain mail, she had taken the goose and wandered on, earning her bread for a while with a troupe of traveling players until at last she reached the marshes of Oncemoon, where the old hermit had taken her in and taught her the secrets of the plants of marsh and meadow. No draught he could concoct, however, had been able to rid Grisaudra of her memories. She would rather relive the battles, hear again the sword blade singing silver toward her face, than relive that homecoming.

Now Grisaudra raised herself on one elbow and felt beneath her pallet for a vial. Catmint and juniper, more powerful than brandy, a drug if taken in a prudent dose, a poison if taken immoderately. Grisaudra allowed herself the smallest of swallows; when it was gone, who knew when she could manage to brew more? She corked and capped the vial and returned it to its hiding place. Soon she had drifted off, amnesiac at least until day should break.

Elric had seen her. At worst, he brooded, she is a cold-blooded poisoner, at best, an unreliable addict. He resolved to determine the contents of the vial at the first opportunity.

The Badger woke from his madness. Elric arose to find him sitting by the fire, his hand shaking as if from age or drunkenness as he raised a cup of tea to his lips.

"You're with us, then ... ?"

The Badger nodded cautiously, as if not sure himself. "It seems I'm safely back." He had washed the sweat and stink away in the stream; his gold hair was dark with water, raked back from his face, and his clothes lay scattered over the hedges. He wore Elric's other trousers and his own leather vest.

Elric quizzed the Badger lightly, without seeming to, ascertaining that the Badger knew his own name as well as Elric's, remembered that he was a knight of Chameol, and recalled visiting Grisaudra's hut. It seemed the fever had not boiled his brain dry.

Yet the Badger himself seemed troubled. "Don't think me an ass," he said suddenly. "It's just that I'm still coming out of a murk. But what is this, and why am I wearing it?"

And he held out the wrist that was cinched with a braided ebony circlet of Caitlin's hair. Elric felt his heart sink, a stone in a well. He wet his lips before he could bring himself to a second examination.

"You have no memory of the bracelet?"

"None."

"Does the name Asaph mean anything to you?"

"Of course! He's the monk who raised me and a knight like you and me."

"Iiliana?"

"Queen of Chameol and your sister."

"Abagtha?"

The Badger frowned. "Something—but I don't—is it her bracelet, then?"

"No. How about the name Cassandra? Calliope? Cressie?"

The Badger only shook his head. "No, not a thing." His face, furrowed in concentration, went suddenly smooth with panic. "Please . . . Tell me—is she my sister?"

"No. Just a friend you knew, once." Elric was afraid to tell him more and frighten the Badger from any memory he might yet retain. To tell a man he had forgotten the woman he loved . . .

"But that's what you asked me to do, make him forget," Grisaudra pointed out. As soon as she was awake, Elric had pulled her aside to acquaint her with this most recent development in their patient.

"But not completely! To him, it would be like losing an eye—or a leg," he amended hastily, suddenly remembering Grisaudra's own eye. "By satisfying his heart's desire, you were to cool his passion enough for him to move about in the world again, for him to sleep in peace."

"And so I did. It was the fever did this to him." Grisaudra jerked her head in the direction where the Badger was saddling the horses.

Elric shook his head. "It's as though someone had taken a pair of shears and snipped out the part of his memory with her in it."

❦

What was this woman the Badger could not remember? A tall creature, sleek and supple as a cat, her face the blue milk of marble in moonlight, set with mismatched seer's eyes. Her hair was a cascade of inky silk, grown out from the shearing it had been given by an eel-seller's knife, sold in barter for a map. He had forgotten the throat and wrists it had been impossible for him to kiss without remembering the bells placed there by the fearful and superstitious.

The Badger had forgotten all this, forgotten the day they met, when she had bitten and kicked him, forgotten how slowly, slowly her shrugs and sullen stares had turned to more solemn gazes and even smiles. He did not remember the morning he had first awakened to find her in his arms, no longer reluctant in any way, holding back nothing of herself. The memory of that kiss was gone as surely as if the kiss itself had never been. Now it lay, curled tight as an acorn, waiting within the halves of its woody locket, waiting buried beneath great frozen drifts of forgetfulness.

Poor Grisaudra remembered all this and more. Elric, out of cruelty or a disinclination to intervene, had said nothing when the Badger had offered Grisaudra a seat before him on the piebald Motley. So she had to ride with the Badger's arms circled round her holding the reins, like a country bride. And how could she object? If he couldn't remember Caitlin, the Badger couldn't be expected to believe in the ghost of her memory.

But it was her own memory of a warm, corporeal embrace that played itself over and over again in her mind.

The welt where she had hit her head had subsided and was no longer tender, but Grisaudra's heart—so long hardened against any siege—was beginning to feel tender for the first time in years.

Darting glances at the conjurer from where he rode a few paces to the side, Elric began to regret having ever visited the hut in the middle of the marsh. We would all have been better off, he thought, if I had simply let him wrap his head in cheesecloth. As it was, the red-haired knight was afraid he would soon have a lovesick herb-woman on his hands as well as an amnesiac knight. If he didn't already.

∽◦∾

Newt guided Caitlin along the corridor, following in Ordella's footsteps. The salamander's eyes gleamed, and he tightened his grip on Caitlin's shoulder.

"It might be best *not* to walk in the front door."

"Very well. We'll go in the back way." Caitlin pulled aside the tapestries that lined the hallway until she found one that hid a door. The knob turned in her hand, and the door opened silently on elven hinges.

They were clearly in a nursery. Caitlin's heart beat wildly as she crept up to the first cradle, where a transparent globe of fireflies hung to amuse the infant. But when she drew the gauzy curtain aside, a yellow goblin stare met her eyes.

"There is no need to look in the other cradles," Newt told her. "This is where they keep the changelings until they are ready to make the exchange."

But Caitlin had known, though her heart rose up against the knowing, that Bram was not in any of the cradles. She would have known in a minute, would have smelled his damp, dark hair and the radiating sweetness from under his chin and the creases of his plump knees, the faint waxiness of the sleepy-sticks in his eyes. There had only been a wet-matches-and-burnt-sugar smell of goblin, which the elves disguised under a liberal sprinkling of crushed orange blossom and clove water.

And before she could turn away in disappointment, Caitlin was assailed by the memory of another smell, of

leather and clean brass and wood smoke, the smell of the
Badger's riding jacket. For the first time since Bram had
vanished, Caitlin broke down and wept, for Bram had been
her comfort for that other loss. Now she felt keenly the
twin bereavement, and her arms ached for Bram and the
Badger both.

Suddenly, the salamander was biting her ear, and Caitlin
felt a quickly spreading numbness, and with it a feeling of
well-being, as if Newt had untied the twisted knot of her
heart. She reached up to remove the creature from her
ear, rubbing it under the chin in silent gratitude.

There was a light gasp in the room, and they turned to
see Ylfcwen in the doorway, summoned by the novel
sound of a human woman weeping. Elves only threw tan-
trums, and the closest goblins got to crying was a case of
the hiccoughs.

Ylfcwen quickly regained her composure. "I warrant
you've come about the baby."

"My son," Caitlin said. "Yes, that's my business with
you."

Ylfcwen came up to Caitlin and looked her over at
nearer scrutiny. The elf queen might have felt at a disad-
vantage, wearing pajamas and having her wings rolled in
a silk-and-parchment nightcase, but the idea that she
should ever feel ill at ease had never occurred to her and
it did not do so now. The fact that the pajamas were
embroidered with dragonflies' wings only made the queen
look more otherworldly.

"Come to my chambers, and we will talk about this—
bram—of yours."

Ylfcwen jingled slightly as she moved, from the small
silver bells on her ankles, which made her heavier than
air and enabled her to walk. Although there were chambers with ceilings high enough to allow flight, flying was
undertaken only to keep one's wings fit and for certain
arcane ceremonies. Only if she was having difficulty sleeping did the elf queen slip off her anklets and let herself
drift to the ceiling to drowse in the clouds of incense
amidst the golden murmuring of fireflies.

The gardeners had trained wood violets and lily of the valley to grow along the walls of Ylfcwen's chambers, so that the effect in the high-ceilinged room was of having fallen into a steep pit lined with flowers. Ylfcwen's pet mole slept on the foot of the silken bed. A small table was littered with a great many finely wrought silver instruments used in the care of the queen's wings.

Ylfcwen scooped up the mole and sat where it had been dozing, indicating with a gesture that Caitlin should be seated herself.

Caitlin shook her head. "I would rather you took me to see Bram."

Ylfcwen sighed and struck a silver tuning fork on the end of the bedpost. An elf servant appeared with a flask of amber nectar. Newt murmured in Caitlin's ear, "It might be better for your purposes if you did nothing to offend. Sit and drink with her, and perhaps she will tell you what you want to know."

And perhaps not.

Newt bit the lobe of Caitlin's ear softly, and this time it stung instead of soothed. *Offend her, and it's* certainly *not,* the salamander replied silently.

Ylfcwen held out a silver-and-crystal cup of the liquid. To Caitlin's surprise, it was quite cold and went down aromatic and slightly bitter. Suddenly she felt a need to sit. Ylfcwen refilled Caitlin's glass and then her own. When she had emptied her second glass, the elf queen slipped the bells from her feet, and the earthbound liquor allowed her to lie on the bed without the help of weights. This was her way of showing her earthly visitor she was accepted as an equal.

Ylfcwen's thoughts were hidden behind the veil of her moonstone eyes, those eyes without a dark center. The elf queen regarded Caitlin with sleepy curiosity before she finally spoke.

"The code is quite clear on the matter: The firstborn child of an Otherworld daughter must be named within three days and with a name of the earth only, names of fire and water carrying some risk and names of air being the most dangerous of all. You waited three *weeks* and then you named him Bram, after a bird of the air, and an Otherworld bird at that. You might as well have put him out the door for the dairyman while you were at it."

"Come, come." It was only with effort that Caitlin kept her voice level. "It was your servant-woman, Ordella, who planted that name in the jar. And she, probably, who put a little something in my tea in the morning to muddle my brain a bit and keep me from making up my mind."

Ylfcwen frowned and tugged at the laces of her nightcase. She shrugged her wings out, snapped them open and shut a few times, and began to work at the iridescent scales with a silver tool a little like a nutpick. "She might have and she might not. Those weren't my instructions to her, in any case. She was told to watch carefully, and if the conditions of the code were met, to bring the bram back with her."

Caitlin swirled the bitter amber stuff around in the bottom of her glass. "What does your code have to say about my getting him back?"

"Well, usually you would have to fill out a petition and bribe me for a while with gifts and then perhaps serve a year or two as my personal supplicant. But I am afraid this is not a usual case."

Caitlin stood up, her heart leaping like a hare. "Why, what have you done with him? Where is he? You must tell me!"

Ylfcwen set down the nutpick and picked up a small silver file. "Don't upset yourself so. Think of my best root-wine, wasted on a case of nervous agitation! The bram is quite safe."

"Then let me *see* him."

"I'm afraid that is no longer possible. You see, he has been taken to Drusian."

"Taken where?"

"Oh, not where! Who! To Drusian—to the Master of Sleep and Desire."

6

FOLDEROL'S BAND

Since the defeat of the Pentaclists and the routing of the
monks from the temples, the thirteen kingdoms had fallen
into disarray. As queen of Chameol, Iiliana faced a daunt-
ing task: to convince her subjects that Chameol was
more than the shroud of mystery and legend that had for centuries surrounded it. The wild tales of an enchanted isle
had long been Chameol's shield and disguise; now they
threatened to usurp its very power. Iiliana found it hard
to convince thirteen feuding kings to bow to the rule of a
mysterious island ruled by hermit women with unpronounceable names, where the arts of the sword were not
merely uncultivated but shunned. Iiliana spent much of
her time dispatching knights to snuff out kindling rebel-
lions and ambassadors to soothe the tempers of kings. The
age of darkness was over, but it would take time before
the thirteen splintered kingdoms emerged united into an
age of light.

When the bell towers of the temples had toppled, the
old tenets of the Pentacle had toppled with them—the
bans on magic and free-lance sorcery not the least among
them. Competition was fierce, and where aspiring sorcer-
ors and apothecaries had neither the talent nor the guile

to make a living, they soon gave their energies over to
another, more lucrative calling. Roving bands of highwaymen and deserters were joined on the roads by itiner-
ant troupes of acrobats and palm readers, and there was
often more to liken them to the robbers than to distinguish them.

Chief among these bands, whether reckoned by quantity
(sheer numbers of tent pegs, juggler's bats, flea-bitten animals, and more flea-bitten trainers) or quality (the spectacular absurdity of its freaks, the unsurpassed ineptitude of
its jugglers, the sheer moral decrepitude of its owner) was
the ragtag ensemble that answered to the bark of an old
sailor and hired sword named Folderol.

For a while, the ranks had thinned; the talking pig had
eaten some bad chestnuts and died, the tumbling dwarves
had defected to a rival troupe for better wages, and his
star attraction, the leopard-woman, had retired to join her
sister-in-law in a dressmaking enterprise. But none of
these setbacks had stopped Folderol for very long. He sat
in his tent, his gouty foot raised on a folding footstool,
counting the evening's receipts. Not bad, he thought, and
better for that new boy. A strange little creature, hair like
milkweed, so quiet you'd think he was mute, too tiny even
to carry the chestnut roaster through the throng. But he
could still work the crowd; the box in Folderol's lap
showed the booty: an assortment of gold coins, two
watches, four snuffboxes, and a small, gilt-over-silver hearing trumpet. Folderol tweaked his grizzled calico whiskers
pensively, weighing the benefits to his accounts book of
keeping the boy on against his own unease around Nix's
partner.

This was Ulfra, a young woman in an old soldier's uniform and a gilt-and-paste crown, first seen driving seven
wolves before her along the road, Nix perched on the
shoulders of the largest, a silver giant that must have been
three-quarters Direwolf. Ulfra's slight, slope-shouldered
stance and bent knees, like those of a dog walking on its
hind legs, and the careful way she had to wrap consonants
around the howl that rode through the middle of her

speech made Folderol think Ulfra must be at least a quarter Direwolf herself.

With short barks and growls Ulfra had put the pack through their paces, getting them to walk first on their hind legs, then on their front ones. They would run in a ring within a ring, Nix leaping from wolf to wolf as though they were stepping-stones. As a finale, Ulfra took tidbits of meat between her lips, and the wolves put their paws on her shoulders to kiss her without harming her at all.

This act had since been greatly refined and expanded to include the wolves singing in rounds, finishing with a pantomime of Ulfra and the largest wolf as a wife and husband at breakfast, ending with the juggling of goose eggs. SEE ULFRA THE WOLF-GIRL, the sign outside the tent read. RAISED BY DIREWOLVES AND BROUGHT TO THE COURT OF THE KING. NO WHIPS, NO SWORDS, HER FEMININE CHARMS HER ONLY PROTECTION. WITH NIX, THE ALBINO DEAF-MUTE, WHO HAS NOT THE SPEECH OF MEN BUT CAN SING WITH THE WOLVES. The sign did not begin to hint at the sound the wolves made, voices raised in eerie song, and rising through them the boy's soprano, pure and clear as melted ice. There was nothing sad about the wolves, the way there was about the dancing bears in their muzzles or the old toothless lion or the swaybacked horse wheezing beneath the burden of the overweight acrobat. Rather, there was the feeling as you watched Ulfra and her wolves that the whole act was a pantomime, a jest at the expense of the human onlookers. Sitting back on their haunches, panting through toothy grins, the wolves seemed hugely amused at their audience.

Ulfra herself had prospered. She and Nix shared a tent with their wolves, and when she was not performing, Ulfra could be found there, reclining on a couch of sleeping wolves, enjoying a meal of very rare meat from Nix's fingers or a pipe of clove. She treated the fledgling daredevil rider and veteran pickpocket as if he were a cub of hers, cuffing his ear if he did something tiresome, pinning him still with an elbow while she licked his face and hair. No human words were ever uttered in that tent, Nix and Ulfra finding it more convenient to converse in growls and low

yelps, though you did hear Nix singing in that voice of
melting mountain ice, singing of the wind in the wood and
the deeds of old wolf warriors.

Folderol turned all this over in his mind as if it were a
rich matron's jeweled pillbox that had gotten mixed in with
the day's take of copper coins. As uneasy as Ulfra made
him, the wolf-girl had been good for Folderol's wallet.
Plucking a silver whisker from his beard and feeling magnanimous, the old rogue resolved to buy Ulfra a roast lamb
in the next large town and some caramels for Nix.

He might have pulled more of his beard out than that
had Folderol known Nix was skimming a fifth of the gate
from the coin box nightly. Folderol might have ended up
completely clean-chinned had he suspected that Ulfra's
crown was not gilt and paste at all but gold, and gold with
emeralds and rubies at that.

❧

Grisaudra might have been more grateful to have someone else's dreams to dream to keep her from her own
nightmares. There were any number of things she could
have dreamed about to keep her from a good night's rest:
the night on the battlefield, for instance, that the young
soldier she adored had discovered that she was not a boy
and had joined with the others in tossing the bundle of
her clothes over her head, and had broken her shield, so
that when the sword had come singing down there had
been no way to protect herself. Or she might have
dreamed again of the way the old Oncemoon wizard had
died, having said too lightly a forbidden spell to call forth
the shadows.

Grisaudra hardly minded riding on Motley and having
to bear hours on end trapped within the circle of the reins
and the Badger's arms. She found it soothing, for despite
Elric's disapproval and his dire, cryptic remarks about all
being lost over honey and a wasp, the Badger liked to sing
softly as they rode. He had a sweet tenor and sang funny
riddle songs, silly ones with endless verses, so that before
she knew it they were finding a place to camp for the
night. It was then Grisaudra began to mind, watching the
Badger currycomb the horses, rubbing Motley's stiff knee,

holding an apple in his teeth for the grey mare, Maud. *That* was a trial, watching him bend to clean the horses' shoes of stones from the road. It almost made her grateful for Elric's bickering about her inability to cook.

"Well, what do you want, when you won't let me add any herbs to the pot?"

"What, and wake up to find the soup's changed us into frogs? No thank you!" And he took the potato away and peeled it himself. Grisaudra seethed and in her mind brewed a tea for Elric of monkshood, which takes men's speech away, and wintersweet, to give him an exquisite pain.

So she should have been grateful to dream so pleasantly of the Badger's eyes gazing at her as if they saw something beautiful, his arms slipping around her, then under her, lifting her clear of the floor, clear of the earth.

Grisaudra should have been grateful. But she wasn't, not even a little bit.

❧

A pigeon had come to Chameol, bidding Elric to follow a troupe of acrobats traveling in red wagons. The knights and their reluctant damsel headed west, following the harvest to the sea. Crafty rovers, too, would follow the harvest to villages where fattened flocks and ripening fields had filled many a pocket with coins that burned like coals.

Their disguises were at the ready, their pretenses well rehearsed. Elric was to be a juggler, Grisaudra a fortune-teller, the Badger an acrobatic rider.

Grisaudra could sew as well as she could cook, which is to say not well at all. Though Elric knew this, he made Grisaudra fit the Badger's tight tunic.

"It's too tight!" the Badger protested.

"It can't be—look," Grisaudra said, seizing a fold of loose fabric in her hand and tugging on it.

"Not there—*here*," the Badger said, and pulled at the leotard where it cut him in the crotch.

Grisaudra, who seemed incapable of it, blushed, although it might have been in fury at Elric, who sat across the fire, laughing. The Badger's fragile sense of dignity collapsed, and nothing they could say would make him consent to so much as a sequin adorning his costume.

Elric insisted on supervising the construction of Grisaudra's disguise himself. He found an owl's nest and fashioned for the conjurer a cap of twigs and feathers, fitting close around her skull, curling around her ears, and coming to a peak in the middle of her forehead. To the tunic of chain mail Elric tied a dozen strange charms: dice in a net bag; a mouse skin complete with ears and tail; four tiny dolls tied from horsehair; half a rusty scissors; the blue-and-white handle of a broken cup; the lens from a spyglass; the joker from a pack of cards; and a child's green glove they had spotted lying in the road.

Grisaudra would not let him tie on the last charm, a twig of bittersweet. He argued that the red berries and yellow blossoms set off the green of the glove nicely.

"You'll spoil the scheme."

"And you'll spoil things you haven't dreamed of, meddling with herbs you've no inkling about."

"Why—what's bittersweet signify?"

She wouldn't answer, only turned to admire her cap of owl's feathers in the Badger's shaving glass. Turned half from him, Grisaudra showed to Elric the side of her face with the good eye and the unscarred cheek, so that as she turned and preened for her reflection, you might have thought her a young girl, too young for more serious games, intent on a game of dress up.

It was the Badger who pointed out the significance of the charms.

"Think—a playing card, dice, a child's glove—all the leavings of a carnival, the sweepings revelers leave behind them at a fair. We're on the heels of our acrobats, you may rely on it."

And it was so. The sun was going down, and they were standing at the top of a hill where the road began its descent into a town, when Grisaudra stretched out a hand and showed them the low, crouching shapes of the tents and the glimmer of campfires. Elric held the lens of the spyglass to his eye and squinted, then pronounced that the wagons were red indeed.

*   *   *

The flap of the largest tent was lifted at their whistle by the shortest, widest man they had ever seen, as if a giant had been compressed by great force into a pudding mold. This burly figure had been giving Folderol his nightly massage, and the trouper sat up on his cot, pink from his bath and wearing a towel.

Folderol nodded the strongman his leave to go. "Not hiring," was all he said to his guests, but he looked them up and down with interest anyway. When he learned their specialties, Folderol had to work hard to give a convincing display of indifference. His own daredevil rider wanted sacking; he had never quite recovered from a bad fall, and after the accident he became ever more partial to gin. Folderol had been trying to secure a reliable fortune-teller for years, and this girl looked the genuine article. Now, if he could only convince the juggler to go on in an apron and cap as the bearded dutchess. Folderol had jugglers coming out of his ears, but such an attraction as the leopard-woman had been would make him rich as a king, or an archduke at the very least.

❧

Myrrhlock stared into the fire as if he were a creature from the darkest recesses, cold-blooded by nature, that must drink its daily dose of fire and warmth to survive. His face and name were known to Chameol; it had been necessary to take a new shape entirely, and the effort of maintaining the illusion exhausted him. So it was he faced the fire not in the new disguise, or in the twisted shape centuries of spell casting had made of his soul, but in the human form that had once been his true nature, in the far-off century that had been his prime. The face was pale, curiously ageless, hairless, remarkable for its cleft lip. Myrrhlock had removed the goblinstone cap, and underneath it the veins of his skull were raised as if irritated by his broodings.

He stared into the fire as though he sought to find his next action revealed there. His position was, for a time, secure; only the slightest spell of suggestion had been required to establish in the minds of Folderol and his band that Myrrhlock, in his new form, had long been a member of the troupe.

A young girl and a stableboy had nearly undone him; Myrrhlock would not make the error of underestimation again. The conjurer from the marsh was in all likelihood harmless, but there was no sense in chancing again that sort of miscalculation. If he could gain an ally while eliminating an enemy, so much the better. Grisaudra would be the monkey, then, that he would send down into the mine after the dark gem he sought.

Out of long practice, the Necromancer no longer needed to say the shape-changing spell aloud; he had only to brood on the runes for it to effect the transformation. Myrrhlock pulled his cloak over his head to shield himself from the light until the metamorphosis was complete. It took something less than a minute before he pushed the hood back and bent to wake Iimogen where she lay asleep at his feet.

It was no more than another minute before she was on her way, clutching the twin to Grisaudra's vial.

Myrrhlock sighed, trying to get comfortable in the shape of his latest disguise. It was not so tall as the shape he was used to, and it was old; the joints ached. He stretched his new hands toward the fire, thought of Grisaudra, and smiled. In order to capture his gem, he must first secure his monkey.

❧

The horses whickered and shifted their weight nervously as Iimogen slipped between them, her young, pale face flashing in the shadows like a small moon. As she drew near to the spot where Grisaudra lay sleeping, Iimogen stepped on a twig and Grisaudra stirred. Iimogen pressed her thumbs lightly to her own eyelids and chanted softly, "Heavy, heavy, three times heavy!" Grisaudra mumbled something half-formed, then sank back into a deep, otherworldly slumber.

Iimogen felt under the pallet, her hand closing around the vial and drawing it out carefully, though there was no danger in waking Grisaudra now. In its place Iimogen left the twin vial, colored and flavored with juniper to match the other but containing another, more singular ingredient. Before she left, Iimogen murmured in the sleeping conjurer's ear. Then she was gone, the only shadow of her passing a ripple of alarm that passed from the nervous horses to the branches of the trees and the fire that flared up suddenly from the slumbering coals.

Grisaudra woke before dawn, her brow damp with sweat. She winced as she sat up and clutched her stomach. It cramped as though she had been given poison. Elric would hear of this in the morning; it was his lousy stew that had done it. Grisaudra had promised herself to be sparing with the cordial; already, when she held it to the light, the vial showed itself only half-full. But these pains were truly awful! She really felt as though she would die unless she had one swallow, comforting and ever so small.

The vision seized her so quickly after she lifted the vial to her lips that it seemed to come out of the bottle itself, like a vapor of evil embodied. It was Myrrhlock, appearing not as the Necromancer with the harelip, nor in his present guise, but in his true form. Centuries of buying off death by eating poison had made of his soul a hideous, scaled thing with unseeing, somehow all-seeing eyes and a mouth of flame.

Grisaudra was held fast by a fascination that was part loathing and part awe. She understood as she stood quaking before him that she was meant to serve him and need not really fear him. That was why she had been made as she had; that was why she had been marked by the sword, so that she might serve one such as this. These thoughts flowed into Grisaudra's mind cold and pure and brilliant as quicksilver, so that she believed they were her own.

The mouth of flame spoke, and the words flared around Grisaudra, bathing her in blue fire.

"Grisaudra, see yourself as you are, as you will be, if you serve me. Look!"

The flames receded and, as though she stood before a looking glass, Grisaudra saw herself unscarred, both eyes grey and wide with light, her unmarred features young and lovely, framed in hair the pale gold of ashwood.

Part of Grisaudra remembered the old wizard of the marsh and a warning he had given her. The way he had died. "No—"

Even with the powerful drug within the drug, Grisaudra still struggled against Myrrhlock. Beauty was nothing to her; it would take a greater prize than comeliness to sway her.

A greater prize Myrrhlock had. The fire flared up to envelop her again, but this time it swirled and formed a figure in fire, the blue flames cooling to reveal a dream-Badger, his limbs still edged with a fiery aura. In his eyes there was desire, and what's more there was love, not for Caitlin, but for her, Grisaudra.

The flames extinguished themselves with a hiss, and the illusion was gone. Grisaudra was weeping. "No."

"Yes. You were made by me, and I made him for you, as your reward.

"But first, you must serve me."

It was as though all her life a cord bound Grisaudra's heart, bound it so tightly that it pained her, and now that cord had suddenly been cut. With that release, Grisaudra opened her eyes and answered him.

7

IN THE GEMFIELDS

Iiliana lay sprawled on the sofa in her chambers, her bronze hair flaming up the sofa back. The queen's eyes smoldered, and she leveled the full fury of her gaze on the goblin in the chair across the room.

Grimald's chin was doubled onto his chubby goblin neck, and his yellow eyes were full of a catlike satisfaction with his day's mischief. Grimald had put in a good morning's work: Iiliana had left him sleeping in the arbor seat only to find, ten minutes later, that he had caught a robin that had hopped too near and pulled out its tail feathers. In the kitchen, where they were making him a new sugar teat, he had managed to pull a whole basin of cooling jam down upon the floor. How he had gotten his little goblin hands into the sewing basket, Iiliana could not imagine. As she handed over the ruined tatters of her best dressing gown to stuff a pillow, Iiliana thought ruefully that it was a hard way to be reminded that a goblin was not a baby, that it grew twice as fast as a human child and had strength to match its cunning.

Still, there was no way to punish him. He was a baby, even if a goblin baby, and too young, or too otherworldly, to warrant a spanking, as much as his actions begged for one.

They had discovered by accident that the goblin could not abide two things, and these were dogs of any size or breed and water. In order to bathe him they had at last to resort to a kind of scouring powder made of sawdust, talcum, and rose petals. Now, when Iiliana had to turn her attention from the goblin for a moment, she left it in the guard of the old toothless mastiff, Pomamber. When the changeling was in the care of the household, the nurse on duty was issued a large sugar shaker full of water, and as soon as the goblin's eyes began to gleam a little too brightly with the contemplation of mischief, the nurse was to sprinkle him with water vigorously, as if he were a newly planted radish patch. The goblin's face would crumple into an expression of alarm and dismay, and it would chew contritely on its thumb for about half an hour.

It was at best, Iiliana thought from her place on the sofa, a temporary truce. Caitlin alone seemed to have any sway with the creature; as soon as Caitlin woke from her nap, she would consult her. Caitlin had fallen into a deep sleep, and for now Iiliana was loath to wake her.

Iiliana was preoccupied by the changeling, or she might have noticed something odd about Caitlin as she lay curled within the warm arm of sunshine from the window. The small mole that had formerly marked her neck beneath her right ear was now to be found beneath the left, and the bruise on her arm where she had hit it on the edge of the washstand had vanished, though a bruise just like it had appeared suddenly on the other arm. If Caitlin had been awake, Iiliana would have seen that her eyes had changed, or rather exchanged, colors: The blue was now green and vice versa. If Iiliana had held a mirror to Caitlin's lips, it would not have misted but darkened, as if a candle flame had been held to it. And a finger touched to the mirror would have shown it to be not soot but quicksilver.

The book of incantations lay beneath the glass, forgotten. Iiliana had replaced the dome over the book without noticing the opening to which the wind had turned. The gilt of the miniature shone as though fresh from the artist's brush, though this was a part of the book Iiliana had not yet restored. The illustration had been given an entire page, and it showed Caitlin in a golden robe, holding the goblin baby to a mirror. Reflected in the mirror was Ylfcwen, clad in silver and white, holding Bram up to the other side of the mirror. In the distance, on Caitlin's side, all the inhabitants of Chameol could be seen, lying where sleep had overtaken them, the gardener with her shears, the milkmaid upon the milking stool, her cheek pressed to the cow's flank. The border of the illustration was a tangled pattern of acrobats and monkeys.

Iiliana yawned, suddenly unaccountably tired. Or not so unaccountably, considering the chase the changeling had been leading her. She could use a nap, at that.

"Pomamber," she called. But the mastiff, asleep by the door, could not be roused. Without a reliable guard for the goblin, Iiliana dared not close her eyes. The sun showed it was early afternoon; she would wake Caitlin. Caitlin knew how to keep the little fiend in line.

But the queen's eyelids were already shut fast.

⌁

Ylfcwen yawned. "It's just not possible," she said again, as if explaining something self-evident to a very small child.

"He's *mine*; he's my *son*. Don't tell me what is and isn't possible!" Caitlin's fist came down on the vanity, making the silver wing-trimmers and bottles of scent dance. Ylfcwen's opal eyes widened at this display of high feeling. She reached out with a pale, translucent arm and righted a toppled bottle.

"It is not possible for *me* to retrieve the bram. If you feel so strongly about it"—Ylfcwen's tone suggested that feeling strongly was as distasteful as smelling strongly—"you can petition Drusian yourself."

The wrath drained from Caitlin's face, leaving it smooth with sorrow. "Just tell me what I have to do."

The elf queen regarded Caitlin with the sleepy interest that was the closest emotion she had to pity. "It's quite irregular, you know. I myself have not had an audience with Drusian in seventy years or so."

"He will see me."

Ylfcwen raised the silver arch of one eyebrow and laughed, not the formal chuckle used in court, but the intimate laugh used among friends and equals; this distinction, however, was lost on Caitlin. "Stay a little longer among us. Then we'll see whether your confidence will flourish or wither. Don't mistake me! Your determination becomes you. But a pretty dress can become you and still let you perish of the cold."

"I once made my bed in a soldier's barrow under the moor. I've endured winters beyond your imagining. I've known the cold, milady. It's not the cold I fear."

Ylfcwen's opal eyes held Caitlin's uncanny ones in a long gaze. The elf queen was one of the few creatures, human or not, who could bear to hold that look for long. Then Ylfcwen bent and opened a small cabinet by the side of her bed. She extracted and laid out upon the coverlet a small jeweled book, a velvet pouch embroidered with gold thread and pearls, and a small crystal vial on a silver chain.

"The way to Drusian's chambers will take you through the gemfields. The miners serve me, but the other denizens are sworn to Drusian. The jeweled book is the courtbook, outlining elvish manners and laws; it may assist you when it comes to the goblins and some others you might find. It was my mother's copy, but it is still up-to-date. The bag contains jewels. Where a knowledge of etiquette and the legal code will not aid you, a bribe often will."

"And the vial?"

Ylfcwen picked up her cosmetic scissors and used them to cut a brilliant yellow orchid from the vine twined in her bedstead. She slipped the orchid into the crystal vial and filled the vial with water from a dropper. "This," she said, slipping the silver chain around Caitlin's neck, "is a canary orchid. It breathes even as you do and will sense any deadly ethers in the mines before you can."

Then Ylfcwen went to one of the flower-covered walls of her chamber and opened a hidden door that swung inward with a scraping sound of stone on stone. Elvish engineers would have made a noiseless door, but this was not a door fashioned by elven hands but by others far more ancient, so that the door's scraping was borne by the elves with a little awe.

"Your way is forward," the elf queen said. "Farther I cannot lead you."

Caitlin stepped up to the threshold; it was utterly dark. "Will you light my way, or is that beyond your means as well?"

Ylfcwen chuckled, her laugh the sound of a wayward silver shuttlecock falling into a secret, forgotten well. "If you can't outwit the dark, airling, you've no hope at all of matching wits with Drusian. No, really, it is just that I have no matches on me. All I can send you off with is this." And she placed on Caitlin's cheek a kiss so cold it burned, and when the frosty mark faded, it would leave Caitlin with a smooth, silvery scar, as if she had glued a small mirror to her cheek after some fad of the court.

It occurred to Caitlin, as the heavy stone door scraped shut again, the possibility of treachery, that a creature without scruples would also lack conscience, and that this chamber could well lead nowhere except to her own death.

"But I thought this was only a dream," Newt said disconcertingly in her ear.

"If you're going to talk," said Caitlin, "say something useful. How to light the passage, for instance."

It turned out there was no need; another useful trait of the canary orchid was that it gave off as a product of its respiration a yellow glow as bright as a lamp.

"Ylfcwen was right," Caitlin said. "The only way *is* forward."

The mine tunnel was nothing like the main corridor. There were no tapestries here. The walls were adorned with the haphazard mosaic of uncut gems, nodes of rubies, sapphires, and emeralds imprisoned in the rock. The floor of the passage was smooth, worn to a high polish by the feet of goblin miners.

Ylfcwen's court etiquette was bound as a girdle book, the binding along the spine brought to a tail that could be tied to the belt, handy for surreptitious consultations during banquets and other problematic social occasions. If he hung by his tail from Caitlin's belt, Newt could read aloud to Caitlin as she walked along the passage.

"Ah," he said, finding the entry he wanted. "Here's a good place to begin."

Goblins

> The old notions about goblins, that they spring sponta-
> neously from coal dust and wet kindling, or that they
> can spoil milk by looking at it, are now universally dis-
> credited, and no one who doesn't wish to look a fool
> can afford any longer to subscribe to them. In fact, the
> only things that can be said to be true about all goblins
> are these: They are the offspring of elves and humans,
> a human mother being the more usual case, but
> instances of an elvish mother and a human father are
> not unknown. Like mules, goblins are sterile, but any
> other comparisons to the intelligence and brute
> strength of pack animals are without foundation. The
> most common goblin features—a ruddy complexion and
> yellow feline eyes—are various enough to include bluer
> complexions and green or lavender eyes. Goblins, when
> not deprived through prejudice of a secure childhood
> and sound education, display sharp wits and keen
> minds, often excelling at wrestling, chess, and the writ-
> ing of satirical plays.

Caitlin gave a small shudder, remembering one of her last conversations with the Badger: *A mooncalf, that's what I am. Now do you see? The blood is bad; bad blood will tell. Monsters breed only monsters.*

"Come now," said Newt, breaking into her thoughts. "He looks nothing like a goblin. You're the one with the uncanny looks. You're the one with a bluish cast to your skin. A cousin on your mother's side, perhaps?"

"Hush," said Caitlin. "I want to hear something else. Read what it says about reading other people's thoughts without permission."

The wild horses of Chameol had wandered brazenly into Iiliana's own vegetable garden and had eaten the last of the lettuces. No one had come to chase them away because all of Chameol was asleep.

The dog lay curled a few feet from the cat it had been chasing when it had been overtaken by the unconquerable urge to sleep. The crows that had been dining on the pie left to cool on the windowsill had fallen asleep on the spot; inside, the pastry cook had pillowed her head on her floury arms while the tarts in the oven hardened into blackened and inedible tiles. In the laundry, the pressers slept on drifts of linen, in clouds of lavender, dreaming of shirts that ironed themselves. Iiliana dozed on the couch in her chambers, dreaming of besting her brother in a snowball fight.

Only the changeling was awake. Grimald sat wedged upright in the chair by pillows, eyeing the mastiff at the door with dismay. Although no one had come to reswaddle him, the goblin did not need changing, for like an owl, a goblin is loath to soil its own nest and will hold its water for days on end, expelling only a few dry pellets. Old wives' tales to the contrary, goblins do not have two stomachs, but they can go for a short time without food, subsisting on the stores of fat that suit them for the cold work of the mines. But despite this natural advantage, Grimald was growing hungry. His ears quivering with the effort, the goblin baby listened with all his might, sifting the several thousand distinct sounds of late afternoon on the island as if turning over the catch from a teeming net. But hard as he listened, Grimald could not make out the singular footfall, the one voice he hungered for above all others. Try as he might, Grimald could not hear Caitlin.

With that knowledge a curious thing happened. Some of the ruddiness left the goblin face, and two fat, golden, resinous tears worked their way out of the corners of those feline eyes. The goblin's silent keening grew greater until at last he opened his mouth and let out a mute and miserable howl. From the depths of her dreaming, the great mastiff covered her ears with her paws and whined.

Pomamber alone of all the inhabitants on Chameol could hear the changeling cry.

⮹⮺

After he finished the entry on goblins, Newt turned to the first section of the jeweled book, which dealt with niceties of elvish dress.

Attire

Audiences at court call for dress appropriate to the occasion, the rank and station of the person who is to be presented, and the season. One does not go without a wingcase after the first orchid harvest; likewise, it is in poor taste indeed to be seen in any more wing-dressing than a light dusting of crushed pearl *before* it. Binding the wings tightly to the back with linen or lamé is a fashion now deemed not only unattractive but decidedly unhealthy as well. Clipped wings are a certain sign of at least a juvenile delinquent, if not a hard-ened criminal.

"Heavens!" said Caitlin. "And me in my nightclothes."

"And your toenails want trimming," added Newt. In annoyance, Caitlin transferred the salamander to her shoulder and firmly shut the book.

The canary orchid around her neck illuminated the passage in front of Caitlin for ten strides before the light lost its battle with the pitchy blackness. Far off could be heard the ringing of goblin pickaxes on stone and the high, metallic zithering of mine cars on steel runners.

But where are the miners? Caitlin wondered. The tunnel led on straight ahead, while the echoes seemed to come from every side.

"They're mining gems, not coal. If gems were so common, I dare say they would put up signs: EMERALDS AHEAD, SAPPHIRES FOR THE TAKING. As it is, I suppose they're none too eager for you to know where they are."

Caitlin was about to pinch the salamander's tail when she stopped in her tracks, cringing out of instinct, her arms raised against the deadly pounce of some invisible beast. The light of the canary orchid had suddenly picked out of the darkness a thousand fierce and glowing eyes, as if five hundred lions, leopards, and panthers had been imprisoned underground to guard the elven gems.

"It's all right," said Newt in her ear. "They're only stones."

The salamander was right. In this chamber the miners had exposed the deposits of tiger's eye and polished them until they were as luminous and brilliant as amber glass, leaving them embedded in the rough stone of the cavern walls to startle—and warn?—unwary and unwelcome trespassers. Holding high the orchid in its vial, Caitlin could read some runes above her on the wall. They were odd, familiar yet unknown, something like common cat language and yet unlike it. The best Caitlin could make of them was *Hear, O Wanderer, of the great grief of Pj'aurinoor, and the manner of the death of Pj'inkinoor, her beloved.*

"Those are surely not elvish names, nor goblin, either," she murmured.

"No," Newt agreed. "I would say we have come to the first of the guardians we were told about."

"Or warned about . . . ?"

Newt bit the lobe of Caitlin's ear, not, it seemed, either to chastise or to comfort her, but to vent his own nervousness.

"But whatever lies ahead of us, Bram is there also, and so there I have to be." With this Caitlin stepped forward into the chamber, and the thousand tiger's eyes followed her movements. There was a carved ivory portal set into the rock, and Caitlin was about to step across the threshold when Newt's voice, urgent in her ear, made her stop.

"Look again! This is no *mortal* gateway."

Where there had been a moment before a simple ivory arch there now stretched open a pair of gigantic jaws, twelve feet from the sharp point of an upper tooth to its mate below. The ivory seemed quite solid, then just as suddenly it seemed to be made of mist, and the arch was a simple arch again.

The chamber shook with a rumbling, the thunder, perhaps, of a distant rockfall. Perhaps.

Caitlin sat on the cavern floor in front of the arch and began to weep, softly at first and then louder.

The rumbling ceased.

"Why weep ye?" asked a voice played on all the lowest notes of a bass fiddle.

Caitlin raised her head, her face wet with tears. "I weep for Pj'inkinoor, beloved of Pj'aurinoor. I fear he alone could have helped me with my quest."

The ivory arch melted away in mist to show there was no door at all but a pit from which there rose a pungent gas. The light of the canary orchid dimmed and nearly went out.

"There is a passageway to the right," said Newt.

Caitlin found it, hidden in shadow. She had to stoop to enter it, but after a few feet the passage opened into an immense tabernacle of stone, its vast vaulted roof out of sight. The chamber was lit as brilliantly as a summer noon, and the light seemed to come from the sole occupant and the source of the voice, a tigress whose length from ear to tip of tail was that of a village street. Sitting up, the tigress might have eaten sherbet from the crow's nest of a great sailing ship.

All the amber fire of the thousand gems was caught in each of the creature's eyes, and both of these were fixed on Caitlin, so that she almost believed her gown would catch fire from the heat of the stare. The rumble rose again, breaking on its highest note into the deep, musical voice.

"Beg ye no boons of Pj'inkinoor, mortal, for murderers have wiped their boots on his fine stripes and made of his ears tents for their armies. Beg of me, of Pj'aurinoor'j'aurinji, his beloved and mate."

8

TIGER'S EYE

Folderol let his hands run through the pile of coins on the tablecloth, scooping up double handfuls and letting them spill again onto the cloth, his mouth in the center of his calico beard pursed into a rosy O. Suddenly his eye fell upon Nix, and the old rogue's face underwent elastic contortions from startled alarm to bald-faced greed to murderous cunning, ending in an oily, unnatural smile that was an attempt at beneficence.

Nix's feet were twined around the rungs of the stool as if he were a vine that had grown there, his milkweed hair raked up into tufts where he had twisted it, waiting for Folderol to count out the money and hand him his and Ulfra's share.

"Well, we didn't do as well as yesterday, m'lad, but none too shabbily, all the same. No, not shabby at all. No doubt it's the bad meat that's put the wolves off their form; once they're back on their feet, we'll really be raking it in."

In fact, the take had been considerably larger than the day before, and Folderol would have been cheating them had Nix not already hidden a bootful of coins, mostly silver, in an iron kettle sunk into the earth in one corner of Ulfra's tent.

Muttering and chuckling to himself, Folderol swept a share of the coins off the table into a small sack. Turning to the table behind, he cut a good portion from last night's joint of mutton and handed both sack and meat to Nix.

"Get along with you—that is, before the meat gets cold." As soon as Nix had slipped through the tent flap, Folderol leapt up, knocking over his chair and careening around the room in a crazy waltz. He kicked off a boot and swung it in a circle over his head, the other hand clapped to his mouth, his eyes bugging with a suppressed shout of glee.

~~~

In the tent, in the bunk below Elric's, the Badger wrestled with a dream, his face pearled with a cold sweat and his hair dark with it. In the dream, he was imprisoned in a tower by a beautiful enchantress. Though her silken hood hid her face, her voice told him of her cold, irresistible beauty. Every day she came to his cell with a jeweled casket and taunted him to tell her its contents.

"Then you will be free," she said.

But he could not even tell her his name. At last, with a cold laugh, she opened the casket and revealed a braided coil of hair, black as ink, tied into a noose.

The Badger woke and flung off the blankets, and without really waking from the dream he found himself across the room at the table, knife in hand, trying to cut the bracelet free. In a second, Elric was beside him, knocking the blade from his hand, a stricken look on his face, as if the Badger had been about to put the knife to his own flesh.

"Please." The Badger's eyes were bright, as with a fever, or with fear. "I must cut it off! You must let me!"

"No. I would as soon let you cut your throat."

"I see her in my dreams . . . she's evil, pure evil . . . and when she opens the box, it's not a bracelet anymore; it's a noose. . . ."

Elric shook his head, picked up the knife, and set it out of reach. "I can't say where the dreams come from, but they are false. Cut the bracelet off and you cut loose your anchor to reason and happiness, perhaps even to life itself."

The Badger had no more fight left in him. He meekly let Elric lead him back to bed, and he drank the dose of brandy poured out for him without complaint, slipping almost immediately into a profound slumber.

Elric stood over him, watching his features take on in sleep the smooth innocence and simple beauty of a child's, the haunted look gone, as if he were a stableboy again, asleep in the hay of the stable loft.

"He *can't* forget her!" he said aloud. Then he felt a gaze upon him and turned to see Grisaudra watching him from the entrance to the tent, a strange expression on her face.

"He had a nightmare," Elric said. "Go back to sleep."

She seemed to be about to object but turned quietly and went back to her own tent. Elric thought it unlike her to pass up an argument. He hid the brandy and went back to bed himself.

In the morning, the Badger woke and went to feed the horses. He slipped loose bridles on the animals and led them to the watering troughs, where he found Ulfra giving Nix a bath. Sniffing loudly at him that morning, Ulfra had suddenly seized the boy and hauled him off for a rough scrubbing, cuffing him lightly with the palm of her hand if he squirmed too much, working up a lather with cold water and saddle soap.

Ulfra looked up as the Badger approached, her dark hair hanging over one eye, the piercing blue of the other striking a chord somewhere deep within the Badger. Then she shook the hair from her eyes and smiled, a white-toothed grimace and a shrugging of the scalp that was still more wolf than woman.

While her attention was thus distracted, Nix ducked from her grasp and fled, streaming water. The Badger hardly noticed, as his gaze was fixed on Ulfra. She had discarded her soldier's uniform for this chore; as her soaked shift clung to her, the Badger suddenly saw a ghost, tall and dark, wading into the dark surf of the moonlit sea.

The wolf-girl casually spat some saddle soap from her

mouth, regarding the Badger curiously from the corner of her eye. He busied himself with the horses, but once Ulfra had gone he clung to the back of the mare, Maud, seeing the figure turn in the surf to cast a glance toward the shore. Her hair was dark but shorn, and while one eye was blue its mate was green. A name played on the tip of his tongue, and then it was gone.

"Are you all right?"

It was Grisaudra, carrying on her arm a basket of goldenrod gathered by the roadside. She had put on a blue cap, and the chill on the morning air had put a hint of roses in her cheeks, so that from a certain angle she might have been a pretty girl of twelve. But the Badger seemed hardly to see her, and when his eyes focused on her face he scowled in annoyance; at the first sound of her voice the vision of the figure in the surf had vanished.

"I'm fine—why shouldn't I be?" he snapped. "Now I've got work to do—as you do."

Grisaudra held her composure until she had rounded the corner of the shed where the horses were stabled. But as soon as she was out of sight, she broke into a run, blinded by tears, and stood sobbing out behind the cooking tent. In a moment she recovered herself and was about to splash her face with rainwater from the barrel when she caught sight of her reflection.

She was the Grisaudra of Myrrhlock's vision; her hood fallen back, hair framing her features in a mist of pale gold. She stood gazing at the reflection until her tears had dried and her breaths came evenly once more. Then Grisaudra gathered up the scattered goldenrod and went to change into her costume for the first performance of the afternoon.

Elric, in the kitchen to beg some matches, stood in the shadows just inside the tent, his pipe gone cold in his hand, watching her go.

❧

Pj'aurinoor regarded Caitlin out of liquid amber eyes. "What is it that brought ye to the gemfields of Pj'aurinoor, daughter of light?"

Caitlin knelt in the courtyard formed by the great paws

and roofed by the vast chin, a hanging garden of ebony and amber fur. "I am looking for my firstborn and only child."

Pj'aurinoor lashed her tail against the cavern wall, roaring a great oath. A small rock slide rained harmlessly onto the tiger's massive head. Newt, disliking the roaring or mindful of falling rocks, had crept into Caitlin's pocket and was curled there tighter than a stone.

"Hunters!" Pj'aurinoor roared once more. "They took all my children, one by one. My firstborn canopies a queen's bed; now that lady sleeps her widow's sleep beneath that peerless pelt. The others hang in the halls of palaces and fortresses from here to Twelfthmoon. And the youngest, my sweet j'aurinji, dreams at the bottom of the sea, with the cameleopard and gryphon, bound for an idle king's menagerie. Hunters!" The whiplash of Pj'aurinoor's tail upset a pile of crowns and boots in one corner of the chamber. "How did thy child come to be taken?"

"Ylfcwen's servant took him in the night and left a changeling in his place."

The tiger's roar subsided into a low rumble, and she nodded thoughtfully. "A new mother, ye were late giving him a name and then listened to the murmurings of an elvish nursemaid. I have heard the tale before. Where was thy mother, that she did not warn thee of this?"

"The only mother I knew was an old spell-seller in the Weirdwood. The way of the birds she did teach me, but not the ways of men, let alone those of Ylfcwen's race."

"But thyself should have known this, otherworld daughter! Or would ye not heed what was before thy seer's eyes? Where is thy child now?"

"Ylfcwen says he has been taken to Drusian, but who and where he is no one will tell me."

The great tail ceased its lashing and the tiger's throat seemed to have run dry of roars. After a pause Pj'aurinoor spoke.

"Drusian is the Master of Sleep and Desire, whose palace lies two fields beyond this one, past the sapphires and the serpentine. But I fear, daughter of light, that if it *is* Drusian that has claimed thy child, thy best path lies upward, past hope and grieving. Ye are yet young; there will be other cubs."

Caitlin's jaw trembled a little before she lifted it defiantly toward Pj'aurinoor.

"Is that what you did when your youngest was taken? Give up hope?"

"I went and slew the hunters and left only their boots and crowns. But they were hunters; they were mortal. They were not Drusian."

"Is he past beseeching, then?"

"Child, ye would as likely snare the moon in a net of cobweb as to bring back from that chamber what Drusian has claimed." The great chin lowered, and a purring passed through Caitlin like a tremor, leaving her calm and content, so that she could have curled up in the amber fur and slept her life away.

"But I must try," she said, her words muffled by the tiger's fur.

"Yes. The children of light must always do thus: rename the world and reinvent water."

"What would I be, then, if I didn't try?" Caitlin's finger traced an ebony stripe on the tiger's jaw. "His hair is just this color, but softer. . . ."

The tiger sighed, a low moan, making her whiskers tremble. "Enough. Child, Drusian rules sleep and desire and rules over such creatures of the shadows as me. I guard this first portal and am sworn to let no human feet trespass here. But if ye were to give me something in payment, it would be no trespass but a toll, and no fault would Drusian be able to find with me. Have ye anything to give?"

"No crowns or boots, I fear. Gems and a book."

Pj'aurinoor snorted her distaste. "Stones and dry leaves—what are these to such as me? Have ye nothing else?"

Caitlin felt in her pocket, and when her fingers closed around the salamander she got a nip, as if to say, Think again! "Just a piece of glass from the sea."

"The flower around thy neck I would take, otherworld daughter. Is it a singing orchid?"

"A canary orchid, but it has not sung for me—more's the pity. But I can't give it up—it's my only light and breath in the gemfields."

Pj'aurinoor lowered her velvet nose, which Caitlin could not have spanned with her hands, to take in the scent of the orchid. Caitlin was lost in a forest of black and amber shadows that smelled of oranges that have lain too long in the sun, sweet and rummy with an edge of tartness. She remembered a morning on Chameol, kissing the Badger, the perfumed oil from an orange rind still on his mouth and hands.

"It has no scent," said the tiger.

"No. Nor a song, either. And I am in no better voice than the flower, I fear. But I can speak you a tale, if I can't sing it in verses. What do you like in a tale? A hunter meeting a grisly end?"

"No—I favor any kind of tale, as long as it has rabbits in it. Ye have told me how the babe was taken, but not how he was gotten. Tell me of thy j'aurinji, thy beloved."

So Caitlin lay in the space between two of the great tiger's toes and told a tale of love found and love lost, how we discover what we love only in the moment that it is taken from us, and learn that the only way to be true to what we love is sometimes to surrender it.

"How lost and how surrendered?"

It was more than Caitlin could bear, to speak of the nights she had nursed the Badger back from the threshold of death, wresting him from the grip of a gilt-and-quick-silver poison. She had made profane promises to the night, to the wolves and the trees and the moon, so that when he woke from the fever she had gambled away everything but two fingers on her right hand.

But she told Pj'aurinoor all of it, how, as they had ridden on toward Ninthstile, she had spent each hour expecting the wolves to come claim their share of her and the branches to pluck out her eyes. The trees whispered but did not reach for her; the wolves howled but did not come within the circle of the fire; and the moon only showed her, in the inky surface of a patch of water, a sight Caitlin had never before seen: the face of a woman in love.

"And how did ye lose him again, child?"

"I found I could not have him and also have knowledge of what I was, what my eyes had made me. I could retain my memory of him but never be with him. Or I might live in the world as if I had never known him. In the end, there was no choice." Caitlin paused, her own face striped by Pj'aurinoor's whiskers, cast into shadows by the canary orchid. Her mouth curled into a small smile. "What a memory it turned out to be! Seven pounds of memory, squalling fit to raise the dead and a shock of hair so black it belonged on a crow—"

The musical thunder of Pj'aurinoor's roar stopped her. "Tell me no more of this tale, daughter of light. Tell me some other, with a sweeter moral to it." The great golden eyes widened into lamps of fire. "Tell me a tale with *rabbits* in it."

❧

"You're sure this will come off?"

Elric twisted around on the stool where he sat, stripped to the waist, an elaborate pattern sketched on his back in charcoal. Grisaudra sat behind him, a crimson-tipped quill poised in one hand.

"Perfectly." She began to fill in the part of the pattern that covered Elric's left shoulder blade, a tangled pattern of roses.

"It's as much as your life is worth if it isn't. Ow!"

"Sorry, but you mustn't move, or I can't answer either for the injury to your back or to the finished effort." Grisaudra consulted the pattern on the table. It was the Badger's handiwork. Within the border of roses he had drawn a figure in a yellow dress, her hair a tangled crown of living eels. In one hand she held a bloodied sword, in the other a red rose.

It was Folderol's idea that the troupe's latest addition should not be merely a bearded duchess, but a duchess with a tattoo. It was he who had seen some of the drawings the Badger made on the backs of old broadsides advertising the leopard-woman who had left to take up dressmaking: horses so lifelike they seemed to rear from the page. Folderol had soon commissioned his trick rider to design a tattoo "fit to make brave men swoon and bring speech to the tongues of the mute." The finished design fit the bill admirably, with a few alterations. The Badger's original drawing had shown the figure's foot resting on a severed head, but Folderol had prevailed upon him to change it to a dragon, which he felt had a more spectacular effect.

Folderol had not seen the other drawings the Badger had made and hid beneath his cot, drawings of the same face over and over from different aspects, but always obscured—by shadow, an upflung arm, a mass of unruly hair—from the viewer's full gaze. It was only Elric who noticed that the severed head in the original pattern for the tattoo bore a disturbing resemblance to the Badger. *Perhaps*, thought Elric as his back began slowly to bloom with roses, *if he draws long enough, he'll sort it all out and remember that she was anything but a fiend.* For Elric was somehow sure this was not the strange malady at work, but the Badger's befuddled brain trying to make sense of his shattered memories. The drawings were perhaps the best way for him to confront and disarm his demons. They might even be the only way.

❦

Nix had wandered from the place where the troupe was camped and slipped into a farmer's fields. For a while he stood looking at a lamb that had strayed from the rest of the flock, weighing whether it was better to kill it here and have to drag it home or to lead it back and risk someone hearing it bleat. The wolves would much prefer the latter method. At last Nix settled for a couple of geese, twisting their necks when he caught them and stuffing them into a sack. Ulfra liked nothing better than a nice crispy goose, and she let him lick the grease from her fingers.

It was outside the kitchen tent, where he was going to swipe a knife and an onion, that Nix saw something he was not intended to see.

Over a rain barrel was draped a black cloak lined with silk in a pattern of poppies. Nix had no sooner noticed the cloak when a young woman, her clouded-honey hair all disheveled and her eyes wild with terror, came pelting around the corner of the tent. She glanced wildly about her, looking at Nix but right through him, searching the air as if she sought to escape her pursuer through an invisible door.

Just then a man turned the corner after her, the shaven skin of his skull seamed with veins but his features themselves strangely youthful—perhaps it was the quizzical twist given to his mouth by a harelip. He called out a name, and the young woman fell with a gasp to the ground, as if he had thrown a dagger in her back.

The man with the harelip stepped up to her. Snatching the cloak from atop the barrel, he draped the girl in it, muttering a few twisted words in a long-dead rune tongue. The young woman struggled within the folds of the cloak, but she was completely enveloped in it and could not cast it off. She struggled less and less, and her body seemed to shrink with her waning will. The harelipped man picked up what was now a small, fluttering bundle, wrapped the cloak more firmly round it, and turned away, the bundle under one arm.

Nix brought the geese to Ulfra, who cooked and ate them with relish, casting worried glances at Nix as she dispatched the birds. She drew him close to see if a pain or ache had put him out of sorts and caught the unmistakable smell of the Otherworld.

Ulfra curled her lip in distaste and gave Nix over to the eldest she-wolf to be bathed until he should smell neither of the one world nor the Otherworld, but of snow on silver fur, of cooling mutton tallow, of a new-snuffed match. Until, in other words, he should smell completely and entirely of Wolf, and nothing but Wolf.

9

THE LION TAMER

He blended into the crowd that had come to watch Ulfra put the wolves through their paces, the children making themselves sick on pickled plums and greasy doughnuts, the comely and uncomely there alike to gloat over the freaks, the jaded in search of a fleeting thrill, the timid standing in line for their penny's dose of excitement.

The man in question was grey from his soft felt cap to the dust that covered his boots. His beard and his complexion were grey, as if he were a chimney sweep who could never quite manage to wash all the chimney black away. The only thing about him that was not grey was the color of his eyes. They were black, like soot on a mirror, absorbing everything they saw and casting nothing back. No one seemed to notice him except the vendor who sold him a doughnut, and he remembered him only for the length of the transaction before forgetting him utterly.

He watched with mild curiosity as Nix placed his head in the wolf's mouth and barely raised an eyebrow when the Badger circled the ring backward, leaning from the saddle, a match in his mouth, to strike a light against the sole of the boot of a man in the front row. But when

Grisaudra entered the tent and called for a volunteer from the audience, the man was genuinely taken aback.

"Her!" the grey man said under his breath.

Out of instinct, his hand went to the raised welt of an old scar on his arm. He slipped from the tent and followed the gaudy painted signs to the tent of the tattooed duchess. A sign declared the tattooed duchess to be absent and assured the throngs she would return with five minutes; the man ignored it and slipped inside.

The duchess sat resplendent in a gown of puce silk trimmed with a dark green fringe, enjoying a pipe of clove between showings, her tattoo hidden beneath a shawl. Beneath ginger eyebrows the eyes of fetching grey registered a glimmer of recognition.

"I'm sorry, the tattoo is off view; I'm on my break."

"That's quite all right. It's just that I hate crowds—the smell of hot lard from the doughnut cart was making me sick." While his tone was nonchalant, the black eyes silently asked whether they could freely speak; in answer, the tattooed duchess nodded.

"Something is very wrong on Chameol."

Fear grabbed Elric by the throat, but his eyes were blank when he raised them to the other knight.

"How so?"

"For over a week now, the messenger pigeons we send have not returned. I need hardly tell you, that has never happened."

It had once. One pigeon he had dispatched to Chameol had been delivered to his own door the next morning on a silver plate. The danger was always there. "What else?"

"We sent a swimmer out to try the old ruse of a boy drowning, to draw the dolphins and tie a message to the collar of one of their number. They did not come. But the boy told us he heard them making a strange call."

"In distress?"

"No—almost like snoring, he said it was, if dolphins could do such a thing."

The duchess stroked her jaw in a strangely mannish gesture, absently pulling at her corset where it pinched.

"Someone must land on Chameol and see what is befallen them."

"But the Code forbids us to land on Chameol—"

"Yes, normally; but now the need is dire. Clearly, someone must land and send us a message. Have him take precautions against poisonous vapors. He is not to drink or eat anything on the island. A pair of earplugs might be prudent."

The grey man nodded. "There's something else, though. Your fortune-teller, the one with the scar."

"She's a conjurer from the Oncemoon Marsh. Why, do you know her?"

"Yes, but not from the marsh. I knew her fifteen years ago, in the border wars. She was just a kid then, disguised as a boy. It was just before she took the sword in her face that we found out. Little idiot, she stepped in front of the soldier the blow was meant for, a silly sack of vanities, a would-be hero with a pretty face. He was far from grateful; the type seldom is. Her scar was as good as the mark of the devil, as far as he was concerned.

"Anyway, she was sent away with the shroud maker, and next time a sword came looking for that ass's neck there was no one so disposed to step in front of it. It almost broke my heart, the look on her face as she trudged off with that old ghoul. God, to think of her at the mercy of a man who'd sell the gold fillings out of a dead man's mouth. She was a really beautiful kid before her face got in the way of the business edge of a sword."

∽∾

That evening the Badger was tending to the horses, polishing their coats to a high gloss, then settling down to do the same for the brass bits on the tack. The old lion tamer, Hodge, sat down nearby to watch.

Cleaning tack was the one activity that felt wholly natural to the Badger. In everything else that he did, there was a weird echo, an odd feeling that he ought to be remembering something. This happened several times a day, as he was watching Nix comb and plait Ulfra's hair by the pump or when he caught sight of a woman in the crowd wearing a particular shade of blue-green. Sitting down to a supper of hard-boiled eggs and the heel of a loaf, the Badger's heart rose in his throat as if it would leap out his mouth. With the brass polish and the rag, there was none of that.

Old Hodge smoked his pipe and watched. The old lion tamer cut an odd figure, with the wild ginger-and-silver mane that fringed his bald pate. He had wide-spaced, narrow eyes and a nose flattened in a long-ago brawl, which combined with his enormous ragged ears to make him look three-quarters lion himself.

Indeed, Hodge was much more frightening to look at than his lion. The broadsides showed Rollo the Man-Eater with a magnificent mane and razor fangs, his eyes great orbs of flame. The true portrait was something rather different. Rollo the Man-Eater was balding around the ears; his belly drooped low to the ground, and in his agitation around crowds he had chewed the tassel off the end of his tail. A very well kept secret (or so Hodge thought) was that the creature wore false teeth and that the great hunks of raw meat delivered to the lion's cage each day were quietly taken by Hodge to be tenderized with a mallet and put through a food mill. And it was not uncommon to find Nix napping, curled head to knees in the fur of the lion's breast, or braiding dried posies of bluebonnets into the thinning mane.

"Where is it you come from? You ride a horse as if you were born to the saddle, but there's something in your way of speaking and the way you hold yourself. You're no stableboy and not even an acrobat, no matter how well you ride."

The Badger shrugged. "I had a mother who had rather grand ideas for me—she sent me off to the monks for an education, and there I much preferred the horses to the homilies. When I wouldn't take the cowl, they sent me off to make my way in the world." All of this was true, but it left out the essential fact that he was now a knight of the court of Chameol. He trusted Hodge; in a way, he reminded the Badger of Asaph, the monk from the abbey at Thirdmoon who had turned out to be a knight after all. But trusting someone and confiding in them were two different things, and the vows the Badger had taken were quite specific about the difference.

Hodge nodded, exhaling a plume of clove smoke. "Ah. So it was the monks who taught you to play the recorder and to draw so true to likeness." Here he gestured to some drawings tacked to the tent pole, of Nix asleep in the lion's embrace, of Elric in full duchess regalia, and one of Ulfra, her arms thrown around the neck of the old she-wolf.

The Badger laughed. "Hardly! Whatever I learned about music and drawing I learned in *spite* of the monks. Or in spite of most of them. The skills they taught were of a different sort altogether. How to sing on an empty stomach at two o'clock in the morning without yawning or letting your stomach growl. Wake me in the middle of the night sometime, and you'll see. Before my feet have hit the floor I'll be on the second verse of a hymn."

Hodge raised an eyebrow in surprise. "To have known you this last week I would never have guessed you had such a laugh in you. What—or who—has made you so sober and so before your time?"

The Badger's smile vanished, and he bent to his work again. "You find me sober?"

"Uncommonly so, for a man young in years, fair-featured, his body untroubled by injury or disease. I can say none of those things with any truth about myself."

"If I am sober, what makes you think there's anything or anyone behind it?"

"Hard to say, though I suppose it has something to do with the way you are forever twisting that bracelet around on your wrist." Hodge gestured with the stem of his pipe, and the Badger abruptly stopped his absent worrying of the bracelet.

"Yes," Hodge went on mildly, as though discussing nothing more important than the shapes to be found in a passing cloud. "It would explain much, that bracelet. Why you haven't a smile or a glance for the legions of maidens swooning for you. Why you can't tear your eyes away from the wolf-girl."

An image rose in the Badger's brain of an old hag selling

eels from a basket. She held in her hand not a writhing eel but a silky skein of ebony hair. Then the memory was gone like a candle snuffed out in a sigh of breath. The Badger came to himself again to realize the sigh had been his own and to find the lion tamer looking at him with mingled remorse and alarm.

"Forgive me." Hodge knocked the contents of his pipe into the fire and flexed his knee, stiff from sitting. "I had no right to dig up those things you have taken such pains to bury. Now I had best go and see what young Nix has been doing with Rollo—probably dressing him up as the tattooed duchess, if I know Nix."

As soon as the lion tamer was gone, the Badger dropped bridle and rag to the floor, pressing the wrist with the bracelet hard between his eyes, willing the vision to return. "Your name! Damn you! Why, *why* can't I remember your name?"

❧

Nix had stolen six toffy apples from the batch meant to be hawked to that night's audience and had lounged in a gluttony-induced stupor while Rollo licked the toffy from his apple, trying not to glue his false teeth together. The wildly content lion licked Nix's face as often as he licked the apple, finding as much toffy in the one place as in the other.

One of the troupe's cats wandered into the lion's cage to pick over the remains of Rollo's dinner. She was a pretty cat with curious markings, orange with black stocking feet and a harlequin mask over her eyes.

"Pretty imp!" said Nix, reaching for her. She fled at his touch, slipping through the bars of the cage and back behind the kitchen tent, where a crow was hopping about, pecking at crusts and cawing a litany of discontent. The racket brought out the cook, a plucked chicken under her arm and a knife in her hand. The old woman cast a sour glance over the boy. She cursed the cat and the crow, kicking the former and throwing a flowered cloth over the other, tucking it under her arm and disappearing into the kitchen tent with it. Nix made a face, his eyes wide.

"Crow pie!" he said to Rollo, who was much more interested in Nix's toffy apple.

That was not, however, to be the crow's fate. For the moment, the cook tethered it to a perch with a piece of twine, muttering a binding spell just in case the bird took it into its head to nip through the butcher's string. The crow hung its head and took up a low cawing that sounded strangely like a woman sobbing. Even more surprising than the tears welling in the bird's eyes was the fact that those eyes were blue. The cook gave the crow a piece of dry cake spread with conserve of violets, or of something that color, and soon the bird had put head under wing.

❧

It was an hour before the evening's performance, but the contrivances on which a convincing performance depended—sulphur pots, a sheep's bladder, concealed wires—lay in a jumble where Grisaudra had flung them the night before.

She ought to have been putting on her fortune-teller's garb, but Grisaudra sat instead dressed only in her shift, practicing her shuffle with a deck of marked tarot cards. Every time she tried to arch the cards within her hands to bring the interleaved halves together, the deck perversely would spring from Grisaudra's grasp and spell out a fortune of nonsense all over the earthen floor of the tent.

The dice she managed better. The hermit in the marsh had made them for her, carved of mulberry wood for wisdom. He had taught her to use them, too, rolling them to foretell gassy marsh fires or the clinging Oncemoon mists that brought chills, fever, and madness. One thing the dice would never tell her, though, and that was where her family had gone.

Now, as Grisaudra spoke the Badger's name, they came up mustard, for indifference, and ivy, for fidelity.

"Pish-posh! That's off the mark, certainly. Here," she said to herself, "I'll roll them for Elric, and then I'll *know* if they're warped or wormy."

So she said Elric's name over the dice in her cupped hands, shook and tumbled them over the felt-topped camp table. This time they came up borage, for bluntness and courage, and lavender, for distrust.

"That's more on the mark. So, which is it? Indifferent to whom and faithful to whom?" Grisaudra did not throw the dice a third time, not at all sure she wanted a clearer answer to her question.

❧

It was a velvet cloak, faced with silk in a pattern of poppies. Unable to sleep, Hodge had found the cloak on a midnight excursion to the camp pantry. The cloak was hung on a nail behind a net of onions. The lining threw back the lamp's gleam and caught the lion tamer's eye. Hodge worked the bundle loose and shook out its folds.

"Very pretty! Just the thing for the greatest lion tamer in the thirteen kingdoms. A puzzle what it's doing here— can it be the cook's? Does she mean to make rags of it? It falls to Hodge, then, to rescue it. Such a cloak as this is not meant to languish on a pantry hook among the onions."

Pausing to help himself to bacon and cheese, Hodge put on the cloak and wore it back to his tent. Once there, he took out the shears he used to trim Rollo's mane, cut the hood from the cloak, and, turning it inside out, fashioned himself a turban, fastening it with an old shoe buckle.

"Yes—much better to have it pattern side out, as pretty a silk as this. It's a bit dizzying, though. Puts me in mind of the wallpaper favored by a certain hothouse variety of lady. Now, what to do with the rest of it?" He held the cloak up, turning it this way and that, tugging it on the bias to test the stretch, draping it around his middle.

"No—too thick altogether to make a decent sash. Perhaps pantaloons? I'll need to get some butcher paper from the kitchen and cheesecloth to make a test pair with."

The cook looked him over sullenly but handed over the paper, letting him cut all he wanted from the bolt of cheesecloth himself. All the same, Hodge couldn't help wishing as he returned to his own tent that Folderol would find someone else to be the cook. The bread was always hard as bricks, the milk sour, the potatoes green and hard.

And her soups, no matter that they burned the roof of your mouth, never seemed to fill or even warm you.

Hodge was not handy with patterns, and it was not too late when he threw the scissors down with a curse and a yawn.

"Glory, I'm weary! This will wait until tomorrow." With that he threw himself down on his cot, too tired even to remove the poppy-covered turban from his head.

Toward morning, Ulfra woke and sat up, shrugging off the blanket of sleeping wolves. Drawing on her ragged soldier's coat but not bothering to button it or to put on shoes, she crept out into the paling night to look for Nix.

He was curled at the sleeping lion's breast, shivering with cold and fright, as if her light tread and the rasp of the cage door had wakened him from a nightmare. His thin arms went automatically about Ulfra's neck, and he buried his white, milkweed-tufted head under her chin. Ulfra bared her teeth at the smell of Otherworld, strong all around the lion's cage. On close inspection, however, Nix seemed to have encountered no terror in the night any more dangerous than a toffy apple.

Ulfra carried the boy back to their tent and tucked the sleeping wolves well around him. Even though he was half-asleep, she fed Nix some rum and milk with a spoon before climbing into bed herself.

But Ulfra slept no more that night. She lay wakeful, shivering at the whistle of the wolves' snoring, starting every time Nix twitched in a dream. When at last it came, never had a creature of moonlight and shadow been so glad of morning.

Hodge was not missed until he failed to appear for the afternoon's first performance. Folderol stormed into Hodge's tent, prepared to sack him for drunkenness, only to find the lion tamer dead where he had fallen.

"Mauled," he said, tossing back a second tumbler of brandy. "Damn, we'll have to poison the lion, and I'll have lost them both. What a rotten morning's work this has been!"

"But surely not Rollo," said the Badger. "For the love of reason, he hasn't a sound tooth in his head!"

Folderol had to admit that. What was more, the lion's false teeth were found on Hodge's nightstand, where he had left them after giving them a nightly polish.

"And surely even *you* don't believe Rollo took his teeth out and polished them and left them there," said Elric.

Folderol frowned. "I might not believe it, and you might not believe it, but the whole rest of the troupe is frightened enough to credit anything just now. It's easier for them to believe in a wild beast returning to his man-eating ways than to believe one of us slipped in with a knife to do him in."

But when Folderol went to the lion's cage, he found the door open and no sign of Rollo. The orange cat sat curled inside the lion's dish, licking the last traces of Rollo's supper from her fur. Nix was questioned, but no amount of bullying or promises of toffy apples could get him to admit to letting the lion out of his cage. The boy only squatted in the dust, placing the doll's saucer span of his hand in the dint, as deep and wide as a soup plate, that was Rollo's paw print.

10

SAPPHIRE

The knight dispatched to Chameol was a recent recruit,
an attempt of Iiliana's to rehabilitate some of the Cavekin,
the cast-off children dwelling in caves by the sea and living
off the jetsam from shipwrecks. When any among their
number began to show signs of "getting big," he or she
was unceremoniously turned out into the world, supplying
the thirteen kingdoms with a steady stream of pickpockets,
horse thieves, and fourth-rate tutors and governesses.

Fiddle, as he was called, had grown half a foot during
a summer spent in the saddle and in the classroom, losing
his weird Cavekin gibberish and mastering the thirteen
dialects of the kingdoms. His sunburn had faded to a rich
nut brown, and the attentions of a barber and a dentist
had worked wonders. Unlike most Cavekin, Fiddle liked
the water and could swim like an otter. This had been the
chief factor in his being chosen over all the other knights
to investigate the strange silence on Chameol. Scavenging
among shipwrecks had made Fiddle an expert diver adept
at maneuvering between splintered hulls and slippery submerged rocks.

He treaded water now just off the hidden bay. There
was no sign of the dolphins, only a lone seal barking at

the sun the way an innkeeper's mongrel barks at the moon. The mournful sound, more than the cold water, made Fiddle shiver.

There were stairs cut into the cliff face, slick with the moss it was someone's daily chore to scour away; Fiddle slipped and nearly tobogganed halfway down again on his belly. He was more careful after that but wished he might have scaled the cliff itself, a simple enough feat for him but one forbidden, as it would have made him too conspicuous.

He scaled the garden wall and dropped silently to all fours in the soft grass, grown quite high. There was a thick silence, as though he were underwater. Ass! he said to himself, shrugging off the creepy feeling. It's only because the birds aren't singing.

Why was it, then, that his heart beat faster the closer he drew to the palace itself? It was white, scoured bright as coral by the sunlight, and there was something about the way the shadows played on its galleries and porches that reminded him of the ghostly hull of a wreck underwater. Around him in the garden the ferns swayed in the breeze as if the swells of the sea and not the wind stirred them, and out of the corner of one eye Fiddle took a shower of leaves for the sudden kite's swerve and plummet of a school of fish.

The Cavekin knew the sea often kept the best treasures for herself, and so a few of their number who had grown big were allowed to remain so long as they agreed to dive to the wrecks and bring back highly prized commodities: crocks of gooseberry jam, knives still keen and bright, and the checkerboard they used to divine solutions to all matters of dispute.

Fiddle himself had grown past the mark on the cave wall at which even most divers were cast out. He had been suffered to remain because he knew the wrecks so well and came back with his net bags full of riches: silver spoons, a hand mirror, a waterlogged ham. But one day he came back empty-handed and would never dive again, though he never told anyone why. He had swum through one splintered hull only to come upon a bunk room of drowned sailors, snoring water, counting fish, and dreaming of their last breath of air.

Now he half expected to turn a corner in the palace and find them again, and when he saw the first roomful of sleepers his heart nearly leapt from his mouth in fright.

"You fool, Fiddle!" he said aloud. "They're only sleeping."

But it was a sleep from which he could awaken none of them. He slammed windows, stamped around the room, hurled a basin to the floor, and still they slept on. And, half because he remembered it from some old story, but mostly because they were all extremely pretty girls his own age, he tiptoed around the room and kissed them all as they slept.

"It takes a prince, I suppose," he said, shrugging. Fiddle left that room, but not before he had kissed the prettiest again, just to make sure.

He tore down the halls, forgetting all knightly caution, hallooing at the top of his lungs, when he turned into a doorway and found himself in the chamber where Caitlin lay asleep. It was a long moment, his heart thrumming, that he stood by the door, summoning the courage to approach the bed where her blue-black hair lay spread on the pillow. When at last he did, Fiddle was too scared to kiss her and could only step up and shake her. But his hand passed all the way through her shoulder, though she looked solid enough, and he felt the mattress beneath. The hair stood up on the back of Fiddle's neck, and he backed out of the room on tiptoe.

The cheek had quite gone out of him by the time he found Iiliana. Her room was full of pigeons, perched on the frame of the mirror and on the canopy of the bed and even on Iiliana's shoulders where she dozed on the sofa. Each bird wore an unanswered message on its leg. Fiddle did not need to read them to know what they said. Some of the pigeons, having eaten everything else in the room, had started to peck at the cakes of rouge and crumbs of talc on Iiliana's dresser.

Grimald was asleep, too, though out of exhaustion rather

than enchantment; his squalling had worn out even a goblin's considerable stamina. Fiddle looked at him and, not seeing his goblin's eyes, thought him only a particularly ugly baby.

Fiddle roused Pomamber, murmuring in her ear a promise of giblets and gravy. The mastiff padded down the hall after her newfound benefactor, it taking something much stronger than enchantment to keep a dog and a boy from ransacking a pantry when the whole of a household is asleep.

∞

Caitlin and Newt left Pj'aurinoor half asleep, her eyes narrowed to crescent moons, growling happily into her whiskers about rabbits.

As Caitlin made her way out of the fields of tiger's eye, Newt twined his tail tightly in Caitlin's belt and read aloud another passage from Ylfcwen's court etiquette.

Tipping

It is a grave insult to tip anyone of full elvish blood, and customs vary widely regarding gratuities for goblins. One can never go wrong, however, in leaving a tip for weavers and other human interlopers. The preferred currency is dried jasmine flowers or dragonfly wings; when the interloper has accrued his weight in these, he may purchase his freedom, a plain brown suit of clothes, and passage to the surface. In practice, this is seldom done, since most interlopers returning to the human realm are taken for madmen and conducted to the nearest asylum. (An exception to the rule about tipping among elves is granted on the evening before the feast ushering in the orchid harvest, on which occasion elven young give their elders silver pieces of human minting, which are then melted down and fashioned into useful implements.)

The passage made Caitlin shiver, for it put her in mind of a man she had seen once, in the days she lived in a barrow on the moor. She had met him in the marketplace;

he was raving outside a baker's shop. His skin had a phosphorescent pallor and his eyes an uneasy brightness, and he wore a suit of clothes the color of earth. He had not fled at the sight of her, a witch in bells, and when out of pity Caitlin had pressed on him some of her own bread he had laughed, filling her hands with glimmering moondust from his pockets: wilted flowers giving off a crushed fragrance, a powder of dragonfly's wings.

A nip on her earlobe brought her back to herself. Newt had regained his perch on her shoulder to murmur, "Where are we?"

Caitlin held up the canary orchid; its glow brightened but showed nothing but the same passageway, paved with uncut gems, such as they had traveled along since leaving Ylfcwen. *How much further it is we have no way of knowing,* she thought. Caitlin had a sudden uneasy vision of herself emerging at last into the final chamber, an old woman, to find Bram already a grown man with no memory of his mother.

Enough of such elvish thoughts. Newt chided her gently, but did not bite Caitlin's ear. *As the elf queen said, our only way lies forward.*

❧

It was a workday like any other. The goblins descended by cart into the depths of the gemfields and upon reaching the appointed site assembled in rows, while their captain led them through the oath of allegiance. Then Ylfcwen's silver banner was raised on a pulley set into the rock, the canary orchids set into recesses in the wall, and pickaxes began to ring on the stone.

They were working emeralds today. The captain sorted the rough stones by size and grade, the poorer ones destined for a workshop that would turn them into chips for mosaics and beads for embroidery. Gems larger than a fist were set aside to be taken to Ylfcwen; all the rest were piled into carts to be sent to the lapidary.

One goblin, taller than the rest, paused to lean on his pickax, listening to the sound of the mine carts on the runners, remembering the tales his father had once told him of sleigh rides through the snows of Ninthmoon that made him deaf with the wind and numb from the cold and blinded by the eddying snow. His father was one of the weavers, his mother none less than Ylfcwen herself; with such a pedigree the goblin might have remained at court and enjoyed all the privileges and favors due one of the queen's favorites. But he preferred the company of goblins to that of elves; the whole court seemed to him to reek of the slow decay of orchids, and the sight of his father, blank eyes in a face flushed with root wine, made his blood rage.

The miner picked up his ax and soon fell into the rhythm of the other pickaxes. He had not struck a dozen blows when the captain blew a short blast on a whistle pitched too high for human ears, and the lamps were doused and the goblins took cover under the rubble and in side tunnels. The elf queen's son did not grumble with the rest, though he didn't like these trespasser drills any more than the others.

On this occasion it proved not to be a drill. A human tread echoed in the tunnel, and the miner barely had time to shrink into the darkness when a woman passed within a few inches of his hiding place. The canary orchid around her neck showed the woman's face, a perfect moonstone set with a sapphire and an emerald. She was soon lost in the shadows along the tunnel, and in a moment two long shrills of the whistle declared the all clear. Soon the miner had entered into speculation with his neighbors as to what the lunch cart would bring that day.

∾

Bram woke in a black, chill silence, drew a breath to cry, and could only sigh and shudder.

A hand, white as death and cold as stone, drew over the child a blanket of ravens' feathers. Bram's eyes closed as though they had been drawn shut, and he slept.

On a nearby table lay an inlaid game board, and on it stood game pieces of ebony and lemonwood. A mirror of crystal, highly polished and hinged like a book, stood open in a bookstand. On the pages images and words formed, swirled, and reformed. When the hand reached out to touch the page, the image was frozen: Caitlin lifting the canary orchid to light the tunnel, Grisaudra tattooing Elric's back, Ulfra and Nix resting among the wolves, Grimald and Iiliana sleeping while a cloud of pigeons rose and settled around them.

The hand rose again to lift a game piece of ebony, moving it from a part of the game board set with tiger's eyes to a part inlaid with sapphire. Bram stirred and sleepily kicked the blanket of feathers from his legs. The hand, veins empty of the blood of humans or of elves, a hand enormously old but without the signs of age, drew the blanket of raven feathers carefully back into place.

❧

Everything before Caitlin suddenly turned blue. The tunnel opened into a wide chamber paved with cobalt and lighted through panels of blue stone set into the ceiling. It was like being beneath the waves; Caitlin felt a sudden memory of weightlessness and the embrace of sea-flax and the seal's bristly kiss.

The floor of the chamber, too, might have been at the bottom of the sea rather than deep within the earth: old sea chests gaped to show rusty maws full of pearls, and the strange shapes of the rocks might have been coral. There was a large rock in the corner that looked exactly like an old man bent over a book.

Just then the rock looked up, and Caitlin started so that Newt lost his grip and barely caught hold of the hem of her robe on the way down.

"You're not blue," he said in a voice of displeasure. The old man was blue, with a face like blue cheese and eyes like cornflowers and fingernails so dark he might have lived on nothing but blueberries. What of his hair was not covered by a pointed cap was the blue of wood smoke. Even his tongue was blue.

"Just the one eye, I'm afraid," she said. "These must be Ylfcwen's sapphire fields."

"Oh, not Ylfcwen's!" The old man blushed indigo. "No one owns these fields but Drusian. Ylfcwen may by rights mine them, but she by no means *owns* them. What is your name, then?"

"Caitlin."

"You may call me Cerulean: it's as good as any of the others. Have you any blue blood in you?"

"I was left in the woods as a baby, so it's as likely to be blue as any other color. It's certainly blue now, from cold if nothing else."

Cerulean stirred up the blue fire and bade her come forward to warm herself at it. As she stretched her hands toward the heat, Caitlin saw Cerulean had been writing in a great book. The old man drew a blotter over the page before she could do more than see it was an inventory written in blue ink in a small, neat hand.

"Just some jottings—only my little game. Are you quite warm now?"

"Yes—am I far from Drusian's chambers?"

Cerulean would not meet Caitlin's eye as he answered. "Oh, one would always hope to be far from those chambers! You are quite near, if you really mean to reach them. What business do you have there?"

"Something of my own to reclaim. Are you a toll-taker for him, too?"

Cerulean sighed. "No—nothing that happy! I stole from Drusian something of incalculable age and immense power—pawned my soul for it. A stone—"

"A sapphire—?"

The old man's eyes snapped, and he shook his head. "More than a sapphire! The Bluenose—the seer's stone smuggled out of Th'teenmoon by the queen who was young Unger's bride. She dressed as a crone and hid the gem in a potato. It was lifetimes later I chanced on it— and stole it. But not from human hands; at least, not living ones. I was a relic-seller then—a grave robber, to call the calling by its true name."

Caitlin remembered another relic-seller she had known, and her hand went out of habit to the spot at her throat where her catstone had once nestled. Instead of touching the amulet, her hand closed on Newt, who had curled his feet in the lacings of her bodice and was pretending to be a pewter brooch of a dragon.

"As a punishment, Drusian set me to a task so immense I shall never finish it: to complete *The Book of Blue*."

Caitlin knew of it: a long nonsense poem begun by a king mad with grief for his dead bride, a young queen with blue eyes. It was a book long lost, sought out by seers who in reading it hoped to find wisdom among the madness. Between love poems to his wife, the king had begun a catalog of blueness, a list of all the shades, from smoke to steel to thin milk, a census of everything blue.

"It would have been easier to set me counting all the stars in the heavens or all the grains of sand on the shores of the sea. Take *blue-cap*, now. It can signify a serving maid, a titmouse, a cornflower, a kind of ale, or a sort of worthless blue stone."

Caitlin's mind was hatching a plan; whether it was to be successful rested on whether Cerulean still possessed the soul of a relic-seller.

"What would you give," she asked, "for the name of a new blue thing?"

"Much, if there was such a thing. But"—here Cerulean sighed—"I wouldn't wager much on it."

"Would you wager passage to Drusian's chambers?"

Cerulean took off and twisted his pointed cap, as if trying to wring an answer out of it, then punched it into a cone again and pulled it down over his ears. "Not to those chambers. You must pass through the field of serpentine first. But I will tell you the secret for passing safely to Drusian's very portal. In return you must name something blue that is new to me."

"And if I cannot?"

"Then you must take my place and copy out for me a page of *The Book of Blue*." Cerulean rubbed his hands together. "Agreed?"

Caitlin smiled crookedly. "Beware such barters, old man. I bartered with a relic-seller once and lost. But the relic-seller lost even more. If I relieve you, how do I know you'll come back or that I won't finish the page to find a few hundred years have passed? Remember, my business is with Drusian. Surely," she said, lowering her voice a notch, "you would not risk his wrath?"

Cerulean wadded his cap into a ball. "You would copy only a page—so that I might creep so far as the edge of the sapphire field and glimpse a bit of something green. . . ."

Looking around the chamber, Caitlin felt a pang for him, imagining how relentless the press of blue must be on Cerulean's eye—as well as on his reason.

"Very well," the chronicler of blue said, composing himself a bit. "Let's begin. Tell me of something blue."

Caitlin's eye fell first on the blue columns of *The Book of Blue*. "On Chamool, there is an ancient runebook and in it—"

Cerulean interrupted her with an impatient wave of his hand. "Yes, yes, yes: three ribbons, one-green-one-silver-one-blue, and a forget-me-not pressed by you when you were six years old between the eighty-second and eighty-third pages. And a blue moth that met its end napping on page four hundred one." Cerulean looked at Caitlin balefully. "I thought you were going to tell me something *new.*"

Newt's teeth nipped Caitlin, pinching her through the stuff of her gown. *You ought to know better than to underestimate a relic-seller. That's how you lost your amulet the first time.*

Well, if you're quite through napping, you might lend a hand, she answered crossly. *Some seer's glass you are.*

Newt's only answer was to fill Caitlin's mind with a picture of her old barrow on the moor and of a long-dead warrior's ring set with a blue stone. Again, the words were hardly out of Caitlin's mouth when Cerulean broke into her tale.

"—and inscribed To ALFRED, with a small chip on the stone." Cerulean flipped through a few pages of *The Book of Blue* and ran a finger down a column. "Here it is, under 'Tokens of Affection, Miscellaneous Rings.' "

Caitlin began to despair a little, and in her nervousness her hand crept to the spot where her cat amulet had lain, closing on the glass salamander. Instantly, she was among the seals again, in the gold and dark-green fronds of the sea-flax, hearing the seal speech she had so quickly forgotten, understanding it again. What she heard was a tale like a remembered dream. Submerged in so much blueness,

Caitlin's green eye seemed to give out the only light in the room.

"Not a year ago a bundle was thrown from a sailing ship, the *Double Dolphin,* some oddments wrapped up in cloth and tied with a leather lace."

"You are going to tell me, I suppose, what was in the bundle?"

"Two things, I know: the others I can guess. A prayerbook, to give it the weight to take it to the bottom; a recorder, broken in half. Two things I would stake my life were in it: two glass marbles, one green, the other blue. This bundle sank to the bottom of the Strait of Chameol, where it came to rest at last in the belly of a whale, and it rests there still."

This was not entirely true. Unknown to Caitlin, the undigestible bundle had caused the whale a great deal of discomfort, and after a few hours of indigestion the creature had expelled the bundle with such force that it split open. The prayerbook had sunk to the bottom, puzzling the ancient eels before it was furred over with sea grass. One marble, the green one, made a fisherman rich, for many would pay to wonder at a lobster pulled from the sea with a glass eye. Of the blue one, nothing more was known, above or below the waves.

It was enough for Cerulean. Well pleased, he blued his tongue with the nib of his pen (or inked his nib on his tongue), and entered the story of the marble in his venerable catalog, under "Talismans, Lost and Mislaid."

Caitlin had heard the tale from the seals, and her own knowledge of the Badger had filled in the missing details. If he had had hair enough to cut or a sealskin to shed, he would have undertaken such a metamorphosis. As it was, the only way he could think of to purge his heart was to send every remnant of the past, every memory of Thirdmoon and especially of Caitlin, to find its rest among the coral porches and watery gardens of the sealfolk.

Cerulean had to touch her shoulder to bring her to herself and tell her the safe way through the fields of serpentine.

"Do not trust your eyes there, not even if they're seer's

eyes. What is down is up, and what is not can seem very real. Do not go forward or backward, left or right, but in the one direction you think you cannot go, for that is the only safe way."

That was all the warning he would give her; when Caitlin left him, she was still uncertain whether Serpentine was a gem or a person or some other kind of creature. She did not guess it named all three.

"So," Newt said, when they had left Cerulean to his task. "What sort of seer's glass do you think I am now?"

"Still an odd one. You've shown me the past as often as you've shown me the future."

"Hmm." Newt twined his toes in Caitlin's hair. "The one world doesn't know what the Otherworld is doing."

"What is that supposed to mean?"

"Just that running pell-mell into the Otherworld may bring you up short, face-to-face with your past. There was a time before these walls were built, when the one world and the Otherworld were the same, when memory of the future was not a gift given to seers alone. Though I wonder, sometimes, whether you have such a gift at all, to rise to Ylfcwen's bait like a whippet after a stuffed hare."

"Bait? What do you mean?"

"Has your love of Bram so blinded you that you can't see you're the prize they want?"

And no matter how Caitlin cajoled and threatened him, Newt would say no more; he curled tight into a ball and went to sleep.

THE FIRE-EATER

It was a source of no little amusement to the rest of Folderol's band that Pyle, the fire-eater, did not like any spice in his food. He waved away the pepper mill and would not partake of anything that was hot to the palate; none, in other words, of the Badger's favorite foods. To the Badger, raised on such abbey fare as suet pudding, the spices and relishes of the taverns and courts had been a revelation. Grisaudra had brewed him a bottle of hot sauce to render the cook's green potatoes and watery soups edible.

"Well!" said the Badger, swinging a leg over the bench where thin, sallow Pyle was sitting. "If it isn't the fire-eater who would eat no fire!"

"Wait and see," Pyle replied with placid good humor. "When you go, the apothecary will open you up and find your stomach as full of holes as a sieve."

The Badger grinned and uncorked the bottle. Across the table, Elric eyed the concoction and tried to conceal his unease. He did not like the idea of Grisaudra brewing potions for anybody, even if the only power they had was to raise a blister on the roof of one's mouth. He had been able to think of no way to caution the Badger without alerting Grisaudra, and there had been no opportunity to replace the stuff with a bottle of pepper sauce bought in town. So far, the Badger had suffered no ill effects from this latest potion of Grisaudra's. Apparently all the spell-seller had added to the mixture of vinegar and honey and pepper was her own devotion.

The fourth ingredient seemed to have had as little an effect as the other three. The only object that seemed to excite the Badger's imagination was Ulfra. There was something about her, something in her wolvish gait, in the mane of dark hair, in the narrowed ice-blue wolvish eyes, that was a magnet for his gaze. The Badger scolded himself: *She, just a child, and half-wolf at that.* But the sight of her, wandering the edge of the camp at dawn or dusk, dressed in her soldier's coat, her arm around the neck of the old mother wolf, made the Badger's throat go dry.

One of the acrobats, Magda, had taken Ulfra under her wing and taught her some tumbling tricks. In the process Ulfra had lost some of her bent-kneed gait and had begun to walk with a grace that said "woman" as much as "wolf." Magda had given Ulfra the present of a hairbrush, which Ulfra used on the wolves until shown a better use for it one day after an accident with some honey. Once Nix had coaxed the worst of the snarls out, Ulfra found she enjoyed having her hair brushed. She rejected Magda's well-meant gift of a gown but did surrender her soldier's coat for a riding kit, breeches, and a fitted jacket of green leather.

But Folderol did not want his wild wolf-girl to look too tame, lest the troupe's take suffer, so before she entered the ring Ulfra took her hair out of its plait and used a little honey hairdressing to lend the proper feral dishevelment.

Neither Elric nor Grisaudra was much pleased with the blossoming of the wolf-girl. Elric worried that Caitlin's memory could not hope to regain its place in the Badger's heart if Ulfra had replaced her there. To Grisaudra, Ulfra was a dangerous rival for the Badger's affections, nearly as like Caitlin as any apparition Grisaudra could conjure with all her drops and potions.

That evening Elric stopped by Grisaudra's tent while the Badger was giving the horses their evening hot bran and cod-liver oil. He found the conjurer seated at a small folding table, her marked cards spread out before her in the crossed-star pattern of a love-fortune. As Elric came in, she swept the cards into her lap and looked up.

He did not wait for an invitation but drew a chair to the table and took his seat. "I think it's time we gave the Badger another dose of those drops of yours."

Grisaudra looked genuinely startled. "Why?"

"Have you watched him lately?" *But then, when did you ever tear your eyes away?* He takes his eyes from her long enough to catch a good wink's sleep. I swear, if she were to dive off the edge of a cliff he'd plunge right over it after her."

Grisaudra stared thoughtfully into the fire. "You said the only cure for his amnesia would be for him to remember her on his own."

"Well, if we don't do something soon, he may *never* remember her. He'll fall in love with Ulfra and raise a pack of howling brats with noses too sharp and ears too big to be canny."

Grisaudra abruptly stood and began snatching bundles of dried herbs from the tent pole as if racing to take washing down from the line before a storm. She began to crumble the herbs between her hands into a bowl.

"I've never used the drops twice on anybody before. There's no telling what might happen."

Elric laughed unkindly. "No, no telling *what* might happen! Heaven forbid, he might even *remember* her."

Grisaudra did not look up, but she stopped rolling the dried leaves between her palms to crush them. "And just what do you mean by that, pray tell?"

"Oh, come now, Grisaudra. Tell me, which is it you take me for, a blind man or a fool?"

"Mad, for as much sense as you're making at the moment."

"All right, I'll spell it out for you: You won't give the Badger the drops because he might remember Caitlin, and where would that leave you?"

She laughed. "I was wrong. You're mad *and* a fool."

"I think not. I've been watching you ever since you

showed up so conveniently when he was taken with fever.
I was afraid that pepper sauce you'd brewed up for him
was poison, but now I know it can't be anything stronger
than a love posset. God, what an idiot I was to take the
poor wretch to you in the first place!" The look on her
face was something awful, but Elric's tongue had run away
with him, and he could not stop.

Grisaudra flung out an arm blindly in Elric's direction
and sent the bowl of herbs skating off the end of the table,
scattering pottery and releasing the bruised fragrance of
late-summer meadow. The blood seemed to drain from
her face, and she gripped the edge of the table so tightly
that the veins stood out in her hands like cords.

"Couldn't I say the same of you?" she said in a low
voice. "Perhaps Ulfra will bring Caitlin's memory to life
again and leave you no chance to woo her yourself. But
with the drops, there would be the chance he could be
made to believe Ulfra *was* Caitlin. . . ."

"You're crazier than even I gave you credit for being."

She laughed. "It's no use denying it, Elric. I didn't need
to steal a hair from your pillow to divine *that*. Did you
know that you talk in your sleep? Shall I tell you what
you say?"

He lunged for her across the table but succeeded only
in toppling the wooden rack of vials that held the various
extracts and oils Grisaudra used for composing her drops.
Elric turned his head too late and caught the splash of
stinging liquid in his eyes.

Grisaudra grabbed the pitcher of rainwater and tried to
bathe his eyes, but Elric shook her off.

"You'd better let me. Heaven knows what's got in your
eyes out of that mess."

He only stared at her with an awful look. What he saw,
Grisaudra could only guess; the accident had married
changeable oils and distilled marsh vapors that she herself
would never have dared combine. They stood and stared
at each other in a terrible silence, and then he turned and
was gone.

Grisaudra began to sweep up the scattered herbs to see
whether there was anything worth saving. But the smell

of their crushed sweetness conjured up her own imaginings, in which the Badger and a summer meadow figured greatly, so that the sight of the chair Elric had overturned made the conjurer burst into bitter tears.

❧

It was a mercy to Elric to find the Badger absent from the tent they shared. God! He was shaking like a man who had seen a murder or done one. In the bit of mirrored glass that hung over the basin he looked murdering mad.

"Damn her!" Whether he was damning Grisaudra for her shrewdness or Caitlin for unwittingly making a misery of his life, Elric himself wasn't sure.

Had he really allowed himself to fall in love with her? And was he really so mean of spirit and small of heart to wish the Badger's memory away, so that with time and persuasion Caitlin might be taught to love another? On Chameol, even to speak such a thing would be enough to lose him his knighthood, earn him banishment. This was the mystery, though: that Elric had long felt himself a man stripped of his best reason for living, had felt dishonored, disowned, and disgraced, a man banished to the edge of madness. Would he really have come so close to striking Grisaudra if she in turn had not struck a nerve?

The Badger came in from tending to the horses and looked at Elric curiously.

"Are you all right?"

"Do I look otherwise?"

"A little ragged around the edges. You winced when I came in."

He pleaded an earache and had to force down the toddy the Badger brought him, had to swallow, too, the gossip the Badger told him to mask his concern. The Badger had sweetened the wine with honey, but Elric thought the bitter taste of his guilt would choke him all the same. He wished he might forget for a little while the woman another man must be brought to remember loving.

The drops, after all, had only shown him Caitlin stumbling through the snow, a pack of farmers' hounds at her heels. As the toddy lulled Elric off to a fitful doze, the scene continued in his dreams, only now it was Ulfra leading her wolves on a chase through the winter woods.

After he had dosed his patient, the Badger went out. He found Pyle at the makeshift forge set up to shoe the horses.

"I was a farrier, you know, before I fell in with Folderol. But I didn't like it much. There wasn't a living to be made in horseshoes, and I hated to feed my family with bread made from swords and armor." Pyle laughed, turning a small piece of iron he was working in the fire. "In the end, though, I was put in debtor's prison, and when I got out my wife and children had moved on. The Widow Pyle, they called her! I suppose when you go to debtor's prison you *are* as good as dead."

Pyle took the tongs from the fire and did some delicate hammering and cajoling of the hot metal, returning it to the fire briefly before plunging it into the trough of water.

"That is a good way to start, if you've any ambition to be a fire-eater. You have to know the uses of fire before you can begin to master its fancies and deceits. There," he said, "I think we can take a look now."

It was not a cloak pin, as the Badger had thought, but a hair clasp formed of an intricate iron knot.

"Here," said Pyle, handing the Badger the tongs, "take a closer look."

In the lamplight the Badger could see in the pattern of whorls and knots the stylized head of a wolf.

"For Ulfra?"

"Yes. I thought these recent improvements should be encouraged. I have a bit of a soft spot for Ulfra; she reminds me of one of my daughters." Pyle took the ornament and turned it over in his hands, hands too callused and scarred over to be burned. Then the fire-eater threw back his head and laughed, a robust guffaw surprising from one so thin and sallow. "Ah, yes," he said, wiping his eyes. "She does remind me of Penny. Penny never *would* wash."

The Badger stood and shivered at the sight of the smoke and steam rising in the mingled lights of the lamp and the moon. The smell of hot iron had brought streaming back a hundred kindred sensations from his days at the abbey: the smell, like burnt hair, of the hot shoe put to the hoof; the whine of the knives on the knifegrinder's stone; bells calling him to prayers; the cock's crow, to chores; and the whispered absolution of the old mare in his ear.

The memory struck him with the force of an actual blow: the nape of a woman's neck where the plait begins, the back of the neck of a woman seated before him on a horse.

The vision was gone as quickly as it had come; even as he tried to fix the picture in his mind it was lost, the edges lost first in a grey mist and finally in a black shadow.

Pyle's hand on his shoulder brought the Badger back to himself. Pyle looked at him closely.

"Seen a ghost?"

"In a manner of speaking."

He turned away from Pyle's tale of a knifegrinder turned sword swallower as soon as he could without being rude. Once out of sight, the Badger paused to lean against a sign he had painted for Folderol, showing Ulfra dressed in a wolf's skin. YOU MARVELED AT THE LEOPARD-WOMAN, the sign bawled in crimson lettering. NOW BE ASTONISHED AT THE WILD WOLF-GIRL AND HER PACK OF DIREWOLVES.

The Badger rubbed the inside of his forearms, suddenly remembering the rasp of rough wool against his skin as he had reached his arms around her to hold the reins. The wind had blown the sting of sea salt into his eyes and whipped strands of ebony hair into his face. The Badger stared at his own handiwork, the picture meant to draw crowds to see Ulfra. It was really nothing like her. Too old, for one thing; for another, Nix had upset the blue paint pot, so the Badger had had to use green for the other eye. No, it was nothing like Ulfra at all.

❧

Nix liked to watch Pyle swallow his "savory," the small bit of fire he ate for luck before going to bed. He would take a little lamp oil and brandy in his mouth, then ignite the mixture from a flaming torch. The amount had to be exact, so that the fire would have burned itself out without burning through to his tongue and throat. Each time he did this, whether for practice or before paying patrons, Pyle would swallow a spoonful or so of lamp oil, and over the years this had taken its toll on his liver. This was the reason he took no artificial fire with his meat. In a short time Pyle knew his liver would force him to give up this line of work and go back to shoeing horses.

Pyle now exhaled a curling stream of fire several feet into the air with no more concern than if it had been a plume of pipe smoke. Blowing fire rings was one feat he vowed to do before he retired, but as yet he had not mastered it.

The fire now out, Nix handed Pyle a tumbler of milk. This ruined the effect onstage, but in practice Pyle allowed himself the soothing tonic.

"You're surely a strange kid. Why don't you ever say anything, I wonder?" the fire-eater mused aloud. The brandy worked Pyle's brain as much as the lamp oil vexed his liver, but Nix ignored this address and only put out a finger to nudge the torch and tickle the flask of lamp oil and brandy.

"I bet you could tell some tales, if you wanted, you and the wolf-girl. And so could I, if I had a mind. Queer doings I've seen around here, queer indeed. No fewer than two knights of Chameol hiding out in Folderol's band—and I should know; I was one myself, once, and would be still, if I'd a steadier head and a stouter heart. And both these knights traveling, mind you, in the company of a Once-moon spell-seller with the face of an angel the devil took a dislike to. More of that one is for sale than her spells, unless I'm very mistaken, and I mean her soul, not just her famous curative embraces!"

Nix blinked and only sighed as Pyle confiscated the flask of lamp oil and brandy and offered the boy the rest of the milk instead. Nix drank, his hands small around the tumbler and his eyes huge over the rim of it.

"Knights of Chameol. I could indeed tell them a thing or two." Pyle rubbed his chin and let out his odd, outsized guffaw. "Yes, I've half a mind to— Come, lad, help me put all this away. I've an errand to run to our friend the duchess."

∽

Pyle's summons found the duchess still awake.

"All right, I'm up! No—we'll talk outside. You've awakened the dead, but one of the living's still asleep, at least."

Leaving the Badger to his slumbers, they went outside.

"And what is this errand that's so important that you must rob me of my beauty sleep?"

"A proposition."

"Oh my. Tell on."

"Oh, I shall," Pyle murmured into his collar. "I've a barter for you. Some information in return for a favor."

Elric shrugged; he'd come out without a shirt, and the shrug made the woman tattooed on his back appear to shudder, her tresses of living eels to writhe. "Tell me what sort of favor you think I have in my power to grant. As far as money goes, I'm afraid you'll find me a duchess much gone down in the world."

"No, something minted in a richer metal. A knighthood."

Elric bowed, grinning. "In the Order of Gawk and Grimace?" These were the caricature knights of the puppet shows.

"Indeed not. In the Order of Chameol itself."

Keeping his face carefully the same, Elric laughed. "They're one and the same: a child's fancy and a fool's figment. Come, man; whatever it is you've been drinking, I want a sip!"

Pyle snapped his fingers and a flame sprang up and danced in his palm; he snapped them again and it was gone. Elric felt the hair rise on the back of his neck.

Pyle wagged a scolding finger at him. "Now, now. What would Iiliana say to hear you speak so?"

The lady on Elric's back tossed her eerie curls again. "You've robbed some old magician of his tricks, bribed some drunken fool of a few meaningless passwords, and you've taken some wild notion that it should all mean something to me. Tell me how I should be impressed."

Pyle took out a pipe and lit it with a snap of his fingers.

"Is that a brother's love, to call his sister a meaningless password?"

Elric wondered through the layer of cold composure that lay over his panic how on earth Pyle could have learned any of it. The harlequin cat—the one that liked to kill songbirds—hissed and scared Elric out of his wits. He swore and kicked it away, thinking, I never even saw it. Where did it come from?

"Think, brother!" Pyle whispered urgently. "How else could I know these things? Why else would I live this wretched life, but that long ago I was sworn to Chameol and fell from her favor? All my life is now come to this: to win back what I once lost through cowardice and folly. And now I have found the means to do it. Have you never noticed the tent neither Ulfra nor Nix nor any of that pack will go near? The rats don't gnaw at the tent pole, and the moths leave the canvas alone. If you've a nose for smells of the inhuman kind—and eating fire has that effect on the sinuses—it reeks."

"Of Otherworld?"

Pyle shook his head, sober himself. "Of evil."

∽∾

The Badger woke to a strange noise, and slowly came to recognize it as scissors on paper. When he opened his eyes, he found it was Nix, sitting cross-legged in the middle of the tent, cutting out masks.

"That's quite a pile of masks you have there. Couldn't you sleep?"

Nix shook his head and held his handiwork up to his face. The first mask, hardly surprisingly, was a wolf with bared fangs and a lolling tongue. "Grrrrrrrrrrr!" said Nix.

The Badger allowed himself to be rent limb from limb. "Very nice. And this one?"

The second turned out to be the woman from the tattoo, each eel in her hairstyle cut out individually and fixed in a slot so that by pulling on a thread Nix could make them writhe very well. For all its mechanical ingenuity and vivid coloring, the Badger only shuddered and said nothing to praise it.

This mask held a surprise, however: a face painted on

the reverse, framed not with living eels but with hair of
jet shot with indigo. It was a pity the boy was not at court,
the Badger thought. He had a future as a portrait painter.

Nix moved a paper strip in its groove, and the eyes in
the mask changed color, from twins of icy blue to a mismatched pair of blue and green. The lady held the Badger's gaze with her own changeable one and planted on
his cheek a paper kiss.

"And what of this last one, the one you were working
on, Nix?"

It was a demon, a monster. More than that, it was an
evil intelligence: a face seamed with veins and scars, the
lip cleft, the tongue in the mouth purple as a serpent's.
The Badger stared at it with the horror not of nightmare
but of recognition. He tore it from the boy's face and cast
it into the fire.

Nix watched it curl to a lace of embers and ash. He
sighed the stuttering sigh of a child exhausted by its own
crying, even though his eyes were dry. Then he crawled
into the Badger's lap and buried his small snowy head
under the Badger's chin.

The Badger rocked the boy until he felt Nix's breathing
lapse into the easy canter of sleep. Still holding the sleeping boy, he wandered around the tent, lighting lamps and
muttering all the old childhood prayers he could remember, until, closer to dawn than to midnight, Elric returned
to the tent.

❧

The Badger dreamed.

He was in a prison cell, and Nix was at the grate in the
street. The Badger of the dream passed something through
the bars into Nix's small hand: two marbles, one green
and one blue.

"Find her."

He woke and found Ulfra standing over him, gazing
down at Nix where he slept, curled up in a blanket like a
motherless puppy, at the foot of the Badger's cot. She
bent to nuzzle the snowy hair, take the boy's pulse behind
his ear with her kiss. Her look to the Badger said, *Just
this once.* Then she was gone.

Find her, echoed the dream in his brain. But was it a dream, after all, or a memory?

∽∾∾

In the kitchen tent, the cook was composing a strange salad. She had gone to the town in the afternoon and stolen some greens from walled gardens; the rest of her medley she had plucked from the roadside as she made her way back to Folderol's camp.

"Here's rocket, for deceit, and moon-ruled purslane," the old woman recited, tearing the greenery between her hands. "And basil for spite and grief-struck marigold. Yes, this will do me very well." Then she dressed it all with oil and wormwood vinegar and set it by under a damp cloth to keep fresh while she prepared the rest of the meal.

The crow looked down from where it was steaming its feathers above the sighing kettle and murmured something that sounded like, "Pity, have pity-pity!" The cat wound round the cook's ankles, mewling a song of ruthlessness and begging for giblets.

∽∾∾

At lunch the Badger leaned over and peered jealously at Pyle's plate.

"Salad! Where did you get *salad*?"

Pyle winked at Grisaudra and kept forking the lightly oiled greenery into his mouth. A dish covered with a towel had appeared outside his tent with a note in a womanly hand: *Here is something more wholesome than anything to come out of the kitchen. From one who wishes you well.* Who but the herbwoman would have done such a thing? He would have to ask her what she had dressed it with: the flavor teased his tongue, its name just out of reach.

The Badger fished in his pockets. "Here, man—a half-silver for a bite of that. What do you say?"

The fire-eater's only answer was to throw back his head and plunge his fork, wrapped with the last leaf of rocket, halfway down his throat, as if swallowing a sword.

Grisaudra was puzzled. Why had he winked? She certainly knew too much about herbs to jumble them together in dangerous juxtapositions in a salad. Well, if people wanted to traipse through the countryside and graze on medicinals like a flock of sheep, Grisaudra supposed they would have to live with the consequences. She herself would rather have eaten fire, or worse, than rocket and marigold and basil together.

The hour before the first performance found Elric transforming himself into the duchess and the Badger tying bells to the horses' harnesses when a loud commotion erupted outside.

The troupe had gathered at the point where the river flowed closest the camp. A figure could be seen struggling in the strong current.

Grisaudra was standing apart from the rest, with Ulfra and Nix, when they came up.

"Who is it?"

"Pyle—"

"What happened?"

"He ran past, screaming and beating at his clothes, as though he were on fire, but there wasn't a spark—"

The Badger dove into the water and fought to free the fire-eater from the deadly river; like a ravenous giant, the river had been known to swallow barges and herds of cattle whole. Twice he had him, only to have the stronger pull of the river wrench the limp form from his grasp. Then Pyle was gone, and he himself was a prisoner of the water's grip.

And suddenly the Badger was battling the water for possession of his own memory. It was as if he struggled to break the cold and numbing embrace of a sorceress, the eels roping around his neck like a noose. In some watery pool, her captive, the beauty from the other side of Nix's mask, called out to him, a plea for help or a warning.

"No—let her go!" The Badger tried to cry out, but the river rushed into his mouth and silenced him. The enchantress drew a heavy dark curtain of water over his head, and he was swallowed by a great blackness, through which a blinding white light seemed to split his skull. Before the water hurtled him into unconsciousness, the Badger saw the two faces merge and melt into one, saw the evil face swallowed up in and consumed by the beauty

of the other. As his lungs filled with a great breath of the
river, the Badger knew there was only one woman and
that evil knew no part of her.

They fished the Badger out of the river on the end of
a pruning hook; of Pyle there was no longer any sign. The
Badger was at first more dead than alive, but by the time
most of the water had been pumped out of him the living
half had gained the upper hand. He opened his eyes,
which focused neither on Elric nor Grisaudra, who were
bending near, but on Ulfra. He spat river and spoke.

"Caitlin," he said.

12

SERPENTINE

Ylfcwen sat up in bed, snapping her wings open and shut while she thought. *Snap. Snap. Snap.* It was a terrible habit, of which her mother had tried with every ruse to break her. *You'll tear them right off if you keep that up!* Ylfcwen began to chew a thumbnail instead.

At last the elf queen rose and went to the wall covered with a living tapestry of violets. She parted the leaves to reveal a silver mirror black with tarnish. Ylfcwen breathed on the mirror to mist it, then knelt before it.

"Liege Drusian, I beg audience with you."

"Yes, daughter."

"The changeling we sent Above will die soon."

"As it must be with all goblins in the realm of men, once the substitution has been discovered."

Ylfcwen bit her lip. "But only if the human child remains with me. You have claimed this—this bram for yourself. What am I to get out of the bargain?"

"You did not cherish this goblin when you dispatched Ordella to effect the deception."

"No. One does not *cherish* a goblin, exactly. But one does not like to *waste* them."

The mirror went black, and the leaves and heads of the

violets curled toward it to conceal it again, indicating that this audience was at an end.

"Liege Drusian."

The mirror lightened a little, and the violets appeared to lift their heads.

"I would like permission to go Above."

"To what end?"

"To bring back what is mine."

∽∾

Though Caitlin and Newt did not consult it on the matter, the court etiquette had this to say on royal excursions to the realms of light and air.

Going Above

Members of court, when receiving a special dispensation to venture Above, must go forth dressed as if banished, in clothes the color of earth, though for the queen herself leaf green is permissible. To venture forth in full court dress of elven silk is not only ostentatious but dangerous, unless one wishes to live out the balance of one's allotted ten score and twenty as a sideshow or lap pet. Only two elf queens have ever been known to venture to the surface. Ygwynyd, having banished her human lover, was astonished to find she loved him and went to dwell with him as a human woman. The infamous Yvyola abandoned the court out of boredom and was last sighted running an inn on the coast near Chameol, where she lived under the name of Emma.

Ylfcwen settled on a suit of loam-colored fur, a cane, and round green spectacles; with her strange opal eyes she felt it wisest to move in the human world as a blind beggar woman. It would be a most useful disguise for, posing as one unseeing, she might move in the mortal world almost unseen.

Ylfcwen searched her mother's trinket box for some old silver coins, which she ordered melted down and reminted after the current fashion. She removed from her ivory hands all her jeweled rings and elvish seals of state and hung them from her waist in an old goatskin purse along with the coins. Then Ylfcwen stood back and laughed at herself in the looking glass.

"Yes, we have long fancied the idea of a holiday on Chameol!"

☙

Cerulean's directions brought Newt and Caitlin through a maze of side tunnels, and the stone walls on either side gradually changed hue, from deepest sapphire through a myriad of teals and aquamarines to the brilliant green of serpentine. Newt clambered from his napping place in Caitlin's pocket to her shoulder, where he bit her hard enough behind the ear to break the skin.

"Ow!" She put up a hand to the bite, which had already gone warmly pins and needles. "What was that for?"

"A little preventative. There are things here that will bite you with a far worse effect."

"Vipers?"

"Among other things." Newt did not elaborate on what these were, leaving Caitlin to conjure them in her own mind in dreadful variety.

It appeared that Serpentine, unlike Pj'aurinoor and Cerulean, did not boast a lofty chamber. Rather, the passage in front of them was suddenly honeycombed green rock, a maze of boxwood hedges turned to stone by some enchantment. Caitlin could not help but remember another maze and roses in the snow at Ninthstile. The memory of that brush with evil made her shudder.

Courage, Newt's mind murmured into her own. *You will need it here.*

Cerulean's odd words came back to her: "Do not go forward or backward, left or right, but in the one direction you think you cannot go, for that is the only safe way." There were forks in the tunnel to her left and right and a wall of green stone straight ahead. Caitlin walked straight ahead, and as she neared the wall, it suddenly was no longer made of stone but of living vipers, poised to strike. With her next footstep the vipers changed to stout briar branches, forming a solid wall of thorns, embedded with the armor of heroes lost in the attempt to cut through it. Caitlin was not a foot away when the wall shifted for the third time and became a barrier of white-hot steel. In the blast of heat Caitlin felt her eyelashes singe, and her tongue and eyes seemed on fire, leaving her mute and blind. "Nothing is as it seems," Cerulean's voice said in her mind. Blindly, Caitlin stepped forward into the white heat.

The wall vanished at her touch like mist, and she was facing another fork in the tunnel, with three choices this time instead of two. Behind her there was suddenly a wall and seemingly no return from the way she had come.

Why was it everything suddenly reminded her of something from the past? The maze at Ninthstile, the chamber of the dragon Ormr, and now the catacombs known as the Devil's Sieve.

Maybe that is the real weapon, Caitlin thought. *To keep me lost in a maze of my own memories, of places I was once, so I can't keep my mind on where I am now.* "Newt, I am going to close my eyes, and you must dowse my way for me."

"Do you think it wise to enter Serpentine's lair with your eyes closed?"

"Maybe not the wisest way, but it seems to me the only way."

"All right, then. Forward."

But simply closing her eyes was not enough to outwit the hallucinations. With her first step Caitlin felt herself slip from a cliff's edge and plummet through space. Newt's voice in her ear next steered her to the right, and her feet seemed to sink into the deadly ooze of a bog. The salamander then guided her around a bit of hanging rock.

"Duck your head," Newt said. "That's it. Now go to your left. . . ."

But before Caitlin could move, a voice, silky and sibilant, coiled around her in the darkness.

"If you please, watch where you step."

Caitlin opened her eyes to look full into the unblinking gaze of a pair of small black eyes. These were set rather too far apart to be human, in a long, flat head covered with jewellike scales. Two pinholes marked the nose; the mouth was wide and lipless. Of ears there was no evidence. The body itself took a more human shape, though there was a superfluity of arms, and the torso was covered with emerald scales. The lower half was draped in a voluminous robe of silk, the whole creature propped up on a heap of cushions brocaded in green-and-gold silk.

They had apparently interrupted a meal. Caitlin caught sight of a dish of quails' eggs before Serpentine drew a cloth over the rest.

"You will excuse me if I don't offer you any. For some reason, humans find my diet repulsive."

"Don't stop on my account. I doubt I would find it so. I have had to eat strange things myself out of necessity."

"That is kind of you, but then, you did not see what was in the other dishes." One of the arms beckoned Caitlin to a seat among the cushions, then offered a dish of pickled hummingbirds' eggs. When these were refused, Serpentine took one herself. "You intrigue me no little amount. No one has ever ventured so far into my lair, not even a seer."

"Not even Drusian?"

The glittering dark eyes betrayed no surprise. "No, Drusian would not honor me in such a manner. When I have a need, I solicit an audience. My needs have been few; we have a long and honorable understanding, Drusian and I."

"You both deal in death."

"No, in sleep and in desire and in dreams. You know the tales? Some are just that: only tales; but a surprising number are true. You are a seer; you know the ancient ones used dream adders to induce their oracular trances. I have been worshipped in ages past, in times far distant, by races whose names would mean nothing to you. But no longer. The greatest boons I have granted these five hundred years have been sleep for the dying, peaceful dreams for the mad, a cordial for the lovesick."

"A deadly cordial for something so fleeting as desire."

"Love may be fleeting, but that makes the desire of the moment no less powerful. The lover will give anything to win her object. What is the risk, when compared with the end?"

"Love can be won, surely, through other means than using venom to enslave the heart."

"Perhaps it eases the lover's ache as much as it relieves the invalid's pain or the madman's delirium."

Caitlin could not answer. She had needed such a venom, or something like it, herself, that first night alone on Chameol, when she thought grief and misgiving and love would surely kill her.

"But it would not avail me now," she said at last. "There is nothing among your rare drugs to ease this ache. It's love that is paining me, though I dare say I will be ill and mad before it is through with me."

The small dark eyes fixed on her contemplatively. "What sort of loss is it that grieves you?"

"That of a child vanished."

Serpentine nodded. "Yes, you feel these things more keenly, having your offspring one or two at a time. If you had them in broods, you might not miss one so much." Serpentine shifted on her pillows and adjusted her silken robe, trying to make herself comfortable and realizing true comfort in her present situation was impossible. "Do you have an idea who has taken your child?"

"Drusian himself."

The black eyes glittered. "Himself? Are you so sure of that?"

"I know Ylfcwen sent a serving-woman to fetch my son away, and Ylfcwen serves none but Drusian."

"But you seem so certain it was at the master's bidding. Has it never occurred to you that it might have been Iiliana who ordered it?"

"Iiliana!"

"Who else had your trust? Who else the opportunity and the authority to order it?"

"But what reason could she have had?"

"You might better ask which reason of a thousand. A child must always claim you above all other oaths and allegiances. A son might become a weapon against Chameol, a pawn to sway you toward Myrrhlock and the other side. And simply in himself, Bram must diminish that part of yourself that you could give over to serve Chameol and serve Iiliana."

Caitlin's mind spun with images: Iiliana bending over the cradle, Iiliana telling her Ordella had gone. "No—"

"No? Very well. I will not mention the other explanation."

"What do you mean?"

"That Bram is not your son."

Caitlin laughed. "That is impossible!"

"Is it? Hear me, otherworld daughter. Bram is the child they put into your arms, but Grimald is the son you gave life. Remember the Badger's words: *Mooncalves breed only mooncalves.* What other sort of son could he father, the product of an unnatural union himself? The tanner's daughter's son, and the tanner's son—"

Caitlin looked into Serpentine's eyes. "So! Is *that* your game? Taking my own fears and feeding them, then reciting them back to me? You take an inchworm of suspicion and turn it into a serpent of fear run mad. My fears become your weapon against me."

Serpentine shifted her weight, adjusting the robe. "I hope you have no idea of my interceding on your behalf with the master. My sense of courtesy, as well as the understanding between us, would prevent it."

"All I desire is safe passage to his chamber, where I can plead my case."

Serpentine gestured with an emerald hand. "It is not in my power to prevent you. You will excuse my not showing you out? I am sitting on my brood, and I expect they will begin to hatch quite shortly. Do watch where you step."

∽∾

Fiddle and Pomamber lay sprawled in the pantry, the youth's head pillowed on the mastiff's shaggy flank. Fiddle's hand trailed in a bowl of gooseberries and cream, and Pomamber's jaws were closed around the bone from a joint of mutton. They were surrounded by the other litter of their repast: crusts from a number of custard tarts, a rope of sausages liberated from its hook, emptied pots of jam, the ruin of a meat pie. The dog and boy were not so much asleep as sated into a stupor.

Pomamber woke first, and her altered breathing woke the boy. They both sniffed the air, both caught the scent that said first "stranger" and then said "Otherworld." Cautiously, Fiddle lifted the latch on the pantry door and the pair padded on silent feet down the deserted hallway, hoping they would find the otherworldly intruder before it found them.

Ylfcwen had come not by boat but by way of the tunnel beneath the Strait of Chameol itself, a passageway so ancient Ylfcwen's own surveys placed it on the other side of the island entirely. The trapdoor had not opened on daylight in a good five hundred years; at last, lying on her back in the tunnel and giving it a solid kick with both feet at once, Ylfcwen was able to break the corroded hinges. She found herself in the grape arbor of the garden below Caitlin's bedroom window, eye to eye with a raven.

She settled her claim to the grape arbor by throwing a slipper at the raven. When she had dusted herself off a bit, Ylfcwen looked around, thinking the mortal race knew little enough about the art of horticulture. That ridiculous fish pond, with its dreadful fountain! Those tousled vines were badly in need of restraint, and the shaggy beds of lamb's ear wanted a firm hand with the pruning shears. How anyone could think to put those roses in that spot was more than Ylfcwen could imagine. They might *survive* there, but certainly they could never *thrive*. She raised her glance from the neglected rosebush to the walls of the palace, feeling a strange and unaccustomed pang. If such was their husbandry of flowers, what could they be expected to do with a goblin, which was as thorny but no less delicate in its way?

She made her way first to the chamber where the mirror Caitlin lay sleeping. It was in that chamber that the smell of goblin lay heaviest. Ylfcwen kneeled by the empty basket in the alcove and swept up some crumbs the pigeons had missed. Macaroons! Had she fed him macaroons? If she had, it was bad, very bad. How much further it might have gone, Ylfcwen hated to think. It was a bad enough sign that the scent of goblin was strongest in a room where the goblin wasn't.

A quick survey of the rooms told her the whole household was asleep. This was not a charm of Ordella's making, Ylfcwen knew. When a changeling was exchanged for a human child, no charm was necessary any stronger than a raven's feather hung by a red thread from an eastern rafter to keep the dogs from barking. Such a deep sleep as Ylfcwen now observed was another matter entirely. It was not just about a simple exchanging of a goblin for a baby, no; it presaged the awakening of one who had slept a far more ancient sleep. Looking about her at the bodies of the sleepers, Ylfcwen shivered, remembering a passage from her elvish catechism:

In that time the slumbering world shall waken, and the waking world shall be cast into a great sleep, and the doorway between the one world and the other shall be closed forevermore, and none shall thereafter pass between them. For in those days the royal exile shall end, the ancient court shall rise once more from its biding-place, and all present things shall be banished, and all things known overthrown.

Ylfcwen knitted her brow, pondering the possibility of an extended visit in the mortal world.

When she entered Iiliana's chamber and saw the goblin lying asleep, Ylfcwen felt her heart sink. She had only to pinch him awake and look into his yellow eyes to know the worst. He had been fed macaroons and nursed at the breast, and rocked and lullabied and dandled on the knee, no doubt. Even all that would not have been enough to make Ylfcwen abandon hope; he might have been rehabilitated, in time. But from the look in the yellow eyes she knew she was too late. Even in a short space of time they had named him and begun to love him, and now he was more human than goblin. A human child could be dosed with drops and catechized and brought along with a mild mixture of nectar and root wine. But once a goblin child had known human love, it was no use trying to get it back.

A goblin enlightened, or "brought to air," as the saying went, could see through the enchantments of the Otherworld and could not be made to work at the looms of the court or the mines of the gemfields. They sooner or later went mad or died in a most troublesome fashion.

The elf queen went out into the hallway feeling lightheaded. Light poisoning, probably. She would find a dark closet and close her eyes and take a sip from the flask of root wine she had brought with her.

To her astonishment, the door of the first linen closet she tried opened to reveal a frightened boy and a large dog, quaking beneath an eiderdown. To Fiddle, who had been expecting a demon, the sight of Ylfcwen was still unsettling; with her dark spectacles and strange fur garments, she was like one of the blind mice from the nursery rhyme, come looking with a carving knife for the thief who had robbed her pantry.

Ylfcwen removed her spectacles to look at her prize more closely. Fiddle was a good height and practically grown into a man of the size and variety the elf queen most favored. This would make up a little for the loss of the goblin baby. In a year or two, he could begin his studies of the court etiquette and the elvish tongues, and by his seventh year in the Otherworld he might even sit for the examination to become her consort, if she hadn't tired of him by then.

Fiddle stood transfixed by the smooth opal gaze, seeing in the rose-and-green fire of its depths the fulfillment of every vague yearning, feeling the same way he felt at the moment of waking from a particularly pleasant dream. Looking into the elf queen's eyes, Fiddle even began to think that his waking life must be illusory and the life of dreams the true existence. The opal eyes said this was indeed so. She was holding out her hand, and in it there was the silver jigger cap of the pocket flask, full of something heady and bitter, something Fiddle knew he shouldn't drink.

Pomamber, who had been standing whimpering and quaking with fear, took this opportunity to bolt. This roused Fiddle to his senses again, and he pelted out of the linen closet after the mastiff as if all the demons of the Otherworld were after him.

Ylfcwen sighed. "These mortals! Why do I trouble with them? One might as well tie a napkin on a jackrabbit and teach it to eat lettuce with a fork."

It seemed a shame to have made the journey and have to return so soon with nothing to show for her trouble, so Ylfcwen resolved to see as much of the country Above as she could, just in case it turned out to be her only visit. She found a boat tied up in a hidden harbor, a pretty, light craft just the right size and color for her, tugging at its moorings like a high-spirited greyhound eager to be off. Ylfcwen settled her cane and bundle in one end and arranged herself at the other.

"Take me to the nearest landfall," she commanded.

The boat obeyed.

∽∾

At the first turning Caitlin was lost again in the windings of the tunnels and would not have been able to swear to the direction from which she had come.

Newt twisted a lock of hair near Caitlin's ear; he did this, she had found, when he was thinking.

"I was wondering that, too," she said.

"All right, thought reader. Tell me what I was wondering."

"Why Serpentine let us off so easily. And where were all these vipers you were so worried about?"

"As for the one, she was busied with her brood. And as for the others, it seems we are to be allowed to pass unharmed. For the vipers answer to Serpentine, and she answers to Drusian."

"Well, I wonder when we will come to these doors. We've had steel and fire and vipers' heads already. What possibly can be left, I can't imagine."

"Eldrin of Tenthmoon."

"Who was he?"

"A king. He craved power over past, present, and future, so at his bidding his court magician built him a cabinet of yew. It had three doors, one of which opened into the past, one on the present, and the third on the future."

"And where did his cabinet take him?"

"Well, the chamber had a flaw in its design, or the magician had a sense of humor that the king did not appreciate, for there was no telling which of the doors of the cabinet opened on which aspect. The king, in his displeasure, turned the magician out of his house, but he could not bring himself to destroy the cabinet. He locked it in a tower room, thinking that someday he might discover its mystery."

"Don't tell me. The king has three daughters, and each in turn stumbles upon the forbidden room. The eldest vanishes into the past, the next-to-eldest into the future, so the youngest returns to the present unknown to her own father, and she is married off to a swineherd."

"You would have made a good storyteller."

"Am I right, then?"

"In most particulars. The eldest was sent back five hundred years and became a wealthy spice trader. The middle one was sent forward only about fifty years and had to live out her life as a widow without ever having known her husband or much else of life. The youngest was returned unknown to the father, but she was not married off to a swineherd. When a strange young woman appeared in his court, claiming to be his daughter, the king ordered her imprisoned in the tower room."

"And what happened to her?"

"Oh, she lived out her life there, unable to decide whether the fate that awaited her through any of the doors would improve upon the one known to her, however dreary."

Caitlin had paused on a threshold once before. Through the first door a life had awaited her on Chameol fulfilling her seer's gifts, in which she might remember the Badger but live ever apart from him. Through the second door lay a life as an ordinary woman, her otherworld sight stripped from her, with no memory of Chameol or the Badger.

But now that she had made her choice and passed through the first door, not even the consolation of Bram was to be allowed her. Caitlin was more certain than ever now that the Master ruled not only sleep and dreams and desires but death itself, and that with every lost hour her chances of reclaiming her son dwindled. She saw them as the canary orchid, wilting and dimming in the dark, and it was not only Bram she was losing; it was love and light itself. Her life would be spent on Chameol as its seer, higher in rank even than Iiliana, with all the mysteries of the ancient runebooks to solve. In her mind, Caitlin saw herself as an old woman, bent over a dusty tome, alone in a tower room. She was the image of her old guardian, Abagtha, gnarled and twisted like an old tree in the wind, bleached grey.

No, thought Caitlin, she would return to the sea and live her life out neither as Caitlin the woman nor Caitlin the seer, but as some third creature, beyond speech, lulled in the heavy sighing of the billows.

"Yes," she said suddenly. "There must be a *third* door." A way to live not in the past or in the future but in the present.

Something fell to the stones paving the tunnel. It was Newt, suddenly glass again. He had brought her as far as he could bring her. Caitlin slipped the glass salamander into her pocket. With the next step the light of the canary orchid guttered as if in a strong gust and went out.

"All right!" she said to the darkness. "What will satisfy you? You have everything of mine. You have taken my son, denied me my only guide and companion, even extinguished my light. Well, I have half of my reason left and nearly all my wits. We'll see how far they can take me in the dark before you claim them, too."

∽◦∾

In the chamber the crystal book swirled with illegible words, ink and oil in water, forming and reforming but never quite taking shape. Amidst the cryptic, changeable runes, pictures formed briefly on the crystal leaves. There appeared in turn a woman who might have been Caitlin or Ulfra, a smaller bent figure that might have been Grisaudra or Ordella, a baby that might have been a goblin. Then the translucent pages dimmed and went blank.

A ghostly hand moved a piece on the game board from a region inlaid with green stone to a golden circle in the center.

Bram stirred under the blanket of ravens' feathers and cried weakly. The hand reached out and gently smoothed the dark hair. The child gazed into eyes that seemed to hold all the light in the world captive in their orbs; the sight calmed him, and he reached out with a chubby hand to touch the bright rings: one of tiger's eye, one of sapphire, and one of serpentine. Bram was lifted from his cradle and held up so he could see the pictures take shape on the pages of the crystal book.

A voice roused the stillness in the chamber, the wind singing of light in a cave that had never known the sun.

"Hush, sweetling. Look, here is your mother, come for you. It will not be long now."

13

THE SNAKE CHARMER

The arrangement would have suited Folderol perfectly, if it had not been for the snakes. In all other respects, Hessie would have made an admirable Mistress Folderol. She was well-featured, even-tempered, no more voluptuous than was becoming, and a good manager of money. If she had been anything but the troupe's snake charmer, he would have made her his wife at the first opportunity. But the old rogue's imagination conjured too many serpents— sleeping in his boot toes, basking among the cushions in his favorite chair—to make the idea completely attractive.

Hessie privately thought it was just as well that she made her living the way she did, for she was not at all certain being Mistress Folderol would have agreed with her. But for all that he was a foolish, vain, thieving kind of man, toward Hessie herself the old rogue was generous, affectionate, and flattering in the right proportion. She might have had a younger man with better teeth, but would a younger man have massaged her feet after a long day? Whenever Folderol tried her patience, she had only to tweak his beard and tease that she would turn him into a snake.

"Oh ho, turn me into a snake, she says. Ha, ha!"

"Well," she would say with a shrug, "how do you think I tamed all these others?"

Hessie took great pride in the fact that she used none of the customary snake charmer's ruses in her performance. The fangs of her adders were intact and had not been plugged with wax. Neither were their jaws sewn shut, and the poison glands had not been cut out or tied off. Hessie relied instead on the curious docility of snakes in captivity and the occasional saucer of milk laced with laudanum.

Their morning and evening feedings had come to coincide with the donning and doffing of their mistress's professional costume, including a gilt headdress and matching fingernails, which together lent an aura of mystery with just the right touch of the sinister. Hessie sat at her dressing table now, dissolving the spirit gum that held the gold talons in place and talking to the snakes, a habit she had fallen into almost without realizing it. The largest and oldest adder, Arabella, already fed, had coiled herself gently around Hessie's throat, apparently intent on the process of talon removal.

"Sybella, don't be so greedy. Give your brother a chance. Oliver, you mustn't be so timid; you'll starve to death if you wait your turn that way. Which do you think I should have made up, Arabella, the olive or the lavender?" Hessie's old confidante, the leopard-woman, had been by with sketches and swatches for Hessie's new costumes, a present Hessie insisted that Folderol had promised her. And didn't she deserve it?

"The trouble with the olive is, while it sets *you* off well, Arabella, it makes *me* look sallow. Perhaps if I wore a scarf of some other color nearer my face it would offset it a little. That crimson silk, perhaps. Yes, that might answer very well."

Hessie had been on an errand to the kitchen tent to fetch milk for the snakes when she first sensed something was awry. It wasn't just that the milk the woman had given her was sour and Hessie had finally had to buy her milk from an obliging farm woman who had an equally obliging cow. No, it was the cat, the strange harlequin cat that spurned milk and catnip and mice and seemed to take its only pleasure in tormenting that poor crow. Something was very wrong with that cat, Hessie was sure.

Folderol had only laughed. "Nothing wrong with it—it doesn't care for the necklace you wear, is all."

"Arabella was back in my tent, having a nap. There is something very wrong with that cook, too, I tell you."

"Well, I can't fire her. She's worked for me—" Folderol tugged his calico beard a moment in consternation. "I can't remember how long, but long enough anyway."

Hessie couldn't remember when the woman had come to cook for the troupe. She seemed to think there had been someone else quite recently, but the face and name of that other cook seemed to have been erased somehow from her mind. Surely, her memory wasn't *that* bad? Then the present sullen woman must have been there as long as Hessie had—mustn't she?

The leopard-woman came, and Hessie told her to make up the olive with a crimson trim. Soon Hessie found herself standing on a stool, cradling a bolt of silk in her arms, its train wound about her like a cocoon.

"Tell me, Tansy, who was the cook when you were here?"

The leopard-woman looked up, her muzzle abristle with pins as if with whiskers. "Have you been drinking some of that milk you give your snakes? Who was the cook when I was here, she asks! Why, can you have forgotten our dear Toby?"

Coil by coil, something deep within the snake charmer's memory stirred: the kindly knife thrower who had one day lost his courage and had to put his talent with cutlery to another purpose. "Toby! Of course—how could I ever have forgotten him?"

"I can't imagine. Oh, Hessie, he used to make old FeatherAll so jealous, the way he fed you like a pet."

"His hash and eggs. What I wouldn't give for the man's hash and eggs. I don't even remember him leaving, Tansy. Where did Toby go?"

"Well, he left after I went to set up the shop. I only

heard about it when I ran into him later. He said it was the oddest thing, that he had gone into the kitchen tent one morning and found a strange woman there—strange-foreign and strange-peculiar—and when he went to complain, old Folly-and-Brawl told him he didn't know what he was talking about, that the woman had been with him for years. Now, *there's* someone who doctors his saucer of milk in the evening."

Hessie thought nothing, not even the better part of a barrel of stout, could have made Folderol sack his old friend Toby. How could they both—they and all the rest of the troupe—have forgotten him so easily? And what had possessed Folderol to hire that dour old woman, with her pressed-leek soups and cinder-coated chickens?

❧

The candle had burned until the flame finally drowned in its own wax. It was light, then, anyway. The Badger stretched and pushed back his chair; he would have set down his pencil, worn now to a stub, but his hand was cramped around it, and he could not let it go.

The tabletop in front of him was littered with drawings, sheets covered front and back with dozens of small sketches, Caitlin over and over, as his mind's eye was now able to recall her: standing in a market square, wearing a collar of bells; sprawled in a corridor in a billowing silk dress with a litter of kittens in her lap; stooping in the curling shallow foam of the moonlit sea; Caitlin having her hair cut off by the old eel-seller, the eel-seller who had been Elric in disguise. All night he had scrawled in a desperate haste, lest his memory should leave him again in an hour. Now that the danger seemed safely past, he could use a shave and a bath.

The tapping of the razor on the edge of the basin woke Elric, who had fallen asleep a little before dawn, assured by then that the Badger's frantic scribbling was a sign of further mending, not further mischief. By the time Elric had bathed as well, the drawings had been put away, and the Badger had begun to fill a fresh sheet with his stable shorthand of a monk's script.

"Take a rest, man. Think of your eyes, if you won't have pity on your body or your brain."

The Badger put out his lower lip and blew a shock of hair out of his eyes. "I'm all right. It's just that we've wasted so much time, and we don't know much more than we knew the day we went to see the shoemaker." He crumpled the paper and raised his arm to throw it into the fire, but Elric took it from him and smoothed it out on the table to read it. The Badger had drawn two overlapping circles, one labeled "Oncemoon" and one labeled "Folderol's T." In the first circle he had written the names of the mad and missing in Oncemoon: Tilda and her father, the shoemaker; the mayor; and the merchant. In the other circle he had written the names of Hodge and Pyle. Where the circles overlapped, the Badger had written his own name.

Elric glanced at the younger knight sharply. "Why your name?"

The Badger's eyes were bright with sleeplessness or dread. "Think about it: I'm the only thing that links the two sets of events."

Elric shook his head and took the pencil from the Badger, or what was left of the pencil; while he spoke, the Badger had been whittling it with his knife, and it was now not much more than a splinter. Without a word, Elric added a name to the space where the circles met.

The Badger frowned. "Grisaudra? But she hasn't been touched by the malady."

"Hasn't she?" Elric was thinking of the look he had seen in her eyes that day he had been coming out of the kitchen tent with matches. "Come, Badger. It's high time we had a talk with Grisaudra."

∽◦∾

The flames had nearly consumed the cap of owl's feathers; the marked tarot deck and the wooden dice were already ashes. The contents of all her vials and bottles had been emptied into the river. Now the same icy water that had shocked the Badger into memory dyed the dreams of pike and perch and trout all the colors of a wizard's paint box. Her catmint and juniper cordial had gone as well, for it might have deadened her pain, and Grisaudra wanted to feel anguish in each fresh variety it presented.

All hope had vanished with that one word: *Caitlin*. But that one word had done far more than dash her hopes: It had opened her eyes to the nature and extent of her own folly. She stood in front of the mirror, forcing herself to gaze on her reflection there. Her eye and scar now appeared as more than a disfigurement of nature; they seemed to her the outward sign of a disfigured soul. It was not the Badger's eyes that haunted her now, but Elric's, as cold, grey, and unforgiving as steel.

Self-loathing is a bitter medicine, and too great a dose can work greater evil than it cures. At last Grisaudra turned away from the mirror and began to place in her pockets those few things she had brought with her from Oncemoon. She had only meant to travel with the Badger until his memory could be returned, and while she doubted his "hauntings" would ever really cease, Grisaudra saw nothing to be gained in staying another hour among the troupe.

As she belted her tunic of chain mail about her once more, she was girding her spirit as well for her return to the marsh. Back in her hut with the cat and the pigs, Grisaudra wished she could be certain of banishing from her mind not only the Badger but Elric as well. His face— and the look of horror the accidental dose of drops had brought to it—had begun to haunt her sleep and to frequent her more familiar nightmares. Suddenly the mocking face of the handsome young soldier was his; the shroud maker leered with those grey eyes, and it was Elric who wielded the sword as it swung toward her, singing of steely death. It was the look in the eyes that woke her, a look that said he believed the worst of her. If he thought such dire things about her now, what would he think if he knew the whole of it? And what, Grisaudra asked herself crossly, does his good opinion mean to you? He is a wormwood kind of man, six pints of bile and bitterness sewn up in a human hide. But the truth of it was that somehow his good opinion had come to mean a great deal, and the more he distrusted her the more Grisaudra longed to gain his trust. *Caitlin:* That one word had wakened something else than shame in her; it had killed one hope but had brought to life a hope of another sort.

To cure herself of this way of thinking, Grisaudra removed from her pockets the charms Elric had tied to her fortune-teller's getup. In the fire, the small green glove curled into a fist in the flames, grasping at ashes. The faces on the playing cards grew beards of fire until finally the features were lost in flame.

She would fill her pockets with things harmless in their usefulness, incapable of rousing her to memory or dreams. A slice of cold pigeon pie, some cheese, a bit of bread. The bread was moldy, and it was as she held it in her hand, poised to throw it away, that Grisaudra was struck by a thought so startling and overpowering that she gasped and sat, staring at the green crust in her hand.

"Of course—of course! But that means—oh, I must tell Elric!"

The scream of the harlequin cat nearly made her jump out of her skin. It arched its back in the opening of her tent, hissing and yowling with a sound that made Grisaudra shudder.

"You hideous thing!" She stood with a shoe in her hand but could not bring herself to throw it. "Grisaudra!" she said sternly to herself. "Surely, you're not afraid of that cat!"

Instantly, she knew she was greatly afraid of it indeed. She held the shoe tightly against her chest and began to back away, feeling behind her for a willow switch, her walking stick, for anything. Her hand closed not on a stick, but on something sleek and feathered. She spun about, frightening the crow out of its wits, so that the one shrieked and the other croaked in fright. Without knowing why, Grisaudra dropped the shoe and clutched the bird to her. Its beak hung open with fright and it shuddered in her arms. Grisaudra held it tightly in front of her, as if it were a charm against the cat.

"Let it go." The hooded figure in the shadow of the tent flap was the wrong height for the cook, though the voice was not unlike hers. Grisaudra blinked and rubbed her eyes with the back of one hand; the figure before her seemed to shimmer and change. Surely it was taller. It drew closer and in a different voice spoke again. "Let it go, Grisaudra of Oncemoon, and the prize I promised you can still be yours."

Her heart was beating as fast as the bird's, but her voice came calmly enough when called. "No, thank you. It seemed a bad bargain when I thought about it: a husband with a brain so addled he could think *me* a beauty."

"It would be as I showed you: You would be beautiful and he would love you."

"No. Being in thrall is rather different from being in love, I think."

"It is Caitlin who has enthralled him, but he will recover from it. But will you surrender him to her so easily, Grisaudra, if I tell you she is dead?"

Grisaudra sank slowly to the floor. The crow in her arms gave out a strange human moan. "She can't be . . ."

"She is dead, or as good as dead. If she does not lose her life, she will certainly lose her reason. She will not be the first seer to go mad; there is an asylumful in Tenthmoon."

He had come up to her as he spoke, and as he took the crow from her arms his hood fell back. He was Myrrhlock, not the old Necromancer with the seamed skull and harelip and terrible eyes, but Myrrhlock as he must have been before pride and will were twisted into something old and evil. This was a flawless face, perfect in proportion and shape; only its utter coldness kept it from being wholly beautiful. The strange, mercurial eyes compensated for this lack; their magnetic gaze made it impossible for Grisaudra to look away. In his arms the crow seemed barely to breathe, its eyes nearly shut.

Myrrhlock cupped her chin in his hand and spoke to her gently, soberly, soothing away a child's nightmare. "This same I can do for you, Grisaudra. But you must serve me. We will take Chameol together. The army is nearly raised to do it. And once there, I will have need of another seer."

Dimly, she remembered what it was she had to tell

Elric. But her chain-mail tunic seemed a suit of lead; like Myrrhlock's eyes it weighed her down. She could not move or speak; she drew a breath to speak and only sobbed.

"Sweet." His hand traced the line where her scar had been, once. "Come to the mirror and see how pretty you are."

As he drew Grisaudra to her feet, the crow suddenly struggled free, and in five beats of its great clumsy wings had cleared the cat's grasping claws and gained the yard.

The crow knew the tent it wanted. It landed on the snake charmer's dressing table, sending curling tongs and bottles of spirit gum flying.

"Goodness!" Hessie exclaimed. "You poor thing. Has that cat been tormenting you again?"

The bird hopped and flapped on the table, stamping in impatience, sending up clouds of talc and sequins. "Errk! Ergkg! Erkot. Errk-KOT! Ergt. Erg-GIT!"

Hessie laughed and shook her head. "All right! Heavens, what has that animal been doing to you? Yes, yes, erkit-erkit to you, too." Hessie's eyes suddenly grew thoughtful, and she recalled something from the days before she had lulled snakes with laudanum, when she had welcomed babies with lullabies and wiped the sweat from their mothers' brows. Even as Hessie didn't like to use tricks with her snakes, she had not liked to dose women in their childbed. But from time to time there had come a case of particular difficulty, and she had reluctantly reached for a certain, singular remedy.

"What—oh! Oh, it can't be! Crows can't—but if you are—and you mean—then—"

The snake charmer sat down in the chair, petting the agitated bird to calm it. Her mind spun with thoughts too wild to entertain but too dire to cast aside. Could it really be that the whole troupe had been under some enchantment, to make them forget Toby and accept a stranger unquestioningly? Could Hodge and Pyle have stumbled on the truth and so met their deaths? It was madness, wild imagination, nothing more. But if it wasn't . . .

Whom could she tell? Perhaps someone who had never

known Toby—the bearded woman and the young dare-devil rider. They both had something about them—a watchfulness, a keenness of the eye—that said they were more than they seemed, that they might be trusted. Yes, she would tell them.

Hessie scooped up the bird and coaxed it into one of the wicker hampers she used for carrying the adders.

"Now, not a peep out of you until I say so, and then you had better repeat your little performance, or I shall look a jolly fool."

∽∾∽

Elric and the Badger stared first at Hessie and then at the crow. The one stood with her hands on her hips, blushing, while the other perched on the table, hunched and ruffled and muttering low to itself.

Hessie sighed. "Come *on* dearie, before they have me carted off to the loony bin!"

The crow growled, spinning out the sound oddly. "Errrrrr—"

"That's it! Now, tell them just what you told me."

The feathers went down a little, and the crow began to mutter faster. "Errrrrrr. Git, git, git. Erkot. Er-KOT. Ergt. Errrrrrrr-git. Er-GIT."

"There!" Hessie looked from the Badger to Elric and back again. "Did you hear that?"

Elric grinned helplessly. "Clear as a bell. Errrrr. Git, git, git. Erkot, Ergt, Ergit. An irregular verb if ever I heard one. Must have been a schoolmaster's pet." He reached over to nudge the Badger in the ribs, but the younger knight's face showed him uninclined to laugh. Elric watched in amazement as the Badger's face lit up like a lamp, then watched incredulous as he seized Hessie, spun her around in a giddy dance, and kissed her.

"It's erkot, erkit, ERGOT! Sweet heaven, it *is* ergot!"

Elric was wide-eyed and slack-jawed. "What on earth has gotten into you?"

"Ergot, ergot! It's the cause of the madness, Elric, don't you see? It explains the Oncemoon business; it explains my fever; it explains everything!"

But Hessie had a stitch in her side and a worry in her

brain. "Stop, oh, stop, please! Badger, seriously." He let her go, and she bent double, gripping her side. "Don't you see what it means?" she panted. "Someone has killed Hodge and Pyle. Who knows who might be next?"

Elric's face was white and mirthless when he caught the Badger's gaze. "Where's Grisaudra?"

They found her tent empty.

"She's only run away," Elric said bitterly, nudging an overturned chair with the toe of his boot.

The Badger shook his head. "She's gone, but not willingly, Elric. Would she have left her chain-mail tunic, or gone without her herb belt?"

Hessie frowned. "This makes me uneasy. Let's go to the kitchen tent."

There was no sign of the cook or the cat. Where there had been not an hour before pots and crockery—or at least the illusion of them—there was now the glass jumble of an alchemist's chamber. What bread there was had staled to bricks, the milk had turned to cheese in the pail; it seemed most of the food to leave that kitchen had been soup from stones and chops conjured from sawdust and cardboard, with enough meal mixed in to keep body and soul together, and charmed so the troupe would not feel their hunger too much.

Elric had put out a hand to pick up an alembic full of a purplish distillation when Hessie stopped him with a harsh word.

"Careful how you handle that—ergot can be given through the skin as well as on the tongue."

Elric drew back his hand. "What is this ergot, then, and how do you know so much about it?"

"It's a powerful drug, distilled from diseased rye. In its mildest form it's used to dose women in labor; I was a midwife once, and that was how I first came to know it. But after I gave up midwifery and before I took up snakes, I worked for a time for an undertaker, a sometime barber and surgeon, who taught me all manner of things that lie between medicine and magic. He taught me how a pure dose, even a small one, could convulse the gut, disorder speech, summon apparitions."

Elric turned to the Badger. "And how did *you* come to know of it? Don't tell me you learned midwifery in the monkery!"

"No—but sometimes a handful of molded rye would ease a mare having a hard time of it with a breech foal." The Badger shook his head. "I wonder I didn't think of it before."

"Why should you have?" Elric said. "For that matter, *how* could you have? Perhaps that was why you got the fever—to keep you from remembering."

Hessie called to them from the corner. "Here. I may have found something."

It lay glittering in the sawdust in the corner of the tent, a hollow glass bell covered with prickles like a chestnut.

"Hollow, like a viper's tooth. That must be how the dose was given."

"Yes," said Elric, scrubbing thoughtfully at the hair at the nape of his neck. "No good to trust to such an irregular method of dosage as the supply of rye grain. No, once the accidental dose was given, it had to be administered regularly."

The Badger's look grew grimmer. "We must be off, then, before the trail is cold. Grisaudra is in great peril."

"I know," Elric said quietly, but with a hint of temper, so that the Badger raised an eyebrow and Hessie looked at him with fresh and mildly startled eyes.

The mongrel potion in his eyes had continued to dye Elric's dreams odd colors. Last night they had showed him Grisaudra struggling to free herself from the unwanted embrace of the shroud maker. She had been forced at last to use a dagger in her own defense and to hide from her pursuers among the bodies in their shrouds. Elric had lain awake afterward wondering if he might have misjudged her completely, and if so, what other secrets the conjurer of Oncemoon Marsh kept hidden behind that wall of rage and pain.

Then Hessie looked around, her brow knit with worry. "What can it mean? The crow is gone."

∽∾

Poppies. They were the last thing Grisaudra saw before she felt a sudden, sharp pricking behind her ear, before the darkness engulfed her and she felt herself lifted on a great rush of air.

She seemed to be flying, borne at a great height over a field of rye, where row on row of dark-robed figures were scything the grain, their arms swinging the curved blades in unison. The second field was charred and blackened, the smoke and steam still hissing from the ruins as if the wind of flame had just raced over it. The ground grew nearer as she was borne over the third field, close enough for her to make out the litter of bodies, looters moving among the fallen, erratic but purposeful as ants.

At last she began to descend. Below her there took shape an isolated group of dark buildings within a high wall. A convent, a prison, a castle? Grisaudra sank nearer and saw it was none of these, for she had come close enough to see the banner that flew from the bell tower: a hand and a stone. These were not nuns or prisoners or princes. This was a house of lepers.

She floated down so softly that Grisaudra wondered for the first time whether she had died and this was the next world. It had so far looked exactly like the only other world Grisaudra had known, but all her life had been a string of cruel jokes, and this might prove to be just another such.

She found herself beneath the vaulted roof of a great hall without any memory of how she had arrived there. The weight on her shoulders proved to be a heavy dark cloak lined with silk in a pattern of poppies; despite its heavy folds, she felt chilled to the marrow. In a mirror framed by tapers, Grisaudra caught sight of herself: unmarred, flushed with the ripe bloom of youth, the candles' glow turning her ash-pale hair bright and insubstantial as moonlight.

"You see, Grisaudra, that I keep my promises."

Myrrhlock stood before her, and behind him stood rank on rank of silent figures in lepers' robes, with blue glass globes around their necks like lepers' bells.

The Necromancer's magic had conjured the very picture of the Badger, down to the smallest points: a tiny scar above one eye from a distant childhood accident; the nick in his ear left by an overaffectionate mare. But the eyes were not the Badger's eyes. Myrrhlock could copy their meadow-sky blue but not the clear, laughing light that came from them. Grisaudra shuddered, remembering how the old hermit of Oncemoon Marsh had met his end, a shape-changing spell got half-right. Finding him, she had run out into the mist, too frightened to venture back for days. By then, there had been nothing left of him.

Now the figure before her wavered and went transparent; for a breath's space she saw a double image: the false Badger and Myrrhlock both. But the Necromancer was weary; the harelip cleft his face from brow to chin, his eyes were dull and his cheeks hollow, as though his face had fallen in on itself, eaten away with evil. Even here, in this sanctuary of his own making, the Necromancer's powers were waning. Grisaudra clung to this thought as Myrrhlock took her hand and drew her through the crowd. The ranks of robed figures parted noiselessly to make way for them.

As they passed into a smaller chamber Myrrhlock gave up the Badger's form entirely and put on a cap of blue goblinstone. He seemed immediately soothed and stretched out a hand to indicate that Grisaudra should be seated. She shook her head, and the Necromancer laughed softly, though not gently.

"Ah. I understand this gesture, I think. You will not sit at my feet, you will not bow to me, you mean to show me that I am not your master. Very good! Very good—then let's see you put off that cloak."

She could not, no matter how she tugged at the clasp. Only at Myrrhlock's word—a word old out of meaning, dreadful to the ear—did the cloak of poppies fall from her shoulders to lie in a crimson wreath around her feet.

The Necromancer retrieved the cloak and folded it carefully. "Quite a treasure, this. The dreamcloak of Yolanda of Twelvemoon, the half-elf queen who was as beautiful as she was mad. I had heard tales of such a cloak but feared the moths would have gotten the best of it after all these centuries. Imagine my delight when I chanced on it. It was being worn by a beggar woman in the madhouse where I first took asylum. Here, you can see where it had to be mended after the foolish lion tamer took his shears to it. It was bad enough that he might make a patchwork of it, worse still if he should show it to someone who would recognize it for what it was. But in making a turban of it, Hodge unwittingly fashioned a dream-cap with the power to summon death itself from his own imagination.

"Now, the fire-eater, he was another matter. He was rash enough to try to barter my little secret to your friend Elric in exchange for a knighthood. So, I mixed up a leaf or two of salad, rocket dressed with—but you can guess what it was dressed with."

Grisaudra felt heavy with dread, her leaden tongue barely able to form speech. "You killed them. . . ."

Myrrhlock raised a finger, a master correcting a student. "No, their own foolishness, their own weakness did them in. The lion tamer's heart was overwound with fear; he died of fright. The fire-eater met his end at the hands of his own imagination."

"And I—how shall I meet my end?"

The goblinstone caught the firelight as the Necromancer shook his head. "You have nothing to fear from me, Grisaudra. You are too valuable to me. You see, the stable-boy will follow you out of a displaced sense of heroism. He will bear a message for me to Chameol." The Necromancer laughed, showing poison-stained teeth and a purple, hanged-man's tongue. "Quite a small vial will be enough. Iiliana opens all her messages herself."

14

DRUSIAN

At first Caitlin thought the chamber was empty. She stood in the center and turned slowly around, taking in the gem-laden game board, the blank pages of the crystal book, and the empty throne, hewn of rock, on which there rested a single raven's feather. Off to one side there was a scrape and shuffle and a baby's muffled cry.

"Bram!" The name tore from Caitlin's throat and struck her ear strangely in the echo, as though someone else had cried it.

A high-pitched shriek of laughter split the chamber, followed by an unintelligible muttering, the sounds together the two things that formed her own most ancient memory: the chiding, wild, and unreasoned voice of her guardian and keeper. At the sound, Caitlin forgot everything, her eyes filling with tears of childhood, tears of rage.

"Abagtha! He's mine! You give him back to me! You had no right to take him, no right!"

A quieter shriek echoed off the walls of the room, so that it was impossible to tell the direction from which it had come. The chamber offered no crevice or hiding place that Caitlin could see, only shadows.

The familiar mutter began to form words in the voice

351

she knew so well. "Hee-eee, Eee-hee-he-he-heeeeeeeeee! Hee-eee-ah-ah-ah! Childling, I have your sweet babykin, your hairless pink pup. A sweet-smelling morsel he is, and toothsome, I'd wager. Hee-eee-eee!" Now Caitlin could hear Bram's voice rising with the witch's in a wail.

Caitlin knew how to speak to the old woman's unreason. "You can't have the amulet; it's gone. But I have another trinket, 'Batha, something you'll like even better. A seer's glass from the ancient ones under the sea. Come see!"

As she spoke, Caitlin struggled to remember that her old guardian was long dead, that the figure before her was some illusion, but the moment she saw the familiar figure, bent and hideous but beloved all the same, Caitlin's heart leapt up. Then she saw Bram.

His sojourn in the Otherworld had taken the roses from his cheeks; he was not so plump as he had been and had lost something of his lively humor, but as soon as his sweet, solemn face fastened on Caitlin's own, he began to squirm and chortle. Caitlin drew the glass salamander from her pocket and held it out to the old woman. Her heart was beating so loudly in her ears she could hardly hear her own words.

"Give him to me. He is only a baby, a noisemaker and a bothersome crock-breaker. This is far better, a bargain. Give him to me!"

Abagtha's ancient eyes looked from the luminous ornament in Caitlin's hand to the dark crown of the small head lying in the crook of her arm. She needed only a moment to weigh her choice before she snatched the ornament, nearly dropping Bram as she made the exchange.

It vanished the moment Caitlin took the child into her arms, the dull ache that had swollen her heart since the hour of Bram's loss. With hands trembling from impatience as much as from dread, she undid the elvish swaddling cloth and looked Bram over swiftly for marks of a changeling's initiation or a claim of royal ownership. But it seemed Ylfcwen's handmaidens had done nothing more dire to him than to fit his little ears wiih gold-foil peaks, after court fashion. Caitlin sighed and buried her face in the plump crease where his neck met his shoulder, the smell of his sweet baby hair summoning up the moment Iiliana had first put him in her arms. Bram's happy crowing turned into a hiccough, his breathing fell into the easy cadence of slumber, and his tiny fist curled around a lock of his mother's hair.

Caitlin raised her eyes to chastise Abagtha and looked instead into a pair of dazzling, luminous eyes that were the only lively thing in a figure that seemed carved of marble. Caitlin's arms closed more tightly around Bram.

Even folded, the enormous wings reached halfway to the roof of the chamber. The raven-black feathers were stark against the marble pallor of the skin, so that the being whose wings these were might have been a fantastic beast from out of Abagtha's book of incantations—half woman, half gryphon. Where there should have been talons, there were graceful, ghostly hands, and where there ought to have been a woman's eyes, there were strange, knowing, luminous orbs that turned on Caitlin a gaze neither human nor inhuman.

It was out of weariness and astonishment rather than reverence that Caitlin sank to the floor, Bram cradled in her arms.

"Drusian."

"None other."

"But they called you Master."

"There is no word in the ancient rune tongues for mistress." The wings stirred and raised a slight wind. "And if there were, it would name only half of me." Drusian's brilliant eyes fell to the glass salamander in her hands. She turned it over and over, as if seeking a secret catch that once opened would reveal an ancient treasure.

"What is it, really?" Caitlin asked.

"A seer's glass, as you thought. But it is more than that, the touchstone of a longer-lost, more-forbidden art. It is a shape-changer's lodestone to her true shape."

"What became of Newt?"

"He had brought you to me, which was all he was made to do."

"Made? But that glass was shaped long before I was born."

"Yes, but made in the hope of your coming. Did Abagtha never teach you the meaning and power of names? Chameol is named for the chameleon, the lizard that changes its colors."

"A salamander is not a chameleon."

"No—but when she was still young her enemies laid siege to Chameol, sought out her children, and destroyed them. It was wiser for the children of Chameol to choose a different symbol by which they could know one another. What could be more natural than to choose the salamander, the creature that can survive the heart of the fire? But my tale gets ahead of itself. Listen, otherworld daughter, and I will tell you what I am—and what you are meant to be."

For some minutes the wings had been growing smaller so that now, folded tightly, they were completely hidden behind Drusian's back. As the great wings had shrunk, the pallid skin had grown rosy, taking on the likeness of flesh in the bloom of health. The eyes had lost some of their brilliance, so that when Drusian reached out to the pages of the crystal book and made some adjustments Caitlin could not see, the crystal leaves began to glow like a lamp until they lit the whole chamber. When Caitlin looked back at Drusian, the pale winged figure was gone. She faced instead a human woman clad in flowing robes in the style Caitlin knew only from books on the Elder Age. Drusian's hair was broadly streaked with silver, the cunning of her eyes softened with age to wisdom. Drusian's hand fingered the ivory seal's-head amulet around her neck, and as she did so Caitlin saw her upper arms bore the tattooed runes of a shape-changer. Caitlin felt unsettled; something in those dark, bright eyes was familiar.

"Yes." Drusian smiled. "You think you know me, and you are right."

"It was you who had the glass salamander brought to me as a seal's love-gift. . . ."

"No, the glass salamander had been lost for generations, until that same lovesick seal found it."

"But you took Bram, knowing I would follow and hoping I would bring the glass salamander."

"There is some truth in your version of things—but not *all* the truth. Have you never heard of that old shape-changer's trick, sleight-of-shape? The glass salamander has been in your pocket all this time. It was I, in Newt's form, who guided you. But that was not the only form I took. I was Pj'aurinoor and Cerulean—even Serpentine."

Caitlin's eyes held a gathering storm. "Is it too much for me to ask why?"

Drusian's smile was gentle. "I should wonder only if you didn't. What do you know of the Elder Age?"

"All Iiliana could teach me. The Elders were of the time before the Pentacle, before Myrrhlock became Necromancer."

"You have been to the Devil's Sieve and seen the carvings there."

Caitlin searched Drusian's eyes for a hint of the shape-changer's purpose. "Can you read minds, then, as well as change your shape? Or do you have spies to learn these things?"

"As it happens, neither. But I do have my crystal book." Drusian put out a hand to touch the page, and there upon the crystal leaves the Badger led a blindfolded Caitlin through the catacomb maze of the Devil's Sieve. Then the picture changed to show fantastic pictures carved on the walls of the catacombs, pictures of airy palaces in the clouds, coral mansions beneath the waves.

"There is a story to be read in those pictures, if you knew it," said Drusian. "Shall I tell it to you? You must know two things before I begin: Chameol was not always an island; even as I once had a twin, so did she, and her twin with mine perished the same day beneath the waves. Also you must know there was once only one world, and the race that became Ylfcwen's people dwelled Above, before there was an Otherworld."

Bram had awakened and was looking intently from Drusian's face to Caitlin's, as if he understood what they were saying. The question rose suddenly, disturbing and unbidden, in Caitlin's mind, how much of the Otherworld Bram would carry with him when he returned to the realm of air and light. She noticed with a start that his eyes, which had been an indeterminate color at birth, had become the same blue as his father's. To see the Badger's eyes gazing out at her from Bram's face was unsettling, and Caitlin turned her attention back to Drusian's tale.

"Long ago, Chameol was not an island, but a city within a city, where the highest of all the arts were kept and nurtured. Outside her walls unpaved pilgrim's roads descended to the wide avenues and boulevards of Iule, with its bright guildhalls and busy harbor, and the palace like a rosy pearl in the setting sun.

"Chameol and Iule together linked what you know as the near and far Moons, which were then states of a single kingdom. My father's kingdom." Shadows of emotion stirred on Drusian's features, her eyes clouding over with submerged rage, surfacing grief. "In bringing us into the world, our mother was ushered from it. I drew my first breath five minutes before my twin, and she had not breathed her first before we were made motherless.

"Our grieving father named us, giving me Drusian, after the Elder word for the weeping willow. My sister he called Nairne, the Elder word for ashes.

"From birth I was taught that I was heir to the crown of Iule, and that in time I should climb the steps to the throne and take my place there. I had long lessons at a young age, in diplomacy and governance, but all the time I was supposed to be memorizing borders and rates of exchange I was thinking of the walled city that had been my mother's home. She was one of the 'walled women,' those who had chosen a life apart from the larger world of palace and guildhall, pursuing those magic arts that were even then and ever since the province of women. But then, you can recite them as well as I."

The words fell from Caitlin's lips, familiar as a prayer, and in this moment oddly comforting. "Naming, to call something by its true name; Healing, to cultivate the saving herbs; Summoning, to call forth man and beast; Changing, to change one shape for another; and Seeing, which is not a learned art but one bestowed."

Drusian smiled. "Like you, I could recite them in my sleep, though if my father had caught me, it would have meant a tanning. For he wanted me to have nothing to do with 'the witches behind the wa'l,' as he called them.

"But Chameol was as irresistible to me as the first sight of my mother had been to my father. So it was that on my sixteenth birthday, instead of being feasted and heralded as the next head to wear the crown of Iule, I ate a simple supper with my father and Nairne and my old nurse, and when we had eaten I wept and left them, for the next morning I should be trothed, not to any man in the kingdom, but to Chameol, and within her walls I should live the balance of my days, perfecting the ancient arts. So, the crown of Iule would fall to Nairne.

"For the first year Nairne grieved for me and would see no one, devoting herself to her painting and her loom. A year passed from the time of my going away, and Nairne was fitful in the palace, choosing to walk by the sea where we had gathered starfish and played a mermaid game as children. Borrowing her handmaiden's plain cloak, the king's daughter could walk without attracting notice, lost amidst the bustle of the port, free to watch the ships come and go.

"Another winter and summer passed away, ushering in the third year of my apprenticeship within Chameol's walls. Nairne turned her hands to the garden, coaxing along the lilies, husbanding the roses. At last, our father went to her in the garden and pointed to the flowers, blazing in their late-summer glory. Think of the winter! he chided her, and be mindful of the frost. How can you tend the flowers with more care than you give the House of Iule? If you do not marry, Nairne, Iule will be as a garden without a gardener, lost to the birds and weeds and in the end forgotten and paved over.

"Nairne lay on the ground after he had gone and wept, and when she had dried her tears she cut every bloom and blossom from its stem and bore them to the king's room, laying them at his feet and saying, send who you will; I will see these suitors. But promise me that the choice will be mine alone.

"A procession then began of suitors seeking the hand of the king's daughter. Some wished to be king of Iule;

others wished to be a husband to Nairne, for her grieving had lent her face a sweet and holy sadness that many mistook for mere beauty. But one among the suitors was unswayed by Nairne's charms; he wished to rule Iule only, to ruin her—a wolf among the lambs. But to Nairne, who had never known a wolf, he alone of all the suitors was handsome, he alone knew the workings of her heart, knew them indeed better than Nairne did herself, or so she wrote me: 'When he looks into my eyes, sister, I feel him look into my very soul.' I was not alarmed, as I would have been had I seen the man and seen what he was. But I had only Nairne's foolish, love-stricken letters, which told me of nothing more serious than an infatuation my father should surely see for what it was and just as surely quash.

"It was my old nurse who alerted me to the danger, both of us risking much in meeting at Chameol's gate. I learned that Nairne's suitor had presented himself at the court as a magician, for over his speaking mirrors and tarot decks he could, in the chaperone's presence, lean close to Nairne and whisper in her ear in a manner no other suitor would dare. As a member of the royal household, he could sit across from Nairne at table and ply her with tales of romance and mystery. Gravely worried, my nurse stole away one evening to meet me, begging me to come and see matters for myself. A summoner, she called him, which is a very old name for a necromancer. I was not very worried until she uttered the word, but when she said 'summoner,' my heart was chilled as it had never been, and I knew I must see Nairne's suitor myself. I agreed to steal away that evening, dressed in beggar's rags, arranging that my nurse should meet me at a gate and hide me in the banqueting hall."

Drusian paused, and for a moment Caitlin saw in the shape-changer's human eyes a trace of that other, inhuman brilliance, and Drusian's face took on some of the pallor of her other form.

"You must understand the nature of my position within the walls of Chameol. I was a third-year apprentice, it is true, but I was also the king's daughter, and accorded nearly the same honor as was given to the Keepers of the

Arts, those women who knew the secrets of the four Learned Arts and of the Art above Arts, Seeing. The Keeper of Changing was in failing health, and in the spring of that year she had called me to the bed to which she was confined and told me that I was to study with her alone that year, and upon her death I was to become a Keeper and a changer of shapes.

"Within my year of study I was to speak to no one and speak of nothing that was of Iule and the world outside, lest I unwittingly betray Chameol. The process of becoming a Keeper was fraught with danger, for in power lay temptation, and in temptation lay the life of Chameol itself. It was on penalty of banishment—stripped of her name, her health, her power to summon, her true shape, and sometimes of sight itself—that a Keeper passed outside the walls of Chameol. I knew this penalty well, for in her youth my nurse had dwelt in Chameol, apprenticed to a Keeper, and had failed the final test. But my love of Nairne and my fear for my sister and Iule both gave me the measure of courage I lacked."

The scene she had summoned to mind was still vivid and repelling to its teller, and Drusian's expression changed to one of remembered loathing. "I found them not in the banqueting hall, but in one of the smaller dining chambers, our father absent and no chaperone but the oldest servant, a woman completely deaf and nearly blind, to wait on them. I barely knew the woman seated there as Nairne, so changed was she, dressed in robes so unseemly my father should never have allowed them. But it was her expression more than her manner of dress that was most altered. She was deep in the thrall of the man who sat close at her side, feeding her from a dish of honey-eyed figs.

"I entered the room with a swiftly beating heart, for despite my beggar's garb it seemed impossible that my twin should not know me. But she met my eyes with a cold gaze and such an expression of peevish ill nature and selfish vanity that it was I who did not know my own twin. Nairne had not a cruel bone in her body nor a thoughtless drop of blood; Nairne lived to please others and grieved to offend. But this was no longer the sister whose life I had shared, heartbeat for heartbeat, from the cradle. I had only to look into her eyes to see that.

"My costume fooled even Nairne; she did not recognize me, but curtly demanded how I had gained entrance and what business I had there. 'Though I am hungry, I do not beg,' I answered her. 'Let me tell your fortune in return for the scraps you would throw to the dogs.'

"Any child of my father would instantly have offered a seat at table and would have fetched the best meat and drink the palace had to offer, for our father treated the least of his visitors as he did the greatest of them. But it flattered this new Nairne to have her fortune told. While I laid the cards out upon the damask cloth the eyes of the magician never once left me, and as I placed the cards in the four corners of the table for the four winds, I fought to keep my hands from trembling, for I knew now what kind of man this was. Every feature of his face was graven in my mind and has never been erased: the coldest eyes I ever have seen, a mouth split with cruelty. It was not to win Nairne's hand that he had come to Iule; it was not a queen or even a crown that he sought. This was the destroyer, the murderer of hope, whose coming had been foretold."

Caitlin lifted her eyes, as if suddenly recalled to memory and startled to speech. The words came to her lips of their own accord: *"To this day they say that if the spinner in the wood is ever awakened, the murder of love and life itself shall be avenged—"*

Drusian's eyes gleamed bright with tears, and she smiled down on Bram as he lay in Caitlin's arms. *"—and the world set aright.* Daughter of light and air! This is at last the night that shall dawn on a new Iule! But I neglect my tale. Listen. These words shall raise up the two things I loved best in all the world: Nairne, my sister, and Iule, my home.

"At Nairne's bidding, then, I spread out the cards and read from them the fortune that came into my head, but still the cards spoke true as any seer: sorrow by water and a long banishment. At these words the Necromancer smiled and pressed Nairne's hand as though to comfort her, but I knew his true meaning! It took all my love for my twin, all my will not to strike him and call him by what he was. But I held my tongue and told Nairne's fortune. When I had done, I was rewarded not with meat nor even with crusts but with some rancid trimmings not fit for pigs. For these I expressed my gratitude and bowed my way out of the room. In the shadows I waited until I had stopped trembling, and casting off my costume I climbed the stairs to my father's apartments. I found him alone.

"One look and I knew the worst. The summoner could not have gained such a place of favor at Nairne's side without the king's assent, so his objections somehow had been overcome, his blessing obtained by poisoning his mind.

"My father was seated at the table, a small ivory portrait of my mother before him, a casket of jewels on its side, its treasure spilling over the tabletop: our mother's wedding jewels and Nairne's dowry. A tall flask stood at hand, nearly empty, and the king greeted me with a warmth that came as much from the wine as from his heart.

"He rose unsteadily and kissed me, pleased that I had come for my sister's wedding. Argue as I might, I could not convince him that Nairne's suitor was a summoner and the sworn enemy of Iule. At one point I could see a struggle play over his features as he fought to remember, as some word of mine sparked a fleeting memory. But the wine—and whatever had been mulled with it—had done its work. The king's animated spirit, his intelligent humor, his very soul had been emptied out, and the enemy of Iule had filled him with a draught of his own concocting, so that his veins ran with a forgetfulness that had completely unbalanced his mind. The king was mad.

"I climbed the pilgrim's path to Chameol in the dead of night, beneath a watchful, foreboding moon. I slipped through the gates and into my bed undetected—at least undetected by any mortal gaze. But the summoner watched me, in some form he found it handy to assume. Perhaps it was the marble statue in the garden, whose eyes seemed to gleam at me as I passed. But I think it was a raven's shape he took.

"That night I lay awake, pondering how to free my sister and my homeland from the evil influence that had fallen over them. At last I lit a lamp and stole away to the library that held the five Books of the Keepers, which none but a Keeper could touch. If an uninitiated hand touched one of the tomes, the silver clasps would burn, and if an untutored eye fell on the pages within, the runes themselves would begin to shriek and howl, for the spells kept therein were some of them deadly, and the arts of Summoning and Changing not to be taken lightly. But I had been well taught and knew to dust my hands and the books with powder of bookworm and was thus able to consult the books without raising an alarm. I found the spell I needed, though I shuddered to read it, and only when I had memorized it did I douse my light and steal back to my own chamber.

"The day dawned that was to see Nairne married to the summoner. My sister woke with an unaccountable urge to walk by the sea. Her bridegroom grew suspicious and listened intently at her window to discern whether she were being summoned, but he could hear nothing, for it was I who summoned her with her own soul's name, which no ear but her own could hear and which she could no wise resist. When she had made her way down to the sea, she walked straight into the waves, and though her handmaidens wept and cried out to her, she heeded nothing but my summons. Out Nairne walked into the embrace of the waves, and thus Nairne appeared to vanish.

"The frightened handmaidens ran back to the palace and related what they had seen. The bridegroom came with them to the shore, where they found Nairne nearly drowned on the beach.

"Or so they thought, for it was I, needing only a small changing spell to become my twin, after all. And what of Nairne? She had been given the shape of a seal and was safely hidden in the sea-flax beds until all danger was past and I could come for her.

"They revived me and brought me back to my father's

house, and for two days the wedding was put off. On the third day I could feign illness no longer, and the marriage was performed. There was some part of the king that was not mad, that had not been conquered, and on hearing the oaths exchanged, this part of him ceased to struggle with his mad, enslaved soul. So my wedding night was spent in a vigil at the king's bedside, and by morning's light my shoulders were heavy with the weight of grief and my brow bowed beneath the crown of Iule.

"When my father had been laid to rest, I begged my husband that I should walk in the garden alone with my thoughts, and he agreed. I worried that in my grief my mind should grow distracted and the spell's thread break. Nairne's fate and Iule's depended on my firmity of mind. So I strolled in the garden and paused to sit by the statue in the garden, a likeness of my mother in marble planted around with everlasting and laurel and rosemary. For a dark hour my courage failed me, and I wept. I did not see the raven come to light on the shoulder of the statue.

"Grief made me careless, and when I heard my name called in Nairne's sweet voice I looked up, straight into the summoner's eyes, an answer on my lips. And it was that answer that imprisoned me, for when I reached back with my hand to steady myself, and touched the marble, I became it, statue and raven both, as you saw me. And Nairne, with no one to free her or guess her fate, was likewise doomed.

"Myrrhlock—for that was the summoner's name—had one last task ahead of him: the destruction of Iule itself. From the depths of the earth he summoned forth fire and tremors, and in an hour the city itself had sunk beneath the waves. Chameol he could not destroy, for her magic was a match for him. He had in mind for Chameol another fate. Iule should be forgotten utterly, the very name erased without a trace. Chameol should live in legend only, an island kingdom whose very existence should be ever disbelieved. And so the house and name of Iule were forgotten even by Chameol herself, and the Arts abandoned.

"Without the just hand of Iule to guide them, the surrounding lands were broken up into the Thirteen Moons, and the age of the Pentacle dawned. It was a dark time for Chameol. The Keepers fled, taking four of the five Books with them. One by one, the Keepers themselves and the Books they guarded succumbed to time and forgetfulness and the tooth of the worm. The books' remaining pages were scattered, cut into fragments that were sold as relics or for spells. Some of the pages survived and were bound together with remnants from other volumes into a book that passed from thief to trader and was so lost, its own magic reduced to a remedy for toothache. Keepers! Better you should be dust than live to see your books so, bound in pigskin and iron."

A look of amazement spread over Caitlin's features. "Abagtha's book . . . the book of incantations . . ."

"Just so."

"But you said there were five Books. What happened to the fifth?"

Drusian pointed to the crystal book, whose pages glowed with a steady light. "It was the Book of Seeing. Ylfcwen's people knew its value and brought it here for safekeeping."

"So that was why you summoned me, to fetch the last Book of the Keepers. . . ."

"Only partly. When Iule sank beneath the waves, a great chasm split the kingdom, creating a world underground. Eventually the magic banished from the one world found a place in the other. Ylfcwen and her kind are beyond the dominion either of good or evil, but when Iule fell and Chameol was sunk in mist they deemed the gemfields a better home for their kind than the world of men. I fled with them to bide my time until the day should come for my and Iule's release. Century on century I have sat in this dark chamber, ruling the Otherworld but a prisoner of it, a tribute of gems laid at my feet when all I desired was my freedom."

"And I was summoned to release you."

"No—there was no need to Summon you. It was enough to take Bram. Love alone brought you here. If you had harbored any other motive, you would never have found me. For love's sake Iule was lost. Love alone can raise her. But it must be done willingly, and you must know what it will cost you."

Drusian reached out to touch the crystal book. The leaves came to life with the scene of an ancient palace, the marble walls hung with tapestries of sea-flax and carpeted with scarlet coral. Schools of golden fish slanted in the windows and across the rooms like shafts of sunlight.

"This is my father's house, which lies now beneath the waters of the strait of Chameol. Fetch me the crown of Iule: once it is raised from the sea, Myrrhlock will be destroyed and I shall be freed from my prison in the Otherworld. I am too old to take my true form Above, but once free of Myrrhlock's spell I can change my form for all time. It is my wish to join Nairne and her kind."

Caitlin pondered the shape-changer's words in silence, her eyes rapt on the shifting image of the watery palace. One of the toppled statues had lost an arm, and the figure, a woman, gazed sorrowfully down on an exquisite marble of a child. The laughing boy reached out over his mother's disembodied arm, his fingers outstretched to grasp the tails of passing fish. Caitlin tore her eyes away, as if wrestling with a powerful charm. "If I do this," she said slowly, "am I free to return with my son to Chameol?"

"Yes, but there is a risk—" Drusian was suddenly alert to a more present danger. Bram had reached a hand out to touch the tempting pictures that swirled on the crystal pages. Drusian siezed him by his plump wrist and drew his hand away as if from a hot stove. "Ah, ah! Careful he doesn't touch the pages, or he'll be in Iule before you."

"That will never do," Caitlin said, kissing Bram on his furrowed brow. "No—don't cry. Here—Drusian will let you borrow her throne, and here's a feather for you to play with. Don't be a goblin."

Her back was barely turned before Bram had found a better toy. The jeweled game board was too great a temptation, and it was just within his reach. His chubby hand reached for an ebony pawn, but he only knocked it over. It rolled from the golden circle across the game board, through squares inlaid with serpentine and sapphire and tiger's eye, finally coming to rest in one of the numbered squares set with silver that formed the border of the game board.

Drusian passed a hand over the pages of the crystal book, and the vision of Iule vanished, replaced by a blue as still as the surface of a pond.

"When you have the crown, call for me and I will be summoned. You will find Bram in the place from which he was first taken. When you are ready—"

"—I am ready."

"Touch the pages of the book."

Caitlin obeyed. The calm reflection of the crystal pages broke at her touch into ripples. In the next second Caitlin felt herself plummet into space, then into water.

The pages of the crystal book went dark, and the chamber rang with a clear tone, a note struck on a tuning fork. Only then did Drusian see the mischief Bram had worked on the game board. The shape-changer gazed with horror at the ebony piece where it had come to rest in a silver square engraved with Ylfcwen's seal and the number seven.

"Seven years! Child, child, what have you wrought! What a grief you've brought on your mother now!"

15

THE CLOAK
AND THE CROWN

"It's the only way."

Elric wheeled on the Badger, his face taut with fear. "How can you know that? It's poison—it could kill us or, if it spares our bodies, kill our souls and minds and anything else that makes us human—makes us other than what *he* is."

Between them on the rough trestle table, in a silver-and-crystal cordial glass, lay a few thimblesful of purple liquor. But more lay between them than that: There was an understanding that somehow they had changed places, that the Badger had emerged from his fever and the clutches of the river bright as a finely honed sword, tempered in the fire and cooled in the water to a shining keenness. Elric's face was graven with care, and his quarrel with Grisaudra had sorely shaken his belief in himself, as a man and as a knight.

The Badger shook his head stubbornly. "You may be right, but it is the only hope we have to find Myrrhlock—and save Grisaudra."

Hessie spoke from the shadows. "I'm afraid he's right,

Elric. Whatever else that swallow may do, it will certainly take you to Myrrhlock and Grisaudra." The snake charmer stepped forward, unclasping what looked like a jeweled necklace. The string of bright green gems lay brightly in her palm, then lifted its head to regard them through eyes of jet.

"The apothecary asp . . ." Elric murmured.

"You know it? Then you also know its bite cures all other poisons. It can lead the hopeless back from the brink of death itself. Except for one: To anyone who lives on poison itself, on evil and hatred—to him this bite is the only death."

Elric's grey eyes narrowed. "Come, Hessie—you were once more than a midwife. How, where, did you learn these things?"

Hessie laughed. "Sometime, perhaps, I shall tell you. But it is a long tale that will take no shortening, and now the lack we feel so keenly is time." She fastened the asp around Elric's wrist, where the reptile resumed its uncanny resemblance to a precious coil paved with green gems. Then Hessie kissed them each solemnly, Elric upon the cheek and the Badger upon his brow, as a mother kisses her soldier sons before they go off to battle. And so the charmer of snakes and other things of the shadows left them, and on her going the tent fell into a profound darkness, though outside it was broadest day. The lamp, its wick burned low, struggled to hold the shadows back from a feeble circle of light.

Within the circle Elric and the Badger sat silent and immobile until the Badger reached out and picked up the small silver-and-crystal glass, raising it to his lips and letting a few beads of the strange liquor pass over his tongue. Then he handed the glass to Elric, who did the same, and so they passed the glass back and forth until the deadly cordial was gone, each man riveting his gaze on the other, watching for some sign that the potion had worked its way into their veins.

"Nothing," said Elric at last, when some half an hour had passed with no observable change in either man's face or in the objects in the tent around them. "It must need a spell to set it off. Or else this batch has lost its potency."

"No, it is still quite potent," the Badger said calmly. He had gone very white and sweat had begun to bead his brow. "Turn around—softly, now!"

Behind them, casting an eerie glow in the dimness of the tent, stood a watery apparition dragging a tangled burden of waterweeds, rotting barge ropes, and torn fishing nets. Ghostly water streamed over the floor of the tent, giving up a wet-rot smell of river, but wetting nothing.

"Pyle!" Elric said.

"Or what our imaginations—or this potion—have raised of him," the Badger murmured.

It was the fire-eater, somewhat the worse for his time in the river: a fishhook snagged one ear, and his left foot was hopelessly snared in an eel trap. The ghost gazed mournfully from Elric to the Badger, as if struggling to regain the speech that the river had taken away. Already the apparition grew paler, and both Pyle and the train of weeds and rope behind him began to rise slowly to the middle of the room, as though borne upward by a rising tide.

And he was gone, leaving nothing behind but a pronounced smell of river and a fainter note of kerosene.

When Pyle's ghost had gone, the Badger sat with his lips pressed tightly together, his boot heels knocking on the rungs of his chair, reliving in his mind the struggle with the current that had nearly taken his life. Then he felt Elric's hands on his shoulders, shaking him.

"No! I'm all right—I was thinking of Hodge, of that face when I saw it last."

But it was the lion and not his tamer who next appeared, his massive paws treading the air a foot above the tent floor. As Rollo wagged his head from side to side, the beams of his eyes gleamed forth like chinks of light from a watchman's lantern. This was not the rheumatic, toothless lion who had allowed a child to braid wildflowers into his mane. This was the man-eater that Rollo had never been in life, and he paced closer to the two knights with a furious fire burning in his eyes.

But already the spectral lion had begun to dissolve. Indeed, the lion's haunches had faded to near transparency, and his forelimbs rolled away into mist; the paws themselves had disappeared completely.

The rest of the apparition went out like a match, with a lingering smell of singed fur.

Something very strange had happened to the tent. The rushes strewn on the floor stood on end, green again and alive with the peeping of frogs and crickets. The tent poles had grown bark, the onions hanging from them turned to moss and the hams to roosting owls. Elric and the Badger strained to see the other side of the tent and the sunlight and air they knew must be there, but they could see nothing. They were no longer in the kitchen tent. The chairs in which they had lately sat were gone; the two knights found themselves on a small island in the middle of the Oncemoon Marsh.

A figure approached them through the mist, a will-o'-the-wisp in human form, the long white neck garlanded with swanthistle, knees ghostly behind a skirt of whispering rushflower.

Their imaginations, aided by the ergot cordial, had called forth Tillie as she never was. It was not a vacant, drowned stare that caught their wary eyes but an owl's, flashing like silver disks in the moonlight. In her hands she was weaving a rope of frog grass, the sharp blades cutting her fingers.

She was sighted like an owl but mute as a swan. With her roughened fingertips she reached out to touch the Badger's cheek; the sensation, light as a cobweb, made him shiver. He reached up to grasp that hand, but his fingers closed on air.

The eerie light in her eyes dimmed, and for a moment that owllike gaze seemed human. She turned to Elric as if in appeal, and all of a sudden it was Grisaudra who stood there, a rope of borage belted around her tunic of chain mail.

Grisaudra seized his hand tightly in her own and looked intently into his eyes. "Courage," she whispered, and pressed her lips to the palm of his hand. And was gone.

The Badger stared for a moment before he found his voice.

"Are you all right?"

Elric could not answer, could only look at his hand, which bore a clear impression of chain mail and a strange silvery blister, something his mother used to call an elf kiss.

The mist had lifted and revealed them not in Oncemoon Marsh, but in the chill flagstone hallway of some long-abandoned fortress. High up in the stone walls were windows of leaded glass in the pattern of a pentacle. But despite the windows and the austere silence, this was no temple, nor was it a castle, unless it was a temple to loneliness or a castle for ghosts. Not a breath of air stirred, and it was cold, cold as the grave.

Elric was the first to place the smell, the acrid vapor from pitch pots, the smoke thought to prevent the spread of contagion. Lepers' robes of grey wool lay piled in an open chest, in readiness for new inmates, and from hooks on the wall hung lepers' bells.

"It *seems* real enough," the Badger murmured. The draft under the door was cold, likewise the torch threw forth heat and light. "I can feel the wool and smell the pitch. I am either very sane or very, very mad."

Elric shook his head, "We are somewhere other than the tent. How far we have wandered—how long we have been gone—there is no way of knowing. But if everything else is an illusion, the danger, at any rate, is real."

"Oh, it is real indeed!"

Myrrhlock stood before them, the hood of the silk-and-velvet cloak pushed back to reveal a skullcap of goblinstone. His hands rested on the shoulders of a slight figure neither Elric nor the Badger could at first recognize. The cloak of poppies fell forward from the Necromancer's shoulders and enveloped her as though it were the embodiment of the spell that held her.

Grisaudra was clothed in an unearthly beauty, a changeable aura that shone from her in hues of moonsilver and alabaster, so that her hair and skin and robes seemed to be made of the same changeable and precious matter. All

that was left of the Grisaudra they had known were her
eyes, and these regarded them blankly, betraying nothing.
Behind her, in endless rows, pressed an army of grey-
robed figures, hoods obscuring their faces so it was
impossible to tell what sort of beings these were, innocent captives or unspeakable creatures called forth from
regions unnamed.

The smooth, cool scales of the apothecary asp seemed to
burn Elric's skin. Surely it would burn through his sleeve.
Myrrhlock would see it, and they would be lost. But the
Necromancer's gaze never strayed from the Badger's face,
his eyes bright with a cold, malevolent light.

"I have looked forward to this meeting, tanner's son.
This time I think you shall find me better armed."

~∞~

The world was all blue-green. She was afloat in the
waves, twined fast in the billows of sea-flax, unable to tell
whether her form was seal or human or to distinguish sea
from sky. Caitlin fastened her gaze on two fishermen's
floats, and the world steadied. Then the floats grew nearer
and became two whiskered faces she knew well. Nairne's
guards swam up to her, barking a greeting. Their sharp
but gentle teeth cut the bonds of sea-flax. As soon as
Caitlin was free, the seals turned and dove, leading the
way down into Nairne's kingdom, ribbons of silver bubbles
streaming in their wake. With a strong kick from the waist,
Caitlin plummeted after them.

Down they went through the perpetual, blue-green twilight. Caitlin's first sight of Iule was a graveyard of ships
speared on the uppermost spires of the city like so many
paper pinwheels, their wrecks turning slowly this way and
that in the current. They sank silently past silent bell towers
and the ghostly domes of Iule's guildhalls. In the dim
green light Caitlin glimpsed wonderful things—a sunken
garden overgrown with sea flowers of dazzling hues: seal
peonies and eel lilies. This was the garden where Nairne
had once tended her roses. But there was not time enough
to pause, not breath enough for anything but her one task.

Caitlin's seal escort led her through the maze of sunken
buildings, through corridors whose tapestries had rotted

away only to be replaced by a bright, living cloth of mosses and lacy sea fans. Through a carpet of scarlet coral Caitlin glimpsed bright mosaics: a tiger rampant, the figure of a wizard in blue robes, and a figure that might have been a mermaid or some other siren—half-woman, half-serpent.

She knew the chamber when she found it by the marble child, broken from the statue of its mother. Why had the sight so disturbed her before, when she had seen it outlined upon the crystal pages of Drusian's book? There was nothing here to worry or perturb her. Her sight dimmed and her lungs burned, and the gentle water lulled her, telling her to heed the loving call of the legion of the drowned. *Breathe me,* said the sea, *a place has been kept for you here in my coral chambers.*

"Seal's song" was the sailors' name for it, the light-headedness that makes the drowning one cease to struggle. But it was the seals who saved her, rousing her from forgetfulness with nips, reviving her with bubbles of air trapped in their thick pelts. Clinging to the neck of one seal, Caitlin spied the crown of Iule.

It was bent and corroded, so crusted with coral that the carvings were nearly undecipherable. But Drusian's crystal book had shown Caitlin the crown as it had lain on the brows of the monarchs of Iule: the golden band of mulberry leaves, signifying wisdom, and above them panels representing each of the five arts of the Keepers.

Caitlin seized the crown, her lungs burning for air, but she had no strength to kick, and the sea took up its chant with the pounding blood in her ears. Nairne's guards pressed in close, gently bearing her form between them, up through the spires of that green and silent kingdom to the realm of light and air.

～⁓～

"It was very simple, once I had conceived it. After all, who would suspect the bread?"

Elric and the Badger had been brought to chambers high in the tower of the leper house. These were Myrrhlock's own rooms; the ergot was distilled elsewhere, but a small table held a number of decanters, alembics, and vials of the distilled poisons on which the Necromancer fed. There was no bed; to such a creature as Myrrhlock, repose came in some form other than sleep. A fire burned on the hearth, but for utility rather than warmth. The only human comfort in the room was the chair in which Grisaudra now sat, impassive and serene, a crow perched on the chair back by her ear, a cat dozing in her lap.

Myrrhlock went to the table and busied himself with a dropper and vial.

"You put most of the pieces of the puzzle together very well. I congratulate you on that, and as a token of my esteem I will fit together the rest for you.

"Something such as I am cannot easily be destroyed. From Ninthstile I made my way to this place, where I could disguise myself without attracting notice. I happened on the ergot by accident. It is a blight that occurs in nature, and it happened that the local grain merchant unloaded his diseased rye on the leper house, thinking it the least exacting of his customers. There broke out among the inmates at this place an epidemic, which many did not survive. The connection between the disease and the grain was made by no one else; they attributed the symptoms to their leprosy and the madness to despair. Those who were spared fled in terror.

"For my part, I had chanced on the tool of my revenge. All that winter in the solitude of this place I tended my seedling rye, and in the spring I set out, selling the tainted grain to farmers, and where necessary burning crops and granaries in order to create a demand for my wares. And once the dose was given, it was simple enough to call them. They were like pigeons coming home to roost. And so I gained two things: I gathered to me a silent army against the time I should have need of them, an army of a kind that should never be suspected. And I had created the very kind of disturbance I knew should bring one or two of Iiliana's best knights." The Necromancer's harelip curled into a smile. "And here you are."

Elric's gaze was fastened on Grisaudra as he tried to read her eyes. Had she sold her soul? It seemed to him they held something of the old Grisaudra, if nothing more than her thinly veiled loathing of him. Their eyes locked for a brief moment in some recognition before she bowed her head, her attention all for her cat. Why should I have expected anything else, Elric thought, too weary to be bitter. And I, what would I do, if someone offered me everlasting beauty, even everlasting youth? With her lot in life, why should she believe in some abstract good of mine? He has won, and we have lost.

"So you will kill us," he said aloud.

"No, only you. The stableboy will carry a message for me to Chameol, after which Grisaudra may do with him what she will."

Grisaudra's eyes were fixed on the smooth plait of Caitlin's hair that cinched the Badger's wrist. Then she raised her eyes to his and a faint current of understanding passed between them.

Grisaudra stood, and the aura wavered like a flame.

"*No.*"

The word seemed to cut her; she winced with pain, and the illusion of beauty faltered, showing a glimpse of the old Grisaudra. Myrrhlock turned on her, uttering a bitter word in a rune tongue. She fell to the ground as if under the force of a blow.

"It is not for you any longer, Grisaudra, to say no or yes to anything. The yes you gave when you swore to serve me was the last that was yours to give or withhold."

The face Grisaudra raised from the floor once more bore a scar across it. "No."

The Necromancer's wrath was turned as much inward on his own mismeasure as it was turned outward on Grisaudra's defiance. Myrrhlock spoke another rune word, and Grisaudra crumpled under the force of it, the aura writhing around her like a sheet of flame. The beauty her soul had purchased melted away like mist, leaving her as she had been the day Elric had first brought the Badger to her for a love cure.

At the window, a pigeon landed on the sill in a ruffle of wind, folding over her back wings that caught the light with the green and gold of mother-of-pearl. Myrrhlock whirled toward the sound, and in the second his back was turned Elric lunged forward, the apothecary asp in his hand like a small jeweled dagger.

Swinging back to face this newer threat, Myrrhlock upset the table and its array of deadly liquors. Elric's feet went out from under him, and a torrent of poison and shattered glass rained onto his head. The Badger sprang forward and with Grisaudra's aid pulled Elric unconscious from the debris. The bite meant for Myrrhlock spared Elric instead, but the asp had spent its own life in the saving sting.

Suddenly the room was ablaze with light, a brilliance borne on a rush of wind, wings threshing light from the very air. And there was in the room a presence, something more terrible than an angel and too beautiful to behold. The face was a woman's face, full of a holy wrath and sorrow, the smooth brow banded with a crown of leaves wrought in gold.

"Yes, I am Drusian released! I am your doom, Myrrhlock, come for you."

Myrrhlock's features were rigid with terror, and he groped behind him blindly for the cloak of poppies, as if it could shield him from that awful gaze. But his hand closed only on the back of the claw-foot chair.

The winged creature spoke three names as softly as a prayer. "For Myhrra, then, and for Tybitha, and for my beloved Nairne, I summon and bind you for all time."

It was the spell Myrrhlock had used in the royal garden, ages past, to bind Drusian. He instantly became the thing his hand had closed on. The Badger stared, hardly able to grasp the transformation before him. Drusian had summoned a demon of wood, the expression frozen in a howl of defeat as though a craftsman's painstaking had carved it there. It was like the Necromancer in every respect but the hands: They were changed to lion's paws, each clutching in its talons a wooden sphere. Already the wood was riddled with wormholes, and before his eyes the Badger watched Myrrhlock fall to dust. Then an acrid smoke rose up from the floor, and a sour smell of acid, and even the dust was gone.

The wind rose again and the blinding light, and then

the crown clattered to the floor, and the only sound was that of the pigeon beating its way homeward to Nairne's kingdom.

When at last they could tear their eyes from the window, Grisaudra and the Badger were startled to see, huddled on the hearth in each other's arms, two girls, where there had a moment before been a crow and a cat. Grisaudra came to herself first, and going up to them took each by the hand and led them from that place.

The Badger first retrieved the crown, wrapping it in the cloak of poppies; the one thing he meant to save and the other see destroyed. Then he lifted Elric on his back and followed.

16

HOMECOMING

Slumped at his counting table, Folderol held his head in his hands and groaned. Hessie and the Badger stood before him and traded a glance.

"You can't blame me," Hessie chided gently. "How can you expect me to pass up an offer to head my own troupe? I have myself to think of, you know, and my old age to provide for. And if a few of the troupe choose to follow me, well, that's their right, now, isn't it?"

Folderol only groaned. "Gone. All of it! Gone, gone. Oh, whoahoah-iz-meeee . . ."

Hessie's patient voice took on an edge. "Here now," she said tartly, "aren't you taking this all a little hard? After all, you haven't lost everyone. You'll still have all the troupe you had a few weeks ago, save me."

Folderol raised his head and glowered balefully at her. "It's the gold!" he barked. "They took it—took it all, every cent I owned."

"Who took it?"

"That damn-cur wolf-girl and that wretched albino pup of hers. Blast them! Blast and damn 'em!" Folderol thumped the table with his fist, making the calico tufts he had torn from his beard leap on the felt tabletop like

378

trained dogs. "I'd hidden it, but that little white rat nosed it out. It's gone, and now they're gone, and the rest of the filthy pack with them." He lowered his head again and moaned. He raised a hand and waved them away. "Go, go, all of you. Take the whole troupe. I can't pay them; they'll all leave anyhow."

Ulfra and Nix had left early that morning, with the pack of wolves and a bootful of gold, and in a few days had made their way to the edge of the great forest known as the Weirdwood. The pledge that bound the wolves to Ulfra's service had expired, and under the terms of their oath the pack was returning to their first wild home. Poor Nix hung on the neck of the she-wolf until Ulfra dragged him off. Some of the younger wolves, ones who had spent most of their short lives in the wolf-girl's service, stood around silently, ears flattened against their heads and heads sunk between their shoulders as if uncertain what trick Ulfra wanted of them. Their elders had only to catch the nutmeggy smell of the rain-damp loam before they struck out for the cover of the ancient and knowing trees. The eldest wolf turned and called to the stragglers, who hurried after. They were soon lost in the thicket of shadows. Nix's whimper broke into an unhappy wail. Ulfra cuffed him, but not too roughly, and he fell in at her side as they turned and retraced their way to the town.

Near the outskirts they began to pass some farmhouses. Each time they passed a long, low building of peat and thatch Ulfra would lift her head and sniff deeply. Nix's spirits lifted, and he smacked his lips, thinking Ulfra meant to steal a pig for them to roast. The third time she sniffed, Ulfra smelled the something she was looking for. She pinned a coin purse to Nix's shirtfront and began to chase him with businesslike cuffs and snarls toward the house.

At first Nix raced and laughed, thinking it a game, but the wallop that landed on his left ear convinced him otherwise. The boy began to whimper and then to cry. Ulfra was unrelenting. Lights appeared in the unglazed windows of the farmhouse; then the door opened and let a heavy slab of yellow light out into the dark yard.

The wolf-girl's gaze locked with the boy's, and the unyielding blue fire he saw there told him he was beaten. Nix swallowed his whimper and without a backward glance walked toward the dark figure framed in the blazing light of the farmhouse doorway.

As the closing door narrowed the light to slivers and chinks around the doorjamb and hinges, Ulfra's shoulders slumped. She stood in the thick shadows of the yard, resisting the call of the wolves that rode the highest pitch of the wind. At last Ulfra set out on the road again, walking away from the last fields and hedgerows to the town, with its smell of soot and wash water on cobblestones and the sweat of horses and men.

"Is it that fox after the hens again, Tom?" the farmer's wife called to her husband.

"No," the householder said, shaking his head. "The damndest thing. Come see."

The farmer stood and looked from the snowy hair of the boy before him to the six gold coins gleaming in his hand. Without a word he handed the note to his wife.

It was written on the back of a bill advertising a band of traveling acrobats. *Take Wondrous and Amazing Care of NIX, The Albino Deaf Mute!* it said in unsteady printing.

The couple stood a moment in silent contemplation of all this. The howl of their seventh and youngest child brought the woman to her senses first, and she took Nix by the hand.

"Come on, then," she said with a sigh, "and see how you like my wondrous and amazing soup."

❧

Ylfcwen groaned, stretching her feet toward Emma's fire, her stomach heavy with the meat and drink that humans favor: lamb stewed with onions and rosemary; chunks of dark, seedy bread; golden ale tasting of apples and summer.

"No wonder mortals don't fly. Even if they had the wings for it, with food like this they could never leave the ground."

"Mmm," was all Emma said in agreement. She had lived

a long time among mortal men and women and found her visitor from the Otherworld an unsettling, almost embarrassing, reminder of the past. Her own days at the elvish court seemed impossibly distant. Among her neighbors Emma was well liked but not entirely respectable, running as she did a rooming house renowned as much for the bed boarders got as for the board. Unknown to her neighbors, Emma's boarders were all knights of Chameol, thankful for a place to let down their guises for an evening of good company.

"Be careful," she said to her guest, "not to eat too much of it, if your design is to return Below. It will make you heavy and dull and give you human cares. I am used to these things and now prefer them, but they might not agree with your constitution as well as they do mine. If you plan on returning to court, you had best not delay."

Ylfcwen sighed. "It was not my intention to go back without a human child as compensation for the goblin I lost. But it's proved to be much more difficult than I imagined. I had never realized what contrary creatures these mortals are."

"Yes." Emma smiled at some memory of her own. "That they are."

The stew had settled a little, and now that she was less painfully full of dinner, Ylfcwen began to grow drowsy and content. Ale had its charms, though it was not root wine. Yes, she thought, it's time I returned to the Otherworld. There will be other chances to find a new favorite and choose a consort. Ylfcwen missed her mole and did not trust her prized orchids to hands other than her own.

Emma was thinking how much better she liked ale than root wine and how she preferred her companions wild from the field and not forced in the hothouse. Over the rim of her glass the elder of the two elf queens looked at her successor and thought she wouldn't have changed places with her for all the world.

∽

Caitlin was in bed. A humming slowly formed into low voices, then into the mutter and chirp of birds. As Caitlin moved her head, light and shadow dappled her closed eyes. She opened them and met Iiliana's worried gaze.

"Thank heaven!" Iiliana said, giving her a white-lipped kiss that was warm, for all that. "What a scare you gave us!"

"I nearly fainted when I found you, lying there so still, with half the bottle of the ergot gone. I couldn't forgive myself, leaving it within your reach like that, when you were distraught out of your mind."

Iiliana was braiding Caitlin's hair. They were seated in the window, and Caitlin was gazing down into the garden as if into the bottom of the sea, as if the birds on the lawn were strange fish moving among the languid fronds. She spoke, but slowly, the way she had when she had first returned to Chameol from her sojourn among the seals, before she lost her seal speech.

"Distraught?"

"About your son," Iiliana said gently.

"Bram."

Iiliana looked startled. "Oh, no! He's quite fine. It was the other, the twin—"

"Twin," Caitlin repeated dully.

Iiliana took Caitlin's hand and squeezed it. "Yes. You remember. They were twin boys, only one did not live long. You named the other one Bram. His wet nurse is bringing him in to see you. He's missed his mother."

The baby they put in her arms was Grimald. Not quite the Grimald she remembered, really, but Grimald all the same. His golden eyes were green now, flecked with gold, his face ruddy only from crying, and the nurse remarked that his milk teeth had fallen out since Caitlin had taken ill.

"He's fussy, 'cause he's teething. We found nothing soothes him as much as a macaroon in a little milk."

Caitlin mused on words remembered, scraps of a dream: *Be careful what you choose to tell them, for those who return from the Otherworld are never more to be believed.* Could it have been merely a dream, an overdose of ergot? The evidence in her arms, where the changeling slept as innocent as any human child, seemed undeniable. But where had the silvery mark on Caitlin's forehead come from? Fever marks were known, but not one so perfectly made. Caitlin traced the outline of it in the mirror, wondering at it. It had almost the outline of a kiss.

So Caitlin might have remembered it always, an unacknowledged and unreasoning grief driving her to madness. But then they found Fiddle.

After his brush with Ylfcwen he had fled to the cheese caves and had been hiding there ever since, only surfacing when an unvaried diet of cheese began to pall.

"Well, it solves the mystery of the larder, anyway," Iiliana said and listened with increasing astonishment as Fiddle related, over a plate of custard tarts, all that he had witnessed of Chameol's sleep.

◆◇◆

Outside it was bitterly cold, and an unforgiving wind swung the shingle on its hinges with a mournful sound. Inside the cobbler thought she might as well take the sign down. It certainly didn't bring in any custom, and at least she would be spared having to listen to it at night.

There came a knock at the door. It was late; the cobbler had put away her work and had settled down in front of the fire with her accounts. She sighed and rose to answer the door, not very much surprised at the lateness of the call. Her creditors had been known to rouse her from her bed past midnight to demand payment.

It was not a creditor at all, but a ghost, "Mama," it said, and fell upon her neck.

In all the commotion of laughter and tears the cobbler did not notice the second figure still hanging in the doorway. Tillie finally pulled Iimogen forward. The cobbler needed no explanation and without hesitation gave Iimogen the same kiss and embrace she had bestowed on her own daughter.

"Now come in, girls, and get by the fire. Heavens, it's a bitter night, and I've kept you standing in the doorway. Come in and get into some warm things while I stir up the fire."

Her hands were so unsteady with the shock of joy that she dropped and broke the old blue teapot and burned the bread twice, but at last they were settled by the fire with tea and rarebit.

The cobbler put her hand to Tillie's cheek and traced the lines of the scratches still visible there.

"What happened to you? Did a cat do this?"

Tillie glanced at Iimogen, but the younger girl had dropped off where she sat, her face flushed from the fire, the dog licking her hand where it hung down.

"No—they're nothing more than briar scratches." Tillie rose from her chair yawning and gave her mother a kiss. "Now I think we ought to get Iimogen to bed."

17

LOVE REGAINED

For the first weeks of Elric's blindness, Grisaudra nursed him. She endured his ill temper and complaints with no perceptible resentment, ever silent but never cold, gentle yet not tender. He sometimes hardly knew she had been in the room, as though she were one of the invisible servants of the monster prince in a fairy tale. Elric's despair raged within him, and he struck out once, sending a bowl of compresses to the floor with a crash.

"Leave it!" he hissed through his teeth, hearing her kneel to pick up the pieces. "I'm blind; leave it! Can't you see it's useless!"

Grisaudra reached out to calm him, and at the touch of her hands on his shoulders he flailed his arms, choking with fury. "Don't touch me! Leave me—I don't want your pity!"

It was so silent for a moment he thought she had left the room. Then he heard the whisper of her clothes as she knelt again and the soft chime of the shards against each other in her hand as she gathered them up, heard the sound of the cloth wrung out at the basin. Her voice spoke at last from the doorway.

"I should have thought that you of all people, Elric, would know the difference between pity and love."

He sat alone the rest of that day, but she did not return. Love—what did she mean, love? What, love him? She could not have meant that; it was madness to consider it. But, though his mind turned her words over and over until the coals had become a heap of cold ash, Elric could winnow no other meaning from them.

At last he stumbled up from his chair and, creeping around the room, felt along the mantelpiece and cupboards until he found the matches and tinderbox. He revived the fire, filled the kettle from the pail by the door, and brewed himself some tea.

The hour was very late when he heard her come back into the room. When Elric felt her hand on his brow, testing him for fever, he quickly seized Grisaudra by the wrist and held her fast.

"What did you mean this morning?"

"You know very well. Are you so surprised?"

"No." He drew her down into the chair beside him. "I must have known for a long time, though I denied it. Imagine my dread and terror today, when I realized what was happening. And you—do you find the idea distasteful?"

In answer she took his hand and placed it over her heart so he could feel it beating swiftly as the wings of a bird. Elric ran his hands lightly over her face, wiping away her sudden tears with the side of his thumb, tracing her upper and lower lip before kissing her, as if relearning by touch what wonder was, and delight, reinventing joy. In that room time seemed to stand still, unable to touch them. The fire lay dead on the hearth, but they were not cold.

In the chair, he held Grisaudra close, smoothing and resmoothing the warm whorl of her ear.

"You must be certain," he said at last. "My eyes may be payment enough to buy me from my vows to Chameol, but Iiliana may yet find a use for her blind knight. Could you live with that?"

Grisaudra laid her head upon his breast. "Yes. I have

thought it through and through. I only worry that when you regain your sight you will change your mind. My voice is pleasing enough, but not so that it would overcome my face."

"And that is your only reservation?"

"The only one worth mentioning. We are very much alike, Elric. If we do not hate each other, what else is left for us but love?"

When the day came and Elric's eyes were unbandaged, it was still uncertain whether his sight should ever fully return. For the time being he saw dimly and greenly through a pair of thick, dark spectacles. When he was ready to travel, they set off together for Oncemoon to retrieve her belongings from the hut in the marsh.

They were camped for the night a few days from Oncemoon when Grisaudra left Elric to refill their water bottles and search the hedgerow for nests and mushrooms so they might have an omelet for their supper. She set off across the fields, stepping over the hedges and stiles, her heart light as she watched wild geese pass overhead, calling to each other. The air was sharp with cold and peat smoke from farmers' cottages.

The evening was beginning to settle down upon the gentle hills when in the failing light Grisaudra came upon a tinker's family camped in the field. Three older children ran around pulling the tail feathers of the tethered geese. Their mother shouted at them without looking up from the potatoes she was peeling, trading a remark with the grandmother, who was tending two younger children and a pig. Nearby, the father had set up a makeshift forge and was reshoeing the cart-horse.

Grisaudra hid herself, though she need not have. Her family would not have known her, even without the scar. She realized with a shock that the tinker was not her father but her eldest brother, so that her mother must be the old grannie, the younger woman, her brother's wife. And that tall girl, the one pulling the two rough-and-tumble boys apart, that must be her baby sister, Olma. . . .

They did not see her. Grisaudra moved away and quickly filled the water jug at a brooklet, realizing she had left Elric too long alone. When she got back to the place where they had made their own camp for the night, Grisaudra found Elric smoking his pipe and roasting chestnuts in the fire. She knelt beside him to warm her hands. He reached out and touched her cheek.

"You were out in the fields a long time."

"Yes."

"You're cold. Are you sure you're all right?"

Grisaudra shuddered uncontrollably. "I must have caught a chill. I had better go to sleep."

But his hands were on her face, and she could not keep Elric from reading with his fingers the high feeling written there.

"What happened? Did you see something, or is this just cold feet, now we are so close to home?"

"Oh no! Not that." She kissed him anxiously. "Not that! I ran across a band of robbers camped in the field. I don't think they saw me."

He was silent for a long moment, his hands heavy on her shoulders. "Grisaudra," he said at last. "You're free to go with them. You're not bound to me. I can make my way on my own."

"Why should I want to go off with a band of robbers?" she said, trying to make herself angry with him but failing, finding herself holding him tightly where they knelt by the fire.

"Why should you tie yourself to a blind man?"

"Hush—forget them, as they have forgotten me. They gave me up for dead long ago. Now it's my turn to lay their ghosts to rest."

❧

Autumn had rusted the leaves of the arbor and brought a bite to the air that made it too cool to sit out, but sit out Caitlin did. She sat on the cold stone bench, a small book open in her lap, watching Bram-who-was-Grimald asleep at her feet in the wicker cradle, thinking he would soon outgrow it. Pomamber dozed nearby, one eye half-open, to see that no ravens stole the tarnished and raveled silver ribbon that marked the place in her mistress's book or the bright gilded laces that bound small bells to the baby's slippers.

While searching for a wayward hair comb, Caitlin had found the book wedged between the head of her bed and the wall. It was a girdlebook, small enough to be obscured by the flat of her hand, its covers thick with a dust that clung and glittered like crushed dragonflies' wings. The cover was set with bits of colored glass, and the clasp that bound it was cheap tin. Upon opening the book, Caitlin was annoyed to find it blank.

Iiliana had never seen it and had no idea where it could have come from.

"It's certainly not from my library. Perhaps one of the girls was making a diary. Take it; it's no earthly use to me, I'm sure."

Caitlin took it, found a pen and some ink, and began that afternoon to fill the pages with her smallest hand, stopping when the overwound spring of her script gave her hand a cramp. She meant to write out all she could remember of Ylfcwen's court etiquette. Her recall of it was already imperfect. Whole long passages, like scenes from a dream, appeared amid entries on proper elvish wedding toasts and the baking of funeral cakes. It was as though she were gazing into the mirrored surface of a pond, glimpsing beneath the glassy reflection of sky and clouds the lurk of carp and turtle.

There were few things, anymore, that she *was* certain of. The beads of wax from her taper sank to the bottom of the basin in meaningless lumps; the flames of the white tapers stretched into smoky tongues, guttered, and went out. Caitlin was forced to take her search for omens elsewhere. Every day now she left Grimald with Iiliana, and walked—sometimes to the marshes where the wild island horses appeared and disappeared among the black and wizened trees like grey and silver ghosts. Other days she wandered to the rockiest part of the sea's edge and stood for hours, listening for the mournful bark of a seal calling her name. Today the wind off the straits chilled her to the bone, and it was dark when at last she made her way back to the palace.

She found Iiliana sprawled on the carpet by the fire, teasing the baby with a bronze tassel of her hair, as if he were a cat. Iiliana needed only one look at Caitlin's lips, blue with cold, to send for an egg beaten with rum. Caitlin was made to drink it down under the queen's watchful eye and afterward to allow a balm of soothing herbs to be rubbed into her chilled limbs. Iiliana frowned at her patient.

"You'll brood yourself sick again if you're not careful."

Caitlin raked a hand through her hair. The fire and rum had warmed and numbed her, but neither they nor the balm could reach deep enough to heal the grief that really ailed her. Caitlin leaned her head on Iiliana's shoulder. "Sometimes I think I've lost my reason, my wits as well as my purpose for being."

"That's only natural. The tug of the Otherworld is strong and not easy to shake off. You were deep in the grip of the ergot, and it will be a while before you are securely back among us. For the time being, I think it would be better if you walked a little less often in the marsh and along the shore. These lonely melancholies can't be good for you."

One day, walking with Grimald in the garden, Caitlin came upon strange marks on the ground, footprints that shimmered though the frost had burned off the rest of the garden. She followed the footprints through the garden until she came to their source, an ancient trapdoor. Then Caitlin blinked and looked again, and it was only a patch of bare ground with an oddly gnarled root that resembled an iron ring.

That night she sat up late, writing in her elvish book, and fell asleep upon her pen. Caitlin woke to find her nightshirt and the blotter blooming with ink roses. Wiping a smudge from her cheek, she saw with growing astonishment that the page before her, which had been blank the night before, had been filled in her own script while she slept. This is what she read:

Gaming, Debts, and Indentureship

Gambling is a great court pastime, and most obligations acquired in this manner are repaid in story or in song, two of the most highly prized commodities. Gold and silver are rarely used. A special sort of betting is used in connection with the servitude of humans and goblins, and with human children brought into the court in an exchange. A game board of ebony is inlaid with gems to represent the gemfields of the Otherworld, and the indentured is represented by a carved piece of wood or stone. Through skill and chance the player must complete a circuit of the board in a given number of moves, without landing on the region of the board claimed for the queen. If a player lands on a square without a number, he merely loses the game. Should a player land on a square bearing a number, however, the player's servitude is extended by a corresponding number of years.

When she had read it, Caitlin's memory of all that had passed in Drusian's chamber returned, and she knew the meaning of the passage. The seer of Chameol laid her head on her arms and wept, for her memory regained and for the son she had lost.

ॐ

Iiliana started at the sight of the man in the doorway. He was dressed in the dark, close-fitting clothes of a high-wayman, the black cloth silvered with a crust of salt water. Seen from the darkened doorway, his eyes were a startling blue in a face the shadows made dark as a miner's. The eyes told Iiliana all she needed to know. The queen crossed the room swiftly, as if to embrace him. Then she saw the crown in his hand and the cloak over his arm and fell to her knees, afraid to ask the price that had been paid for them.

The Badger spoke through lips blistered by the wind and sun. "Myrrhlock is no more." He placed his burdens, the one shining, the other seeming to gather to it all the light, at Iiliana's feet and then sank to the floor, all his strength gone. Iiliana raised her eyes, a silent question written in her features.

"Elric lives," the Badger said. "But he gave his sight, Iiliana. I left him in the hands of a capable nurse."

Iiliana shed the last thread of her queenly demeanor and burst into tears of mingled sorrow and relief. The Badger let her weep for a time before he asked the question most on his own mind.

"Where is she?"

He found Caitlin asleep. The book had fallen shut in her lap, and the hood of her cloak had slipped back, loosing her hair to the wind, which teased it out in tendrils around her face. The Badger crouched the better part of an hour among the leaves of the arbor, afraid to wake her and find that he was asleep himself and this was but another dream. So rapt was he that it was some minutes before he noticed the cradle at her feet.

"I *am* dreaming," he muttered, stepping forward from his hiding place and gingerly lifting the swaddled child from the wicker cradle. One look at Grimald's golden-green eyes and slightly pointed ears and the Badger knew this was his mooncalf, his firstborn son.

"Hello!" he said under his breath. "And who are you?"

"His name is Grimald."

Caitlin was sitting up, rubbing the kinks from her neck, her eyes roaming over the changes his absence had made in the Badger, the way his eyes seemed polished with sleeplessness, the restless poise of his limbs, ready to flee: the marks of a knight of Chameol or someone haunted by a ghost.

The Badger could not tear his eyes from her face. Even flushed from sleep, Caitlin's features were suffused with a tender sorrow that made her lovely to behold. For a long moment, beholding her was all he could do. At last the Badger stepped forward and placed Grimald in Caitlin's arms.

"A funny name for a baby. Better for an old man than a boy. But it suits him. How did you choose it?" While the Badger said this, he cautiously twined the fingers of his hand in Caitlin's.

"He named himself, in an odd way," she replied so softly that he hardly heard her. Her fingers closed around his. "Do you know the thing for which I will never forgive myself?" she said suddenly. "Sending you away the way I did, without telling you how much I loved you."

At that he broke down and wept.

Iiliana barred the household from the hallway leading to Caitlin's rooms, but the precaution was unnecessary. Upon retiring, the Badger fell soundly asleep and spent the night of their reunion in the most profound slumber he had enjoyed in a year, while Pomamber guarded Grimald in his cradle at the foot of the bed.

But Caitlin slept less soundly. Toward dawn she dreamed of Ylfcwen's court and of the room where mortal interlopers wove tapestries to color and warm the walls of elvish stone. A weaver was working on a tapestry of a monastery. Looking over his shoulder, Caitlin could see the beehives, the stables, and, off behind the garden wall, the orange grove. Here was the stableboy, asleep under a tree, and a fat monk hurrying up to summon him to prayers. Caitlin knew the weaver before the dream showed his face: It was the Badger. His face was pale and blank with hopelessness, and his hands worked the loom mechanically.

The dream showed the approach of a jeweled foot and an intricate hem; attired so regally, who could it be but Ylfcwen? An ivory hand reached out and came to rest on the Badger's shoulder, a gesture of possessiveness, not of lover to beloved, but of master to pet.

"When you are finished with this one, bring it to my chamber," said the queen.

"Yes, milady." Eyes followed the elf queen's retreat down the hall, eyes as blue with scorn as the sapphires on the train of her gown.

But the figure they followed was Caitlin.

The Badger woke to find Caitlin crouching on the cold floor, her knees drawn up, racked with silent sobs. At once he was beside her, his arms around her, kissing her face through the screen of her hair. He helped her back into the bed and settled her among the pillows.

"It was awful," she whispered.

"Tell me."

In halting but unsparing words she related her dream. When she finished, her eyes were glazed with tears, her mouth a grimace of pain. "Get out, go, before I make you hate me—"

"Caitlin." He smoothed the hair gently from her face. "I couldn't hate you, any more than I could forget you. Not that I didn't do my best. But when I tried, every part of me rebelled against it, Cait. I love you. I have to live my life beside you. You must believe that."

She could only nod her head mutely. He kissed her lightly on her mouth.

"It was so real," she murmured.

"No," he said, pulling her close. "This is."

The Badger knew there were nightmares in his past he could never bring himself to share with her. His own turn would come, he knew, to wake in the night, the name of fear on his lips. But they would neither of them wake alone, ever again.

◦◦◦

Caitlin woke late in the morning without first remembering her nightmare and lay awhile sleepily, thinking the Badger and his words part of a dream.

Then she remembered and turned to watch him dreaming beside her. Her eyes roamed over him, noting the creases care had carved beneath his eyes, the way his mouth was soft with sleep, the new beard glittering on his jaw. Then Caitlin saw on his wrist the bracelet of her hair, plaited so tightly it gleamed as smooth and polished as steel. She shuddered, thinking of manacles and bells, and slipped from the bed without waking him.

Hello, she mouthed to Grimald in his wicker cradle. Grimald made an *O* of his mouth back at her. She placed her finger to her mouth, miming for silence, picked up the changeling, and carried him to Iiliana's rooms.

Iiliana was at her dresser, her bronze hair unbound and

streaming over her shoulders. She looked up as Caitlin came in and waved her to a seat on the bed.

"There's something on the tray by the bed, if you're hungry. I haven't looked yet."

Caitlin lay on her back, holding Grimald overhead. He didn't crow, like most babies, but his golden-green eyes got wider and wider. Caitlin kissed him and set him down. The tray held a pitcher of milk and a plate of rolls. She tore a roll in two, dipped one half in milk before giving it to Grimald, and ate the other.

Iiliana finished dressing her hair and turned to Caitlin. "How are you this morning?"

Caitlin did not answer immediately. "If I had to answer only for today—then, happy."

"And for tomorrow?"

Caitlin shook her head. "I'm afraid. How can it work? My work is here, while as a man he can't even remain on the island. Not to mention the vows he took as a knight of Chameol." She laughed. "It's like the plot to a penny romance. Star-crossed, and then some."

"Mmm." Iiliana frowned hard at the tray before picking up the jam pot and a spoon. "I'll say two things, then— with my mouth full. First, he already loves that child, and you're sadly mistaken if you think you'll be able to separate them. Second, Chameol is not the island she was anymore. She can't be, now we know of Iule. I think the days of our cloister are over and that the vows of our knights must be reviewed." Iiliana put another spoonful of jam into her mouth and looked into Caitlin's startled eyes with an expression of utmost innocence.

18

THE BOY
WITH AMBER EYES

The Direwolves watched the progress deeper into the Weirdwood of a dog and three humans: a mated pair and a youngling. The mingled scents, human and goblin, confused the watchers, and they sat back on their haunches, keen-eyed but not venturing any nearer.

Caitlin walked a little ahead, carrying the bundle with the small jeweled book and a few other volumes from Chameol's library, Iiliana's gifts to them on the occasion of their wedding and leave-taking. Caitlin had chosen first a book on the powers and properties of stones, and second, a bestiary—chiefly for the quaint and cunning pictures of seals that the monk, who must once have been a sailor, had added to the margins of the text. For his part, the Badger had chosen a treatise on the treatment of various equine maladies and an encyclopedia of common childhood ailments. For these he had passed up a book with wonderful color plates of a joust and had lingered only briefly over an atlas with folding maps the size of tablecloths.

"It's a different sort of life we're going to," he had said to Caitlin, showing her his choices rather sheepishly.

Though what use he hoped to make of the horse book in the Weirdwood, Caitlin couldn't imagine. His beloved piebald, Motley, was to remain behind on Chameol to bring fresh blood to the stock of horses that ran wild in the marshes. The dappled horse had whickered a good-bye into his master's neck, mouthing his hair as if it were part of the farewell offering of meadow-sweet hay.

The horse would not have liked the Weirdwood; the grasping branches of the trees, the watchfulness of owls would not have agreed with Motley at all, the Badger thought as he followed Caitlin, carrying Grimald before him snug in a bunting. Caitlin's dark cloak made it hard to see her as she slipped with native ease through the trees, and the Badger was glad of the mastiff, one of Pomamber's daughters.

Caitlin had been afraid she would not be able to find it, but every twig and stone seemed to know her and point the way.

"Here," she said, coming to a stop in a clearing and turning in a slow circle. "It should be right—there!"

The red door was green with moss, but the key was where she had left it, under a stone. Inside, the house of her childhood was gone, and in its place was a ruin looted not by human hands but by squirrels and owls and time; mattresses spilled rotting straw, drawers were turned out, porcelain jars smashed, the tiles of the hearth dug up in a search for nuts. In the pantry, jars of mushrooms, ground roots, and dried lizards were tumbled everywhere, and what had not been eaten had been taken for nest material.

Caitlin leaned her head on the Badger's shoulder.

"I didn't expect it to be this bad."

"Well," he said thoughtfully, glancing around. "I've cleaned many a stall in my day. It's not so bad. First thing we do, let's light a fire."

By the time it was dark they had a livable room, beaten, swept, and scoured. They laid a cloth on the floor by the hearth, until the chairs could be mended, and made a supper out of cheese and dried apples. On the old bookstand the repaired book of incantations lay in stately repose, and if Abagtha's spirit was still in that house, it was appeased.

Caitlin drowsed, Grimald in her arms, the Badger's arms around her. The upper room would become hers, and she planned to outfit it for her new task: reconstructing the five Books of the Keepers. She would sell spells and remedies enough to buy all the books she required. Against the other wall she would fix a niche for her candles and basins and other tools of divination. And she wanted to add a window to look out through the branches to the sky and stars and, not least of all, to admit pigeons bearing news of Chameol.

The old root cellar was to be the Badger's, and he had already measured it out in paces and found it large enough to hold a small printing press. Mending tack had made him handy with a needle, and he meant to try his hand at making books.

The Badger shook Caitlin awake gently, kissing her ear. "It's late—"

Outside, the Direwolves settled down in their dens contentedly. Things were well: Magic had returned to the Weirdwood. The owls nodded their agreement, and the wind in the trees muttered about it.

In the oak with the red door, the Badger had made up the bed and placed Grimald in the middle of it. Caitlin climbed in after, yawning as she took down her hair. The Badger sat on the edge of the bed, kicking off his boots.

"I meant to ask you before, Cait. What is that trapdoor in the cellar?"

But Caitlin was already asleep.

❧

Ulfra stood before the window, looking out into the filthy streets of Moorsedge. A little towheaded boy, just Nix's size a year ago, was running up the street with some apples he had stolen from under the apple-seller's nose. Ulfra let the curtain fall.

The leopard-woman looked up from her sewing. "Why don't you take a walk? You can finish those hems later."

Ulfra shook her head. "I haven't done my lessons today."

Tansy shrugged. "Suit yourself. There's cold mutton, if you want it; the joint end's rarer, the way you like it. You can have it at the little table, by the fire."

The girl (the wolf had nearly gone out of her) cut herself some meat and bread and settled down by the fire with her paper and pencil. It was certainly easier to get wolves to jump through hoops than to get a pencil to go in the direction you wanted it to go. She copied out some sentences and fell to staring raptly at the fire and at the way it made the deep marmalade-colored stuff of her dress glow like fire itself. Ulfra still preferred trousers, and she liked to put her hair up under a cap and take the dog out for a long walk, searching all the lanes and hedges, though she never meant to, for a small boy with white hair.

∽⁕∾

The letters flew up in the air; the silver letter opener and letter tray clattered to the floor. The courtier hurriedly kneeled and began to collect the scattered correspondence.

"There is *one* thing, madam, that demands your attention."

Ylfcwen arched an eyebrow at *demands*. "Leave them," she said, removing her pet mole from a pigeonhole of her writing desk. It snuggled sleepily into her hand. "I'll read them later. But first I shall have a bath."

Elves do not need to bathe, the *Elvish Book of Court Etiquette* tells us; they lack the glands to make it a necessity, and life Below makes the practice impractical. For the queen, however, almost anything could be arranged, and there was a little-used chamber where hot springs had been piped into a tiled pool. This was hastily scoured and filled, some orchid crystals found, and a large, soft robe recovered from an old wedding chest.

Ylfcwen settled into the water happily. At Emma's, even having to boil her own water and lug the heavy kettle up the stairs to the tub, she had taken no fewer than three baths a day. The discovery of bathing almost made up for the loss of both Bram and Grimald.

She got out before her wings were too waterlogged and left a trail of silvery wet footprints the length of the hall to her room. There, in the center of the bed, lay the thing that most demanded the elf queen's attention.

He was pink and plump with health; she gave him a good pinch to see that there was nothing wrong with his lungs. Then Ylfcwen lifted Bram squalling into her arms, an unaccustomed smile tugging at one corner of her mouth.

"Well, little raven, we must see if we can find you a nice rattle."

EPILOGUE

"Nix!"

At the woodpile Nix wedged the ax into the chopping block, seized an armful of kindling, and ran with it back to the house. Seven years of Mistress Goody's amazing and wonderful soup could not make him big, but he had grown wiry and strong for his size.

"Oh, good, you remembered the kindling. Just put it in the box and hurry up. We're taking this lot in to market, and you're to help me with the stall."

They loaded the cart with sausages, hams, and crocks of pickles and jam. Mistress Goody liked to have Nix along when she took her goods to market; he could make change quick as a wink and always knew which customer had slipped an extra sausage into her marketing basket. She loved the boy as well as she did any of her other children, and it worried her that she had never heard him laugh, though when asked he always denied that he was unhappy. Well, the boy had always been a mystery, as unexpected though welcome as the money that arrived anonymously for him every month to keep him in shoes and coats, and as the bundle of dresses that had arrived once for her and all the girls.

They got a stall in an excellent location and set out their wares. Soon the marketplace was abustle with early morning marketers, and Mistress Goody and Nix were kept very busy until eleven o'clock. Things had just slowed down when two wealthy women came up to the stall, one wearing a hat that veiled her face, her arm linked with that of her companion, a woman whose bright gaze danced from under the brim of her fashionable hat. The companion pointed to the Goodys' stall with an elegant, gloved hand.

"Oh, look, Tansy. Sausages! Shall we get some? I'm tired of partridge; we'll dine on sausages and beans tonight."

The voice that issued from behind the veil had a light lisp. "Yes, but let me; I haven't haggled in a long time."

While Tansy began to bargain with Mistress Goody, her pretty companion began to turn over the crocks of preserves. "How much are these?" she asked, without looking up.

"Tuppence," Nix whispered hoarsely around the heart sticking in his throat.

It was then Ulfra looked up and gazed for a long time at the wondrous and amazing changes time had made in her Nix. At last she smiled and drew a gold coin from her purse.

"I'll take two of the plum and one of the pear, please."

⌁

It was that seventh year also that a boy came out of nowhere, a boy just Grimald's height, with raven-dark hair and amber eyes. Caitlin found him when she was out gathering mushrooms, the silvery, fragile kind that spring up in the night and are gone by the time the sun is very high. She came upon the boy curled asleep in a pile of leaves, his face stained with tears.

Caitlin brought him back to the oak with the red door and fed him, but she did not ask him too many questions, knowing all she needed for the moment from the silver ring on his finger, the muddy amber of his eyes. They took him in and treated him as their son. Grimald was not pleased at the start with this intruder, but the rivalry faded in time. His new companion was awfully good at digging moles from their burrows and always knew where to find a cave to play in, and Grimald began to believe having a brother was not such a bad thing after all.

The Books
of the Keepers

To the Keepers of the Books—
Barbara Lucas, Marcia Marshall, Ruth
Mortimer, and Irene Rouse—this book is
affectionately dedicated.

Contents

Contents

1

THE CONSORT PENDING

The Consort Royal and Most High, Pending Examination,
woke long before Morag was due to rouse him and lay in
bed studying the ceiling of his room. This was vaulted,
plaster over solid rock, painted with a cracked and much-
faded map of the known world.

From Ylfcwen's palace in the center, tunnels and canals
in gold and silver leaf wound past gemfields and pomegranate groves to the outlands held by the Goblin Pretender. The border of the ceiling where it met the four
walls was a pale blue void, an arid home to wingless monsters. This was the world beyond the elvish kingdom, the
mortal realm known simply as Above.

In the schoolroom there was an anatomy book with colored woodblocks of elves and goblins. Of these he saw
living examples around him every day. Elves had wings
and six-chambered hearts that pumped pale violet blood
beneath their nearly colorless skin. Their bones were long
and hollow, like a bird's. Goblins were by contrast more
feline, with peaked ears and yellow eyes. They were wingless, their hearts had five chambers, and their blood was
not purple but red. It gave them a ruddy complexion.

Their bones were solid. This made them strong and well suited to work in the gemfields.

The anatomy did not devote a colored woodblock to humans, so the boy was forced to study himself in the looking glass. He felt his shoulder blades nightly for signs of fledging—did he only imagine an itching there? His own blood was a puzzle. When he held his hand up to the light, the blood beneath his skin seemed blue; but when he pricked his finger, it welled up in little ruby beads.

If he stared at the map for a long time without blinking and then closed his eyes, the Consort Pending could see a ghost of it on the backs of his eyelids. Before the image faded, he would try to see what lay beyond the void. But, try as he might, he could never make out a thing.

He only realized that Morag had come into the room when the golden light of a daylamp slowly spread across the ceiling. The goblin nurse went around the room extinguishing the nightlamps.

The stronger light of the daylamp showed a familiar crease of worry in one corner of Morag's mouth. She sat on the edge of the bed and mussed the boy's hair.

"Pending, I wish you wouldn't brood over that old ceiling."

The boy held his arms straight above his head. "Why?"

She pulled off his nightshirt and folded it carefully, shaking her head. "It should have been painted over long ago."

He laughed. "I'm glad it wasn't! How bored poor Tomus would be then, when he's sent to my room without dinner." Tomus was the goblin whipping boy whose lot it was to receive the royal punishments. As often as not, the Consort Pending sneaked in to serve the punishment with him, and they would lie on their backs and gaze at the ceiling, taking turns making up stories about the wonders to be found Above.

"The monsters will give you nightmares."

"They don't frighten me. Besides, I'm quite certain there aren't any monsters Above."

"And what makes you so sure?" she asked, smiling.

He had opened his mouth to answer when Morag suddenly stood and twitched smooth her smock, her eyes darting to the door.

Vervain swept into the room, her silks crackling as if with displeasure. "In future, Morag, please see that His Most Highness is not in a draft when he is being relieved of his nightclothes." She turned to the boy, her annoyed expression replaced by one of practiced inoffensiveness. "Most High, your bath awaits."

The boy pulled on his robe as he ran and they presently heard the slap of water against the side of the bath as he got in.

Morag made as if to pass with an armload of bed linen when Vervain's fingers closed on her arm. "Must we have another talk about overfamiliarity?"

If she shook inwardly, Morag preserved an outward calm. The goblin nurse looked the elvish governess in the eye. "No."

"Then don't let me catch you sitting on the edge of his bed again. Remember, he is the Consort Pending."

Morag lifted her chin a fraction of an inch. "But a boy, just the same!"

Vervain shook her head. "No—not to you, not even to me. He is the Consort-in-Waiting."

Being goblin, Morag could not cry, and her eyes glittered with a hot grief they could not shed. She turned and went into the adjoining bath to see that the Consort Pending washed behind his ears and did not splash more water on the floor than was seemly. Being a relatively recent addition to that section of the palace, the bath had no decoration, on the ceiling or otherwise, that could present any danger to a young imagination.

Vervain went into the schoolroom and began laying out pens and ink and parchment. Taking the Chronicles down from the shelf, she opened the massive volume to that morning's history lesson—the Goblin Revolt and Schism. Vervain shook her head; they would never get to the next lesson if the Consort did not memorize his Goblin Pretenders.

Vervain was worried. Someone had been telling the boy tales of Above, and she was unpleasantly certain who it must be. Even if Morag were capable of such foolhardiness, she had never ventured beyond the palace itself and so could not have told the boy anything. No, the boy had been sneaking off to the mines again. He'd heard those stories at Ethold's very knee. It was brash and unpardonable and could not go on.

Above all, Ylfcwen must never learn of it.

The Consort Pending came into the room, dressed in his everyday robes of dark blue damask with silver buttons. His dark hair, damp and carefully brushed by Morag, was already beginning to rise up in a cowlick. Sliding into his seat, the boy saw that the Chronicles lay open and made a face.

"Most High, I must risk an impertinence and ask you a question, and you must do your best to answer me candidly. I know you would never tell an untruth, but omitting to tell me the truth could have grave consequences."

The boy blinked and, sensing something more was wanted, slowly nodded.

"Have you been down to the mines? No"—she held up a hand—"it was wrong of me to ask. You need not answer. Only let me say this: If you were to go down to the mines, and if the queen should hear of it, it would not go well with Morag. It would be thought that she had encouraged you to go. You would not want Morag to get into trouble on your account, would you, Most High?"

The boy frowned, staring at the list of Goblin Pretenders. "No, Vervain."

"Then the next time you want a diversion, you must tell me. We'll pack a lunch and go on an excursion. Would that please you?"

The boy had been staring at the chart of the Goblin Pretenders without really seeing it. Now he raised eyes clouded with worry. "Yes. But, Vervain—"

"Yes, Most High. What is it?"

"Can't we begin with the rune tables today, instead of the Goblin Pretenders?"

∽

Ylfcwen reclined on her silver grasshopper lounge and sighed as her dresser laid out wing case after wing case on the end of the bed.

"One would never guess that elves were supposed to be known for their needlework," said the queen. "Is this *all*?"

The dresser was that rarest of creatures, the elf given to plumpness, and she was pink and panting from the exertion of climbing up and down the ladders of the queen's closets. She gazed down at the dozens of wing cases ranged over the bed and upon velvets spread over all the tables and the floor. There were wing cases made of gilded parchment, wing cases encrusted with powdered dragonflies' wings, wing cases of cloth of gold stuck with beads of glittering jet. There were wing cases of spun silver and hammered pearl, of jeweled damask and hummingbird feathers. There were wing cases of cobwebby silk stiffened with a sizing of crushed opal and varnish. None of them would do, and there were no wing cases left to show the queen.

"No, madam," lied the dresser. "There is one more." And she disappeared into the maze of closets as if to fetch it. Returning from the closet empty-handed, she had caught up a wing case neatly as she passed the foot of the bed.

It was old, worked in a style long passed from favor. Midnight-blue silk was embroidered with pearls in a pattern of lilies of the valley. The pearls were only second-best, and at the corners the silk covering was worn shiny with age.

"It's perfect. Absolutely perfect," said the queen with a sigh. "Honestly, you are such a pea brain! Why by all Below didn't you show me this one first?"

The dresser had. She merely murmured an apology as she laced the queen into the wing case.

The queen's morning promised to pass in the usual tedium. Over breakfast her numerologist determined that it was not an auspicious day to visit the shrine of her ancestors at the center of the sacred underground lake.

Ylfcwen was disappointed. She loved visiting the shrine;

it was a rare opportunity to use her silver barge. The ceremony itself was especially pretty: the relighting of the ether torches and the dedication of the gifts. And a feast to follow, involving many courses and the pandemonium of the right-of-seat, a ritual form of musical chairs.

She dragged her attention back to her numerologist, only to discover that he had left and that it was now her rune caster who sat beside her, advising her on the unlucky words she should avoid that day.

"Oh, by Above and Below and All-in-Between!" she snapped. "I might as well stay in bed!"

Since the Royal Household Agency had conducted the last purge of goblin spies, there had been no one interesting to talk to. There were no ambassadors or envoys to receive. She had all day to amuse herself before anything really entertaining could be counted on to happen. Her orchid arrangements and her watercolor scrolls had become tedious. The book she had been reading was being repaired, her pet mole having chewed out the binding. She could always rearrange the tapestries in the Great Hall or, rather, have the stewards rearrange them while she sat by eating pistachio cake soaked in root wine. But the queen was too restless to do even that.

Ylfcwen stopped picking at the silver embroidery on her gossamer robe and looked up.

"Where is the child?"

One of her myriad attendants, indistinguishable from all the rest, answered. "With Vervain, madam, in the northwest schoolroom."

"Let him be summoned. No, stop. I shall go myself."

She took one of the dilapidated corridors, part of an extensive network that was under constant repair. It had been years since she had come this way. Didn't it turn here? Yes, it did. Then you went down the corridor and made—a left?—yes, a left. It all came back to her. And suddenly there it was, as clean and tidy as if it had been waiting for her—the spy hole with its shutter, the folding stool with its worn tapestry cushion.

Ylfcwen settled herself and put her hand into her pocket for the cake she had taken from the secret store in her night table. It was nursery food—a marmalade tart from the boy's schoolroom tray—and she was ashamed at having taken it. Morag alone knew of the habit and deliberately left the Consort Pending's tray unattended to give Ylfcwen the chance to lift a few sweets. The cook would never have insulted the queen by preparing such a childish treat.

In the reign of an ancestral queen, when the palace had been much smaller, what was at present the northwest schoolroom had been a council chamber. Then the spy hole had given many an elvish queen a chance to find out what her trusted advisers said about her behind her back. At least one Goblin Pretender had met his end because of it. Through it Ylfcwen had spied on her own son, her Aethyr. It had been a young mother's only chance to see her child out from under the watchful eyes of his keepers, the ever-present instruments of the Royal Household Agency. The queen's interest in the present young scholar scowling over his Goblin Pretenders was altogether different. Ylfcwen pressed her eye to the spy hole.

The boy had worked one foot free from his slipper. With his stocking toes he was fiddling with a loose rung on his chair. The governess was intoning a list of names, pausing now and then to prompt her pupil and getting no response.

At last Vervain shook her head. "That's enough for today. But you must promise me, Most High, that you will at least *look* at the lesson before we begin. The sooner you learn the Goblin Pretenders, the faster we can move on to something else."

"But Vervain, *why* must I know all the Goblin Pretenders?"

The elvish governess considered this rather treasonous question a moment before she answered. "Tell me your full name, Most High."

"The Consort Royal and Most High, Pending Examination."

"Can you tell me what the last part means?"

"It means that I am the Consort Pending."

Vervain folded her hands over her grey smock. "It means, Most High, that you *will* be the consort once you are examined. You will not be examined until your seventh birthday. If the result is satisfactory, you will become the queen's Consort Apparent. And, when you are old enough, you will be crowned Consort Royal."

The boy drew in his bottom lip and considered this. "But, Vervain—"

"Yes, Most High?"

"What if I don't pass the examination?"

"Then you will have to study six years more and take it again on your thirteenth birthday."

The boy's eyes widened so that the whites were visible all the way around the amber irises in the middle.

Vervain bit her lower lip to suppress a smile. "With your permission, Most High, I will withdraw. Morag has your lunch ready. We will take your afternoon lessons in the orchid nursery. Bring your brushes and colors, and make sure Morag has your painting smock for you."

The boy slid off his chair and ran from the room.

Ylfcwen closed the shutter over the spy hole. She suspected the goblin nurse of feeding the boy the same meals the miners had. She frowned, thinking of coarse goblin food flavored with things that grew in the outlands, hard by the borders with Above: cavern figs, cave swift smoked with cloves and roasted with the stunted onions that grew in the dark. The queen sighed and thought of her own likely lunch: some mossy salad, pale hothouse fruit, pistachio cake, and wine. The queen brooded on this a moment, then lifted her chin. A headache was in order. Yes, she was quite sure she felt a headache coming on. She would retire to her bed, where there were at least two marmalade tarts in the drawer of the nightstand.

But it was not to be. She was accosted by the director of the Royal Household Agency. She was too near him to pretend to be out of earshot. In the moment that she hesitated, considering whether to duck behind a tapestry, he was upon her. There was no escaping.

"Madam, there are still some matters that need to be decided for the Consort's examination."

"Surely not. The preparations began four years ago. What by all Below can be left to do?"

"The examination clothes for yourself and the Consort Pending remain to be commissioned. And there *are* still a few legal difficulties that must be resolved favorably before all can proceed."

"These legal difficulties," she said in her cold, smooth, silver voice, "tell me, exactly how—*difficult*—are they?"

The director paled; she could see him trying to think of the most inoffensive words in which to couch the unpleasantness. "There has never before been a case of a consort being examined when the mortal mother was yet living and retained memory of her child."

Ylfcwen's face was as seamless as a mirror. Her enormous eyes studied the director as though he were a moth found among her precious silks. She was assessing the potential damage. At last she said only, "I am not unfamiliar with the particulars of the case." The goblin sent to replace the human child had not "taken." When discovered, the changeling had not been exposed to the elements, but named and, worse, loved. "I suppose you want me in a room somewhere, to sign things. Tell my dresser to fetch the signet ring."

"If you will pardon the liberty, madam, I have brought the necessary papers with me." He held out a sheaf of large, limp, closely written pages. "The Authorization of Royal Commission for the Consort's examination suit."

Ylfcwen took the papers and scanned them. "Is it not irregular? He must be at least seven to sit for the examination."

"That is so. But, as it happens, the terms of his indenture expire when he turns seven years and seven hours old. We have looked over the regulations most carefully and have found a most fortunate exception. He may begin the exam while he is six, so long as he *turns* seven years old before he finishes it. It is possible for him to be examined a few hours before his indenture ends; in that case, he then forfeits his birthright to return Above. Of course, it will not be put to him that way." The director of the

Royal Household Agency cleared his throat. "If madam will sign . . ."

Ylfcwen paid him no heed. She was remembering her son on his seventh birthday. Nothing had been spared in the lavish preparations and gifts, the most fantastic of which had been a revolving kaleidoscope room. When the time came for him to make a wish over the cinder cake before it was cast into the fire, the boy was nowhere to be found. He turned up at last under a couch, playing with a wooden top a goblin nurse had given him.

∽∽∾

Vervain waited until Pending was twenty minutes late before dispatching servants to find him and remind him of the drawing lesson. The search proved futile. Morag reported the boy had bolted his lunch and beat from the room like a bat from Above.

"Boys will be boys," she said, biting off a thread from her mending, "even if they are Consorts-in-Waiting."

Vervain swallowed her chagrin. "Well, he's nowhere to be found. For all anyone can tell, he's turned into a mole and disappeared down a tunnel."

She was not far wrong.

∽∽∾

It had all started several months earlier with a game of hide-and-go-seek. His goblin whipping boy, Tomus, had been the seeker and, even with the consort's head start to offset goblin intuition, Tomus had found him six times running. Determined not to be found again, Pending had hidden himself in one of the old dumbwaiters left over from another regime when, afraid of being poisoned, the queen of the time had dinner laid in dozens of decoy dining rooms to outwit the Pretender of her day.

He had been congratulating himself on his latest hiding place when the dumbwaiter began a rapid descent, plummeting past all the inhabited levels of the palace, past unseen basement storerooms and armories and kennels, so that he thought he must be moving toward the very middle of the world itself. This, everyone knew, was filled with the Ether of Life and molten gold. The boy bit his lip and prepared to be gilded alive.

The dumbwaiter had come to a rusty halt, and someone on the other side—some creature of the ethereal interior, impervious to the temperature of molten gold—had cursed the dumbwaiter doors while trying to open them. When they opened at last, the boy looked with astonishment upon a broad face grimed with soot. Recovering from his own astonishment, the goblin yelled to the others.

"That Alma! Come look at what she's sent for our supper! If is isn't the Consort Pending's whipping boy!"

The tallest of the other miners came over.

"Whipping boy, nothing. That's the Consort Pending himself. No mistaking Vervain's handiwork." He threw back his head and laughed. "And he's sat on Alma's best pie."

That was how he first met Ethold. At the miners' insistence, he had joined them in a lunch of flattened mole pie. Contrary to Ylfcwen's suspicions, the miners ate food from the queen's own larders, prepared in the palace kitchens by the queen's own second sauce cook, a goblin lass by the name of Alma.

Hours later, after singing many goblin songs whose words were cleaned up for his benefit, and drinking much strong tea with a slug of root wine in it, he had tiptoed through the palace to find Morag had fed his dinner to Tomus and put Tomus to bed in his place so that Vervain would not guess he was gone.

"Pending, I won't give you Tomus's whipping, but you do deserve it, you know you do! They'd flay me alive for speaking to you so, but mercy, someone has to tell you. If Vervain had discovered Tomus, do you have any idea what would have happened to him?" And she had fed him Tomus's dinner, and put him to bed on Tomus's pallet, and Vervain was never the wiser.

∽∾

This day, while Vervain waited for him in the orchid nursery, Pending found the miners engrossed in a game of cat's eye, a drinking game played with somersault tumblers. Instead of a pedestal, these tumblers ended in a metal cage that enclosed a pair of dice. When the glass was filled the player emptied it in a swallow and set the

glass upside down in front of him; the dice sealed in the
cage showed a number or a "wild" rune. One miner, no
doubt losing, accused another of having weighted his glass
so that the dice always came up elevens.

A fight seemed about to break out. Ethold looked up
and caught the boy's eye.

"That's enough, boys. Here, Pinch; take over my hand."
With that he got up and came over to Pending.

"Well, it's been some time since you've paid a visit.
Vervain must have been holding your nose to the whetstone." Ethold put out a hand and felt the boy's nose.
"Yes, it's noticeably sharper." Then he felt the back of the
boy's head. "She *is* cramming you full of wisdom. Here,
feel it yourself."

Pending laughed and knocked Ethold's hand away. "Not
so crammed as all that!" He related his problems with the
Goblin Pretenders.

"Just remember, That Which Is Required Is Forbidden," Ethold said. At the boy's blank look, he repeated
himself. "That Which Is Required Is Forbidden. It's a
memory device: Each word begins with the first letter of
one of the goblin kings, in order from the first king to
the last."

A light dawned and Pending broke into a grin. "Tab-
ardyr, Waerleg, Irlkin, Roleg, Ivo, Fustaugh!"

"Ah, we'll make a goblin of you yet!" muttered Ethold
under his breath.

"But, Ethold—"

"Yes, Pending?"

"You called them kings, but Vervain calls them the Goblin Pretenders. Who is right?"

Ethold shook his head. "For as long as anyone can
remember, the elvish queens have been fighting the goblin kings."

"What are they fighting about?"

"It's very complicated, Pending. The elvish queens say
they have ever and always been fighting to defend the
throne, while the goblins claim only to be fighting for their
freedom. But listen: When you are with Vervain or anyone

else from the palace, you must call them the Goblin Pretenders and nothing else, understand? Much hangs on your learning that lesson."

～∽～

Ethold waited at the appointed place. The person he was meeting was late. It would have been nice to have a pipe while he waited, but he could not chance it. The queen's spies were everywhere, and clove smoke was a giveaway. No one in Ylfcwen's court would smoke anything so goblin. So Ethold stood in the half-light of a dimmed miner's torch and waited.

If he had so desired, Ethold might have lived at court with all the rank and privilege due a noble, even one of goblin blood. Ethold could pass for a full elf: he was uncommonly tall and lithe, lacking the florid complexion and stocky build of most goblins. His complexion had, in the poetic phrase of the court, "the kiss of the pomegranate" with none of its stain. His eyes, catlike only in their slant and intensity, were a mutable violet. Like all goblins, he possessed great physical grace and stamina as well as strategic intuition. These qualities made him a formidable opponent at wrestling and chess—and war.

Ethold had been at war with the queen for eleven years. To mention his name at court was an offense punishable by banishment; he had gone over to the side of the Goblin Pretender.

At some point, one of them must falter and bring the confrontation to an end. But it would not be soon; a similar blood feud several dynasties back had lasted nearly two centuries. There was plenty of time for Ethold and his followers to lard the queen's treasuries with counterfeit gems and set cave-ins at certain key tunnels in the gemfields. The rebels had allies within the palace itself. It was such a one that he awaited now, in the hour before the lighting of the daylamps.

The darkness of the tunnel gave up the form of a woman. They greeted one another with the secret sign of their cause. Even when safely in the shadows, she did not push back the hood of her cloak.

"I am suspected," she said.

He darted a glance down the tunnel behind her. "Followed?"

"No, I am almost certain I was not. But suspected, yes."

"Have they any proof?"

"No, but you and I both know that with Ylfcwen, suspicion is as good as fact—or better. Ethold . . . I have been thinking. I had better not come anymore."

His laugh was full of affection. "You've been thinking too hard."

Her voice shook and she tried to steady it, speaking clear and low. "No, hear me! Someone else could serve in my place. The risk is too great—"

"And you are too valuable to us." He slipped his hands inside the hood on either side of her face. "And you're quite indispensable to *me*."

It was an uncomradely kiss. She turned her head and mumbled into his shoulder.

"I should go. They will miss me. . . ."

"As I will." His eyes glowed amethyst in the dark.

"Before you make me forget, here's this." She drew a linen-bound notebook from her cloak.

He slipped the notebook inside his shirt. "You're right about one thing, sweet. We'll have to be more careful. We'll change the place and time we meet. I won't send word to you for a while, for safety's sake. In the meantime, my thoughts are with you."

"And mine with you." She took a different tunnel, slipping back into the darkness. She did not look back, and soon had disappeared from his sight.

When he was safe in his bunk in the miners' barracks, Ethold drew out the notebook. It was full of elvish runes in a child's hand—not any child's hand, but the schoolboy script of the Consort Pending himself. Handwriting exercises, nonsense sentences, maxims of an arcane schoolroom etiquette. The boy had struggled to shape the court script, with its clawed feet and hooked tails. The assignment had been constructed to force the boy to work on the most troublesome characters:

Crimp the crusts and cut the crinkled cakes.
Weave wet willow wands for weary wasps.
Quiz the queen about the quick, queer quest.
Bury the busy, bright blossoms, bumblebee. . . .

Ethold took out a small wheel fashioned from two circles of stiff paper, one large and one small, pinned
together in the middle. A crescent-shaped window had
been cut in the smaller circle. He turned the wheel so
that a certain number showed through the window. Now,
each goblin rune on the outer wheel was aligned with an
elvish rune on the inner one. Ethold glanced at the first
page of the notebook, then at the wheel, and began to fill
in a blank sheet of paper.

The palace is busy with preparations for the examination of the Consort. Ylfcwen has commanded the Mistress of the Stones and the Woman of the Rings to lay
out all the royal jewels so that they may be sent out to
be cleaned and mended in preparation for the ceremony. In addition, the queen has sent a servant Above
to engage a tailor to make the examination suit for the
Consort Pending. This presents us with an excellent
opportunity to strike. . . .

2

THE DRESSMAKER'S APPRENTICE HAS A DREAM

The dressmaker's apprentice rarely dreamed anymore of her former life among the wolves.

At first, the memories had padded tirelessly after her. Not the recent past, with the circus troupe, or even the years at court before that, but her very earliest recollections—of the den; the warm, solid body of the old she-wolf; her first sight of winter trees silvered by an ice storm.

Seven years since, Ulfra had left Folderol's troupe and settled in Moorsedge, coming to live with Tansy over the dressmaker's shop at the sign of the Cat's Face, named for the curious appearance of its owner, a former attraction with the same circus. She had been the leopard-woman, and her countenance had about it all that the name implied: Coarse black hair covered her face except for the tip of her small, flat nose, which was white and pink. Her prominent upper jaw formed a kind of muzzle; because of it she spoke with a soft lisp. "All I lack to make the illusion complete are whiskers and a tail," she once told Ulfra, "and that old rogue Folderol tried to make me put them on, too."

Ulfra came to her new living at the age of twelve, more than a little rough around the edges. Before she could be entrusted with the shears or the heavy tailor's iron called a goose, Ulfra had to master the rudiments of acceptable behavior. Tansy taught her apprentice not to take meat from the spit before it had been carved at table, not to bare her teeth whenever a strange man came into the room, and, most difficult of all, to submit as meekly as she could to the indignities of soap and hot water, and the hated hair comb and nailbrush.

None of these things had come easily. Ulfra's snarl had driven more than one customer from the premises, and before she learned the rules of the house, Tansy would come down to supper to find the joint had been divided among Ulfra and the neighborhood dogs.

Ulfra was now nearly twenty-one. Looking at her, with her hair smoothed back, dressed in her spotless blue smock, few guessed her strange beginnings. But even now, when being introduced to a stranger, she pressed her lips together to suppress a wolfish grimace.

Tansy and Ulfra's conversation had about it an understated affection not found in many families, let alone between master and apprentice. Ulfra had a bedchamber of her own tucked up beneath the eaves. When her work was done she had the run of the house until Tansy called her to supper by the fire in their common sitting room. The leopard-woman took delight in being read to; many an evening in bitter weather Ulfra would oblige, with a traveler's tale, if it were a book of her choosing, or something with a good heroine, if Tansy's.

On a fine evening Tansy would take up her heavy walking stick and Ulfra would fetch their cloaks and they would walk along the lamplit streets and out of town, far enough down the road for the darkness to close in and show them the teeming stars.

Sometimes on these walks Ulfra's contentment would swell without warning into the keenest joy. Afterward she would crawl late to bed and sleep a bottomless sleep. If she dreamed a dream, wolves figured in it not at all.

Tansy's old friend and confidante Lady Twixtwain came one evening to sup with them in their rooms above the Cat's Face. Ulfra helped her out of her cloak and hat. Lady Twixtwain's person was very large and exquisitely dressed, her humor unfailingly good, her tongue and wits sharp, her face reckoned among the two or three most beautiful in the thirteen kingdoms.

"Ulfra, my sweet, will you kindly take Opaline along to the kitchen for her tisane?"

"Have a peek at dinner, too, will you?" said Tansy. "If it's ready, you can just dish it up."

Opaline was Lady Twixtwain's aging and adored greyhound, who carried around her neck a purse containing her mistress's smelling salts and snuff, rouge and brandy. Ulfra unbuckled the purse and led the dog to the kitchen, where a bowl of chamomile steeped in milk was keeping warm.

Lady Twixtwain watched Ulfra go. When she was out of earshot, her ladyship began to peel the snowy kid gloves from her hands.

"She is much improved, my dear, very much improved. I commend you."

Tansy protested. "I have only tried to show her the advantages of mastering a craft and of sharpening the mind."

Lady Twixtwain considered this, her head tipped to one side. "In some cases, the only way to accomplish one's end is through a slow bringing along. But really, Tansy, you have succeeded admirably. She is lovely and natural without being at all false or coarse."

"I should hope she is still her own person."

"Oh, my, yes. That she is and will always be, have no fear of *that*."

Tansy shook her head. "I am afraid this is a hermitish life for a young woman. I go out so little, myself; my friends come to me. Our circle is small—outside of our patrons and one or two servants, I am her sole companion. It's a pity she should spend her youth making gowns for the daughters of merchants and councilmen without enjoying the same advantages. Though, to tell the truth, she never seems to envy them. She might be nine, not twenty, for all the interest she shows in the opposite sex."

Lady Twixtwain nodded thoughtfully. "Perhaps she is a winter's rose and will blossom when all hope of it has been given up. It's only natural, considering what her life had been. Think how much further she had to come than most young girls. When she *does* lose her heart, I think it will be wholeheartedly, with the same quiet passion she brings to everything."

"I hope you're right." The leopard-woman rose and went to the fire, taking and lighting a taper from the mantelpiece. She touched the taper to the wicks of the tall candles in the center of a card table laid for three. "I can't abide the thought of her breaking her heart," she said, shaking her head. "After all, I stripped away all the wildness that protected her. I made it possible for her to be terribly wounded."

Lady Twixtwain smiled. "But how else is love possible?"

Tansy rose and went to the hearth, where three plates were keeping warm. Wrapping her hand in the folds of her skirt, she transferred the hot plates to the table. "May I tell you something?"

"You mean, will I keep a secret?" Lady Twixtwain heaved a sigh. "It goes against my grain, but I shall."

Tansy first went and listened at the door. Ulfra's voice carried faintly, answered by Opaline's happy yelp. Taking her seat again, the leopard-woman began her tale.

"It was market day a few weeks past. We went out walking. I had bought her a hat, her first. Though she protested fiercely at the expense, I could tell she was quite pleased. It was very becoming, but with it on, she suddenly became unlike herself—coy and giddy.

"Well, we stopped at a stall where a farm woman was selling her wares. Ulfra said she was sick of partridge, why didn't we have sausages. It was a joke: Actually, business had been slower than usual, and we'd been dining on nothing but beans for a month. I began to barter with the woman and Ulfra asked the boy about the jam."

"Wait. Whose boy?"

"The farm woman's son, I supposed. I only glanced over for a second. I was wearing my veil, but I could still see him. He was about twelve or thirteen, small, wiry, brown as a nut, with strange, white hair."

"Wait. My feeble brain begins to stir. Wasn't there a mute with her in the circus? An albino, if my memory serves me?"

Tansy nodded. "Though, from what Ulfra has told me, he was neither mute nor albino. His name was Nix. And that is all she has told me of him in seven years."

"Did she speak to him?"

"Only what she had to, to buy the jam. It was plain to me she knew him. His face was a terrible thing to see. She smiled and thanked him; he handed her the jam; we left. And do you know, she hasn't worn the hat since, nor will she touch the jam. We never speak of it."

"Small seams," Lady Twixtwain said under her breath. This was a signal used by tailors to mean: The person you are talking about is coming into the room.

Tansy busied herself with the saltcellar.

Ulfra entered the room carrying the supper on a tray. Lady Twixtwain smiled.

"You had better hold that tray a little higher, or Opaline will have those chops out from under your nose."

Ulfra awakened the following morning to find Opaline asleep at the foot of her bed. When the game of spoilfive ran on after dinner, the old dog would follow Ulfra up to bed and nap until Lady Twixtwain went home. The game must have gone on very late indeed.

Opaline opened her eyes, licked Ulfra's hand, and yawned. Watching her made Ulfra yawn, too, and she laughed.

"Good morning," she said, scratching the dog behind the ears. Opaline beat her tail on the coverlet politely, but her plaintive look said, It is past my breakfast time.

They padded downstairs together, where they found plum cake and hot wine keeping warm, and a note from Tansy.

> Hope you both slept well. Opaline looked so sweet we
> didn't have the heart to wake her. I've taken the court

gowns to Lady Alders in Blackswan Street for the final
fitting. Please pick up the order at the button maker
and then drop Opaline off at Lady T.'s—she has gone
to the baths for the rest of the morning to lick her
wounds. (Ha!)

Ulfra smiled; Lady Twixtwain always retreated to the
public baths when Tansy had beaten her badly at cards.

They went out into the street. Moorsedge had been in
decline for many years, a rough town on the border of the
downs. Then one year the king's only son had come to
hunt and stayed. He had reopened the long-closed palace
built by an earlier king as a refuge for his queen during
a drawn-out civil war. The prince's set had flocked to
Moorsedge, and the merchants had followed them. Biding
his time until the crown should be his, the prince indulged
his tastes for the theater and other amusements.

It was the last market day before a holiday, and the
streets were thronged with merchants selling tinware, live
ducks, bottles and corks, melons, sausages, ribbons, flour,
copper saucepans, cheeses, and hothouse grapes. One
could have scissors sharpened, chickens plucked, boots
mended, teeth pulled, keys made, curses removed. The air
was filled with the fragrant steam and smoke from a stall
where you could buy a paper cone filled with tiny, sweet
crabs, dipped in batter and fried whole.

Ulfra had to drag Opaline away from the crab stall,
where the dog was in danger of being nipped on the nose.
They made their way to the button maker's, where Ulfra
picked up the parcel. When that account was settled, she
went from case to case in the tiny shop, looking for some
buttons for the bodice she was making as a surprise for
Tansy. At last she bought some of jet and amber in the
shape of bees.

She had spent more time deciding on her buttons than
she meant and hurried through the streets, with Opaline
casting anxious looks up at her, as if to ask why they were
in such a hurry.

As they turned into Lady Twixtwain's street, Opaline

pulled up short, so frantic with fear that she tried to clamber up into Ulfra's arms.

In the cobbled yard, a slight, weasely man was baiting a wolf. If the wolf had not been muzzled and hobbled, it would not have been much of a match. A crowd of well-dressed onlookers watched from balconies and doorways, drinking wine and cheering the man on.

The wolf was too spent to resist as the man poked it in the ribs with a sharp stick. It lay glaring up at its tormentor. Then it caught sight of Ulfra and began a strange, high keening, a mingled greeting and plea.

Ulfra rushed up and struck the stick from the man's hand. The crowd roared. Scarlet with anger, the man grabbed her shoulder. She seized his thumb smartly and bent it backward so that he shrieked and let her go.

Ulfra knelt by the wolf and started to loosen the hobble. The crowd saw what she was about and their shouts faded quickly to a nervous murmuring. The courtyard quickly emptied, echoing with the clatter of many doors and shutters being fastened at once.

The animal was but half-grown, rope-sore and frightened, but Ulfra found no open wounds. She ran her hands over the wolf to reassure it, speaking to it low in her throat, in the whines and growls of wolf speech.

Keeping a safe distance, the man clutched his thumb and protested. "That's our wolf. There's a gold bounty on it! It's as good as stealing, what you're doing! My master will have you flogged for thievery—and for breaking my thumb!"

"Be careful what you say, William," said a new voice. "She looks capable of doing a little flogging herself."

Ulfra turned to see the newcomer. In the doorway of the inn stood a man of blunt, bearlike features and build, with a weather-roughened face above a grizzled beard. He held a goblet in one hand and a napkin was tucked under his chin, draped incongruously over the iron-studded leather breastplate of a professional hunter.

He was, in fact, the king's own huntsman. Seeing her there, her ice blue eyes the match of the wolf's, the animal calm and trusting in her arms, he was not about to tell her so.

"She's broken my thumb," the first man complained again.

"It's the least you deserved," Ulfra snapped.

"Yes, William, it is the least you deserved. Never tease a wolf. You had no way of telling if the muzzle would hold."

Ulfra stared blue daggers at him. "Is that his wrongdoing? Carelessness, and not cruelty?"

"Madam, that is my wolf. I intend to collect the bounty on it, in the name of the king. If you have some argument with that, then come with me, and we shall let the king decide the matter."

The huntsman smiled and held out his hands. The wolf curled its lip and growled low in its throat. Ulfra spoke to it in wolf speech; the animal flattened its ears in submission.

"This is a Direwolf," Ulfra said. "It is untouchable under the king's or any other law. If you harm it, you will answer to the Direwolves."

The huntsman frowned and considered. He had eaten a large meal; he wanted to finish his wine and have a pipe and a nap. He did not want to stand here arguing with a wolf-eyed girl.

"It is asking me to let it go so that it can kill you," she added. "It says you killed its mother with a trap."

"Tell it," he replied, carefully biting off each word, "that its mother and her kind have been killing the king's deer."

"It is the wolves' wood and their deer."

He saw that she would not be moved. "Take it. Take it back to the damned wood. But I promise you this: If I catch it again, I will skin it myself on the spot."

Ulfra nodded, coaxed Opaline from her hiding place under a stairway, and left, carrying the wolf in her arms.

The huntsman watched her go. "William, never interrupt my meal in this manner again," he said, and went back in to his repast. But his venison had lost its savor, and his hand, when he reached for the wine, trembled.

One spectator had not fled when Ulfra untied the wolf. He stood now as he had when the scene first unfolded, leaning against a rainspout in rumpled clothes the color of earth, a strange green hat perched on his head. He waited

until the huntsman and his kennel master had left. Then the
odd spectator bent and retrieved something from the ground,
a parcel no bigger than a loaf of bread: the buttons, forgotten
in the scuffle. The parcel was labeled in ink:

T. PANTER, DRESSMAKER
AT THE SIGN OF THE CAT'S FACE
EVERLASTING LANE

"Oh, my heavens!"

Tansy stood in the doorway to the sitting room and
gazed in dismay at the scene before her. A half-grown
wolf lay on the sofa, its paws bandaged, taking bits of raw
liver from Ulfra's hand.

"It's all right," said Ulfra. "I've put down a cloth to
catch anything he drops."

"Oh, Ulfra!"

"He's not strong enough to travel. He would never make
it back to the wood on his own."

"Oh, my." Tansy ventured into the room and gingerly
took a seat. "But who will take him there? No—you cannot
think of going."

Ulfra shook her head. "I won't need to. When he is
well, the others will come for him."

Tansy stared. The wolf stared back, then rested its head
on the sofa cushion and grinned at her, tongue lolling.

"All right," she said, "but please make it—make *him*
understand the rules of the house. And I think it best that
our customers do not make his acquaintance."

The next day there came to the Cat's Face an odd customer. They were in the workroom when the bell rang;
Ulfra set down the hissing iron goose and went into the
outer room.

The person on the other side of the counter was remarkable even by the standards of the Cat's Face, a man of
birdlike slightness and grace, dressed all in brown. He
held in one hand a hat of ivy green. His face was outwardly
stoic, with the merest hint of mirth about the eyes. These
Ulfra took at first to be blue, but then realized that they

were in fact silver and were only casting back the color of her work smock.

"May I be of some service?"

"I require a suit of clothes for a boy of not quite seven years." The silver eyes roamed over the room, changing hue as they settled on various garments on display, drinking in a brilliant court dress in cloth of gold before turning on Ulfra a gaze as full of liquid fire as a cat's. "I am prepared to pay handsomely." One birdlike hand disappeared into a pocket and reappeared with a purse. Five-sided silver coins spilled onto the counter with a musical clatter. It was a currency unfamiliar to Ulfra, but in her circus days she had learned never to turn up her nose at other people's money.

"For such a sum you could have something handsome indeed. What is the occasion?"

"An examination."

Ulfra thought that odd, but held her tongue. She knew there was nothing of the kind in stock; among all their youngest patrons, there were no boys of seven. Then she remembered a commission recently completed for an old friend from Tansy's circus days. Ulfra fetched the suit and slipped it onto the smallest wooden form in the shop. She did not mention that it had been made for a dwarf.

It was black velvet, faced with cream silk and lavishly trimmed with lace and pearls.

"So heavy!" marveled the stranger.

"Yes. There are over one hundred pearls on it. Will something like this do?"

The odd customer smiled. "Something like it will answer our requirements most admirably."

Ulfra reached to get the heavy pattern register down from the shelf behind her. When she turned back to the counter she was alone, and the suit had vanished.

Ulfra returned to the workroom and took up the hissing goose.

"Who was it?" Tansy asked.

Ulfra started to say "A thief," but heard herself say instead, "The strangest person."

*   *   *

That night Ulfra was roused from sleep by a loud rapping noise. She lay in bed, breathing as though still asleep, listening intently. The sound seemed to be coming from the heavy, dark wardrobe on the other side of the room. Easing off the blankets, Ulfra rolled out of bed, landing softly on the floor. Still in a crouch, she crept noiselessly across the room.

The wardrobe had stood in a neglected corner of the workroom until recently, when Tansy had decided Ulfra required a wardrobe of her own. They had aired it out and rubbed it with beeswax and lemon oil and hired six strong men to haul it upstairs. It was extremely heavy and very old—here and there the intricate carvings had been worn smooth, and the wood was black with age.

As she reached out to touch it, the knocking suddenly ceased. Ulfra stood staring at the heavy doors of the wardrobe, a prickling at the back of her neck keeping her from flinging them wide.

"Open, please," said a voice, muffled by wool and silk and damask. Fear gave way to indignation. Ulfra threw open the doors with a bang.

Inside, standing among her clothes, was the odd customer from the shop. His mousy suit had been replaced by a magnificent costume of white silk. He bowed low, the sleeves of his blue and silver overrobe sweeping the ground.

"I am sent at the queen's bidding to bring you back to the court Below," said he. "Will you come of your own free will?"

Ulfra laughed. "I should be very surprised if the back of my wardrobe was the way to the court of the elves. Tell me, when did you manage to hide in there? And why did you steal the suit?"

He smiled. "The suit will be returned. It is because it so pleased the queen that your services have been engaged. Will you come of your own free will?"

The tone of his voice and the cool gleam of his quicksilver eyes were together so compelling that Ulfra found herself nodding. In a wink he had seized her hand and was drawing her into the wardrobe. What had always been a solid panel at the back of the wardrobe had become a brick wall set with a small door. The messenger in blue and silver opened it and helped Ulfra down a narrow staircase. They passed into a clean and spacious tunnel lit with ether. The silver gaslight showed walls covered with rich tapestries, surpassing in skill any Ulfra had seen, even at court.

The messenger led Ulfra to a room where elvish hand-maidens gave her a silk coat with trailing sleeves to slip over her muslin nightdress. Returned to the custody of the messenger, she was led finally into a chamber that held a strange group of personages.

In the center, seated in a chair that was very grand yet not quite a throne, was an elf woman of extraordinary beauty. Her opal eyes betrayed both boredom with the situation and the hope that it might yet prove diverting. She held in her lap a small, furry creature, which Ulfra at first took for a rabbit, then saw was a mole.

To the queen's right stood an elvish woman whose bearing and clothing bespoke a position more of merit than birth. A close handmaiden or, more likely, a governess. Ulfra thought she was anxious, hiding something. Guilt, or fear.

At the queen's other hand stood a lean, elvish man with a face so expressionless it seemed a mask. Even his eyes were unreal, and they kept a sort of loathsome watchfulness, as a carrion crow keeps on a flock. Nastily keen for opportunity—that was it. Ulfra disliked him.

By far the most compelling person in the room was the boy seated at the feet of the queen. He sat on a small miniature of the queen's chair, and the queen's hand rested on his shoulder with the same lazy air of possession with which she petted the mole.

To judge by his face, he was no more than six, dressed after the elvish custom in many underrobes of sheer silk and an overrobe of heavy damask. This outermost robe was deep blue, embroidered in silver thread with a pattern of fireflies and lamps. For want of sun, his skin had grown almost as translucent as that of the queen. His legs seemed too long for the rest of him, as though enforced inactivity had thwarted a natural sturdiness of limb. He stared at

Ulfra, trying his best to pass it off as mere gazing and not succeeding. The stare from his odd, amber-colored eyes was the only warm thing in the room.

The lean man took a step forward and read rapidly from a parchment. Then a set of papers was passed to the queen, who added her signature and seal. Once the wax was cool, the man nodded to the governess, who relieved the boy of his layered ceremonial robes. He stood before them in his smallclothes, unembarrassed. Ulfra assumed he was used to being dressed and undressed at the whim of his elders. A measuring tape was presented to her on a small cushion. Ulfra took it and began to measure the boy, stretching the tape taut along his shoulder and then down his back from the end of his neck to the bottom of his spine. He laughed when she measured his inseam, and his laugh, at least, was not pale and thin from lack of use. Like the look in his eyes, it spread through the room like the warmth of a fire.

"Does it tickle?" she wanted to ask, but in this dream she apparently had no power of speech. Still, the boy seemed to understand her, for he nodded and smiled.

The measurements taken, contracts were produced and she was made to sign the papers in several places. The queen extended her hand, and Ulfra knelt to kiss the signet ring, startled at the sting of the cold elvish silver. Then the original messenger appeared and led her away. Over her shoulder she caught sight of the boy as he lifted his chin so that the governess could button him all the way up. Ulfra thought he winked.

The messenger walked so quickly down the corridor that Ulfra could barely keep up. They passed the changing room without a pause, and she was about to ask if she should return her borrowed robe when she suddenly woke up.

Sunlight was slanting through the dormer window; from the foot of the bed the wolf watched her. For a moment she forgot where she was. Tansy came in with a cup of tea, and Ulfra laughed and related her dream.

"Isn't it funny? When I woke up I was so confused

that I thought it was yesterday and that Opaline had been changed into a wolf!"

Tansy did not laugh, but went and examined the wardrobe.

An odd feeling came over Ulfra as she watched the leopard-woman push aside the hanging clothes and rap the back of the wardrobe with her knuckles.

"Tansy!"

The leopard-woman came and sat on the bed. "I'm sorry; I don't mean to frighten you. It's just that you're not the first person to have an odd dream after spending a night in the same room with that wardrobe. It came down in my mother's family, from a relative said to be one of the Banished. It was careless of me to give it to you."

"But it was a dream!"

Tansy shook her head. "I'm afraid not." She drew from her pocket a small folded paper. "This was tacked to the door when I came back from the baker's."

It was parchment, folded into a tight square and sealed with wax. Ulfra stared at the sign embossed in the wax and felt her lip; where she had kissed the signet ring, there was a small spot blistered from cold. She broke the seal and unfolded the parchment.

The sheet was large and closely written in a runish hand. At the bottom someone had signed a large letter Y with a flourish. Beside it, in her own hand, was written her name.

Tansy shook her head. "This is no rune hand I've ever seen. Look at the tails on the runes. Perhaps Lady Twix-twain will know someone who can translate it. In the meantime, we'll have that damn thing"—she nodded at the wardrobe—"hauled back downstairs!"

"No." Ulfra half shrugged, half shuddered, as if shaking off a chill. "I remember what it says. It's a contract for a court suit for a small boy, to be made in black velvet, with silver buttons. I must complete it before the new moon, but I may only work by moonlight, and in silence. I remember how the last part goes: 'And lest my task should come to grief, No man so much as touch a sleeve.' "

Tansy stared. "Well," she said when she found her voice again, "in that case, you had best go back to bed and get some sleep. You have your work cut out for you."

3

THE GOBLIN PRETENDER

"Tomus. Tomus!"

Tomus's dim form stirred at the foot of the bed.

"What?" he answered, his voice thick with sleep.

"What's a consort?"

Tomus yawned. It was the deepest part of the night and they both should have been fast asleep.

"Dunno. Nothing good."

"What happened to the last one?"

"The R.H.A. declared him an Official Disgrace—you can't speak his name anymore and it was erased from all the royal books. You know, the heavy ones."

"The Chronicles."

"Yeah, those. In the hall, where there should be a picture of the last Consort, there's a tapestry of some old battle."

"Was he banished Above?"

Tomus yawned. "I can't remember. I think he became one of the weavers."

He had no better luck with Morag the following morning.

"What's a consort?"

Morag smiled her half smile, the way she did just before she was about to tell him something that was half true.

"Well . . . I suppose it's a little like Vervain's elixir: a necessary unpleasantness." The Universal Mineral Elixir for Complaints Royal, Goblin, and Mortal was a thick, bitter syrup compounded of root wine, honey, and herbs.

"Who are the weavers?"

This time Morag's hands paused in their gathering-up of a blue stocking. She cast a brief glance at the boy, then swiftly pulled the gathered stocking over his toes and heel, past his ankle, and up to his knee. "Why ever should you want to know about weavers, Pending?"

"I've never heard anyone mention them before. I wondered where they were."

Morag smoothed the stocking up to his knee. "They're off in one end of the palace, Pending. No one goes there. There's not much to see but some dusty old tapestries."

"What do the weavers do, then?"

"Mostly they repair the seats of chairs and things." She sat back on her heels and smiled, staring off into the air behind Pending's head. "By all Below, I haven't thought of them in years. My family lived in quarters quite near the workrooms. When I was a girl, I used to fall asleep to the noise of the looms."

"Are they really all mad?"

"Gracious, Pending! Where do you get all these questions? Has Tomus been filling your head with nonsense?"

"Morag," he said sternly, "this is *very* important. Are they all mad?"

She looked at him, then at the door. Something in her face relaxed slightly and something else in it tensed.

"Some. Not all."

"Were they mad when they became weavers, or did the weaving make them mad?"

"I can't say. And now," she added in a tone that marked the matter closed, "you know as much as I do about weavers."

He didn't believe her.

❧

It is a lesser-known trait of the elvish race that it harbors a superstitious dread of throwing anything away. The lower levels of Ylfcwen's palace were honeycombed with store-rooms dating to the Early Epochs. Ethold and Pending had brought a picnic by dumbwaiter to one of them, spreading their feast on the floor among broken tag ends of furniture and dusty, rolled-up carpets.

They came upon an entire royal barge wrapped in muslin like a gigantic moth in its cocoon. Ethold discovered a child-sized copy of the barge, complete with movable oars. There was even a wooden elf queen with rooted silk hair and real dragonfly's wings. Ethold gently worked the wings back and forth. The fifth time Pending said his name, he looked up.

"I'm sorry, Pending. What did you say?"

"I asked if you knew anything about the weavers."

Ethold nodded. He fitted the elf queen into the throne of her barge and, rewrapping the whole, placed it carefully back on the pile of forgotten playthings.

"That's a funny coincidence, Pending. I was just going to take you to see them."

They passed through what seemed like miles of corridors, through heavy curtains that hid much older passageways.

"Tomus and I play hide-and-go-seek everywhere. We've never gone anywhere near *these* tunnels."

"Well, I'm sure Tomus has his orders," said Ethold.

They came to a small door set in the tunnel wall. It was barred and locked. Ethold took out a set of keys, identical to the set Vervain wore on a ribbon at her waist.

Pending stared. "Those are keys from the Royal House-hold Agency!" It was a high crime to steal or duplicate keys to the palace.

"Very observant, Pending. Could you speak more softly? It wouldn't go well with me if we were to be discovered."

Ethold turned one of the keys in the first lock and carefully drew back the bolts. He laid an ear to the remaining lock.

"Charmed. They must know I have keys and are hoping I will trip an alarm." Ethold drew from his pocket a pouch of silvery-grey dust and blew a pinch of it into the final lock.

The door opened soundlessly, at least to the boy's

human ears. Ethold paused, listening for something Pending couldn't hear.

"Forward, quietly. No whispering; it carries. Just keep your voice low, the way I do."

The door opened into a large workroom, empty but obviously still used; it smelled of lamps lately extinguished. Taking up one end of the room was a huge loom upon which a carpet was taking shape. It was unlike any of the tapestries that hung in the halls of the palace. Those weavings showed royal processions or represented the feasts of the elvish calendar: the dedication of the gifts, the blessing of the mines, the festival of the fireflies. This tapestry was something else altogether.

Cords of silk, knotted one strand at a time, formed an intricate pattern of twined leaves and flowers. The blossoms shown were unlike any Pending had seen or sketched in the extensive palace hothouses and nurseries.

Ethold fingered a small, white, heart-shaped flower. "They only bloom Above."

Stepping closer to see the weave, Pending saw brilliant flies and glossy beetles, perfect to the smallest detail, as though nature and not the weaver's skill had made them. The carpet was cool to his touch and gave off a smell of crushed flowers and something he could not name.

"Sunshine," Ethold said, as though reading his thoughts. "Sunshine burning the dew off a meadow."

Pending looked at him blankly.

"Ah. Dew—how do I explain? It's a kind of rain that springs from the ground. Here, there is something else I have to show you."

At the other end of the workroom a low door opened on a bunk room, narrow and poorly lit, the air blue with the smoke of dreamlily. In the middle of the floor a few weavers shared a common water pipe. Others lay stretched on low cots around the room, dozing until it was time to return to the looms.

"Can they hear us?"

"Yes, but only as you hear your own breathing without paying it any mind. They don't know peace or pain—just oblivion. Their wages are paid in dreamlily, which dulls their wants and obliterates their cares. Even when they earn their freedom and can return Above, they seldom go. This is the only life they remember."

Only one of the weavers took any notice of them. Seated apart from the others at a small table, he was thumbing through a thick sheaf of papers. He glanced at them and went back to his papers.

"That's the timekeeper," Ethold's voice said in the boy's ear. "He assigns the work and doles out the dreamlily."

Ethold and Pending returned to the storeroom, but the picnic had lost its savor. Pending climbed into the royal barge and sat banging his heels against the base of the gilded throne.

Ethold climbed in and sat at the boy's feet. He picked up the toy barge and worked one of its oars. "There is something I must tell you, Pending."

"About the weavers?"

"Yes. But not just about them." He paused, as if searching for the right words for what he had to say. "The first weavers were human, like you. They came Below by accident and were given a place at the looms. Some married elves of the lower ranks, and their goblin children were sent to work in the gemfields. The gems they harvested made the elvish queens wealthy.

"One year a fever came. Many weavers and miners died. Suddenly there were fewer of them to work the looms and the mines. The elves could make do without tapestries, but gems were the lifeblood of the realm.

"So the queen of that time sent a servant Above to take a human child and leave a goblin infant in its place. This was the first changeling. More followed. Some became weavers, gem cutters. One changeling, a tavern keeper's son, became the queen's cellar master. One became the first human Consort. They had a son, and for the first time, there was a goblin of royal blood. When that son grew up, he began to wonder why it was that the weavers lived as they did and why goblins worked the mines to make elves rich.

"That was the beginning of the Goblin Wars."

Ethold came out of his tale as if out of a fog, startled to find himself seated in a decrepit old barge with faded cushions and cracked gilt. He looked at Pending and shook his head.

"They'll have raised the alarm for you hours ago. I had better get you back."

They gathered up the scattered plates and knives. Rather than wrap up the rest of the cake, Ethold broke it in two and crammed half into Pending's mouth.

"Eefold," said the boy, muffled by cake.

"Whmmf?"

Pending swallowed. "There was something else you were going to tell me. Not about the weavers."

Ethold shook his head. "Another time."

"We have it on the most reliable confidence that the Pretender has planted a spy in our midst."

Ylfcwen was trying to teach her pet mole to open pistachio nuts for her. She paused and looked up. "Why must I be concerned with it? That's what the Agency is for."

The director's face was smooth and professionally expressionless. "In another situation, we would not have had to involve madam. But, regrettably in this case, the infiltrator is one of madam's own personal attendants. The Consort Pending himself has unwittingly carried messages."

The queen held up a hand. "You know I'd rather have a tooth pulled than speak of such things. Just take care of it in the usual manner. I wish to hear no more about it."

The director bent low in a deep obeisance and noiselessly removed himself from the royal chamber.

The queen looked down. Her pet mole had eaten all the pistachio nuts. She had picked up the creature and was cradling it beneath her chin when it came to her, what the director reminded her of: a statue before the sculptor had gotten around to the features.

A chill crept over her, and she called for hot root wine.

Ethold waited an hour, and still she did not come. He had given up hope of her when a hooded figure approached. At the last moment his hand went up to make sure his mask covered his eyes. She made the secret sign, and he returned it.

"Well met," he said.

"Well met. Why the mask?"

"A sensible precaution." He laughed, shaking his head. "Tonight I had the strangest fancy that you had been found out and replaced by an agent of the R.H.A."

She laughed and pulled her hood a little closer around her face. "A strange fancy indeed."

"You do not sound like yourself. Have you caught a cold? Here, let me feel if you have a fever."

As he reached out a hand she drew back, then lunged forward in an attempt to snatch off the mask. He seized her wrist in a tight grip. The imposter twisted but could not break free. The hood fell back to reveal the queen's Mistress of the Stones—an agent of the R.H.A.

"Don't feel bad—it very nearly worked. You were the right height and size. Even the voice wasn't too bad. You couldn't help it if your feet gave you away." His voice grew cold and quiet. "Now, listen and listen well: Tell your director to inform the queen that we will not be turned back by so shabby a ruse."

He released her, and she fled on the feet that had betrayed her. Like all agents of the R.H.A., she had a completely silent footfall, but her feet were too big to be those of the woman she was impersonating.

If they knew the secret sign, then they might know the rest. He thought of his love. She had been found out; it would not go well with her. She had, as they all did, a poison pellet. By now she had surely taken it. Ethold pulled the mask from his face and stared at the strip of black bandage, fighting back a choking terror that rose in his throat. He sank to the floor of the tunnel in a crouch, clutching his head in his hands.

Surely, she had taken it.

❧

The suit was done.

Almost all of the silver had gone to purchase the pearls

and the silver thread. Tansy had let her have the velvet and lace as an advance on her allowance.

The workmanship was particularly fine. Tansy counted twenty stitches to the inch on the seams and gave up counting on the buttonholes.

The leopard-woman glanced at her apprentice. Ulfra was somewhat thinner and her hair wanted washing, but her face brimmed with an exhausted elation usually seen in women who have just given birth.

"And six hours to spare!" Ulfra said through a great yawn.

Tansy folded the suit and laid it in the box. "I have to admit, I had my doubts you could finish it in such a short space of time. You certainly deserve a rest. Why don't you have a bath," she said, "and I'll fry you a chop."

But Ulfra was fast asleep, her head on the worktable. Tansy tucked her in on the workroom sofa with a hot brick at her feet, then gave the suit a final pressing before wrapping it. She wondered where to leave the parcel— the messenger hadn't said—before deciding the wardrobe was the most logical place. Tansy wrote out the bill and slid it beneath the cord that bound the box, then placed it on a high shelf and closed the wardrobe doors.

In the morning, the box was gone, but the bill remained, beneath a large sum in new-minted silver. At the bottom someone had added in pencil, "Many thanks. It suits perfectly."

⌘

Things, animate and inanimate, that make the passage from the one world to the Otherworld often undergo a transformation. The arrival of the examination suit was anxiously awaited, and when it arrived it was unwrapped with no little trepidation. Ylfcwen was quite pleased; at a Royal Examination long ago, a suit of ermine had fared badly, arriving as no more than a moth-eaten muff.

The examinee was forbidden to wear the suit before the appointed day, so the goblin whipping boy was fetched to model the suit before the queen.

Ylfcwen lay on her lounge and gazed at the suit; Tomus squirmed and was pinched by the queen's dresser.

"One sleeve is a little longer than the other," observed the queen.

The dresser cleared her throat. "Rather, madam, one is a little shorter so the examinee shall not get ink upon his cuff."

"Ah," replied the queen. But she no longer saw the suit, for she was remembering her fourth husband and only beloved as he looked the day he was examined. Above, he had been a soldier turned highwayman, sentenced to hang for his misdeeds. The day before he was to be led to the gallows, he had tunneled from his cell into the Otherworld.

He had an eye for gems, and was being trained for work as a gem cutter when he caught the queen's eye. A tall man of fine form, with red-gold hair like pale flames and eyes so dark a blue that they seemed black ice.

A mortal tailor, long since dust, had fashioned a suit to the style of the day: blue-and-gold brocade touched with snowy ermine and lined with crimson silk. In it, he had seemed all fire and air and light, a fearsome angel summoned from the blue void at the edge of the world. She had stitched the examination answers into his cuff herself. There was no sense taking chances when you were up against the R.H.A. When it was over and the crown was on his brow, she had held to his lips the silver cup of forgetfulness. Then she had inscribed his name in the registry beside her own, the fourth Consort Royal, and, she devoutly wished, the last.

But mortal love is a fickle thing. Deprived of light and air and freedom, the new Consort did not thrive. Perhaps he took no joy in riches freely given, only in those stolen in the night. Perhaps he had drunk too deeply from the cup—her hand *had* been unsteady. From the occasional medicinal tipple, he took to soaking up cordials of root wine and stronger stuff. He grew suspicious and fearful and, in the end, quite mad, a ravaged figure roaming the corridors in tattered raiments. At some point, he had become a ghost. The actual point at which he ceased to number among the living was difficult to determine. By then he had become a weaver.

∽∾∽

The director of the R.H.A. had just asked a question. Ylfcwen shut her eyes and snored a subtle snore. After much whispered discussion, they left the room. When the sound of their withdrawing subsided, she opened one eye. The whipping boy was sitting there, like a forgotten comb or shoehorn: something not thought of until it was required.

"Come," she said. "Sit here."

Tomus clambered up into her lap.

Ylfcwen trained her opalescent eyes on him. "You thought I would be bony."

He returned her gaze unblinkingly.

"I am very light, you see. Without weights or root wine I lack the gravity to touch the floor. As I grow older it will get worse. I will grow less and less substantial, until I am overwhelmed by a compulsion to fly. At that time my reign will come to an end, and a new queen will be crowned in my place."

Not sure what to say, Tomus said nothing at all.

Ylfcwen's arms crept around the goblin boy. Late one night her son had slipped from his handlers and she had left the Consort Royal to his root wine to meet the boy in a forgotten storeroom. For an hour mother and child had huddled in a silent embrace, each lulled by the heartbeat of the other, until the handlers found them and pried them apart. After that, she saw her son very little. There had been a sudden increase in documents requiring her urgent attention; the documents had been very long.

The director of the R.H.A. reappeared. He stood and stared at the sight of the queen holding the palace whipping boy upon her knee.

"Madam."

Ylfcwen opened one eye. "Surely it has occurred to you that I do not wish to be disturbed."

"This is most unseemly—"

"*I shall do what pleases me.* And it pleases me that this child should sit on my knee as my own could never do."

A rare expression crossed the director's face. It had something in it of glee and something else of malice. Then it was gone.

"It is about your son, madam, that I must speak with you."

~∞~

Vervain was late for the Consort Pending's appointed geometry lesson. To pass the time, Pending dragged the heavy Chronicles from their high shelf, nearly toppling down the library steps in the process. To his disappointment, there was nothing about weavers, but there was an interesting entry under *Consort*.

> In the twelfth year of the Fifth Cycle of the Tenth Epoch of the Dynasty of the Lily, her supreme and divine majesty Ylfcwen, daughter of Yvaine, granddaughter of Ylyssia, great-granddaughter of Ygwynyd, took to her a mortal wanderer who, beseeching her with a comely face and plaintive way with a harp, had escaped indenture at the looms. Crowning him Consort, she bore of him a son, named ▆▆▆▆ [here something had been blotted out by the censors of the Royal Household Agency] who was raised to take his place as the first king in three Epochs. In his sixteenth year, however, ▆▆▆▆ spurned his place at his mother's side and entered a self-imposed exile Above, where he lives to this day as a mortal man. The queen's Consort was so grieved at his son's behavior that he drowned himself in the sacred lake. Since that day, there has been no other Consort Royal.

Try as he might, Pending could not lift the censor's blot. He even tried a little of Vervain's Universal Mineral Elixir on the end of his pencil eraser, to no avail. No doubt the ink had been charmed. Pending was peacefully engaged in mixing hot candle wax and spit into ink lifter when he heard a disembodied voice call his name.

"Ethold? Where are you?"

"Over by the bookshelves. There's an old spy hole. Put your ear to it."

Pending obeyed.

"Listen carefully, Pending. There isn't time for long explanations. Vervain has been arrested by the R.H.A."

"Arrested!"

"They have charged her with being a spy for the goblins. She had been an agent of the R.H.A., but she was swayed to our cause by you, Pending. She couldn't bear to see you become the next Consort."

Pending's eyes filled with hot tears. "Can't we save her?"

"No, Pending. But you must listen carefully and do exactly as I say. Go back to your room as if nothing has happened. Tomus will be waiting for you. Change clothes with him; he will take you to the tunnel that leads to the underground lake. I'll meet you there."

"But—Morag—"

"I'm sorry, Pending. It would be too dangerous. You can send word to her after. Now you must hurry."

∽◦∾

In Pending's clothes, Tomus looked remarkably like a Consort Pending.

"Do I look like a whipping boy?" asked Pending.

Tomus squinted at him. "You'll do. Here—Ethold said to give you this." He handed him a bundle. "Now we've got to be quick. Follow me."

They left the main corridors for the less-used passageways.

"Tomus. When he showed me the weaving rooms, Ethold said you never took me there because you had your orders. Whose orders?"

"The R.H.A. Don't give me that look—I wasn't *with* them; I just pretended to be. Vervain used you to send messages, but she was afraid that if she did it too often she would be found out. So sometimes she used me, in the dumbwaiter. If I was caught, I was to say I was playing hide-and-go-seek with you."

They had come to a branching of tunnels.

"Here's where I leave you. Ethold will meet you here." The whipping boy put out his hand. Pending grasped it and shook it.

"Maybe they won't find you out and you'll have to sit for that examination. And that's another thing—you knew what a consort was all the time!"

Tomus shrugged. "Maybe I did. Now I have to get back, before you're missed. Good luck."

And he was gone back down the tunnel, the way they had come.

Pending was shifting from foot to foot, thinking that whipping boys' clothes weren't quite as warm as those for consorts pending, when Ethold appeared, carrying a bundle like his own. He was changed. It was not just the light and echo of the tunnel; something about his face and voice was not the same.

But he came up smiling and rubbed Pending's hands in his own great ones to warm them.

"Have you grown cold waiting? I'm sorry—I had some loose ends to tie up. Now tell me, can you swim?"

"Only a little."

"No matter. I can swim for us both, as long as you can hold your breath. Can you do that?"

"Yes, but where are we going?"

"Above, through the underground lake."

❧

Morag discovered the substitution at once, but was too frightened to say anything. She gave Tomus a bath and put him to bed early and told the director of the R.H.A. that the Consort Pending was upset about Vervain, having been close to his governess. Morag could not tell whether he believed her.

She stood in the doorway and watched the goblin boy sleep. He was some relation of hers, distantly descended from the same human ancestor, a renowned goldsmith who had had quite a way with the ladies of the elvish court. The human features were uppermost in him. Could it work, could he possibly pass for the human boy? But even if he did, how was she to explain the absence of the goblin whipping boy?

There came a soft knock at the door, and she found herself staring down at a goblin boy just Tomus's height. Armon's boy, Fegyn, if her memory served her right.

"Let me guess: You are the new whipping boy."

He smiled shyly and nodded.

Morag opened the door wider. "You'd best get to bed,

then. I am sure the Consort Pending will explain your duties in the morning."

∽◦∾

Ylfcwen retired to her chamber to find a parcel on the foot of her bed. It was about the size of a shoe and was wound tightly with fine muslin. The object was familiar but unexpected, as though it were something she had seen in a dream and had not expected to encounter while waking.

She sat cross-legged on the bed and unwrapped it. It was a perfect model of the royal barge, beautifully carved and gilded. On the throne sat a tiny elf queen with rooted silk hair and real dragonfly's wings.

There was a slip of paper rolled tight and tucked into one of the oarlocks.

Mother,

I know when I have been bested so I will for a little time withdraw. I have wounds to lick. Perhaps the rarer air Above will restore me. It is said to have such powers.

You will forgive me, I think, for taking the boy. Perhaps you will eventually thank me. For a while I have suspected it was not a consort you saw in him but a less rebellious son. But he has a mother and he shall be returned to her. You will find another left in his place—a sort of changeling. You may think it a poor joke, and perhaps it is. Yet with the advantages you can give him, he might prove devoted enough.

When the R.H.A. came to you, did you know it was Vervain? I like to think they kept it from you. You didn't love her as I did, but I don't believe Vervain ever disappointed you. You must admit, the absence of disappointment has a faint whiff of love about it.

Until we meet again, I am your well-meaning son,
Ethold-that-was-Aethyr

Ylfcwen furled the note and hid it in the hollow handle of her ivory wing burnisher. She was feeling light-bodied and poured herself a glass of root wine but did not drink it. She lay back on the bed and gazed at the walls of her bedchamber, covered with a tapestry of living violets. She did feel very peculiar, as though the air disagreed with her. Perhaps she needed to fly a little. She slipped off the ankle weights and drifted to the vaulted ceiling.

I must tell the dresser to have it dusted up here, she thought dreamily. There were fewer fireflies than she remembered from her last flight, and more cobwebs and moths, but it was pleasant all the same.

It seemed a shame about the suit. By the time they had coached the new Consort for examination, a new suit would be required. But perhaps there would be no Consort at all. If it weren't for the fact that goblins were sterile, she would almost have suspected Tomus the whipping boy of being Vervain and Ethold's son. She was sometimes struck by the fact that she had so far escaped having a grandchild, despite her rapidly advancing years. Four marriages and only one child to show for it, and him the Goblin Pretender. It was too much.

∽∾

The sacred lake glittered cold and smooth as a facet of onyx. Its shores were littered with drifts of dried jasmine flowers from the most recent dedication of the gifts. Far off at the lake's center, Pending could make out the cold gleam of the shrine's silver spires.

"There's a long dive to a tunnel, and at the end of that a shorter dive that will bring us Above." Ethold was tying their bundles tightly to his back. "The other routes will be watched, but they don't remember this one. If we're traced, they will assume we drowned."

Pending shivered. They had stripped to their small-clothes for the dive, and this place was still and cold. "Then we're not coming back? Not ever?"

It was then that Ethold sat him on one of the carved stone seats and told him of his real name and his mortal mother. He pictured a house with spires at the edge of the blue void, surrounded by all the flowers from the weavers' carpet. His mother was at the door. Her face was a little like Vervain's and a little like Morag's, and her hair was rooted silk.

Ethold had led him to the point along the shore where the water was deepest. They were standing on the brink. Ethold's voice was telling him to fill his lungs, to hold on tight and jump at the count of three.

There was no splash. The cold waters of the lake closed around them.

4

THE HOUSE IN THE WOOD

As it happened, Pending's mortal mother lived not on the edge of a blue void but in the heart of a great and ancient forest that divided the three realms of Twinmoon to the north, Thirdmoon to the east, and Fourthmoon to the west. This was the Weirdwood, its green twilight ruled by the Direwolves and watched over by the silent flights of owls. At its center stood a massive oak, set with a red door, that had once been home to a witch. These days there were different tenants, the Binders and their boy.

It was early morning on a cold spring day. A man and boy emerged from the thick growth of hemlocks into the small clearing surrounding the oak. Binder's hair glinted gold in the weak sunshine; his darker beard was well trimmed and he wore round spectacles. The boy was about seven. His face peeked out from a blue hood, apples in his cheeks from the cold, his eyes an odd, pale brown.

The man had a basket strapped to his back; the boy carried five trout on a string. They paused by the door to use the boot scraper (added since the witch's time) and let themselves in.

The boy took off his coat. Beneath the hood, his hair was the deep russet of a fox's tail and stood up in unruly peaks. His eyes were not pale brown after all, but yellow as a cat's. His ears were small and flat to his head and slightly pointed. He was, in other words, a goblin child. He went and stirred up the fire.

Binder shrugged the basket off onto the table and began to remove its contents: a honeycomb wrapped in leaves, some speckled eggs packed in spongy moss to keep them from breaking, and a number of more ordinary parcels: butter, cheese, candles, a piece of soap.

"When you've put the kettle on, why don't you clean those fish?" said Binder over his shoulder. "Out by the stump would be a good place."

The boy fetched the scaling knife and took up the string of trout. He turned back at the door. "After, can I go see Sleeker?"

"Yes, but don't be long. We'll have breakfast soon. If I know your mother, she hasn't taken so much as a cup of tea."

The boy nodded and went out.

Binder put away the provisions and went down the twisty, narrow stairs. The tiny room had once been a root cellar; now it held a finishing stove, sewing frame, and lying press. Beneath his short beard and behind his wire spectacles, Binder had the look of the perpetual wanderer come to rest. He once had been a knight of Chameol; now he was a binder and mender of books.

He lit the finishing stove and set the glue pot on it to warm, then went upstairs, where the water had come to a boil. He brewed a pot of woodmint tea and took it up the ladder to the room nestled among the oak's upper-most branches.

From the look of the workroom, it seemed as though the old witch was still in residence. Among the pots of shade-loving herbs that lined the windowsill were lizards in bottles, moths on velvet, eggshells speckled like stones, and the eerie, white masks, no bigger than acorns, that were the skulls of shrews and mice.

At a worktable piled with books and papers, Caitlin sat bent over a sheet covered with runes. Seer's eyes, one blue, one green, gazed out from a face pale by nature and made more so by overwork. She had wound a length of her blue-black hair around one hand and was tugging at it absently as she worked. Binder noticed a pair of hair combs—his present to her on their last anniversary—lying on the worktable and smiled. She was always complaining of her hair and threatening to cut it. He told her that if she did, she would never get anything done; she could only think, he chided her, while tugging at her hair.

Binder handed her a cup of tea. She shook her head, as if coming out of a spell, muttered thanks, and took a scalding swallow.

He watched as some color returned to her cheeks. "How goes it?" he asked, nodding toward the book.

Caitlin grimaced. "Not so well. As soon as I think I've got the hang of it, the text shifts and changes. I suppose it's just eyestrain, but I'd swear the damn runes are doing it on purpose."

Behind the spectacles his eyes gleamed dangerously. "Well, if you *will* stay up all night and not come to bed—"

"If I recall correctly, you were the one who fell asleep taking his boots off. I came to bed to find you snoring away, one boot on and one boot off."

"No changing the subject," he said, taking the tea from her hand and holding it out of her reach. "You have been sadly derelict in your wifely duties."

Caitlin smiled and reached for her tea. "You know very well that I wouldn't know a wifely duty if it bit me on the nose. Let me have my tea and I promise to be more tractable. Ow!"

A wifely duty had bitten her on the nose. A skirmish broke out, and they fell to the floor with a bump. The tea spilled and went unnoticed.

She laid a finger on his lips. "Before this goes any further—where's Grimald?"

He kissed her finger. "Looking for his otter. Damn!" He sat up, raking a hand through his hair so that it stood on end. "I told him not to be long."

Before she could answer, there arrived at the window a pigeon with a green band on one leg. Caitlin went to the window. As she was unfastening the capsule on the bird's leg, she caught her husband's eye.

"I'm sorry—it's from Iiliana."

He gave the bird a dark look and smiled wryly. "It's all right. I have fish to fry." He swung down the ladder and out of sight.

She placed the pigeon in a cage and gave it seed and water, then sat down to read the message from Chameol's former queen, now its High Counsel and Ambassador to the Thirteen Kingdoms.

> My dear,
> I am in Twelvemoon, heaven help me, trying to sort out which of the late monarch's offspring has a legitimate claim to the throne. There are a great many contenders from both sides of the blanket, as they say, and I will be detained here until the turning of the year. I am very sorry, and not just for the dreariness of life here. It's past time you visited me and Chameol. The sun and sea would do you good and, besides, we could put our heads together about the books.
> —Iiliana
> P.S. The library here yielded nothing about the runes you sent. The best I can do is confirm your suspicion that they are not a living rune tongue. They are most likely Iulian.

When she left the isle of Chameol, where she had been apprenticed as a seer, Caitlin brought with her the ancient book of incantations that had belonged to old Abagtha, her late guardian and the original tenant of the oak with the red door. The book held the secrets of the long-lost kingdom of Iule, long buried beneath the waves by the necromancer Myrrhlock. Now that the wizard had been defeated, the secrets of Iule remained to be uncovered. Chameol had been the kingdom's seat of learning, with a library of fabulous books, the jewels of which were four powerful books of magic: the Books of Naming, Healing, Summoning, and Changing. When Iule sank beneath the sea, the Keepers of the Books had smuggled them from

Chameol. It was said that in the centuries since, they had been broken up and sold for relics; the pages that survived had been stitched together by some long-dead owner into Abagtha's book of incantations.

Tackling the runes had been a penance of a kind, a compensation to Iiliana for abandoning Chameol and life as a seer. Raising Grimald in the harsh Weirdwood, there had not been much time for runes at first. Now they were a welcome obsession. In the hours she sat occupied with them, Caitlin did not dwell on the fact that her seer's gift had abandoned her. Since her marriage her visions had grown less and less frequent. Two years ago, they had stopped altogether after the death from fever of her only daughter, Rowan. The runes had that power, at least: They kept her private ghosts and demons at bay.

Caitlin sighed and glanced at the piles on the worktable, pages from Abagtha's book, which had been pulled to pieces. The leaves were sorted by kind into four piles. Some were richly illuminated in brilliant reds and blues and burnished gold leaf. Some were closely written in crabbed, dark runes. Others flowed with an elegant cursive hand, with cryptic diagrams and marginal notes in red. The last pile held leaves from an herbal, so lifelike that it seemed the plants were not painted but pressed between the pages.

As she looked at them, Caitlin felt compelled to resume her work; the impenetrable runes seemed to exert a strange pull on her mind, and in the green light from the window, the pages seemed to cast a faint, irresistible glow.

But as the smell of frying trout reached her from below, a pang hit her in the pit of the stomach, equal parts guilt and hunger. Caitlin went down the ladder.

Grimald was laying the table. Besides the smoking hot trout, there was sour rye bread, a cheese, and applesauce. Caitlin bent to kiss the boy's forehead.

"Did you find Sleeker?"

Grimald shook his head. "It's days since I saw him. I'm thinking—I'm thinking maybe a wolf got him." He said it matter-of-factly, but she knew how he really felt. The otter had been hand-raised since before his eyes were open. He was not truly wild and not as wary of the wood as he should be. A Direwolf would make short work of him.

"Oh, I don't know about that," she said. "After all, he's grown now. Maybe it was time for him to find his ladylove and settle down."

Binder set the platter of fish on the table. "Just think: If he's being shy with *you*, he'll be that much safer around wolves and such."

This seemed to cheer the boy, and he held out his plate.

❧

Grimald had cleared the table and gone back out into the wood. He had his lessons at night by the fire; as long as it was light, the Weirdwood was his teacher. Now that it was beginning to thaw, there were shrew skulls to be dug up and nets to check for bats.

And otters to look for, Binder and Caitlin thought as they watched him go. Binder divided the last of the tea between their cups.

"Do you think a wolf really got Sleeker?" he asked at last.

She shrugged. "By now Grimald knows the wood almost as well as I do. But I don't think even he knows. You always hope they will get to be a little older before they first lose something they love."

They both fell silent, thinking of Rowan. If she had lived, she would now be five. Caitlin had stayed by the child's sickbed until she, too, fell ill. To keep the boy from the infection, Binder had walked him to the nearest farm. When he returned at last with help, Caitlin was delirious and the fever had settled in little Rowan's lungs. She was buried in a quiet, mossy spot marked with a white stone and grown over with lilies-of-the-wood.

They had each blamed themselves and, in the worst moments of their grief, each other. They thought of leaving the wood. Binder had been unable to set himself up as a printer, and to keep body and soul together, Caitlin had had to bottle herb remedies to sell in the nearest market town. Her researches into the runes had been abandoned. Grimald had developed night terrors and could only sleep if one of them spent the night beside him.

Then Grimald had ruined one of her books, a volume borrowed from Iiliana's library at Chameol. In mending the broken spine and torn pages, Binder found a craft that could support them. Once a month he collected mending from an old bookbinder whose fingers were grown too stiff to keep up with all the work. Caitlin still bottled enough simples to pay for the little books of gold leaf for the binding and new shoes for Grimald.

Binder laced his fingers with hers and gave her hand a squeeze.

"Back to work, I'm afraid. I promised Femius I'd have the next lot for him a little early. One's a real bear—thirteen fold-out charts in need of patching."

"So much for my wifely duties. Well, I have a letter to answer and runes to crack."

He shook his head at her. "For heaven's sake, try to get some sleep first."

When he had gone down to the bindery, Caitlin went back up to the workroom, pausing at the basin to bathe her eyes. Her reflection in the glass was a reproach. Though Binder would never say it, she looked more than tired. Her face was lined with weariness. She cursed the runes under her breath. For their sake she was ruining her health, straining her husband's affection, neglecting her child, and wearing away her sanity—yet their meaning remained just beyond her reach.

He's right, she thought, I *do* need a nap. She kicked off her shoes and stretched out on the cot. The runes still danced before her eyes, but she made herself draw even breaths, imagining a vine of ornament growing over the runes, shutting them out. Between the leaves of the vine she imagined a door. She opened it and saw the gardens of Chameol, Iiliana seated on a stone bench reading a book. Seeing Caitlin, the High Counsel of Chameol smiled and held out the book so that Caitlin could read the cover: *Ancient Rune Tongues Explained.*

Caitlin walked toward her.

⟡

There never was a colder place or one more lonely than the half-frozen spring hidden by a deep thicket in the heart of the wood. In its black surface, last fall's leaves were frozen in a thin glaze of ice. Grimald knelt on the bank, a dark, wet bundle in his arms.

He had found Sleeker. One of the otter's hind legs had been crushed by the jaws of a trap. He had bound the leg as best he could, but Sleeker had stopped moving. Grimald was sure Sleeker was dead; as soon as he was done with his good-byes, he would bury him.

"Hello. What have you got there?" said a voice softly.

Grimald had not heard the man approach. He was young and clean-shaven, his hair pulled back in a lock beneath a wide-brimmed hat. He wore a heavy traveling cloak and carried a pack.

Without ceremony he crouched beside Grimald and examined Sleeker with hands that were as kind and gentle as his voice.

"I think he's dead," Grimald said, shuddering with cold.

"No—not quite. It's good you tied up his leg the way you did. Here, we'll bathe him in the spring and then take him back. He's your pet? You live in the Weirdwood, then?"

Grimald nodded. He watched the man pick up the wounded otter and break the thin ice to bathe the injured leg. The boy turned his face from the sight of the otter's teeth bared in a grimace of pain. When he looked back, the man had wrapped the otter in the folds of his cloak.

"What's your name?"

"Grimald."

"Well, Grimald, I'm Fell. It's a lucky thing I found you, for I'm lost. I'd be grateful for a chance to warm myself before I make my way out of the wood."

⌖

Binder met them at the door, his heart in his throat. He had not seen Grimald, only a man bearing down on the house, a bundle wrapped in his cloak.

"Sweet heaven, you scared me witless. Get inside before you freeze solid."

Caitlin appeared at the top of the stair, barefoot, clutching her box of remedies.

As his father helped him out of his wet clothes, Grimald shook his head, his teeth chattering. "No—Sleeker first—"

Fell gave a loud yell. He had just received an otter bite on the hand. He handed Sleeker over to the boy, who had struggled from Binder's grasp. Speechless, the boy nuzzled his face in the creature's fur. Sleeker gave a weak *prrt-prrt* of contentment.

Caitlin examined the young man's hand. Luckily the otter was tame to start with and weak from his own wound; an otter bite can break bones. She did not tell the young man this. When the bite was dressed she turned her attention to the otter.

"It's a simple fracture. If we can keep him still and warm, it should mend. Grimald, go cut me some green wood for a splint."

Grimald let his father bundle him in dry clothes. Dwarfed in one of Binder's wool shirts and clumsy in his mother's boots, the boy stomped out, glad of something to do.

As Binder pressed a cup of hot rum into his hands, Fell turned to Caitlin with a stunned look. "But the trap . . . that leg was badly crushed. I saw it. And when we came up to the house, he had stopped moving. I was sure the creature was dead."

Caitlin shook her head. "It was hard even for me to tell, with the blood and the fur around the wound. It must have looked a lot worse to you. But tell me, how did *you* happen into the middle of all this?"

The young man blushed. "I set off to seek my fortune. I'm afraid I got lost." He lifted his chin. "My late father was a goldsmith; I am the youngest of his sons. Between them, my brothers have spent what fortune there was. I am hoping to find a trade. I came to the Weirdwood looking for a binder I was told lived here."

"My husband is the bookbinder, if it's that kind of binding you want."

"It is. So I am not lost, after all."

Binder shook his head. "Even if we could offer room and board, I couldn't take on an apprentice. I'm not a master yet myself; I rely on the binder in town to give me what work I have. Besides, to become apprenticed you need to be sixteen."

Fell drew himself up. "I'm nineteen! Nearly twenty." Without the wide-brimmed hat and cloak, he was revealed as the youth he was—tall for his age but slight of frame.

Binder smiled and tried to repair the slight. "Then you are more skilled with a razor than I was at your age. No offense."

"None taken."

Caitlin looked at Fell closely. He was telling the truth, as far as it went. But his clothes, though simple, were very well made, not those of a youngest son without prospects. Some impediment other than lack of fortune stood in his way.

Fell seemed uneasy beneath her gaze. He turned down their invitation to stay to supper, reaching for his hat.

"I have no wish to outstay my welcome."

"Nonsense; your cloak is not yet dry. If you can't stay to supper, at least let me show you the workshop. You'll still have time to reach the edge of wood before dark."

Once in the workroom, Fell's shyness fell away, and his features grew almost animated as he asked questions about the tools and materials. Binder watched him thoughtfully. At last Fell's departure could be put off no longer, and they ascended to the kitchen to retrieve the cloak, now dry.

"Bookbinding's hardly the only trade you could learn," said Binder. "I hear there is a good living to made as an engraver." He gave Fell the name of an artisan in the town.

"Thank you. I am sorry you cannot take an apprentice, sir, for I feel we should have got on well. Good day to you."

"Best of luck to you."

He bowed his way out. Through the window they could see him saying his farewell to Grimald where the boy was cutting splints of green ash.

"It's a shame, in a way," said Binder. "He would have been a friend to Grimald."

"Yes," was all Caitlin said. She did not like to tell her

husband so, but she thought the young man more secretive than shy and, no matter what his story, he was no poor youngest son.

That night, Caitlin came late to bed, hours after her husband had carried Grimald up to the workroom to kiss her good night. She crept down the ladder to the room they shared, a tiny chamber taken up almost entirely by the bed and the heavy chest at its foot. Binder had made shelves for the curved wall at the head of the bed, the brackets carved in a pattern of ivy and fitted to hold candles. She placed her candle in the headboard.

He had fallen asleep half dressed, without climbing all the way beneath the covers. One hand still clutched his spectacles. Caitlin eased them from his grasp and laid them on one of the shelves. Hurrying in the chill of the room, she changed into her nightclothes and climbed into bed. At this slight movement he turned toward her, still deep in sleep, burrowing his face into the warmth between her neck and shoulder.

She lifted her head and gazed at him for a time before she blew out the candle, thinking, searching his face for traces of her lost Rowan and of another child, the son whose place Grimald had taken, whose place he could never take. Binder had changed—in name, for one: Only she called him Badger now. To Grimald he was Baba. To others he gave a new name, Matthew Binder. In appearance, too, he was altered. The close work of the bindery and the scant light of the Weirdwood had taken their toll on his eyes—thus the fine lines in their outer corners and the wire-rimmed spectacles. He had grown the beard during the dark days surrounding Rowan's illness and death. He wore it now, years later, less a badge of grief, more a kind of remembrance.

Binder had never believed that Grimald was a changeling. As the child grew and began more and more to resemble a goblin, he remained convinced that Grimald was his child. And in many ways human love *had* made the boy human. Caitlin was resolved to tell him—and loath to.

So she alone knew, knew and remembered. Dark-haired Bram, her firstborn, her first-lost. Rowan had been flaxen-haired, a rebuke to her hope that Bram somehow might be reborn in their second child. No sooner had she begun to love her daughter for the gift she was than she was taken, too.

That was why she came late to bed, well after Binder was asleep: to deny herself the comfort and solace of her husband's arms, to atone for trying to remake Bram, to make certain there would be no more grieving for another lost child.

She blew out the candle and lay back in bed, turning her back to him, hugging her knees. With effort she emptied her mind of all thoughts, slowing her breaths until at last she drifted off. In sleep, he drew nearer again, matching his posture to hers limb for limb, twining his fingers in her loose hair.

&

Pending was cold, so cold he burned with it. He did not remember surfacing; he did not remember setting foot Above. Cold made all his senses shrink until they were a shuddering core in his numb body. A voice came to him faintly. Hot liquid passed between his lips, like root wine, but not so bitter.

He came to briefly and struggled to sit up but could not. This frightened him, until he saw that he was only weighed down by heavy furs. He was in a small space with irregular walls and a roof only a few feet above his head. There was a strange, thick smell made up of many other smells; it was not unpleasant. He was aware of being warm. Eyes glinted at him in the darkness. Goblin eyes.

"Here. Take this," said Ethold's voice. The boy heard the light scrape of a spoon against the side of a bowl.

He had never tasted anything like it, but it was hot and sweet and thick and delicious. He ate every spoonful and fell back upon his bed into a deep sleep.

&

Binder stood and scowled at the open cupboards.

"Did you give Fell any food?"

Caitlin looked up from the floor, where she and Grimald

were sprawled over a game of his invention called liar's checkers. "No, why? Is anything missing?"

Binder shook his head. "Yes. Odd things. At first it was a crock of honey here, a loaf of bread there. I figured you'd gone on one of your midnight cupboard raids."

She smiled. "I see. Go on."

"Then some cider went missing—and the bottles turned up, empty. We're low on candles, and I know I bought enough to last another three weeks. And just yesterday I set some applesauce on the table by the window to cool, and a little while later it was gone, bowl and all."

Grimald captured the last of her dried lizards, winning the game, but Caitlin didn't seem to notice.

"Come to think of it," she said, sitting up, "someone's been at my herb garden, too. I thought it was rabbits, but it was too regular for that. And they were peculiar herbs— things a rabbit wouldn't eat."

"But medicinal?" said Binder.

"Not in themselves. They'd have to be boiled with—"

"Cider, perhaps, and honey?"

"Yes. What will you do?"

"Hang some sausages up in the shed. A neighbor's a neighbor, invisible or not." He put on his coat and went out.

"Who's invisible?" Grimald asked.

"No one. Your father only means that we've never seen the person who's been taking the food. Now, are you going to give *me* a chance to win a game and redeem myself?"

"All right."

"Well, I get the lucky piece this time. Fair's fair."

∽≫

Pending opened his eyes, and for the first time in days he could really see and hear and smell and think. He lay on a bed of furs in a small room with earthen walls and a low earthen ceiling from which tree roots protruded like crooked beams. Through the low, arched entrance he could see Ethold outside, crouched by a smoky fire.

He struggled out from under the heavy covers and found his clothes. When he got to the door the light of the clearing struck his eyes and made him dizzy.

Ethold looked up from the cider he was warming. "Well, Bram, how are you feeling?"

The boy remembered what Ethold had told him at the edge of the underground lake. This was his new name, his real name. It sounded strange.

"Achy. The light hurts my eyes. Did I almost drown?"

"No, you made the dive beautifully. But coming Above affects people differently. You got a bad case of light sickness, on top of a nasty cold. Here. Drink this." Ethold handed him a cup of cider with honey and herbs.

"Is it a wolves' den?" he asked, after he had swallowed. There had been pictures of wolves in the Fabulous Bestiary Vervain had given him for his fifth birthday.

"No, a poacher's den, I think."

"Is this were we are going to live?"

Ethold's eyes were unreadable. "No. The poacher will want it back. You're going to live with your mother."

Then Bram remembered. The light sickness had driven it from his mind. Anticipation and a sick dread gave him a queasy feeling in the pit of his stomach. He spoke around the knot that had formed in his throat. "Where will *you* go?"

"Away, to a new life." The goblin stared into the coals, then looked up at the boy, his amethyst eyes bright. "I will have a new name, like you."

Bram opened his mouth to ask another question, but Ethold gave the smallest shake of his head. Then the goblin opened wide his arms and the boy stepped into them. The hot knot in his throat untied itself, unraveling in hoarse sobs that echoed in the little clearing. Even muffled by the goblin's coat, it was a dismal sound.

❦

It was early and grey. Though she had been up for hours, Caitlin had not been able to get anything done. Binder and Grimald had gone off before dawn to walk to the nearest farm; the Harriers' mare had had twin foals.

The house, indeed the whole wood, seemed to ache with stillness; Caitlin fought a temptation to leap and stamp and shout to dispel it. There was something uncanny, almost otherworldly about the heavy quiet. It was as if, once alone with her, the runes were trying to speak. The air hummed with the silence that was almost itself a sound.

She got up from her worktable and went to the basin to wash her face, glad of the noise the water made pouring from the bright blue pitcher. As she bent to cup the cold water in her hands, there rose in her mind a fragment of a remembered dream: a woman seated in a garden, holding out a book. It was the garden on Chameol, the woman was Iiliana (no mistaking those coppery tresses), and the cover of the book read *Ancient Rune Tongues Explained*.

Caitlin sank to a crouch on the floor, the basin, the room, everything else forgotten. Could she remember the rest of the dream? She had been awakened abruptly, when Fell and Grimald had brought the wounded otter into the house, and had not thought of it since. As a seer on Chameol, she had been trained to remember and interpret her dreams, even to summon them. Since Rowan's death she had all but abandoned the practice, but it was as much a part of her as memory and needed only to be called on. She called on it now.

She was back in the garden at Chameol. Iiliana was sitting on a stone bench, reading. She walked toward her. Iiliana held out the book. She took it. It was heavy, much too heavy for its size. She opened it, but it was unreadable. The runes upon the page shifted and buzzed before her eyes, then slowly resolved into the shapes of bees, circling on a blank page.

She turned to Iiliana to complain that the book was full of bees, but Iiliana was gone. In her place on the stone seat sat a boy of seven or so, with black hair and eyes as amber as honey. He gazed at her solemnly and held out his hands, which were full of jasmine petals.

No sooner had she taken the flowers from his outstretched hands than the bees began to desert *Ancient Rune Tongues Explained* for the sweet, papery petals. When the last bee had left the page, ghostly shapes could be seen to form there, the shadows of the shadows of runes.

And there the dream ended. Caitlin let loose a shout of frustration.

"It can't end there! It simply can't!"

She went downstairs and put the empty kettle on the fire. When it squealed immediately in protest she took it off the fire, filled it, and stood a minute staring at it. Then she emptied the kettle and put it away. She took up her cloak and a basket and left the house.

It was really still too early to gather mushrooms. As she walked through the wood she listened intently for a twig snap, a sleepy birdcall, any sound breaking through the oppressive stillness, the great held breath of the Weirdwood.

The place where she usually found the best mushrooms was not far from the mossy bank where Rowan was buried, but Caitlin did not stop to visit the grave. Her errand, begun out of exasperation, somehow had become too important to be put off. When at last she reached the spot, she understood why. There were no mushrooms after all, only a small boy, curled up asleep at the base of a tree, his grimy face streaked with tears.

Caitlin stood a long time, wondering at him: at his hair, sooty as a raven's wing; at the strange silver ring upon his finger. She stood clutching her empty basket, afraid to wake him lest he should prove a trick of her dreams, another taunt of the runes.

At last she did reach forward and gently shook him by the shoulder. They looked at one another, each a little afraid, and then the boy held out his hand and she took it and led him through the wood all the long way home.

～∞～

Binder looked from one boy to the other and saw the truth of it, the truth she had tried to make him see from the beginning. Despite his amber eyes, there could be little doubt that this boy, with his pallid skin and blue-black hair, was Caitlin's child. And the more he looked, the more Binder believed it must be his son. That hair was hers, but the cowlick and forehead, nose and chin were his own.

As Grimald had grown, Binder had stubbornly ignored

the boy's peaked ears, his yellow eyes, his fox-red hair. He could not believe the boy a goblin or suspect he was some other man's child. It was less confusing, less painful, to continue to accept him as his own. Besides, he loved the boy.

Now the changelings (for his eyes told him they were) stood before him, of an age, of a height, one unmistakably goblin, the other so clearly human. The boys looked at him, the dark one waiting for him to speak, the ruddy one waiting for him to make everything right.

He could not make everything right (which for Grimald meant returning things to the way they had been a half hour ago, before Caitlin came in the door with Bram). But he could still speak.

"Welcome—Bram." He cleared his throat and began again. "Welcome home. All right—fish traps. First we'll go check the fish traps, and then I suppose we had better get started building you a bed."

5

SOME ALTERATIONS ARE MADE

Ulfra had been mistaken about the injured wolf. Several weeks passed, and the other wolves did not come for it. As the wolf regained its strength it became harder and harder to conceal it from customers. Still worse, Lady Twixtwain refused to cross the threshold while the wolf was in residence; so she wrote from the sanctuary of her well-appointed house in Goldenmouth Street.

> I know Ulfra would not let the creature harm me, but I can't make my poor Opaline understand that it will not harm her. And I cannot think of leaving her behind. It seems the only solution is for you to come to my house for our next game of cards.

"Dinner at Lady Twixtwain's!" Ulfra's eyes shone. She had been in bed with the measles the last time an invitation had been extended. The tales Tansy had brought back of painted ceilings and a glassed-in fish pond had only sharpened her disappointment.

Now Tansy shook her head. "The wolf can't be left

alone. You'll have to stay home and look after him. A half-grown wolf can get into too much mischief in the workshop."

There had already been an unfortunate incident involving a ball gown decorated with plumes. The feathers gave the dress the appearance of a startled bird rising up in flight. How else, Ulfra argued, could a wolf have been expected to act?

She had not won the argument then and she did not win it now.

So this evening found her home alone. The wolf had denned himself in underneath the workshop sofa; there came to Ulfra, as she sat at the drawing table with her sketches, the crunching of his teeth on a bone.

Since the episode of the examination suit, not a day had passed in which Ulfra had not revisited Ylfcwen's court. These were not mere daydreams—they struck her imagination with a force daydreams do not have, and they stayed with her, begging to be put down in pencil, chalk, whatever was at hand. Later, she put them down in watercolors, filling sketchbook after sketchbook with vivid renderings of fabrics so delicate of pattern that they seemed to shift and shimmer beneath the eye.

Page after page blossomed with gossamer silks of peacock and canary, rich brocades of ruby and emerald and silver-shot azure. Her pencil struggled to capture the intricate shape of a silver buckle before the vision fled from her mind. Then there were ear bobs, carved buttons, elaborate clasps, and a strange article of which she could make no sense—something of starched linen, laced like a corset but shaped like an archer's quiver.

Sighing, Ulfra erased, redrew a line, and began a sketch in the pattern of a gold brocade. She hoped it was not an article of underclothing. Something told her that gold brocade was just the thing, and more and more lately, Ulfra found herself paying attention to that something. She set the sheet aside to dry, feeling a bit guilty that she had spent the whole evening doodling, neglecting the rack of dresses that needed finishing. She cast a final glance at the sketch, wondering what the strange corset-quiver could be.

The something that guided her hand chose not to inform her that it was an elvish wing case.

She was about to start sewing tiny jet beads onto the bodice of a gown when the wolf growled. It was an alarm growl, and Ulfra turned to look.

The wolf was at the window, intent on something in the street outside. His ears were laid flat along his head.

Sewing on the tiny jet beads, each no bigger than a grain of rice, promised to be tedious indeed, so Ulfra was glad enough of a reason to set them aside. She went to the window and drew back the curtain just a little so that no one in the street would notice.

It had rained a little while ago. The cobblestones glistened under the light of the lamps, and the gutters of the house opposite still dripped. A few passersby, huddled against the damp, hurried on their way to late dinners. After a moment it became clear that one figure was not hurrying to dinner or anything else. He was loitering in a doorway across the street and a few doors down from the Cat's Face. His cloak was pulled close around him against the creeping damp.

The wolf had known him at once by his smell, a curious blend of boar grease and oil of bitter-orange. Unlike the wolf, Ulfra could not catch a scent through a closed window and across a rainy street. She recognized the man by his shape: a great bear balanced on its hind legs. It was the king's huntsman.

The wolf's growl changed to a wheedling sort of whimper. Let me out, he was plainly saying. Oh, just let me out.

"It would only be trouble if I did." She forgot to speak in Wolf, but by her tone of voice she made herself understood. The wolf reluctantly rested its muzzle on the sill.

She wondered what the huntsman was doing here. He wasn't looking in her direction; she didn't think he knew the Cat's Face from any other shop. If he did, he wouldn't be standing in the light where she could see him.

Just then the door of the house opposite opened and a young man stepped out. The lamplight picked out the gleam of a silver button, a lace cuff. Though he was the shorter and slighter, this other man managed to be commanding, even next to the bearish figure of the huntsman. In the tailoring trade, one learned to notice how people carried themselves. This man carried himself like a nobleman. (Though sometimes one couldn't tell: There was a wellborn customer of theirs who bore himself as though bound for the gallows and another, a reformed highwayman, who carried himself as though he were destined to wear the crown.)

A sudden gust of wind worried and tugged at the young man's cloak, and Ulfra saw a flash of purple silk. The sumptuary laws decreed that only those of royal blood could wear purple. So he carries himself like a prince for good reason, she thought.

Lady Twixtwain had told them tales of the crown prince, how he had made a double-faced cloak that he could turn inside out and so go unnoticed when visiting his mistress, "an—*unpedigreed* woman, shall we say?" The prince had recently become betrothed to a suitable princess, well dowered, sufficiently pretty, and moderately clever. The commission of his wedding clothes was hotly sought after by the Cat's Face and its competitors.

"And there are some," Lady Twixtwain had said, "who would gladly sew *themselves* into the linings of his clothes, if they could manage it."

At that point, Tansy had abruptly sent Ulfra to buy thread, so she had been unable to satisfy her curiosity on the matter of the prince's clothes and their interesting linings.

Prince and huntsman moved off down the street. Ulfra let the curtain fall back into place, but did not return to the tiresome little jet beads. She stood there, absently stroking the wolf and thinking.

❧

The farmyard was strewn with the litter from a wedding. Flowers had been trampled into the sawdust, and one of the garlands to which guests had tied money and good wishes had come untied and trailed in the dirt. In one corner of the yard, the dogs fought over the tag end of a ham. Farmer Goody had said farewell to the last straggler and fled to the barn to smoke a pipe, digest his ale, and ponder in solitude the solemn sums lavished on the nuptials of his youngest daughter.

Hazel had some months before grown past the pencil mark on the pantry door, the acknowledged signal that it was time for her to leave the household and make a home of her own. Happily, a love match had been arranged with the neighbors' second son, and an hour ago the new bride, not yet sixteen, had driven off in a cart to her new life.

Nix sulked. Though Hazel had been his favorite, he had not gone outside to see her off, and as she waved from the wagon, the new Mistress Brown had cried as though her heart would break. Now Nix sat alone with Mistress Goody in the kitchen, helping her clean up the remains of the wedding feast. Neither said a word, but their thoughts ran along the same lines: Nix would never grow past the notch.

Mistress Goody could not be displeased at this prospect. For all his small size, Nix was sturdy and clever, unquarrelsome, and a wizard with money. Mistress Goody's income had increased twelvefold since she had put Nix in charge of the eggs and butter, and as for the jam and pickles, well, they had taken off like a house afire.

Nix had appeared on their doorstep out of the dusk seven years before, a strange note and a purse full of money pinned to his shirt. The note had been written on the back of a bill for a troupe of acrobats. "Take good and amazing care of Nix, the albino deaf-mute," it had said. He had been six, perhaps seven years old, with odd hair as white as an old man's and so soft-spoken that at first they had thought he really was mute.

Farm life had made him sturdier and browner, so his milkweed-pale hair stood out with striking whiteness. Like any boy his age, he was all elbows and knees, but for months now he had not grown any taller. It was a mystery, but then everything about Nix was a mystery. He never spoke of the days before his arrival on their doorstep. When pressed, he retreated to a dumb stare. So they had not pressed him, grateful for the money that arrived at regular intervals, enough to keep him in shoes and pay for the bonesetter when he fell from the apple tree retrieving Hazel's cat.

∽

Dusk had fallen when Farmer Goody strode in, grim-faced. The chairs were still against the wall and the floor was invitingly bare. Wordlessly he seized his startled wife and spun her across the farmhouse floor in a country dance.

"Tom!" she protested. "Did the ale bring this on?"

"Can't a man—a newly impoverished man—dance with his own wife?"

"But the floor still has to be scrubbed. I can't leave it for Nell. She won't do it properly. It has to be *scoured*— people have been treading ham rind and beer into it all afternoon."

"Hush, woman."

"But I'm out of breath."

He laughed. "But never out of words, damn you. Hush, I tell you, and dance."

Nix picked himself up from his chair by the fire and went out into the farmyard. The youngest Goodys, seven-year-old Pippin and nine-year-old Jack, were upstairs sleeping the uneasy sleep of boys who had discovered that it was possible to consume too many sweets at one sitting.

The dusky sky was already thick with stars, large and low to the earth. In the western half of the sky the world curved away to a thin crescent of purple and gold. The air was chilly and Nix wished for his woolen shirt.

It had been an evening like this one, the day Ulfra had left him here. When she had picked out the Goody farm, he had thought at first that she meant to steal a pig, but a cuff on the ear had taught him otherwise.

The Goodys had taken him in and raised him as one of their own. But it had not been the same. He missed life on the road with Folderol's band, picking pockets, performing with the wolves. For the first year after he came to them, Mistress Goody would come downstairs in the morning to find Nix curled on the floor with the dogs. When he had been Nix, the Albino Deaf-Mute, his bed had not been a pallet of straw but a drowsing heap of wolves.

Nix looked up at the sky and found the group of stars called the Greater Wolf. Ulfra had been named for its brightest star; Nix was in the habit of wishing on it.

"Please, I want to grow," he said. "Not just past the mark on the pantry door. I want to be *tall*."

The wolf star shone no brighter or dimmer and stayed exactly (as far as Nix could tell) in the part of the sky where it had always been.

It had granted a wish of his once before. He had wished to see Ulfra, and promptly the wolf star had produced her, grandly dressed, turning over crocks of jam at the Goodys' stall in the marketplace. She had recognized him but had not spoken to him except to buy three crocks of jam. There had been nothing of wolf left about her. Worst of all, she had overpaid for her purchase, so he thought she had lost all her sense, along with her good wolf smell.

Still, it had shown that the wolf star granted wishes. Nix turned and started back toward the house.

⁓

The lamplighter had just started his rounds, putting out the lamps. The night owls of the town had barely gone to their beds, passing in the lane the early birds, laborers and tradesmen whose day began before dawn.

In the bleary half light, the baker's boy hurried past shuttered inns and the grey, sleepy fronts of houses. His mistress would have set the loaves for a last rising before she went to bed. It was his job to put those in the oven and form the loaves for the next baking. Today was to be a busier day than usual. It was the eve of a feast; there were seedy loaves to make, and sweet braids, and a special holiday loaf in the shape of a crown. He rounded the corner to the street where the bakery stood and stopped short at the sight before him.

Eight wolves trotted swiftly at the heels of a ninth, a great she-wolf, grizzled black and silver. They made a perfect triangle but for the back row, where there were three wolves instead of four.

The baker's boy shrank back against the wall, but the wolves took no notice of him, loping past in silence.

After they had gone, the boy let himself into the bakery and set about his tasks. He was a little rattled; though he did not burn the bread, he shaped the seedy bread into braids and the sweet bread into round loaves, instead of the other way around.

⋙⋘

The wolves reached the Sign of the Cat's Face and sat down on the cobblestones, still in formation. The she-wolf went to the front door and scratched on it with her claws—too lightly to wake Tansy, or even Ulfra, but just loudly enough to wake the wolf inside. In a trice he was at the front door. There he sat back on his haunches and gave a whimper, for the door was latched and bolted. He communicated this fact through the keyhole to the she-wolf.

The other wolves, overhearing, lay down to wait. One of them yawned, and was bitten on the ear by his neighbor for bad manners.

The she-wolf tasted the air. By the smell of him, the lamplighter was still several blocks away. There was time. *Draw the bolt with your teeth*, she explained in Wolf, *then press the latch with your paws.*

The younger wolf saw how this was possible and, after several tries, got it right. He took his spot in the fourth row, and swiftly the pack moved out of town. No human had seen them except the baker's boy. The baker would shake her head at the seeded braid and the sweet round loaf and sell them anyway. And, from one end of town to the other, householders would wonder why their cats perched on the highest beams, fur on end, impervious to coaxing or saucers of milk.

Tansy, when she came downstairs, assumed that she herself had left the door unbolted. Only after they realized that the wolf was missing did Ulfra find the scratches on the front door.

⋙⋘

Lady Twixtwain paid a visit that very afternoon. Opaline stood in the doorway uncertainly. Though the house had been well aired and the rugs beaten, there was still a faint whiff about the place that made the dog tremble. But on seeing Ulfra she overcame her fear and came inside, beating her tail against the carpet apologetically.

"No, no tea, thank you," said Lady Twixtwain. "Now the only thing I take is this water." She held up a small, stoppered flask. "If you have a little wine . . ."

Tansy rose to fetch some.

"The man I see about my foot recommended it most highly," said Lady Twixtwain, pouring a fingerful of the water into the glass provided. "It purifies the blood, sweetens the breath, promotes concentration, *and*"—she filled the glass the rest of the way with wine—"improves the complexion."

"I can see it does," said Tansy. "Your complexion is *very* much improved."

"But does it help your foot, Lady Twixtwain?" asked Ulfra. Lady Twixtwain had handed the flask to her. Its label, covered with crabbed writing in brown ink, did not mention afflictions of the hands and feet.

"Alas, no. I must sleep with them above my head, he says, and bathe the left in milk and the right in vinegar."

"But your right foot is not afflicted," said Tansy.

"I thought the same thing, but he set me straight. The humors in my feet have become imbalanced, you see. It is all very complicated."

"And expensive?"

"Oh, not half so expensive as I feared. And I do not mind the taste at all. Now, Ulfra my dear. You were going to show me the sketches you made for my dress for the masked ball."

"I have them here." Ulfra took out her watercolor board, to which several drawings were pinned.

"*Ah.* A charmer of snakes. Oh, how well you have drawn me! And Opaline peeking out from under my skirts.

"And here I am as Night, I presume? A celestial look. See, Tansy, she has made my skirt out of a comet's tail. Alas, I fear it would not be proper to wear in front of royalty."

Lady Twixtwain admired in turn sketches of herself as

a black swan on a lily pond (complete with embroidered frogs, dragonflies, and carp), an aviary (a cage of gold wire worn over a skirt embroidered with birds), and the personification of a rose—a gown of the palest ivory silk over green hose, embroidered with crystal beads of dew.

"And what is this?"

It was one of Ulfra's doodles, a gown of layered silk in blue-violet and cloth of gold, with a strange corset-quiver affair on the back, and a strange staff topped with a jeweled orb.

"Ylfcwen—the queen of the elves," Ulfra said, the something of her daydreams speaking for her.

"It will answer handsomely, though we will have to change the colors. I wouldn't want to be fined for breaking the sumptuary laws. But tell me, what is the strange apparatus on the back?"

And at once Ulfra knew. "It's a wing case." In her mind she was already envisioning how it might work, how a small cord, when pulled, would release the wings of stiffened gauze.

∽∾

"Grimald!"

Grimald drew further into the shadows of the shed and held his breath. The door hinge squealed and a patch of dim light slid across the earthen floor in front of his hiding place. His father's boots strode into view.

"You'll have to come out sooner or later. It might as well be now."

Grimald made a face. He was sorry now that he'd chosen this hiding place. The hollow oak down by the stream would have been better. He knew how to live in the wood. A bundle was ready under his bed. He knew how to light a fire and keep it alive. He knew where all the fish traps were, and the beehives, and the places the wood-hens laid their eggs. He and Sleeker would live by the stream.

"Come on," said his father, drawing him by one arm from his hiding place. "That's enough of this."

Bram was at the table with Caitlin, helping with the week's bread, when the door opened and Binder entered, steering Grimald before him.

"Tell your brother you're sorry."

Grimald glowered. He was not sorry and he certainly had meant it. Then he caught his mother's eye. He mumbled something in the direction of the new boy.

Binder shook him gently by the shoulder. "Again, with feeling, and look at him this time."

"I'm sorry I locked you in the cellar."

"And?"

"And I'm sorry I put a walkingstick in your bed."

Caitlin made a face. "Oh, Grimald."

"It gets worse," Binder said. "Go on."

"And I'm sorry I put grubs in your porridge."

"That's better. Now, you, say you forgive him."

Bram raised sullen eyes to Binder's. "But I don't, and I won't lie and say I do."

Grimald wriggled from his father's grasp. "I take it back! I'm not sorry at all and I'll do it again!"

The taunt was on the tip of Bram's tongue—the elvish slur for goblins—when Bram caught a fierce glance from Caitlin. Then he thought of Ethold, and shame soured the word in his mouth.

"All right, that's enough. Grimald, no more trips to see the Harriers' foals. As for you, Bram, you're as much in the wrong as he. Lights out for you early the rest of the week."

The boy's sullen look was gone. His face wore a look of blank misery. His only pleasure was reading.

"Now I want the two of you to go together and get the water and wood for tomorrow. No, Grimald, not another word. Go on."

In silence they went, Grimald abristle with suppressed fury, Bram unreadable. When they had gone, Caitlin shook her head. "I can't really blame either of them. Think how they must feel. All of a sudden I bring home this strange boy and expect them to behave like brothers."

"That's just the problem. They *are* behaving like brothers."

"But grubs in the porridge. It has to stop." Caitlin slashed the tops of the shaped loaves and slid them onto the floured shingle, ready for the outdoor oven.

"What about these?" Binder said, pointing to two smaller loaves.

"Bram made them. They need a second rising."

Binder looked at one of the loaves and then picked it up to examine it closely. Carefully, he pulled the dough apart.

"Oh, Badger, you'll ruin it. He spent a lot of time getting it right."

"In a way." He held out the halves of the unbaked loaf for her to see. Embedded in the dough were some dozen fat, white grubs.

That night Grimald lay in bed and plotted his escape and fell asleep to pleasant dreams of living by the stream with Sleeker.

In the other bed, across the chalk line that divided the small room in two, Bram lay awake trying to remember faces. Ethold's was still clear in his mind, but Tomus's and Vervain's and even Morag's were not so easy.

He stared at the ceiling and willed himself to remember.

Hours later Caitlin paused in the doorway to look in on them where they slept. Grimald slept on his stomach, his breathing slow and heavy. Bram's face was turned to the wall. She thought he was awake but let him feign sleep, going up to her own bed.

Binder opened his eyes when she came in.

"Go back to sleep."

"I wasn't really asleep. What time is it?"

"Late." She undid her braid swiftly and, too tired to be bothered with brushing it, got into bed with her hair loose around her shoulders.

Binder reached out and looped a few strands behind her ear.

"A silver one . . ."

"More than one, thanks to the boys."

"And other things." The litany went unuttered but understood: the isolation, the death of Rowan, their marriage.

She smiled, working a dab of greenish paste into her roughened hands. "Ah—this is a well-worn theme. My life of ease as a seer on Chameol, revered, serene, and *chaste*."

"Something like that." The warmed beeswax released its

scent and he breathed in the green perfume of balm and woodmint. At least the scars on her hands could be seen.

"If you think my hands wouldn't have been callused on Chameol, then you don't know Iiliana." She blew out the candle.

She never feigned sleep to deceive her husband. It was to lull herself into sleep, to turn her mind from incessant worries, that she turned her back, slowed her breathing.

Since the day she had found him in the woods, Caitlin had spent sleepless nights thinking of all the ways Bram might come to harm. In secret, because she was ashamed, she had schooled herself in all the old lore of mortals released from the Otherworld. She read up on the shaking fever called elf's dance and the ailments known together as elf's kiss, manifested as fainting spells and fits of paralysis that came on and passed with the new moon.

Those were no more than superstitious tales. What she could not shrug off were the recurring references to changeling sight, Otherworld visions manifested in childhood that led to blindness, madness, and death before the age of twelve.

Binder was not asleep either. He knew she was only pretending to be, for reasons he did not like to think about. But, asleep or not, she was beside him. In seven years, they had not driven each other to madness or violence or flight.

And that was a balm, of a kind.

∽◦∾

Lady Twixtwain's costume was a great success. The final color scheme was silver-and-blue brocade reversing to magenta. Ulfra had sacrificed the spring mechanisms from several mousetraps before perfecting wings that would unfurl when a hidden string was pulled.

Lady Twixtwain had created a sensation. The crown prince himself had come over to compliment her ("*much* to the chagrin of his bride-to-be"), and within the week a woman of any social standing could not be seen at court without a wing case. Mechanical wings were not a part of the new fad; the cases were used instead to hide everything from illicit love letters and unfinished needlework to the emergency pair of silk hose or the secret flask of gin.

Ulfra's designs were much copied by other tailors around town, but the Cat's Face got the lion's share of the business in wing cases. Tansy was perplexed but uncomplaining, and gamely produced a new design on a weekly basis.

They had to hire three women to handle all the work. When the house next door was vacated, they expanded into it. Amid the workmen and plasterers they stood and toasted their new good fortune with expensive wine, casting their glasses into the unfinished fireplace.

"We're rich," Tansy said, wonderingly.

"No," said Ulfra, with an uncharacteristic giggle. "We're *extremely* rich."

A workman came up to them, hair and face whitened by plaster to the aspect of an unkempt ghost. He spoke in a thick Se'enmoon accent. "Summun left this inna dur."

Tansy took the proffered letter, a heavy vellum packet sealed with red wax. She broke the seal and scanned the letter's contents, then sank down on the plaster-strewn floor in shock. Ulfra picked up the letter where Tansy had let it fall.

Let it be known that, by royal appointment, the tailoring establishment known as the Cat's Face, with premises in Everlasting Lane, has been awarded the commission to make the wedding clothes for His Most Serene Highness, Prince Berthold of Twinmoon. (Details of said commission will be forthcoming from the Valet Royal.)

6

BARTER AND TRADE

The fad for wing cases had played itself out, but over the course of the next nine months, the name of the Cat's Face became so imprinted on the fashionable mind that anything produced by their shop became a mania in its own right.

First came black velvet mitts called cat's-paws; then sheer, stiff embroidered sleeves called dragonflies' wings; and then a fad for women to go about in blue tunics— the Elf-Prince look, they had called it.

Meanwhile, Tansy and Ulfra worked on the prince's wedding clothes. This included the actual suit of clothes he was to be married in and a cloak with a long train, as well as his traveling clothes for the year-long pilgrimage he and his bride would undertake while the new summer palace was being constructed.

At the start, nine months had seemed more than ample for the work to be completed. That was before they made the acquaintance of the Valet Royal. A strict procedure had to be adhered to; sketches and patterns and embroidery designs examined, approved, and notarized; dyes formulated and fabrics certified; workers bonded and sworn to secrecy.

There were to be two formal winter suits (best and second-best), two formal summer suits (ditto), five costumes for attending the theater, six different dancing costumes, and various outfits suited for sleigh riding, falconing, hunting, fencing, and sampling the hot springs at Se'enmoon.

Bolts were only rolled out to impress clients; to choose fabrics, Tansy and Ulfra referred to large ledgers. Pinned to the felt pages were swatches of fabric, with notations of the shelves in the workroom where the bolts could be found, as well as which customers had garments made up in them already. This was to reduce the chance of embarrassment at balls, where a guest might find, to her chagrin, that her next-door neighbor had a dress made out of the same fabric.

Ulfra let her fingers skim the surface of the fabrics, mulling over nap and color and weft and weight. There were light cambrics, soft challis, and chambray for shirts and blouses and underskirts; an ivy-green damask worked in a pattern of vines and leaves, another in pale grey with a pattern of doves and roses; fine dimity for starched collars and sleeves; rubbed silks tender as doeskin; rich silk luster and delicate messaline; precious sarcenet and shot silk.

At last she found what she was looking for: wool combed from black mountain sheep, woven with silk into a light, flexible fabric of lustrous silver-black. This Ulfra chose to make the prince's hunting coat.

She sat down with her watercolors to sketch out the embroidery that would band the hem and sleeves: hunters on horseback and their hounds, twined with branches and leaves. The buttons would be horn in silver mounts: one a fox, one a boar, one a stag.

Ulfra worked, unaware of Tansy's scrutiny from across the workroom. The leopard-woman studied her former apprentice; her apprenticeship had ended on her twenty-first birthday. She was now a master tailor, entitled to all the rights of the guild. As a birthday present, Tansy had made her a full partner in the business.

"You realize," she had told her, "that you are a very

wealthy young woman. You need not remain with me to make your way in the world."

"But what else would I do?"

"Your painting, for one thing. Explore life outside this damned workroom, for another. You could be presented at court."

Ulfra had shook her head stubbornly. She had known the wild Weirdwood in winter, when it was left to the wolves; she had known life at the court of mad King Milo and life on the road with Folderol's band. And she wanted none of it. She wanted only to be left alone with her sketches.

Tansy looked at her now and turned things over in her head. A farce was being staged in the town, playing to packed houses. It featured a girl tailor at an establishment called the Dog's Muzzle. The prince was lampooned, too; he wore a cloak of mourning that reversed to a wedding suit. Tansy badly wanted to see it, but could not bring herself to. Lady Twixtwain urged her to go (she herself had been three times), but to Tansy it seemed somehow disloyal.

Ulfra sat and sketched. In a portfolio case under her mattress she kept sketches she did not show Tansy, scenes of the Weirdwood and life with Folderol's troupe, and sketches of a boy with strange, pale eyes and a shock of unkempt hair, milkweed white.

One such sketch, of this odd child with his arms around the shaggy neck of an old she-wolf, was tacked to the back panel of the cedar clothespress in Ulfra's bedchamber. There she retreated to sleep and think, the din of hawkers' cries and the rattle of cart wheels on cobblestones muffled by the thick woolen folds. Breathing in the mingled lavender and cedar, Ulfra would sleep, dreaming, as she had not done for years, of wolves.

The clothespress featured a false bottom. Tansy might have known of its existence, but it would never occur to her to look for anything there. In the hidden cavity, Ulfra kept the relics of her past life. A small strongbox held a strange inventory: strung on a leather lace, two teeth, one from a human child and one from a wolf cub; a small velvet pouch full of large, fine pearls; a handbill, luridly illustrated, advertising "The Wolf-Girl, her Ferocious Direwolves, and the Albino Deaf-Mute"; several large, colored spangles and dyed plumes, as from a gaudy costume; the coiled, translucent skin shed by a snake, and, the most recent addition, a carefully folded handbill advertising *The Dog's Muzzle*.

✦

Neither Caitlin nor Binder could recall exactly when the chalk line had disappeared. Apparently, a truce had been in effect for some time when, stooping to pick up a vole's skull that had rolled under Grimald's bed, Caitlin noticed the line had been rubbed out. It seemed not to be the act of a deliberate hand, but of feet scuffing back and forth over the disputed border.

By the end of the first three months, the boys had advanced from tolerance to cautious overtures of friendship. By the end of six months, they had begun a commerce in mantis egg cases, moths, and owl pellets; and soon after that, they developed a private language, in which they traded secrets. Now they went together to visit Sleeker at the creek.

As the months passed the boys grew ever more different in both looks and temperament. Grimald was more foxlike than ever, ruddy and mischievous, nearly impossible to catch red-handed at anything. His temper was hot, his fancy impulsive. He could climb any tree in the Weirdwood and had once crept the length of a rotten branch to rescue a nest of owlets. His greatest joy was helping Binder tool a leather binding in gold leaf. It was marvelous how such a chatterbox and creature of impulse could sit still for hours on end in perfect silence. He was just learning how to stitch gathered pages together in the sewing frame.

Bram was the cool one, quieter, more likely to bide his time than to act in the heat of the moment. If Grimald was the fox, then Bram was the owl: watchful, silent. Many nights he would seem to be dozing by the fire but afterward could repeat to Caitlin every word that had been spoken. When he did lose his temper, Bram was capable of a cold rage, and when he laughed (which he did even more rarely), it was a sweet sound, a sound Caitlin liked to hear above every other. His keenest enjoyment came from the hours he spent sitting motionless in Caitlin's workroom, watching her restore the vivid, gilded pictures in the margins of books.

∽◦⌒

There came one day to the oak with the red door a strange figure, frail more from illness than age, his reddish hair thinning and the soles of his shoes almost worn away. His shabby coat of red and gold brocade was cinched by a stout leather belt with a heavy silver clasp. Beneath the coat his shirt was riddled with moth holes, the collar and cuffs foxed with brown stains. One ear was ragged, as if the moths had moved on to it after finishing the shirt.

"Is the binder about?" he asked. His voice was surprisingly sure and sound, as if it had been spared the forces that had ravaged the rest of him. His eyes, too, were clear and bright.

"If it's books you want bound, then I can help you," answered Binder. Occasionally a determined customer would track him down in the Weirdwood. The present visitor, however, did not seem to be a man of great means.

"I have some scraps to sell, bits and pieces of old books, good enough for patching things up."

He opened a satchel that stank of must. Inside were sorry remnants that had once been books, a sad catalogue of fates: books worried by dogs or gnawed by mice, books with the boards and spines charred away to the bare cords, books swollen and splayed from lying in the rain, their pages obliterated by mildew. Oddly, none had been damaged by bookworms.

Binder selected two or three books whose leaves could be used to mend other books. He also took a crudely sewn volume of scraps, thinking to make it into a practice rune book for the boys.

As payment, he offered the bookman six coppers and the hospitality of their pantry. Grimald hurried down to the cellar for a pitcher of cold cider.

The ragged bookman sat and ate steadily without

uttering more than a sigh or grunt as Binder refilled his plate. At last he pushed the plate away and wiped his mouth carefully with his napkin; one could guess from the state of his sleeve that this was not his usual habit.

"Tell your wife she makes a good crab-apple pickle."

"Actually, I do. Thank you all the same." Binder nodded at the stranger's satchel. "Business any good?"

"Middling, alas, middling." The man drained his cider mug and smiled at Grimald when the boy refilled it. "Mind you, middling is a damn sight better than business has been for years. Some of those, the burned ones, were pulled from bonfires back when a man could be flayed for reading in the wrong rune tongue. When I think what was lost . . ."

"Do you know rune tongues? You must stay and meet Cait. She's been studying runes these last seven years. She'll be glad of the company of someone who can speak the language, if you know what I mean. She's in town at the moment."

A spark of interest flickered in the visitor's eyes, but he shook his head. "I can't wait. I must see a man today on urgent business. Payment on a debt, alas. But if she will visit me in town, we might talk of runish things. Have you a pencil?"

Binder found paper and pencil, and the bookman labored some time with these. When at last he sat back, the paper and the man's hands were both much begrimed with pencil lead. Beneath the smudges the sheet was covered with odd markings.

The bookman rubbed his hands together. "She will understand that. I need not trouble you longer, I think." But his eye strayed toward the pitcher of cider.

"Well, if you can't stay for another cup, will you take a jug with you?"

The bookman protested, but the short of it was that Grimald was sent down again, returning this time with a corked jug, and the visitor went on his way.

⤔

Caitlin and Bram returned at dusk, laden with supplies. Caitlin set out on the table several bundles of smooth calfskin in blue and red and green, tiny pots of pigment from the apothecary, a new bloodstone burnisher, spools of stout thread. Binder's eyes scanned the goods as if looking for some object he did not see; he opened his mouth and closed it again without saying anything.

"What," said Caitlin sharply, "not satisfied with all that? Everything *there* is for you except the little pots of color for *my* work. Isn't that so, Bram?"

"Well," said the boy, "there *is* this." He drew out a small bundle, no bigger than a pencil.

Binder seized it and happily undid the cloth tapes of a doeskin pouch. Inside were six new finishing tools, made to his own design by a metalworker in the town.

Grimald hung back until Caitlin gave him a smile and said, "Right coat pocket." He dug a hand in and drew it out, clutching a tiny book of gold leaf.

Caitlin picked up the bookman's note, then sat down to work her way through the runes.

"Who—" She looked up, but Binder and Grimald were gone, down to the binding room to try out the new tools on some scrap leather.

Bram rubbed his eyes. "Pickles and cider."

"What did you say?"

"A funny man—all red and gold—with a ragged ear." Bram pointed to the chair Caitlin was sitting in. "He sat there. I can see where he was. Da gave him pickles, and Grimald brought him cider."

Caitlin spoke calmly, though her heart was beating fast. "Come here a moment. You can tell me about the man later. Right now I want to see those poor eyes you keep rubbing."

∽

Getting ready for bed, she told Binder about it.

"Now I can see them, all the signs he showed before that I didn't *want* to see. But at this distance—"

Binder removed his glasses and polished them before setting them out of the way on the carved headboard. "Are you so sure it's such a bad thing? Couldn't Iiliana teach him, the way she taught you?"

She shook her head. "It isn't the same kind of sight. He

wasn't just seeing what could happen or what would happen. He spoke as though the bookman were still in the room—as if he saw him in the chair where I was sitting." She paused, gathering words. "Some people who have been Below can see—auras, _presences_—the way a wild animal can 'see' a scent. These people can see traces of the Otherworld."

Binder looked at her closely, narrowing his nearsighted eyes. "You're not telling me everything."

"I don't know everything."

"May I have that in writing, please?"

Her reply was wordless. He was taken aback (though not unpleasantly), and replied in kind, feelingly.

So she banished from that room for a little while the cold shadow that was her dread.

❧

The Binders had another visitor before the week was out. A prosperous guild master arrived on a cold autumn morning.

He was a well-fed man who had once made his living with his hands and now made it with his wits; a man who had married late or perhaps for a second time, to judge from the ring upon his finger: A young man might buy such a thing for his bride, but not for himself, and it was not old enough to be an heirloom. All in all, thought Binder, a man much risen up in the world. He grew hopeful in the anticipation of well-paying work.

But his hopes were dashed as soon as the guild master spoke.

"I have a daughter of marriageable age who is, shall we say, recalcitrant. In all other matters, she is sweet-tempered, but the merest mention of matrimony turns her into a shrew." The guild master smiled bitterly and turned his own wedding band upon its finger. "I had been told that you sold potions, and I hoped . . ." He let his words trail off, embarrassed to be dealing for such goods at a hermit's hut in the middle of the Weirdwood.

"I don't handle that kind of binding," said Binder. "But you're in luck. The spellbinder of the house is at home."

❧

Caitlin listened to the man without sympathy. She did not go in for love potions. Compared to real feeling, they were an unsatisfactory substitute, a cheat. She only prepared them for couples who had fallen out of love with one another, and then only half-strength. When it came to love, she found the mortal mind capable of sufficient magic of its own.

"Why do you think your daughter needs such a potion?"

"She will not marry." The guild master paced the workroom, taking up a shrew's skull and putting it down again with distaste.

"She will not marry the man of your choosing?"

"A man of mine or her or the man in the moon's choosing. She does not wish to marry. She is the elder of my two daughters. There is a legal difficulty. If she marries, she will inherit a small fortune from my father's estate. She was his favorite grandchild. If she does not marry, the fortune will enrich a charity house for orphans. In either case, my younger daughter, the child of my second marriage, is dowerless, dependent on the generosity of her sister."

"You appear prosperous. I should think a dowry for your younger daughter within your means."

"Money does not make itself. I have a workshop to run, two sons to educate and set up in life. I must maintain a house in town."

"And no doubt your wife is expensive to maintain."

The guild master blustered and changed colors. "You do not see how it is."

"No, I see precisely how it is. There is nothing wrong with your elder daughter that I have a cure for. Good day. And watch your step going down."

⌇

The king's huntsman glanced around the darkened gallery of the theater and felt beneath his coat for his dagger. The prince insisted on attending performances in disguise, even though he could command a performance at the palace when the fancy struck him. It was foolhardy, but Galt understood the impulse. After the finery of court—men and women starched and laced, wigged and perfumed within an inch of their lives—it was something of a relief to come to this place, to feast the eyes on women whose figures had never seen a stay, their complexions florid, not from the rouge pot, but from hard work and a little too much gin. From the cheap seats there rose a ripe smell mingled with the bitter steam of the roasted chestnuts being hawked up and down the aisle. It was a barn smell, a clean stink. Galt liked it.

The crown prince sat back in his box, his cloak turned purple side in, brooding into a cup of ale. To say that he was unhappy at the prospect of his approaching marriage did not do justice to the prince's mood. He was in a sour, princely sulk. His affianced bride was undeniably beautiful, of the best bloodlines, and had been schooled in all the arts deemed appropriate for a marriageable princess. She could make small talk in six languages, sing and play the harp, and draw in perspective. In short, her manners had been developed at the expense of her mind. "She is," the prince complained in private, "incapable of *having* an opinion, much less expressing it."

His father-in-law had, however, formed an opinion about his daughter's married life and had expressed it to the prince in no uncertain terms through the dowry negotiators. When their life together commenced, he expected the prince to give up many things, the chief among these being the theater "and all that attends it." "All that attends it," of course, meant his mistress, Lucivia, a woman of irregular reputation, who lived in Everlasting Lane.

Now the players strolled onstage, and the prince was able for the space of a few hours to forget his marital worries.

The Dog's Muzzle; or, *The Tailor's Business* was a fine bit of farce, with barbs aimed to skewer lords and ladies of fashion and the tailors who lived off them. At one point the heroine, Modesty, and her sister, Pulchritude, entered with velvet cats' tails peeking beneath their skirts. While the audience roared, the hero, Prince Lovelorn, entered with his friend, a huntsman named Gout.

The prince swore in Galt's ear. "By all the honey in heaven above, if it isn't you, my old friend!"

Galt watched as Gout tried unsuccessfully to plead his case to Pulchritude. He grinned back at the prince uncomfortably. Beneath his leather vest Galt began to sweat. But worse was to come.

The girl tailor entered, wearing wolf's ears and carrying enormous tin shears that were half her height. She began to give Gout advice on how to win Pulchritude's heart, and convinced him to strip to his smallclothes in order to be measured. While his back was turned she produced, with much winking at the stands, a "measuring tape," and when Gout turned around again she thrashed him about the head and ears with a stout leather strap, singing,

> "Beat a wolf, sir, wolf, sir, wolf, sir,
> (Beat a wolf, sir, wolf, sir, wolf!)
> Come a day, sir, day, sir (yes, sir!),
> The wolf will come and beat—on—you."

The audience roared its approval. The crown prince glanced at his friend. The huntsman was tight-lipped. The incident of Ulfra and the injured wolf had, over the months, taken on a life of its own. No one seemed to remember that it had not been the huntsman himself who had baited the wolf. Poor Galt would never live it down.

But it so happened that the playwright had been magnanimous. In the end, the thing had a happy ending, and the huntsman Gout was married off to Pulchritude. It was the girl tailor, though, who wed the prince. Modesty, wearing her cat's-tail finery, was pursued and eaten by wolves.

It was, after all, a farce.

When the crowd had thinned somewhat, the prince and Galt left the theater by a back door. The prince cast sidelong glances at his friend as they wound their way to the guild district and Everlasting Lane.

"A nice bit of work. My sides quite ache. I had not realized my little tailor had achieved this degree of fame."

"I did not know the Dog's Muzzle was your tailor. Anyway, whatever fame your tailor has achieved has come from her dealings with you."

"You sell yourself short, my friend. Surely her fame

comes from that incident with the wolf. Ah—now I have offended you. But you *will* allow me to lose to you at dice, and make up for it.

"Now let us quicken our steps; 'All That Attends' is keeping supper hot for us."

❧

The cast of *The Dog's Muzzle* trooped into a tavern, where their supper had been laid by the innkeeper. There were jugs of cream-and-black ale, smoking-hot meat pies, cheese-and-leek tart, and a boiled pudding called drunken lords. It was midnight, and the actors were in high spirits. They would sit, eating and drinking and otherwise making merry, till dawn.

The part of the girl tailor was actually played by a sly-faced boy of fourteen who used the name Trammel. He strode to the head of the long table and handed to its sole occupant a purse.

"Your fee, sir!" he said, with a smart bow. It was a little too smart; something about Lord Gobeleyn made Trammel uneasy. He did not smirk or joke with him, as he did with the others. Lord Gobeleyn was the author of *The Dog's Muzzle*, and in a way held the fate of all the actors in one hand.

Lord Gobeleyn smiled the smallest wisp of a smile and waved a negligent hand at the repast. The company sat and fell to.

Their author and benefactor did not eat, but filled and refilled his cup from the jugs of ale. Lord Gobeleyn had an otherworldly capacity for drink, known colloquially as "a goblin's leg." In truth, Lord Gobeleyn had not one goblin leg but two, neither of them hollow.

7

SOME SUITORS, KEEN AND RELUCTANT

Royalty cannot be stuck with a pin. A prince who must
be fitted with enough traveling clothes for a year-long pilgrimage must have a manikin to take his place at those
fittings where the garments are stuck through with pins
like some vestment from a torture chamber. A prince, of
course, must have a living manikin.

The prince's present manikin had grown up in the palace kitchen, turning the spit, until one day all the young
men of likely height and breadth had been summoned
into the courtyard to be measured.

It was not bad work. He must eat what the prince ate
and exert himself as the prince exerted himself—at riding,
falconry, dance, everything—on the theory that by living
like the prince, he would keep the prince's figure.

This evening the prince was dining with his lady in
Everlasting Lane. The prince's manikin, by name of Tod,
was finishing his supper by the kitchen fire, in the company of the maid.

From the other room there came a loud crash and clatter of glass and metal and crockery, as though a supper

tray had toppled to the floor. Gales of laughter reached
the two by the kitchen fire. Lily got up, but Lucivia's voice
from the other side of the door stopped the maid with
her hand on the knob.

"Never mind, Lily—I've got it."

The maid retook her seat. "Now, you don't suppose the
prince was exerting himself, do you?" Lily said, all innocence. She and the prince's manikin had an understanding
of their own. He removed her hand from his knee.

"Hold a moment; let me finish this pie. I get measured tomorrow."

※

It was not Lily but the pie that undid him. That one
slice, eaten by the fire, was not the culprit; it was all the
slices of pie that had come before. For, exert himself as
he would, Tod could not eat pie as the prince ate it and
keep the prince's figure. The next day the Valet Royal
weighed him, and he was found wanting—or, rather, found
not wanting enough.

"It's back to the turning spit, I guess," he told Lily. "I
don't suppose I'll be back." There would be another manikin; wasn't their understanding at an end?

Lily burst into angry tears. "You have another thing
coming, Tod William, if you think I'll let you exert yourself
with anyone but me!"

And, in the end, it was all right. He and Lily kept their
understanding and, when it suddenly became necessary
that they tie the marriage knot, Lily's mistress made her
a nice settlement. Tod was pleased with the way things
turned out. The falconing thing had been all right, but he
had never been keen on the dancing.

※

After he had wished on the wolf star, Nix had started
to grow. Within two months Nix had shot up four inches
and added half again to his weight. Within six months, he
had not only grown past the mark on the pantry door but
past the door frame itself. He had to duck his head when
Mistress Goody asked him to hand something down from
the top pantry shelf. Silently he cut and hauled wood,
lugged pails of water for the wash, and scoured the stables.

Watching him, Mistress Goody shook her head and marveled.

"Late grower," said her husband. "Some start out runty and catch up later. Think how much of your good soup has gone down that gullet!"

She thought it was something other than her soup: magic or sheer will, maybe some of each. With a heavy heart she knelt by her blanket chest and took out a parcel of plain brown paper. Inside was a boy's coat and shirt of fine linen. They had arrived six months earlier, with a modest sum in silver and a dress for Mistress Goody. The coat and shirt were hopelessly small.

"But yours, all the same," she said, laying them before him. "There was always a little money, too, which we used for your care. But I saved whatever was left. It's a nice sum and will get you settled somewhere."

Nix nodded. He raised the coat to his nose and breathed in. It smelled faintly of dust and lavender and the old cat that liked to nap in the blanket chest if it was left open. Beneath those smells rode another—old, familiar, but faint. Too faint.

Nix let out his breath with a sigh and opened his eyes to see Mistress Goody looking at him strangely.

"Thanks, Mummer."

Her eyes smarted; he hardly called her by that name anymore.

"I packed you a meal for the road," she said, handing him a tin box.

He nodded and added it to his pack with the clothes. The silver he added to his purse, which he wore around his neck beneath his shirt. Then he kissed her good-bye and left. Through the window she saw him cross the turnip patch to the field where her husband was mending the fence.

"And not even one of mine!" she said, weeping, watching them embrace, Nix now a few inches taller than her husband.

So he left them not quite eight years after he came.

❧

In the most prosperous (and therefore respectable) quarter of the town, a house presented a demure aspect

to the street. In the smaller of its two dining rooms Niccolaus, engraver and guild master, sat at the head of his
breakfast table and surveyed the scene before him. It was
prosperous and respectable. His two young sons, Albert
and Bastian, were attacking the sausages with vigor. Columba, his daughter from his second marriage, was break-
fasting on cream puffs, careful not to spoil either her gown
or her artfully applied complexion. His wife Ermingrude's
delicate disposition forbade breaking her fast before sup-
pertime. She sat at the foot of the table, sipping limeflower
tea while she read a letter from her sister.

The merchant frowned. "Where is Iona?"

His family looked up from their respective preoccupa-
tions and stared. Columba laughed shortly.

"Where is she ever, father?"

Niccolaus waved away the servant who had stepped forward to distract him with smoked trout. "Call her again."

His wife set down her tea. "She has been summoned
three times already, my lord."

Niccolaus pushed back his heavy chair, startling the
small dog curled asleep beneath it. "Then I shall go myself
a fourth time!" He strode from the room.

Ermingrude sighed and nibbled a dry rusk. The boys
went back to sawing sausage into the lengths that could
be crammed into their mouths most efficiently. Columba
admired her reflection in the back of her spoon, licked
some stray sugar from her little finger, and smiled.

Iona was in her attic bedroom, bent over a block of
boxwood, the handle of a burin cradled in one hand. She
wore fingerless gloves over hands ingrained with ink and
covered with innumerable nicks and tiny scars in various
stages of healing. Her hair was pulled indifferently back
with a plain black ribbon, and the only pigment on her
face was a smudge of ink where she had wiped her brow.
Her lips were chapped; she bit the lower one as she
worked. From time to time, she blew wood chips from her
work and held the block up to the light from the window.

It was a sunny room, and pleasant, but one would not
have called it clean. One wall had been covered with cork,
and to this were pinned prints in various stages of comple-

tion. Efforts that had pleased their maker less lay wadded
in drifts under the workbench. A neglected tray held an
all-but-uneaten meal—last night's perhaps; perhaps the
night before's. Under the workbench a tabby cat was picking clean the bones of a chicken wing. On the worktable
beside Iona lay an apple core, so browned it might have
been carved of wood. If it were, thought Niccolaus, studying the scene from the topmost stair, his elder daughter
might pay some attention to it.

"Iona."

She blew a final shower of wood curls from the block
before looking up. "Hello, father." She reached for her
spectacles and wiped them on her smock. A look of dismay
came over her features. "Oh, dear—have I missed
dinner?"

"Not dinner. Breakfast. Tell me, what is it that so
absorbs you this morning?"

Iona held up the block. Half of it, still uncarved, bore
a charcoal transfer pattern; the other half had been transformed into a scene of an underwater palace, with a queen
upon an underwater throne surrounded by sea serpents
and a garden of watery ferns.

Iona happily pushed back a lock of hair. Her sleeves
were rolled up and both elbows were black where she had
leaned on the inking table. "It's one of a series of blocks
on tales from the Elder Age. When Columba and mother
and I went to the sea, I visited the new water gardens to
make sketches and called on an elderly gentleman in the
old quarter who keeps specimens from the deep. It was
the first holiday I ever really enjoyed, Papa."

"Yes." Niccolaus sighed. "Your sister told me about it."
They had been unable to get Iona to dress respectably for
meals at the inn, and so had had to hire a small villa to
keep her scandalous behavior from pubic view. He took
the block from his daughter's hand.

"The work is quite good. But tell me, what use do you
think it will be to you? The trade will pass to Bastian, as
my eldest son."

"I know, Father—that is both customary and right. I

only ask to keep my small room and to be allowed to do my part to pay my keep."

"Until you marry, you mean."

Iona laughed and shook her head. "Oh, Papa! Me, marry? Who would have such an oddball as I am? What man would take a wife who burns the roast because she is bent over a block of wood all the day long? I would rock the dog in the cradle and throw my child a bone."

"Silence!" Niccolaus brought his fist down on the table, making the tools rattle and the curls of wood jump. Iona flinched.

"What—what have I said?"

"I will hear no more shocking nonsense! I will not have you make a laughingstock of the family, and I will not have Columba's position imperiled by your willful disobedience!"

"Willful disobedience! Papa, that is not just! I have missed a meal or two, but that is hardly disobedience!"

Niccolaus held up a hand. "The fault is entirely my own. You are my firstborn child, and for many years, for lack of a son, I taught you my craft, proud to have such an apt pupil in my daughter. But it was one thing when you were eight or ten or even twelve. When you were fourteen I hoped you would turn your energies to more seemly pursuits, such as Columba has always preferred. Nothing, it seems, can make you take an interest in the impression you make on others or how you present the family face to society."

Iona flushed scarlet. "The family face! What in hell is the family face, may I ask?"

"Here it is, profane willfulness! Can you deny it?"

"Not willfulness, Father. Indignation! Would you have me give up all you taught me and devote all my time to adjusting the lace of my cuffs and painting moles on my cheek?"

"No! I would have you marry!"

"And perhaps I *will* someday, when the time and the man are right. But what and who am I harming up here? I hurt no one."

"And how is Columba supposed to marry? She is the

younger; no respectable young woman marries before her elder sister. And what man of good name would marry into a family with such an infamous eccentric?"

Iona studied her father's face as though something had become clear to her. "Obviously, some man of good name *has* asked her. Which is it, the paper merchant's prodigal son or the not-so-young duke? Let me see—which would most benefit the family? A prosperous match ensuring a supply of fine paper at a substantial discount, or marriage to a generous patron under whose protection the house is sure to prosper?" She sat down at her workbench and took up her block. "I see from your face that I am right in part, if not all. Willful, disobedient Iona must marry so that Columba can make an advantageous match. Now I understand."

Niccolaus raised a hand to strike her and for a moment froze with his hand in midair. Then he took the half-carved block from her hands and cast it into the grate.

Iona did not stir. "The fire went out long ago. And if it had burned, I would simply begin again. Not out of willfulness—but because I can't *not* do this work you taught me to love."

∽∾∾

"It was *so* mortifying, Mother!"

Columba leaned toward the mirror to examine her beauty spot. Her father often marveled that the spot appeared and disappeared and was never to be seen before noon.

"There she was in the high street at two o'clock in the afternoon with her hair loose, hanging on the arm of some old bearded fool. I was with friends, so of course I had to pretend I didn't know her. She didn't see me, but I was mortified just the same. She was wearing an enormous black smock that flapped behind her, like some great black goose. And spectacles! I swear I would rather be struck stone blind than be seen in the street wearing spectacles. *Can't* you say something to her?"

Ermingrude lay back upon her cushions. "Oh, she never listens to me. Only her father can get anything out of her."

Columba darted a glance at her mother in the mirror,

then began to apply a rosy stain to her lips from a small gilded pot.

"I only hope that Mathias does not lose all hope of me and find himself an heiress. He might marry that merchant's daughter, the one with vulgar dimples whose father sells those gorgeous silks we saw in that shop in Thistledown Street."

"That reminds me," said Ermingrude. "Aren't you due for a fitting today for your new gown? We will go directly. Smuggs is done with your hair. Iona will come, too. Your father has declared she is to have a new gown from the Cat's Face."

Columba was not pleased and had to redraw her mouth.

⸎

While his wife and daughters were occupied on the premises of the Cat's Face, Niccolaus was engrossed across the street in a business transaction of great importance.

"Where did you find him?"

"It does not matter where," said the marriage broker. "He finds your terms acceptable."

"I must at least know the name of his family."

The marriage broker laughed, a low, throaty chuckle. She refilled their glasses with plum brandy, colorless, tart, and strong. As she poured, a few dark gems winked on her fingers. "Do you want a young man of spotless reputation or a young man with a fine family name? If you must have both, it will cost you."

"So long as he is not a thief or a scoundrel."

Lucivia gazed at her customer dispassionately. "I will vouch that he is not."

"Well, then." Niccolaus picked up the sheaf of papers and signed them where Lucivia indicated.

"It's all set, then—he will come for his interview tomorrow at four o'clock."

"How will I know him?"

"He will know you."

⸎

"It is really going to happen," said the prince.

"What?" Lucivia looked up from her accounts. She was seated at the window, and the morning light played on her face and hair. It was not a young face, but it was, in the prince's experience, surpassingly beautiful.

"My marriage." The prince spoke from the bed on the other side of the room. The clothes he had worn to the theater the night before had been cleaned and pressed and lay awaiting him when he should emerge from his bath, which steamed behind a screen in front of the fire.

"Well then." Lucivia dipped her pen into the inkwell and bent her head over the account book. "I don't see what is so startling about that. Several hundred people have it as their full-time occupation. It would be a wonder if it did not come about."

The prince sighed. "I know. It was seeing the sketches for my wedding clothes nearly complete. I wish I was at least indifferent to her. It would be preferable to finding her unbearable."

"You have had my professional opinion on this subject before. Didn't we agree not to speak of it between ourselves?"

"We did indeed." Rather than getting up and having his bath, the prince poured himself another cup of tea. He always postponed his bath at Lucivia's. Bathing meant getting dressed, and getting dressed meant leaving. "I wish I could marry you—"

Lucivia threw down her pen with a laugh.

"No, don't laugh. I wish I could marry you instead—"

"As if I would have you," she chided.

"And I most heartily wish you would make my wretched wife-to-be a brilliant match with someone else."

She came over and took the teacup from his hand.

"Stop talking such nonsense. You are a prince and she is a princess. What could be more eminently suitable? I am a marriage broker. With what I know, I would not be any man's wife. Our present arrangement suits me as it is; if you must give me up, so be it. Now, are you going to get into that bath or not? If Rose has to lug any more water upstairs, you'll have her to answer to."

⋙⋘

Niccolaus watched the tall young man circle the room, scrutinizing every tapestry and silver ornament. He had not removed his hat upon entering and did not surrender his cloak. A servant, hovering expectantly, cleared his throat. The young man spoke over his shoulder.

"Your servant seems to have a cough," he remarked thoughtfully.

Niccolaus waved the servant away.

The young man stopped by the window. In the courtyard below, two women could be seen making a circuit of the garden. The younger wore a grey smock and her hair hung loose, the color called gilt-and-ashes. At one point the older woman took the younger's elbow and spoke earnestly in her ear. The young woman pulled away, casting her eyes up to the very window where the young man stood watching. Startled, he withdrew from the window. The young woman strode from the courtyard, her arms held stiffly at her sides, fists clenched. The older woman trotted after.

The young man let the curtain fall into place. "At what price?"

Niccolaus cleared his throat. "My advisers in such matters have drawn up an inventory of the proposed dowry." He placed the document on the table between them. The young man reached over and picked it up.

"'One linen press ... one bed with tapestry curtains ... one ebony-and-silver clothes chest . . . one dozen silver plates and goblets . . . one small coffer of assorted books . . . silver-and-ivory dressing-table set . . .'" He looked up. "This is overgenerous. The sum you mentioned would be more than sufficient."

"Nay, sir," said a woman's voice, "it is not compensation enough."

In the doorway stood the young woman from the courtyard; her hair had been tied back and her grey smock removed to show a dress of blue silk damask. Though the blue became her, someone had pinned to the neck a bit of lace frippery. With the distaste of a cat ridding itself of a bow, Iona snatched off the collar and cast it onto a chair.

"No, not half compensation enough to make up for the sacrifice of saddling oneself with such a virago!" She seized the dowry list and laughed out loud. "Oh, Father! A cradle! You *do* have great plans for this match!"

The young man looked at her with renewed interest. Niccolaus hastened to repair the damage.

"Master Fell, allow me to present my daughter Iona and my wife, Ermingrude."

Iona nodded. Ermingrude held her hand out to be kissed. When Fell instead seized it and gave it a vigorous shake, she colored deeply but recovered herself. "Master Fell of . . .?"

"Just Fell. Of no fixed abode." He turned back to the window. The sky had opened up, and the orange trees and fountain of the courtyard were obscured by grey curtains of rain. A servant ran out into the downpour to fetch something that had been left on a stone seat. Gloves, perhaps.

Niccolaus cleared his throat. "Master Fell."

The young man once again dragged his gaze from the window and gave his attention to his proposed father-in-law. Iona studied him with interest. As it was, she found him repellent only on principle; he was tall enough and broad enough in the shoulders. His nose was just shy of straight and his chin not quite square, but these flaws made him more attractive rather than less. He was cleanshaven, his light brown hair pulled back in a lock. His grey eyes were serious without being sober, perhaps because he always appeared on the verge of a smile without seeming to smirk. He gave the impression of one perpetually alert and pleasantly surprised by everything around him.

"I hope I satisfy."

"Whether I am satisfied hardly enters into the matter, I think. It is my father you must please. I am sorry if you find me ill-mannered; I was only curious to see the sort of man I am to be appended to."

There it was: a fleeting smile. "We shall get stares in the street, going about joined at the hip."

❦

Nix walked into the town as the inns were putting up their shutters. He followed his nose until he found a place that reminded him of the Goody farm: sweet straw and clean horse dung. He slept that night where cart horses were stabled and drank from the animals' trough.

As he lay in the straw, Nix let the smells of the town waft over him, sorting them over in his memory, looking for one small scent, a certain faint note. But among all the smells of the town, hot coals and cold embers, sour beer and overcooked cabbage, soot and dishwater, fresh pig's blood and new sawdust, horse sweat and human piss, he did not smell the one smell he was searching for. He did not smell so much as a whisker of wolf.

Nix rose at dawn to look for work as a laborer. The streets were just coming to life as he walked past the taverns and inns, oblivious to the many bills and notices that plastered their sides, many overlapping and obscured by mud and whitewash.

Once such bill extolled the virtues of a new play, *The Dog's Muzzle*. Another called all young men "of sound limb and good character," urging them to report to the Valet Royal in order to be weighed and measured for possible work in the king's palace.

Nix saw neither.

"Know anyone needs a laborer?" he asked of a man loading barrels into a cart.

"Try the Tart's Nose," said the man, and guffawed at some private joke.

"He means the Turtle and Rose," said another. "It's a tavern across from the theater in the Compass. The owner wants someone to help him hoist the wine casks and such. From the size of you, you'll do."

Following their directions, Nix made his way to the circle known as Compass Street. The Turtle and Rose was not in the best part of town, and Nix's purse with its silver coins was not as well hidden beneath his shirt as it ought to have been. All along the street, people apparently engaged in their own business traded winks and nods.

The tavern was not yet open. Even as Nix raised his hand to knock on the shutter of the tavern, someone kicked his feet out from under him and threw a sack over his head. Then he saw stars, and not the kind for wishing on.

He came to in an alley alongside the Turtle and Rose, just as someone in an upper story tipped a pan of wash water out the window. Nix sat and dripped, knowing without looking that the silver was gone.

"It might have been worse," said a voice. "It might have been the chamber pot."

A well-groomed man stood over him, remarkable for his violet eyes, which sparkled in the dim alleyway. His clothes showed him to be a man of no small means: His coat was as black and glossy as a horse's hide, and his immaculate cuffs gleamed in the dimness.

Nix could not place the man's accent, but he trusted him on instinct. When a gloved hand was extended, Nix took it and was hauled to his feet.

"That's a nasty gash. It should be looked to. And here is Winsom with the carriage. Will you accept the hospitality of my house? It is some distance, but you can be better looked after there. Heaven knows, Winsom can look after a gash."

So Nix began his singular education under the roof of Lord Gobeleyn.

8

TEA AND TALES

The twenty-third Lord Gobeleyn lived behind a high wall
in a district of town where guildhalls and artisans' workshops outnumbered houses. Here twenty-two previous
Goblin Pretenders had retired in defeat, each assuming
the wealth, title, and house of his predecessor. The wall
presented to the street a face of bare grey stone festooned
with iron spikes. This appearance led passersby to speculate about the mysterious house and its even more mysterious occupant. Such a wall bespoke vast wealth, cold
splendor, vicious hounds; gargoyles on either side of the
gate suggested that something worse than mastiffs awaited
the unlucky trespasser. The truth was rather different.

The garden side of the wall was inlaid with an intricate
mosaic, nearly covered over by ivy. The mansion itself, of
pale russet stone, rambled in porches and terraces down
to the hothouses of tousled roses and sleepy peonies. An
unseen fountain burbled; from a hidden dovecote came a
low cooing and the soft flutter of wings.

Lord Gobeleyn sat on one of the terraces, bundled like
an invalid in several dressing gowns, his feet clad not in
slippers but in boots, in case he should be overtaken by
an urge to walk in the garden before first being overtaken

by an urge to get dressed. His pale, red-gold hair stood up on his head like flames; his eyes, a violet of startling intensity, were set deep in a face that had lost some of its high color to fatigue or illness. His face was a poor-fitting mask of languor; through the gaps one could occasionally glimpse the features beneath. His eyes especially gave him away, for they brimmed with remembered loss and ever-present pain, a keen violet sorrow.

Beside him a sideboard on wheels held a silver urn the size of a small child. This contained a quantity of tea strong enough to tan a mule skin. Close at hand sat a cut-glass dish of jam. No one of his acquaintance had ever observed Lord Gobeleyn to take any more nourishment than tea. This was, of course, romantic exaggeration on the part of both admirers and detractors, for he did take the occasional sardine on toast or egg beaten with brandy.

A smock-clad someone appeared, short of person, round of shoulder, bland of face. Nothing of this someone's appearance or manner, neither hair nor voice nor bearing, revealed whether this was Lord Gobeleyn's footman, valet, or housekeeper.

"Lord."

"Yes, Winsom."

"The young man is now presentable. Shall I present him?"

"Has he been fed?"

"Yes, my lord. I also took the liberty, while his clothes were drying, to avail him of some of your own, as well as a glass of the brandy."

"Then bring him to me."

Nix was brought before him, his recently washed hair drying in white peaks around the expertly bandaged gash. He wore some of his benefactor's old fencing clothes: a full white shirt gathered loosely at the wrists and neck and straight black trousers tucked into high, glossy boots. As he walked out onto the terrace, Nix caught his reflection in a looking glass and stared.

"It is a difference, is it not? Please sit by me. Will you have tea or more brandy?"

"Tea," said Nix.

"Just the thing for an insult to the skull. Winsom will attest that tea has done wonders for me. Was I a shadow of my present self when you met me, Winsom?"

"You were, sir."

"Did tea do wonders for me?"

"It did, sir."

"Most people," said Lord Gobeleyn, filling a bowl with tea and spooning jam into it, "make the mistake of not brewing it long enough. It should steep overnight at the very least. You want it full strength. Here—have a swig of this and tell me what you think."

Nix took a sip and felt, in the words of Mistress Goody, his eyelashes straighten and his spine curl.

"It is strong."

"Long brewing makes all the difference. Now tell me how you came to be lying in the alley of the Turtle and Rose."

Nix began his story, from the time he left the Goodys.

Lord Gobeleyn raised a hand. "Begin," he said, "at the beginning."

So Nix began again, this time with his earliest memory: a beggar and guttersnipe eating stolen bread. Through chance he had met Ulfra, who was then living at the court of mad King Milo.

"When Milo went mad for good, we joined Folderol's troupe with the wolves. And this was all right for a while, for we had all the geese we wanted and we were setting some gold aside. Then the contract with the wolves ran out, and we had to return them to the Weirdwood, and on the way back she left me with the Goodys." The tea (or those violet eyes) had loosened Nix's tongue; he had never spoken so much at one stretch in his life.

Lord Gobeleyn seemed to follow this disjointed narrative perfectly. He made no connection, however, between the wolf trainer of Nix's tale and the heroine of *The Dog's Muzzle*.

"And now you have come in search of her."

Nix nodded.

"So you know where she is living?"

Nix shook his head.

"Well, then. I would suggest to you the following plan. The lady you describe has some means, for she has sent you money and fine presents. In order to circulate—to go around in such company as she keeps—you must learn some things you may not have needed to know on the Goody farm, things with which I am intimately acquainted. I would be happy to teach them to you and to take you to such places as she is likely to be."

This was a kingdom unknown to Nix. "Where is that?"

Lord Gobeleyn shrugged expressively. "The court, the theater, the baths, the falcon grounds, the tailor."

"Will it take a long time to reach it? I would like to begin at once."

Nix's benefactor shook his head. "It is not far, but there is much we must do to prepare. You must first learn the language."

Nix felt his heart sink. He was clever enough to realize he was not clever enough. "What language is that?"

"Conversation."

Iona could not make Fell out, not at all.

His manners were curious, to say the least. He was taciturn to the point of rudeness, and when he did speak he was so blunt that she wondered whether some mockery underlay his seemingly simple words. Iona suspected Fell kept his hat and gloves on when they met only to irk her and spent all their conversations gazing out the window only to test her patience.

While he was not unhandsome, there was in Fell's look nothing that strived to please. There was a subtle anticipation in his every word and gesture, as though he were prepared to fight or fly or, at any moment, turn into something else entirely, as though released from a spell.

Iona laughed at herself. And what would Fell turn into? A prince, or a tusked beast in ermine and velvet? Had she to choose, Iona thought she would much prefer a beast for a husband. Humming, she sketched a well-dressed beast on the back of a proof.

She was so engaged when there came a knock. Iona turned from her work to see Fell ducking his head to clear the low doorway. As she followed his gaze around the room, Iona blushed, seeing as through his eyes the clothes draped over the furniture, the unemptied basin from her sponge bath, yesterday's stockings discarded in a snarl in the middle of the floor.

"I'm sorry," said Fell. "You are at work."

She wiped her inky hands on her smock. "That's all right. I was going to stop in a bit anyway. I keep a little stove hidden up here so that I don't have to bother anyone when I only want some tea. Father would never allow it—certain I'd burn the house down while they all slept."

Fell smiled. "No, if *you* were ever to burn anything to the ground, it would not be accidentally. Well, if you're quite sure I won't bother you . . ." He lifted the cat from the chair and sat down.

She brought out the small, tabletop brazier and lit it. All the cups that did not leak had been used for mixing ink. While she was wiping out the two least objectionable, Fell picked up the heavy folder of finished prints.

"May I see?"

Fell had already untied the cloth tapes that held the folder shut, and Iona could only murmur her assent.

He leafed through the folder, examining each print carefully, hardly noticing when she pressed the cup into his hand. He did not look up except to hold a print to the light, nor speak except to ask how a certain effect had been achieved. When he had gone through the entire folder once, he turned the pile over and gave his attention to certain prints again, admiring a print of a warrior woman, helm on one hip, sword aloft. Iona sat in agony and watched him.

At length he set the folder aside.

"I asked your father's permission to speak with you alone, but he does not know what I plan to say to you. I know you do not wish this marriage. You see me as a fortune hunter, and I cannot deny it. All I can do is offer you compelling reasons why this match is in your own best interest, as well as mine.

"I offer you this: marriage in name only. You will keep your own workroom and, if you so desire, a separate bed-

chamber. You may come and go as you wish, travel abroad
as you wish. I only ask that you spend part of the year
under the same roof with me. I should add that, legally,
I may not share in your marriage portion unless we reside
together at least six months and one day of each year."

Iona could not at first reply. "Forgive me if I seem
ungrateful. This does not strike me as a happy prospect."

He bowed. "I misunderstood you. When we met, I
received the strongest impression that the idea of marriage
to anyone was repellent to you."

"It is," she said uncertainly.

"Then the plan I have outlined must be the least objectionable form of matrimony imaginable. You could do
exactly as you pleased."

She looked at him, her eyes narrowed more out of suspicion than nearsightedness. "There are plenty of marriageable maidens with larger dowries and better manners than
mine. Why me? What do you get out of the bargain?"

Fell shifted his grey gaze out the window, where
pigeons were fluttering and cooing among the decorative
chimney pots. The noise they made, rising and falling
among the red-tiled roofs, was at once soothing and
mournful, a sad cradle song. "When we met, you seemed
so determined against the match that I thought there was
nothing for it but to withdraw. But it seemed to me, Iona,
that your father would eventually attach you against your
will to someone without my views on marriage. I suggest
that you stand a better chance of happiness under the
arrangement I describe."

"How gallant of you!"

He raised an eyebrow. "Is it? When I first came up
these stairs today, it was to tell you I was abandoning my
suit. You seemed to have so much spirit that I doubted
the arrangement would work at all."

She laughed bitterly. "Then you admit I *am* a shrew."

Fell shook his head. "No. You need the only thing I
cannot bring to the match."

"And what, may I ask, is that?"

"Love."

She had no answer. He set his cup on the dresser and

rose to leave. When he was halfway to the first landing, Fell turned and called back up to her where she stood at the top of the stairs.

"By the way—your warrior woman. You have given her left hand a right-handed thumb."

"What?"

"The hand that is holding the sword—the thumb is the wrong way around." He turned and went down the rest of the stairs.

When her mortification had passed, Iona gave rein to her temper. "I wouldn't marry you if you were the very *last* man Above or Below or in All-in-Between!"

This did not seem to surprise her cat, who reclosed one eye and returned to a dream of plump, flightless sparrows.

Iona turned and took up her own, untouched, tea. It was stone cold and tasted emphatically of ink. Fell had drunk two cups of it without complaint.

◦◦◦

"Let's see, now," said the old apothecary, rummaging in a wooden box full of bits of glass and wire. "I seem to remember I got some small ones in."

Caitlin did not like to think about how the apothecary came by the secondhand spectacles: At best, she got them from starving widows parting with a last memento; at worst, from unscrupulous grave diggers. Or perhaps the old woman procured them herself, through the occasional embalming she did on the side. Easy enough to substitute plain glass for the valuable lenses—the embalmed tell no tales.

Bram's eyes were much worse. As the episodes of changeling sight had become more frequent, his eyesight had dimmed. He suffered from frequent headaches and had to lie down for part of each day.

At last the old woman pulled a pair of spectacles from the box, spat delicately on each lens, and polished them with a filthy cloth.

"You, boy—leave that be and come here."

Bram left the stuffed owl with its single dusty glass eye and went to Caitlin's side. The apothecary set the spectacles on the bridge of the boy's nose and hooked the wires over his ears. The old woman was as grimy as her tiny shop, the whorls of her fingertips ingrained with dirt, but she had a clean smell, sharp with juniper and fir smoke, sweet with beeswax and mint.

Bram was fascinated by her large ears. The pendulous lobe of the left was hung with a lizard's foot, the right with a glass owl's eye. As her ears came into focus, he saw inside them tufts of grey hair. Startled, he stepped back. The apothecary cackled.

"Ah, he sees—sees how ugly I am!"

Bram grinned uncertainly back at her, glad of Caitlin's hand on his shoulder.

"What do we owe you, besides our thanks?"

The old woman waved her hand, dismissing the notion. "Just bring me some of those wood herbs you dry, next time you come. I am getting too creaky in the knees to bother with them myself."

"Done. Say thank you, Bram."

They had barely reached the corner when he burst out, "Did you see the hair in her ears?"

Caitlin smiled. "Yes, I did. It was good of you not to ask her about it."

"I don't think she would have minded."

"Probably not, but it'll do you good to practice your manners. Heaven knows you don't practice them at home. Now, I have one more call to make before we go. You can come with me or meet me back here in an hour. You have so much to see with your brand-new specs."

Bram weighed his options. He could go to the canal and watch the floating market, the brightly painted boats stacked with tubs of live turtles and wicker baskets of crabs and eels. Or he could go to the square, where the old men who idled in the tavern doorways would buy him lime punch if he beat them at checkers. Lime punch was a delicacy unknown to the Binder table. Bram was very fond of it and very good at checkers.

"Where are *you* going?" he asked, nibbling his thumbnail.

"To see a book peddler."

"Then I'll come with you."

☙

The bookman's directions led them to an unlikely street. Caitlin was beginning to think she had mistranslated the runes when Bram spotted a shingle hanging from the uppermost story of a tall, narrow house.

☞
BOOKS
BOUGHT
&
SOLD

They climbed the narrow staircase until they reached a door. A small shutter set in this at eye level was closed. Tacked below the shutter was a notice, written out in an elegant hand.

BEMBO GILL, BOOKSELLER
*Books may be left on consignment,
but the Owner reserves the right to
examine them for bookworms, &c.,
before they are brought onto the
premises. Sweetmeats out of wrapper,
uncorked bottles (esp. ink), &c.,
must be surrendered to the Owner
upon entry. Live animals are to be
left in the yard.*
☞ALL PIPES Must Be PUT OUT☜

While they were reading this notice, Caitlin became aware that they were being observed through the small shutter. At once the shutter slid closed and the door was opened. The bookman peered out at them.

"Master Gill?" said Caitlin.

"Yes, yes, but please call me Bembo. No one calls me Gill, let alone Master."

"It's Caitlin Binder. You left a note with my husband."

"Ah, yes. Come in—I have been expecting you—your husband gave me to understand you have an interest in runes." He turned a sharp eye on Bram. "You—little man. Have you got any candy in your pockets, hmm? Peppermint whistles? Treacle mousetraps? Larks' tongues?"

"I haven't even got *pockets*," Bram protested.

"Well, that's all right, then. Come in, come in. And watch your step!"

They entered a maze, a room filled halfway to the rafters with books. The floor was covered in piles waist deep, through which the bookman threaded his way. Caitlin caught glimpses of heavy oaken boards set with iron bosses, slim volumes bound in creamy vellum. There were atlases that were taller than Bram, and a book small enough to fit entirely into the palm of his hand. Bembo fetched it from the glass case where it lay with other tiny volumes, none quite as small.

"It's a treatise on bees, written by a monk. This is not his smallest book; he wrote subsequent volumes on ants, fleas, and mites. Eventually he went stone blind."

Bram turned the tiny pages, each no bigger than his thumbprint. The bees were shown life-size and, at the end of the book, there was a fold-out cutaway diagram of a hive.

"A lovely thing, a lovely thing," muttered Bembo, returning it to its glass case. "Now, will you take a little tea? Never mind that smell—it's only camphor, to keep the bookworms away. The tea is verbena, very nice verbena, at that." He looked from Caitlin to Bram anxiously and was relieved when the offer was accepted.

They emerged from the maze to find a worktable. At least, a worktable could be deduced from the four legs that supported the heaps of parcels and papers awaiting the bookman's attention. Mismatched and mended chairs were ranged around the fire that burned in the grate.

Bembo put the kettle on and began to scrounge around for three uncracked cups with handles.

"Little man," he said over his shoulder, as he searched for spoons, "will you fill the dish with milk and put it on the floor? I've not been around to the fishmonger today, and the mice have been scarce of late."

A pie tin and a covered crock of milk sat on the dresser. Bram filled the dish and set it on the floor. He was immediately up to his ankles in cats: big, middling, and tiny; tortoiseshell, smoke, marmalade, and harlequin; a few missing bits of ears or tails; several with extra toes. There had been no sign of the cats among the stacks of books, though Caitlin now recognized the shop's faint oily smell to be the odor of sardines long since eaten.

"Keep the mice down, you know. A mouse would rather eat the glue out of a bookbinding, I think, than a whole Six'moon cheddar. Have a seat—tea's ready. That's the secret to good tea, you know. Mustn't let it steep too long."

The tea was scalding, fragrant, and pale green; Caitlin sipped hers cautiously and studied their host. He did not square exactly with Binder's description of an impoverished man selling ruined books. The bee treatise alone might have made him a rich man, but he fed his cats better than he fed himself.

As if reading her thoughts, Bembo spoke.

"The problem, you see, is that no one reads. In these sorry times, the purpose of a book is to show everyone else that you are rich or learned or devout or well connected. See that pile over there?" Bembo indicated a pile of books tied in bundles; they were all of a size, all bound in vellum. "Those don't open. They are wood blocks covered with sheepskin and gilded along the edges. And others are just old bindings. Back when the rune tongues were banned, you could have your eyes put out for reading the wrong book. So they tore out the offending pages and sewed new ones in. That atlas? It was used by a horse breeder to record the bloodlines of his stallions. And this, this was once a bestiary. Now it is the account ledger from a pawnbroker."

It seemed to Caitlin that the time had come to broach the real purpose of her visit.

"What do you know of the Books of the Keepers?"

"Well, that depends," Bembo said, without a hint of craftiness. "What do *you* know of them?"

Caitlin was caught up short by this but soon recovered herself. "Not counting the Book of Seeing, there are four of them: the Book of Naming, the Book of Healing, the Book of Summoning, and the Book of Changing. They were written during the Elder Age, before Chameol was an island, when it was a cloister on a hill above the lost kingdom of Iulc."

"Go on."

Bram settled back, tucking his feet up under him and blowing on his tea contentedly. His mother told good stories, and the best ones began "Long ago, in the Elder Age . . ."

Caitlin suspected she couldn't tell the bookseller anything new, but resolved to leave nothing out all the same.

"In the Elder Age, when this world and the Otherworld were one, Chameol was a cloister, a walled city within the royal seat of Iule. The women of the cloister were dedicated to knowledge and the Elder Arts, what we call magic. The Keepers' task was to study the Books and guard them, for the magic they contained could be dangerous in the hands of the unwitting. Each book was protected by a powerful spell.

"The Book of Naming set forth the art of calling things—stones, beasts, herbs, winds, beings mortal and immortal—by their true names. It was bound in ivory that had been carved in the shapes of fabulous beasts. It was protected by wailing runes that would bray and howl and shriek when the book was opened without permission. Its Keeper was Gudule, who is shown in later books holding a pen and inkhorn.

"The Book of Healing was the grandmother of all herbals, for all those that survive today descend from it, sickly children though they are. The pattern of its binding was a knot garden, planted with precious stones and set around a silver fountain. It was protected by its pictures. The hemlock on the page was deadly and the thorns and nettles could catch and sting. Edda kept it; she is always shown holding a branch of the elder tree.

"The Book of Summoning taught how to use a true name to summon forth winds and water, men and beasts. In some fables from the Elder Age, the Book of Summoning is used to return wayward husbands to their wives and children. Chroniclers say it was bound in gold set with six cameos of the four winds and the sun and moon. Its protective magic was the loss, bit by bit, of the power of speech: The reader first began to stutter, became tongue-tied, lost his voice, and eventually turned mute. Its Keeper was Orisyn, who is shown with, or as, a wood thrush.

"The last book is the Book of Changing, the art of exchanging one shape for another. Fables have survived with nonsense morals: 'It is easier to change an ass into an angel than a priest into a pin.' It seems that changes from animate to inanimate were more difficult to pull off than worldly to otherworldly. Since the book itself could shift its shape, nothing is known of its appearance. It was said to be protected by shifting runes that could not be read or copied. Its Keeper, Thyllyln, is usually shown as a chameleon, the lizard that changes its color. The least of the arts of changing, those of stealth and disguise, were kept alive by the brotherhood known as the Knights of Chameol."

Caitlin, feeling a little parched from so much talking, drained her cup. Bembo looked at her expectantly.

"Oh, do go on, please," he said.

"I'm afraid that's all I really know about them. I seem to have found out more what they aren't than what they are."

Bembo looked embarrassed. "I'm sorry, I have misunderstood. Your husband told me you had been studying runes these seven years."

"So I have, with precious little to show for it. I have been working from an old book of incantations, pages from each of the Books bound together. But whether because the Books are not complete or because I am not initiated, the runes will not speak to me."

Bembo's distress became acute. He bit his thumbnail and shifted in his chair as if it were acrawl with ants.

"But you know—you *must* know . . ."

Caitlin felt an odd sensation of extreme impatience mingled with dread. "What? Tell me!"

"The Books as you described them to me are quite right. Nothing wrong there. But you do understand—you must know—the rune books you have been working from are only copies."

Caitlin shook her head. She could not have understood him. "What?"

"They are copies. They are from the Elder Age, all right, and the Keepers charmed them, but they are copies." Seeing her face still incomprehending, Bembo bit his lip and searched the ceiling for words. He found the word he wanted and looked back at her, beaming triumphantly.

"They are decoys. Fakes."

9

MISAPPREHENSIONS

Bram looked anxiously from Bembo to his mother. Bembo looked at Caitlin. Caitlin's gaze seemed transfixed by an invisible object suspended some six inches from her face. Over her features there played a range of emotions, all strong and none simple.

"Fakes," she repeated at last, trying the word gingerly on her tongue, as though the power of speech were new and strange.

"Yes," said Bembo doubtfully. "I am very much afraid so, yes."

"Ah. *Ah*." Caitlin collapsed in laughter. Bram joined in, and then Bembo, and the three laughed for several minutes on end.

Caitlin wiped mirth from her eyes. "You have just told me I have wasted seven years' study on fakes, and yet, I feel like a new woman. How do you explain that?"

Bembo shrugged. "Now you know why you weren't getting anywhere with them."

Caitlin shook her head. "But it still doesn't make sense. Scraps from the Books became my old guardian's book of incantations. If they were fakes, how could she use them to perform magic?"

Bembo scratched his head thoughtfully. "The fakes had to fool magicians of no mean talent. Nonsense books, mere puzzles, would have been found out. The fakes had to be convincing. From other books of incantations that have come my way, it seems that portions of the real Books were copied over with mistakes put in and some essentials left out, a powerful cryptic spell cast over it all. Some of the spells would work, others would not. Failures would be put down to copyists' flubs. You and many others have spent lifetimes"—Caitlin smiled ruefully—"trying to decipher them, with nothing to warn you that you did not have a real Book."

"So the real Books were destroyed after all."

Bembo shrugged. "Who can say? Me, I think not. The Keepers were crafty. I think they made up those tales of their own demise and the Books being scattered. Why bother to look for something you think has been digested by bookworms? I think they hid the Books in plain sight so that they would be sure to be found and used again. But the real books were charmed, so they could be found only by one with a pure motive."

Bembo suddenly fixed his gaze on Bram, who had been squirming in his seat for some minutes.

"Speak up, boy! No need to burst your bladder. There is a little closet at the bottom of the stairs."

Bram scampered from the room.

Caitlin saw her chance. "You know so much about old books. Why—"

"So why am I so poor? Ah, that question has been simmering in your eyes since I showed you the bee treatise, I think." The bookseller undid one cuff and rolled up his sleeve. The length of his arm from shoulder to elbow bore an elaborate tattoo.

Caitlin had seen the ancient pattern once before; there was no mistaking the design.

"A shape changer!"

Bembo protested, tugging his sleeve back into place. "Heavens, no. It's nothing so honorable, I'm afraid: a pawn mark, a sort of receipt, if you will, for my true shape." He sighed. "I was once a—well, I came from a very old family, and I was, shall we say, a *wealthy* man. Through an unbridled love of books I became hopelessly indebted to a pawnbroker. He dealt in shapes as well as books, so to settle my debt, I pawned my true form to him."

Caitlin wavered between crediting and disbelieving his story. Shape shifting had fallen from common practice hundreds of years since. "I thought it was a lost art."

Bembo smiled, and his eyes shone as if with a brilliant vision. What does he see? wondered Caitlin, and in his eyes she fancied she saw reflected the spires of his ancient city, its glittering port. "Not in *my* kingdom, it wasn't."

It was time to go; when Bram returned, Caitlin made their apologies. As he saw them out, Bembo said thoughtfully, "Not to say, of course, that the fakes might not have a clue or two in them. Watch your step on the way down— the railing's coming away from the wall."

On the long walk home, Caitlin remembered a story she had heard at Abagtha's knee, of an ancient king who pawned his true shape in order to own the Book of Wisdom. She told it to Bram as they reached the edge to the Weirdwood.

"And so the magician granted his wish, and turned the king into a book. . . ."

∽⌒∾

There was nothing quite so tiresome, thought Columba as she sat on the couch of the front room of the Cat's Face, as watching someone else buying clothes. Beside her Ermingrude reclined with her feet propped up, fearfully regarding the proceedings from beneath a damp compress.

"All this white is giving me a miserable headache."

"We must have seen every bolt of white cloth in the thirteen kingdoms," said Columba with a sigh.

"No," said Tansy crisply, unrolling yet another. "Only the best of them."

There were blue-whites like snow under moonlight, green-whites like jasmine in shadow, pink-whites like the wannest rose. There were swan's-breast velvets, moth-wing muslins, and a sheer, stiff silk that crackled with the fire of opals.

Iona agonized. Columba's boredom was palpable. She

must pick something. She must decide. Anyway, you may never wear it, she told herself. She could still call the wedding off, so it hardly mattered which.

"This one." She fingered the bolt of jasmine silk.

Tansy held a length of it next to Iona's cheek and nodded.

"Yes—this will be very nice. The color sets off the roses in your cheeks. A simple round neck, I think. And the sleeves should not be too long. Just past the elbow."

Ermingrude protested. "But her hands are so unsightly—cover her wrists, at least."

Her hands *were* unsightly, scarred from the burin and ingrained with ink. Iona scowled and hid them behind her back.

Tansy was firm. "You have very fine hands, long and well shaped. I get a special sort of soap from the dyer. It will get that ink out from under your nails. No, the sleeve must barely cover your elbow." The leopard-woman jotted some measurements on a sketch.

Now that the Cat's Face was well established, Tansy saw customers without a veil. As the leopard-woman calculated the length of silk required for each of several designs, Iona studied her, trying to commit to memory as much as she could. She had that morning prepared a new block of boxwood; as soon as she got back home Iona meant to begin a portrait of the cat-faced tailor.

Tansy caught Iona gazing at her and smiled. "No lace for you, I think. Just some roses worked in silk. And real ones in your hair."

Ermingrude could not decide on a pattern. Certainly the one that used the least silk; but she did not want to be thought cheap. Yet it was important that Iona not outshine Columba. At last a middle-priced design was selected.

Columba had to be shaken out of a reverie of her own wedding clothes: the watery, opal silk, so encrusted with crushed pearl that the dress would stand up on its own. And golden slippers for her feet.

In the street Iona felt a rush of happiness: Her ordeal was over for the moment. Soon she would be home, working on her block.

"I hope that silk will not make you look sallow," said Ermingrude.

"I imagine Master Fell will go through with the ceremony if it makes her look three days dead," murmured Columba.

Iona ignored this remark, but the barb had drawn blood. And at home, in the attic workroom, she stared at the paper pattern for Tansy's portrait, unable to carve the first line in the boxwood block. Lulled by the sound of the pigeons on the rooftops, she sat and brooded on Fell's strange proposal. Amid these thoughts there cropped up unbidden images of herself at the altar in her wedding finery.

Annoyed, Iona bent over her drawing.

∽∾

Iona's betrothed was across town, in his lodgings over the Turtle and Rose. He shared a rented room with an actor in the troupe, a lad who was always out drinking his night's pay or sleeping it off. This suited Fell; he liked his privacy. For an extra penny the landlady brought meals up on a tray so that he need not eat in the tavern dining room.

As lodgers went, Fell was unfailingly sober, untroublesome, cool-tempered, and thoroughly odd. His half of the small attic room was strewn with rag pickings, scraps of paper, and boxes of scrap lead. Sweeping the room out, the landlady had discovered drawings of an odd contraption under the mattress.

"A what?" asked her husband, the keeper of the Turtle.

"An odd contraption. Like what you put people on, to stretch the truth out of them."

"A rack!" The landlord laughed until he had to dab his eyes. "Ah, I've married a madwoman. Our tenant, building a rack in the attic. Hee hee!"

His lady pressed her lips together in a thin line. "All right then, Maxwell Hunt. We will just see!"

∽∾

Nix sat and stared at the objects before him. The mental concentration made the sweat stand out on his lip like nail heads. His glance strayed down to the fresh cherries on his plate, then back to the implements. He pleaded wordlessly with his inquisitors, but Lord Gobeleyn seemed engrossed with his fingernails; Winsom, as usual, was a cipher.

Nix picked up the larger of two spoons, scooped up a cherry, and conveyed it to his mouth without mishap. He managed not to choke on the pit, but then held it on his tongue, aware that something more was wanted. Lord Gobeleyn's glance seemed to lift a fraction of an inch and fasten itself on the spoon in Nix's hand. Nix spat the cherrystone onto the spoon and lowered it to his plate.

Winsom nodded and began to clear away the discarded dishes and linens. Gobeleyn applauded and poured out the brandy, which the boy swallowed entirely. When Winsom had left the room, Lord Gobeleyn leaned over and said in a conspiratorial whisper, "I must admit I feared for you, my boy, that fourth course, before the second soup. Stouter men than you have fallen to fish in jelly."

Nix rose from the table on unsteady legs. He collapsed into a chair with a second brandy. At length he opened his eyes and nodded curtly, as though to his executioner.

Lord Gobeleyn hesitated. "We *can* continue tomorrow. . . ."

"No! I'm ready."

"All right, then." Lord Gobeleyn poured himself a brandy and studied the ceiling for a moment. "A woman drops her fan. Do you pick it up?"

"Yes, but I don't return it to her hand. That would mean I was consenting to a tryst. I place it where she can see it, say, on a table. Unless her husband is watching, in which case I leave it where it is."

"Good. Now, suppose you do want to accept her offer and her husband is watching?"

"I pick up the fan and return it to her later."

"Any exceptions?"

"The queen or her chief lady-in-waiting. In that case, I leave the fan where it is and show up for the tryst."

"Good."

"But Gobeleyn, what if I don't want to?"

"Have a tryst? Well, in that case there are only two courses of action available to you. Under the influence of wine, you may pretend to fall asleep. Or assume a degree of innocence that suggests you haven't the slightest idea what she expects of you. Neither strategy, I should caution you, is foolproof. If a fan should fall at your feet, don't scruple too much before you pick it up."

Nix yawned widely. "Go on. Duels . . ."

But Lord Gobeleyn had not outlined the first problem when his pupil gave out a faint snore.

Winsom returned for the table linen and paused to remove the glass from Nix's hand and place it out of harm's way.

Lord Gobeleyn studied Nix thoughtfully.

"No luck tracing this mysterious wolf-girl of his?"

"No, my lord."

"It is too bad, you know. I begin to think I was wrong about the source of her money. Perhaps she is dead of consumption or drink or languishing in a brothel."

"It strikes me, my lord, from his description of her, that she is rather resourceful enough to have escaped that fate."

Lord Gobeleyn smiled. "As usual, Winsom, you are full of abundant good sense. Of course she is, and he will find her. Love will have its lovers. And I shall do my part to keep him from the arms of ladies-in-waiting, even if I have to pick up all the dropped fans in the thirteen kingdoms to do it."

"I am sure you are equal to the task, my lord."

"Sometimes, Winsom, I suspect you of making remarks at my expense."

"Never, my lord. Good night, my lord."

"Good night. Leave the brandy."

❧

"Madam, I told him you were otherwise engaged, but he would not wait!"

Rose—successor to the departed Lily, now Mistress Tod William—looked daggers over one shoulder. A pale young man stood behind her in a state of barely concealed agitation, running his slender fingers ceaselessly around the brim of his hat.

Lucivia pulled her silken wrapper more closely about her and shut the door to her inner bedchamber. "It's all right, Rose; you may go. Bring up some hot wine." She turned to her visitor. "Unless you'd rather have something stronger?"

The young man turned and shook his head. It was Fell.

The door closed after Rose, but Fell waited until he heard her making noise in the scullery below to speak.

"Are we alone?"

"If I am alone at this hour I am usually up working. It is all right; he sleeps." She chucked him lightly under the chin. "Now, tell me. What brings you here, with such a look?"

Fell was all smooth composure. "I can't go through with it."

She made a face of sympathy and disappointment. "Is there something about the bride or her situation that does not meet your expectations?"

"No. Everything about her and her situation is as you told me it would be. It's just that—" Here the composure faltered, and Fell drew a ragged breath. "I find myself unequal."

Lucivia smiled. "Nonsense. Never were two more alike, more equal, than you and Iona. These are mere jitters."

Fell shook his head, a little angry. "I see nothing to joke about."

"I was not joking."

"She should not have her affections, her heart, her very life trifled with. It is too much—"

He broke off. Rose had entered with the hot wine. When her mistress had tasted and approved it, the maid withdrew.

Fell opened his mouth to continue, but Lucivia held up a hand. "Drink your wine first. It is late, and I fear you have come through the streets in foul weather. Think carefully, I urge you. Are you really so ready to relinquish your suit?"

"I do not see what choice I have."

"Are you so willing to go back on our contract?"

Fell's spine stiffened and he set his wine down cautiously. He laughed shortly.

"You would not hold me to it! Not with what I know about you."

"Oh, I most certainly would. What you know about me is nothing to who I know. You swore to fulfill a solemn promise. If I release you from our bargain, it will cost you the advance in silver upon the dowry. If I were in your shoes, I should not find it an attractive prospect. Besides, my sweet, where is the hardship in it? So she is not complacent; she *is* very rich." She could not resist a final needling. "All you have to do is be a man."

This final insult was too much. Fell pushed past her out of the room, bowling over Rose, who was engaged in a useless rearrangement of the hall linen chest.

In his haste Fell had knocked the wine cup from Lucivia's hand, and the contents had splashed upon her silk wrapper. She gave a hoarse shout of frustration.

"Love?" called the prince from the inner room.

Instantly she snatched up the paper knife from the writing table by the window and was upon the floor. The shaft of a paper knife protruded between her rib cage and armpit, and a ghastly stain spread pinkly over her heart, smelling faintly of cloves.

Such was the sight that met the prince's eyes as he entered from the bedchamber. With an oath he knelt and slipped an arm beneath her to raise her.

She opened one eye, and with a shout of fright he let her fall back on the floor. The truth dawned across his face like a black eye.

"Damn you, Lucy!"

She clutched herself, shaking with mirth. "Oh, I have banged my elbow, and now I shall break a rib laughing! Darling, you looked so sweet. Really, are you *very* angry with me? How could I resist such an opportunity? My best silk wrapper is ruined. I might at least get a smile out of it."

A frightened Rose peeked in at the door, but an oath from the prince sent her scurrying out again.

Lucivia put off the stained wrapper, and stood by the fire in nothing but a moth-wing muslin gown. "Will you get me my other wrapper?"

"Certainly not."

She made a face and crossed to the inner room. As she passed, he caught her by the arm and pulled her back into a kiss.

"Fiend," she murmured.

His reply was the barest exhalation: "Witch."

～∞～

Rose had soon told the tale of the hired bridegroom to her own Matthias, who related it to his cousin Lam at the tavern, who told it to his mistress, who waited upon Lady Littlefoot, who told it to the ostler, who told it to his ladylove, who was Columba's own maid, who told it to the housekeeper as they were counting out the linens purchased for the wedding feast.

"Even with the dowry what it is, he won't have her. They say he wanted more money to go through with it."

"Well, it doesn't surprise me. After the first mistress died, the master let her run wild. She was indulged something awful. Once grown, it's hard to bring such a creature to heel. You can comb her hair and put her in a nice gown, but that doesn't give her nice ways."

Unknown to them, Iona had curled up in the window seat of her favorite alcove, the arras pulled across it for privacy. Her book had slipped from her hand, and she sat frozen where she was. When the last napkin had been counted, the two servants moved away.

Iona pulled back the curtain, dizzy and sick to her stomach. She stood, uncertain where to go, wishing she could vanish on the spot and never have to see any inmate of that house again.

Then she began to get very, very angry. A quarter of an hour later, she had put on her black cloak and packed a bag with her tools, any jewelry she could sell, all her money. Once out of sight of the house, she had soot to smear her face, wax to black out one tooth. She would go about as a beggar woman.

She came down from her attic room and met Ermingrude in the hall.

"Why on earth have you got your cloak on indoors?"

"I—I'm going out to make sketches."

"Well, you'll have to make them later. Your betrothed has paid you a visit."

Iona curled her hand confidentially upon her stepmother's arm. "Oh, dearest, will you let us alone a little? The wedding is so soon and we have spent so little time in one another's company, that I fear he will seem a stranger to me on my wedding night. Will you give us half an hour alone?"

This seemed to Ermingrude a very pretty sentiment, and she assented. Fell was shown to the same room overlooking the courtyard where he had first been received.

Iona was seated by the window, looking uncommonly pretty. Her temper had put her in a high color; her ash-gold hair lay in charming disorder about her shoulders, and an unaccustomed brightness lit her eyes.

Fell had brought a posy of geraniums picked from the window boxes of the Turtle and Rose. Iona held them to her nose and inhaled their spicy fragrance and smiled in a way Fell found disquieting.

"Rumors have reached me about a certain business arrangement concerning myself," she said.

Fell swore under his breath. "The damn maid . . ."

"How quickly you defend yourself!" She rose and began to pace the room. Fell picked up the discarded posy and idly plucked the flowers from their stems. Petals began to pattern the carpet.

"You are not in a state of mind to credit what I say."

"I'll thank you not to speculate on my state of mind."

"Your state of mind is closer to my own than you might think."

"Do I really seem such an idiot to you? Did you think I would not learn that you had been bribed to marry me?"

Fell sighed. "My dear, you scruple too much. What else is marriage? What else is a dowry? What else is the entire ridiculous custom but bribery, deceit, and civilized indentureship?"

"Don't make fun of me. I suppose this woman, this marriage broker, is your mistress."

Fell began to laugh in a way that made Iona regret her

words. Her composure broke, and in her anger and confusion she began to cry.

Fell sat quietly where he was. When the storm had passed he laid the flower stems upon the table.

"The date is set for two weeks hence. I can't deny anything you have said, except to say that you have put the wrong color on it. I honestly believe this match is the best thing for each of us."

"Then why did you want to be released from it?"

"I feared you might mistake my motives and take it into your head to run away."

"And if I should?"

"For one, I think the scandal would make your father wash his hands of you. There would be no coming home in a fortnight. Shall I tell you how penniless young women make their living in this town?"

Iona did not reply, but picked at her sleeve.

"In any case," Fell continued, "you would have to leave all your prints behind, and Columba would be sure to burn them out of spite."

He got up from the chair and went to the door.

"I know you don't believe me, Iona, but my motives are purer than the driven snow."

"Yes," she said, raising her head. "Why should I believe you?"

"Don't believe me. Just trust me."

He left, and she listened as his footsteps echoed down the hall and ceased. After a time the shadows in the room lengthened, and the light from the windows began to dim.

Ermingrude entered and made a small exclamation. She lit a candelabra and set it on the table next to the piles of flower stems and petals.

In the candlelight, Iona's face showed traces of her tears. Ermingrude might be languid to a fault, but she was not entirely unobservant.

"Oh, dear, it has not gone well, has it? Did you quarrel?"

Iona laughed. "Yes, you might say that."

"Well, a quarrel is a sight better than indifference, I dare say."

Iona sighed. "I suppose it is."

∽◦∽

When at last the Keepers broke their centuries' silence and spoke to Caitlin across the chasm of ages, it was in the form of a small, crimson scrap of linen.

It was late, the boys long since asleep. She heard Binder go up to bed. She stretched and thought only fleetingly about joining him. She was restoring a page from an herbal, a leaf copied perhaps from the ancient Book of Healing itself. Many of the colors Caitlin used in repairing the illumination came brush-ready in small pots, already mixed with gum. Some colors, however, were left over from the dyers' trade. For these, scraps of linen were soaked in dye again and again until saturated. Caitlin then only had to set a clothlet in a dish and add a little egg white and water to achieve the pigment.

As Caitlin touched her brush to the wet clothlet in the dish and watched the color spread into the surrounding glair, she froze, and began to make a list in her mind. Woad blue, whelk purple, yellow buckthorn and saffron, green woodbine—all came in clothlets. There had been a cloth-making industry on Chameol. What if there had been a connection between the illuminators and the dyers?

She imagined Chameol under siege, the Keepers persecuted. Suppose the Keepers had *not* fled after all, but continued to practice their arts in secret, while engaging in other trades. The women who sewed the bindings of the books could have turned their skill with a needle to tailoring easily enough; the illuminators and woodblock carvers might turn their talents to dyeing and printing cloth. The binders, skilled in cutting and paring leather, might have become glovers and cobblers. And the scribes themselves might have turned their pens to pattern making and the design of embroidery.

Caitlin wrote out a short message and fixed it to the capsule of a pigeon's leg. Saying a short charm against owls, she released the bird into the Weirdwood night, and with a few wing beats it was gone, bound for Chameol. She remained at the window a few moments, thinking, before she went down to bed.

Bram was waiting for her. Wordlessly, he crawled into her arms.

"Nightmare?"

He nodded. He didn't want to talk about them, usually. But now for some reason he spoke.

"I dreamed Grimald was beneath the ice.... He was all made of glass. I could see his heart inside. And his eyes ..."

She kissed the top of his head. She wanted to tell him there was no reason to worry, that everything would be all right, that Grimald would be fine, but she could not tell him any of those things.

All she said was, "Do you want to sleep with us tonight?"

He nodded and scrambled into the bed; only when he had been badly frightened did he take her up on this offer. He normally disdained it as babyish. A small creeping fear bit at her heart as she got into bed after him.

He had settled down and was dropping off to sleep again when she realized that Binder was awake, watching them. In the dark his eyes glittered with some wordless mix of emotions that made her heart ache: weariness, love, regret.

She leaned over their sleeping son and kissed her husband's eyes to close them, then his pulse above his ear, and the warm spot just behind it.

"You'll wake him...." he murmured.

"Oh, he's dead to the world." She yawned into his shoulder. "I had to banish that look in your eyes."

"Is it gone?"

She had to admit that it was.

"Then go to sleep."

10

THE FINAL FITTING

Winter was beginning to close in on the Weirdwood. The days grew shorter, and with every passing day Bram's sight was growing dimmer. Every afternoon Caitlin made him lie down in the dark with compresses on his eyes. To a boy whose chief pleasure came from reading, this was torture in its cruelest form, and before the first week was out he was wild with boredom. Grimald took pity on him and sat with him during the hours of his enforced blindness, trying to distract him with stories: how many brown bats were in their nets, how their mother had finally outwitted the mice who had been chewing the glue on the new bindings, by reversing a spell that eased toothache.

Bram seemed to be listening, but during Grimald's tale his hand crept up to the blindfold that bound the compresses to his eyes. Caitlin's voice came to them sharply from the kitchen, where she was steeping herbs for compresses.

"Bram—you'll only have to wear them longer tomorrow."

He made a face and let his hand fall down to pick at the embroidery of the coverlet.

"I had a dream," he said. "About the palace."

Grimald knew which palace he meant. He sat and waited for him to go on, if he was going to. Bram hardly ever talked about life before he came to the oak with the red door.

Bram spoke quickly and distinctly, the way people sometimes do in the grip of a fever. "I was in the dumbwaiter, the one they put the food on. It ran between all the levels of the palace. I was in it, and it was falling very fast—my heart felt like it was going to come out of my mouth. Then it stopped, and the doors opened, and I was looking out at the furnace room. There were all these goblins, and the fire made all their faces sooty. Ethold was there, and I called out to him, but he didn't hear me. Then one of the other goblins heard me and turned around. He had your face."

Grimald shifted in his chair. Bram sounded serious—not at all like he was pulling his leg. Like he meant it, like he believed what he was saying.

"Did I say anything?" he asked, laughing uneasily.

"No, I woke up right after that."

In truth, the dream had continued. Grimald the dream miner handed Bram a lump of dull black ore and told him to polish it. He dutifully polished it and polished it, and at last it took on a glossy sheen and passed from gold through several other colors, until at last it became clear, a crystal heart, five-chambered. A goblin heart.

But when he went to show it to Grimald, he saw that his brother's eyes had turned filmy and white, like fish eyes. There was a hole in his chest, and he was dead.

&

Caitlin had carried her tea to her workroom and was halfway through the cup when a pigeon arrived, carrying a letter from Chameol.

When she had unfastened the tube and unrolled the tiny scroll, she saw that the lengthy message had been written in Iiliana's best flea's-eye script. She fetched her hand lens, a birthday present from Binder.

"That's better," she muttered as the words sprang into view.

Cait, my dear,
This will not be as long a letter as I would wish, since

I have much to do to prepare for an expedition to the northern isles.

A shipwreck off the Chameol coast was raised six years ago, but the inventory of the artifacts was completed only last year. To judge from the contents of the ship's hold, the crafts of dyer, weaver, embroiderer, cobbler, and tailor were represented upon Iule. That is, if the ship was leaving port with Iulian goods and not arriving with them from somewhere else. (From the surviving documents that we have been able to decipher, it seems likely that this was so.)

One of the objects retrieved from the wreck was a waterproof money box belonging to a cloth merchant from a town in Sixmoon called Madderfields. Madderfields was the country name of a town later known as Isle-of-Praise, a possible corruption of "Iule be raised," the last words of a famous heretic. The box contained some documents wrapped in oilskin, including receipts from dyers, weavers, and tailors. There were notes on the receipts, apparently written by the merchant, that bore a strong resemblance to a script known only from a fragment found at the old library on Chameol. A network of merchants might have avoided the heretics' pyre by conducting meetings under the guise of trade. And, as you guessed, keeping their bookmaking skills alive.

Curiously, one of the receipts was from a tailor's establishment in a town called Moorsedge—perhaps yours? It was marked, "At the sign of the Shears, Lasting Lane."

I hope that gives you something to grab on to. I eagerly await news of further discoveries. Give my best love to Badger and the boys. I am glad the nets I sent met with your bat catchers' approval.

> Many blessings,
> Iiliana

Caitlin rolled the message and placed it in one of the tiny pigeonholes of the tiny writing desk Binder had made for her when she had despaired of finding a misplaced message from Iiliana. Just the size for a mouse scribe, it had been carved from a single piece of cherry, rubbed with beeswax till it shone like satin. Musing on the mystery of the clothlets, Caitlin pressed a hidden catch. A panel slid back, revealing two glass marbles, blue and green. *Your witch eyes*, his voice said in her brain. The words were spoken with wry affection, vinegared with impatience and something else: the fear that has wonder in it.

Caitlin tried to sort out the facts she was sure of. Before the kingdom of Iule sank beneath the waves, its artisans had carried on trade with a town known as Madderfields. When Iule sank, leaving only Chameol above the waves, all trade had ceased. The town of Madderfields became Isle-of-Praise, a reference not just to Iule but to Chameol itself. Had a secret society of artisans kept the arts of the Keepers alive, or was she letting wishful thinking get the better of her?

But why in Moorsedge, so far from the channel that separated Chameol from the kingdoms of the near Moons?

She closed the hidden compartment and set the mouse-sized desk into a niche in the wall by the window seat. Ink was a disaster around old books; she did most of her letter writing at the window seat, where there were cubby holes to hold her pen and ink and paper.

From the window she could see that Binder had sent the boys out to do their late-day chores. Bram moved through the garden, pulling turnips from the frosty ground for the soup while, further off, Grimald gathered kindling. As she looked at Bram, a wave of cold seemed to grip her limbs and make her heart sink, as though some monstrous shadow had passed over the house, boding ill for all who lived in it.

She had not lately divined with a candle and a basin, afraid of the shape the wax might take in water—the rune for "stone," the rune for "dark."

❧

Binder looked up from the book he was mending, took off his spectacles, and rubbed the bridge of his nose.

"If you start for town this late, you won't be back tonight."

"No. If I deliver some of the finished books, it should buy me a bed for the night."

She caught his glance; wordlessly it spoke the words his tongue shied from, the irony of her buying a bed in the town with the money he earned mending bindings. Her face burned.

"It's important. I can't explain—"

"No. I know. The books that are done are on the shelf; the addresses are inside. And yes, I'll make sure he wears the compresses." He smiled. "I might try them myself." With the spectacles replaced, his eyes seemed resigned and reproachful.

"I'll be back tomorrow night," she said, frowning unconsciously.

"I didn't think you wouldn't be." He said it a little too quietly.

"I only meant that I'll dose you myself when I get home."

"Is that a promise?"

"A threat . . . as you should know by now."

She kissed him and was gone.

❧

The prince soaked in his bath. Not the tub before his mistress's fireplace, but the extravagant gold structure with dolphin-head spouts at the palace.

He soaked and he brooded, and as he soaked, his broodings began to shape themselves into a rough plan. If a manikin could stand in for him at his fittings, why not at the wedding ceremony itself? The reluctant bridegroom sank back into a pleasant reverie of abdication, elopement, and wedded bliss in a shepherd's hut high on some mountain meadow.

Only, he could not put Lucivia's face on the shepherdess. When he conjured the shepherdess in his mind, she had a simple, vacant look, and when he succeeded in calling Lucivia to mind, she was not in the neat little hut but at her table by the window, doing accounts.

The Valet Royal entered carrying a robe. Pages followed, bearing linen, hose, and the royal smallclothes.

"Highness, the tailor awaits."

The prince was most curious to meet his tailor. All the previous transactions had been conducted through the Valet Royal, and all the early fittings on the manikin. She was nothing like the hellion of *The Dog's Muzzle*, this serious young woman, stoic in her deep blue smock. She was accompanied by a veiled woman. He nodded at her, indicating his permission to remove the veil, but the odd figure only nodded back at him in a disconcerting fashion. The Valet Royal stepped forward and whispered in the prince's ear.

"Oh, well, then," said the prince, as he crimsoned to the ears, "in that case, she may remain veiled."

Only the king's wedding suit itself remained to be completed, and this had progressed to the point at which it must be fitted to the prince's own person. In any case, the royal manikin still had not been replaced.

The prince hated finery, or at least the silliness in it. His own clothes were invariably dark and plain. The only concession to sumptuosity that he made was the purple lining of his cloak. So the Valet Royal held his breath as the nuptial suit, basted together, was eased over the royal head. No one noticed the note to the embroiderers pinned to one sleeve.

The heavy blue silk was covered all over with stars in gold thread. The sleeves were not ridiculously large, nor was the skirt of the tunic overpleated.

"Golden hose?" asked the Valet Royal.

"Blue," replied the tailor.

"Ah. Yes. Simplicity itself."

The prince regarded his reflection as the tailor made adjustments to the sleeves. He did not look like himself, but everyone—his father, his friend, his mistress—told him that this was what he must be.

"For the ceremony itself there is a cloak with a train. We brought a sketch and a swatch with the embroidery. Your Highness will see it is white velvet embroidered with suns and comets. It reverses to royal blue."

The Valet Royal held his breath and the pages looked at their feet. The prince himself cast a startled look at the tailor. The whole palace knew of the reversible cloak the prince wore when visiting his mistress, but no one spoke of it. The girl did not appear to mean any disrespect. His look seemed to discomfit her.

"The blue side is impervious to rain," she explained.

"Ah," said the prince.

"And at the collar . . . ?" said the Valet Royal.

"Properly, nothing. Perhaps a bit of ermine." Ulfra cast a sidelong glance at the prince to see if she had overstepped.

The prince only nodded absently. "Are you through? Can I—can *we*—get out of this thing now?"

It was then that the only pin, the one in the note to the embroiderers on the sleeve, scratched the prince's arm.

The pages and Valet Royal and tailor stood in appalled silence. The prince swore mildly and seized the nearest cloth to swab the blood beading the length of the scratch.

"Red after all, like the rest of ours," said a voice in the doorway.

"Ah, Galt. We've managed to cut ourselves on a pin."

It was only then that the king's huntsman saw the tailor. As their eyes met, Ulfra saw the silver wolf pelt fastened around Galt's shoulders.

He waited for a glancing blow from some sharp, wicked shears or at least a tongue lashing. But she said nothing. The dangerous brightness in her eyes suddenly welled up as tears.

"My lord, you must forgive me," she whispered to the prince and, turning, fled from the room.

With a gesture of his hand, the prince dismissed the Valet Royal and the assorted pages. "Stay," he said to the leopard-woman.

"She meant no insult, my lord prince." The slightly lisping voice that issued from behind the veil unnerved the prince. "Your huntsman wears a wolf skin. My young partner has an abiding kinship with that animal. To her, the sight of a wolf skin is abhorrent. Forgive me; I cannot offer you a better explanation without betraying a trust. Now I must go to her."

When they were alone, the prince clutched his arm and stared at his friend in amazement.

"Galt! Either our eyes deceive us, or you're nursing something of a passion for our tailor. Oh, I see I have salted a wound. Come, I'll make it up to you, in pints."

∽◦∾

Lord Gobeleyn was unwell. Winsom ministered to him, bringing him an egg beaten in brandy and possets of sweet woodruff. When Winsom rubbed a strong-smelling ointment into his chest and Lord Gobeleyn did not protest, Nix knew his benefactor was very ill indeed.

Nix hovered anxiously until Winsom banished him to the other end of the house, where he made faces in the hall of mirrors and practiced his dance steps with the fencing dummy.

At last he carried the dummy back to the fencing salon and hung it on its hook. Giving his dancing partner a parting kiss, he set to with his foil. It was an uneven match; a thrust from his sword gored the headless torso, and Nix stood transfixed, watching the sawdust trickle down onto the highly polished floor.

The sight and smell of the sawdust had recalled to Nix his days among Folderol's troupe and the sawdust put down in the ring, woody, sweet, and sharp. Other memories came flooding back: counting out their stolen gold, Ulfra letting him have the wishbone from the roast goose, sleeping in the crook of her arm upon a bed of wolves, Ulfra singing to him in Wolf under her breath.

Nix licked the sweat from his upper lip and replaced the foil in the rack on the far wall. His hand trembled slightly, and his knees seemed about to go out from under him.

As he passed through the hall he glanced at a clock face and saw that he had spent not one hour in the fencing salon but three. Nix was suddenly aware of a ravening hunger. He called out, but no one appeared. Winsom was still with Lord Gobeleyn. After some hesitation, Nix sought out Winsom's pantry, a plot of holy ground some twelve paces by eight that even Lord Gobeleyn himself dared not violate. The pantry was small and serenely ordered, the crockery and copper and knives cunningly arranged and gleaming. On an upright wooden chair beside the only window lay a long letter in a language Nix did not know.

Nix cut himself some cold meat and ate it where he stood, with the single-mindedness of one who is starving. But as his hunger ebbed, his restlessness returned. He could not stand to remember, or think or feel. And he was afraid— afraid he would never find Ulfra, afraid Lord Gobeleyn would die. So he must not feel, he must not think.

He would go to the Turtle and Rose.

When they reached the Cat's Face, Ulfra, as was her wont, shrugged off all Tansy's attempts to talk about the fitting. She pleaded a headache, took a teaspoonful of poppy syrup, and went to bed.

Tansy turned at last to the wedding clothes for the rich engraver's daughter, a task that could be neglected no longer. She was just turning under the neck facing when a knock came at the door. She gently set the gown aside, careful not to bruise the delicate jasmine silk. She hoped it would not be the little boys who knocked at the Cat's Face hoping the leopard-woman would answer the door. They sometimes pulled the trick five or six times in a single day.

It proved to be something else entirely. Well worth setting the gown aside for, Tansy thought, sizing up her visitor's odd smock and trousers and her seer's eyes.

The visitor was apologetic. "I should come again tomorrow. You have an illness in the house."

Tansy looked at the visitor intently. "So we do—though how it is known to you, I cannot fathom."

Caitlin smiled. "I work with herbs, and my sense of smell is rather acute. I smelled poppy syrup as I came in the door."

"The illness is not serious—indignation and heartache in equal parts."

"May I presume upon you a little while, then? I have come a long way, not to engage your services but to ask some questions I believe you—or this house—may be able to answer."

This struck the leopard-woman as a sound proposition. Besides, she liked the look of her visitor. Once you have worked in a circus, you give little weight to superstitious nonsense about seer's eyes. Tansy possessed a cat sense, and was able to judge trustworthiness at a glance; the woman on her doorstep could be trusted. Besides, her curiosity had been aroused.

"Will you come in, then, and sit?"

The Cat's Face had been recently refurbished and now boasted an elaborate room for greeting clients. Tansy led her visitor instead to the small sitting room still favored for privacy and comfort. A fire burned in the grate to keep the autumn chill at bay. The leopard-woman waved Caitlin to a deep chair.

Tansy listened intently as Caitlin explained about the Books and the Keepers and the shipwreck off the coast of Chameol, interrupting her only once to get up and nudge the fire when it fell into a slumber.

"You see," Caitlin said, "I believe that these Keepers scattered, but kept their book arts alive by working as tailors. And the papers found in the shipwreck seem to point to Everlasting Lane."

Tansy retook her seat upon the sofa. "Well, there has been a tailor on this spot as long as anyone can remember. This whole district was once called Tailor's Nine. We are the only surviving establishment."

"Have you come across any old documents—letters, ledgers? Anything at all?"

"There are some old pattern books. All patterns and client measurements are written in tailor's code, to keep trade secrets. But these are different. They seem to be written in runes, though I know only a smattering of the under-tongues, as my mother used to call them. They are curiosities, really—we leave them because they give a sense of history to the place, but it would be hard to remove them even if we wanted to—they are chained to the workroom wall."

"May I see them?"

"Of course."

The ground floor of the Cat's Face was deserted. To celebrate the occasion of the all-important royal fitting, Tansy had given all the workers a bonus and the day off. The workroom was a place of cheerful disorder, bright with bolts of fabric, its walls covered with Ulfra's sketches for current commissions, and populated by headless muslin-and-sawdust torsos in various states of undress. While the room seemed alive with color and industry, it was also unmistakably old—very, very old. Its age radiated from the flagstone tiles beneath Caitlin's feet, from the massive beams of the half-timbered ceiling, from the far wall of dark, smooth stone.

"The latest renovations to the room are at least two hundred years old. I was told by the last owner that the oldest things in it are that low counter over against the wall and this smoothing iron, what we call a goose, after the way the handle curves. The books are over here."

She led Caitlin to the far wall. This was of dark grey stone, worn smooth as glass. Half its length was fitted with wooden drawers and bins that held buttons, ribbon, thread, and such. The rest of the wall was given over to the shelves that held the pattern books.

Six of these were obviously older than the rest, massive volumes bound in oak boards fastened with iron clasps. Each was chained to an iron ring in the original wall. A low trestle lay against the wall to help in consulting the heavy pattern books. Upon this Tansy laid open one of the old books.

"We never have been able to make sense of the runes, though it's become a sort of rite of passage in the trade, when the apprentices become journeymen, for them to try to tell what the runes say."

"How would anyone know the difference?"

"Legend has it that when the runes are translated, a fabulous treasure will appear. The apprentice first makes a wish, then opens the book and points to a passage while blindfolded. Then the blindfold is removed and the apprentice must try to translate the passage she has pointed to." Tansy smiled at her visitor. "Would you like to have a try?"

"I would very much indeed. Do I have to be blindfolded, or can I just close my eyes?"

"You know as much as I do about it—no one has ever succeeded in disclosing a treasure."

Caitlin covered her eyes with one hand and brought the index finger of the other down in a slow spiral onto the open pattern book. She opened her eyes.

The page was crabbed with runes that she recognized as numbers, with occasional words in between.

"They are only measurements, after all," she cried in disappointment. "This is the word for waist, here is shoulder, here is elbow. The spot where my finger came down says 'Waist, eleven; neck, twenty-three; elbow, nineteen; shoulder, six.'"

Tansy laughed and shook her head. "But those are nonsense measurements! A neck twice as much around as a waist."

Caitlin looked at the page more closely. The passage on which her finger had landed was repeated several other places on the same page. She flipped forward and backward in the book and found the passage appeared again. An apprentice picking a passage at random was likelier than not to hit upon the nonsense measurements. But why?

She copied down the passage and closed the book.

"Thank you. I believe I may have found what I have been seeking, if I can only make meaning of it. Now, let us tend to your patient."

Caitlin might have remembered Ulfra as the wild wolf-girl she had encountered many years ago at the court of the boy-king Milo. But the occasion did not arise: Ulfra was not in her bed. The covers had been thrown back violently. Wherever she had gone, she had gone in her nightclothes—her robe still lay upon the end of the bed.

"Does she walk in her sleep?" Caitlin asked.

"No—but in extremes of fatigue or distress she sometimes goes off and hides. I don't look for her. There is something animal in it—she dens herself up to tend to her wounds, and I let her."

∽

Ulfra was asleep in the cedar clothespress, the contents of the strongbox scattered about. She had been working feverishly on a drawing of Nix, not as the boy she had known and cared for as a wolf might her cub, but Nix as he must be now, at thirteen or fourteen. She could not get the features right, as if her brain refused to frame them, refused to admit the passage of time, of change itself. The drawing lay crumpled beneath her now as she slept.

In her dream she wore the prince's hunting costume and rode a dappled grey through a dense forest. This was the Weirdwood, home to the Direwolves. Galt rode at her side, and when they reined in the mounts on the forest path, the horses put their muzzles together in a companionable nickering. From the underbrush the Direwolves watched and, when they passed, lifted their muzzles in a mournful cry.

They were hunting a white hart. Ahead of them the hounds caught the scent of the quarry and broke into a run. Galt spurred his horse and called to Ulfra. As she urged her horse forward through the trees, branches snatched at the folds of her cloak. Unsnagging it, Ulfra saw that it was lined with wolf's fur. The waving branch spooked her horse, and as it broke into a gallop she struggled to hold the reins in one hand and undo the cloak with the other. Glancing down, she saw that the toggle was made of wolf's teeth.

Ahead, the hounds had cornered their quarry in a glade and were milling in a circle around it, keeping up a high, keening cry. The hart was a magnificent creature, with antlers of burnished gold and a milk-white coat that seemed to gather up all the light of the wood. From the center of the circle where the dogs had hemmed it in, the hart struck out at its tormenters with golden hooves.

Galt drew his horse up bedside hers and, drawing an arrow from his own quiver, fitted it in her bow. Leaning from his saddle, he set his grizzled cheek against her fair one and showed her how to set the bowstring in the arrow's notch and, holding his fingers over her own, helped her hold the bow steady while she drew the arrow back.

The arrow sang true to its target and struck the animal in the throat, near its massive shoulders. Blood began to spout like a ruby fountain. Not the way it really would, she thought as she slipped from her horse in the dream, but the way a painter would paint it.

She ran to the animal where it had fallen. Its eyes rolled

wildly, then fell on her: blue eyes, uncannily pale. At once the animal grew calm and laid its head meekly in her lap, as though it knew her for a friend.

It was gravely wounded; Ulfra knew it would die unless she could retrieve the arrow and stanch the bleeding. As she seized the shaft of the arrow and tried to wrench it from the wound, it was suddenly not the hart's shoulder but a man's, though still unearthly white. She gazed down into her lap and saw the face she had not been able to draw, the face of her beloved Nix. His strange white hair was streaked with sweat and his face spattered with blood from the wound.

"The spring will heal me," he said, "if you hurry." When he spoke, his tongue was slick with dark blood. Dread brought Ulfra's heart to her throat.

"Where is it? You must tell me where it is!"

Ulfra was suddenly awake, her heart pounding, the very words in her throat. She sat up and leaned her head against the cedar panels of the clothespress until her heart slowed its frantic beat. But though her breaths were less ragged, her mind was still gripped by confusion. What did the dream mean? Was she supposed to find the spring? Was Nix her one true love? Or was she meant to right the wrong she had done by abandoning him at the farmhouse?

Lady Twixtwain would know what to do. Changing by feel in the fragrant clothespress, Ulfra put on thief's black and a black hood to cover her hair. Since the notoriety of *The Dog's Muzzle* and the success of the Cat's Face, she could not walk the streets anymore without attracting a crowd. So the hood and thief's clothes had gotten to be a habit when she wanted to go about her business unmolested. Besides, she knew Tansy would think this a feverish fancy and insist she stay in bed. Ulfra's errand could not wait until morning. It was almost the supper hour, and Tansy would be putting her feet up. It was now or never.

She climbed from the bedroom window to the drainpipe, slid down the drainpipe to the street, glanced up and down the alleyway, and was gone.

11

SOME SUITS ARE PRESSED

The physician was tall and gaunt; beneath his paper white complexion the blood flowed in his veins as purple as ink. He closed his bag and went to wash his hands at the basin. He enjoyed a thriving practice, for he was both skillful and discreet and did not disclose his patients' identities or the curious natures of their ailments.

Winsom stepped forward to collect the basin of dark blood and the crimsoned toweling.

"When you are done," said the physician, from where he stood at the elegant marble washstand, "I want to speak to you in the hallway."

Winsom gazed down at Lord Gobeleyn. Drained of blood, his naturally ruddy face was as white as the pillowcase beneath it, and his outflung arm black and blue where the physician's sharp lancet had probed for a vein. The faithful servant's eyes filled with tears that could not be shed.

In the hallway, the physician spoke quickly in low tones, so as not to awaken the invalid.

"It is his heart. Some goblins—more often boys born to mortal fathers and elvish mothers—are born with a weakness of the heart. It is not life-threatening so long as they

550

remain in the Otherworld. But should they venture Above, the consequences are grave. In infants and boys, the heart weakens gradually, until death is inevitable, though often masked by some other illness, such as whooping cough. In older boys and men, the course of the ailment can be slowed somewhat, by avoiding exercise and eating a spartan diet. But the onset of the weakening can only be postponed, not prevented. Once it begins, its course is rapid and severe. The only cure lies in returning immediatcly Below."

"That is quite impossible."

"Then he has a month at the outside, perhaps as little as a week. I can at least make him comfortable. Rouse him every four hours and make him drink a dilute solution of this elixir. I have written out the proportions. Make sure it is well shaken before he drinks it. One of these blue vials broken under his nose will rouse him; do the same with one of the black, and he will sleep. He should sleep comfortably enough. But be careful that he does not harm himself. He will soon cease to think or feel anything real going on about him and will live only in the past. He may have nightmares or rave in his sleep. He may ask to see people who are long dead. Humor him."

Winsom nodded dully. "Is there nothing else I can do to ease him?"

The doctor shot a glance at Winsom. "Unstop the proverbial Spring of the Dead and dip him in it! I must go on now to attend a lying-in."

Winsom nodded and showed the man out, then returned to the sickbed. Lord Gobeleyn opened fevered eyes that looked up vacantly at the ceiling without focusing.

"The boy . . . I must save the boy. . . ."

Winsom broke open one of the black vials, and Lord Gobeleyn sank back into unconsciousness.

❧

The Turtle and Rose was not crowded, in part because the cast of *The Dog's Muzzle* was busy rehearsing a new entertainment, a masque in celebration of the prince's approaching nuptials. In an alcove of the inn that afforded the greatest degree of privacy, Galt and the prince were savoring a jug of cream-and-black. At least, the prince was enjoying it. Galt was in a mood, and the prince knew better than to jolly him out of it, though he could not help making an observation.

"Has it ever occurred to you that the reason you cannot bring yourself to speak to her has nothing to do with wolves or even her wolfish ways?"

"No. But I suspect it has occurred to you. Pray"—Galt cracked a walnut in his fist—"enlighten me."

The prince gazed up at the rafters as if every beam were carved with words of wisdom. The ale had ever so slightly loosened his tongue, else he would have been more heedful of the gleam in Galt's eye.

"It's that you have always surrounded yourself with a certain kind of female company not inclined to the art of conversation, and so have no conversation yourself."

Galt gave the prince a baleful glance, refilled his tankard, and pushed the jug away. "Again," he said softly. At once the landlord was at their table. The empty jug was swiftly removed and a full one set down in its place.

"And how do you know what kind of female company I keep?" he asked when the tavern keeper had moved off to supervise the tapping of a cask of wine.

"I know that you are a not-too-frequent but generous patron of the better sort of courtesan, and that you favor those who, while young and comely, are not given to idle chat."

Galt's mouth twisted into a ghost of a smile. "Unlike a king, a king's huntsman can only choose so far. He must content himself with the selection available to a man of his rank and means."

The prince perceived that the conversation had passed beyond playful bandying to something else. He searched his friend's face for a moment before he spoke, and when he did he chose his words carefully.

"I begin to suspect that you believe yourself incapable of engaging a woman except through a business transaction. Or is it your own affections that fail to be engaged?"

"You mistake me, my friend. I like to leave my heart at

the door in such transactions. My affections were engaged once. I did not care for it."

"I see. So the unscrupulous might slit your throat and make off with your purse, but they will never wound you *here*." The prince leaned over and tapped Galt soundly on his leather breastplate.

Galt brushed the hand off with a soft hiss. "Tread softly!"

The prince held up his hands, palms outward. "On cat feet," he murmured.

Galt stared into his black ale. "When I was young—younger than you are now—I married, only to discover my affections had been sadly misplaced. But my wife was so beautiful and her ways so sweet that I could not believe she was capable of deceiving me with another. One day, while hunting boar, my arrow went astray and killed the man rumor called her lover. When she heard the news she took poison." He looked at the prince's face and smiled. "You see, she did not believe I could miss my mark."

∽∾

Three flights above this conversation, Fell was seated at the unsteady table that served alike as washstand, boot stand, and writing desk in the small, ill-furnished room. On this occasion it was a writing desk. He sat with his pen poised over the sheet, biting his thumb and staring out the window at the distant rooftops, imagining the prospect as seen from Iona's attic window, pigeons rising and falling among the ornate chimney pots.

Before him on the half-filled sheet was a list.

REOPENING THE HOUSE
- ✧ Air out trunk (check for moths)
- ✧ Candles, firewood, cat's meat
- ✧ Wine (Where is key to cellar?)
- ✧ Count linens
- ✧ Have extra set of keys made for I.
- ✧ Pawnbroker for Mother's jewels (Get garnet ring reset for I.? Can this be done in three days?)
- ✧ Have press delivered (Do this at night?)

Fell turned his attention from the view to his list and began to draw on the bottom of the piece of paper. A few minutes' sketching produced Iona in wedding clothes beside an altar covered with flowers. Then, after a pause during which he stared off into space, Fell erased the flowers. In their place he drew his own effigy in armor, stretched out on a low tomb. Then he filled in Iona's gown with black.

Beneath this he wrote: "Make arrangements for death (Check on dowry, arrange funeral, decide on day—how soon after wedding?)"

～

Dusk was beginning to gather. The narrow streets, with their houses so close that a man could lean out his window and light the pipe of his neighbor next door, were sinking into an enveloping darkness, dispelled here and there by the hopeful work of lamplighters making their rounds. Through these streets Ulfra made her way, her thief's garb allowing her to pass within feet of others unnoticed, her face hidden by the close hood.

As it happened, Galt had veered from the route to his lodgings to persuade an apothecary just shuttering his shop to sell him a headache powder. The premises of this obliging merchant were in the same street as the button makers Ulfra had visited the day she had rescued the young wolf, and lay quite close to Lady Twixtwain's house.

Cutting through an alley to shorten his way home (his head was pounding now; damn that last pint) Galt spied a figure in black trying the back door of a house in Goldenmouth Street.

With the ease of one plucking a rabbit from a snare, he stepped forward and seized the housebreaker by the nape of the neck.

"Let's have a look at you," he said. Pulling back the hood, he was astonished to find himself face-to-face with the prince's female tailor.

"You!" Galt gave a stifled cry, half shout and half laugh, and released her so abruptly that Ulfra fell back on the slick cobblestones. Realizing this was not winning conduct on the part of a suitor, the huntsman hauled her to her feet and suddenly found himself holding her tightly by the wrists, mesmerized by those wolf's eyes.

It is never advisable to kiss a wolf, but that is what Galt did. Taken completely off her guard, Ulfra stood frozen with her fists clenched. When she regained her wits she found she could not shake off his grip. At last Ulfra wrenched her head to one side with a snarl that issued from some place low in her throat. It was a murderous sound—enraged, uncanny, and not quite human.

Galt released her wrists as though they were red-hot pokers. He felt as though he had been pulled from a seething cauldron only to be plunged into an icy deep: His bones sang, his eyes dimmed, and he found himself suddenly drenched with a cold sweat.

She stood before him a girl again, her face damp with tears of outrage, dragging the back of her hand across her mouth. The wolf had receded from her eyes, leaving them indignant and confused.

Her lower lip was bloodied. Galt found a handkerchief and stepped forward to press it to her lip, then placed her fingers over the bandage so that she could hold it herself.

"I'm sorry," he said.

She shook her head and removed the handkerchief to speak, trying the words out gingerly. "It happened when I turned my head."

"I'm sorry," he repeated.

Neither of them had stepped away. It only wanted a glance for an invisible spark to cross the gap between them. Neither knew afterward who had moved first into a kiss that tasted of blood and tears and the Turtle and Rose's best cream-and-black.

Then, with a sudden exclamation, she ducked down and out of his arms, loose-boned as a mink shrugging out of a trap. Before he realized what was happening, she was gone.

What had happened was this: Just as she was about to abandon all caution, Ulfra's hands had closed on the lining of Galt's cloak.

∽

The prince left the Turtle and Rose and began to make his way to Everlasting Lane. He had turned from the alley into the wider street when he was nearly bowled over by a strange young man, long-limbed and impeccably dressed, except for the omission of gloves and the less-than-fashionable disarray of his collar and cuffs.

Nix was winded, but between ragged breaths he gasped a hasty apology and made as if to run past.

The prince, staring at him, did not release the boy's shoulders. His mind whirled with new-sprung possibilities. "You are the very thing! No, never mind that, I'm fine. Here, hold your arm out."

Nix did so, a little wonderingly, but obeying the easy command in the prince's tone.

They were of a height, their shoulders an equal span, and their arms so alike that if they had been cast in bronze, one could not tell which was the model and which the copy.

"If our faces were anything alike, I should begin to fear for my throne," the prince muttered. "Instead, I begin to hope for my happiness." The prince drew a card from his pocket, scrawled something on it, and handed it to Nix. "Present this at the palace and tell them you are to see the Valet Royal. You will be well paid for your trouble."

❧

Lady Twixtwain saw at once how it stood with Ulfra.

She had been quite surprised to discover Ulfra on her doorstep, since Ulfra had both a key to the kitchen door and a standing invitation to let herself in and make herself at home until Lady Twixtwain should emerge from any of a number of baths, naps, changes of wardrobe, and small cosmetic adjustments that made up her daily domestic routine.

Taking the girl firmly in hand, she set her before the fire and gave her a clean compress for her lip, a little of her miracle tonic on a silk handkerchief that smelled faintly of scent. Ulfra haltingly related first her dream and then the encounter with Galt. Lady Twixtwain listened to the girl's expressions of repulsion and loathing for Galt and her bitter self-recriminations with an increasingly unsympathetic ear.

"My dear," she sighed. "I beg you, don't waste perfectly

good indignation on the matter! It is quite commonplace to love and loathe the same person by turns, and often both at once. And, if I may further shock your nice sensibilities, you can even be in love with more than one person at the same time."

Ulfra squirmed a little where she sat, looking extremely ill at ease. "I can't believe that."

"Well, you ought to. It has been the way of the world since time began. You may very well hate this man with all your reason, nay, even with all your heart, but your blood may sing another tune! Tell me the truth: Did you find his kiss loathsome?"

Ulfra stared down at the handkerchief in her hand. "Yes! No . . . not the second time."

"From what you have just told me, I surmise a few things. You had only just discovered in this dream that you love this lost boy—Nix, is it?—and before you can come to tell me, you find yourself in the arms of the man you most loathe in the world. And now you are feeling guilty and afraid that you have been unfaithful to this Nix of yours. My dear, you are all of twenty-one, and never yet kissed? It is too much for him to expect for you to be untouched by other lips. It would be a crime against nature. It is *beyond the pale*."

Thinking she had perhaps taken the topic as far as was wise for the time being, Lady Twixtwain took the conversation in a different direction.

"Here—let me have a look at that lip."

Dutifully, Ulfra removed the compress. The bleeding had stopped. Indeed, it was impossible to tell where the cut had been.

"There. Did I not tell you my water works miracles? Now kiss me, my dear, and then up to bed with you. I will send word to Tansy that you are staying with me tonight. Heaven only knows what other adventures you might have on your way home."

❧

"I tell you, it solves everything!"

The prince spoke these words with great passion and more than a little annoyance that they seemed to carry no great persuasion for his mistress, who sighed and moved to dip her pen into the ornate inkwell.

In a fit of unbidden temper the prince shoved the inkwell away, making a great blot on the page of accounts to which Lucivia had been devoting herself. She looked up at him with an expression of intense exasperation.

"All right, that is it. I have had quite enough, thank you, for this evening. Uninvited, you present yourself during the very hours which we have agreed I am to be left to myself. You then outstay your thin welcome, bend my ear with some harebrained scheme of hiring a manikin to stand in for you at your wedding, and now you have undone an hour's tedious accounting! Really, I have half—no, three-quarters—of a mind to turn you out altogether. No, not a word, I am quite serious. I am tired of your peevish behavior. How can I state it more clearly than I have done? I will not marry you, under any circumstances!"

His eyes flashed with anger. "Don't scruple about my feelings! Let me have it, madam!"

"All right, then. You do not consider it possible that I should have any business of my own that is more important than your personal and immediate gratification. Simply because you are in a mood you expect that I should cancel all other appointments, set aside important work that must be done, and devote myself to soothing your wounded self-regard."

"What other appointments at this hour, may I be allowed to know!"

Her eyes flashed. "Oh, you are most infuriating! If a woman's attention, let alone her affection, is not engaged entirely, heaven knows she can only be bestowing it upon some other *man!* She cannot possibly be engaged in business, or the running of her household, or even her own *thoughts!*"

"That is an unkind cut, Lucy," he said wearily.

"If it is unkind, it is only because it is the truth." She paused to catch her breath and smiled at him wryly. "Believe me, my sweet: We would not suit. We are too different, and ours are not the differences that complement, but those that detract. My ambition, my independence of mind, would only make you unhappy; I am utterly incapable of the sentimentality you so like to credit me with. You would do far better to resign yourself to the bride that I have spent so much time and energy procuring for you."

A stark and dreadful realization was beginning to take form in the prince's fevered brain. "How can I love another, after you?"

This at last made her laugh. "But you do not love me, goose. You are *in love* with me, and only with the part of me that is pliant and pleasing and dresses itself in scent and silk. And that is not who I am the other sixteen hours of the day. If I *were* to marry, it would be to a grey old man who would allow me a good night's sleep."

The prince stood and looked at her, acutely aware that nothing between them could be as it had been before. His eyes had been opened—not to her true nature, which she had never concealed from him, but to his own.

Her anger had passed. She looked at him with affection and reached up to lay her palm upon his heated face.

"Unlace me," she said. "I have something to show you."

When the bodice was unlaced and her back laid bare, Lucivia pulled aside her heavy tresses and revealed the mark, wine-dark and the size of his outstretched palm, that spread between her shoulder blades in the shape of a butterfly.

"What do you see?"

"Your scar," he said dully, "where your brother scalded you in the bath." He thought he heard a note of pity in her voice, and it made him afraid.

"I told you that because it was what you would believe. A discreet surgeon made that scar. Yes, I paid him to do it. Wing removal is a far more common operation than you might think. There," she said gently. "I've told you." She shrugged back into her bodice and turned to face him.

"That is what they removed from me. Now you know what I am. If you will not heed my other reasons, you must heed that one. Go on—leave me. Rose will lace me up again. She is finally getting good at it, the little idiot."

* * *

The prince dragged his feet up the gilded staircase to his bedroom, where his page kept a sleepy vigil in case his master should make a rare appearance in his own bed before the small hours of the morning.

"Will you bathe, Your Highness?" inquired the Valet Royal.

"No."

"Have you dined?"

"No."

"Have—"

"No! Leave me. I want nothing."

When he was alone, the prince went out onto his balcony to breathe the night air, then came back in and rummaged in the drawer of the massive writing table, never used, that made up part of the princely appointments of the royal bedchamber.

He drew out a packet of documents and took them over to the bed to read: a series of formal letters, from his future father-in-law, and the marriage contract and its many codicils and legal appendages, on thick curling parchment much covered with red wax seals. Among all these papers there was only one short note from his appointed bride, a few lines in a girlish hand. Her accomplishments, the enclosed note told him, included not only the lute and harp, but the mastery of several languages and a decided proficiency at embroidery.

With these documents there was a small ivory box set with diamonds, which, when its catch was sprung, revealed a portrait of his betrothed. She was very young, with quantities of glossy, soft brown hair caught up in a net of pearls. The painter had given her wide-set brown eyes a wet luster; this, with her slightly upturned nose and small chin, gave her the inbred look of a spaniel a little too highly strung.

∽∾

Three days passed, and on the eve of Iona's wedding a package arrived at a house in the most prosperous and respectable quarter of the town. The servant left the enormous parcel in the hallway and went to tell the mistress of the house of its arrival.

Ermingrude set down her letter and her spaniel and her bowl of tea and scurried to the hallway, exclaiming and calling for Columba to come and look, the thing had indeed come in time, and who would have expected it?

Ermingrude and Columba and the housekeeper had spent some minutes exclaiming over the workmanship of the dress and wondering how its folds could be conveyed in a carriage without crushing the delicate embroidery, when they realized the bride herself was not among them.

"How like her," said Columba. "If my sister is one thing, it is not *vain*. Shall I find her?"

"Yes, do. You would think she would think of me and be a little bit anxious for my sake. She seems to me such an unnatural child."

"I should hope so, madam, since she is not yours," murmured Columba, gliding out the door.

She found her half sister in her attic room, packing the last of her inks and tools and blocks into a special crate. Iona had removed all her prints from the walls and placed them in the special case that Fell had given her as a token of their engagement. She had thought it a little wrong of her to accept it, but she had not really known what else to do. And it had come in very handy.

"How nice this place looks, now that you've picked it all up," said Columba, leaning in the doorway but disdaining to cross the threshold.

Iona glanced around. "Really? To me it looks rather bare."

Privately Columba thought the room could best be made into quarters for a live-in seamstress. Her own marriage was to follow Iona's at the minimum respectable distance of three months. It would be uncommonly handy to have her own private dressmaker installed at her mother's house, working full-time on her own marriage clothes.

"Your dress has come at last. We were all looking at it this past half hour before we noticed you weren't with us."

⌘

Columba had to admit that she had been wrong about the silk. The jasmine white did not make Iona look sallow at all. Rather, it brought the roses out in her cheeks and made her hair glitter like gold leaf glimpsed in a dim chapel.

"My dear, you are quite a vision," said Ermingrude from the couch, where a back spasm had sent her. "Who would have imagined it? Your father was quite right to make you eat a piece of bloody beef once a week. It has done wonders for your complexion."

Iona gazed silently at her reflection in the glass. The dress was marvelous. The cut of the bodice worked wonders, the silk clinging here, skimming there, and finally flaring below her hips in a full skirt. The gown was embroidered all over with intertwined jasmine vines.

The housekeeper appeared in the doorway.

"This was just delivered, madam."

"This" turned out to be another parcel, addressed to Iona, bearing no return address. When the paper was removed it was revealed to be a small box of horn, carved with a motif of doves.

"It looks old," said Ermingrude, wondering if it might be valuable.

"No—he made it himself," Iona said softly. She had recognized the doves for pigeons, and the design on the box as the view from her own window, with its maze of chimney pots.

"Open it, silly," said Columba impatiently. "Of course, it's your ring!"

It was a fine red stone in a setting of reddish gold that curled up around the stone like leaves of ivy.

"It's only a garnet, after all. He might at least have gotten you a ruby," said Columba.

"Be quiet," Iona whispered, turning the ring over in her hand. The inside of the band was engraved. She held it to the light to read the inscription.

It said, "For Iona," and nothing more.

12

A GOBLIN HEART

The vows were sworn, the marriage feast over, the guests dispersed. Good-byes were said, and the small chest containing Iona's clothes was loaded into the carriage.

As part of Iona's dowry, her father had intended to make the couple a present of a modest house close to his own, with a dozen or so rooms. But Fell quietly insisted on a house with only eight rooms, on the fringe of the artists' quarter. No argument could move him on this point, and rather than see his daughter settled in a still less respectable part of town, Niccolaus grudgingly conceded. Fell had engaged the servants himself, claiming that he was quite particular about the management of his household.

As they rode in silence through the streets of the city, it occurred to Iona that it was no longer her wedding night but early in the morning hours of the first day of her married life.

Fell sat with his face turned to the carriage window. She thought that perhaps he had fallen asleep. Something in the set of his shoulders bespoke a profound weariness, an intense fatigue he hid from the world when awake.

Shyly Iona stretched out a hand and touched her husband's shoulder.

The carriage had stopped, and Fell stirred, from sleep or contemplation, and turned to her. His face was unreadable, but in the pale lamplight it seemed young and uncertain. He smiled at her wryly.

"Your new home, madam."

In the hallway the sleepy housekeeper helped them from their cloaks. Iona glimpsed crates and trunks and furniture draped in cloths.

Fell knelt to pick up a large cat that was weaving between his legs. He buried his face in its plush grey fur, and for a moment she did not recognize him, so unaccustomed was she to seeing an expression approaching tenderness on his face.

He set the cat down and cast a quick glance at Iona, seeing the draped forms of the hall through her eyes. "I thought you would want to arrange the furnishings to your own liking." Fell turned to the housekeeper and ordered hot wine. "Bring it to madam's bedroom."

The housekeeper led the way up the staircase. Fell paused at a different door along the passage.

"I'll join you when I've bathed and changed." He dropped a kiss on her cheek.

Iona paused in the hallway, suddenly feeling oddly disembodied and confused. The housekeeper waited, holding the lantern aloft. Iona hurried to catch up, lifting the heavy skirts of her wedding clothes.

The housekeeper showed her into a spacious room furnished with a clothespress, a writing table, and a carved bed hung with silk curtains. In an alcove, a cushioned seat looked out through leaded windows to the park below.

"Shall I help you out of your dress, madam?"

"No—yes. If you would just undo the back, I can manage on my own."

When the woman had gone Iona washed her face at the basin and combed out her hair. When she went to change the heavy wedding dress for her nightclothes, she found that her mother (or possibly Columba, in a fit of spite) had substituted for her maidenly nightdress another of diaphanous muslin that, in the candlelight, was entirely transparent. None of her other clothes had been unpacked, so Iona left her shift on. The housekeeper returned with a tray containing a jug of spiced wine and two goblets. Iona filled a goblet with a fingerful of wine and tossed it down. Her throat was parched. Unconsciously, she wiped her palms on her shift.

She could not bring herself to wait on the bed, so she sat in the window seat and looked out at the park below, angry at herself for being so nervous. She had made her bargain, and now she must live by it. Columba's taunting words about wedding nights rang in her ears and made her cheeks burn. Opening the window a crack, she inhaled the cool night air. Behind her a door opened and softly closed again. Iona turned around.

At first Iona thought no one was there. Then she realized the door she had heard was not the door to the hallway but the smaller door that led to an adjoining room. Beside this there stood a woman.

She was tall, with features too striking to be comely on a woman. Her best features were her light brown hair and her large grey eyes. She wore an elegant silk gown of deepest blue, the dress not of a servant or relative but of the mistress of the house.

Iona rose on legs that were unsteady, her mind racing from possibility to possibility as down a corridor of locked doors: This was Fell's sister, his cousin, his mistress, his secret wife. Her mind wrestled with each possibility and weighed it against the evidence of her eyes. The awful truth dawned on her.

This *was* Fell, got up in woman's clothing.

"You!" she said weakly.

"Yes," said Fell, coming forward and helping her back onto the window seat. "I am sorry to give you such a shock. Would it help you to drink some wine?"

Iona looked at him in the light, and suddenly her mind made the last leap to the truth. Fell was a woman.

Something rose in Iona's throat, but whether it was a shout or a sob or a peal of laughter, neither occupant of the room was to know. Before she could utter it Iona slumped over in a faint.

∽∾

Lady Twixtwain's miracle tonic had as its source a spring in the heart of the Weirdwood—the same spring that provided a measure of flood control for the network of subterranean canals that wound their way to Ylfcwen's palace.

Things were not well with the elf queen. Spies of the Royal Household Agency had caught her in an abandoned ballroom, about to let go of the chandelier and attempt an illicit solo flight. Ylfcwen had been placed under house arrest, confined to her room while her former numerologist and rune caster set about divining the name of her successor. They had even replaced her silver ankle bells with iron anklets that locked with a key.

This the director of the Royal Household Agency put around his neck on a ribbon. It lay upon the front of his robe beside all the other keys, the ones to the lapidary and gemarium, interrogation rooms, and the passages that led Above.

"You may still ring for anything you require," he said through the door, when she was locked into her royal bedchamber.

She tested the bell cord to see if it would indeed be answered. Minutes passed, then an hour. The director had perhaps meant to be sarcastic.

Hours passed in the dark; she did not light any lamps. When the fireflies died she doubted they would replace them. At last the door opened, and her faithful dresser entered bearing a tray; behind her trailed an elf guard in full armor. This struck Ylfcwen as rather excessive; with the weights on her ankles she could barely walk, much less bolt for her freedom.

Without meeting her mistress's eyes, the dresser set the tray on the nightstand and left the room. The door was relocked.

Ylfcwen pounced on the tray. Its contents proved disappointing: a flask of water and a heel of coarse bread—not even goblin bread, thank you, but the stuff they fed the weavers.

With a sigh, Ylfcwen closed her eyes and brought a piece of the bread to her lips. As she did so, the queen thought very hard about marmalade tarts, and from there her thoughts moved rapidly to the secondary larders and other storerooms that honeycombed the lower levels of the palace. The possibility of forgotten provisions for some upcoming festival gave the tasteless bread some savor.

Then she remembered something else that lay forgotten in the storerooms.

An opportunity presented itself more quickly than she had dared hope, in the form of her faithful dresser, who took pity on her mistress and brought her a glass of root wine and a jasmine cake. Out of pity, she even unlocked her mistress's weights and replaced them with the jeweled anklets. While she was bending to this task, Ylfcwen brought the tray down on the dresser's head.

As Ylfcwen bound her hand and foot with the cords from several wing cases, the queen took pains to make her boundless gratitude clear.

"It will not go too badly with you. After all, you didn't cooperate in the least."

Above her gag, the dresser blinked.

Not wishing this faithful servant to starve, Ylfcwen removed the gag and fed her captive the root wine and jasmine cake. "I dare say they will find you before long." Ylfcwen added thoughtfully, easing the ring of keys from the dresser's belt.

Ylfcwen did not change into the earth brown clothes that were the required attire for elf royalty Above. She would not be returning, so what were the rules to her? Instead, she donned one of her favorite gowns. She seemed to remember being married in it, once, to whatever-his-name-was, Aethyr's father. It was a gown fit to fly in, fashioned of silk gauze hardly more substantial than breath, to which clung a frost of opal dust and crushed pearl. By some happy unlikelihood it still fit.

Her heart beating swiftly, Ylfcwen let herself out by the hidden door in the closet, behind the shoe rack. She lit a small lamp and stepped down into the cool, slightly damp air of a narrow staircase.

∽◦∾

Grimald was in his father's workshop, making a birthday present for his mother, a small tooled girdle book that she could tie to her belt while working in the garden, with blank pages so that she could write in it the spells to keep the rusts and blights, worms and rabbits away.

He was vaguely aware that it was growing colder and that he was getting sleepy, but so intent was he on his work that he did not pay it much attention. By the time the punch and hammer fell from his hands, he had lapsed into something between sleep and death.

Looking for her husband, Caitlin found him, his usually ruddy face blue with cold. For one long, terrible moment she could hear no heartbeat in the boy's chest.

Binder came running, unable to make out his wife's words but hearing in her shout an urgency that filled him with dread. Grimald was already stirring and saying he was all right, but he did not protest when he was put to bed hours before the usual time.

"That was no faint," Binder said under his breath.

Caitlin started to answer, but burst into tears instead, giving way at last to exhaustion and panic. For weeks gnawing fears had robbed her of sleep at night. By day she was to be found divining with wax in a basin of water, in a fruitless attempt to see what fate would befall Bram. She saw now why the basin had not answered her; it had been Grimald who was marked for misfortune. Remorse made her heartsick; she felt weak and wanted to retch.

He led her to a chair, strangely calm himself, soothing her.

"Shhh ... shhh ... listen. Cait, look at me. It will turn out all right. You'll leave tomorrow, the three of you—I'll put you and the boys on a boat to Chameol. Iiliana will know what to do. I'll close the house and follow as soon as I can."

She nodded, holding fiercely to his hand.

"Oh, Badger ... I haven't loved him as I should have. First I was mourning Bram, then Rowan—"

He gave her a gentle shake. "Hush. No more of this."

It was only then that they noticed Bram sitting quietly

in one corner of the kitchen, his eyes strangely magnified by the lenses of his spectacles.

"Go to bed," said Binder. "I'll be up in a little bit to tuck you in. Go on."

Wordlessly he went, like a clockwork boy.

~❦~

The next day dawned cold, with a film of ice on the water pail. Binder had been up all night, first packing, then relieving Caitlin at Grimald's bedside. Caitlin had been to bed for an hour or two at his insistence. At dawn she was in the garden, covering with moss those herbs that would survive the winter, harvesting what would not. She seemed relieved to have a plan of action and eager to have the journey already behind her.

The boys had been told they were going to Chameol, to see their Aunt Iiliana. Each was allowed to take a few of his special things, so long as they were not heavy. Grimald was agonizing over his choice: He wanted to bring his vole's skull but was afraid he might lose it. In the end he decided to leave it behind in favor of the playing pieces for liar's checkers, good for passing time on the voyage.

"I was on a ship before," he said suddenly.

Bram glanced up from his own packing, an uneasy expression on his face. "Were you?"

Grimald stared past Bram, as though at a memory, a shadow just behind him. "And it was a boat, really, made of wicker, like an eel trap. I was just a baby. Mama was with me—" He stopped, frowning.

Behind his spectacles Bram's eyes were strangely bright. "No. Someone else. A woman with hands like paws."

"Yes . . . Her name was—"

"Ordella."

The boys looked at one another, each frightened: Grimald at remembering what common sense told him he could not possibly recall, Bram at his changeling visions. For in his mind had risen, clear as life, the picture of a small, scurrying woman whose smile showed a row of pointed teeth. To her breast she clutched an eel trap containing a baby with yellow eyes, a baby that did not, could not cry.

"You were there, too," whispered Grimald.

Bram nodded. "Yes. She brought you, and took me away."

Suddenly, Grimald knew everything, knew why his skin was ruddy and his hair neither fair nor ink-black but fox-red, knew why his mother sometimes looked at him the way she did, why his parents argued about him, why once, long ago, he had caught his father crying.

And he was running, down the stairs, out of the house, through the herb garden and into the woods, running without seeing, running without feeling his feet on the ground or his heart pounding in his chest, feeling nothing but his ragged breaths and the drumbeat of his blood in his head, beating a chant: *Changeling. Goblin. Changeling.*

The branches of the trees reached out to catch at him, stinging his face. A twig caught him in the eye, but he ran on, tripping over roots, stubbing his toes on fallen branches and stones, running toward nothing, away from everything, as though he could change the truth by running into some other version of it. He would run straight into the Otherworld from which he had come, to which he belonged, to which he had always really belonged.

He foot landed on something slick, and before he realized his misstep he had broken through a glaze of ice and plunged into freezing water. As he fell, his head struck an overhanging rock, and Grimald sank, unconscious, beneath the surface.

❧

It is always prudent, where there are wolves, to hunt with a companion who can repel an attack should one somehow become unhorsed. When Galt suddenly decided to go hunting in the Weirdwood, he went alone, liking his own company little enough as it was and not wanting anyone else's. He took with him a bow and arrow capable of bringing down a stag but hardly a Direwolf.

As he rode he remembered with discomfort his encounter with the girl tailor. He remembered the wolfish snarl that had come out of her throat and half imagined he was being watched by Direwolves as he rode.

Which he was.

A sentry posted at the first fringe of trees had signaled an alert, which had passed through the ranks back to the lieutenant.

A wolfskinner! snarled the final messenger, a young male.

How foolish of him to venture into the wood, said the lieutenant, wonderingly.

Shall we kill him?

No—for now, watch him well. But show nothing—not your yellow eyes, not your white fangs.

When she heard the news, the matriarch of the Dire-wolves sang under her breath a song in Old Wolf, a sweet ritual song of revenge.

Now the pack flanked the intruder on three sides, hidden by the brush and bracken. Normally, Galt would have sensed their presence and taken steps to prevent an ambush, but his mind was occupied with other thoughts than hunting.

He was both desperate to see Ulfra again and terrified at the thought of seeing her. For the first time in his life, Galt had not the slightest idea what course of action he should follow. At the end of yet another sleepless night in which he had pondered it all for the hundredth time, Galt had saddled his own horse well before dawn and ridden out without a word to anyone as to where he was bound.

He was quite certain he was losing his mind. What else could explain the irrational thoughts that had beset him, thoughts of attaching himself to the most unsuitable female imaginable? She had bewitched him; that was the only explanation for it. He had given the fur-lined cloak to his housekeeper with instructions to burn it. Whether this was an attempt to win favor with the girl tailor or a mere preface to throwing himself on the same pyre, Galt had no idea.

Night air, unhappy liaisons, too much ale, the moon—all these things had no doubt driven him mad. Perhaps killing a deer would make all right with the world.

So he rode out. The wolves stayed well back, just close enough to keep him in sight.

The horse first? signaled the lieutenant of the left flank to the she-wolf.

Yes. But save the man for me.

Before Galt knew what was happening, the wolves appeared out of nowhere, more than forty of them, assembling on the path as though conjured from mist and shadow. Two wolves seized Galt's mount by her forelegs, while a third dispatched the unfortunate beast with a bite to the neck. With a shriek the horse sank to her knees beneath her rider, dead.

Galt screamed curses at the wolves, but they pressed so close that he had no room to fit an arrow to his bow. Then a wolf lunged at the bow and bit the string clear through. Unhorsed and unarmed, Galt prepared to die and racked his brain for a prayer, any prayer. But all that came to mind were oaths, and those profane.

Stay, said the she-wolf sharply.

The wolves suddenly drew back, flattening their ears in deference and glancing quizzically at the matriarch of the pack.

Don't you smell it? said the she-wolf, stepping up to sniff Galt's beard, his sleeve, his gauntlet. *She has left the mark of Her blood on him. He is Hers alone to kill.*

The left lieutenant stepped forward to smell for himself. *So it is.*

They apologized for the bowstring and the horse, then turned and dissolved back into the wood the way they had come.

It was some time before Galt was able to summon the presence of mind to slide from the saddle and find a stream to slake a throat parched with fear. That, and wash off the blood of his poor mare.

As he bathed, the prayers of his childhood came flooding over him, and he knelt in the cold water, muttering them feverishly, one after the other, wishing he had some offering to leave behind on the bank to mark this spot for future pilgrimages. At last he unbuckled his hunting knife and buried it in the streambed, where its jeweled hilt glittered beneath the swiftly moving water, bright with cold.

Upstream, something else glittered and caught his eye. Galt glanced up and was instantly transfixed by the sight that met his eyes.

A golden barge was just turning the bend in the stream. Its gilded prow burned in the sunshine of the clearing, casting back the bright sparkle of the stream, and its pennants fluttered in the breeze. But none of these rivaled the brilliance of the beautiful navigator.

The streambed was too shallow to be easily negotiated, and Ylfcwen had been obliged to abandon her throne to pole the barge around the corner. The effort had undone her silver hair from its careful arrangement, and the exertion had brought the lavender blood to her cheeks. A single silver droplet of elvin sweat sparkled like a bead of quicksilver below her queenly nose.

The barge made the turn and drifted further downstream before it came to a halt, its keel stuck in the pebbly bottom. For the first time the elf queen noticed the man bending his knee to her on the shore.

"Don't sit there staring," she snapped. "Help me get this thing up onto the bank."

Something in those opal eyes drove every thought but obedience from Galt's brain. Shoulder to shoulder (hers came only to his elbow), they pushed with all their might until the gilded prow of the barge had nosed onto the muddy bank. Then Ylfcwen scrambled back aboard and threw Galt the end of a cable. Together they dragged the boat the rest of the way out of the water.

"Cover it," she panted, and Galt did as he was told, disguising the barge with moss and ferns.

Ylfcwen was looking quite disheveled. There were twigs in her hair, and the hem of her skirt was dragging with the weight of water and mud. Paying Galt no more heed than if he were a dog or horse, she stripped off the dress; the wet jeweled silk made a strange sound as it was peeled off, a little like corn being husked and a little like ice cracking on a lake.

"Your handkerchief," she said to him, holding out her hand.

He surrendered it, and she spread it on the bank so

that she could kneel without muddying her knees, and washed the dress out in the water, wrung it out, and draped it over a branch to dry. Then, using the surface of the water as her looking glass, she put her hair to rights.

Elvish fabrics are strong and dry almost instantly; when Ylfcwen went to feel her dress it was dry enough to put on again.

She handed Galt back his handkerchief.

"Hook me." At his blank look she stared at him closely, wondering suddenly if he were simple or mad. "The hook at the top—I can't reach it. Fasten it."

He did so, and only then did he notice the wings, veined and iridescent, beginning to unfurl like new lilies. Their facets, catching the sparkle of the stream, were so like the texture of her gown as to be indistinguishable from it. Ylfcwen kicked off her jeweled ankle weights and floated up to hover above Galt's head, level with the top of a silver birch.

"Keep the weights, if you like," she called down to him. "They will fetch a fine sum. A reward for your trouble."

"I am much obliged to you," he said. At least his mouth formed the words; his throat didn't seem to be working.

She ascended in a lazy spiral, threading her way between the lower branches and finally through a hole in the canopy of the uppermost boughs, startling a bird from its perch. She hovered there, high above the Weirdwood, enjoying her first good aerial view of the world Above in several mortal lifetimes. The countryside was so cunning, with its hedgerows and fields dotted with haystacks. Beyond the fields a town lifted dull red chimneys and white spires to the sky. Far off, the palace glittered, bright banners tugging in the breeze.

Ylfcwen turned her wings this way and that until she caught a balmy current of rising air, and let herself be lofted higher and higher, carried westward, more or less in the direction of the palace.

≈

By the time Binder found him, Grimald was past saving, past even the saving of the otherworldly arts. Binder hoisted him onto his back—so much lighter than a load of firewood—and carried him back to the house.

They gently laid him out on the kitchen table. Caitlin mutely went about lighting all the candles in the house. This time, she would do the fitting thing and stay up with the body the first night. She moved as though in a trance—unseeing, unhearing, unknowing. From a chair by the hearth, Binder lifted a haggard face to watch her.

"Stop it, Cait." His words came out in a hoarse whisper.

She looked at him blankly and then turned back to the next candle.

"I couldn't for Rowan. I have to now."

As Caitlin lit the candle on the table near where Binder was sitting, he blew it out, and her taper as well.

She began to cry, shuddering with mute sobbing. He took her arm and gave her the chair and brought a blanket and a dose of something that tasted of bitter herbs and gin.

"It won't make me sleep?"

"No."

She sipped it, then half rose from the chair. "Bram . . ."

"It's all right. He's asleep in bed." He looked at her, then kissed her wrists. "I'll look in on him."

Bram was in bed, but not asleep. He was staring at the ceiling above his bed, trying to remember how the map went, over his bed in Ylfcwen's palace. Start at the center: Ylfcwen's palace. Now add the tunnels in gold, and the canals in silver. Then the gemfields and the hothouses and the firefly hatcheries and the pomegranate orchards. And then the wingless monsters, and the blue void.

But an unwanted thought intruded, no matter how hard he concentrated. Maybe you went to the blue void when you died. Maybe Grimald was there now, being tormented by wingless monsters.

He wondered what dying was like. He remembered his long dive when he and Ethold had escaped through the sacred lake, how his lungs had burned for want of air, how easy it had seemed at the time to simply breathe the water, but how some part of him had resisted the water, how some part of him had remembered what air was, and light, and life. And then there had been the beckoning surface, and the light beyond it.

By the time Binder looked in on him, Bram was asleep, twisted in the covers, one leg hanging out of bed. He still had his spectacles on. Binder removed them and put them on the table. Then he untangled the blanket and tucked the boy in.

Grimald's knapsack still lay on the other bed. The pieces to liar's checkers lay scattered on the bed; some lay on the floor. Before leaving the room, Binder picked up the much-prized vole's skull where it lay among the other treasures.

He first went down to the workroom to get a length of bookbinder's ribbon on which to thread the small skull. When he came back into the kitchen, the fire had died down and Caitlin was fast asleep. He took the empty mug from her lap and set it on the shelf.

The fire had kept the body warm. When he lifted Grimald's head to slip the ribbon over it, the boy's neck was warm to the touch. In the glow cast by the coals, Grimald's body seemed a statue on a tomb, still as marble, but for his hair. This had dried in the heat of the room and was standing up in fox-red wisps, the same in death as it had been in life.

Binder lit a taper from the coals and went around the room, relighting candles.

13

REVELATIONS

Iona sat in her room and thought. She had come out of her swoon to find that her shift had been changed for a warm, soft nightshirt, much like the one Columba had replaced with the bit of diaphanous nonsense. She had been tucked into the great curtained bed. Beside the bed there was a tray on legs, which held a covered dish and a selection of books: some ballads (long banned and very hard to find) and a natural history with colored woodcuts.

She was most of the way through the natural history when she thought to look under the cover of the dish. The silver dome, when lifted, revealed a plate of cold partridge, cheese, and pickles, and a note:

> I know I cannot possibly explain *myself*, but when you are ready, will you at least let me explain my motives?
>
> Your friend,
> Fel

"And well you ought to," Iona muttered, picking up a pickle and going back to a passage on the spinning mechanism of spiders. When she had finished the book, she ate the partridge and then slept a little, until she awakened to a knock at the door.

It was the housekeeper, looking not at all surprised.

"The mistress—Master Fell that was—wishes me to tell yourself that she has gone out and expects to be gone for some hours and most strenuously urges you to make yourself at home in the rest of the house." This speech delivered, the woman craned her neck slightly, as if to peer around the doorjamb. "May I air the bedding?"

Iona dug down to the bottom of her trunk for her most worn-out muslin and her stained workroom smock with the large pockets. In this armor, she ventured downstairs.

By day the rooms were airy and flooded with light. There was no great dining hall, but a smaller salon with a table that might seat eight comfortably. This opened into a modest library whose shelves gaped here and there. The gaps, however, were free of dust; the books had perhaps been recently sold. If the choicest volumes had been pawned, Iona longed to know what they must have been, for the selection that remained was splendid, if small.

She came next to a workroom, much of which was taken up by a massive wooden contraption. A wooden frame slid into place beneath an iron plate held in place between two huge beams. A lever turned a giant screw and lowered the plate until it touched the wooden frame.

Why, she thought, it's like the press I use for my prints. But the plate in place on the bed of the press was like no woodblock she had ever seen. Small, irregular pieces of metal had been fitted together in rows within a wooden frame, with thin pieces of lead between each row. After some study, Iona realized that the individual pieces of metal were runes, carved backward in raised relief.

"What do you think?" said a voice at the door.

It was Fell—or Fel, as she had written it—in man's dress again. Iona tried to muster some indignation, but only said, "How is it done?"

"They are cast, actually. First I carve the letter on a steel punch, then strike the punch into soft metal, usually copper or brass. Then I pour hot lead in."

Iona nodded, running her hand over the surface of the strange metal block. "So you can reuse them—you only have to carve them once."

Fel smiled. "Exactly."

"The press must have cost a fortune."

"A small one, anyway: most of your dowry. I hoped you wouldn't mind." Fel had taken off her hat and gloves and now shook out her light brown hair. "Do you mind if I don't change? I confess I've come to prefer this attire."

"Who am I to dictate to my lord and master?" Iona thought she had spoken without sarcasm, but Fel blushed furiously.

"I suppose I have put off this explanation long enough. Here, let's go to the library."

"At first, I did it for the most selfish of reasons: money, and my freedom." She smiled. "For me, they were the same. I was the youngest child of a goldsmith, and his only daughter. He died, and my brothers were some of them dicers and all of them bad at business. So there was no dowry for me; nothing for me but to make the best marriage I could.

"And I could not bear it! My father had taught me his trade; I was a skilled metalworker, so I thought that perhaps I could make my own living. But no guild would have me. And I was no beauty: The only offers for my hand were from men my father's age—or older.

"In desperation, I sought out a marriage broker. She suggested that, while I could not pass for a beauty, I might make a credible man. I am overtall, wide of shoulder, slight of hip; my hair is mouse brown; my feet, hands, nose, all unwomanly large. Grievous flaws in the figure of a woman, they are favored in a man." Fel paused in her story, as though struggling to find the words to make her case before a judge.

"Will you believe me, poor deceived Iona, that when I first heard it I thought it a heartless, a reckless scheme? But her arguments were compelling, and so I found myself watching you from that upstairs window. And once I saw you, I knew marriage to the sort of suitors who had courted me would—not *break;* there would be no breaking *you*—but somehow *reduce* you. You, your work, would never have been the same. I couldn't bear to see that happen."

Iona had sat quietly, letting Fel's words wash over her. At last she turned up a face devoid of expression.

"What is your real name, then?"

"Felicity. But my brothers always called me Fel."

Iona smiled wanly. "There was something all along that seemed ... out of kilter. The way you shunned strong light; you never took your hat off, or your gloves. . . ."

"Yes. I had to keep my face in shadow as much as possible, and while my hands are large, my wrists are a woman's." Fel laughed. "The *hardest* thing was not losing my temper with you! My speaking voice is low enough, but when I'm really angry it climbs an octave. Honestly, sometimes you were incredibly—"

"Provoking?"

"Well, yes."

"It's all right. Other people have told me the same thing." She was silent for a moment, running her finger along the brim of the soft hat.

"You might have let me in on it, you know."

"The broker forbade me—if the match should not come off, or if you should confide in a maid, it would have meant an end to the scheme for all the others."

"The others!" A smile tugged at the corner of Iona's mouth. "I see. What happens now?"

"Well, in a few weeks, I will meet with an untimely accident. . . ."

Iona looked at Fel, uncertain whether she was serious. Then she began to understand.

∽

Entering the pantry, the unflappable Winsom dropped the sickroom tray in startlement.

Seated at the table by the window was an elf, her wings furled and folded neatly across her back. She had recently flown: The wings were flushed with violet blood, making them shimmer like opals. The gown she wore, an ethereal confection of silk and crushed pearl, was hardly seemly.

Her presence had a strange effect on the objects in the pantry; beside her, the copper jam kettle on the wall took on the appearance of a gong, and the ranged jars of spices seemed offerings at an altar.

Ylfcwen set down the letter (from Winsom's second cousin Elga), now bedribbled with pink stains. At her elbow, the bowl of fruit Winsom had saved to make a plum flummox was sadly depleted. Ylfcwen licked plum juice from her fingers and bent to pick up the medicine bottle that had skittered across the tiles to stop at her feet. She read the label, sniffed the cork, and made a face.

"Good heavens! If *that's* what you're dosing him with, no wonder he's at death's door." She sighed. "I suppose I had better see him."

Winsom gathered enough wits to object. "The doctor said no one was to see him."

"Well, obviously he didn't mean me. I'm royal and I'm a relation. Last I knew, that gave me some kind of rank in the sickroom."

❧

"Ethold."

Lord Gobeleyn heard his goblin name and opened his eyes.

"Mother. Majesty. I am honored on two counts."

"You look dreadful."

"Do I? I wouldn't know. Winsom is superstitious about mirrors in sickrooms." Speaking was an effort; he had to close his eyes.

"With what that quack is dosing you with, they should fit you for a shroud and be done with it. I wouldn't let him near a hangnail of mine."

"Have you a better plan of treatment?"

"A remedy never known to fail. You will return Below at once."

He searched her features for a clue to her humor and swore softly. "I believe you mean it," he said wonderingly. "Tell me, what has brought about this change of heart?"

She related the story of her house arrest. In the middle of her tale, Ethold fell into a fit of convulsive, silent coughing. She leaned forward, an anxious feeling in the pit of her stomach. Then she realized he was laughing.

"That poor hunter's face! I wish I had seen you in that barge."

"I don't see what's so funny."

"No, you wouldn't." Suddenly all the laughter left his eyes. "It's a pity that you didn't come a few days ago."

"Why is that?"

"It might still have made a difference. But there's no helping it, now. I'm dying."

Cold fear bit at Ylfcwen's heart. "A dramatic gesture, I'll grant you, but completely unnecessary under the circumstances. I am prepared to abdicate so that you can take the crown."

"But I don't want the crown. I've lived Below as the Pretender and I didn't fancy it. I don't imagine I'd like Goblin King any better. Besides, I'm ready to die. I *want* to die."

She placed her hands over his mouth in alarm. "Don't say that!"

He removed her hands. "Listen to me. I am tired of living. I've been half alive since Vervain died. The only thing that kept me going was getting Pending away from you and the Royal Household Agency."

"You are not going to die," Ylfcwen said peevishly. "I won't permit it."

"Then I am afraid I will have to disobey you," Ethold said, a wraith of a smile playing over his lips. "But promise me something. There is a boy. He came to town to look for someone. He went down the wrong alley and was fleeced by some thugs. I took him in. His name is Nix."

Ylfcwen discovered that swallowing had become uncomfortable. "Nix," she repeated, and her voice sounded thick and unfamiliar. Was she crying?

"He needs to be taken in hand, or he'll fall in with a bad lot. Take care of him. He won't heed Winsom, but he'll heed you. Mother! Are you paying attention at all?"

"Yes, yes: Won't heed Winsom; a bad lot." Her sleeve of crushed pearl was useless as a handkerchief. The tears rolled down her cheeks unchecked.

"Then promise me you'll look after him."

She promised, and Ethold fell back against the pillows, satisfied. The conversation had sapped him, and the light behind his eyes seemed dimmer.

"I brought something for you," she said. She unwrapped the toy barge and placed it on the coverlet where he could see it.

He smiled and took her hand. When Ylfcwen felt his pulse, the last of her hope slipped away. His pulse was rapid and uneven. It grew weaker beneath her fingers, and after a few minutes it stopped.

Ylfcwen sat and looked at his features; they were peaceful, and for the first time she saw in them a likeness to herself. She tried to rise from her seat on the edge of the bed, but lead seemed to flow in her veins; she couldn't move. The Royal Household Agency published a pamphlet on the Correct Forms of Grief and the Degrees of Mourning. She had been made to commit it to memory as a girl and could remember none of it now, only a rumor of a queen long ago who, out of grief for her dead consort, had torn out her own wings and gone to wander Above.

Well, she was already Above, so there seemed no need to tear out her wings. She had the distinct feeling they were going to come in handy still. She could have used a short flight around the garden to clear her head, but there was that boy to deal with and that person in the pantry to tell. Ylfcwen went to find them, not missing the light silver music of her old ankle weights, for her feet were heavy enough now.

❧

What woke Caitlin was the sound of the last candle guttering out in its own wax. She sat upright in the chair for some minutes, trying to remember how she had fallen asleep there. Then her eyes fell on the body on the table. Before she could shut them out, the events of the previous day flooded into her mind.

She rose from the chair and went to look in on Bram. Binder had fallen asleep beside him; the two pairs of spectacles lay side by side on the table between the beds.

She went back to the kitchen and forced herself to

approach the table. After she made herself take the first look, it wasn't as bad as she'd feared. Grimald's body was as ruddy in death as it had been in life. The fall through the ice had left no mark: There was not a scrape or a bruise on him.

Caitlin went to the chest and took out towels and a length of clean linen for a winding sheet. From the cupboard she took the funeral herbs she would need, beeswax for filling his ears and nostrils, and a seed cake for his mouth. Then she set some water to warm, not the water hauled daily from the stream, but the springwater she kept in a covered pail for compounding her herbal tonics. It did not matter to Grimald whether the water was cold or not. She was only warming it so that her own hands were not frozen as she bathed him.

When the water had warmed enough, Caitlin dipped in the sponge and began to wash him, singing lightly under her breath. She did not sing the proper songs, the ancient ones handed down to be sung during these chores. And she did not sing mournful songs. Instead she sang a cradle tune about the fox in the moon. That was what she had called him when he got a dreamy look on his face: her fox in the moon.

Suddenly she snatched her hand back as if burned: *His eyes were open.*

She let out her breath slowly, willing her heart back to a slow rhythm. She had lifted Grimald's head to wash the back of his neck; the movement had probably caused his eyes to open. Much as she hated to, she should find some coins to put on them. Caitlin reached over to draw the eyelids down again.

The eyes followed the movement of her hand.

Suddenly she remembered the toothache spell she had cast on the mice. Her voice shaking, she began to sing the ancient washing song backwards. It took all her concentration to reverse the notes and syllables, and she almost forgot to breathe as she did it. When she finished the washing song, she began the sheet-winding song. On the second verse, a muscle convulsed in the boy's throat.

At this sign she lifted him from the table and struck

him sharply between the shoulder blades. A trickle of dark water escaped his lips, but there was no other response. The eyes, when she looked at them, were fixed and glassy.

Had it been her imagination after all, fatigue, a trick of grief? Perhaps the eyes had moved, not with life, but with some last twitch of liveliness when all other life had fled the body. It was known for bodies to play such tricks, the lungs to draw a sudden disconcerting breath when the body was rolled in the sheet.

After a moment she collected herself and resumed the task of bathing him, passing the sponge over his face, tenderly washing his eyelids. She had not wrung enough water from the sponge; some of it ran down his cheeks and chin, into his ears and parted lips.

He frowned and coughed. His eyes flickered open, and the light of memory was in them, and reason's spark. He had been restored to her, through some miracle, just as he was.

Caitlin found she was weeping and laughing at the same time.

"My little fox! You always did hate water in your ears. . . ."

⤝⤞

Binder remembered Sleeker, and how the otter's wounds had vanished after being washed with springwater. Then Caitlin recalled visitors to the spring, gathering the water in bottles. It was a cure-all, they had told her. Good for the blood and the complexion and the circulation of the feet. Caitlin saw no harm in letting them collect as much as they needed for their remedies. She had even seen it for sale in the town, in bottles marked "Miracle Revivifying Tonic."

But now Caitlin wondered whether it was more than good, pure water. When Grimald was able, they took the boys and set out for the spring.

Two things struck her immediately as they approached the pool. The first was the moss: Beneath a crust of frost it was still green and living. The second was a turtle resting near the water's edge. Its shell had been damaged, perhaps in a tug-of-war between two fox kits. The damage should have killed it, but the edges of the shell showed signs of mending.

They all took sticks and began to break up the ice that covered the pool. Beneath the ice the water was perfectly clear; they could see to the bottom, which appeared to be covered with moss.

"It's tiled!" said Binder. Sure enough, here and there where the moss was thin, a pattern was visible of squares fitted together.

Caitlin began to dance on the edge in impatience. "And I think I know what's underneath those tiles!"

"Mother," said Bram suddenly, "let me dive. I did before, when I came up from Below. I held my breath a long time, and the water was at least as cold as this."

Binder was unpersuaded and Caitlin was of two minds. In the end it was Grimald who convinced them.

"It's magic, isn't it? I don't think he *can* drown in it. Besides, we can tie a rope around him, and if he gets into trouble, he can pull on it, and we will pull him up."

Bram was diving back to the Otherworld, his hand held tight in Ethold's, the dark waters closing around him. The water seemed to shimmer with light, and the light was a kind of music, the tremor of a string that had been plucked. He didn't need to kick; the water drew him down.

It was easy to pull the moss away. The square tiles formed the border of a mosaic; in it, a woman stood by a fountain at the center of a maze. In one hand she held an elder branch. Her other hand pointed to the ground at her feet.

The tile she was pointing to was larger than the rest, and it had a half circle cut out of one edge. Bram wedged his thumb into the space and pulled up the tile.

Beneath the tile there was a metal box, its lid free of rust and embossed with runes. It was too heavy to lift, but the iron ring in its center seemed sound. Bram untied the rope from around his waist and fastened it to the iron box. Hoping his knot would hold, he gave the rope three sharp tugs, and the box began its ascent to the surface. Bram followed it, kicking for all he was worth.

It took all Caitlin's determination not to open the box on the spot. They had to get Bram home to a warm fire, and she wanted to have her tools beside her—if the book disintegrated when she opened it, there would be a better chance of saving a portion of it.

Both boys were bundled into the big chair and given cider as hot as they could drink it. Caitlin brought down her tools—the soft, small brushes and bone paper knife—while Binder spread a cloth over the kitchen table.

The box was set on the cloth and examined. It had no visible hinges or clasp. Caitlin read the runes on the lid: "And they shall all be healed, made visible and made one."

It was hard to read the rest of the runes; while the box was not rusted, it was discolored. Caitlin took a soft cloth and began to rub the remaining runes clean. With the slight pressure a catch slid out from a recess. Caitlin pressed it, and the top panel of the box sprang up, revealing a leather book satchel.

The boys leaped out of the chair and pressed close.

"It's dry!" Caitlin said wonderingly.

Binder reached in and took out the satchel. It was the kind once used to carry sacred books, in the days when reading was forbidden, when books were used to bless crops and launch ships and cure cattle of disease.

"Careful," Caitlin murmured. "It may be protected by some kind of mischief."

Binder shook his head. "No. We found it: we unlocked the box. I think we're home free." He undid the buckle and drew out the book.

The sight of it drove the power of speech from them, and they could only stand and gaze in wonder.

The Book of Healing was bound in boards covered with silver. The cover showed a knot garden with a fountain at its center. The flowers in the garden were worked in pearls and precious stones. On the petals of a rose rested a topaz-and-onyx bee no bigger than a barley grain. The herbs were all accurate. They found feverfew, and harefoot, and sweet balm.

"Open it!" said Bram, his eyes shining.

"Yes," said Grimald. "Open it!"

The pages were pristine and intact. Plant after plant leapt from the pages as if it had been pressed between them and not merely painted: allheal, hedge-maids, pretty mugget, ruffet, stinking goosefoot, wake-robin. The colors of the plants were fresh and intense, and as the pages were turned they seemed to give off a crushed green smell. Beside each plant was a column of strange runes that listed the animal that had dominion over the plant, its mortal and elvish names, and the phase of the moon during which it was most potent.

Binder, looking up, saw Bram reading over his mother's shoulder. Bram had taken off his spectacles to dive; they were in Binder's pocket, forgotten. Binder started to say something, then checked himself as Bram turned to Grimald, eyes bright.

"This one's called goblin's ears!"

14

A CHANGE OF HEART

Berthold William Alfonse, Crown Prince of Twinmoon, was wed to his highly suitable princess in a ceremony that lasted three days; the toasting, feasting, and general making merry would go on for twenty-one days, a dizzying succession of masked balls, pageants, and almsgiving, during which prodigious amounts of wine and roast meat were made away with and much royal goodwill dispensed to the needy. There were commemorative statues to unveil and almshouses to dedicate. The palace's vast menagerie and gardens would be open to all and sundry. But no event would draw a larger crowd of gawkers than the ritual burning of the marriage bed.

The special gilded bed in which the newlyweds had spent their wedding night was dragged to the center of the tourney fields and set alight. Fireworks sewn into the mattress exploded and lit up the night sky. With every explosion the crowd roared and toasted the royal couple's babes-to-be. From carts, vendors sold cakes called burn-the-beds: Sweet with orange rind and dense with seeds, they were dipped in ale between toasts.

The prince stood on the balcony of the palace and watched the fireworks. Theirs was a predicament, he had to admit, but they would extricate themselves from it somehow. In public they would, of course, have to keep up appearances, but how they conducted their lives in private was no one's business but their own. After a tasteful interval, they could move to separate bedchambers. Then she might conduct herself as she pleased, so long as she was discreet.

But he had been unable to make the matter understood to his young bride. Behind him, she sat on the real marriage bed and wept quietly.

"Don't," he said without turning around. "Please don't."

She began to sob in earnest, hot tears falling from her dark spaniel eyes.

He went and sat beside her on the bed and chafed her hand. "Here; dry your eyes. We'll just have to make the best of this. I don't like it any more than you do."

The crying had brought some color into her face, and the tears had stuck her eyelashes together in little clumps that were curiously fetching. She gazed up at him, her face flushed and her girlish bosom heaving. Berthold took pity on her, and kissed her.

She kissed him back, an unpracticed but wholehearted kiss. The feel of her tiny shoulders beneath his hands drove reasonable arguments, separate bedchambers, and tasteful intervals from the prince's mind. For a moment, he ceased to hear the sizzle and bang of fireworks out on the old tournament grounds.

He pushed her gently but firmly away. It had been a lapse, that was all. He would be careful not to forget himself again.

But the princess's eye had in it a gleam that had not been there before, and in the lift of her pretty chin there was a suggestion of pleased stubbornness. She was a lever who had found her fulcrum, and was now confident that she could move her boulder. She poured her husband a glass of wine and drew him toward the window.

"Whatever you think best, Berthold. But may we watch the fireworks just a little while longer, before we retire?"

◇◇◇

A light veil of mist was falling as the mourners gathered in a remote corner of the graveyard, hard against a hillside and rather more overgrown than the rest. The motley band stood around an open coffin. The keeper of the Turtle and Rose was there, and Trammel, the boy actor, with the rest of the troupe. Winsom was there, with Nix and an odd woman none of the actors knew, the hood of a cloak pulled close around her face.

Lord Gobeleyn had expressed his wish to be buried according to the rites of the theater. One by one the mourners filed by the casket, which in accordance with custom contained a coffin bell, a precaution against interring those who were not yet dead. Each mourner dropped a small offering into the coffin, took up the pen provided and made his mark in the ink upon the winding sheet, and finally slapped the bell. When it was Nix's turn, he found affectionate insults scrawled all over the shroud. Nix dropped his own offering (a handful of sawdust from the fencing dummy and a few cherry pits) and stepped away. He was surprised to feel Winsom slip a hand into his— small, warm, and surprisingly strong.

Lord Gobeleyn was not in fact inside the winding sheet. His place had been taken by a man who had gotten drunk during the prince's wedding and drowned in a fountain. Ylfcwen would rather have given her son a funeral in the elvish style, sent him across the sacred lake in a burning barge, but she had been unable to think of a way to get Ethold's body to the barge's hiding place in the wood. Then Ylfcwen had seen the preparations for the royal marriage-bed burning. She thought he would have liked the joke of it, and the rockets, and the revelry swirling around him.

The coffin was closed and lifted onto the shoulders of the actors, who slid it into place in the crypt where all the past lords of the House of Gobeleyn slept their eternal sleep. As they walked from the hillside, Ylfcwen linked her arm with Nix's.

∽∾

Very early on the morning after the burial, the funeral party at the Turtle and Rose began to break up. Trammel, who had raised countless toasts to speed the new ghost to its rest, was loudly protesting the end of the party and cajoling the mourners to raise their glasses a last time.

While he was less conspicuous, Nix was far worse for drink. Winsom brought the carriage around, and, supporting Nix between them, the landlord and Ylfcwen began to lead Nix to the door. Plastered beside the entrance to the tavern was a handbill.

"It's just an old notice—a call from the Valet Royal for manikins," said Winsom. "They stopped looking long ago."

Nix shook his head vehemently. "No, no! The other . . ."

Over his protests, they firmly led him to the carriage and bundled him in.

"*Dog's Muzzle* . . . ," he whispered fervently, gazing up at Ylfcwen with an imploring look.

"Yes, yes, dog's muzzle," said Ylfcwen soothingly, tucking a robe around him before seating herself at the other end of the carriage. Watching him fencing, she had begun to think that Nix would need only a little grooming in order to make a Consort. But she was a queen without a court, and besides, she had promised to find his what's-it—his Ulfra—for him. It was a pity. With that otherworldly coloring and talent for fencing, Nix figured in her daydreams less as a Consort than as an agent of revenge against the director of the Royal Household Agency.

She glanced over at him, sliding her feet farther over to one side. He did not *look* as though he would be sick, but one could never tell, and her new kid slippers had come dear.

This was the thing that had caused Nix such agitation: Next to the handbill calling for manikins was an old notice announcing the final performances of *The Dog's Muzzle*. Unlike the original playbills, which had featured the girl tailor in a dog mask, leaning on giant shears, the final version showed her wearing wolf's ears, flogging the character of Gout. The cartoon was captioned with a verse from the play that had become a popular expression around town:

> Come a day, sir, yes, sir,
> The wolf will come and beat on you!

But later the cream-and-black had blotted the words from Nix's brain, and the cartoon was forgotten.

～～

In the space of a few days, their little household had fallen into a comfortable constellation. Ylfcwen had resigned herself to the prospect of having her wings painfully bound to her back, when Winsom remembered the fashion for wing cases. Thus attired, she might move in society accepted as a mortal woman, Lady Gobeleyn, sister of the deceased.

Ylfcwen's wings had been the least of her worries. She lived in dread of Nix leaving her to try his hand with the actors. If Nix left, Winsom would soon follow, and she would be alone. She said her Fates every night and lit a candle against them leaving.

One afternoon, as she strolled along the long, vaulted gallery of mirrors, she had suddenly been seized by an irresistible urge to try out her wings. The effect was rather nice: endless copies of herself reflected back into eternity in the glass. She executed a slow roll and tumble, and her mirror selves did likewise, like the view through a kaleidoscope room. When she had grown a little too dizzy doing this, she flew up to inspect the fresco on the ceiling. As she had suspected, the elves were badly done, their expressions annoyingly insipid, their wings anatomically inaccurate.

A muffled cry had made her glance down. She saw Nix, standing stock-still in a shaft of mote-heavy sunlight, as though overtaken where he stood by a shower of molten gold. The sight of his uplifted face, the rapture on it and the wonder, let Ylfcwen know that she had made her first conquest.

～～

Ulfra was alone in the workroom of the Cat's Face. It was their customary closing day, and Tansy was spending it with Lady Twixtwain. Ulfra had begged off—since their last conversation, she had been mildly dreading seeing Lady Twixtwain again, though, if pressed, Ulfra could not have said why.

Things were much upset at the house in Goldenmouth

Street; Lady Twixtwain was having new carpets put down, and when the old ones were pulled up, the floors beneath were found to be wormy. So she had the floorers in; the clamor of hammers and scraping of planes on wood seemed to sound throughout the house long after the workmen had gone home. Both Opaline and her owner were in a state of high nervous agitation, but it was the dog who was sent to stay at the Cat's Face. "After all," said Lady Twixtwain, "someone has to make sure the carpenters don't sham the work or raid the wine cellar."

So, because Lady Twixtwain had a horror of slanted floors and tables with wobbly legs, Ulfra was in the workroom trying to figure out where a dress had gone wrong, and Opaline was curled up asleep on the rug near the workroom stove.

"What in heaven," muttered Ulfra, turning the garment around in her lap. It was a mess of muslin pattern, grey wool, pins, chalk lines, and loose basted stitches. It had been abandoned by the frustrated seamstress, and Ulfra had to straighten the garment out before the scheduled fitting the next day.

She had just begun to sort it out when Opaline lifted her head from the carpet and whimpered softly. The next moment, the shop bell rang. Ulfra picked up a stitch ripper and bent over her task; the shop was closed, and besides, it was after hours. Whoever it was would have to come back the next day.

Then she saw Opaline looking at her reproachfully.

"Oh, all right!" she said, setting down the dress. "I needed a stretch anyway."

For a moment she did not recognize him without the wolf-skin cloak. He'd been to a barber; his beard was newly trimmed. He still smelled of the leather (though he no longer wore the breastplate) and more faintly of the wine he had drunk with dinner, and the bayberry lotion with which the barber had anointed him. And there was something else—the faint tang of Otherworld.

"I've come for a shirt," said Galt.

"We're closed," she said.

"I know."

It was damp there, on the step. "You had better come in," she said grudgingly.

She was all business and did her best not to catch his eye as she rolled out bolts of muslin.

"This one isn't cheap, but it's the best in the shop. Is this shirt for every day or a celebration?"

"I hope for a celebration."

"Then I would make it up in this, if you like. It's brushed, so it has a slight nap on one side."

"I like it very much."

"You haven't felt it."

"I don't need to," he said gently.

Ulfra replaced the bolt in its bin. "You had better take your shirt off so I can try some pattern shirts on you."

As he unbuttoned the shirt, Ulfra wondered at the exquisite workmanship. It was made of humble muslin, but a skilled hand had fashioned those buttonholes. Looking up, she saw that Galt was more than usually florid.

"My sister makes them for me. She used to be a nun."

"She makes a fine buttonhole." He removed the shirt, and she was startled to see an irregular scar, pink and raised, among the grizzled hairs of his chest.

"I didn't always wear a breastplate," he said. "I once wrestled a boar and it caught me with a tusk." He smiled, recalling her words in the courtyard the day he had first seen her. "From the boar's point of view, I suppose it was the least I deserved."

She handed him a pattern shirt made up in inexpensive muslin. "Here, try this one." When he had put it on, she stood back and looked at him with a critical eye.

"That looks well on you. A little less fullness in the sleeves, I think, and the neck should be let out. I don't think it needs any decoration but the tuck work."

Galt considered his reflection in the mirror. "No, I don't think the king's guard will haul me in for breaking the sumptuary laws."

"Are you going to wear it at court?"

"I plan to wear it to a wedding."

His meaning was lost on her. Ulfra placed half a dozen pins in her mouth. Tansy was always scolding her, saying she would swallow a pin one of these days, but she hated wearing a pincushion on her wrist. She reached for the sleeve, to mark the spot where she would take it in. His hand came up and covered hers; it surprised her, that his hand was so warm. Suddenly she was overcome by a feeling strong and sharp; it was not fear, though it made her heart race, and it was not pain, though there was at its center a sweet ache.

"Look at me," he whispered. And at last she did, looked full into the depths of his dark eyes, and saw there the reflection of something so unlikely, so unexpected, that it was wonderful beyond imagining.

Galt reached up and very slowly began to draw the pins from between her lips, for it is a dicey business to kiss someone whose mouth is full of pins.

∽

"Things are all in an uproar," Tansy said. She was standing at the window, watching the passersby in Goldenmouth Street and seeing none of them. "I am sure I don't know what to do."

It was the day after Galt's visit to the Cat's Face, and Tansy and Ulfra had spent much of the night in earnest conversation.

"Now *there's* something to consider," said Lady Twixtwain thoughtfully. "Can two people even *have* an uproar? Wouldn't you ideally have to have at least three or four to do it properly?"

They were standing in Lady Twixtwain's house, in a spacious salon sadly denuded of its elegant furnishings. Beneath their feet the new floors had been sanded and rubbed with beeswax to a glassy sheen. Lady Twixtwain bent down and placed Opaline's ball in the center of the floor. After a second's hesitation, the ball rolled slowly but with gathering speed to one corner of the room. Lady Twixtwain pressed her lips together in a grim smile.

"Ah! I suspected as much, but I did not like to say anything until I had made my little test. But my woes are beside the point. Will she marry him, do you think?"

"Who knows? But what will happen to the Cat's Face, if she does? Our reputation rests on her fame, not mine.

What am I, without the prince's girl tailor?" Tansy put a hand to her mouth. "Listen to me! I should be wishing her happy."

"She is unschooled in love. When the novelty has worn off, perhaps this attachment will seem less compelling. I think Galt knows that and will not rush her to an answer."

"I fear she will rush him! I hate to think what might have happened, if I had not come home when I did."

Lady Twixtwain laughed at her friend. "Tansy! Listen to yourself!"

Tears welled in the leopard-woman's eyes. "I would not see her hurt, not for anything in the world."

"No, of course not. And if he is half as much in love with her as you suggest, neither would Galt. I will come and have a talk with her, but I can't stay long. I have carpenters to murder."

They found Ulfra filling the window with the half-models of the prince's wedding clothes. The royal commission had specified that the Cat's Face should make all the clothes half-size for an exhibition that would travel the length of the kingdom, raising money for the new almshouses and asylums. Ulfra had painted a woodland scene and poised the half-models around it on wire forms riding wire horses. A wire hawk paused on a gauntlet, ready to chase down a wire pigeon suspended from a string.

"It's marvelous!" said Tansy. "But how in heaven's name did you manage all this by yourself?"

"I'm not sure," Ulfra said, working another costume over its wire form. "I wanted something to do with my hands, I suppose."

Inside they found that the fabric in the bins had been reorganized by color, the floor swept, and the stove polished. A box of spangles, buttons, and beads had been turned out on the counter, where Ulfra had begun to sort them.

Tansy covered her mouth and sank into a chair, and Lady Twixtwain began to laugh.

"If it isn't Ella Cinders, sorting lentils from the ashes!" She seized Ulfra's hands and examined them closely. "Just as I thought. You're coming out in calluses, and there's stoveblack under your nails. Come, young woman," she said, taking her firmly by the elbow, "you and I are going to have a little chat."

"Well, do you *want* to marry him?"

"I don't know!" Ulfra said. "I can't leave the Cat's Face, and Tansy."

"Of course, you needn't marry him. A young woman in your position should not underestimate the importance of her independence. Especially if she has brains behind her pretty face."

"He says he will wait and ask me again in a year."

Lady Twixtwain smiled and laid a hand on Ulfra's cheek. "Then he is braver than I gave him credit for. Or more foolish."

But Lady Twixtwain saw something in the girl's eyes that made her think Galt would like Ulfra's answer when at last she gave it.

∽∾

The time came for Master Fell to meet his untimely demise. After much discussion, Felicity and Iona agreed Fell should be killed in an accident with the printing press. That way, no one would question the sealed coffin. They fashioned a body out of bars of lead wrapped in paper and linen and dressed in some of Fell's clothes.

"Are you sure it's heavy enough?" asked Iona.

"I was *pressed* to death!" cried Fel. "How heavy could I *be*?"

Burial took place in the part of the graveyard reserved for the grander tombs and vaults. Niccolaus and Ermingrude stood to one side with Columba and her betrothed, while Iona stepped forward to strew rose petals on the coffin. Another young woman, dressed in the green mourning reserved for relatives, stepped up and emptied a vial of ashes-of-roses over the open grave.

"Who is that?" Columba whispered.

"Some female relative of Fell's," said Ermingrude. "A sister, I think, just come from the nunnery."

Behind this conversation stood Lucivia, heavily veiled. She was watching the two mourners with some satisfaction.

The match seemed to have been a good one, and she liked to see her newlyweds doing well. She had heard that the young widow planned to carry on the work of Fell's printing shop. Broadsides had appeared in town announcing the opening of a press available "to print small volumes at modest cost with quality rivaling any copyist." Lucivia already had another match planned, between the youngest daughter of a wealthy ship's captain and a young woman with a great gift for music but without prospects for making a prosperous marriage.

Marriage seemed finally to be agreeing with Berthold, a fact that relieved the matchmaker considerably. As the court gossip mill ground it, the crown princess had stood up to her father and said that she intended to accompany the prince to the theater. They had their own private box, and so there could be nothing improper in it. Lucivia had gone herself and had been gratified to see the way the prince let his hand casually rest on the princess's knee. It seemed Berthold had finally realized the benefits of his situation.

The grave diggers stepped forward and tossed the first spadeful of earth onto the lid of the coffin.

"How I like that sound," Fel whispered to Iona behind her handkerchief. "Freedom!"

"Hold it till we get home, can't you? I think Columba suspects."

But Columba had worries of her own. Her affianced husband was a man of business, and he had expressed concern about the cost of her planned bridal attire. To pay a king's ransom for a gown to be worn but a few hours was madness, he said. Did she want them in the poorhouse before the vows were even said? Had she any idea what an ell of swansdown silk cost? As much as a carriage! She should prevail upon her father to make them a gift of the money, instead. So there was to be no watered-silk gown with pearled bodice, no elfsbreath overskirt with opal finish, no otter-skin gloves, no fur-trimmed traveling cloak.

He had already thrown down the gauntlet, saying he thought she might be married in Iona's gown, *made over*.

She quite hated him already.

⌘

There was great excitement in the Binder household as they prepared for a long-postponed visit from Iiliana. The Book of Healing was to be returned to Chameol, and the Binder family was going to accompany Iiliana on the voyage. The Book would be installed in the library at Chameol amid great celebrations.

Everything was ready for the visit. The various interior surfaces of the house had been swept, scoured, or polished. Provisions had been laid in: nestled in the coals of the hearth, an iron kettle of duck, sausage, and beans was beginning to release a mouthwatering aroma. The boys, already keyed to a high pitch of excitement, began to squabble over the pinecone animals they were making to decorate the dinner table.

"Take it back!" said Grimald, twisting his brother's arm.

"No! It *does* look like a skunk. Who ever saw a fox with legs that short?"

Badger looked up from the antlers he was whittling. "You two need to take the edge off your tempers before you cut yourselves. Here—why don't you go down by the stream and gather some moss for the animals to stand on? You can check the fish traps while you're at it."

They went off, after being sternly admonished not to tease the snapping turtle. Binder picked up Grimald's fox and smiled. It *did* look like a skunk.

⌘

Caitlin despaired of turning her workroom into a bedchamber befitting a former queen of Chameol. At last she sat down on the bed to catch her breath, casting a critical glance around the room. A linen runner transformed the ink-stained worktable into a washstand for the ewer and basin. The cot where she took her naps had been covered with a feather bed and counterpane borrowed from the Harrier farm. An earthenware pitcher held black branches with small scarlet berries. Not palatial, she thought, but it has a homely charm.

A crown of red hair appeared at the top of the ladder, followed immediately by Iiliana's laughing eyes.

"Careful!" cried Caitlin, as she was caught up in a fierce embrace. "I'm filthy."

"Never mind—I've been two weeks on a ship—I'm no rose myself," said Iiliana, holding Caitlin at arm's length. "My dear, my dear! How it mends my ragged soul to see you!"

Caitlin felt a sudden stab of relief that was as keen as anguish, and had to turn away. "Nice of Badger to tell me you'd arrived! Wasn't he downstairs?"

"I wanted to surprise you. Besides, I had a long letter for him from Elric, and he was instantly engrossed." A former knight of Chameol, Elric was Iiliana's brother and Binder's dearest friend.

"But I can't contain myself another minute," said Iiliana. "Take me to the *Book!*"

The Book of Healing was in the bindery among the roots of the oak with the red door. Powerful enchantments had spared it the ravages of flood, fire, and bookworms; eight-year-old boys, however, were another matter, and Caitlin had not been about to take chances.

Iiliana sat before the Book a long time, turning its pages silently, so that a casual observer might have thought it was a book she knew well. She asked once for more light and took from her pocket a jeweler's glass, which she fitted to her eye in order to examine a detail of one of the marginal paintings. At last she leaned back with a great sigh and sat a long time with her eyes closed. Just as Caitlin was beginning to wonder whether she had fallen asleep, Iiliana's eyes opened. They were full of tears.

"Well," she said in an unsteady voice, wiping them on her sleeve. "I could stand to wash my face, change my linen, and drink a pot of tea."

∽∾

"I have to admit, once the excitement wore off I was a little disappointed. I had hoped to find all four books together."

They had taken their tea out into the clearing to enjoy the last rays of light.

Iiliana bit her lip. "What was the rhyme on the cover? They shall be healed and made visible? Maybe we need to heal something before the others will come out of hiding."

"The strange thing is, I don't read that particular rune script well at all, yet I knew what the words meant. I understood what was *written* even when I couldn't make out the *writing*."

"I noticed that, too. The Keepers didn't know who would eventually find the book. Suppose they thought that reading might die out entirely. So they added a charm to help the reader along. We know of charms to keep someone from reading what they aren't meant to see. It only stands to reason that there would be an opposite kind of spell."

Just then the boys returned from the stream. Bram hung back as Grimald threw himself on Iiliana with a great, triumphant bellow. Her braids pulled down from their circlet and hanging to her waist, Iiliana lifted Grimald's hands from her eyes long enough to glance at Bram.

"Unhand me!" she said to Grimald, who wanted to know whether her ship had encountered whirlpools or sea monsters on the voyage. "Yes, the sea unicorns bored an enormous hole in the bow, and then we were sucked into the whirlpool. We had to take turns plugging the hole and bailing to get afloat again."

It was late when they sat down to supper. Down the middle of the table, the strip of moss had been arranged with ferns and pebbles in a miniature landscape, through which wandered the pinecone animals, one in front of each place. Binder had a badger, Caitlin a doe, Bram the disputed fox/skunk, Grimald an otter, and Iiliana a stag and boar (since the boys could not agree who should make the animal for the guest, they both had). Small rushlights flickered the length of the table, shining on the crockery.

After dinner, Caitlin sat and watched Iiliana as she brushed out her braids, her magnificent copper hair streaming over her shoulders in the flickering rushlight. She kept up a steady stream of jokes with Grimald on her left, quietly winning over Bram on her right.

What if our lots were reversed? Caitlin wondered. What if it were me sitting there, home triumphant from a mission to Twelvemoon, playing aunt to someone else's children? Before she could shut her mind to it, the troublesome thought had crept into her mind: What if she had remained on Chameol, had never married? She could have raised Grimald by herself, on Chameol. And there would never have been Rowan.

But with the thought came a sudden certainty: If she had not lost Rowan, Bram would never have been restored to her.

She drank her cider and caught Binder looking at her. He took her hand and pressed it gently.

"Wishing you were a seer on Chameol?"

"A little. Does it show?"

"A little." In the rushlight his blue eyes gave nothing away.

It was well past midnight when they finally went to bed. He was restless beside her, and the darkness between them seemed vast and thick with unspoken questions: Once on Chameol, would she want to remain? If it hadn't been for the boys, would she have left long ago?

But he did not speak then, so she did not have to find answers. She lay awake, listening to his troubled breathing slow and change its pace as he sank into sleep. When sleep came for her, Caitlin dreamed, as she so often did, of visiting Rowan's grave. When she arrived at the spot where they had buried her, she found the moss rolled back and the grave empty. Sitting nearby, washing her tail, was a vixen, the ruling animal of the fabled herb known as cheat-grave, named for its ability to bring people back from death's door.

"Where has she gone?" asked Caitlin.

"To the moon," replied the vixen. "She was really the moon's child. You could not have kept her."

Caitlin tried to curl up in the grave, but it was too small. As she tried in vain to pull in her elbows and knees, the vixen gazed down at her, head cocked to one side.

"*That* won't work," observed the vixen. "You will have to make your bed among the living."

Caitlin awoke and lay in the dark with the dream still vivid in her mind, using all her will not to get up and go through the woods to visit the grave.

Beside her Binder stirred.

"What is it? What's wrong?"

"Nothing. A dream."

"With you, a dream is never nothing." He meant it in jest, but it was a jest with a rueful edge. "I'm sorry." Trying to kiss her in the dark, he missed her mouth and laughed. "I can't see a damned thing! Where *are* you?"

"Right here," she said, and felt her heartbeat quicken.

When Caitlin finally awakened for the second time, it was late morning. She left Binder to sleep and made her way to the kitchen, where she found Iiliana yawning over her tea.

"I hope the boys didn't have you out checking bat nets at dawn."

"They did, but I was awake anyway. I confess I was up all night, poring over the book, half afraid it would disappear before I'd finished reading it, like Ella Cinders's carriage at midnight." Over the rim of her cup, Iiliana's eyes laughed disconcertingly. "You look as though you spent a sleepless night yourself."

Caitlin was maddened to feel herself blush like a new bride. "I never could hide anything from you."

"Forgive me—I can't help teasing. It makes me happy to see you lose sleep for a good cause." Iiliana searched her face. "Or am I wrong?"

Caitlin shook her head. "No. He and I have had our rough patches. I think we smoothed them out a little last night. What's this?"

On the table was a scrap of paper on which was written a short column of letters and numbers:

w 11

n 23

e 19

s 6

"Where did this turn up?" asked Caitlin.

"It fell out of the looking-glass frame when I was washing my face. I wanted to ask you what it meant."

"It's the tailor's riddle I wrote you about. 'Waist, eleven; neck, twenty-three; elbow, nineteen; shoulder, six.'"

"Oh, now I see. When I read it, I took them for the points of the compass."

Caitlin sank slowly into the other chair, a curious expression on her face. "Tiliana . . ."

"What? What did I say?"

"Of *course* they seemed like nonsense. They aren't tailor's measurements at all!"

15

THE TAILOR'S RIDDLE

"Upon my soul!" cried Bembo Gill, "if it isn't a pigeon among the cats!"

The unexpected messenger had landed on the sill, met one yellow-eyed feline stare, and had promptly flown to perch on the highest rafter, where it trained on the bookseller a beady eye, as if to say, Now what?

After rummaging in the tangle on the landing, Bembo finally unearthed the stepladder used to retrieve books from the highest shelves. It brought him level with the rafter. There was a capsule affixed to the pigeon's leg.

> Master Gill,
> If I may beg a favor, would you call on the proprietors of the Cat's Face in Everlasting Lane and tell them that I plan to pay them a visit tomorrow at noon on an urgent matter of great mutual interest? (Can you come, too? It involves the Books.)
>
> Your servant, C. Binder

Bembo seized the pigeon firmly and made his way back down the ladder. Holding the bird out of reach of the swarming cats, he went to the window.

"I imagine you will find your way home the same way you found me," he said as he released it. It was true, he thought: A pigeon under a spell looks much the same as any other.

∽∾

When they set eyes on the leopard-woman, Bram and Grimald stared and stared until Binder spoke to them sharply.

"Close your mouths, both of you, before you catch a fly! Excuse them," he said to Tansy. "They know better."

"Oh, let them look," she replied. "Can you blame them? Besides, I'm used to being stared at. After all, I made my living from it."

Another consequence of her days as a curiosity with Folderol's circus was that Tansy took the extraordinary in stride. She made a curtsey to Iiliana, High Counsel of Chameol and Ambassador to the Thirteen Kingdoms, as though she were any other customer, and nodded to Bembo Gill, not in the least put off by his moth-eaten attire or ragged ear. She heard Caitlin's story of the Book at the bottom of the spring with interest but no great show of surprise; Caitlin might as well have been describing the design of a gown she had seen.

"Let me see if I have this right," said Tansy carefully. "You think they changed *west* to *waist* and *north* to *neck*, in the hope that some apprentice through the years would notice that the measurements were nonsense."

"Yes," said Caitlin. "Only no one did. Even if they did notice the measurements were nonsense, they still had to figure out what they really stood for—points on the compass. Now, my guess is that the numbers stand for paces, or maybe tiles. I don't suppose this is the original floor?"

"I can't say for certain, but it *is* very old. The tile layer we had in to do the new rooms had not seen its like."

The stone tiles were black and smooth, so tightly joined that there was not room to fit an eyelash between them.

"Then I think it would be tiles, not paces. Now, if only we knew where to begin."

"The room isn't square," said Binder, who had been silently counting tiles. "It's longer than it is wide."

"The right wall was moved in to make a closet," said Tansy.

"Then the original center of the room . . . was about here," said Binder, pausing at the spot.

Caitlin kneeled to examine the tile. "No different from the rest."

Bembo Gill began to laugh. "Look up!"

At regular intervals along the ceiling, there were hooks for hanging lamps; the iron of the hook directly overhead had been worked in the shape of a hand pointing down.

Starting with the tile below the hook, Grimald and Bram counted out the tiles: eleven west, twenty-three north, nineteen east, six south. Incised very faintly on the surface of the last tile was a hand pointing up.

Like the tile at the bottom of the spring, this had a thumbhole cut from one edge. It proved to be hinged to the tile next to it and lifted quite easily. They all crowded around to see.

There was an iron strongbox, the twin to the one that had been pulled from the spring in the Weirdwood. Caitlin let out her breath; she had been half expecting to find a tiny staircase spiraling down into the Otherworld.

The box was laid on the worktable. It was not so discolored as the first; the dark, glossy metal seemed untouched by time. The lid bore a different inscription: "That which was destroyed shall be recalled from dreams and longing."

Like the first, it had no latch. Unlike the first, no amount of polishing would open it. Caitlin tried, then Iiliana, and so on around the room.

"I don't seem to have the magic touch either, I'm afraid," said Ulfra, handing the box back to Caitlin.

At these words Bembo jumped as though stuck with a pin. He traded a meaningful glance with Caitlin: He was the only person in the room with a changed shape.

"That just leaves Bembo, I think," she said, handing him the box.

At the bookman's touch, the hidden clasp sprang open, revealing a book satchel like the first. The book he removed from it was bound in plain oak boards.

"It doesn't look like one of the Books of the Keepers," said Caitlin.

"Well, we'll know as soon as I get this clasp undone," said Binder.

"Not one of the Books, but something better!" said Bembo, rubbing his hands together. Caitlin looked at him; he had had just that gleam in his eye once before, when speaking of the love of books that had cost him his true shape. He turned now to Iiliana. "It's nothing less, I'll wager, than the catalogue of the lost library of Iule."

"That's done it," said Binder, as the clasp gave way.

It was as simple within as it was without: The pages were closely written in black ink, with no decoration of any kind. It appeared to be a list of books. The pages were ruled, divided into columns for the title, author, and donor of each volume. At the end of each entry some words had been added by a different pen in an ink that was somewhat browner.

"Oak gall," said Binder.

"These runes were written by a second scribe and, if I'm not mistaken, in great haste," said Iiliana.

Caitlin bent over Iiliana's shoulder. "In the hours before the Keepers fled?"

"Maybe they tell where the books were hidden," said Grimald.

"One would think so," said Iiliana. "Unfortunately, I've never seen this particular rune tongue before and I haven't the slightest idea what this says."

"I can read them."

Bram had spoken without meaning to and now, finding them all looking at him, he stared, tongue-tied, at the floor.

"Go on," Bembo urged gently. "You can read them. . . ."

His tongue suddenly loosened, and the words tumbled out in a hurry. "They're elvish. The Chronicles were written in them. I had to do my lessons in them every day. I can still read them." He pointed to the first line. "It says, 'In the name of the blessed sage Thyllyln, who kept and hid you, I bid you appear.'"

His words echoed in the workroom, then faded away,

leaving them standing in a charged silence they were afraid to break. Then Iiliana laughed.

"Gracious, I half expected—"

She was interrupted by a cry of surprise from Tansy, who stood pointing at the padded board used for pressing clothes.

"The goose! Everyone, look at the goose!"

Sitting upright on its stand, the tailor's iron had begun to glow and hiss. Soon the glow had spread and deepened until the whole iron was fire red. The hissing rapidly rose to a kettle's screech, and soon the iron was white-hot. The screech grew so loud that the boys covered their ears. Then suddenly it ended in an explosive pop that made them all jump.

When the steam cleared, the goose had vanished. In its place was a book, its cream vellum cover decorated with a chameleon worked in gold leaf.

"The Book of Changing," said Iiliana, reaching for it.

"Careful," said Tansy. "It's still hot."

When it had cooled, they let Bram open it. "After all, you summoned it," said Iiliana.

Twice he reached for it, and both times snatched back his hands at the last minute. "You do it," he whispered to Grimald.

The covers were quite cool now. Grimald undid the metal clasps that held the book shut and turned to the first page.

"It's ruined!" he said, dismayed.

At first glance it seemed that the book had been damaged by water. The runes were meaningless blots of ink, the pictures in the margins random smears of pigment, as though the colors had run in the rain. But as they watched they saw the runes dissolving and reforming before their eyes.

"The famous shifting runes . . . ," said Iiliana.

"Yes, the ones that have driven so many scholars mad," said Caitlin. She turned to Tansy. "Have you got two small mirrors I can borrow?"

Reflected in the second mirror, the runes sat still long enough to be read and the swirls of color in the margins resolved into wonderful illuminations: A serpent with a dog's head chased its tail; a gryphon played cuckoo in a raven's nest; monkeys in armor jousted astride unicorns. But most wonderful of all, the illuminations were constantly remaking themselves. As they watched, the dog-headed serpent succeeded in swallowing its tail and disappeared entirely.

At last Caitlin returned the book to its satchel, and Bram read aloud the charm for the next entry in the catalog.

" 'In the name of the blessed sage Gudule, who kept and hid you, I bid you appear.' "

Nothing happened, or for a few minutes it seemed that nothing had happened. Then Ulfra noticed that one of the old pattern books kept at the back of the shop had fallen from its shelf and was hanging suspended from its chain. It was no longer a pattern book, but a volume bound between covers of ivory carved with all manner of fantastic beasts.

"Careful," said Iiliana, as Caitlin reached for the clasps that held the book shut. "If my memory serves me, the Keepers protected this Book with wailing runes."

"Don't worry," said Bembo, producing a small vial from one pocket. "Powdered bookworm. I always carry a little with me, just in case. Really!" he said, catching Binder's doubtful look. "You never know when it might come in handy."

The book was dusted with the antidote, and when it was opened, the wailing runes were mostly subdued, though they whispered and muttered among themselves. The Book of Naming was a catalogue of the names of things: all the beasts and birds, the stones and gems, the seas and rivers, the winds and stars. The Book had fallen open to "The Creatures of the Air." In addition to remarkably lifelike portraits of goshawks, swallowtails, and mute swans, the artisan had painted dodos, the phoenix, dragons, and a strange creature of mortal form that carried tall, feathered wings folded behind its back. The outer surface of the wings was a glossy black, the inner surface iridescent. Each creature's name was written underneath its picture in four rune tongues: ancient mortal, the elvish tongue that Bram had been translating for them, and two others Iiliana didn't recognize.

"I think this one might be goblin, but it's not one of my rune tongues. And this other one—from the accents, it must surely be Longaevi."

"What is Longaevi?" asked Grimald.

"The language of the Longaevi, the Long-lived Ones," said Iiliana. "The old stories say they were a winged race older than the elves. They got their name because they lived much longer than you or me."

"What happened to them?" asked Grimald.

"No one knows. One cradle tale says they built their houses too near the sun and were banished to the Land of Night. Some people think they fled from the Pentaclists and settled in the far north, beyond where our maps end."

"They weren't in my anatomy book," said Bram. "It just showed elves and goblins."

Unable to contain his exasperation, Grimald punched his brother in the arm. "We swore, no secrets! You never told me!"

Bram rubbed his arm thoughtfully. "It was just an old schoolbook." He looked up into his mother's face. "Wasn't it?"

Caitlin bent down and gathered Bram to her with one arm, snaring Grimald in the crook of the other, and hugged them so fiercely that they protested.

"I think we should stop," said Iiliana. "I know I'm all out, and Bram can't read all those charms aloud. We can come back tomorrow." She turned to Tansy and Ulfra. "That is, if it won't disturb your work too much?"

"Heavens, who could sew after this?" said Tansy, "Besides, the work will wait."

"But will our ship?" said Binder. "We sail for Chameol the day after tomorrow."

"We'll sail," said Iiliana. "The books have stayed hidden this long; they should be safe a little longer. The Keepers knew what they were about."

It was agreed that they would stay the night in town; Bram would teach Caitlin and Iiliana to sound out the charms so that they could retrieve as many books as possible the following day.

"Here's the thing," mused Tansy. "With all the festivities for the prince's wedding, the inns are full. I'd gladly put you up myself, if only I had enough beds."

"That's all right," said Iiliana. "We have a place to stay." The Knights of Chameol kept safe houses in every village and town throughout the thirteen Moons. Thus, a beleaguered knight might find sleep in the hay over a buttery in Twinmoon, or between fine linen sheets in a nobleman's summer house in Fifthmoon, or upon a pile of sails and nets in a fisherman's shack in Eightmoon, all of them refuge for those engaged in the struggle against the evil Necromancer. Now that Myrrhlock had been destroyed, the Knights had been dispersed, but the network of houses remained in place, ready like the Knights against the day when they would be called to serve again. Lately Iiliana had been turning some of the safe houses to new uses.

At the corner, they parted from Bembo Gill, who could not be persuaded to sup with them. As Caitlin watched him walk away down the street, she felt a vague foreboding, though she could not have given it a name. At her side, Bram slipped his hand into hers, and she gave it a squeeze.

"Does he have to go? Can't he come with us?"

"No, he had to feed his cats." But the words rang hollow as she said them.

As though he sensed this, Bram ran after Bembo, who heard the rapid approach of footsteps on the paving stones and turned around.

"Here, here! What demon's at your heels?"

"Don't go!" Bram gasped the words, choked by sudden tears.

"I must. I will be going away on a journey, and there is much I have to do to prepare for it." Bembo smiled a fond, sad smile. He no longer seemed a befuddled shopkeeper; now his eyes were sharp and wise, and in their depths Bram saw something ancient and strange that made him shiver.

The bookman reached into his pocket and withdrew a

small object wrapped in a handkerchief. "Now, now, no tears! Here is something for your mother. Will you give it to her, with my thanks?" He pressed the handkerchief into Bram's hand.

Bram took the handkerchief and nodded, too heartsore to speak. He clutched it tightly, watching Bembo's retreating back until the bookman turned a corner and was gone. There was a faint buzzing coming from the handkerchief-wrapped something. Carefully Bram undid the loose knot.

It was the bee treatise.

❧

"Madam, there are visitors downstairs to see you."

Lucivia set down her pen and glanced at the clock; it was an unfashionable hour when most people could be expected to be lying down before the theater.

"Visitors? More than one?"

"Two ladies, a gentleman, and two boys. The one lady, she asked me to bring you this, with her compliments."

Lucivia scanned the note, then slid it beneath her blotter.

"I'll be right down. And you can lay out my blue silk with the pearl fringe."

"Madam?" Rose wavered in the doorway.

"Why? Weren't you able to get out that mud stain on the hem?"

"Yes, of course, madam. It's just that, well, that's your court dress, madam."

"Yes, Rose, and I would like you to lay it out, please."

Burning with curiosity, Rose did so, wondering which of the guests was of sufficient rank for her mistress to dress at this uncivil hour, and what the note had said. She would not have been much enlightened to learn that it contained two words ("Surprise . . . Iiliana") and nothing more.

"My dear!"

Lucivia crossed the room to Iiliana and embraced her. "Poor Rose was staring at your note so hard that I thought it would spontaneously ignite. This *is* a surprise, and such a happy one!"

"Pardon the hour and inconvenience." Iiliana introduced Caitlin and Binder, without explaining their connection to Chameol. She did not need to; one glance at Caitlin's seer's eyes told Lucivia her entire story. She remembered a ballad that had been popular some seven years ago that told of a seer who had left Chameol to wed a knight and live in the Weirdwood.

"These must be your boys," she said. But that redhead was surely a goblin, Lucivia thought, watching them all agog at such wonders as gilded mirrors, tasseled footstools with clawed bear feet, and an embroidered screen depicting the mining of gems. The dark one was mortal, but he had the unmistakable stamp of the Otherworld on him. "Rose, I think you might make a bath ready in the blue salon. In the meantime, why don't you show our young gentlemen guests the theater?"

Before his marriage, the prince had made a gift to Lucivia of a model theater, complete with scenes for *The Dog's Muzzle*. In addition to miniature figures of the prince and Gout, there was a little Modesty pursued by a pack of small, flocked wolves, and the girl tailor had a tiny pair of tin shears that snipped. After twenty minutes, a faint howling reached the others from down the hall, followed by the sounds of happy mayhem.

The Books had been locked into Lucivia's strong room for safekeeping, and while Rose was supervising the business of the bath, Lucivia brought a bottle of wine from the cellar and prepared a rarebit and toast over the sitting-room fire. Iiliana saw the royal crest on the wax that sealed the wine bottle and smiled. It was a vintage put up expressly to celebrate the prince's wedding.

"You're looking very well," Iiliana observed. "Matchmaking must agree with you."

"Yes, I suppose it does. The enterprise certainly has surpassed my dearest hopes for success."

"But that's outrageous!" Binder protested when the nature of her matchmaking was explained to him. "If men are such hopeless creatures, you might as well wall us all in and have done with any pretense."

"It seems to me," said Lucivia, "that the walls are already up. They are the marriage laws. They are invisible walls, it is true, but they are all but insurmountable to a young woman without a dowry. Unless she has a way to earn her living, she must marry it. What is badly needed is a guild for women, where they can learn their own trades." She smiled. "Besides, from my vantage point, I see little risk of mortalkind dying off anytime in the near future."

But Iiliana was not about to let the shuttlecock lie, and she and Binder began to trade rapid volleys. Caitlin sat a little to one side, lulled by the fire and deep in thought, letting the good-natured argument wash over her.

It was late when at last they retired. Rose had long since bathed the boys and put them to bed. When Caitlin paused to look in on them, they lay at angles in the great canopied bed, each clutching one of the theater's tiny players.

The air of the room was stale and close, and Caitlin crossed the room, dodging stray wolves and bits of scenery, to open the shutters to the night breeze. She stayed there longer than she meant to, enjoying the cool air on her cheek. The runes had rotted her brain, she thought sadly. Time was, she would have been able to tell what was out of kilter. *Leave the cloister at your peril, that's what I'll tell the next aspiring seer I meet. Your eyes'll cloud over and your brain will turn to sponge.*

The night watchman passed beneath the window, crying his singsong "All's well," but the words sounded tinny and false. No, she thought suddenly, all's *not* well. *That's what I felt when Bembo said good-bye.* Suddenly she wanted another look at the Books.

The book satchels had been locked in Lucivia's strong room, a small, windowless closet with an iron door where she kept her clients' dowries (as well as her own considerable commissions). Its shelves held fabulous sums of gold and equally fabulous gems. Lucivia had given the key to

Iiliana before retiring, and the High Counsel had made her bed on a cot just outside the door.

Iiliana had just unpinned her hair; it streamed down her shoulders like a sheet of flame. She paused with her brush in midair as Caitlin appeared.

"I thought you had gone to bed." She gave Caitlin a more searching look and set down the brush. "What's wrong?"

"Perhaps nothing. I'm probably being a silly goose, but I won't be able to sleep unless I have one last peek at the Books."

Iiliana took the key from around her neck and unlocked the massive door. At once a curious sound met their ears, as a child raving in a fever or an old woman delirious with pain. "Something's awakened the runes," said Iiliana. "Here, help me get the door open."

Despite its weight, the door opened easily. As soon as Caitlin drew it from the satchel, the Book of Naming began to wail in earnest.

"What a din," said Iiliana, covering her ears. "Let's hope the king doesn't call out the guard."

"I forgot about the powdered bookworm," said Caitlin, turning the pages until she came to the section titled "The Creatures of the Air." The picture of the Longaevi was just as she remembered it. Then what had caused her such unease? She turned over the leaf.

There, in the margins, the artist had painted the story of a nobleman who loved books so much that he sold his true shape to a pawnbroker. So the man she knew as Bembo Gill was very likely a Longaevi prince, and a prince probably impatient to resume his true form.

"Of course!" Her hands trembled as she unbuckled the other satchel. The book she drew out was not the Book of Changing but a manual on bell ringing.

Iiliana sank onto the cot and clutched her head.

"How could it have happened?" she moaned. "I saw Lucivia lock the door myself. How could anyone have gotten past me?"

"I don't think anyone did," said Caitlin. "I think the books were switched before we ever left the tailor's shop."

"By whom?"

Caitlin took a deep breath. "Iiliana—there is something I should have told you about Bembo Gill."

But before she could begin, she saw Binder looming in the doorway, boots in hand, his clothes half buttoned and buckled. "Bram's not in bed."

"But I left them both asleep," said Caitlin.

"Grimald woke up and found him gone."

"Sweet heaven, the window . . ."

Binder swore, stamping his foot down into his boot. "How far is it to Bembo's shop?"

❧

Bembo opened the shutter and peered down at Bram. "Got any peppermint whistles? Treacle mousetraps? Larks' tongues?"

Bram could only shake his head.

"That's all right, then," said Bembo, holding open the door.

Bram walked in and sat down on the stool by the ink-stained worktable.

"I'm sorry I can't make you any tea. I sold the kettle this afternoon so that I could feed the cats before I left. Though they will have to fend for themselves, anyway."

"Why did you switch the books?" said Bram, staring at his hands.

"You noticed that, did you? Why didn't you say anything then?"

"I thought you might bring it back when you were done."

"Your mother would have thought to look here eventually. I imagine she's on her way already. If she's noticed you've gone missing, too."

"Why did you take the Book?" Bram looked up, eyes dull with anger and confusion. "I could have memorized the spell for you."

"I wouldn't have let you. Shape changing is not a pretty thing, and it can be perilous, especially for one like me, who has been held in another shape so long. No, changing one's shape is best done alone, in the dead of night, when little boys are safe abed."

Bram folded his arms tightly and hooked his ankles around the legs of the stool.

"An immovable object, are you?" said Bembo. "Oh, dear. Well, it can't be helped. I've no time to argue." Clutching the Book of Changing with one hand, the book-man mounted the stepladder and unlatched the skylight.

"Where are you going?" Bram called.

"First? The roof."

Bram hesitated for a moment, then scrambled after him.

Bembo held up a finger to test the direction of the wind, nodded, and opened the Book of Changing. In order to read the shifting runes, he had rigged a pair of make-shift spectacles fitted with double lenses cut from his shaving mirror. It made him look like a madman, or a wizard. He began to recite the spell in a strange tongue. It was rough on the ear at first, but grew ever more musical.

Bram had been expecting "Abracadabra!" and an explosion like the one in the tailor's shop, but for a long time Bembo's chanting seemed to have no effect at all. Then Bram noticed something growing out of the neck of Bembo's shirt and out of his cuffs, greenish black, like a statue being covered with ivy.

It was the shape changer's tattoo, growing and changing and remaking itself the way the runes and pictures on the page of the Book did. Before long, every inch of Bembo's skin was covered by the tattoo, and as he chanted, Bram could see that his tongue was tattooed, and even the palms of his hands, and his eyelids. Then Bram couldn't see him anymore; his body was enveloped in a greenish black cloud with an acrid, inky smell that burned Bram's throat and made him hide his eyes in his sleeve.

On and on Bembo chanted. His voice changed and was not a human voice anymore, as though the words were issuing from a different throat. Bram opened his eyes and saw that the cloud had become a dancing sheet of green flame and that the figure in the center of the flame was no longer Bembo Gill.

The chanting ended abruptly, and the flame snuffed itself out, leaving a little oily, greenish soot around the feet of the creature Bembo had become. Like a man, but not a man, he was wrapped in a strange cloak. He raised his head, and Bram saw a sharp, dark face with brilliant eyes, ancient eyes. Then the creature shook off the cloak, and the wind caught it and spread it, and the cloak was a pair of wings that blotted out the sky.

The wind from the wings as they beat blew Bram's hair back from his face, and the look from the eyes froze him where he was, unable to speak or move or breathe. The creature fixed him with that look, then rose from the roof in a single smooth motion, catching the southerly wind in the broad sail of those enormous wings, rapidly rising higher and higher, until the dark wings disappeared against the cloud-driven, moonless night.

A single word came down from the shadow that guttered against the sky. Even from that height it was so clear that it might have been whispered in Bram's ear: "Farewell."

Bram lay a long time on the roof, crying for wonder first, then for grief, then for Ethold, then for Bembo, until all the tears were gone. His face and hands were filmed with a greenish soot; he wiped them on his shirt, then picked himself up and dusted himself off. After he had done the same for the Book of Changing, he climbed with it back down the ladder and sat down on the stool to wait. It was not long before a carriage rattled in the lane outside. Feet hammered on the stairs, fists rained on the door, voices he knew called his name.

He got up to let them in.

Epilogue

Three Years Later

If the truth were known, Galt missed sitting in the three-penny seats at the theater. He had never got used to sitting in the box like a nobleman. For that matter, he had not got used to being a nobleman. The prince was now King Berthold, and six months ago he had bestowed on his friend and huntsman the title and lands of Lord Weirdwood. This afforded his wife no little amusement.

"You will have to pay the wolves a rent," she said. "After all, it *is* their wood." Her tone was gently chiding, but she spoke the truth. So the day after he was elevated to the nobility, Galt walked into the Weirdwood and left one of the king's peacocks, smuggled from the palace grounds in a picnic basket. He tethered the bird to a tree and walked back out of the wood.

The Direwolves did not eat the peacock right away, but bit its tether and let it wander through the wood, fattening on acorns.

A few weeks more, said the she-wolf contentedly. She liked peacock, especially when her lieutenant plucked it for her. *Remind me to give them u gift in return, when she has her first youngling.*

∾∾

"How often do I have to pay rent?" Galt asked Ulfra the next night.

They were dressing for the theater, and she paused, holding the two ends of her necklace poised behind her neck.

"Quarterly," she said thoughtfully.

He took the ends of the necklace from her fingers and fastened them deftly, then kissed the nape of her neck. "Sooner or later the gamekeeper at the palace is bound to count the peacocks and come up short."

"Yes, but by then the wolves will be content with a peacock feather and a suckling calf."

He was never quite sure when she was serious. Sometimes he suspected it was that very uncertainty that lent spice to their married life.

It was the first performance of a new play celebrating the first birthday of the Princess Ivy-Ysolde, and the theater boxes were full of lords and ladies in their best finery—the finest of it from the workrooms of the Cat's Face, tailors to the king and queen. But none of the patrons were more elegantly turned out than the strange couple in the box two down from Lord and Lady Weirdwood's.

The woman was of indeterminate age—her hair was silver, but her face was remarkably unlined. There was not a crease or wrinkle anywhere upon her translucent skin. Her long black gloves appeared to have been painted on her alabaster arms, and on her white throat a necklace of peerless sapphires smoldered with a deep blue fire. Her gown was heavy brushed silk, the inky blue known as black swan. When she turned to speak to her companion, its expertly draped folds glittered with a black dew of tiny jet beads.

Ulfra leaned over to whisper in Galt's ear.

"Who is that lady? She is very familiar."

Galt had come to think of his encounter with the elf queen as a revelation or a dream. Besides, rouged and dressed in silk, Ylfcwen looked passably mortal. "Lady Gobeleyn. The man I've never set eyes on, but from the way I've heard him described, he must be her young ward,

Lord Motley. I know very little about him except that he is supposed to be a wicked hand at cards. Around town they call him Lord Piebald."

It was plain to see how he had gotten the nickname. The hair on his head was snow white, but his closely trimmed beard was coal black. Between these extremes, his eyes were a startling blue—and somehow startlingly familiar. When they met her gaze, those unsettling eyes made Ulfra jump. But it could not be Nix: He was too tall and too old. His clothes were cut in simple good taste, but the jeweled pin that fastened his plain neck cloth could have bought several gowns at the Cat's Face.

The play had started. Ulfra turned her head and watched the brightly lit scene unfold; the rich colors of the costumes; the exaggerated, pink-and-white painted faces of the actors. She let the laughter wash over her, but the first act passed, and she could not have said what it was about.

After the play the royal couple gave a supper at the small summer palace built for the young queen's use on a quiet bend of the river. There was dancing and music, and at midnight the sleeping princess was brought out to be admired. The king led Galt off to see the aviary, which had a pair of nesting falcons.

"The oddest thing happened yesterday," said Berthold, unlocking the first of the gates to the aviary.

"How so?"

"Well, a madman was brought before me. He had been caught outside the palace gates, and his pockets were crammed with gems, the like of which I've never seen before. The palace guards assumed he had stolen them from the palace, but they were far finer than any gems in *my* crown, and besides, they were all uncut. The man was raving, clear out of his head, going on about how he was the king of the elves, that there was a price on his head, that there had been an uprising in the gemfields, and that a new Pretender was leading a revolt."

"What did you do with him?"

"Waved my hand, granted him amnesty, and told him we would hide him until the danger had passed. He's in the new asylum."

They had come to the second gate, beyond which lay the seven interlocking greenhouse pavilions that formed the Queen's Aviary. The king paused, key in the lock.

"Hear that? Those are the peacocks. You can hear them in the palace, they're that loud. Filomena insisted I move them, when her time was near. She said it sounded like children being murdered in their beds. She didn't think it could be good for the child."

"It doesn't seem to have harmed her."

"No. She is beautiful, isn't she? But, there's another odd thing. One of the peacocks is missing."

Ulfra was unaccountably restless and wandered out onto a balcony to enjoy the cool night air. Overhead the constellations wheeled their way across the heavens, the wolf star chasing the hind it would never catch. Below, willows on the river's bank bent to listen to the song of the moving water. A climbing vine on the wall gave off a sweet perfume; the smell of it made her heartsore.

Suddenly she smelled something else, so faint it was barely perceptible among the tangled scents from the ballroom behind her—the burning tapers and the mingled perfumes and pomades of the dancers as they exerted themselves. This smell was faint: an after-dinner clove held between the cheek and gum and fresh sawdust from the floor of a fencing salon. It reminded her keenly of the sawdust in the ring of Folderol's ragtag circus.

A man was standing at the other end of the balcony. He stepped forward, and the light of the ballroom fell upon his face. It was Lord Motley. At the sight of him Ulfra turned away, leaning out over the balcony to breathe the air from the river and clear the smell of him from her head.

"Are you all right?" he said with mild alarm.

She did not at first reply, and when she finally found her voice it came out in an urgent whisper.

"I had to do it, I *had* to."

"I know. I did think it was a rotten trick at first, but they were good people. They took good care of me."

"We couldn't live forever, picking pockets and stealing

geese, always on the road. I wanted you to stay in one place. And I—I wanted to learn how to read and write and speak like a woman instead of a wolf."

She was overtaken by a sudden storm of tears. For a few minutes he waited to see if she would cry herself out. When she began to cry harder, he drew her away from the balcony, away from the lamplit windows, into the shadows and into his embrace. For a little while they clung to one another, while the river ran by below them. In a willow tree a whippoorwill sang to the moon's broken reflection in the running water.

Little by little her sobs subsided, and at last she stepped away. He offered his handkerchief; she accepted it wordlessly and dried her eyes.

"Don't be shy, have a good honk," he said. "I've got handkerchiefs by the dozen now."

She laughed and blew her nose loudly. "You're so *tall*. All those shirts I sent—they never fit you."

"They did at first. Before I grew."

"So I see. You look as though you've done very well for yourself."

He shrugged. "A run of good luck, that's all."

"Promise me . . . promise me you won't fleece anyone at cards."

"Don't worry." He laughed. "I'm reformed."

"Yes. But you still smell of Wolf, somehow."

He glanced back at the illuminated windows of the ballroom. "I should go and find her." She knew he meant the silver-haired woman in blue. "Ours is a long way home." He clasped her hand. "Good-bye, then."

"Good-bye—" She was about to say his name in Wolf, but she stopped herself. "Good-bye."

She turned back to the river and remained there a long time, until Galt came to find her, her cloak over his arm.

"You're chilly," he said, chafing her bare shoulders.

"Am I? It was so close in there, with everyone dancing."

He wrapped the cloak around her and paused behind her a moment, his chin resting easily on the top of her head as he gazed up at the night sky. "Got your fill of stars?"

She turned to him, laying her cheek on his shoulder to hide the tears in her eyes. "No."

"Well, let's go home to our own piece of heaven."

❧

Nix quickly rounded up Ylfcwen's cloak and gloves, but it took some time longer for him to round up Ylfcwen. He finally found her in the royal nursery, gazing down at little Ivy-Ysolde where she slept in a curtained cradle. She was beautiful for a mortal child: all porcelain pink and gilt, with dense rose-gold lashes fringing her eyes and soft rose-gold curls on her head. Her small, dimpled fists lay out-flung on the coverlet, and her small red mouth was pursed into a tender rosebud.

"Don't even *think* about it," he said, taking Ylfcwen by the elbow and leading her from the room.

"I wasn't." She was annoyed at the suggestion, all the more so because she had turned the matter over in her own mind and come to the same conclusion.

❧

Out of *W*'s, Iona set down her composing stick, yawned violently, and stretched. Across the shop, Fel looked up from the type for the broadsheet she was inking.

"Tired?"

"Out of sorts." Iona made a face at the shelves of set type, tied within wooden frames. "I *could* put all that away."

"Anything but that! Just make the book shorter. Of course, we can't print it at all unless the paper comes through."

Iona took one of the bundles of type from the shelf and untied it, picking through the lines for *W*'s like a child picking currants out of a pudding. At last she gave a sigh of resignation and began to sort the type into the wooden case before her, rapidly returning each rune to its own pigeonhole.

Fel pulled the first proof of the broadsheet and held it to the light to check the impression.

APPRENTICESHIPS
BY ORDER OF HER ROYAL HIGHNESS QUEEN FILOMENA,
THE QUEEN'S GUILD
HAS BEEN ESTABLISHED TO OFFER APPRENTICESHIPS
TO YOUNG WOMEN IN THE FOLLOWING TRADES:

Apothecary	Pewterer
Bookbinder	Printer
Clock Maker	Silversmith
Cobbler	Tailor
Hatter	Woodblock Engraver

APPLY AT THE QUEEN'S GUILDHALL
NEW GUILD STREET
(OLD JOUSTING FIELDS)

Outside the house where Bembo Gill had kept his shop, there now hung a new shingle. On one side was carved BOOKBINDER and on the other, APOTHECARY.

The house had been divided along similar lines. Living quarters took up the left half of the house, and their respective workshops, the right, the bindery on the upper floor and the apothecary below. In the stairwell, rising fumes of distilled herbs mingled with the smells of warm glue and leather. The apothecary shop shared a hearth with the kitchen of the living quarters. It made it handy when one had to watch the progress of both dinner and a batch of herb simples. There had been confusion only once, when they had had the fever remedy for dinner instead of the soup. None of them had had a cold all that winter.

Bram came in from his round of deliveries and set the basket down on the wooden counter beside the scales and the large jar with the picture of the mandrake man on it. Caitlin looked up from the powder she was grinding.

"That was quick. I hope some of them paid?"

He nodded. "Almost everyone, even the asylum, and they *never* pay their bill." He took a small milk can from the basket and poured some of its contents into a pie dish, which he set on the floor. Cats materialized from all the corners of the shop but not so many as there had been in Bembo's day. Excellent mousers, much in demand, their sale kept both boys in shoes.

He poured the rest of the milk into a bowl and broke a piece of bread into it. Then he bent down to pick up the child, not quite two years old, who was playing under the counter.

"She's got into the dried lizards again," he said accusingly, taking a blue-tongued skink away from the baby and balancing her on his hip. "You have to keep an eye on her."

"I was," Caitlin said. "Besides, dried lizards never hurt me, and I cut my teeth on them. They made me wise."

"Says you." He put the baby in her chair and tucked a napkin around her neck.

"Try one and see, if you don't believe me."

He only made a face and spooned some bread and milk into the baby, waiting to make sure she wasn't holding it in her cheek, ready to spit it out when he wasn't looking. You had to watch her all the time; she was three-quarters imp, Iilie was. He glanced up at the ceiling.

"How's it going up there?"

"I'm not sure. It's been dreadfully quiet. I hope quiet and not too dreadful."

৵

While his father was checking over the binding, Grimald could do little but stare at the worktable. Outwardly he appeared confident and even a little bored, his inward agonies betrayed only in the sidelong glances at his examiner.

This particular binding was the fruit of three years' study at his father's elbow, learning the bookbinder's craft; if it met with approval, Grimald would begin working in the bindery alongside apprentices from the royal guilds, some of them as old as seventeen.

Grimald's sidelong glances told him nothing. Binder had attention only for the book in his hands. The sewing was sturdy but not too stiff; the book opened invitingly in the hands. The vellum had been stretched neatly over the boards, the excess leather at the corners having been pared thin, but not too thin. The rounding of the spine was skillfully done, too, with light, glancing blows of the hammer that left no marks on the vellum. Finally, Binder fitted a jeweler's glass to his right eye and bent to examine the decorations.

Grimald had chosen the scene of the animals exiling the fox to the moon. All the animals had been worked blind, in deep relief, only their crests and hooves and horns touched with gold. The night sky had been stained a deep purple, and clouds scudded over the face of the moon. The fox was in his tiny boat, with its sail furled, telling the first of a hundred tales to forestall his departure. The fox's tale was represented by a thin scroll issuing from his mouth, with some runes on it. Gathered around the boat to listen to the story were the boar and the wolf and stag from the woods, the badger and rabbit and lark from the meadow, the frog and pike and otter from the lake. The bat hung from an overhead branch beside the whippoorwill and the owl.

Binder removed the lens from his eye, replaced his spectacles, and turned to Grimald.

"Six o'clock. You'll eat breakfast with the other apprentices. It won't be as nice as you're used to, but from now on you'll be treated just as I would treat any of the others. Understood?"

Grimald could only nod. Binder's stern expression relaxed into a smile, and he reached out to clasp the boy warmly to him.

"Well done."

∽⌒∽

Back in the apothecary shop, Bram finished giving Iilie her bread and milk, sponged the milk from her upper lip, and set her down among the cats. Then he resumed unpacking the basket, which contained a great many bottles of all shapes and sizes. It was his job to wash them out and scrub off the labels and cut new corks for them.

Caitlin watched him. She was proud that he had doggedly stuck with his studies of herbs, even when it meant bottle washing and bill collecting. In the evenings, after the baby was asleep, he would read her large herbal for hours, poring over its pages as though it were a tale of knights' derring-do. He need not have cut the corks or watched the baby, but he was greatly insulted if either task was taken from him. Grimald complained that his brother's nose was "always in a splint."

Caitlin would have been completely content except for two things. She would rest easier once Iilie had passed her third birthday, for then she would be older than Rowan had lived to be. But part of her would remain restless as long as the Book of Summoning remained lost. She did her best to be philosophical about it. Yet of all the Books, it was the one most likely to stir up trouble. It might be used to summon hail and drought, floods and locusts, and even waking spirits. In Iiliana's opinion, it was better left undiscovered, and at last she had persuaded Caitlin to the same view. So it was that the three remaining Books were installed in the library at Chameol amid great celebration.

And still, and still . . .

∽◦∾

It would have eased Caitlin's mind considerably to know that the Book of Summoning had made its way into one of the lower storage rooms of Ylfcwen's former palace, where it lay in a chest with surplus copies of the *Elf Book of Court Etiquette* and sets of the ten-volume Chronicles. It was fifteen years into the reign of the Goblin King of the New Realm before the party dispatched to inventory the storerooms of the corrupt elvish regime discovered some sixty chests of books. They stood a minute debating: One was in favor of cataloging the books and making a report to the Minister of the Inventory. Another suggested burning the lot. But at last the captain in charge sealed the room and placed a green flag on it so that it would be left for a later inventory in a hundred years' time. And so they moved on to the next storeroom.

"Silver wing implements, assorted," said the captain. "Make a note, then down to the mint with them. And wing cases, assorted. Those can go directly to the furnace."